THE
SINNER

ALSO BY MARTYN WAITES

The Old Religion

THE
SINNER

MARTYN WAITES

**BLACK
STONE**
PUBLISHING

Copyright © 2021 by Martyn Waites
Published in 2021 by Blackstone Publishing
Cover and book design by K. Jones

The characters and events in this book are fictitious.
Any similarity to real persons, living or dead, is coincidental
and not intended by the author.

Printed in the United States of America

ISBN 978-1-982548-78-0
Fiction / Mystery & Detective / General

1 3 5 7 9 10 8 6 4 2

CIP data for this book is available
from the Library of Congress

Blackstone Publishing
31 Mistletoe Rd.
Ashland, OR 97520

www.BlackstonePublishing.com

To Chrissie and Beth, always

A MESSAGE FROM
MARTYN WAITES

Dear Reader,

Hello once again. If you've read *The Old Religion*, that is. And if you have, then thank you so much. I really appreciate you doing so and hope you enjoyed it. Obviously I'd prefer you to love it but if not, then fine. I hope you had some kind of strong reaction to it rather than just, "Meh." Because after all, the opposite of love isn't hate, it's indifference. That's a quote from *Dynasty*.

However, if you haven't read *The Old Religion* and this is your first one of mine, then welcome aboard. I'm very happy to have you. And I hope that feeling is mutual. If you want to know a bit more about me and *The Sinner*, then read on. If you don't, then fine. I'm sure you've got a Netflix subscription or something.

First, here's a bit about me. *The Sinner* is my twentieth novel. Hooray. I've managed to keep going for that long. Most of the novels under my own name have been gritty (I'm contractually obliged to use that word) urban noir settings, mainly in my native North East of England. I've also written eight thrillers under the pseudonym Tania Carver. And I was chosen to write *Angel of Death*—the official sequel to Susan Hill's *The Woman in Black*. I've won awards and been in the bestseller lists, both here and abroad. *The Old Religion* was something of a departure for me. My first novel with a totally rural setting incorporating elements of folk horror. I loved writing it and a sequel was inevitable. However, I didn't want to just repeat myself. I wanted something a little different. The result is *The Sinner*.

Not everyone in prison is guilty. Great tagline for the cover. (I didn't think of it, incidentally. I just handle the bits inside.) And it's kind of true. I used to work in prisons and young offenders institutions as a Writer-in-Residence. The first thing that struck me was just how arbitrary the justice system is. Every single prejudice and cliché that I had was confirmed straightaway. The richer you are, the less time you do and the punishment is inversely in proportion to how much money you have or where you are on the social scale. But I've written elsewhere about that. I'm here to talk about *The Sinner*.

I was aware that it was going to be a follow up to *The Old Religion*, using the same lead character, Tom Killgannon. Whereas the first book had used all these sweeping open spaces, this one would be cramped and claustrophobic. *The Old Religion* played with folk horror. This would have the vibe of a haunted house. I wanted every character (or nearly every character) to be guilty of something. To be haunted—imprisoned, if you will—by their past actions. To be the sinners of the title. Also, and rather incongruously considering it's set in a prison, I wanted an homage, at least in part, to Geoffrey Household's classic novel of rural pursuit, *Rogue Male*. Did I manage? Read the book and find out . . .

By the way, if you would like to hear more from me about *The Sinner* and my other future books, you can visit www.bit.ly/MartynWaitesClub where you can join the Martyn Waites Readers' Club. It only takes a moment, there is no catch and new members will automatically receive an exclusive e-book short story from my previous novel, *The Old Religion*. Your data is private and confidential and will never be passed on to a third party and I promise that I will only be in touch now and again with book news. If you want to unsubscribe, you can of course do that at any time.

However, if you like what you read then please let people know. Social media (I'm on Twitter as @MartynWaites), Amazon, Goodreads, all of that. It really does make a difference for writers.

But enough of my yakkin'. It's time to get banged up with *The Sinner*. Enjoy, dear reader . . .

All the best,
Martyn Waites

PART ONE
GHOSTED

MANCHESTER, MAY 2014

A NIGHT FAR ENOUGH IN THE PAST for stories to be told. But recent enough for those stories to matter.

An old industrial estate and truck stop in the badlands of Stretford. The buildings are mostly empty and vandalized, the tarmac potholed, refilled with debris: broken glass and excrement, canine for the most part. The remaining lights stretched so far apart they looked stranded. The kind of place no one went to voluntarily. It was perfect.

Dean Foley sat in the passenger seat of the BMW X5. Its gleaming black carapace stood out against its surroundings, as inconspicuous as an intellectual at a UK Independence Party meeting.

Foley turned to the man in the driver's seat. "What's the time now?"

The driver checked his watch, tried not to look irritated. "Just gone ten to ten. They'll be here. Don't worry."

"Yeah," said Foley. "I know they will, I know they will."

The tension in the car was palpable.

Foley looked like a bouncer on Love Island. *Short and stocky, he wore expensive clothes that were all label and no style, his hair well-coiffed, teeth the color of Egyptian cotton, skin the color of mahogany. His muscle showed he could handle himself and he had a lightness of step that surprised many. He also had a charismatic salesman's smile that made you feel like you were an instant friend for life. But that smile could turn on a breath, become so fierce and snarling it would be the last thing you'd want to see. And for quite a few it had been.*

Foley sighed. Tried not to pretend he was nervous. "You know," he said, resisting the urge to check his own watch again, *"I don't know why we bother with all this cloak-and-dagger shit. Meetings in the dark in shitholes like this. We should just do it in broad daylight. Get it over with. No one's bothered anymore."*

"You think?" said the driver.

"Yeah," said Foley, warming to his theme. "I mean, protection I've got, the amount of people on my payroll, I could walk into a pub on Deansgate—if they hadn't all been turned into fucking wine bars or craft beer places or some shit—pull out a gun and kill someone. Right then and there. Bang. In front of thirty witnesses. And you know what? I'd get away with it. That's how untouchable I am. That's why all this is just bollocks."

"Yeah," said the driver, "that's what the Krays said. Look what happened to them. And that was before CCTV."

Foley turned to him, his smile a vicious slash in the streetlight. He snorted. "You're a bundle of laughs tonight, aren't you?"

The driver stared straight ahead. "Why would you want to murder someone in a pub on Deansgate?"

"I wouldn't unless they were asking for it, would I?" said Foley, "Then I'd have to. Because that's what it is. You cross me, that's what you get."

"If they've crossed you they wouldn't hang around drinking on Deansgate."

"Then I'd track them down, wouldn't I? Get revenge. They wouldn't get far."

"You know what they say about revenge," said the driver, "you go looking for it, you'd better dig two graves."

Foley stared at him. Then threw back his head and laughed. "Brilliant. Just brilliant. Mick, mate, if I go looking for revenge, I'll need a damned sight more than two."

Mick lapsed back into silence. Foley fidgeted, flicked looks like lit matches all around the truck stop. His gaze came to rest on Mick once more.

"Why are you so miserable tonight, anyway?" asked Foley. "It's like watching Man U when Moyes was in charge."

Mick sighed. More from professional exasperation than boredom. "Just want everything to go right. That's all."

"Everything's cool," said Foley, knee bouncing up and down. "It'll go down fine. Why wouldn't it?"

Silence once more. Both resisted the urge to check the time.

"Hey," said Foley, eventually, "Just think if my old man could see me now . . ." He shook his head at the thought.

"Sitting in some shitty truck stop in Stretford? He'd love that."

"No, you prick, if he could see what I've done, you know, built. Achieved. One of the most successful businessmen in the northwest. If not the country. Respected. And I've done it all myself, haven't I?"

Mick nodded. "You have, Dean."

"Yeah. I have. If he could see what I've achieved . . ."

"He'd still be a miserable bastard."

Foley stared at Mick, the smile falling sharply away. Eyes as hard as stone. No one talks ill of Foley's father, everyone knew that. Foley might have hated him, but that didn't give anyone else the right to join in. He was still Foley's father.

Mick didn't know which way the situation would go. He thought he was close enough to Foley, but the man was so unpredictable that he could have made a misstep. He tried to smile his way out of it.

"Well he would be," said Mick. "You know he would."

Foley kept staring.

Mick tried to shrug. "Just you and me here, Dean."

Gradually the harshness left Foley's eyes and the smile reappeared. He started to laugh, building up to a roar, the kind of coarse, loud laughter you only hear in films when the bad guy tries to convince everyone he's a decent human being with emotions like everyone else. Mick smiled along.

"Oh," said Foley eventually, mirth subsiding, "good one, Mick. Good one."

Mick looked to the front, knowing he had dodged a bullet. Through the windshield he saw activity.

"They're here, boss."

An articulated semi with a shipping container payload was turning into the truck stop, headlights temporarily blinding them, playing along the buildings, making the shadows give up their secrets. Foley's team suddenly visible.

Mick saw the cars too. Four by fours, like the one they were in. Predatory darkling beetles waiting to pounce. Dotted between buildings, waiting. Filled with Foley's men. Mick looked through the windshields, knew them all by name. Then, heart jumping, saw one person in a passenger seat who shouldn't have been there.

"What's she doing here?" he said, pointing at the vehicle that had slipped back into darkness once the headlights moved on.

"Who?" said Foley.

"That girl, in the front seat, over there. What's she doing here?"

"Oh, Hayley. Yeah, she's a good girl. Been proving very useful to the team. Very useful." Another kind of smile. The kind that turned Mick's stomach.

"She shouldn't be here. She's—"

"Hey, what's your problem?" said Foley. "We make the trade, we go our separate ways, we head off somewhere and celebrate. Yeah, maybe Foxy shouldn't have brought her but she's a good kid, it's cool. No problem." Another smile. "She'll be around for the party afterward. Maybe Foxy'll let you have a go, if you want."

Mick felt his anger ramping up. "She shouldn't be here. What if something goes wrong? What if—"

Foley stared at Mick, eyes crinkling. "What you trying to say?"

"Nothing. Nothing at all. Just, she shouldn't be here. That's all."

Foley shook his head. "Right." He smiled. It didn't reach his eyes.

The semi pulled up, stopped dead with a hiss of air brakes. The sound dissipated to a tense silence.

"Here we go, then," said Foley, opening the car door. Mick did likewise.

Foley went around to the back of the car, opened the trunk. Waited while the hydraulic door silently moved upward. Then leaned in, brought out a huge duffel bag.

"Jesus Christ," he said, handing it to Mick. "Carry that, mate, bastard thing's heavy."

"Thought they said it had to be you handing over the money in person?"

"I'm here, aren't I? Get moving. Haven't got all bloody night."

Another four by four pulled into the parking lot, kept its lights on. It parked next to the semi. The doors opened. The backlit silhouettes of two men emerged.

"Here's the Romanians, right on time." Foley laughed, moving forward. "Should get a quote for my new bathroom."

Mick didn't respond. They walked toward the two men. Stopped halfway between the two vehicles. The other men continued toward them. Stopped also.

Mick handed the duffel bag to Foley. He stared back at Mick.

"Just put it down, what the fuck's the matter with you?"

"You take it," said one of the Romanians. "We want you to give it to us. So we know who we are dealing with."

Foley's eyes glittered in the dark. Clearly unhappy about being told what to do. But he picked the bag up, put it in front of his feet. "There. Now where's my stuff?"

"In truck. We will get it. When we have checked money."

He bent down, opened the bag. A smile returned to Foley's face. "Doing it old school, yeah? Notes and that. Unmarked. Thought you'd be all electronic transfer these days. You lot and your cybercrime."

"We like old school," said the other Romanian. "Face to face. Know who you're dealing with. Less to go wrong."

The first Romanian stood up, satisfied that the money was all there. He nodded toward the driver of the semi who went around the back, opened the double doors. They waited in silence while the driver came to join them, a cling-wrapped bundle in his arms.

"The good stuff," said Foley. "Let's have a look." He took the bundle from the driver, took out a knife, dug it in. "It's not like the films," he said. "I'm not going to put this up my nose. If it's as pure as you say it is I'll be off my tits for days. But I'm sure you won't cross me. If you do, I'll know where to find you."

"We not cross you. We want to deal with you. Deal?"

Foley put the package on the ground. "Deal." He stretched out his hand. The Romanian took it. They shook.

"We all happy?" asked Foley.

"One more thing," said Mick.

Foley turned to him, irritation on his face.

"What?"

"Speaking of crossing . . ." He reached behind his back, brought out a pair of PlastiCuffs, slipped them onto Foley's wrists, pulled them tight. Foley was too surprised to react.

"Dean Foley, I am arresting you on the charge of obtaining class A drugs with intent to sell. You do not have—"

Foley found his voice. "What the fuck are you doing? Mick? What the fuck are you doing? What's . . . what's happening? Mick, what the . . ." He turned to the Romanians. "Fucking do something . . ."

"We're with him," said the first Romanian, voice now more Manchester than Bucharest. He drew his automatic from his side holster, pointed it at Foley.

Foley looked around, tried to see his men in their cars but he had been cuffed out of their eyeline.

The second Romanian spoke into a mic hidden in his jacket lapel. "Target apprehended. Letting you out now." He trotted around to the back of the truck, began opening the double doors.

Foley struggled in Mick's grip, managed to turn and shout at the cars.

"It's a fucking set-up! They're law!"

Foley's men were on hair triggers. In response to his call, they jumped out of their cars, pulling their guns from within their jackets. Mick dragged Foley to the ground as his men started running toward them, firing as they came.

"Where's that backup?" Mick yelled to the back of the truck. He saw the second "Romanian," an undercover firearms officer, swing the first of the double doors open, then spin and fall, face creased up in pain, as a bullet ripped through his side.

"Shit," shouted Mick. He looked at the first Romanian. "Get him out of the line of fire, get those doors open. Get the men out, move . . ." Mick's training kicked in. He took his gun out, grabbed Foley, dragged him back to the BMW. Keeping covering fire going all the while. Turning on men who, until seconds ago, had been his closest friends. Or thought they were. Not thinking, just acting, reacting.

The fake Romanian ran around to the back of the truck, pulled at the door. Armed, body-armor-clad police began disgorging. They assessed the situation quickly, found spots to shelter behind, take aim.

Then it was free fire.

The fake Romanian managed to drag his wounded comrade behind the car, knelt, and returned fire.

The police outnumbered Foley's men and outflanked them in professionalism, but Foley's team were vicious, desperate. They had the chance to be the outlaws they'd always imagined themselves to be and they weren't going to go down easily. At least not without taking out as many cops as they could.

Mick ran, dragging Foley across loose gravel and broken glass, *keeping up the covering fire, head down, dodging overhead bullets. He didn't have the benefit of body armor like the uniformed officers did. He just concentrated on the task at hand, didn't allow himself to be drawn into the firefight. Foley screamed all the way, kept up a litany of threats as to what would befall Mick when he got free.*

The police were winning. It was an uneven fight. They found positions, attempted to pick off anyone who came at them. Foley's men were reckless and young, brought up on a diet of video games and self-aggrandizement. They believed they were the indestructible heroes of their own stories. The officers, guns used sparingly, clinically, were proving them wrong. Foley's men were the cannon fodder.

Some of them ran back to their cars, tried to get away. They wouldn't get far. The police had stationed cars at all the exits to the estate. Armed response officers alongside.

As the fighting died down, Mick and Foley reached the BMW. Mick opened the hatchback trunk and lugged a protesting, kicking, swearing Foley inside where the duffle bag had previously been.

"You put me in here where you'd put a fucking dog? Would you?" Mick ignored him.

Foley stopped shouting. He calmed slightly, panting from the exertion. Started asking questions.

"So you're law, are you, Mick? Fucking law? Since when?"

"Since always," said Mick, getting behind the wheel and shutting the door.

"What the fuck?" Foley still had difficulty comprehending what he was hearing. "You're my right-hand man, Mick. We did all this together. You've been with me fucking ages. How can you be law?"

"Because that was my job. I played the long game, Dean."

Foley fell silent. When he spoke his voice was more reflective. "Was it worth it? All the shit you've done? That we've done together? Brothers in fucking arms, was it worth it?"

Mick didn't answer.

Foley's voice took on a plaintive tone. "I trusted you, Mick. I trusted you . . ."

Mick couldn't reply, couldn't listen to any more. It sounded, if Mick concentrated hard enough, as though the man was almost crying.

He locked the car, walked toward the semi, pulled a red bandanna out of his jacket pocket, the previously agreed sign to mark him as police.

Bodies everywhere. Mainly Foley's men, but a couple of police officers had been wounded beyond the reach of their body armor.

He found the duffel bag. It was where it had been left along with the block of cocaine. He stood beside it. It was clear to see who had won.

"He's in the BMW," he said to an armed, uniformed officer striding over to him. "What's the damage?"

"Couple of them badly injured, couple of fatalities. The rest have either run or given themselves up."

Mick nodded. "Good night's work." Then remembered something. "There was a girl in one of the cars. Where's she?"

Sadness always looked worse on the face of a professional. "Driver tried to get away, sir. Looks like she was in the line of fire. Got hit running, apparently."

"Who by? Who hit her?"

"Don't know, sir. Stray bullet, probably."

"What's happened to her?"

"Sorry, sir, did you know her?"

Mick's heart skipped a beat. Then another. His legs became water. He didn't answer. "Get an ambulance, get her seen to . . ."

He tried to run over to where she had been. The officer tried to push him back.

"You don't want to see, sir. Believe me. It's a mess."

Others joined the officer, kept Mick away from the girl's body. He fought them all the way but they were too many for him. Eventually the adrenaline rush subsided. His shoulders slumped. He felt defeated.

"Was she important to you, sir?" said the first officer.

"*My niece. And she shouldn't have been here. She wasn't supposed to be here.*"

"*I'm very sorry sir.*" The officer looked around. He was being called. "*Excuse me sir. I'm needed over there.*"

Mick didn't know whether he had replied to him or not. He just stood there, staring at the carnage. Ambulances were arriving now, their flashing lights adding to the chaos all around. He walked away, back to where he'd left the duffel bag. Stood beside it once more. Looked down at it.

He felt so, so tired.

Of everything.

1

Now

HE WAS ON THE WRONG SIDE of the door. And he hated it.

Movement buffeted him from side to side. He tried to stay still. The room was small, less than three feet all around, and he could easily touch the walls if he wanted to. He didn't. Previous occupants had left their mark in several ways: mucus smeared on all surfaces, graffiti, hardened phlegm on the plexiglass door. Other, darker smears and trails. And the smells: sweat—yes, obviously, that's where the name of the vehicle, the Sweatbox, came from— shit, piss. Like the worst broken-down elevator in the worst tower block in the world. He thought of all the diseases the room might harbor. Then tried to forget it. Couldn't.

There was a gap under the door where a drink could be slid in if he was thirsty. Or a box if he needed to urinate. Beyond that, he was on his own.

But not alone. Another man either side of him, another three men opposite them. Each in his own little room. Unable to talk to each other, almost unable to think, the driver having pushed Kiss FM up to near ear-splitting levels. A small act of sadism or something to keep the driver awake? He didn't know. But he could guess.

The Sweatbox, a miniature jail on wheels, moved through the night.

He knew where he was going. That didn't make the journey

any more endurable. His destination was just as bad. Worse, even. Not for the first time he wished he was home. Or the place he was learning to call home. Building his new life, working on his future. And he could go back to doing that. As long as he did this one thing. And it worked out. Simple.

He shook his head. Yeah. Simple.

The Sweatbox juddered, shook, turned to the left. He tried to look out of the window, twisting his body nearly ninety degrees to do so. No use. Couldn't make anything out. The glass, or the night, too dark. But he had a feeling they would be arriving soon. He sat back, tried to think about anything other than where he was, where he was going. And more importantly, tried not to touch anything.

It didn't take long to reach his destination. He may have nodded off, although given the circumstances he didn't know how. He jolted forward as the Sweatbox came to a standstill. Then remained still, trying to listen for anything above the blare of the radio.

Nothing.

The Sweatbox pulled forward again, came to its final resting place. The radio was silenced. The ringing in his ears was deafening. He waited. It wouldn't be long now.

He was wrong. He sat there for nearly an hour before anyone came for him. He heard voices, the other men in their cells, trying to talk to one another, size each other up, glean information, explore camaraderie, even. With varying degrees of success. He listened, but didn't join in.

Then his door was opened. A prison officer stood there, big and doughy, stretching his uniform, the seedy yellow light in the van making him look like a rancid marshmallow.

"Come on, then. Haven't got all night."

He picked up the four big plastic bags, made his way out of the cell. Followed the officer along the van's narrow corridor and down the steps to the outside world. The air hit him. So cold it woke him immediately. He looked around, tried to make out his surroundings. Saw only dark gray stone against gray sky. Floodlights lit the way toward a door.

"You'll have plenty of time to admire the view," the officer said, pushing him forward.

He gave no resistance, went where he was instructed.

He was marched through to a holding cell. Inside was a row of plastic chairs. Five men sat on them, trying not to touch each other. The others from the Sweatbox, he assumed. He sat down on the nearest chair, dropped his bags in front of him. The door clanged shut as the officer left, the key turning in the lock. He hoped he wouldn't have to get used to that sound. He sat back, head against the wall. Processing. He knew the procedure. Make as little fuss as possible, try to get a cell to himself.

He didn't know how long he was kept there. Time moved at a different rate inside prison. The artificial light told him nothing. Could have been morning by now. Or even afternoon.

The man next to him kept looking at him, attempting eye contact, wanting to talk. He ignored him. The man persisted.

"Nice reception committee, innit?

"I mean I've had worse," the man continued, oblivious to his silence. "First time in this nick?"

He gave only the slightest of nods.

The other man took that as encouragement. "Not that bad, really. Not as bad as it used to be, anyway. Jesus, should have been here then . . ."

He looked at the talking man. Small, gray-haired, features like carved, well-oiled leather. Eyes that weighed odds, made calculations, did deals while he spoke. The speaking, he now saw, just a cover for thinking.

The man looked at him. "Clive," he said.

He didn't answer. Clive smiled.

"Right, I get it. One of those silent types. Fine by me, mate. We all have our own way of coping." He kept looking at him. Kept smiling. "Mind you, with that hair and that beard, they should call you Thor."

He almost smiled at that. It was true he had let his hair and beard grow, and that the sun had lightened it a little. But Thor? That was a stretch. The key turned in the lock. The door opened.

"You're up." Clive nodded as the officer beckoned.

He picked up his plastic bags, followed. The door clanged shut behind him. He was escorted to a reception desk. He stood, bags in hand, before the desk, waiting to be spoken to.

The officer behind the desk looked like she had never smiled in her life. Or had used up her supply long before she'd met him. Hair scraped back from her face, uniform rendering her neither masculine nor feminine. She stared at him, her gaze stern.

"Name?" A question that sounded like a statement.

"Tom Killgannon."

She looked up at him once more. "Welcome to HMP Blackmoor, Killgannon."

2

"WE DON'T LIKE DOING THIS EITHER, if that's any consolation."

It wasn't. Tom had been taken to yet another room, told to strip naked by the prison officer, and searched. His bags had been gone through thoroughly, his personal items examined in minute detail. The officers had stopped at the photos, scrutinized the images, scrutinized him in turn. Guessing relationships, keeping judgements to themselves for now. Mentally filing the images away as potential leverage at a later date. It was intrusive, having his life dismantled and put on show, but nothing compared with what was to come.

"Take a seat," the officer said, pointing to the BOSS chair. The Body Orifice Scanner.

Tom had heard about this and had dreaded experiencing it for himself. Gray and functional looking, it was a full body scanner that checked every cavity for contraband. Humiliating in the extreme, but he had no choice but to submit.

"I've got nothing to hide," said Tom.

"Then you've nothing to worry about."

The chair was switched on. It was something Tom hoped he would never have to endure again.

The experience over, he was told to get dressed and take a seat. He was tired, ready for whatever sleep he could get, but no one seemed in any particular hurry. He sat. The officer opposite him picked up a file from his desk, opened it. He was tall, gray haired. Thin, with large glasses and a mournful expression. He looked more like a funeral director or an unsuccessful dentist than a prison officer. There was no cruelty about him, no harshness. Just a tired professionalism. Then the questions started.

"Where've you come from?"

He had decided to answer questions as monosyllabically as possible. Inmates tried different things when they first arrived. Some played hard, set themselves up as a challenge, tried to intimidate. Others went for cocky, unbreakable. Some, especially the older ones, tried to be chummy with the officers at first, make themselves seem likeable, get privileges in the bank. Tom gave little of himself away. Let them come to him if they wanted something.

"Where've you come from?"

"HMP Long Lartin."

"How long you in for?"

"Two years."

"How long you got left?"

"Eighteen months."

"What level were you on?"

"Enhanced. Yeah. I worked for my privileges. Don't intend to lose them."

The officer read the rest of the file in front of him. Tom waited silently. Eventually the officer looked up. "You'll do all right here, probably. Keep your head down, your nose clean. All of that."

Tom inclined his head to demonstrate he'd heard and understood.

The officer closed the file, studied Tom. "How did you get on in your last prison?"

"Should be all there in the report."

"It is, but I want your opinion."

"Fine," said Tom, talking as if words were difficult, precious things to extract from him.

"No problems with other inmates? Officers?"

"Don't think so. Unless someone's said anything I don't know about."

"No." The officer opened the file once more. "Model prisoner. Says here you're well-educated but you didn't want to go to education classes."

"Couldn't see the need. I've done all that stuff. Didn't want to do art either. Not good at drawing. Or creative writing . . . I don't like making up stories." The irony, thought Tom.

"So you ended up working in the laundry. Why was that?"

"I like wearing clean clothes."

The officer sat back, studied Tom once more. Took in his hair, beard. The tattoos poking out from his rolled-up sweatshirt sleeves. The way Tom held his body, still but not relaxed, like an engine at rest.

"If I may say so," said the officer, voice dropping, "you don't seem like many of the men we get in here. I'm not saying you don't belong, because clearly you do, otherwise you wouldn't be here."

The statement seemed to invite a response so Tom gave a small shrug.

"It says in your file that you committed assault."

"That's what it says."

"A troublesome customer in the pub where you worked."

"You know all this. Why are you asking?"

The officer looked up from his notes. Smiled. Tom's first question. A breakthrough.

"I just want your opinion on what happened, that's all."

Tom shrugged once more. "Rowdy customer got a bit too handsy with the boss. Needed putting in place, that was all."

"And that's the way you see it, is it?"

"What other way is there?"

"Well according to the trial notes, this rowdy customer, as you describe him . . ." He verbally placed quotation marks around the words " . . . was attempting to rape your boss. He had followed her outside to the back of the pub, pinned her up against the wall and was attempting to sexually assault her when you happened upon them."

"Yeah. That's right."

The officer regarded Tom over the tops of his glasses. Like peering out from behind a shield. "Should have got a medal, really."

Tom shrugged. "He needed to be taught a lesson."

"Which is where, it says here, it stepped over the line to assault." The officer nodded. His tone became warmer, conciliatory. "Thin line, that. Very thin. Better barrister, different judge in a different mood on another day . . . there but for the grace of God, isn't it?"

Tom said nothing.

"Anyway, you're here now. My advice? Make the best of it."

Tom nodded.

"Just another couple of questions before I send you along to the medical department. Have you had any suicidal thoughts since you've been in prison?"

"No."

"Dark thoughts? Depression?"

"I'm on antidepressants. Long term."

"Are they working?"

Tom shrugged. "Still here, aren't I?"

"Mental health's a big problem inside. If you feel you can't cope or you need someone to talk to, speak to your personal officer. He'll introduce himself on the wing tomorrow."

Tom gave a small nod.

"Anything else?"

"I want a cell to myself."

The officer smiled. "Don't hold your breath."

Tom nodded.

The officer wrote something in the file, closed it. "Right, that's you done. Off you go to medical. Best of luck."

HE SAT IN HIS CELL, ON THE BED, staring at the wall. It was painted a shade of yellow that looked like a dying, sick sun. The door, huge and riveted, took up most of one wall. On the opposite wall was a barred window, the plexiglass strips, pitted and melted from cigarette burns, gave only the barest of openings to stop inmates from stringing a line from cell to cell in order to pass contraband or reaching through to take whatever had been brought in by drone. The bed was against one wall, opposite that was a cheap table with a small, greasy-screened TV, a plastic chair, a metal, seat-free toilet, and matching metal sink. His bags sat on the floor, unopened.

Whoever had lived in the place before him hadn't been one for cleaning. The floors were dirty, the walls smeared. It stank. That would be one task he would have to undertake immediately.

Medical had presented no problems. He had been passed fit and healthy, ready for work or education. After that he was given his nonsmokers welcome pack—a small carton of orange juice and a few cheap biscuits—and directed to his cell. But not before his allocated phone call.

One call, a duration of two minutes, then cut off whether he had finished or not. Made from the wing phone with everyone else around, not knowing who was listening, both in the vicinity and beyond. Knowing someone could use your words against you if they wanted to. Choose carefully who you want to talk to, what you want to say, he had been advised. Make every second count. He should call Lila. Tell her he was OK. Not to worry. Or Pearl, even. But both of those calls would have to be longer than two minutes. Infinitely longer. And full of things he couldn't say. Instead he dialed another number, one he had learned by heart.

"It's me," said Tom. "I'm in."

"Any problems?"

"None."

"Good. Then get to work."

3

The end of October. Halloween mists and denuded trees. A day that, to all intents and purposes, had started like any other. But Tom, in hindsight, felt it was anything but.

A staunch rationalist, he had always dismissed the slightest hint of superstition. But as he looked out of his bedroom window that morning, part of him—the part that had been awakened by and responded to the untamed, isolated world around him, the part that had allowed the beliefs of locals to influence or at least commingle with his own—was tempted to think there were no coincidences, only omens.

The crows had returned.

Always present to some degree, they now circled the house cawing and screeching, swooping and diving, as if singling Tom out for special treatment. Sitting in the leafless autumn trees, charcoal against the gray sky, like the backdrop to a folk horror movie. The rational part of him dismissed such thoughts as pagan, as voodoo nonsense. But it was a hard unease to shift. The crows were reminding him of what happened seven months before. And with that memory came the unnerving feeling that he had somehow escaped censure for his part in those events. Or at least deferred it. But payment, he felt, would fall due.

He tried to dismiss such thoughts, or at least reduce them to an irritation, noise at the back of his mind. He went downstairs to get on with the day.

Lila was up and about before him. He came into the kitchen to find her eating a slice of toast with butter and Marmite, drinking a mug of tea, and packing her rucksack at the same time.

"Just look after yourself," he said, "don't mind me."

"What d'you mean?" she said through a mouthful of bread. "You're never up at this time."

"Neither are you. Is this a college day?"

"You know it is. Why you even asking?"

Tom thought for a second. "Sorry. Bad dream. Dragged it into the morning with me. Can't remember what day it is."

"You're getting old," she said, taking a gulp of tea. "Right. Got to catch the bus. Laters, taters."

She ruffled his hair as he sat down, picked up her rucksack, and was gone. He smiled as she left. It didn't last long. The slam of the door echoed away to nothing.

His dream. He couldn't remember what it had been about. Just that feeling that something dark and foreboding was gathering like storm clouds. And he was caught in the middle. Then on waking he had seen the crows. Or maybe the crows had wormed their way into his dream, darkening it, wakening him. Omens, Pearl would say. Don't mess with the omens.

He stood up, shaking superstitious nonsense out of his mind, and put the kettle on to make coffee.

Seven months since he had come back from work on a freezing, wet night and found the seventeen-year-old Lila shivering, starving, and soaking wet in his kitchen, on the run from an abusive family, a vicious boyfriend, in genuine fear for her life. Seven months since he had made a decision to help her, putting his own life in danger. Seven months since those events led to the village he had come to call home losing its collective mind in the grip of a murderously deranged demagogue. Tom had helped to pull things back from the brink, but life in the surrounding area wouldn't be the same for a long time. Not now that the neighbors had glimpsed the skulls under their own skins.

In the aftermath he had asked Lila to move in with him. She needed safety, stability, and had nowhere else to go. In doing so, the pair attempted to create some kind of functioning family unit from their mutual dysfunction. On the whole, it had been a positive experience, Tom trying to take his position as the girl's surrogate father, or at least uncle, as lightly as possible. They were a good fit; both damaged, both trying to move forward, hoping in doing so it would help the other. Keeping each other's demons at bay. For the present.

Lila was now taking A levels at Truro College. Tom still worked the bar at the Sail Makers pub in St. Petroc. Trying to live as normal a life as possible. He hoped it would last but suspected it wouldn't. In his experience nothing good did.

He was right.

IT HAPPENED BEFORE LUNCHTIME, before he was due to leave for work. A knock on the door. Tom was sitting in an armchair reading a book, listening to music, a mug of tea by his hand. He stood up, went to answer it. Heard a crow cawing outside.

"Mister . . . Killgannon?" The pause just long enough to inform him: I know your real name. And to give an implicit order: don't play games.

"Who are you?" A shudder went through Tom.

The stranger smiled, stepped aside. There were two of them, one man, one woman. Both wearing the kind of plainclothes that marked them out as just another uniformed branch of the police. The man held up his police ID. "Detective Sergeant Sheridan. And this is Detective Constable Blake." He gestured to the hallway. "May we?"

Tom knew he had no choice. He stood aside.

He followed them into the living room. Sheridan was tall, brown haired, gray suited. Neat looking, like a daytime TV host. Every centimeter the modern, management-trained police officer. Blake was smaller, more lithe, with dark bobbed hair. Her features, while plain, were remarkable. She had the blankness of film stars, gave nothing away, allowed a viewer to superimpose their own opinions on what she was thinking, read what they wanted to see. Good trick for a cop.

"Sit down," said Tom, pointing to the sofa.

They did as Tom turned the music off, sat back down in the armchair. Not wanting to speak first, knowing they were waiting for him to do so, that his question would be their way of gaining the upper hand. He had done it himself enough times.

Sheridan took a laptop out of his briefcase, opened it up. "I expect you're wondering why we're here, Mr. Killgannon?"

"The fishing? Very good this time of year."

Sheridan gave a brief smile. "In a manner of speaking, yes." He found what he wanted on the laptop, gave his full attention to Tom. Blake was looking round the room, making silent judgments.

Tom waited. He hadn't asked if they wanted tea. Neither had suggested it. This wasn't a social call.

Sheridan shot a quick glance round the room. "Nice place you've got here. Not everyone gets this kind of opportunity."

"The price is commensurate with what I was earning previously. Those are the rules. And you should know what I was earning since I was one of you lot. Plus I've put a lot of work into it."

"Yeah, and it's paid off. Very nice."

Tom felt anger rising within him. "Did you just come here to compliment my decor or did you want something else? And how d'you know I'm here?"

"Has your liaison officer talked to you, Mr. Killgannon?" Still saying his name but the tone changing, the pretense of the game slipping. Getting down to business.

"I'm kind of between liaison officers at the moment. I'm sure you know what happened to the last one."

Sheridan said nothing. He was well aware of the events of seven months ago.

"You stuck your head above the parapet," said Sheridan. "Could have been nasty. Left your new identity in tatters. All that work for nothing."

"Well you've found your way here. My identity seems to be an open secret." His anger rose a notch.

"You've been given a fair degree of leeway in the past. Had several blind eyes turned when perhaps they shouldn't have." Something crept into Sheridan's voice. Bitterness? Jealousy? Tom couldn't make it out. "You must have been quite an asset back in the day."

"Can't have been that good if you two have heard of me."

"We've been given your name by the department handling you." Sheridan gave a small laugh. "And you wouldn't believe the hoops we've had to jump through, the forms we've had to sign, the briefings we've had so Tom Killgannon doesn't get given away."

"So it should be. This is my life we're talking about here."

"Oh, absolutely. But you're still down as an active asset. As and when you're needed. And you're needed now, buddy."

Outside the crows continued to caw. This was the call he had always expected. Always dreaded. "What's the job?"

"Noel Cunningham. Know the name?"

Tom frowned, thinking. "Rings a bell."

"Convicted child murderer," said Blake. "Known as the Choirboy Killer because he was a choirmaster. Local to the southwest. Killed seven, but only five bodies have turned up. Won't say where the other two are."

"Until now," continued Sheridan.

"What d'you mean?"

"He's been making noises that he's ready to talk," said Blake.

Her tone of voice gave as much away as her features. "Ready to give up the locations of his final two victims. We want someone there to help him along."

"Why would he do that? Presumably he's never going to be let out so nothing he could say would make any difference."

"His mother's got cancer. The terminal kind. He wants to visit her, be there when she goes, he says. It would be too politically sensitive to let him do that, especially for the amount of time he wants. So we've suggested a bargain. The two dead bodies for the right to be with his mother."

Sheridan nodded. "We've tried getting people from our own team next to him undercover, but without success. They're too well known. Put half of them that's inside there."

"Inside being . . ."

"Blackmoor," said Blake. "Prison. Cunningham's a local boy. The bodies are buried somewhere on the moor. He requested a move to the prison. Said it would jog his memory. He's been there a while now. And nothing's changed."

"So we're going to put someone on the inside," said Sheridan. "Cunningham's not good with authority. Doesn't want to just come out and say it. Plus he's a tricky bastard. We thought it would be more likely for him to open up to one of his peers."

Prison . . . Tom's stomach lurched. He had previously worked undercover with criminals, in gangs . . . But not prison. He had drawn the line at that. Too confined, too easy for something to go wrong. To be found out. And if it did, he'd be stuck there. Or worse.

"Presumably you've read my file, or been briefed on me."

"Yes," said Sheridan.

"Then you'll know I don't do prison work. Never have."

"You've been given a lot of leeway in the past like DS Sheridan said," Blake's voice hardened. "You've had it easy here. Been left alone when someone else wouldn't have been. And that's OK. Give and take, isn't it? But you knew you'd have to pick up the tab one day."

"I don't do prison."

A ghost of a smile crossed Blake's face. "You do now."

"Don't worry," Sheridan said, trying to head off any further conflict, "we'll move you in at night so as not to arouse suspicion among the staff and inmates. Ghosting, it's called."

"Just a minute. The staff? They won't know why I'm there? Who I am?"

"The fewer people the better. Need to know only. I've read your file. That's how you've always chosen to operate. One person in control on the outside, you left on your own. Said it got you the best results."

Tom could say nothing. Sheridan had clearly read his file thoroughly.

"We'd provide you with a cover story, a good one that you'll be able to corroborate and stick to. We could even use this identity to give it a bit of extra reality. Then once you're inside, get close to Cunningham. Once he talks, your job is done. Relay the information to me, we'll get you out of there. Handshakes all round."

Tom thought before answering. "So *if* I do this . . ." He looked at Sheridan. From the expression on his face, Tom didn't think he had a choice. "The debt you mentioned."

"What do you mean?"

"I do this and I'm left alone? For good?"

Sheridan smiled, looked directly at him. "Obviously that decision isn't mine to make, but honestly? I don't see why not."

Tom sighed. He knew what Sheridan's words were worth. Had even been on the same training course that taught him how to lie to another person's face without giving himself away. The room felt claustrophobic, suddenly. Like he was already jailed. "When do I start?"

Blake stood up. Sheridan followed. "No time like the present."

And that was how Tom Killgannon ended up in HMP Blackmoor.

4

It was late afternoon but the darkening sky made it more like night. The sea wind hit the cliff tops around St. Petroc, announcing the arrival of November. The St. Petroc stone circle stood out against the flat horizon, dark gray on light. Lit only by the distant streetlights of the village, a sodium sunset on the horizon.

Two figures sat on a fallen stone, sharing a flashlight between them. The stone had been worn flat over the centuries. Local legend stated it was once used for sacrifices. During the madness seven months ago, it almost had been. Now Tom and Pearl sat there, huddled close. For warmth only, they would have both said had they been asked.

Tom had something to tell her.

"So why have we come up here, then?" Pearl laughed. "Crap idea for a date."

Tom didn't know how to reply. He pretended he hadn't heard her. Nominally she was his boss at the Sail Makers Arms, the pub he worked in. But over the months they had become more than employer and employee. What that was hadn't been fully explored. They weren't lovers but they were more than friends. There was a connection Tom had felt only rarely. Once that might have delighted him. Now the thought scared him.

"Neutral ground," he said. "You know what the pub's like for gossip."

She nodded. Their relationship was often a subject for speculation.

"So you've got something to tell me," she said. "That's what you said in the text. What's all this secretive stuff for?"

He sighed. Thought. Knew he had no option but to tell her straight. "I've got to go away for a bit."

She just stared at him. "Got to?"

"Got to."

"What d'you mean?"

He looked at the ground, checking for any remaining scorch marks in the grass from that night seven months ago. They were barely there. The seasons had covered them. He looked at her. She was very attractive, he thought. Slightly younger than him, dark hair kept quite short, intelligent eyes, a mouth ready to laugh. Trying not to let the recent past define her. She had become so important to his life. He didn't dare believe she would be thinking the same.

"I've got to go. You know my . . . background? How I ended up here?"

Pearl nodded. She was one of the two people he had told the truth to. The other being Lila.

"Well, as part of my deal with them I have to be on call. When they need me."

"And they need you now." Disappointment in her voice.

He nodded. "They've got a job for me." He turned to face her. "And they want you to have a place in it too."

"Me?"

"They've given me a cover story. I just need you to corroborate it for me. If anyone comes looking, you know."

"Might that happen?"

"I doubt it. But don't worry. I've been in touch with an old mate. He's going to be around to keep an eye on things. Just in case someone comes around trying to poke holes in the story."

Her eyes widened. She looked scared. "What the hell's going on? What are you talking about?"

"It's just a precaution, that's all. Standard procedure, the way I used to operate. I'm being doubly safe. It's silly, really. But I have to tell you. Please say if you'd rather not be part of it and they can think of something else."

"What is it?"

He told her. Blackmoor Prison. Noel Cunningham. His plausible cover story and her part in it. And how he would get it done as quickly as possible.

"I'll be back by Christmas. Promise."

"You'd better," she said, grateful for something she could cling to, "or you'll get the sack. Busiest time." She looked at the ground. Her voice became smaller. "I need you there." She tried to smile. It could have broken his heart. "Isn't it dangerous?"

He shook his head. "Not really. I just do what I'm supposed to, get out. Simple as that. It'll be fine. Honestly."

She stared at the ground. He was sure she wasn't looking for scorch marks.

"Never trust anyone who uses the word *honest*."

"Good advice," he said.

She shook her head. "It's just . . . it's a lot to take in. It's . . ." Another shake. "I don't know. It's like normal life has stopped suddenly. And now there's . . . this." She looked up at him, eyes direct, locking. "Do you really have to do it? Isn't there anyone else?"

"I don't know. I seem to be the best qualified, according to them. It's fine. The pub'll keep going."

"It's not the pub I'm worried about."

A wave crashed against the cliff behind them. The sea wind

intensified. She moved toward him. Tom stayed where he was. She took his hand in hers.

"Tom . . ."

"Why do we have to meet out here? Where it's freezing? What's wrong with the living room or the pub?"

They both turned, hands dropping. Lila stood behind them.

"I asked Lila to join us," said Tom. "She needs to know as well. Both of you do."

"Need to know what?" asked Lila. "What's all this about?"

Tom noticed a slight buzz of anger on her words. Was that because she had had to walk all the way to the stone circle or because Pearl was here too? Or was it something else?

"You two announcing your engagement or something? Should I buy a hat?"

Lila sat down on the stone. "Budge up, then. What's happening?"

"Come and join us," said Tom. He smiled but it dissipated quickly. "I wanted you here as well."

"It's freezing."

"OK, then." He looked between the two of them. His gaze settled on Lila. "I've told Pearl about this. Now it's your turn." He sighed, hesitant, as if his next words would make something notional real. Both to them and himself. "I've got to go away for a bit."

It looked like something had shuddered to a halt inside Lila. "Why? Where?"

"It's . . ." He leaned forward, concentrating on his hands rather than looking at either of them. "You know who I am. Or who I used to be." Lila looked like she was about to be told a loved one was terminally ill. Pearl looked like she'd just received the same information.

"I thought this might happen. I dreaded it, to be honest. And it seems I've got no choice."

Lila stared at him. "They're making you work again, aren't they? They've got you a job."

He nodded. "Undercover."

"But you've retired. You told me that."

"Yeah, I have. But I also told you that I have to be available when they want me. Price I pay for being left alone. After what happened here."

"That's not fair. Tell them no."

"I wish I could. I can't, it's not like that."

"Just tell them . . ." Anger and sadness fighting it out with Lila. It looked like a part of her was detaching, drifting away. Tom found it heartbreaking to watch.

"But you're coming back, aren't you? It's not going to be for long."

Tom smiled. "I'll be back as soon as I can. Believe me."

"For Christmas?"

"A long time before then." Hopefully, he thought.

"So where you going then?"

He told her. Everything he had just told Pearl. In as quiet and reasonable a voice as he could manage. Pearl watched Lila, checked her responses. Concern in her eyes.

Time passed. Eventually Lila looked up. "They won't let you in without a cover story. Have you got one?"

"He has," said Pearl. "It's me. A customer overstepped the line and Tom had to put him right."

Anger rose again in Lila. "When did all this happen? When did you decide this and why didn't you tell me earlier?"

"Pearl's just found out now. I had to check with her first, make sure she was OK with it." He glanced across at her. There was something heavy in that look. "Not everyone would have agreed to it. Thank you."

She shrugged, returning a gaze full of unsaid words.

Tom sat back. Looked at Lila. Reached for her hand. She pulled it away.

"No," she said. "Not yet. You don't get to do that yet."

"D'you want to ask me anything?"

Tom could see Lila was angry that he had told Pearl before her. Even if he did need to discuss it with her first. And annoyed at him keeping secrets from her. "Why didn't you tell me sooner?"

"It only happened this week. The plans were advanced before they brought me in. The cover story was already there. They just needed me and Pearl to fit around it. And I wanted to tell you in a place where no one could overhear. Both of you."

Lila tried to take it all in. Didn't reply.

"You're still going to be safe, still living in the house. Nothing's changed."

"Maybe I could move in as well," said Pearl. "Girls together. Might be fun. Or at least company. We could—"

Lila stood up.

"What's the matter?" asked Tom.

"Shut up," she said.

"But—"

"Just shut up." Tears welled in her eyes. She looked angry with herself for allowing that to happen. Tom knew she had felt safe, secure with him. For the first time in a long time. Possibly for as long as she could remember. And now, to her, this safety was gone.

Tom stood up too. Reached out to her. "Lila . . ."

"Leave me alone."

She turned and ran back toward the village, stumbling as her tears blinded her.

Tom and Pearl watched her go.

5

QUINT STEPPED BACK, admired his handiwork. The tent looked sturdy. As deeply pegged as he could manage, it wouldn't take off at the first gust of wind. It might even keep out some of the cold, and the inevitable rain. It was the first time he had pitched a tent for years and he was rather proud of himself.

Slaughter Tor was near the southeast of Blackmoor, all open land, rough rocky outcrops, and at least one standing stone. Quint was always surprised when he encountered something like that. A part of the past intruding into the modern world, reminding people that for all their Wi-Fi, electricity, and vehicles, their lives were brief. But stone, that would endure. Or maybe it was just him. He didn't get out into the country much.

Not that there was much in the way of Wi-Fi or electricity where he was. Quint felt more alone than he had in ages. He knew people came to the country for a break, for contemplation. But he couldn't have cared less. This wasn't a holiday, it was work. And until it was completed, that was all he would focus on.

He had read up on Blackmoor in advance. On where and when he could camp and park. Campsites were to be avoided. The sight of a single black man in a tent was liable to arouse suspicion, if not at the time then afterward. It was the way of remote places, of the kind of people they attracted. Hikers and campers liked camaraderie. Drinks and shared dinners, swapping stories. And they would overcompensate because of the color of his skin against theirs, try to be extra chummy, show they weren't racist by inviting him to join. They wouldn't keep in touch, though. Holidays were one thing, the rest of their lives quite another. He had experienced it before, the casual racism of the middle classes.

So he kept himself to himself. It suited his temperament, suited his needs. Suited the work. He wouldn't crop up in the memories of other campers. He had enough provisions for a few days. He had pitched his tent well away from the roads, out of most people's sight. He could be alone and wait.

Quint walked up to the brow of the hill he was camped under, put his binoculars to his eyes, looked around. Smiled.

There it was. In the distance, but not too far away.

The prison.

6

"KILLGANNON. GET YOUR THINGS TOGETHER. You're moving."

Tom had barely slept so the words didn't wake him. As soon as he lay down on the narrow, uncomfortable bed, the room seemed to get even smaller, the walls closing in. Fears ran around his head, fears he hadn't expected to experience.

The door is locked. What if there's a fire? Or some kind of catastrophe and I'm locked in here forever? What if they don't let me out? Or I'm rumbled and they decide to teach me a lesson?

On and on, his doubts spiraling and deepening, until he stuffed the thin, lumpy pillow into his mouth and stifled a scream.

Everyone has a fear, a defining phobia. Heights, snakes, spiders, illness, whatever. For Tom it was confined spaces. Closed, locked spaces. He'd been claustrophobic ever since he was a small boy. When his sister had taken him on shopping expeditions into Manchester city center, he had hated getting into department store elevators. Expecting them to break down and become suspended tombs as the air ran out, and no one came to save them. Crowding on to buses, trams, or tube trains had been an ordeal, closing his eyes and holding his breath, blocking his ears, and pretending to be anywhere but there. Even taking dares from other kids, to explore old, abandoned pipes and factories, in the wasteland beside the estate where he grew up. He'd always avoided it. But he didn't want anyone else to know, to see it as weakness, so he hit the first person to question his bravery, ensuring that no one else would.

Although he had tried to conquer his fear as he got older, his commando training brought it all back to him. On exercise with a full pack, trying to pull himself through caves and tunnels that he was barely able to squeeze inside without the pack. He tried to channel that fear, use it to motivate him, and hide from the others how terrified he was. Be a leader. And it had worked. This had taught him a valuable life lesson: no one knows what they're doing. Everyone just hides their fear and keeps going.

But now, after one night, those fears had returned. He wished he had never agreed to do this job. No matter the consequences.

It was too late for that now. As the prison officer stood at the door waiting for him, Tom struggled off the bed, his muscles aching from the prone calisthenic workout he had given his body instead of sleep.

"Get your stuff."

"Where am I going? I only just got here."

"This is the induction wing. You stay here till you've been properly allocated. Come on." Sighing as he spoke. Just one more thing on his to do list.

Tom complied, gathered up his meager belongings into trash bags once more, followed the officer out. Relieved to be stretching his legs, if only temporarily.

On the wing, the rest of the inmates were already up. Clad in regulation blue tracksuits, they were being herded to the kitchen to queue up for what smelled like the poor relation of hospital food and looked like slabs of beige stodge designed to keep them full, placid, and pliant. Or that was the theory. Once served their meal they would take their trays back to their cells to eat. And wait to see whether they would be allowed out for the morning jobs or education.

Tom looked at the queuing men but didn't make eye contact with any of them. He didn't want to be seen as issuing a challenge. The men came in all shapes and sizes, mostly with short hair, some with arms and faces full of spidery, homemade tattoos. Drug-sunken features, always-alert eyes, fear hiding behind the threat of violence in every movement.

Tom was led off the wing and through the prison, pausing at every gate, facing the wall, and waiting while the officer unlocked and then relocked as they went. He walked along corridors in silence, the officer's attitude discouraging him from questions or small talk. He used the time to process as much about his surroundings as possible. Orient himself.

His training kicked in: mentally checking for angles where he could be attacked, hallways where he wouldn't be safe, vantage points where he could defend himself if he had to. Committing the layout to his memory, or as much as he could manage.

As they walked the prison became older, like traveling back in time. Walls turned from painted plaster to old brickwork. Light fittings and wall outlets looked less integral to the architecture, more like later additions. The caging and gates they walked through looked overpainted, layered up to disguise and discourage any rust. Cell doors were heavily riveted, reinforced, immovable.

The officer led him up some metal stairs. Tom looked down to the level below. Netting partially obscured the view but he could see one or two track-suited prisoners carrying buckets and mops, pretending not to be interested in this new arrival.

"Here we go."

The officer stopped before a cell door, took out his keys. Tom glanced at the cell's whiteboard telling the name and number of the occupant.

"Cunningham."

Really? Was it that simple?

The officer opened the door. "Stand up, move away from your bed. Got some company for you."

Tom was ushered into the cell.

"Your new home," announced the officer.

Cunningham was on his feet. "I said I didn't want to share. Want to be on my own."

"And I want Beyoncé waiting for me when I get home. Can't always get what you want."

Anger blazed in Cunningham's eyes. "But I said—"

"Take it up with the warden." He walked back through the door, closed it behind him. The sound reverberated away to nothing.

Tom tamped down the rising fear inside him. Locked up again. He turned to Cunningham who was still staring at him.

"Who the fuck are you?"

7

CUNNINGHAM'S FISTS WERE CLENCHED, rage flaring. He was big, bulky. Thick arms, stout legs, but from the way his stomach undulated a few seconds after the rest of him, Tom guessed he hadn't been keeping up his exercise routine. His face was round and red, purple-veined, hair clipped short, stubbled chin, deep-set black eyes. Like an angry gooseberry past its best.

"I wanted to be on my own too," said Tom, unmoving, "but here we are."

Cunningham took a step toward him. Tom remained where he was. He was in better shape than Cunningham, but didn't have his rage. In a confrontation, that wouldn't necessarily be a bad thing. For emphasis he flexed his biceps, his chest. Cunningham didn't move.

The two stared at each other, Tom breathing quietly, Cunningham raggedly, wheezing. Maybe he'll die of a heart attack before he gets the chance to confess, thought Tom. Or even speak.

"Don't think we have much say in the matter," he continued.

Cunningham didn't reply.

"But I've just arrived and I've been put in here. I'm on Enhanced. I worked hard for that. And I'm not going to lose it for anyone." Tom opened his arms. "So give it your best shot, big boy. Here I am."

Cunningham stared, but Tom's words had penetrated. The fire

burned out of his eyes. He looked away, around the cell. Trying to find some way to back down yet still save face.

"Just . . . stay away from me." The words gurgled out quietly. Drained away. Cunningham's mood seemed to have changed completely. Where there had been anger, all Tom could see was wariness, fear perhaps.

Tom regarded him quizzically, noting the change. As if Cunningham's anger had been a learned response from being inside. If in doubt, confront.

"But I still have the top bunk." Sullenly, like a stroppy child.

Tom didn't want to argue. "Your call, mate. You've been here longest."

Cunningham nodded, honor seemingly satisfied.

The Choirmaster Killer. That's what the tabloids had dubbed Noel Cunningham. And they had played that up in every photo they printed. Round faced, cherubic, like the stereotype of an overgrown choirboy. Living with his aged mother. Dressed and groomed by her, by the look of him. Bowl cut and bow tie. Photographs published and studied. Everyone looking for evil behind the jowls.

Tom didn't recognize his new cellmate from the person the tabloids claimed he had been. It was as though being caught had stripped him of whatever camouflage he had used to exist in the real world, sloughing that skin, revealing the pathetic individual underneath. More damaged than dangerous.

He had started by abusing boys in a cathedral choir in Devon. A figure of respect in the local community, an odd one, but nevertheless thought of as harmless. Then children in the area started to go missing. The children were never from the choir. Too dangerous for him to do that. Too many questions asked. But the church did outreach in the local community. And that involved taking under-privileged kids away for weekends and during school holidays. Usually camping on Blackmoor. That was when he had first met them, sized them up. Moved in with a predator's cunning. Picked off the weak, the fragile, the not easily missed. From there, simply befriend them, see them back in town, tell them about other trips to Blackmoor if they were interested. Then take them away with him. Never to be seen again.

The local police eventually put together a pattern that trapped Cunningham. He admitted his crimes, confessed easily, but still refused to say where the bodies were. Or how many there were. But he had always tried to be friendly with men who fit Tom's description. Tall, rugged.

"Always looking for a father figure, according to the psychological profile," Sheridan had told Tom. "To replace the one he never had. You fit the bill. You should be just his type, so to speak."

The tension in the cell had eased. Tom placed his bags on the floor, pointed to the wall. "This shelf mine?"

Cunningham shrugged.

Tom opened his bag, began to unpack. It didn't take him long. Clearly Cunningham was on Enhanced too, having the privileges that came from playing along with the rules. Color TV. PlayStation. A shelf of toiletries. A framed photo of an older woman, smiling.

"That your mother?" said Tom, unpacking his own toiletries.

Cunningham nodded, grunted.

"She looks happy."

Cunningham didn't reply. He had decorated the area around his bed with pictures torn from magazines and newspapers. They were all of beautiful boys who seemed younger than eighteen. Apart from their posing and pouting they had two other things in common. They had crude, swan-like wings drawn on their backs. And their eyes had been clipped out. They looked like dead-eyed angels.

Unnerved, Tom looked away, unpacked a couple of books, placed them spine out next to his toiletries. Took out some underwear, spare joggers, the shirt and suit he had been wearing when he entered the prison. Folded them all up, found a drawer for them. All the while Cunningham pretended not to watch him.

Finally he took out a framed photo of himself and Lila, placed that on the desk by the bed. Cunningham became interested then, couldn't help himself. Tom saw him staring at the photo, unblinking.

"Who's that? Daughter?"

"Niece," said Tom. "She lives with me."

"Does she now." Cunningham didn't—couldn't—hide the leer on his face.

Tom stared at him. "Yeah. She does." The tone of his voice warned Cunningham not to pursue that train of thought. Cunningham complied. At least outwardly. Tom sat down on his bunk. "How long you been here?"

Cunningham grunted. "Six months. She looks very young."

Tom ignored the comment. Wondered instead about the etiquette of asking other prisoners what their crime was. Before he could speak, that decision was taken away from him.

"What are you in for, then?" Cunningham leaned forward.

"Actual bodily harm."

"How come?" Cunningham's expression changed. Like he was waiting to be told a story.

Tom obliged. "I work in a pub. Customer got too handy with my boss. Had to be taught a lesson."

Something crept across Cunningham's face. Tom couldn't describe it. "How handy?"

"Very handy," said Tom in a voice meant to discourage any further investigation. It didn't.

"You mean like trying to . . . you know?"

Tom didn't answer. Cunningham took his silence for agreement, became more excited. "How far did he get?" Then he shook his head as if to dislodge the thoughts growing there. "No, no . . . don't . . . no . . ." He looked up. "Did he get his hands on her . . ."

He couldn't say the words, gestured to his chest, mimed breasts. "Did he?"

Tom stared at him.

"No," said Cunningham, once more, to himself, "No. That's wrong. Don't think it. Don't think about the, the dirty things . . ." His face contorted, struggling. He looked up, a lascivious smile in place. "Then what? Did he force her down?" He clamped his hand over his mouth, eyes wide, as if he couldn't believe what he had just said. "No, it's not right . . . You've been told, Noel, been told . . . you know what happens if you have those kind of thoughts . . ." His voice had changed. Become older, more feminine. He closed his eyes, shook his head once more. Leaned forward, body rocking to and fro. Opened his eyes only when he had finished violently shaking his head. His voice dropped low, scared to say the next words aloud but also defiant. He gave Tom a long, leering smile. "Did he fuck her?"

Years undercover had taught Tom to stay in character, play along with the target rather than impose his own values on a situation. Out of practice, he thought. He swallowed down his revulsion, tried to ignore the thought that this face was the last thing Cunningham's victims ever saw. Kept his eyes hard, his cover intact.

"No one fucks her but me. He learned that the hard way."

His tone of voice had clearly been authoritative enough. Cunningham backed down from any more questions.

"What about you?" The ice was well and truly broken.

Cunningham made a noise that sounded like liquid gravel on the move, but Tom realized it was a laugh. "You don't know me?"

"Should I?"

"You should. Famous, aren't I?"

"Tell me, then."

"I'm a murderer." Cunningham simpered, his eyes shining. Like a child trying to impress by saying the worst thing imaginable.

"Right." Tom's face was as still as stone.

Cunningham looked deflated. Expecting a bigger reaction from Tom. "Who'd you kill, then?"

Cunningham's features became evasive. "Well, that's the thing. That's what they all call me. Murderer. Here. On the wing. Murderer." Said in an angry whisper, followed by a giggle. "Keeps them away from me. Let's me be on my own." He did it again. "Murderer . . . Don't go near him, he might murder you too . . ." Another laugh. "They leave me alone then. Scared. Scared of me."

Tom had seen the other inmates. Cunningham was deluding himself if he thought they were scared of him. He could imagine them leaving him alone, though. Too irritating to bother with.

"So you're not a murderer?"

Cunningham's expression changed again. Sharply. Tom couldn't gauge what it meant but something behind his eyes unnerved him. "Oh, I'm much more than that. Much more . . ."

"Like what?"

Cunningham shook his head, a blissfully sick look on his face. "You wouldn't understand. It's . . . you just wouldn't."

He took his attention away from Tom, went back to the photo of Lila. Stared at it. "You wouldn't understand . . ."

Tom's first impulse was to jump up, hide it. Then smack Cunningham on the head. But he tamped it down. Kept in character.

"So why aren't you on the VP wing?"

Vulnerable prisoners were housed on a separate wing. Usually child killers or pedophiles but not exclusively. Anyone whose life was in danger, a suicide risk or even an ex-cop, they were all put in there.

Cunningham smiled as if he knew something Tom didn't. "Who knows? Maybe they want someone to hurt me here." He leaned forward. "Are you going to hurt me?"

The sick light in Cunningham's eyes told Tom that he might not find that so unappealing.

Tom ignored him, took a paperback out of his bag, lay back on his bunk.

Cunningham just giggled.

Silence fell. Following his outburst Cunningham zoned out, sat slumped, staring at Tom's photo of Lila, a smile twisting the corners of his mouth. He began to sing to himself. Tom couldn't identify it but knew it was something holy. Something befitting an ex-choirmaster.

Tom tried to read but his mind was whirring too much.

8

DEAN FOLEY CLOSED HIS EYES. Tried to relax. Or relax as much as he ever could. Sentries were posted, guards paid off, no one could get to him. No one would dare. But still, the rational part of his brain was telling the other half that this would be the perfect opportunity to attack him. With his guard down. With everything down. The other half of his brain told him to chill. Enjoy it. He tried to listen to that side of his brain. But it didn't really matter. Because at present, a completely different part of his anatomy was doing the thinking.

He opened his eyes, looked down. Kim was doing a grand job. Working his cock with her mouth and hand like a pro, head bobbing up and down like she was nodding to the beat of something only she could hear. She was half in, half out of her prison officer's uniform, enough that she could pull it together if she needed to, but also enough for him to see her magnificent tits as she worked.

Or magnificent for in here. Maybe on the outside he wouldn't look at her twice. A five or a six, probably. But in here everything changed. In here she was a ten. Prison did that to people.

He felt his legs stiffening, breathing becoming harder, harsher. He was coming. Kim sensed it too, bobbed, pulled quicker. Building him up until he couldn't hold it anymore.

He came, gasping and grunting. Kim tried to pull away, get her face, her mouth out of shooting distance, but he was having none of it. He forced her head down onto his cock, pushed his body up toward her as he bucked and spasmed.

Eventually the wave passed and his body eased, moving his hand from her head. She fell backward, red-faced, gasping for breath, chin and mouth wet. He looked down at her, slumped with her tits hanging out, anger, shame, self-loathing in her averted eyes. Christ, what did he see in her? Was she really the best he could do?

He knew the answer to that one.

She stood up, crossed to the sink, rinsed her mouth out, began to gather her uniform around her.

"How's Damon doing?"

"Fine," she said.

"Did you get him into that special school?"

She nodded. "Thanks," she said, eyes not going anywhere near his. "For the money."

He sniffed, sat up. Wiped himself off with a tissue, pulled his jeans back up. "When you next on?"

"Got two days off. Back on Thursday."

"See you then."

She crossed to the closed cell door, knocked. It was pushed inward from the outside. She stepped over the threshold and was gone.

Foley stood up. Got his breath back, sniffed once more. "Baz."

The door opened and a young man stepped inside. In another life he might have been good-looking but not in this one. His face looked like it had suffered severe punishment. His nose had been broken so many times it looked like a useless appendage. His skin was flecked with healed cuts and scars and there was a strange symmetry about his features, like one side was a perfect but unnatural mirror of the other. Despite the damage his once handsome features could still be glimpsed underneath. His face was a road map of where he had been, the underlying handsomeness the path not taken.

"Close the door," said Foley, sitting down in a wooden chair.

The cell was well equipped. A large screen TV in the corner, curtains at the window. The mattress and duvet were a long way from standard prison issue and there was framed artwork on the walls. It wasn't very good art, all landscapes and sunsets, but it was original and it was all signed in the bottom right corner: D. Foley.

Baz stood, waited.

"Everything all right out there?"

"Yes, boss."

"No problems while she was in here?"

"No, boss."

"Good." Foley relaxed. But only slightly. Baz was the best right-hand man he'd ever had. But in prison everyone was vulnerable to attack. "How's business?"

Baz crossed to the table the TV stood on, emptied his pockets. Grubby, creased, screwed-up dollar bills fell out, a few coins. He straightened the bills out, piled up the coins. Foley looked across.

"Hardly worth bothering. But every little bit helps. The next shipment should be in a couple of days. Keep it quiet, I don't want anyone getting tipped off again. Hopefully we've scared off the opposition."

Controlling the supply of drugs in a prison was like controlling the air they all breathed. Everybody wanted it so there was a demand, which was good. But nearly everybody had a way of getting it, which meant there was more than one method of supply, and that made Foley's job even more difficult.

Supply was easy, especially with drones cutting out the hassle of the mules, no longer running the gauntlet of sniffer dogs and body searches, but as he knew, it meant anyone could do it. So if he was to hold on to his monopoly, he had to do it the old-fashioned way. Put the fear of God into them. God being him. And Baz, his representative, who carried out the Lord's work.

When he arrived he had let it be known that he was in charge.

And if anyone didn't like that they could challenge him. But he came inside with money and favors owing and challengers were few and doomed. Now it was well known that no drugs entered the prison without his say so. But that didn't mean everyone stuck to that rule: he still had to get his foot soldiers to teach a lesson or two.

He looked at the pile of money. It was dwindling, no doubt. It always got like that before a new shipment came in. And then it was boom time again. The fact that the prison was privately run helped Foley immeasurably. The entry requirements for these officers were lower than state ones and they consequently attracted a lower quality of officer. Easier to manipulate, bribe. Corrupt.

It was no bother to have a hole cut in a security fence and send one of his runners to the perimeter to pick up packages droned and dropped there. The private officers didn't have the training or the pride in their work. It was easy to get them to look the other way. Or just to have stuff droned right to the cell window. Even better.

Foley had contacts all the way up the northwest to Manchester, which meant he was able to source and supply high quality product. Demands and tastes changed. He was happy to accommodate them. Where it would have been heroin and weed a few years ago, now it was spice, black mamba, and the bastard daddy of them all, annihilation. Super strong synthetic cannabis, that didn't just mellow you out, it sent the user on a psychotic trip. True escape for the mind, even if it was often difficult to come back from. They weren't called zombie drugs for nothing.

Yeah, it fucked people up, but so what? Foley only cared about profits. And that was something he needed now, more than ever.

A knock on the door.

Both Foley and Baz turned. Foley stayed where he was, but Baz moved to the side of the doorway, fists ready. They shared a look. Foley nodded.

"Yeah?" said Foley.

"Someone to see you."

"Who?"

A pause. "Says his name's Clive. Got something for you."

Foley frowned. Did he know a Clive? He searched his memory. Clive . . .

The only Clive he knew was some greasy little scrote from Oldham.

Foley sighed. "Send him in."

The door opened and a hunched little weasel of a man entered. "Hello, Mr. Foley," he said, hands wringing as if holding a cap in Dickensian times, "how are you?"

"All the better for seeing you, Clive. What d'you want?"

Clive smiled, missing the sarcasm. Then he noticed Baz. Frowned, trying to look beyond the ruined face. "I know you, don't I?"

Baz stared at him. Unnerved, Clive turned back to Foley.

"I've . . . I've got something for you, Mr. Foley. Something you're going to like very much."

"What?" A statement rather than a question.

"Well. You'll never guess who I've seen coming into this prison . . ."

9

The cottage was small, but Lila thought it felt even smaller when Tom wasn't there to share it with her. Stifling, even.

She had been studying stuff like that in her Psychology A Level at Truro College so she knew why it was. The same reason that unhappy people don't become miraculously happy when they move somewhere new. They don't change as people. They just take their unaddressed problems with them. That was how it was without Tom to distract her. She was alone with herself and her thoughts. Her doubts, guilt, and fears. And they grew to fill the space. Or the space contracted around them.

That was why she had been so angry when he announced he was going away. Or one of the reasons.

Things had calmed between them before he left. She began to accept what he had to do. Knew he was only doing it reluctantly. He also knew how much he had hurt her by having to go. But he had no choice, and deep down she knew that.

So now she was alone. She hadn't really made any new friends at college. Unsurprising, given what she had been previously. The fact she had turned her life around to attend college at all was astounding enough. Tom had encouraged her to think that what she had endured wouldn't happen again and she could look to the future with confidence. She wasn't sure she believed him—or that he believed it himself—but she was trying. And struggling. Her peers at college all seemed so happy and sure of themselves, their world, their place within it, and their life maps, unaware that things could take a sudden turn for the worse and those rock-solid beliefs could come crashing down. She couldn't be like them, think like them, feel like them. "Just do your best under your own terms," Tom had said. "And if you're worried about not fitting in, just pretend you do. That's what they're all doing. You might not think it but they are. Everyone does it. If there's a secret to life, that's it. Fake it till you make it." So she tried. It had been difficult. Now even more so in his absence.

Meeting Tom had changed her life. And, although she had felt she was being presumptuous, or even tempting fate, she had taken his surname for college enrollment.

"I never found out what your real one is," he had said.

"Killgannon," she had said, smiling. "Like yours."

He had understood.

She made herself a cup of tea, looked out the back window. Autumn had dismantled summer, leaving drifts of wilted leaves and carpets of rotten flowerheads around the garden. Leave it all on the ground, Tom had said. Good compost. Make things grow bigger and stronger come the spring. Lila had dutifully done so, watched as those beautifully lush green branches turned into spider scrawl against the heavy gray sky, waited for those green buds to return. But for now it was the quiet period before the end of the year and winter fully hit, the earth gone into lockdown.

The water boiled, the kettle clicked. She turned away, took a tea bag from the jar in the cupboard.

A knock at the door.

Lila couldn't stop the involuntary shiver that ran through her. No matter how comfortable she got in this place, there was always that threat of a knock at the door. It had happened to Tom. She feared that she would be next.

Another knock.

She turned, headed down the hall. Took a deep breath. Opened the door.

"Just me."

Lila smiled in relief. Another bullet dodged.

"Hi, Pearl."

"I was just passing and . . ." Pearl stopped speaking. "No I wasn't actually. I came to see you."

Lila stood back, let the other woman through. "I was just making a cup of tea."

"Brilliant timing."

They both made their way to the kitchen. Lila took out another mug, another bag. Poured in the water. Tea made, she took it to the table. Pearl had already taken off her coat, sat down.

"Thanks."

Pearl was over ten years older than Lila, with dark hair where Lila's was mousy blond, smart jeans as opposed to Lila's attempts to bring back grunge, and with a poise and self-confidence Lila thought she could never hope to emulate. But the woman was Tom's boss, perhaps more. And they had been through a lot together.

"How you coping?" asked Pearl.

"Fine," said Lila, sitting down opposite her. While it was true that they had shared a lot, Lila was still wary of opening up to her.

"You heard from him?"

Lila shook her head.

"Me neither." Pearl took an experimental sip of her tea, found it too hot, placed it back on the table. "He said it might be difficult."

They sat there in silence. Both, for their own reasons, not wanting to be the first to speak.

"Look," said Pearl, "That offer still stands. Me moving in here."

Tom had asked her again before he left. She had told him she would be fine on her own. Neither had believed her.

"Did Tom ask you to come round?"

"He just wants me to keep an eye on you."

Lila felt anger building inside her at Pearl's words. "What does he expect me to do? Have wild parties? Get into trouble? Run away again?"

Pearl shook her head slowly. Her voice was low, calm. "He was worried about you out here on your own. Just wanted to make sure you were looking after yourself." She smiled. "That you weren't just eating pizza and burgers and drinking Coke all the time."

Lila felt herself redden with a kind of angry amusement. "He said that? Those words?"

Pearl laughed. "Yeah. Is that code, or something?"

Lila smiled. It was the last thing he had said to her before he left. They had gone through the anger and heartache, tried to come out the other side and joke about it. No pizza and burgers and drinking coke all the time. And no boys in your room after ten thirty. Yes sir, she had replied, giving him a mock salute in response. "That's all he said?" she asked.

Pearl shrugged. "Something about boys as well."

"Right."

"I didn't think you needed to hear that bit."

"It's OK. He's already given me that speech."

"Right. But how are you holding up, really?"

Lila took a sip of tea. It was still too hot, but she wanted to drink it anyway. A psychological thing, she thought. "OK. I'm used to looking after myself."

"I know you are. But that's not what I meant. And I don't think it's what he meant, either. He just wanted to make sure you felt safe here." Pearl paused, looked straight at Lila. Hoping her unspoken words would be understood.

They were. Lila had been in trouble when she met Tom. And despite his insistence that those troubles were gone, she still woke up screaming at the things she had done to gain her freedom. The nightmares had become less and less frequent as time went on, but they hadn't completely left her alone.

"I'm OK," said Lila then felt something else was needed. "But thank you."

"No worries." Pearl looked round the kitchen, clearly thinking. She found her tea, drank. "Listen. I've been thinking. Instead of you being here on your own, you could move into the pub with me." Pearl looked at Lila expectantly. Lila said nothing. Pearl continued. "There's plenty of space since Mum and Dad moved out."

Pearl tried to keep her voice as neutral as possible while she said those names, but Lila knew what kind of pain was behind those words. At that moment, she felt a kind of kinship with her. A sisterhood of pain and disappointment. Of being let down by those you should have been able to trust absolutely.

Pearl continued. "I mean, you're on your own with no one to talk to—"

"I want to stay here. This is my home. This is where I live."

Pearl nodded. "Fair enough. OK. I understand." She looked round the kitchen once more. "But you know, it's not just you. On your own, I mean. I am as well."

Lila looked at her curiously.

"I miss him. Lots." She reddened. "He's my friend too, you know." She placed a strange emphasis on the word *friend*. "And it's lonely in the pub without Mum and Dad around. And him especially."

Lila knew what she was saying. For the first time since she had met this woman, Lila felt as though she understood her.

"I said I don't want to move into the pub."

Pearl nodded. "Right. Sure." Head downcast.

"But . . . you could move in here if you like."

Pearl looked up at her. Smiled.

Lila felt her own cheeks redden. "I mean, just while he's away. For company. And that. You know. Like you said. Safer together."

"That's great. Girls' nights in. Drinking tea, watch Netflix. Whatever."

"You'll be lucky to get Netflix here," Lila told her. "We barely have electricity."

Pearl laughed. "Thank you. Look, I know you're still not sure about me, for whatever reason, because of what happened, and yeah, I understand that. But . . ." She sighed. Continued. "We're on the same side. Always have been."

Lila looked at Pearl over the table. Remembered what Tom had said about looking to the future with confidence, trusting things to grow again.

"It gets cold. Better bring some warm sweaters. And some wood for the burner."

Pearl smiled. "Deal."

"And some box sets." Lila smiled too. "Got to find some way to fill these long, dark winter evenings."

"You can count on it."

They both drank their tea. And chatted. Like new friends just getting to know each other.

10

THE DOE WAS LINED UP PERFECTLY. Grazing, away from the rest of the herd, which was usual in this cold weather. Just walking in the woods, coming in and out of the trees, head down looking for food. Then a few quick upward jerks, around, left, right, then, satisfied she was alone, back to foraging.

Quint had spent most of the morning waiting. He had built a blind for himself out of ferns, twigs, and branches. Now he sat inside, unmoving, barely breathing. Wearing his weather-resistant camo gear. Just watching. Waiting. Like he had been trained to do.

Looking down the Schmidt and Bender scope atop his Tikka T3x Hunter. Perfect in low light, which was all there was in this winter forest, even in the middle of the day. It had a range of nearly a quarter of a mile and he was well practiced in its use. Nothing escaped him when he was hunting.

He looked at the deer once more. Lined her up in his sights. That thin black cross, its apex coming to rest on her neck, then moved up ever so slightly, gently, to rest on her head, just behind the ear . . . a clean shot—only one—and it would be over for her. The sound would ring out around the forest, scare away birds, other deer, but it would echo away to nothing. Fading as quickly as the deer's life. Just one shot.

His finger tightened on the trigger.

Just one shot . . .

He took his finger away. Breathed in deeply. Not today. She was lucky. She would live. Go back to the herd, her children, oblivious to how close she had come to the end of her life.

Quint still watched her. Observed her movements. A hunter could learn more about their prey by watching them than by killing them. It made the conclusion of the hunt more satisfying, more complete. A single bullet wasn't always the correct way to do things. Each hunt was individual, it called for an individual kill. Some called for involvement, some for distance. Some led to that incomparable feeling of emotional nourishment, others, unfortunately, not. Most of them didn't, if he was honest. But that didn't stop him hunting. It just made that rarefied high all the more intense when he finally experienced it. And that was what drove him on.

Sometimes, like today, it wasn't necessary to kill. It was enough just to know that he could, that the power of life and death was within him, to use when he wanted to.

A gust of cold wind blew through the forest, moving debris on the forest floor, the branches in the trees. The doe looked round, suddenly skittish. As if sensing her own vulnerability, she turned, moved quickly back to the rest of the herd. Quint took his eye away from the sight. Looked up. Rain was on the wind, slanting in toward him, hitting him side on.

He stood up. There was nothing else to be gained from sitting here now. He had proven his point to himself, and anyway, the moment was broken. Slinging his rifle over his shoulder, he walked back to his tent.

He completed his security tests to ensure no one had tampered with anything. He examined his motorbike. No one had touched it. He walked all around the tent, checking that the patterns of branches and twigs he had arranged hadn't been disturbed. They were still intact. Then finally, he opened the tent. Inside was everything he needed to survive in the wild. The large metal box was still locked. He took the key from around his neck, opened it, inspected its contents. Two handguns. One assault rifle. Ammunition. It was all there. And a manila folder on top. He took the folder out, lay the contents on the bed. Two photographs with names attached. He placed them side by side, studied them.

Pearl Ellacott.

Lila Killgannon.

He nodded to himself, gathered up the written information that went along with them. Read it once more, familiarizing himself with it. Then, once he was sure it had sunk in, he picked everything up, put it back in the file, placed the file back in the box, and locked it.

The rain hit the outside of the tent like hard pellets fired from an air rifle. Quint was hungry. Thirsty. He took out the camping stove, went about making himself something to eat and drink.

Once more way of measuring out time's passing.

II

NIGHT FELL EARLY IN PRISON, at any time of year. The thick brick walls and tiny barred windows on Tom's wing made daylight's attempts to penetrate feeble so its absence wasn't greeted with much fanfare. If it hadn't been for a certain shift in the attitudes of the inmates, the passing of time would have gone unnoticed. Even in the short while Tom had been inside he had noticed it. The same shift animals feel at the zoo after the visitors have stopped staring and left. A collective stillness, not calming or tranquil but tense, coiled. A tightening of muscles, a hardening of features. Eyes looking beyond what could be seen. The inevitable realization that, assuming you'd been allowed out of your cell that day, your tiny bit of freedom was about to be taken away. The cell doors would once again be locked, and you would be back on the wrong side. And when the lights went out, the talking stopped, the cries and shouts died down, you would lie there, locked in the even deeper prison of your own head, alone with only your thoughts, emotions, and fears for company.

Tom understood why there were such high rates of mental illness among prison inmates.

He looked out of his cell window. Blackmoor stretched out onto the horizon, uninviting and bleak. The perfect place to build a prison. Just looking outside was an escape deterrent. A challenge:

Think prison's tough? Get out and come and meet me. A direct coun-
terpoint to his claustrophobic cell. But no less frightening.

He turned away. Cunningham lay on his bunk. The cell door
was open, and out on the wing other inmates were having their
evening association time. Tom had decided not to join in.

THE DAY HAD BEEN ALL ABOUT HIS INDUCTION. Tom, as part of a
group of new inmates, had sat through lectures and presentations
about prison rules, behavioral guidelines, visiting information,
and the courses that were on offer. Cleaning, cooking, business
accounting, none of these appealed to him. He filled in a questionnaire for the education department listing his qualifications
and what he might want to study while he was there.

The irritating inmate from the Sweatbox, Clive, had been in
Tom's group. He had tried to attract Tom's attention, nodding and
waving. Tom had replied with a stoic nod, but Clive persisted. He
contrived to sit next to him through it all.

"Thought that was you, Thor. How you settling in?"

"Fine."

"What wing you on?"

"Not sure yet." Something about the man made Tom not want
to trust him.

"I'm on Heath." He shrugged. "Not bad. Least it's one of the
newer ones."

Tom said nothing. Clive, trying to break the silence again,
looked down at the questionnaire Tom was filling in.

"Know what you want to do, mate?"

"What?" Tom hoped his irritation was showing.

"Put down art. That's a good one in here. Lot of privileges
attached to that. Trust me, it's worth it."

Tom just stared at him.

"It's good, mate, makes the days go quicker. Very therapeutic. And there's competitions. National ones. You can win things. Get out for the day. Get some decent food."

Tom ignored him. Put down astronomy instead, looked at Clive, a challenge in his eyes.

Clive couldn't look directly back at him. His eyes dropped away. Tom relaxed, placed his pen on the table. Clive quickly picked it up and, too fast for Tom to stop him, ticked the box for art on Tom's questionnaire. Tom stared at him.

Clive gave a simpering smile. "Trust me, you . . . you'll want to do it." Nodding, desperate to be believed.

Tom didn't know what Clive's game was but didn't have time to do anything about it. The questionnaires were collected. Clive slunk away back to his own seat.

"See you later," he said.

Tom stared at him, wondering what had just happened.

Rounding the day off was a visit to the prison chaplaincy where a vicar talked to them. He had short gray hair and a wide smile on his weathered, suntanned face. His shirt fastened at the cuffs but didn't hide his tattoos or his well-muscled frame. Ex-army or ex-biker, was Tom's guess. He explained about religion in prison, how all the major ones were catered for. Tom knew that. Also knew how inmates had miraculous conversions if it meant extra time out of their cells on Sundays.

After that Tom was returned to the wing. With Cunningham away doing whatever it was he did during the day, Tom went back to his cell. He tried to make use of the time, so he went through Cunningham's belongings. There wasn't much there. Toiletries, clothing, underwear. All prison issue. A couple of well-worn tabloids left on his bunk, crosswords attempted with letters heavily gone over and altered. No books or magazines. No notebooks, diaries, letters. Nothing. Tom had more stuff with him.

He lay back on his own bunk, thought of home. Of Lila and Pearl. Hoped they were looking after each other. Tried not to miss them too much, told himself it wouldn't be long before they saw him again.

Tried to make himself believe it.

Tom turned away from the window. Cunningham still lay on his bunk, eyes staring at his wall of angels, lips moving with words only he could hear, reciting prayers or hymns to them. He looked again at the open cell door, went out on to the wing.

It was what he had expected it to be. Victorian, he guessed. All worn red brick and heavy metal pipes. Small barred windows looked out onto darkness. The top level that he was on was separated by a metal walkway and landing. A net strung between it and the ground floor.

Men milled about in gray or maroon joggers and sweats, chatting with others. Broken features, wounded eyes hardened with cataracts of fear and violence. All sizing Tom up, giving him a provisional place in the wing hierarchy.

Someone nodded at him. He nodded back. Another couple looked up from the game of cards they were playing as he passed. One bald and covered in tattoos crafted by an artist more enthusiastic than talented, the other tall with graying blond dreadlocks.

"Just got in?" the tattooed one asked him.

Tom nodded. "Overnight yesterday."

The dreadlocked guy looked toward the cell Tom had just left. "Put you in with him, have they? Moaning Myrtle?"

"What d'you mean?"

They smiled between them. The dreadlocked one's teeth looked like they had all been knocked out and reinserted in a random order. "You'll see. Well, you'll hear." Another look around then, as if by secret, tacit agreement, Tom was asked if he wanted to join the game.

"Yeah." He pulled up a chair, sat with them. He wasn't a natural card player, had always dismissed it in the army as a waste of time, but he knew how important it was now. Bonding, sizing each other up. Isolation on the wing could be dangerous.

They asked him questions, he stuck to his script. He asked them questions in return and received equally rehearsed replies. Life stories edited down to short stories, learned off by heart. Painful pasts minted into polished anecdotes. He didn't learn anything of interest but it did him no harm to mix.

He watched the steady stream of inmates queuing to use the wing phone, wondered whether he should call home as well. Decided not to. Lila would be missing him. He was missing her too. And he didn't think it would help to be reminded of the outside world. Not just yet. So he stayed with the card players.

Eventually it was time for lockup. They all got up, and with a minimum of argument, went back to their cells. Tom did the same.

The door slammed shut. Echoed away to nothing. Tom sat down on his bunk.

"Where'd you go?" asked Cunningham.

"Onto the wing for a look round."

Cunningham grunted, turned toward the wall.

"Didn't want to join me?"

Cunningham grunted. "Nothing out there for me. Nobody I want to talk to."

"Because they're scared of a murderer?"

Cunningham didn't answer.

"Just thought it might pass the time. Make things go quicker."

"Things don't go quicker or slower," Cunningham told him. "Things are what they are."

Tom detected a quaver in Cunningham's voice. He dismissed it, picked up his book to read.

"I'm going to read till the lights go off," said Tom. "Good night."
Cunningham didn't reply.

It wasn't long before the cell was in sudden darkness. It took Tom by surprise, but Cunningham audibly gasped. His breathing became heavier, more agitated. Tom closed his eyes. Tried to go to sleep.

THE WHIMPERING AND SOBBING WOKE HIM. He had no way of knowing what time it was, how long he had been asleep. From the uncomfortable position of his neck and the heaviness of his eyes, he didn't think it had been too long. Cunningham was thrashing about on the bunk above.

Tom had no idea if the other man was asleep or awake but he knew now why the other inmates had called him Moaning Myrtle. Tom closed his eyes, tried to ignore him. But all he could hear was Cunningham's crying, his pleading with whoever was in the dark with him to go away, leave him alone.

Tom again tried to tune out.

As he eventually drifted off into a disturbed, uncomfortable sleep, a thought struck him: how long would he be in here before his own night terrors struck?

12

THE COLD CUT THROUGH TOM as he made his way along the paved path. He pulled his sweatshirt around him, turned up the collar on his cheap denim jacket. Mist had settled all around. He could barely see as far as the razor-wire-topped high fences, certainly no further. The prison looked foreboding and abandoned. A sprawling old mansion ripe for a haunting.

He was among a group of prisoners being escorted to the education block, ready for the day's lessons. Two officers hurried along with them, clearly wanting to be done as soon as possible, to get back on the wing with a hot cup of tea inside them. The weather stopped much conversation. Tom liked it that way.

Most of the men he had seen and spoken to the night before were there. He seemed to have been accepted by them, or was at least on friendly nodding terms. Good. He didn't need any unnecessary complications.

The dreadlocked guy, Darren, walked alongside him.

"Moaning Myrtle keep you awake?" he asked, displaying his random teeth.

"You could say that."

Darren laughed. "Say the word, mate, and he's taken care of." He tapped the side of his nose. "For a price, mind."

Tom tried to smile. "I don't think it's come to that. Yet."

Darren shrugged. "Whatever. You'll get a good night's sleep, 's'all I'm saying. Important thing in here."

Tom smiled. "I'll bear that in mind."

They walked on.

Cunningham had woken up before Tom, although Tom hadn't had much sleep. A combination of Cunningham's night terrors and Tom's claustrophobia had seen to that. It seemed like he had only started to drift off as the thin morning light began creeping through the barred windows. And the cell was so hot. He had thought he would be cold initially, seeing how sparse the bedding was, but he had figured without the heating. He knew it wasn't done out of concern for the inmates' welfare, it was at that level to keep them pliant and docile. Same with breakfast: Tom had never eaten such poor quality, carb-laden food in his life. Even in the army.

"Sleep all right?" Tom had asked Cunningham, hearing again in his head those screams, expecting what the answer would be.

Cunningham merely grunted.

Tom persisted. "Not a morning person?"

Another grunt. Cunningham swung his legs off the bunk, farted, made his way to the toilet. Tom turned away toward the window to give him some privacy, and also because the smell was atrocious.

"Where d'you go during the day?" asked Tom. "Education?"

"Business Studies. Accounting. I'm good with numbers. On Sundays I go to church. I sing in the choir."

"Right."

Cunningham finished his ablutions, flushed the toilet. Didn't wash his hands, Tom noted.

Tom was also aware that Cunningham was avoiding looking at him directly. His night terrors, thought Tom. He knows I heard it and he's waiting to see if I'm going to mention it, make something of it. Tom had already decided that if Cunningham introduced the subject, Tom would talk about it, but he wouldn't bring it up himself. Cunningham was making every effort to avoid it.

And now, thanks to weaselly Clive, here he was on the way to his first day as an art student.

The education block was a brick building of indeterminate age but certainly well into the last century. As they approached the officers looked at one another, smiled, then one of them turned to address the group.

"Lot of new faces here, who's just arrived?"

A few grunts, small hand gestures in response.

"Let's go this way, then. Quick detour, bit of history."

Instead of letting them into the main entrance, the officers led them over to a door on the left that looked as though it led into another building. A couple of the inmates raised their eyebrows, knowing what was coming next.

They were taken through a heavy wooden door which was then locked behind them. Tom felt relieved to be out of the cold. The relief was short lived.

"This way."

They were led through another door into a circular room with a tall vaulted ceiling with wooden beams and supports. Stacking chairs and flat tables were piled against the walls, showing that it was a storeroom. It had once been white but it seemed no effort had been given to its upkeep. It felt colder than—or just as cold as—the outside. The wind sang a mournful, plaintive song through gaps in the walls and roof. The officers kept the lights off.

"Think yourself lucky," the first officer said, "that you were never here earlier. Because this is where you'd have ended up, probably."

Tom immediately knew where he was. Something more than cold chilled him.

Some of the other inmates weren't as quick as him. They looked confused.

The other officer spoke. "This is where, until fairly recently, certainly in my lifetime, the executions were carried out. Hangings."

"The topping shed, we call it." The first officer took over, unable to keep the relish from his voice. "The gallows stood here," he said, pointing to the center of the room, "took up most of the space. The condemned man would be marched along, through the door you all came through, into here where he'd stand in front of it, looking at it. Just him and the chaplain, if he wanted him. On his own if he didn't."

"And the executioner," continued the second officer, "would stand at the side here, ready to throw his lever when his victim was in place. He'd walk up to the middle there . . ." He pointed, his gestures becoming as expansive as a tour guide's. " . . . have his hood put on him, and then . . . bang."

"The trapdoor would open and he'd be gone. Neck broken."

"If he was lucky."

"Yeah. If he was lucky. If the executioner had worked out his weight correctly and the height of the drop, otherwise he'd just hang there, slowly strangling and choking to death."

From their tone it was clear which method the officers preferred.

"Anyway," the first one said after a pause, "count yourselves lucky we don't do that anymore."

"Even though it mightn't be a bad idea."

"Very true." They both laughed. "But we can't stand here reminiscing about the good old days. These gentlemen have to get to their classes." The final word a sneer.

There was silence all the way to the education block.

THE ART ROOM WAS SURPRISINGLY LARGE. The walls were covered with artwork of variable quality, but most of it was better than Tom had expected. Their teacher, Mike, a small middle-aged man wearing gray overalls, greeted them all and guided them to their workstations.

"Got some new faces, that's nice." His voice was soft, nonthreatening. "Brushes are over there, pencils there, paper there. Let's stick the radio on, enjoy yourselves while you work. I'm here if you need to ask anything."

The regular inmates made their way to a block of files at the back of the room, took out their work to continue. Mike came over, stood next to Tom.

"New here?"

"Yeah," said Tom.

"What are you interested in, then?"

Tom looked around. There was another delivery of men from a different wing. Just a couple this time. Tom studied their faces then looked around for Clive. Annoyed that he had made him come here. He couldn't see him.

"I don't know. I've never done this before."

Mike smiled. Began to explain the mediums he could work in, the styles he might like to try, the subjects that might inspire him. "We get a lot of lads want to draw landscapes, the outside world. Then take them back to their cells, give them something pretty to look at. That's popular. Or if you want to bring in a photo of a relative or loved one, a son or daughter, perhaps, do a portrait of them. Anything like that. Have a think."

Tom said he would. He thought of the photo of Lila, wondered if he should do a portrait of her. It didn't feel right, somehow.

He was thinking about it as the door opened and another lot of inmates were let in.

"Busy today," said Mike.

Tom watched them enter, looking once again for Clive.

But Clive wasn't there. Instead Tom saw someone who he had believed he would never see again. *Hoped* he would never see again.

Not living, anyway. Someone who hated Tom and had vowed to kill him if their paths ever crossed again. And Tom didn't doubt him. Someone who had forced him to move to a different part of the country, get a different name, lead a different life.

Dean Foley.

13

TOM WANTED TO STARE, but he knew he couldn't give himself away so cheaply. He kept his face devoid of emotion, his eyes fixed on the paper in front of him. He picked up a pencil, twirled it through his fingers, made out he was thinking.

He stole glances when he could. Foley seemed to be well known. Mike scurried up to him, treated him like a valued friend. Guided him to his workspace, asked if he wanted anything. Foley behaved as if this near deference was what he was used to, didn't expect anything other than that. He told Mike he just wanted to get on with what he had been working on. Mike then brought his work over and set it before him. Foley looked at the half-completed painting, and with that Mike was dismissed.

Tom kept studying him. He was older than the last time he had seen him, obviously, but beyond that he didn't look much different. Perhaps bulkier, although prison often did that. Once one of Manchester's most feared drug barons. A man who was never attacked or challenged by his enemies, whose presence was so terrifying that he had the confidence to appear in public without bodyguards. A man who believed he had legitimized his empire, had respect, or the veneer of it, from the community at large. A man who was ultimately betrayed by one of his closest lieutenants when he was revealed to be a police officer working deep undercover. He still carried himself as if his empire was intact, as if his downfall had never happened. As if the person who had betrayed him wasn't at the opposite end of the room.

Tom doodled, making scratches on the paper, head down, his mind—his body—wanting to be somewhere else entirely but knowing he had to keep all his mental and physical receptors open. He was bearded now, his hair longer, but he doubted that would be enough to stop Foley recognizing him. Not with a hatred that deep.

"Need inspiration?"

Tom jumped, looked up. Then quickly down again, hoping he hadn't attracted any attention. "What?"

Mike. Hovering at Tom's side. Smiling, a pleasant, open face.

"I'm . . ." Tom's voice dropped too. If Foley didn't recognize his face he wouldn't miss his voice. Tried to disguise it, neutralize it. "I'm just getting going. Yeah."

"There's books over there," he said, gesturing to a shelf on the other side of the room, the side where Foley sat. "Different kinds. Landscapes, nature. Photos, all of them. Some of the class like to copy them to get going. Want to help yourself?"

"I'm . . . fine at the moment." His words a whispered near hiss. Bent over, he made himself as closed off as possible.

"Well, if you're sure, I'll leave you alone. Anything you need, just ask." Mike walked off.

He must be used to people talking to him like that, Tom thought. They were all prisoners, damaged men. He couldn't imagine anyone being pleased to be there. He pushed everything else from his mind, tried to think. Ran through possibilities as quickly, analytically, as his thumping heart would allow.

What was Foley doing in Blackmoor? And why was he in the art room at the same time as Tom? How big a coincidence was that?

Tom froze. The understanding, the answer to his question made his heart skip a beat. He couldn't believe it but it had to be. The question wasn't what was Foley doing there, it was what was he doing there? Or rather, how did he get there?

Clive.

That ratty little bastard. That's why he had so many questions for him when they arrived. He must have recognized him. Then told Foley.

So who was Clive? And since Clive knew who he was, why hadn't Tom recognized him?

He sneaked another glance at Foley who seemed to be in his own world, happily painting, a smile lifting the edges of his lips as he concentrated.

Tom wasn't fooled. He had seen that look before. Too many times. Up close. Masking what was really going on in the man's mind. Disguising his true intentions. Letting his prey believe they were safe before swooping unexpectedly, violently. Sometimes terminally. Then his face showed a completely different expression. The memory of which still unsettled Tom.

He looked at him again. The man was giving nothing away.

He risked another glance round the room, this time seeing if Clive was there. He wasn't. His absence just added weight to Tom's theory. He felt his anger at Clive rise, competing with his fear of Foley. Tried to tamp down both emotions. Fall back on his training. He couldn't let either of them get the better of him.

So he drew. At first he had no idea what he was doing, just making trembling marks on the paper. But gradually a picture began to emerge. A young woman's face, drawn from memory. Not brilliant or particularly competent, he didn't think, and perhaps the features were only recognizable to himself, but it was heartfelt. Honest. It was what was in his mind right now.

Hayley. His real niece. The one whose death he still felt responsible for.

He glanced up again, that familiar anger mixing with that familiar fear. Foley. He was the one who should be blamed for her death, not him. But that would be too easy, that would give himself a free pass from the pain his actions had caused. And it wouldn't help right now, in this place. So he put his head down again, worked.

Eventually the bell went. It had been one of the longest hours of Tom's life.

Everyone reluctantly stood up, began to tidy their work away. Tom didn't know what to do. Move first and be left waiting for the officers to arrive, mingling with inmates from other wings. Or be last, risking the possibility of attracting attention to himself, have all eyes on him as he dawdled. Perhaps even get a name for it. So he stood up when the rest of them did, tried to hide among the mass of prisoners. But there was a greater problem. To put his work away he had to walk past Foley.

Foley hadn't moved. Head still down, as though the room was his and he was waiting for everyone else to clear so he could have some peace and quiet. Tom edged past his desk, trying not to even acknowledge the man, but at the same time not to make it obvious that he was turning his face from him.

He risked a glance as he passed. Foley's gaze didn't seem to have changed but Tom wasn't so sure. There was an infinitesimal flicker at the corner of his eye, like he had been looking but didn't want to be caught. The expression on his face remained the same. Or was the smile deeper?

Tom's stomach lurched. *He knows*, he thought. *He knows it's me.*

Hands shaking, he put his work away, made for the door where he tried to lose himself among the other inmates.

Soon their escort arrived and he fell in with the men coming out of the classrooms, going back to the same wing.

He didn't look back.

Once on the wing Tom, along with everyone else, was herded into the queue for lunch. Instead he went to the small glass office where most of the officers sat.

"Oi," an officer said, behind him. "You. Over here."

Tom held up his hand. "Just a minute."

The officer didn't want to give up. Tom tried to make his body language unthreatening, but urgent. He kept moving toward the office. The officer inside looked up.

"I need to call my solicitor," Tom told him. "Now."

14

HE DIDN'T GET HIS CALL. Not until later the next day during association time. There were no special rules, no privacy. He had to line up along with everyone else, take his turn on the wing phone, put in his PIN, remember the number he had to call, and hope he had enough credit. Since the mobile number for Sheridan had been given as his solicitor, the wing staff weren't allowed to listen in. But that didn't preclude inmates. Not for the first time Tom wished he had set the terms for this job. Or put up more of a fight not to take it at all.

He had spent the rest of the day avoiding the education block, keeping to himself during association time. The ever-present tension on the wing fed into Tom. Made him nervous, kept him tense. Loss of face, loss of reputation was everything inside, so men concentrated to hear any slight against them, imagined or otherwise, and make restitution for it. Violence and the threat of violence were constant. A wrong look, a wrong word was all it took. Sometimes not even that. A punch, a kick, a headbutt for no reason. Inmates would hide behind their padded doors with homemade weapons, waiting to attack the next person who appeared. Didn't matter who. And those attacks had to be avenged. If someone was the victim of an unprovoked attack, they had to attack someone else or risk looking soft, weak. It didn't matter who. The wing staff treated this as any other day at the office.

After lights out, Cunningham experienced a new night's terrors.

But that wasn't what kept Tom awake. His claustrophobia hadn't abated. He felt panic rise through the darkness. He had tried to reason it away, tell himself he was safer inside the room than outside. But it was what—or rather who—awaited him beyond the door that really kept him awake. The next day he stayed on the wing, even though it meant being locked up all morning. He thought he was safer in his cell.

He had tried to find something he could use as a weapon. He knew inmates could make weapons out of anything, like a malevolent episode of *Blue Peter*, but he didn't have any tools on hand to help him. No lighter to melt his toothbrush, push a razor blade into it. Or even better, two, side by side. Stripe an attacker, make the wound harder to stitch back together. No paperclips either, or Blu Tack. Same principle: break down the paperclips, sharp edges out, push them into Blu Tack, carry it between his knuckles like a scared suburbanite would a car key. Swing a punch, make a lot of painful mess. Especially if he aimed for the eyes. But he had nothing like that. A hot cup of tea overloaded with sugar was useful when flung in an attacker's face: the sugar helped the heat stick and burn. But he couldn't carry that around with him all day. So he stayed in the cell, only venturing out to use the phone.

He dialed the number, waited. Looking around all the time, trying to work out who Foley could have contacted, paid to do Tom damage. Who was avoiding eye contact or whispering, trying not to look at him. Any other time he would have thought he was being paranoid but he had spent enough years undercover to know that there was no such thing. Paranoid feelings had saved his life more than once.

The phone was answered. "I've got a problem," said Tom, trying to keep his head down, turned away from the majority of inmates, his mouth covered just in case anyone could read his lips.

A sigh at the other end of the line. "What?" DS Sheridan's exasperated voice. "I thought I said no communication until you'd got what we needed."

"As I said, there's a problem."

"Well it's down to you then. You have to make Cunningham talk. So work round it."

"It's not about Cunningham."

"What then?" Sheridan couldn't have sounded more bored and irritated if he tried.

Tom put his mouth even closer to the phone. Covered the side of his face with his hand. "Dean Foley."

"Can't hear you."

"Then listen closer. Because I'm not going to speak any louder. Dean Foley. He's in here. And he's made me."

"So?"

Tom tried to keep the anger and desperation out of his voice. Struggled to keep calm. "Read your fucking case files, Sheridan. Find out why him and me don't get on. Then you'll see why we have a problem. A bloody big one."

Silence. When Sheridan eventually spoke there was no hint of his earlier irritation. "You sure about this?"

"Why have I got a new name? Why did I go into hiding? Dean Foley."

Another sigh from Sheridan. Tonally different. "Shit."

"Yeah. Right."

"You sure he's made you?"

"Definitely. And you need to get me out of here. Now. Otherwise I won't be coming out. Ever."

"Leave it with me. I'll see what I can do."

Tom felt that anger, that desperation rise within him once more. "That's it? That's your answer?" He grasped the receiver so hard his knuckles turned white. "My cover's blown and I'm in danger. Don't you understand? We've got to abort. Now. Get me out."

Tom became aware of someone standing next to him. He looked up. One of the inmates from the art room was standing next to him. Staring at him. Tom stared back.

"You goin' to be long?"

"Solicitor," said Tom, mouth suddenly dry.

The inmate gave him an intimidating, unblinking stare.

"I'll be as quick as I can be," said Tom, not backing down but not wanting trouble.

"I'm waitin' as well. Don't be a cunt."

Tom turned. There were several people behind him. All watching to see what he would do next. He turned back to the receiver. "Just do it," he said. "Get me out."

Without waiting for a reply, he put the phone down and broke the connection. Turned to the inmate. "All yours."

He walked slowly back to his cell. Aware all the time of the others around him.

He needed to get out. He needed to find a way to speed up his job, gain Cunningham's trust, get out. He needed—

"All right, mate?" Dreadlocked Darren.

Tom looked up, reverie broken. "Yeah, fine."

Darren scrutinized his face. "Look tired, mate. Myrtle keeping you awake?"

"No it's . . ." Tom looked at the cell, knowing Cunningham would be in it. Looked back at Darren. "Yeah. He is."

Darren smiled. "Want me to do something about it? Cost you, mind."

"What?"

"Twenty Marlboro. Going rate."

Tom looked round, checked no one was listening. "Come over here. Let's talk."

15

DEAN FOLEY WASN'T, by his own admission, a subtle man. Or an overly cautious man. That wasn't to say he was an unintelligent man. Quite the opposite.

Many of his enemies had thought that, given his temperament and proclivities, he was some ignorant Neanderthal who only knew to strike out. How to hurt, not to think. They had used that assumption against him, to underestimated him. They were no longer around to regret that mistake.

He preferred to think of himself as Alexander the Great faced with the Gordian knot. Taking a sword to the most complex puzzle, splitting it down the middle, and moving forward. He knew that some would be surprised he even knew who Alexander the Great was, let alone what he had achieved. He had been to school once. And seen Hollywood films. A couple of people had laughed and pointed out to him that Alexander the Great had been gay. They too were no longer around to contemplate their error of judgment.

So when he saw the man who was now calling himself Tom Killgannon in the art room, he did not confront him. Foley was, in his own mind, responding the best way he knew. Injuries came later. Thinking came first.

He sat slumped in his armchair, watching daytime TV. Endless property programs, shows about moving abroad or to the country.

He would have dismissed them as care-home viewing before but now he was inside. If he was honest with himself, he was becoming hooked. Color images of long white beaches or rolling, bucolic countryside. He even liked the interiors. The freedom to walk from the living room to the kitchen, then out onto the patio. Imagining himself taking a long, leisurely stroll around spacious interiors with the presenters, sometimes thinking of stopping off in one of those bedrooms too. Those presenters were tasty. Young, fit, enthusiastic. But that was secondary. It was the homes he'd grown to love. He'd gone as far as to paint them, hang them on his cell wall.

Looking away from the screen and the paintings around the rest of his cell, that familiar depression would hit once more. The weight of where he was. Yes, he had everything he could possibly get in here but he was paying for it. And the money wouldn't last forever. He knew that. He just hoped it would be there for as long as he was here. He was never going to be released. He just had to make everything as enjoyable as he possibly could. But he knew he would never be able to walk around some spacious country house and call it his own. He'd never drink wine in the kitchen or lounge, putter around in the garden, feel the sun on his face. Not anymore. And that hurt. Those feelings could curdle into anger. Well now he had someone to take it out on.

Tom Killgannon.

The beard had been a surprise. And the long hair. He had always been close cropped, ex-army. Now he looked as though he'd been living in the wild since they last met. But the eyes were the same. He couldn't hide them. That green. Overly sensitive for a muscle-bound thug, showing a depth of intelligence that was rare in the people Foley dealt with. That was why he had recruited him. Knew him to be more than just a physical threat. And he had been right. Tom Killgannon quickly rose up the ranks of Foley's empire until he was one of his most trusted advisors.

Tom Killgannon—ridiculous name—Mick Eccleston was the name Foley knew him by. And the fact that Foley's empire went down so hard and so fast, was all down to Eccleston's testimony. After the trial, Mick had disappeared. He had tried to look for him, spent money and manpower on it, used every contact on any side of the law, but Mick Eccleston was nowhere to be found. The man was a ghost. Then, he discovered Mick had a sister. And that Mick wasn't his real name. Foley kept the sister under surveillance for months, thinking he might contact her, but no. Nothing. Eventually Foley began to believe he was dead, so successfully had he vanished.

He remembered the conversation they had the night Mick betrayed him. About crossing Foley, about running. About revenge. About digging more than two graves. Foley smiled at the memory. This was more than just revenge though. He believed Mick had taken something belonging to him. And now he had the perfect opportunity to ask him where it was. And yes. Revenge. He smiled. Too good. Too good.

He deliberately hadn't said anything in the art room. He knew Mick had recognized him. He had watched him surreptitiously, taking great pleasure as his expression changed from near boredom to abject fear. Mick had even walked past Foley while he was painting and Foley, so good, hadn't even looked up, acknowledged his presence. Perfect. So now he would be back on his wing, terrified of what Foley was going to do next.

A knock at his cell door.

"Who is it?"

"Baz."

"Come in, then."

Foley flicked the remote at the TV, turning the screen to black. The young man with the wrecked face entered. Foley looked up at him from his easy chair. "What d'you got for me?"

Baz began to empty his pockets on the table, taking out crumpled bills, coins. He smoothed out the bills, stacked up the coins. Stood back, waiting for his handiwork to be admired. Foley looked at it.

"Jesus, that it? New shipment not arrived yet?"

"Anytime now. We're making do with what we've got, stretching it as far as it'll go."

Foley took the money, pocketed it, sat back, and regarded Baz once more. "Got a job for you."

"Yes, Mr. Foley." A statement, not a question. Baz would do whatever was asked of him, he was a good, loyal soldier.

"Is Kim on today? Can't remember." Before Baz could answer Foley continued. "Doesn't matter. If not her, one of the other ones. Skippy'll do." He leaned forward, wrote something in a notebook, tore out the page, passed it to Baz. "I want him to find out everything he can about this bloke here. What wing he's on, what he's in for, where he comes from, everything. In fact just tell him to print off his file and bring it along to me. Can you do that?"

"Yeah, Mr. Foley. 'Course."

"Good lad. Oh, and be subtle. Know what that means?"

Baz nodded. Face impassive. "Yes, Mr. Foley."

"Good. Then tell him to come straight back to me when he's got everything, yeah? Soon as."

"Right, Mr. Foley."

Baz waited for his official dismissal then left.

Foley sat back, looked at the black screen, not wanting to put the TV on again. Not just yet. He thought of Alexander the Great, taking his sword to the Gordian knot. Yeah, he could have done that with Mick Eccleston or Tom Killgannon. Had someone take care of him straight away. Have him bleeding out in the showers or the dinner queue by now. But that wouldn't give him anything he wanted. Not the satisfaction he craved, and, more importantly, not the answer to his questions. And that, if he tried to look at the situation objectively, was more important. Or equally as important.

He sat back, smiled to himself. That was the thing about knots: You couldn't always cut through them. Sometimes the joy was in unraveling them slowly.

16

DS SHERIDAN STARED AT THE SCREEN on his desk. Didn't see what was on it. Instead he thought about the phone call from Tom Kill-gannon.

He looked over at Blake. She was sitting at her own desk opposite him, looking into something on her computer, reading glasses on the end of her nose. She wasn't given to displaying much frailty, knowing how difficult it still was for a woman to be treated equally in the police force. So this admission that she couldn't see perfectly was, Sheridan had always believed, a huge one on her part.

He hadn't told Blake or their superior DCI Harmer about the call. He had tried to, but couldn't decide on the best course of action. For both the assignment and Killgannon. He needed help to reach a decision.

He gestured to Blake. "You busy?"

She turned around, closing her screen, taking her glasses off straight away. "Why?"

"We need to talk to the boss."

She frowned. "What about?"

He stood up, looking round the office. "Tell you in a minute. Come on."

Keeping the frown in place, she followed him as he knocked on Harmer's door, waited to be summoned, then entered. DCI Harmer sat behind his desk. He looked like a squash player in a suit, or a well-presented hedge fund manager, about as far away from the rank and file as it was possible to be. He also bore an unfortunate resemblance to a red-haired Muppet, hence the nickname Beaker.

"DS Sheridan. DC Blake. What can I do for you?" He gestured for them to sit.

The office looked like it was waiting to be featured in *Middle Management Monthly* magazine. Sheridan imagined Harmer standing against a filing cabinet, file open in his hands, trophies and framed certificates in shot behind him, smiling sideways at the camera. His mass of red hair untameably unruly, undercutting the confidence he tried to exude. All he needs is googly eyes, thought Sheridan.

"Got a problem, sir." Sheridan was aware of Blake looking at him, still frowning.

"What kind of problem?"

"The Killgannon assignment, Operation Retrieve. He's been compromised."

"What?" said Blake.

Harmer leaned forward. His action was swift but designed not to crease his freshly laundered shirt. His voice serious. No doubting he was a cop now. "In what way?"

Sheridan addressed the two of them. "He worked undercover in Manchester a few years ago. Infiltrated Dean Foley's gang. Got high up, the right-hand man. His testimony put Foley away."

"I know. And a shipment of money went missing, didn't it?" said Harmer.

"It did," said Sheridan. "But the drugs that were due to hit the street were all impounded. The money was never found. Foley swore he didn't have it. Didn't matter. We still made the case against him. Thanks to Killgannon's hard work. The whole network collapsed."

"Commendations all round, yes. So what does this have to do with Operation Retrieve?"

"Foley's in the same prison as Cunningham, sir. And he's made Killgannon as the man who put him there."

Harmer sat back and let out a stream of air, eyes narrowed, face pinched. It was as extreme as he got in showing emotion. "Shit."

"When did this happen?" asked Blake. "Why didn't I know about it?"

"Phone call. Not so long ago," said Sheridan, covering up the fact that it wasn't just immediate, and he had been trying to decide what action to take and had not come up with anything. "I couldn't tell you in the office. Sorry. Anyway, he says he thinks he was recognized, sold out to Foley."

"Is he safe?" asked Blake.

"He doesn't think so. He wants to come out now."

"What about Cunningham?" Harmer this time.

Sheridan shrugged. "We'll have to try again later. Use some-one else. Or get Cunningham transferred, take Killgannon with him." He stopped talking, realizing how ridiculous that sounded.

Harmer stared at the desk. "All that work, all that planning . . ." He looked up. "Why didn't we know this? Wasn't there a risk assessment done? Surely this should have been looked into. Rule one stuff."

"Absolutely," said Blake. "It was done thoroughly. Then I went through the whole thing myself. Double-checked. Nothing, no one was flagged."

"I checked since I got the call," said Sheridan. "Current prison population for Blackmoor. Foley's been there a while."

Blake looked between the two of them. "I don't know how that happened. It shouldn't have happened. Seriously, there's no way that could have happened. No way." Incredulity was giving way to anger.

Harmer sighed, shook his head.

"Look, I know this is all cloak-and-dagger and stuff," said Blake,

"And we have a strict set of guidelines to comply with before putting an operation like this into motion. But could someone have hidden Foley's name from us?"

"Why?" asked Harmer.

"I don't know. Is there some reason he wouldn't show up? Is he some kind of asset? Something going on above our pay grade, perhaps?"

"I don't know," said Harmer. "There shouldn't be. We'd have been told about it before we launched this operation. I'll look into it."

"What do we do in the meantime, sir?" asked Sheridan.

"We've got to get him out," said Blake.

Another sigh from Harmer. "Let's see. How close has Killgannon got to Cunningham?"

"Physically very close. They're sharing a cell."

"Brilliant. Perfect."

"But Killgannon's in fear for his life now. Foley's recognized him. He's just waiting to see what he does next."

"Who in the prison knows that he's one of ours?" asked Harmer.

"No one," cut in Blake. "We didn't want his cover blown or for him to be compromised in any way."

"So you two are his only line to the outside world?"

"It's the way he's always operated, sir," said Sheridan. "He insisted we didn't change that. He's always got results in the past doing it this way."

"So if we got him out, how long would it take to get someone in the same position with Cunningham again?"

"Killgannon is a perfect asset," said Blake. "Might take us months to find a replacement as good. But he's compromised."

"And he might only have a small time to live if Foley gets to him. I've just called a couple of detective mates who know more about Blackmoor than me. Apparently Foley pretty much runs the place. He's still in charge of what's left of his empire, runs it from his cell. And no doubt he's got everything inside sewn up as well. It's his caged city. Killgannon's just a tenant."

Harmer almost smiled. "You should have been a writer, Nick."

Sheridan felt himself redden.

Harmer steepled his fingertips and thought. "I say we keep him where he is," he said eventually.

Sheridan and Blake exchanged glances. "*What?*" said Sheridan.

"We may never get a chance as good as this again," said Harmer. "Not this close. Not without a lot of work. Let's see what Killgannon can get for us. If he gets what we need and we get those locations sooner rather than later, great. We get him out."

"And if Foley gets him first?" asked Sheridan.

Harmer sighed. "It's regrettable, but . . ." He shrugged. "He knew the risks. He's deniable. Like you said, Nick, no one but us knows he's in there. And Blackmoor's one of the privately run prisons. At arm's length from the Home Office if there should be a death. They could take the blame, not us. I'm thinking operationally here."

"Or we get him out," said Sheridan. "Start again with someone else. Keep an asset intact to be used again."

Harmer stared at the desk. "No, we keep him in."

Sheridan frowned. "Sir?"

"Monitor the situation, get regular status reports, updates. If it looks like Foley's getting too close, then we'll pull him out. Straight away. But we have to weigh everything up."

"So what do I tell him?"

"To stay where he is for the time being. We appreciate his situation, but we're at too crucial a juncture to jeopardize the operation. If he does his job efficiently, he'll be out in no time."

Would you like to tell him yourself, sir? thought Sheridan. But he said nothing. Instead he stood up, knowing he was dismissed. "Right, sir. I'll do that."

"Good." Harmer gave a smile. It was the kind Pontius Pilate would have made.

Blake was already out of the door and on the way back to her desk. Sheridan watched her go. He went back to work, knowing that the next phone call he made to Killgannon might be sentencing him to death.

17

Tom had tried, with his limited phone time, to contact Sheridan again but there had been no reply. It was like he was holding his breath. He was still here, in the cell with Cunningham, waiting for Foley to act. Waiting for Cunningham to talk. Waiting for something to happen.

Dinnertime came, and he and Cunningham queued up alongside everyone else for beige carbs. They stood with their plastic trays, plastic mugs. Not speaking to each other or anyone else. His senses were heightened because he knew what was about to happen. It was risky, but he felt he had no choice. He needed to demonstrate to Cunningham that he was on his side. That he could be trusted. And this seemed like the most direct way. And all it would cost him was a packet of Marlboro. Tom didn't smoke but he always carried a few packs with him. They were valuable currency in prison.

Darren came charging out of nowhere, swinging for Cunningham. This wasn't the kind of prison fight in films or TV. There was no warning, no build up. One second he wasn't there, the next he was. And he wasn't backing down. It was the prison way: get as many hits in as possible until everyone else stops staring and catches up, takes action against him.

The suddenness even took Tom by surprise. And he was expecting it.

Darren's fist connected to the side of Cunningham's head. Cunningham, almost too surprised to scream, held his arms up. Darren kept hitting. One side, then the next, not pausing for breath. Getting as much hurt in as he could.

Cunningham went down, curling into a fetal ball, whimpering. Darren stepped in to follow up. He brought back his fist, ready to transmit as much energy as he could down the knotted muscle of his arm and into his fist. And on, to Cunningham's head.

Everyone else, those in the queue, those serving, the officers standing around, stared, too shocked to move. Tom was the first to regain his composure. He stepped up to Darren as fast as he could, grabbed hold of his swinging arm, forced it down by his side.

Darren looked at him, confusion on his face, about to speak.

"Changed my mind," said Tom, so low only Darren could hear, if the blood hadn't been pumping in his ears so much.

Anger blazed in Darren's eyes. He tried with his other arm to swing at Tom. But Tom was ready for him. He placed his foot behind Darren's heel, pushed him backward. He was in midpunch, his body not expecting the sudden change of direction. He stumbled, fell backward. Went sprawling on the floor.

Tom turned to Cunningham, tried to pick him up. "You OK?"

Cunningham looked terrified, didn't seem to trust himself with words.

The guards had come to life and were piling on the prone body of Darren. Tom helped Cunningham to his feet.

"He needs medical assistance. Now."

Guards escorted Cunningham away, found a seat for him to sit on, and assessed the damage. Tom held his hands up, he was no threat. The two men were hauled off separately, Darren kicking and screaming, swearing and cursing in Tom's direction.

Tom gave no resistance. Allowed himself to be led away.

That went about as well as could be expected, he thought.

HE WAS TAKEN to one of the wing classrooms, questioned by staff. He could hear Darren's cries echoing off the walls as he was led off the wing.

"What happened?"

Tom shrugged, made out he was as surprised as they were. "Don't know. We were just standing in line and he comes straight for Cunningham. Starts hitting him. Hard. So I just . . ." Another shrug. "Pushed him away."

The officers stared at him, before going back to their office to check the CCTV, then their bodycams. Everything supported Tom's version of events. He asked what had happened to Darren. He had been sent to the seg—the segregation block. A spell in solitary might calm him down, they said. Eventually they allowed Tom to go back to his cell.

Cunningham was curled up on his bunk. He jumped when the door was opened.

"Only me," said Tom, as the door closed behind him.

Cunningham slowly sat up. Looked down at Tom. The left side of his face was swollen and red.

"Have you had that seen to?" asked Tom.

Cunningham nodded. "They said it would be fine. But it'll hurt tomorrow." He sighed. "Hurts now."

"They give you painkillers?"

Cunningham nodded.

"Good." Tom sat down on his bunk. "Well that was a bit of excitement, wasn't it?"

Cunningham nodded. Still shaken.

Neither man spoke.

"Thank you," Cunningham said eventually, voice small and whispery.

"No problem," said Tom, aiming for lightness. "What friends are for."

Cunningham moved about as if agitated. "Friends?"

"Yeah. We're stuck in here, with each other. We have to make the best of it. And that means being friends. Don't you think?"

Cunningham didn't answer straight away. The bunk started to move. Tom knew he was crying.

Tom lay back. This is what he was again, how he had to act, to live. He had used Darren, lied to him, given him extra, unnecessary hardship to contend with. And now he was lying to Cunningham, all to gain his trust and then drop him afterward when he had what he wanted. Yes, Cunningham was a child murderer but he hadn't started out that way. His life had been shaped and twisted until he had become that. If someone had intervened earlier, he might have been stopped. And now here Tom was, the latest in a long line of people letting him down when he needed help.

This wasn't who Tom wanted to be anymore. Years of being undercover had taught him to weaponize his humanity. Make friends, take lovers. Fake sincerity. Be liked by the right people. Like them in return. And then betray them. Walk away. Tell yourself it didn't affect you. Keep telling yourself that. Then do the whole thing again. And again.

He could truly hate himself for doing this again if he allowed himself to. But he had to keep going. Tell himself—as he so often had in the past—that the end justified the means. Try to believe it this time.

"She's an angel," said Cunningham, breaking his reverie.

"What?"

"Your niece. She's an angel. I'm just looking at her picture now."

He felt something inside him curdle. Swallowed it down. He hated to use the photo of Lila but if it got Cunningham talking, especially now, then he would. And worry about how it made him feel later. "Is she now?"

"Yes. She's pure. Her hair, like angel dust . . ."

"And you like purity, Noel? Yeah?"

"Yes . . . purity. Children have it. It's . . ." Tom felt him moving about on the top bunk, getting into his story. "Fleeting. You have to catch it, capture it. Then it's gone. So fleeting. But beautiful while it lasts. Oh yes, beautiful . . ."

"And what happens when it's gone, Noel?"

Silence in response. It went on so long that Tom thought he had asked the wrong question. But Cunningham had been weighing his words carefully. "It's gone." His voice had changed. Empty of creepy passion, devoid of anything approaching common human- ity. Like a different person had entered the room. "Gone. And you have to dispose of it. You see, you take that purity, keep it, let it nourish you and then . . . it's no good. You have to get rid of it." He laughed. "I can tell you this, now that you're my friend. You can understand."

"Right," said Tom. "And that's what you did, yeah? Got rid of the purity?"

No reply, but from the rocking of the bunk, Tom could feel Cunningham nodding. Or at least he hoped that was what he was doing.

"And where did you do that?"

Cunningham gestured toward the window. "Out there . . ."

Tom felt something shift within him. Like he was onto some- thing. "Where in particular?"

Silence. Tom waited.

A sigh from the top bunk. "I'm tired now. Want to go to sleep. Thank you for being my friend, Tom."

And that was as much as Tom could get out of him.

18

NIGHT IN BLACKMOOR. And again Tom couldn't sleep.

The sounds of unhappy men drifted along the wing, slipping under the heavy metal door like ghosts on wires. Wailing, crying, sobbing, pleading. Other sounds too, harsher ones: calls to *shut the fuck up* and threats of what would happen if they didn't. Back and forth until they tired themselves out, wore themselves down until some form of sleep claimed them. At least some of them.

Tom didn't scream, didn't shout out. He kept his fear locked up inside. Now it was around two in the morning. Cunningham was engaged in his usual nighttime activity. Crying. Tom didn't need to hear the rest of the wing, there was noise enough in this cell. Cunningham had the same dream, or a variation of it, every night. Always apologizing to someone for something. Sobbing that he was sorry. Tom knew he had a lot to apologize for.

"I'm sorry . . . sorry, I . . . I won't . . . I didn't mean to . . ." Then breaking down once more.

All night, it seemed like. Every night.

Driving Tom mad.

Cunningham's constant confessing was getting to Tom in other ways. It made him think of apologies he wanted to make but knew he never could. Especially to Hayley, whose death he would always blame himself for.

His niece, the daughter of the sister who had brought him up in their mother's absence, had started running with a bad crowd, thinking it was an easy way out of her impoverished background, getting involved with a local drug dealer. One who worked with Tom's then target, Dean Foley. And it all came to a head the night that Foley had finally been arrested. Hayley had been where she wasn't supposed to be and had paid the ultimate price. And Tom, knowing it was his operation, blamed himself for her death, even though he hadn't pulled the trigger.

He hadn't been able to contact his sister during or after the trial; it was too dangerous for her. Foley's men were hunting him and he knew they wouldn't hesitate to kill her if it meant getting to him. So he stayed away. And now he was in Witness Protection. He had never spoken to her since. Something else to hate himself for.

It was a part of the reason he had taken Lila in when she was in trouble. Trying to avoid another death, another lost soul. But no matter how many people he helped, it would never remove the guilt. And Cunningham pulled that guilt into focus once more.

Tom tried to push it all to one side, concentrate on his mission. Tried to square the crying with what he knew of Cunningham's past.

"No, please, I . . . I . . ."

Tom sighed and swung himself out of bed. Enough.

"Hey," he said, touching Cunningham on the shoulder, rocking him gently and trying to wake him. "Hey."

Cunningham jumped, startled, almost banging his head on the wall. In the darkness, lit only by the perimeter lights, Tom could see Cunningham staring ahead, eyes fixed on something he couldn't see.

"Cunningham . . ."

Cunningham jumped once more at Tom's touch. Kept staring ahead.

"Give it a rest, mate," Tom said, not knowing what other words would reach him. "I'm trying to sleep down here. Yeah?"

Cunningham didn't blink, just kept staring.

"You OK?"

Cunningham raised a pointed finger, aimed it at the shadowed corner of the cell. "There they are . . ."

"What?"

"There, in the corner . . . can you see them?"

Tom turned. He could make out shadows on the wall. They were substantial, they had depth. It looked like two figures, one standing in front of the other.

"You can see them, can't you? The choir?"

Tom blinked. The figures disappeared. Saw only the silhouettes of the chair and the desk. The outline of the TV against the wall. Cunningham's grinning, eyeless angels. He blinked again. The figures didn't return.

"It's the middle of the night. Your mind's playing tricks on you."

Cunningham turned his head toward Tom. His eyes were lit by a strange, penetrating light. For the first time since he arrived, Tom was afraid of what his cellmate might be capable of.

"You saw them," Cunningham said. "I know you did. You saw them." He pointed again, his hand shaking. "They're here all the time. With me. They hide in the day but come out at night. They sing to me. My requiem. I can never get rid of them. Never. They won't go away . . ."

He screwed his eyes tight shut. Tom saw tears squeezing from the corners. He looked again into the corner of the cell. Saw nothing out of the ordinary.

"Hey, mate," he tried again, "get some sleep. You're not alone here and they won't get you while I'm here."

Cunningham slowly turned to look at him once more. A desperate kind of hope in his wet eyes. "You . . . really? Protect me?"

"Yeah, sure." Tom hoped he wouldn't regret what he was saying.

Knew he was taking a chance doing this. Didn't know which way it could go. "Go to sleep. I'm here."

"Thank . . . thank you . . ." Cunningham's words sounded so pathetic. He laid himself down again, breathing heavily. "You don't know what this means to me . . ."

"Just go to sleep."

It took a while, but Cunningham eventually did. Tom lay there, feeling revulsion at having befriended the man, or having pretended to. But he had done it for the assignment. And more importantly, so he could get a good night's sleep.

Except he couldn't. He lay there listening to Cunningham snore, staring at the corner, watching until those shadows dispersed in the pale morning light.

Trying not to let his own ghosts haunt him.

19

Quint could see why Tom had chosen the house he lived in. It had good vantage points on all sides, anyone approaching it would be seen. If they were watching.

Nestled in a bay beside the village of St. Petroc, the house was one of a few dotted around a shingled slope that led down to the water. The bay itself was quite narrow, curving out to the sea, not wide enough for surfers, barely deep enough to launch any craft. A winding, steep switchback road led to the cliff top. Anyone approaching came down very slowly.

The other houses were mostly summer vacation rentals, appealing to urbanites who wanted the pretense of being cut off from civilization for a week, the inconvenience of getting supplies in, and the novelty of terrible Wi-Fi. They were empty at this time of year, adding to the haunted, desolate feel of the bay. The only house with any lights on was Tom's. The last house on the bay.

Quint had thought long and hard about how to approach it. He thought covert surveillance best, only to find precious little in the way of camouflage. He was sure his motorbike's engine would alert the house's inhabitants. So instead he stayed at the top of the hill, looking down, a discreet pair of binoculars pointing toward the house.

Dawn struggled to rise, and the light within the house was a boon for him. He saw silhouettes move behind windows. Caught glimpses of two different bodies, making their separate ways sluggishly from room to room. He guessed they would be Lila and Pearl. The names in the file. They moved in together while Tom was away. That made sense. Quint could see why Tom would do that.

The front door opened and a figure emerged. Young, female, blond. Lila, he thought. He looked round for somewhere to hide, realized there wasn't anywhere. He was exposed. If she looked up, he would be seen. The girl began to walk toward the road.

He stowed his binoculars in a leather saddlebag, readied himself to put the bike into gear, ride away. Then looked down again. She had disappeared.

He checked on all sides. No sign of her.

Panic rose in his chest. An unfamiliar sensation. Usually he was the one that induced panic in others. Among other emotions. He thought quickly, tried to reach a decision. He would have to go. Come back later, find somewhere he could hide—construct it if necessary—and observe the house more fully. He still had his tent pitched on Blackmoor, perhaps he could bring everything over here and camp out? Would that be more or less conspicuous?

He didn't get any further in his thinking. Because there, right in front of him, was the blond girl walking toward him. He immediately put his head down, trying to hide his identity from her, to pretend there was some mechanical fault and he couldn't get his bike moving.

She paused in her walking, looked at him. "Trouble with your bike?" she said.

He looked up, couldn't avoid it. He had the visor of his helmet up. She saw his face and he saw hers. She was wary of him, suspicious even. He had to do something to counteract that, prove he was no threat. Act.

"Yeah," he said. "I'm camping down the road, I just came for a ride, was looking for shops, stopped for the view . . ." He gestured over the bay where the sun was rising. He shrugged. "Then this happened. Must be the cold, or something."

"Right," Lila said. Her voice still unsure but giving his story the benefit of the doubt. "You want to give it another go?"

"Yeah," he said. He took her in from the corner of his eye. Dressed in a parka and boots, a bag slung over one shoulder, files and books poking from the corner. College. Another quick glance around showed him the stepped footpath, cut into the side of the rock, the lonely looking bus stop she was headed to. "I'll just . . ."

He put his foot down. Hard. The bike sprang into life.

"There you go," she said.

"Yeah." He smiled.

She didn't move.

"I'll be off, then."

"Right." She still hadn't moved.

He put the bike into gear, rode away.

Down the road, deserted at this hour, he glanced behind in the side mirror.

She was still standing there. Watching him go.

20

Tom was too tired to get up. He had barely slept, only drifting for a couple of exhausted hours when the dawn arrived. Now, he just wanted to roll over, stay in bed all day. He didn't even mind having the door locked. At least he would be safer that way. Probably. But he had to get up. He was working, things to do.

He didn't want to open his eyes, though. Or his nostrils, for that matter. Cunningham was sitting on the toilet. From the smell, his body was in as parlous a state as his psyche. The lack of privacy, or dignity, was something Tom didn't think he could ever get used to. He had been in the army and was used to living up close to other men in regimented conditions, but this was worse. He tried to block out the groans Cunningham was making too.

Instead he retreated once more inside his own mind. Tried to think. Plan.

No news from Sheridan and no way to call him until later. He expected to be pulled out any second, but until that happened he had to come up with a way to keep himself safe.

Clive. No surname yet, just that. And he didn't recognize him either. He had tried to place him, gone through as many faces as he could remember from undercover operations, villains he had crossed, but he came up with nothing. Yet it seemed that Clive knew him. Or knew who he used to be. And that kind of knowledge was currency in prison. He couldn't see any other way Foley knew he was here.

The art class. He was supposed to attend again this morning. He couldn't risk it. If Foley said something, did something, it would jeopardize more than just this operation.

The cell door was opened.

"Breakfast. Up you get. Outside, line up."

Tom threw back the covers, got up. He pulled his joggers on, slipped a sweatshirt over his head, laced up his sneakers. His day clothes barely differed from his night clothes. And showers were a rare commodity on the wing. He had begun to smell like every other inmate. A mixture of poorly washed and dried clothing, cheap soap, and sweat. Prison cologne.

He had a quick wash, still holding his nose, brushed his teeth, made his way to the door, and looked out at the wing. All the other prisoners were lining up to receive their food from the kitchen. He joined the queue. Face as neutral, as slack, as possible, his eyes on full alert all the time. He didn't know if Darren had any friends on the wing who wanted retribution for what he'd done to him. And that was without the threat of Foley. The food smelt like bad school dinners. Tasted even worse. But it was that or starve. Again, he thought of the army and was unsurprised that so many ex-soldiers ended up in prison. There was little in the way of lifestyle adjustment to make. Only downward.

Then he stopped dead. He hoped his expression hadn't changed but was sure it had. What he saw threw him off guard. There, about ten people ahead of him. Clive. Queuing up for breakfast.

Tom's mind whirled. Why was Clive on his wing? When had that happened? Must have been overnight. Why the move? Could be any reason. But he knew the main one: Foley wanted Clive to keep an eye on him. A few days ago he might have dismissed that as fanciful but not now. It wasn't a huge leap of the imagination to

think that Foley could do something like that. He still had influence, power, money. Enough to pay off a few officers, for sure.

Tom could do nothing, say nothing. So he just pretended he
hadn't seen him. Tried to look from the corner of his eye, see if
Clive was watching him.

He reached the counter, chose his food, and took it back to
his cell to eat.

Cunningham came in after Tom, sat down, started to eat. The
door was closed behind him.

"Another day," Cunningham said, trying for a smile.

"Yeah," said Tom.

Cunningham finished his food, placed the tray on his bunk.
Stood up, hovered over Tom. It was clear he had something to say,
and Tom knew it had to do with his behavior during the night.
Tom said nothing. Waited.

"It's hard sometimes," Cunningham finally said. "You know.
At night."

"Yeah," said Tom, as noncommittal as he could manage.

Cunningham sighed. "It's hard."

"Yeah," Tom said again. He waited, wanting to grab Cunningham, scream at him: *Just tell me where they are!* But he didn't. Instead
he said, "Do you tell the psychologist about these dreams?"

"Sort of. No, not really. She might . . . I don't know. Laugh or
something. Or send me somewhere worse."

"She won't do any of that. Just tell her. She'll understand." And
hopefully make my job easier, he thought.

Cunningham nodded, said nothing more.

Tom turned on the TV. Breakfast television. Brightly painted
presenters in a brightly painted studio. Compared with the drab-
ness of the cell, it hurt Tom's eyes. He blocked it out, tried to think.

Clive had forced him to put down art on his education choices.
Or rather made the choice for him. But what had Clive put down?

He had seen Clive's form. He tried to visualize the paper, Clive holding the pen in his hand. There were marks against certain subjects. If he could only remember . . .

He opened his eyes again. Got it.

The door opened once more. An officer stood there, clipboard in hand.

"Right. Killgannon, Art. Cunningham, Bookkeeping. Get ready, you're going now."

Tom stood up. "I've made a mistake. Can I change it?"

The officer stared at him, impassive yet angry at the same time. The majority of them seemed to have perfected that look, he thought.

"Please," Tom said. "I'm not trying to cause trouble or make your life difficult. I've just put down the wrong thing. I went to art the other day and hated it. Can I go to the carpentry workshop instead? Please."

"You're not supposed to change like that. You have to do it properly."

"I know. But I don't know who to talk to. It's my first time in here. Please. I'm not messing you around. I've made a genuine mistake."

Tom waited. If that didn't get through to the officer, he would have to try another way. But he wasn't going to the art class today under any circumstances.

The officer sighed, looked at his clipboard. Erased a mark, made one somewhere else. "Go on. Put it down to clerical error. Wouldn't be the first time."

Tom smiled. "Thank you. I appreciate it."

"Get moving, then."

He did.

On the wing the inmates were lining up, getting ready to go to their respective classes and workplaces. Their names and destinations were called out and they left with their officers. Tom saw Clive standing near the back of the line.

"Carpentry shop, this way."

The group started to follow the officer. Tom stepped in with them, coming up next to Clive.

"Hello, Clive. Surprised to see you here. Changed wings, have you?"

Clive jumped. The color drained from his face and it took him a few seconds to regain his powers of speech.

"What . . . what are you doing here? You're—you're supposed to be going to art."

Tom smiled. It was a lot less pleasant than the one he had given the officer. "Change of plan, Clive old son. I'm doing carpentry now."

"But . . . you can't . . ."

"Can't I?"

Tom moved in closer. Grabbed Clive's arm, gave it a squeeze. Clive winced.

"Going to be spending all morning together. I think it's time we had a little chat. Don't you?"

From the expression on his face, Clive clearly didn't agree.

21

THE SAME TWO OFFICERS who had given the tour of the topping shed escorted them to the workshop. There was something different about their attitude, Tom noticed. As though they had been told a secret about him and it had changed their opinion. They weren't scared of him, but they were apprehensive. Tom couldn't decide if they wanted to rush him or back away from him. But they were definitely watching him more closely.

On Foley's payroll.

His closeness to Clive on the walk was making them take even more note. Clive tried to telegraph his fear to them, show them in his eyes and body language that something wasn't right. Tom countered this by seeming as cheerful as possible. The officers were given no excuse to intervene.

As they walked, Tom noticed another inmate coming in the opposite direction. He was unescorted, but that wasn't the most unusual thing about him. His face was covered in scars but strangely overly symmetrical. Like he had placed a mirror too close to one side of his features. He noticed Tom and Clive walking together. Clive just stared at him, as if silently begging him for help. The scarred man ignored him, kept looking at Tom. Then he smiled and was gone.

Tom tried to shake the encounter from his mind. He didn't

know what had just happened but he knew it wasn't a positive development.

They arrived at a prefabricated hut. One of a number erected on a patch of land by the farthest perimeter fence. Some had been turned into offices, some classrooms. Tom entered with the rest of the group. Gave his name, number, and wing to an officer inside, then looked around.

It was like being back at school. Workbenches dotted the room, tools hung in locked cupboards on the walls, felt-tip outlines of each so missing ones could be easily spotted. A couple of full-size lathes. The teacher wearing a gray overall, waiting for everyone to enter.

It was the same as the art room. The regulars went to their benches, took out their work. Went through the procedures to be given tools to work with. Everything counted off, ticks on clipboards. Tom, being new, didn't know what to do or where to go.

"You'll need an induction," said the teacher. Sour looking, middle aged. Nose wrinkled as if perpetually smelling something unpleasant. Talking like he might expire before he's finished his sentence. "There's always a few new ones every week. Just wait there till I've sorted everyone out with work to do." His worn-out features and bitter eyes seemed to resent not only the inmates being there, but the officers and himself as well.

He walked off, made a cursory circuit of the room, nodded at what he saw, then returned to Tom and the other two men with him. They were then given a tour of the room, had the machinery and tools explained to them, given warnings about what would happen if they misbehaved or even worse, misused the tools in any way. He asked whether any of them had experience of working with wood. The other two put their hands up. The teacher took them away, got them started. Tom was once again left on his own.

He saw Clive at the other side of the room, sanding down a

small box. He checked to see if anyone was watching him. They weren't. He went and stood next to him.

"What are you making?" Tom kept his voice as loud and cheerful as possible, as though he and Clive were old mates.

Clive had no option but to respond. "A box."

"I can see that." Laughter from Tom, the funniest joke in the world. "What kind of box?"

"For my granddaughter. Something for her to keep. To remember me by."

"Nice," said Tom, voice still loud. Then he let it drop and moved in so no one else could hear. "I know you're only a small bloke, but I mean. Bit tiny for a coffin, isn't it?"

Clive stared at him.

Tom, unblinking, kept on. "I could work with it, though. If I had to."

He straightened up, smile in place once more. Clive's eyes darted round, hoping someone had heard, but knowing they hadn't.

"So what's going on, Clive?" asked Tom, his voice as conversational as possible. "You set me up with the art class. And you know who with. Now I'm guessing you're not bright enough to pull that one yourself. So why do it?"

"Don't know what you're talking about, mate." Trying desperately not to look at Tom, but to concentrate on his box.

"Yeah you do. You filled in my form. And I know who you're working with. Or rather for. Want me to say his name?"

Clive said nothing. Just kept sanding away.

Tom bent in again, pretended to be admiring Clive's handiwork. Even pointed at a dovetail joint. "You set me up. With Foley, Clive. Didn't you?"

No response.

"I'd go so far as to say that you recognized me as soon as I arrived here. That right?"

Clive kept sanding.

"Then you went straight to Foley, told him I was here. And Foley told you to get me to the art class. How'm I doing so far?"

"Nice . . . nice story." Clive's voice as uneven as his handiwork.

"Yeah. Lovely. And then after that, Foley managed to get you sent over to my wing. Spying on me, Clive? Reporting back? Surely Foley could have got someone else to do that. I'm sure you're not the only one on the payroll."

No response.

"But there's something gnawing at me, Clive. You see, I could well believe you capable of all that. Well believe it. But here's the thing. I've never seen you before in my life, Clive. I'd remember a weaselly little face like yours. Might have even slapped it around a few times. But I've racked and racked my brains and got nothing. So tell me, Clive, where do you know me from?"

Clive stopped sanding, looked up. "You don't scare me," he said, the words barely coming out in between swallows, his Adam's apple bobbing up and down so much it was quivering.

"Your voice says otherwise."

"I'm protected. You're not. Not in here." Voice stronger.

"You're only protected as long as you're useful, Clive. And at the moment you're useful. But only while Foley wants you. When that changes you'll be tossed aside. If you're lucky, that is. Might be worse. Then what'll you do?"

Clive stared at Tom. A weird intensity began to grow in his eyes. As though he was developing bravery.

"You haven't a clue, have you?" said Clive. "Not a clue."

"About what, Clive?"

"About what's going on here. About you. Not a clue." He was on the verge of laughing. A giggling, unhinged laugh. "Have you?"

Tom wanted to keep pressing, find something out, anything that would give him a clue. But his interrogation was cut short.

"Killgannon," shouted a voice from the door.

Tom looked up, startled. "Yeah?"

"Solicitor visit." An officer had come to the door, a slip of paper in his hand.

Tom straightened up. His heart began to beat faster. This was it, he thought. He didn't have to question Clive about anything. That wasn't important now. All that could be dealt with later, when he was on the outside.

Because this was it. Sheridan had come through.

He was going home.

22

THE OFFICER LEFT THE ROOM with a combination of reluctance and relief. Maybe he wanted to listen in, thought Tom, but it was too much to break those rules even for Foley.

The room they met in was part of the admin block, near the warden's office, away from the main body of the prison and any ears or eyes. Solicitor meetings were private, but Sheridan had another reason for the secrecy. As a detective he was no doubt responsible for putting away plenty of the inmates so his cover would be blown the second he walked onto a wing.

Sheridan was already sitting at the desk. Files and briefcase in front of him. Props and set dressing for a solicitor. Tom pulled up a chair to join him. He tried to gauge the detective's face, but Sheridan kept his head down, looking at the desk.

"Thanks for coming," said Tom. "Glad you're taking this seriously."

Sheridan nodded.

"So this is it, then? I'm walking out?" Tom allowed hopefulness to enter his voice.

Sheridan looked up. Tom saw his eyes. And hope died.

He knew that look from his time in the force. The expression an officer assumed to impart bad news, usually when informing a relative of a death. But any bad news would do. Such as telling an innocent prison inmate his appeal had been turned down. Or an undercover officer that he had to stay where he was, even if there was a good chance it would lead to his death. Something like that.

Sheridan sighed. "I thought it better if I came to see you, tell you face to face."

Tom stared, quelling the conflicting emotions rising within him, keeping his voice steady. "I think you've already said it. What the fuck is going on?"

Sheridan leaned across the desk, hands clasped. He looked pained, sounded sincere. If it was just his training showing, then he was very good. But he looked like he meant it. "It's not my decision. Honestly."

"Yes it is, you're in charge of the operation."

"There's . . . I talked to my superior. He wants you to stay. Thinks the threat isn't too great."

"He's not the one inside, though, is he?"

"No, he's not."

"He's not the one whose testimony put someone away for life. A someone who threatened to hunt him down and kill him. And the threats were taken so seriously I was put into witness protection. And now that person is here, inside with me. And he's running this place. And he could have me killed . . ." Tom clicked his fingers. It echoed round the room. Made him realize how low, controlled his voice was. " . . . like that."

"I know."

"So why am I not out of here?"

"Because . . . they want you to make progress with Cunningham. That was the prime directive of the operation."

"But I won't make progress with Cunningham if I'm dead, will I?"

Sheridan looked up, startled. Tom's voice had risen louder than he intended. Tom hoped no one outside had heard that.

He settled back, tried to regain control of his emotions. "Will I?" he repeated.

"Look," said Sheridan, hands raised in a gesture of useless supplication, "I'm on your side. Honestly. I've done a few jobs like this in the past. Never on your scale, obviously, but I know what you're going through."

Tom opened his mouth again. Sheridan cut him off.

"OK, OK, I don't know what you're going through. Not like this. But I can appreciate the pressure you must be under. And I argued your case. I honestly did. I don't think you should be here any more than you do. I want nothing more than for you to walk out with me right now. But—"

"Then do it."

Sheridan stared at him.

"Do it," said Tom. "Stand up, walk to the office, flash your badge, tell them who you are, who I am, and that this operation's been compromised. There'll be a bit of complaining on their part but they'll let us go. They have to." Tom stared at him, unblinking.

Sheridan tried to return the stare. Couldn't. He sighed. "I can't."

"Why not?"

"You know why not. I'd be disobeying orders. I'd—"

"We've gone way beyond that."

"I can't do it." Sheridan's voice began to creep up in volume and shrillness. "I'm sorry. I want to. If it was up to me, I would. But I can't. You know the way these things work."

"Yeah, I do."

"So you'll know that I can't just stop it now. I don't have the authority."

Tom stared, deciding what to say next. Sheridan said nothing. Had nothing more to say.

"You know why I was so good?" Tom said at length. Sheridan didn't reply. "At what I did. Working undercover. You know why?

Because I knew when to dig in. And I knew when to get out. And my handlers respected that. They let me run things my way. Trusted me." Tom leaned forward. "Trust. That's the main thing. That's why I was successful. Because I had trust from my handlers. They knew I was the one on the ground, risking my life. They knew I would do the best damn job I could. Get results. And they trusted me to do it. But they also trusted me when I said I had to be pulled out. If I said a job was going wrong and to get me out, I was out within hours. And that's the difference here. Trust. That's what these kinds of operations are fueled on. And I'm getting fuck all of that from you."

The words hung in the air. Time dragged, prison slow. Eventually Sheridan spoke.

"Like I said, I want you out of here. Right now. But I've been overruled. And there's nothing I can do. I'm sorry."

"So you keep saying."

"I know. And I wish I could do something more."

"Then do something more."

"I can't just walk out of here with you. You know that."

"Then go and talk to your superiors. Tell them I need to get out. Not that it would be a good idea, not perhaps, tell them I *need* to get out. Or I will be killed. Tell them that. Then get me out of here. Straight away. Do it now."

"I will. I promise. But . . ."

"No buts. Get me out of here. I'll try and look after myself until that can happen. But make it quick."

"What are you going to do? How will you protect yourself?"

Tom thought of Darren. Of the scarred man who had stared at him. At the danger he was now in. An idea entered his mind. A stupid, desperate idea that might not even work. But he had nothing better. "Leave it to me," he said. "Just go to your boss and get me out."

Sheridan nodded, then stopped. Like something had just occurred to him. Something unpleasant.

"What?" said Tom, picking up on it. "Something wrong?"

"No, I . . ."

"What? Something's going on. You've just thought of something."

"No . . . leave that to me. I have just thought of something. Let me sort it."

Tom stared at him once again. Trying to appraise Sheridan, work him out. "Is there something you're not telling me, Sheridan?"

"Like what?" Sheridan seemed suddenly shifty.

Tom wasn't going to trust his answers. "I don't know. But something's just occurred to you. And you're not going to tell me."

"It's nothing."

"Even if you think it's nothing, tell me."

"If you can get a confession out of Cunningham that would be great. Your ticket out of here straight away."

"Yeah. That's not going to happen overnight. Just get me out."

"I will," said Sheridan, resolve in his voice.

Sheridan stood up. "I have to go. Please trust me. I'm working to get you out of here. In the meantime, do what you have to do to survive."

"I always do."

THE OFFICER ESCORTED SHERIDAN OUT, another took Tom back to his wing.

No one tried to stop him, assault him, impede him on the journey.

Back on the wing he checked his watch. Dinner in a couple of hours.

Then he could put his plan into action.

23

TOM SPENT THE REST OF THE AFTERNOON locked up by choice. He had long missed lunch by the time his meeting with Sheridan had ended, so he was given a cold coagulated mess on a tray to eat. It remained uneaten. He no longer had an appetite. Cunningham was off the wing, so he remained in his cell alone.

He couldn't read, saw only words dancing on the page, couldn't watch TV, saw only mouths moving but nonsense coming out. Couldn't do anything. Except go over the conversation he had just had with Sheridan, then think about what he was planning to do.

It was a ridiculous, stupid plan. And worst of all, it might not even save him. But it was that or nothing. And nothing would definitely get him killed. Whereas this could buy him a little time. Then it was down to Sheridan.

He was starting to warm toward the detective. He didn't think that would have been possible after their first meeting. Sheridan had been cold, arrogant. But that mask had slipped to reveal a conscientious cop trying to do his job as best he could.

Further thoughts were cut short by the sound of the key in the lock. The door opened.

"Dinnertime," said an officer, walking away before the word was out of his mouth.

Tom stood up. Took a deep breath, exhaled. Another. Exhaled. Ready.

He stepped outside. The walkway of his upstairs cell was narrow, the metal steps downstairs to the food queue clanging and clattering with the footsteps of inmates all moving at once. He looked around, tried to catch sight of the person he wanted. Couldn't see him.

"Hello." Suddenly Cunningham was by his side. Smiling.

"Hey," said Tom, continuing to scan the wing.

Cunningham smiled. "I've been thinking about things."

Tom didn't reply.

"I've been to see the psychologist this afternoon."

"Good for you." Distracted, eyes on the crowd.

"And she says I should open up more. I told her about the night terrors, like you said I should."

Had he? He couldn't remember.

"And she said I should talk to you about them. Especially if you're there to share them. I told her you'd been a friend."

The word still jarred, even though Tom had used it first. "Right."

"Yes." Cunningham was nodding earnestly, the smile still on his face. "A friend. My friend. Because you stopped me getting hurt. And you helped me during the night. And we talked. Remember?"

"Right."

"So she said—"

Tom was aware of a movement on the walkway above him. He looked up. There was the scarred man once more. Smiling the way he had that morning. But now he was joined by someone else.

Dean Foley.

As Tom stared, Foley cocked his finger and thumb, made a gun. Fired. Laughed.

Tom looked round, mind moving quickly. Message received and understood. He was in danger. Immediate danger. He needed to do something about it if he wanted to stay alive.

He looked again at Cunningham. The man had been about to say something. Might it be about the bodies? Could Tom risk it? And what would he do if it was? How would he get the information to Sheridan then?

Then he saw his target. Looked between the two men below, the two above, making his mind up on the spot. "Just a minute," he said and walked off.

Clive was lining up along with the rest of the men returning from the carpentry workshop. Tom pushed in alongside him.

"Oi," came a voice from behind, a huge threat implied for such a small word.

Tom turned. "Won't be a minute. Just want a word with my mate here."

Clive's eyes darted round the room like a swallow trapped in a barn.

"Don't I, Clive?"

"We got nothing more to say."

"We were in the middle of a conversation, weren't we? When I was dragged away. Now what were we talking about?" Tom pretended to think. "Oh yes. You were telling me I didn't have a clue what was going on. Isn't that right, Clive? Yeah?"

Clive looked round once more. If he expected someone to come to his aid, he was going to be disappointed. Others were curious about what was happening, but not enough to intervene.

"So tell me, then," continued Tom. "Tell me what I don't understand."

"There's nothing."

"Oh, come on, Clive. Don't be like that. You've gone all shy. Come on. Tell me." Tom put his arm round Clive's shoulders, began to squeeze.

"Get off me. I'll call one of the guards over. I will."

"Do it," said Tom. "Because I really don't care anymore. I've had enough of this place, of your shit. You think you're protected? We'll see."

Clive turned to him, tried to squirm out of his grip. "I am protected. But you're not." That sick little smile again. "Your days are numbered, mate. Numbered."

"I know that. And I've got nothing to lose. Nothing at all. So if I'm going down, you're coming with me, Clive. Now tell me. What's going on in here? And why are you involved?"

"Oh, that's the thing that really annoys you, isn't it? You don't know me. You don't know what I'm doing here. You're so used to having everything your own way, having every angle thought out that you can't take it when that doesn't happen, when someone pulls one over on you. You hate it, don't you?"

Tom was really beginning to get angry now. He no longer bothered to hide it. "Then tell me. Enlighten me."

"Enlighten you? Oh, la-di-fuckin'-dah. Enlighten you." Clive laughed. Heads began to turn.

Tom felt his face redden with anger. He knew how this conversation was going to end but at least he could try to get something from it. He made one last attempt. "Just tell me, Clive. What's going on. You've got nothing to lose. Just tell me." Hoping that his raised voice was one of anger not begging.

Clive just giggled. Then, with a quick lick of lips, he stopped. Thought. And spoke. "How's your niece, Mick? How's Hayley doing?"

Clive stood back, pleased with his retort. Even more pleased with Tom's reaction.

Tom staggered back as though he had been punched in the heart. Staring all the while at Clive who kept giggling, a small, frightened man enjoying his moment.

He cocked his fingers into a gun, pointed. "Hayley," he mouthed. And Tom lost it.

PART TWO
ISOLATED

FOLEY WAS FINALLY ALONE.

The holding cell in the police station looked and felt exactly the same as it had when the teenage Dean Foley had been repeatedly locked up for finishing too many conversations with his fists. And for starting them that way too. He thought he had come too far to be back but clearly that wasn't the case. And he would have at least the rest of the night to decide how he felt about that.

His high-priced lawyer had been and gone. Arriving with his usual anger and arrogance, throwing profanities and threats around the interview room like grenades, telling the detectives they would just get up and walk out, that they had nothing. His usual tactics, but this time they didn't work. They just stared at him, watched the show. This noted, he shifted his approach. Argued his case, Clarence Darrowed himself through every loophole. Like the well-paid legal whore he was, thought Foley, he tangoed nimbly round every tenuous legal definition, contorted himself into every possible position to dazzle them. Nothing. He didn't scare them anymore. They had Foley bang to rights. His lawyer was a sideshow distraction. He could huff and puff as much as he liked, no way was he blowing their house down. Once he realized that he checked Foley was being looked after to the letter of the law and left.

No joy catching the eyes of his payroll boys and girls either. They wouldn't look at him, speak to him, from which he drew two conclusions.

Firstly, they didn't want to give themselves away, secondly and most importantly, he was fucked and they weren't going down with him.

So, back in the cell, belt, shoes, watch, money, everything gone. Stripped of his assets. No special privileges. Alone. With only his thoughts for company.

Get used to the solitude, Mick had said through the flap in the door as he'd passed by earlier, you're going to have plenty of it.

He had shouted in return, given a full rundown on what he would do to him once he got out of here—and he would be getting out of here—then what he would do to his family and . . . But Mick was long gone by then. So Foley, spent and exhausted, slumped back down on the bench.

Now he had time to think. Plenty of time to think.

Mick Eccleston. Betrayed by Mick Fucking Eccleston. Betrayed.

"Betrayed . . ."

The word sounded overly dramatic spoken aloud. Like Shakespeare or Game of Thrones *or EastEnders or something. But it was the right one. The only one. Betrayal. And by someone he trusted. No, not someone—the person he trusted more than anyone else. The one person he believed would never betray him. It was unreal. Like his life had skipped the rails and he was in some upside-down dream world. He wanted to wake up, for everything to go back to normal again. But that wasn't going to happen.*

Betrayed by a man he had come to regard as a brother. Again, that sounded dramatic but it was true. His own brother—his real one— was long since gone. Spirited away into foster homes and adoption, where their father couldn't get at him anymore.

Dean had gone into foster care too, separated from his brother, because it hadn't been determined whether he had helped his father with the abuse or been trying to prevent it. But Dean didn't want to live in foster homes. Or with his father. So he set out on his own.

His mother had left when he was little. Well, not left, because he could never remember her being there much. Just kind of drifted away. He could remember her smell: dead flower perfume and economy gin. Her taste, when she pushed her face up against his and gave him a great slobbery kiss: sweat, hardened powder, and thick cheap lipstick. He would always rub it away when she had gone. Remove any mark of her, open the door of any room she had been in to get rid of the fumes. She was always going out, always looking for something his father could never provide, she said. One night she went out and didn't come back. Nine-year-old Dean felt plenty of conflicting things about his mother. When she disappeared he just felt relieved, but mostly because his dad had told him that's what he should feel.

"Gone off with a fancy man," said his dad at first. That changed over the years to, "Gone to live in Spain," "Went to see her sister and never came back," "Just didn't want to know us no more." It wasn't until years later that Foley realized his father had been interviewed repeatedly by the police about his mother's disappearance. Sweated for as long as they could legally hold him. Assaulted with telephone directories and rubber pipe in places that hurt but didn't scar. Then let go, only to be brought in again and again, whenever they thought they could turn the screws on him. She never turned up. Dead or alive. Being able to prove nothing, they eventually, reluctantly, left his father alone to get on with his life.

"Never trust the police, son," his bitter father's bitter mantra. "They're a bunch of cunts."

Young Dean took those words to heart.

His father had plenty of other words for Dean too.

"You're fucking nothing. You'll always be fucking nothing."

"Best part of you dribbled down your mother's leg."

"Should have drowned you at birth."

Years later, Dean had driven his Bentley to his father's house to show him what he had made of himself. His father wouldn't let him in. "You're still a fucking nobody. Always will be." Slammed the door on him.

He was the only man Foley couldn't hurt. So he hurt everyone else instead.

Dean Foley was an angry kid. He made that work for him. Eventually he learned how to channel it and became an effective, angry man.

His empire was quickly built. And he needed a right-hand man. Enter Mick Eccleston.

Mick was perfect. Hard when he had to be, clever when he had to be. Deaf, blind, and dumb when he had to be. He became the brother Dean had lost.

They did everything together. Everything. And now this. That's why it hurt so much. More than he could show. He had never had a meaningful relationship with a woman. Sometimes he saw one who made him feel things he couldn't articulate, connected on some lizard level. Put images in his mind of what he wanted to do to her body. So he would. And sometimes pay her afterward. But nothing more than that. Nothing that would get in the way of his work. Or his relationship with Mick.

He thought of what he had said earlier. About shooting someone in a Deansgate bar and getting away with it. About digging more than one grave for revenge. About what Mick had done to him. About what he would do to him as a result of that.

And he thought.

And he thought.

And he thought.

And when the morning arrived and the officer opened the door for his hearing and looked at him, both of them pretended not to notice the tears.

24

LILA STIRRED HER COFFEE, stared ahead at nothing. Morning in the refectory coffee shop on Truro College campus and she was taking a break from her classes. Alone. As usual.

She crumbled her double chocolate muffin into pieces, popped one in her mouth. The campus was still busy this close to Christmas, local day students on predegree courses, just like she was doing, reluctant to say goodbye to their friends and go home. Degree students still doing the rounds of Christmas parties before they disappeared. Lila was apart from all that.

She was invited to parties, drinks in the town with her classmates, and had attended a few. But she still felt she had little in common with them. Because of what she had been through, she couldn't share their self-assurance and certainty about the future. So she went along with them, joined in as much as she could, but found them, for the most part, too young for her. Or at least too naive.

Tom had encouraged her to mix, get to know them. They might not be as bad as she thought. And she had made an effort, but she still preferred her own company at breaks, rather than hearing their opinions on the latest vacuous American TV show they were all watching on Netflix. And not just because she and Tom couldn't get Netflix.

But as the term had progressed, she had reached something of a conclusion. Maybe it wasn't them. Maybe it was her. Yes she was different to them, had had a different set of life experiences, felt older than her years as a result. But maybe she just wanted to fit in and couldn't. Maybe she wanted to be carefree and laugh at everything like they did. To care about dumb stuff like TV shows and Instagram celebrities. To have certainties instead of nothing. Maybe. And the closer she got to that, the harder the divide was to navigate.

Whatever. She sat on her own, drinking her coffee, eating her muffin. Thinking that maybe she should just accept that distance if she couldn't change it. She tried to think about other things. Like the motorcyclist she had seen a couple of days ago at the top of the hill.

Why couldn't she get him out of her head? He had been lost, he said, that was all. Looking for somewhere. Seemed simple enough. So why did she feel like he had been watching her?

She hoped it wasn't because of the color of his skin. True, there weren't many people of color in her part of Cornwall and the ones who were there tended to stand out. But with his Belstaff motorbike jacket and good boots he hadn't looked like a local. Or a tourist for that matter. He looked like he had been working. And that made her uneasy.

Since then she had checked for him while she was on the bus, when she was home, even during the night, getting up to peer into the darkness. She found no trace of him, no evidence he was watching her or the house, but that unease still wouldn't lift. She was glad Pearl was with her most of the time, just for security.

She wished Tom were there. He would know what to do. Or if he didn't, she could comfortably imagine that he did. He was that kind of reassuring presence in her life. She just wished she could talk to him. Maybe she could go and . . .

"Hey," said a voice, "mind if I join you?"

Lila looked up, startled. A girl was standing in front of her.

Dark skinned, pretty, smiling. Lila thought for a moment, recognized her from her sociology class.

"Uh . . . yeah, sit down."

"Looked like you were miles away," said the girl, sitting down opposite, putting her coffee on the table.

"Yeah, I was."

"We're in sociology together, aren't we, with good old Guru George Hearn?"

"Yeah." Lila smiled then looked perplexed. "Guru? Is that what he's called?"

"Yeah the whole class calls him that. Don't you?"

"I'm . . . I hadn't heard." She smiled again. "Guru. Suits him."

"I'm Anju. Don't know if you knew or not. You're . . . Lola?"

"Lila." She said it. Couldn't help herself. There was something about this girl's openness that made her put aside her normal reticence.

"Lila. Right. Where's that from?"

"What d'you mean?"

"Lila. Does it mean something?"

"Dunno."

"Your parents didn't give you that name because of any deep meaning or anything?" Anju laughed as she spoke.

Lila smiled again. It felt like the most smiling she had done in ages. "Obviously you've never met my parents."

Anju laughed again. It sounded so refreshing, unforced. Infectious, even. There was no way this girl had an agenda. No way someone had sent her over to talk to her. At least Lila hoped there wasn't.

"Mine gave me this name, Anju, because it's Hindi for beloved."

"So you're Hindu?"

Another laugh. "No. Muslim. My parents wanted to show just how progressive they were by giving me a Hindi name. I told them, if they really want to show how progressive they were, they should have called me Alison or Sandra, or something like that. They didn't think it was funny."

Lila was starting to enjoy herself for the first time in ages. She made eye contact with Anju. Anju's gaze was direct, intense, even. But not in an unpleasant way. The opposite. Like she just really wanted to see her and be seen by her. So honest Lila dropped her eyes to her crumbled muffin.

"Sorry," said Anju. "I'm stopping you eating."

"No." Lila shook her head, "You're not. I was just having a coffee. The muffin was just something for my fingers to do while I drank."

Anju laughed, again unforced, uninhibited. Lila was really warming to her. "Why are you on your own? You waiting for someone?"

"No," said Lila. "Just . . . dunno. Just on my own."

Anju sat back, regarded Lila inquisitively. "I've been watching you."

Oh God, thought Lila, here it comes. She's mental. I've attracted another mentalist.

"Not like that," said Anju, almost reading her mind, "Not in a stalkery way or anything. Just, you know. I've seen you in class and round here. And you're always alone. Well, most times. But you don't really look lonely."

"What do I look like, then?"

Anju thought, tried to find the right word. "Apart. Separate."

"Yeah?"

"Yeah. Like you're different to the rest of the class. You're mainly in psychology, right?"

Lila nodded. "And sociology. But mainly psychology. So you think I don't fit in? I'm a misfit, is that what you're saying?"

"No. You just seem like you know something they don't. And they might never know it. It's interesting."

Lila sat back, stared at the other girl. Wary now. Not wanting to give up any more of herself. "I know something? Like what?"

A look of worry crossed over Anju's face. "I'm sorry. I'm really sorry. I've spoken out of turn. I get like that. I don't have . . . whatever other people have. A filter? I don't know. I just . . . say things. What I'm thinking. Some people say it makes them uncomfortable. I've done it to you now. Sorry." Anju's face reddened. She picked up her coffee cup, made to go. "I'll leave you alone. Enjoy your muffin."

Lila watched her rise. Something told her if she let her go, she would regret it. She thought quickly, made a decision. She would trust her feelings.

"No, wait. You don't have to go."

Anju paused, looked back at her.

"Sit down. We were getting on all right."

Anju sat back down. "Sorry. I'll make small talk instead. Promise."

Lila smiled. "Who the hell wants small talk?"

Anju smiled too.

And they both laughed.

25

FOLEY STOOD BY THE DOOR, waited patiently for it to be opened. Looking at the floor, his feet, showing a deference, a nervousness even, he never would on the wing.

The door opened. A young woman greeted him, hand on the edge of the frame, looking round, smiling, long hair falling to one side as she did so. "Hello, Dean. Come in."

The accompanying officer nodded at him to enter then walked away. No longer visible, but somewhere nearby. Dean Foley entered the room. The door was closed behind him.

The room was like no other in the prison. It didn't even feel a part of the prison, which was the point. A desk at one end, bookshelves and files against one wall. Modern furniture. Tasteful, not the usual institutional kind. Even some decorations, paintings, flowers. A coffee maker on top of a filing cabinet filling the room with welcoming aromas. Recognizably branded supermarket milk and biscuits in their packaging gave a comforting but slightly melancholic glimpse of the outside world. In the center of the room, two comfortable Ikea armchairs.

Foley knew the procedure. He sat in one. Waited.

"Coffee, Dean?" Doctor Louisa Bradshaw knew the routine. She had established it.

"Please," he said.

She poured a mug of coffee, added milk and one sugar. Foley smiled inwardly at her remembering. She passed it over as she seated herself opposite him.

"Thank you," he said. His voice changed in here, layers of hardness stripped away, revealing something softer. He knew he did it but couldn't help it. Now he no longer wanted to help it. He took a sip of the coffee, then placed it down at his side.

"So how've you been, Dean? How's your week?"

He picked up the mug, took another mouthful. "Interesting, I suppose you might say." Replaced the mug. She was waiting for more. He knew she would be patient with him, wait until he found the right words.

He had never thought he would actually tolerate a visit to the psychologist. Not just tolerate, actually enjoy. Look forward to it, even. It had been one of the terms of his sentence. A reduction in time served if he agreed to address his underlying anger issues. With no choice, he'd agreed. It was the approach his lawyer had taken during his trial. Dean Foley wasn't a villain—not as such—just an angry man trying to make a living the only way he knew how. If he didn't have the anger he might be a more useful member of society. All bullshit and he knew it. But if it reduced his sentence, he would play along.

And it worked. So when he was transferred to HMP Blackmoor he was told that he would be having regular weekly sessions with Doctor Louisa Bradshaw. Fair enough, he thought. He would find a way around that.

But he didn't. He had taken one look at this young woman—pretty but not making the best of herself—and thought she would be a pushover. So he took charge, told her he didn't need all this nonsense, that he was going to use these sessions to contact associates on the outside, check how his empire was running. He'd see she was handsomely compensated.

But this doctor, this young woman, had stood right in front of him and said no. You're not going to do that. You might have your own way everywhere else in this prison but not in this room. And if you think you can try that then I'll refuse to hold these sessions with you and whatever concessions you've managed to achieve for sentence reduction will be null and void, and you'll be back at the beginning. If you're in here you do what you've come for. Or you don't come at all and take the consequences.

Foley had been shocked. No one had spoken to him like that in years, certainly not a woman. He didn't know what to do, how to respond. So he just looked at her speechless. And then did what she told him to do.

And it was the most difficult thing he had ever done in his life.

"In what way interesting?" she said.

"Someone turned up. From my past. Turned up in this prison. The person who's responsible for me being in here, you might say."

Louisa's eyes widened, then quickly regained her professional composure. "Before you say anything else, Dean, I have to remind you of my position here."

"I know. If I confess anything, you have to pass it on. But other than that, everything in here stays in here, right?"

"That's right."

"Well it's no secret. I was betrayed by my right-hand man, who turned out to be an undercover cop. And now he's in here. Supposedly for assault."

"Why d'you say supposedly?"

"Because he's an undercover cop, isn't he? Got to be working on something."

"Not necessarily. He might actually be in here for assault. It was a long time ago. His life might have changed. Have you spoken to him?"

"Not as such." A smile crept onto his face. "But he's seen me. He knows I'm here."

Louisa picked up on the smile straight away. Knew it wasn't a positive development. "And have you attempted to do anything? Take revenge against him?"

She looked at him directly. He tried to avoid her penetrating, unwavering gaze, but couldn't. He could see beyond those eyes, knew decisions were being made about him. Like she knew and understood him better than he did himself. It used to unnerve him. Not anymore. Just made him want to find out what she knew, how she knew it. Wanted to understand himself as well as she seemed to understand him.

"No," he said, eyes dropping away. "I haven't."

"Do you intend to?"

He picked up the mug, took a mouthful of coffee. Tried to hide behind that before answering.

"I . . . don't know."

Louisa sighed. "Your honesty's commendable, at least. But I've got to remind you . . ."

"I know. I'm just trying to tell the truth." He leaned forward in the chair, hands clasped, engaged. "I mean, I looked at him, went onto his wing to see him for myself. Made sure he saw me."

"And?"

Foley shrugged. "He kicked off. Got taken to the seg." He held his hands up. "Nothing to do with me. Honest. Didn't touch him."

"And now what? Are you waiting for him to be released back into the general population?"

He frowned. Twisted his hands in his lap. "I've been thinking about this. For years, really. And honestly? I don't know what I want to do. I mean, I know what I should do. And I'd do it in a heartbeat if I was on the out."

"And what's that?"

"Make him pay. Slowly. Then make sure he couldn't do anything like that again. To anyone."

"And would that satisfy you?"

"Yeah." Quickly, without reflection.

Louisa frowned. "Would it? Really?"

Foley thought. Again, he wanted to be honest with this woman. She demanded it of him. Deserved it. "I . . . It used to. In the past, like. You know? When someone does you a wrong turn, you make them pay for it. Don't think about it, it's just the way it is. You have to do it, it has to happen."

"Why?"

"Because you look weak if you don't. And if you look weak, others'll think you are weak. And they'll attack you. Image, innit? Got to project a strong image or your enemies'll find a way to get you. Like Chinese whispers. Word gets round. Before you know it, everyone's left you for the other side—because there's always another side, always someone who wants to be where you are— and you're on your own. And you won't last long like that. So yeah. You've got to take revenge."

"But you haven't answered the question. Does doing that, taking revenge, satisfy you?"

"I . . ." Foley thought. Hard. "I don't know. I never look at it in those terms. Just what has to be done, you know? You do it without thinking. It's what you have to do."

She gave that penetrating gaze once more and he felt himself shrinking. Sometimes he wanted to shout: "What can you see? What am I really like? To you? To everyone? To me? Tell me . . ." But he never had. Or at least not yet. But he never stopped thinking it, wanting to do it. He might do it one day. But he probably wouldn't. He was too scared to hear the answer.

"So you get no satisfaction from it, is that right?" Her voice calm, as though she had all the answers to the questions she was asking and was waiting to see whether his measured up.

"I've never . . . I don't know. I suppose I must do. Yeah, I must do."

He tried to imagine times in the past, draw those memories out, and examine them in front of her. It was what she had taught him to do in these sessions and he found it so damned painful. Reliving his life. All the pain, tears, hurt, everything. But it was necessary, she had told him. To try and understand who he was now, where he was going from here, he had to discover and acknowledge how he had come to be here. And that meant opening everything up. Everything.

His father. The beatings. The childhood taken away from him by one man's singular cruelty. Making himself so pathetic in front of his father he would turn his vicious, abusive attention to his younger brother. Letting his relief, his silence become complicity. Reliving all of that once more. Stripping himself emotionally bare in front of her.

And the life after that, in care. Foster homes. Institutionalized neglect. Abuse. That anger building up inside him, all the time, waiting for an outlet. Detention centers. Young offender institutions. Feeling something within him die, something fragile, knowing once it was gone it could never be reborn. Then trying to harden himself around it. Not wasting time mourning the man he could have been but embracing the man he had no choice but to become.

Which led him here. And now this question. Did he enjoy his revenge?

He thought back on all the punishment beatings he'd orchestrated, the ones he'd carried out himself. Bones breaking bones, turning flesh into something unrecognizable, getting high off the screams, the prayers, and the pleading. Seeing other faces on the bodies he hurt, older faces. One in particular. Hitting again and again until he had no strength left, until his arms were carved from jelly, until that face disappeared. And that would suffice, that exhaustion. That sense of accomplishment. Until the next time. And the next . . .

"I . . . suppose so." He had tried lying on previous occasions and had been found out straight away. He had done it to look good in her eyes. But he soon realized the only way he could do that was by telling the truth.

"How did it make you feel?"

"Like . . ." Back there again, in some anonymous warehouse or lock-up. Punching a hanging body like he was tenderizing a side of meat. Blood pounding in his ears, the air rank with coppery blood, shouting all the while, drowning out the screams of his victim.

Trying to get rid of that one face.

"I had to keep going," he said, eyes closed, mind somewhere else. "Had to make sure that face went away."

"Which face?"

He opened his eyes. What had he said? He was suddenly sweating, shaking from more than the coffee. He stared at her.

"Which face?" she asked again.

He hadn't known he had said that. She had done it to him again. Forced him to admit something about himself that he hadn't realized he was thinking or feeling.

"You know which one."

"You need to say it."

His voice had shrunk to near a whisper. "My father."

Louisa nodded, as though her hypothesis had been confirmed. There was no triumph in her gaze though, just acknowledgment.

"So all the time you were taking revenge on people you thought had done you wrong, you were trying to attack your father." Not a question, a statement.

He nodded.

"So what are you going to do about this new person? The one you claim is responsible for you being in here?"

"He is responsible." The words whiplash quick, coated in anger.

"Is he? Aren't you ultimately responsible for your own destiny? That's what you've said previously."

Foley didn't answer. He knew to answer either way would incriminate him.

"Dean?"

"I trusted him. And he betrayed me. That's the facts."

"So how did you feel when you saw him again? Did you want to take revenge on him for what he did? Are you planning on doing that? And if you do is it because of what he did to you or who he represents?"

"I . . . I don't know. I really don't know."

"Were you and he close?"

He couldn't look at her, didn't trust himself to speak. He nodded.

"Very close?"

"Brothers," he managed.

"And if you do decide to take revenge on him, this brother figure, for betraying you, how would you do that?"

He frowned at her.

"You've just said that when you administered punishment beatings before you did them personally. Would you do that this time? Could you do that? To someone you considered a brother? Or would you have to get someone else to do it for you?"

He looked at her, frowning.

"Come on, Dean, I'm not stupid. I know the sway you've got in this place. The hold you have over people. You say the word and something would happen to this man."

"That's not—"

"Yes it is true, Dean. We both know that. What I want to know is, what would be the point? For you, I mean. You could have him beaten up, even, I don't know, killed. But what would be the point? He's been out of your life these past, what is it, four years? I'm sure you don't regard him as someone close to you anymore. So what would you gain?"

Foley said nothing.

"Or do you think it's something you have to do yourself? Are you trying to prove something? I mean, you wouldn't be trying to hurt someone who can never be hurt again. It wouldn't be your father. Not this time. And it wouldn't be to save face on the out. So ask yourself. Why would you do it? And what would you gain?"

Foley stared at the floor. The coffee had gone cold. The room felt dark, as though a thunderstorm was about to hit. He felt tired. So, so tired.

"I want to go back to the wing now, please."

HE WAS ESCORTED BY THE SAME OFFICER. Neither attempted conversation. He felt like he had just done six rounds in the ring. The sessions did that to him. On other occasions he had screamed and thrown furniture. Other times he had curled up into a fetal ball and sobbed his heart out. But this time he just felt . . . different. Exhausted, but like a door had been opened inside him and he didn't know which way he should go. All he knew was that he had better regrow his shell by the time they reached his cell.

Public persona back in place, he stepped onto the wing. And almost immediately ran straight into Clive.

Foley took in the other man's disheveled appearance, reddened features, and black eyes. "Well, well, well . . . Killgannon's done a number on you, hasn't he?"

"Yeah," Clive spat through missing teeth. "Got solitary for it, though. Bastard."

Foley laughed. "Come into my room."

The officer led the way to Foley's cell, let them in, then, dismissed, drifted away.

"Tell me what happened."

"I reckon Killgannon thought he was being clever," said Clive.

"Attack me, get put in solitary. So you can't get to him. Or so he thinks, anyway. But you can get him anywhere, can't you, boss?"

Foley said nothing. Heard Louisa's words rattle round his head, spinning so fast they gave him a headache.

He blinked them away. "Why?"

Clive frowned. "Why what?"

"Why did Killgannon go for you?"

"Like I said, so he could get put in solitary. For protection."

"I know that, Clive. I was on the wing and saw it happen. He could have gone for anyone. Why you and not someone else?"

Clive became suddenly impatient to be away from there. He could sense the mood in the cell had changed. "Because I led him to you. And he was angry because of it."

"And that was all?"

"Yeah," said Clive, nervously, "That was all."

Foley stared at him, unflinching. The kind of gaze Louisa had given him.

Clive wilted. "Well, I may have said something to annoy him. Nothing really."

"Like what?"

"Nothing, just . . . to spark him off, see what he would do."

Foley felt his anger rising. "Like what?"

Clive knew he had no choice but to tell the truth. "I mentioned his dead niece. That's all."

Foley turned his back on Clive, walked as far away from him as he could in the cramped space. Clive kept prattling on.

"Shut it." Foley turned back, eyes blazing.

Clive shut it.

Foley's voice, when he spoke, was dangerously calm and low. "That was a bad thing to do, Clive. A very bad thing."

"Yeah, I realize that now, Mr. Foley, but—"

"Don't interrupt. You did a stupid thing. An unnecessary thing."

Clive shook. "I'm . . . I'm sorry . . ."

"So you should be, Clive. And you will be. But first you need to be taught a lesson."

Clive was almost sobbing now. "Why?"

"Because . . ." Foley thought. About his session with Louisa. About what had been said, what he had experienced. The conclusions about himself he had reached. "Because it's what I have to do. Because you've done me wrong and I have to punish you for it. Simple as that." The words said like a learned piece of church ritual. He sighed, felt something slip away inside him.

Clive was openly sobbing.

"Baz."

His right-hand man stepped into the cell.

Put something into it, he thought. "Little task that needs attending to, if you don't mind. Clive here's been a naughty boy and spoken out of turn, upsetting someone very badly. As such he needs to be taught a lesson. Nothing too major, just so he won't do it again."

"What about a fall?" asked Baz.

"Yeah. A high one. With some stairs for a bit of variety."

Baz nodded. Smirked.

"Please, Mr. Foley, no, please . . ."

Foley turned to Clive. Regarded him with contempt. "We're all responsible for our own destinies, Clive. Be a man. Accept responsibility for yours."

Baz dragged Clive out of the cell. Foley heard him pleading all the way up the stairs until, after a little while, his pleading crescendoed into a scream, then silence fell across the whole wing.

He sighed once more. Felt, in his mind's eye, Louisa giving him that stern gaze.

Seeing right inside him.

Even when he closed his eyes, she was still there.

26

DS Nick Sheridan liked to think of himself as a decent man. Conscientious and diligent in his work, always putting in as much effort as he could, a staunch friend and supportive colleague. One of the good guys, making a difference by catching the bad guys. Or women. Or however they preferred to be referred to. He didn't differentiate. At home a loving husband to Carrie and a great father to Chloe and Baxter. He also refereed nonleague football matches. Just a hobby, but one he took seriously, bringing his rigorous sense of right and wrong to bear on the field. He saw it in part as an extension of his police work: creating as fluid and exciting a game as he could while at the same time not allowing impropriety to go unpunished. Rigorously enforcing fair play in all things. So to have doubts about his colleagues and their attitude toward an investigation was no small thing for him. And to actively take steps to investigate for himself was unheard of. It challenged every belief he had been brought up with, the very bedrock of his existence. Nevertheless, something told him to persist. And he listened to that voice.

No police station was ever silent, and Middlemoor, the Exeter headquarters for Devon and Cornwall, was no exception. With its flat-fronted red brick facade and pitched roof, it resembled anything from a redundant Territorial Army base to a factory in

an old Norman Wisdom film. Inside it had been gutted and reno-
vated according to the best practices of every generation of police
commander, every Home Office initiative. Currently the Serious
Crimes Squad worked out of a large open plan first floor office, all
workstations and access cards.

Sheridan was still at his desk even though the rest of his shift
had long since gone home. He was waiting for an unobtrusive time
to start investigating, when he wouldn't attract too much attention
from the night shift.

The office was still well lit, the overhead strip lights and desk lamps
turning the windows into mirrors against the darkness beyond. Night
shift tended to be on call more than day shift, reactive not proactive.
As such he found himself alone in the office. He had made small talk
with the few officers he had encountered, telling them he had reports
and court documents to finish before he could go home. Trading weak
jokes and bonhomie, they left him to it.

He had thought of working from someone else's computer in
case anything was logged but decided that his own would be secure
enough. There was a legitimate reason he was searching for these
things, after all. He logged into the Police National Computer.
Quickly found who he was looking for.

Dean Foley. Plenty on him and what led to his subsequent
imprisonment. But it was less informative than he'd been expecting. Sheridan knew all the facts already. There was only a mention
of Killgannon by the pseudonym Witness M, and a note that
nothing more could be revealed about his identity for fear of being
compromised in the field. It stated that Witness M had infiltrated
Foley's gang under the name of Mick Eccleston and was reporting back to his handlers. It was his first-hand testimony that led
to Foley's arrest and imprisonment for drugs, human trafficking,
assault, robbery, intimidation, extortion, and anything else they
could find to throw at him. And it had stuck.

As he read through something caught his eye. The fact that there had been another undercover officer involved in Foley's gang. Witness N. Witness N had been placed first but hadn't been as successful as Killgannon. For some unspecified reason there was no mention of Witness N anymore. Sheridan tried a search under that name. Came up with nothing.

That was as much as he could discover. The rest he knew, even down to which prison Foley now resided in. Which made Sheridan wonder. Had Harmer not known Killgannon was really Witness M when he assigned him to cozy up to Cunningham? Or had the information somehow slipped through the net? Or the line of thought Sheridan didn't want to pursue but knew he had to: had Beaker known about Foley's presence and still assigned him? Or even worse, assigned him *because* of Foley's presence?

It made no sense. Or none that Sheridan wanted to countenance. He sat back, logged out of the Police National Computer.

What next? He looked over at Harmer's closed door.

He knew what he had to do. And he didn't relish it one bit.

He stood and caught his reflection in the glass. He looked furtive, a criminal about to commit a crime. Felt immediately guilty because of it. Maybe that's all he was. An untrustworthy sneak spying on his colleagues. In a way he hoped so. He wanted to be proved wrong. But there was that inkling again, telling him that he was right. That there was something wrong and he had to find out what it was. No matter how unpleasant the outcome.

He crossed to Harmer's door, tried the handle. Unlocked. He knew he should feel pleased about that but it just made what he had to do all the more unpalatable. He looked round once more even though he was the only person in the office. He felt he was being watched through the night-mirrored windows. Or maybe that was just his sense of guilt again. He stepped in Harmer's office, opened up the screen, tapped in Harmer's password. Finding it had been easy. His porn name. Name of first pet, mother's maiden name. The team had played that game one night in the pub. Harmer, not wanting to appear standoffish, contributed his. Then, still drunk later, let it slip he would use it as his password. Sheridan, good cop that he was, had filed the information away. He never thought he would need to use it, especially under these circumstances.

When requested he typed in "LolaCraddock," which he supposed could have been a real porn name given some adjustment or imagination, and he was in.

But he didn't actually know what he was looking for. He just hoped he would recognize it when he saw it. If he saw it. He still hoped that he was imagining things.

And yet . . .

He scanned the files for anything that looked out of place, anything alluding to the current investigation. Nothing looked out of the ordinary. Everything seemed in order. He was going to leave things at that, reluctant to delve further into a superior's work, when something caught his eye. A file. No. Two files. He checked their names.

Witness M.

Witness N.

Sheridan sat back, heart hammering away.

He had been right. Damn it, he had been right.

He didn't know whether to congratulate himself or commiserate with himself.

He did neither. He opened the files.

27

TOM HEARD THE KEY TURN, the sudden noise resonating around the empty cell. Even though an opened door usually signified the beginning of something, that deep, heavy metal sound seemed more suited to an ending. Maybe it was time for him to leave solitary, Tom thought. Or knowing this place, maybe it was just lunchtime.

Tom sat up on the rudimentary bed, regarded his visitor. A young woman, quite well dressed, looked back at him. She smiled. The gesture seemed more about showing she was no threat than any kind of kindness. Prison wasn't a place where kindness flourished. Or if it did, it was swiftly punished.

"Hi," she said, dismissing the officer who had opened the door for her.

"Have to stay with you," the officer said, unmoving. "Hostage risk."

She turned toward Tom. "You're not going to take me hostage, are you?"

Tom frowned. "Why would I do that?"

She turned to the officer. "I don't think there's anything to worry about."

The officer clearly didn't want to move. "Will you state you're taking full responsibility for your own safety, then?"

"I will."

The officer reluctantly left, but not before saying he'd just be down the corridor.

"Hi," she said again. "I'm Dr. Bradshaw. Louisa."

He nodded. "Tom Killgannon."

"I know." She looked round. The only piece of furniture in the room was the bed. "May I sit down?"

"Be my guest. Didn't know I was getting visitors. I'd have run the vacuum round."

She laughed. It sounded genuine. She sat down at the far end of the bed, away from Tom. He didn't move. The only other seat was the toilet in the corner. "How've you been?"

The question invited a full answer, one Tom was unprepared to share. He had been dragged off the wing as soon as he assaulted Clive. The officers were on him straight away, hitting the alarms for backup and using the kind of restraining techniques he had used in his previous life. Some of them had got in body shots while he was restrained, the clever, sadistic kind that left little or no mark but instantly debilitated him and hurt like hell for ages afterward.

He was dragged straight off to the CSC, the Close Supervision Center or Seg Block as the inmates called it. The place was a prison within a prison, no natural light in the corridors, no way to tell day from night. Once the key was turned and he was left alone, he could have been deep underground for all he knew.

He'd paced the tiny floor until the adrenaline rush wore off then lay on the bed as the pain the officers had inflicted replaced it. And there he had remained. His claustrophobia, already bad in his usual cell, went into overdrive. It was like a cheap public toilet in some brutalist parking lot, tiled walls, disinfected floor, stainless steel pan and washbasin. A bed that provided the barest minimum of comfort. A small window of reinforced glass in the cell door so wing staff could observe him, shatter marked and blood smeared by the force of a thousand fists and headbutts. If his injuries hadn't been so debilitating he would have screamed himself hoarse. Instead he just lay on the bed, trying to hold himself together, eyes closed.

Sometime later that night—he thought it was still night—an officer brought him a tray of food. His first instinct was not to touch it. Foley had people all over the prison, why not the kitchens too? Could it be poisoned? Or worse, could someone in the kitchens have tampered with it just because he was in solitary and they assumed he was a pedophile or a rapist? He knew from urban legend the kinds of things that were put into prison food. Everything from excrement to broken glass.

He had no appetite. Left the tray by the door.

Later, after a fitful spell of sleep, he was awakened by the key in the door and an officer telling him it was time for exercise. He was led out to a small cage, still inside the prison within the prison, and told to walk around it for half an hour. If he wanted a shower now was the time to do so. He did so.

There were other inmates in the exercise cage, some walking, others just standing, staring. All kept apart from each other by the officers. They ranged in looks from the damaged to the dangerous but all seemed to have one thing in common: something missing behind their eyes. Either as the result of their segregation or the reason for it, Tom didn't know. But he avoided eye contact with all of them.

He took his shower, alone, then it was time to go back to his cell. Another tray replaced the untouched one from the night before and he looked at the unappetizing food in its compartments. Some cheap white sliced bread. Something which could have been porridge or wallpaper paste. Two overcooked, shriveled sausages. At least he assumed they were sausages. A plastic cup of milk. He ate the bread, one of the sausages. Left the rest.

And that became his routine. He thought he had been on the Seg Block for at least three days, judging by the number of times the lights had gone out and the number of times he had been allowed out to exercise in the cage. Other inmates came and went, making as much noise and trouble as possible: banging on cell doors, shouting threats, making promises. Like once powerful jungle animals having their agency forcibly removed, reacting the only way they knew how. Their bravado failing to disguise their fear.

Tom had managed to keep his claustrophobia under control by congratulating himself on escaping Foley's attentions. Hoping Sheridan would manage to get him released. But the silence dragged on, the loneliness crept up on him. And with it paranoia. Justified paranoia, he felt.

He wasn't safe here. The door could be opened at any time and anyone could enter and he had no way of stopping them. They could take him somewhere, even beat him up in the cell. Or worse. Alone, Tom imagined it all.

It wasn't just the fear that got to him. There was the enforced time spent with only his psyche for company. Time to reexamine every single event in his life that had led him to this point, every wrong or right move he had ever made. Not just reexamine, but relive. In as much detail as his memory could muster. And, with nothing else to expend its energy on, it could muster a lot. His emotions were in constant turmoil. All he relived were the wrong moves. The costly ones. And no matter what he did, he couldn't get his mind off that track. He understood why so many people in solitary attempted suicide. His claustrophobia ramped up, made him want to throw himself at the walls, batter his way out, scream the place down. But he forced it down, kept it trapped inside him, as he was trapped in the cell. It made him shake constantly. He didn't know how much more of this he could take. Lights out on the wing in a locked room was bad enough. But lights out inside him was a whole new level.

Then the door had actually opened. And Dr. Bradshaw had

entered. At first Tom was relieved to see someone who wasn't in a uniform, someone smiling. But that meant nothing. Someone could have sent her. And that whole hostage thing might have been to lull him into a false sense of security. Or was he just being paranoid? He gave himself the benefit of the doubt.

"So," she said again, "how are you?"

Tom shrugged, not wanting to give anything away to a stranger. Tried to keep his trembling under control.

"Must be difficult for you in here," she said. "I've had a word with the officer outside, said you should at least have something to read to pass the time. Any requests?"

"Sorry, but who are you and why are you here?"

"My mistake. I thought you'd know. I'm the prison psychologist."

"And why have you come to see me?"

She smiled once more but Tom sensed nervousness in that smile. Her eyes darted away from him, down to the right. She's about to lie, Tom thought.

"I do this with everyone who ends up on the CSC. It can be a harsh environment. It's my job to see you're coping. And if you're not, suggest ways which might help."

"Right."

"So how are you coping?"

Tom shrugged.

She said nothing, she was working out another approach. "Noel Cunningham. You know him, right?"

Tom nodded.

"He's been acting out since you've been in here."

"So?"

"He's a . . ." She thought. Seemed to be deciding how much she could say to Tom. Or how much she should say. Or maybe just pretending to do that to get Tom on board. "He's an interesting person. I see a lot of him. When you were brought here he wanted to see me. Said it was urgent. Said it was about you."

Tom waited. Tried not to show any eagerness in what she had to say.

"I think he misses you. He seemed to function better when you shared a cell with him. Said you answered his questions, talked to him. Tried to help him with his night terrors. He seems to have taken a few steps backward since you've been here."

"What d'you want me to do? I thought anything like that was frowned upon in prison?"

She leaned forward, sharply. "Anything like what?"

"I don't know. You said he misses me. That sounds like a red flag if you're thinking of putting me back in with him, don't you?"

"Or it sounds like you were a positive influence on him. Someone who could help make his time inside more bearable."

Tom didn't know what to say next. He didn't know whether to trust this woman—his instinct said not to—but she seemed to be smoothing the way for him to return to the wing and resume his place in a cell with Cunningham. Let him complete his mission and get out. That mission, however, had now taken second place to survival. Stay alive by any means necessary.

Before he could reply, she spoke again. "His mother is very ill, you know."

"Cancer. I know."

"He wants to get out and see her."

Tom said nothing.

"He's made a kind of deal with the warden. Has he mentioned it to you?"

Tom was wary now. If she wants to know something, make her work for it. "Would he have?"

Dr. Bradshaw sat back, regarded him again. Seemed to be making up her mind. She leaned forward again. "He's agreed to give up the whereabouts of the graves of his final two victims on Blackmoor. If he does that and it checks out, he can visit his mother."

"Right. And you're telling me this why?"

"When you're returned to the wing, I can arrange for you to be his cellmate once more."

"Why would you do that?"

"As I said, you're a positive influence on him."

"And you want me to get him to open up about these graves, is that it?"

She smiled. Nodded.

"What about me? What do I get?"

She paused, seemed to study him. "You were in therapy for PTSD before you came in here. On antidepressants. Yet you've not asked to see me or anyone else on the mental health team. Why is that?"

Tom didn't reply. Just felt his heart hammering.

"I think I could help you."

"With what?"

No smile now. Only seriousness. "I saw how you looked at me as I entered. I've observed how you've behaved while I've been in the room with you. I've seen those looks, those reactions before. Prison can be a harsh environment even for those who are used to it. There's help here if you need it. And I think you'd benefit from it."

Tom said nothing.

"Would you like me to recommend you return to the wing? Back with Cunningham? Inmates are usually only here for a few days when they've done what you've done."

"And I be your spy, is that it?"

"It would certainly help in your parole."

Tom thought. The walls of the cell pushing in on him, suffocating.

"OK," he said.

"Good." She crossed to the door, knocked on it a couple of times. It was opened. She turned back to Tom.

"Thank you for talking. I've enjoyed it. I hope you have too." She smiled. "And thank you for not taking me hostage."

The door slammed shut behind her.

28

LILA HAD FINISHED HER COURSEWORK and had no exams but still went into college. Not because she had to, just because she wanted to. She was beginning to enjoy the routine. Having had no structure in her life for so long, to willingly embrace it was quite exciting. Almost an act of rebellion. Pearl and she had settled into a routine of sorts at home too. Lila going to college, Pearl running the pub, both coming home, taking turns cooking, watching TV together. Pearl being the better cook by far but tolerating the meals Lila came up with. Becoming comfortable in each other's company.

However Lila had another reason for still coming into college. To meet the girl who had sat next to her and couldn't make small talk.

Anju had been on Lila's mind a lot since they met a few days ago. The thin Asian girl with the ready smile and the sparkling, I-know-something-you-don't eyes, the dark, shining hair. The way she picked up her coffee cup, those long, sensuous fingers curling round it, bringing it to her lips, enjoying drinking in slow, languid mouthfuls. She'd barely stopped thinking about her. *Couldn't* stop thinking about her.

Lila had tried to explore and understand her feelings for Anju, so strong, so sudden, but wasn't given to that degree of self-examination. She usually pushed everything as far inside as possible where it couldn't hurt her. Tom was the only person she had come close to opening up with. And he wasn't here to listen to her.

Then there had been the text last night:

Coffee tomorrow? - Anju X

She had replied:

Yes.

Oh yes.

She reached the café. There was Anju, sitting at the same table they had sat at last time, two coffees, two muffins in front of her.

Her head propped on one hand as she read a book. She looked up as Lila approached, gave a wave and a smile.

Oh God, thought Lila. Why is my heart racing?

"Hi," said Anju, straightening up and closing her book.

"Hi back," said Lila, returning her smile too. She felt suddenly awkward.

"You going to sit down? I got you a coffee. And a muffin. Waited for you to get here before I started on mine."

"Thanks." Lila put her bag on the table, sat down next to her. The move, bringing her into such close proximity to the other girl, felt exhilarating yet natural. She looked at her once more, aware she hadn't stopped smiling since she saw her. Noticing Anju doing the same thing.

Lila forced herself to look away. "What are you reading? Something for the course?"

"Nah," she replied, picking up the paperback and showing her the cover. "Something for me."

Lila took it, looked at it. "*On the Road*, Jack Kerouac. I've heard of it. Any good?"

"Nah," Anju shook her head. "Supposed to be the kind of novel everyone has to read when they're our age. Meant to open our horizons and make us rebel against our parents and take off looking for art and creativity the rest of our lives."

"And it doesn't?"

She laughed. "Fake as fuck. This guy admits he borrowed money off his mother and took off when his exams were done. Drove round a bit with his mate then wrote it down. It's like what he did in his Easter vacation. And he hates women. Or at least is terrified of them."

"Well that's off the list then." Lila put it down on the table.

"Yeah. I'm not at the end yet, so maybe it all changes. But I doubt it. It's like that other one you're supposed to read and love. *Catcher in the Rye*." She shook her head. "World's moved on, mate."

"Yeah. I read *The Great Gatsby* a couple of years ago," said Lila. "It's really not."

They smiled at each other. Eyes held for that beat too long, neither wanting to be the first to break. But Lila did.

"Thanks for the coffee."

Anju picked up hers, took a sip. Lila watched those long, delicate fingers at work. Fascinated by them.

"What's up?" asked Anju.

"Nothing." She took a sip of her own coffee. She wished she could have matched Anju in the finger stakes but with her bitten, unvarnished nails and her red, scarred hands, there was no way. Those scars told a story. One of desperation and escape. One she didn't want to talk about.

"So what have you been up to?" asked Anju.

"Oh, nothing much. The guy I live with . . ." She stopped herself. "That's wrong. The guy I share a house with is away at the moment. And his . . ." She paused, unsure how to describe Pearl. "Well, friend, I suppose, she's moved in."

"Why?"

"Company, I guess."

"He's not your dad or anything though, is he?"

She shook her head. "Just a guy I share a house with." She looked at Anju once more. Differently this time. "You think it's weird, or something? It's not . . . you know, anything funny."

"Nah, I don't think it's weird. You're in Cornwall, remember. Weirder things than that round here."

Lila definitely interested now. "Like what?"

"My dad's a child psychologist. Some of the things he's seen out in the really remote villages . . ." She shook her head. "I'll tell you about it sometime."

Lila was surprised at how warm a feeling those words gave her. It meant she would be seeing more of Anju. And she really liked the sound of that.

"What's this guy you live with do, then?" asked Anju.

"He's . . . well he sort of runs a bar in the village. St. Petroc."

Anju looked immediately more interested. "St. Petroc? Where there was all that trouble a few months ago?"

"Yeah, that's where we live. Just outside, anyway."

Anju leaned forward. "Did you see any of it happening? There were human sacrifices, weren't there?"

Yeah, thought Lila. It was meant to be me.

"Oh, it's all over now." She sighed. "I think the village's trying to put it in the past. Good for the tourist trade, though. Apparently."

Anju sensed Lila didn't want to talk about it. Sensed there might be something more to her reluctance and let it go. "So," she said instead, "he's not running his bar now? He's away."

"Yeah."

"Coming back for Christmas?"

"Hope so."

Anju sensed the weight behind Lila's words. Leaned in closer. "Something up?"

Lila turned to her. She hadn't known this girl long—barely knew her at all—but she felt there was some kind of connection between the two of them. A deep connection. She felt she could talk to her. But more than that. Tell her secrets that wouldn't be used against her.

"Can I tell you something?"

Anju shrugged. "Yeah. Sure."

"I mean, really tell you something. It's important. You can't tell anyone else. And I mean that."

Anju began to look a little nervous. "What are you saying here, Lila?"

"I just don't want you to tell anyone else. No one. This is really secret. D'you understand?"

"Yeah." She smiled. "I'm not going to say that you can trust me because I've found that everyone who says that turns out to be an untrustworthy little shit. But go on, you can tell me. I don't lie."

Lila thought. There was something about Anju that seemed trustworthy. Honest. She hoped she was right.

"He's in prison."

Anju nodded. "Right. I thought it might be something like that."

Lila jumped forward, lowered her voice. "No, not like that. It's . . . he's working in there."

"A prison officer." Anju's expression said she wondered what the fuss was about.

"No, not like that either."

"What, then?" She laughed. "Is he a spy or something? Working undercover?"

Lila didn't answer. Her expression did the talking for her.

"Seriously? Really?"

Lila shushed her. "Keep your voice down. Yes. He's . . . he does jobs for the police and people. He's doing one now."

Anju sat back. "Wow. Just . . . wow. I was only joking, you know."

"I know. But you've got to keep that a secret. Please."

"Yeah, course. Who'm I going to tell?"

Lila believed her. She had wanted to tell Anju so much, share something important with her. And she had feared that if she did so she would regret it afterward. Hate herself for it. But she didn't. Telling Anju had felt like the most natural thing in the world. The right thing to do.

"D'you go and see him?" asked Anju after a silence.

Lila shook her head. Took a sip of coffee.

"Why not?"

"I dunno, I . . ." Another sip of coffee. "It's selfish of me. I know it is."

"What d'you mean?"

"I just don't want to see him in there because I know it'll depress me. Sitting in that room, behind bars . . . I don't think I could take that."

"But doesn't he want to see you?"

"Yeah, probably. And that just makes it worse. Because then I feel even more guilty. And I feel like such a selfish cow. I hate myself for it."

"Couldn't you go with someone? That friend of his who's staying at yours?"

"I think she feels the same. But she can't go because she's part of his cover story and doesn't want to blow it." She sighed. "I just hope he gets his job done and comes home soon."

Another silence.

"I'll take you," said Anju suddenly.

"What?"

"I've got a car. I mean, I won't come in with you, I'll wait outside, but at least you'd get to see him. And you'd have someone to bring you home so you wouldn't feel lonely."

Anju placed her hand over Lila's. Lila's heart skipped a beat. Neither moved.

"OK, then," said Lila eventually. "Thank you."

"You don't have to thank me. We're friends. It's what we do. Now eat your muffin. Then let's go do something."

Lila smiled. She wanted to eat her muffin. She wanted to drink her coffee.

But she didn't want to move her hand away from Anju's. Ever.

29

SHERIDAN COULD BARELY SIT STILL. Back at work, at his desk, staring at the screen, but hardly seeing it. Mind otherwise occupied with what he had discovered on Harmer's computer.

DCI Harmer had given the go-ahead for Operation Retrieve with Killgannon. But he was also the one who had dismissed Sheridan's concerns for his safety. And now there was this. Harmer was compromised, but Sheridan couldn't say or do anything about it to anyone higher up the chain of command. Especially not concerning how he had come across the information. It would be a huge black mark against him, potentially even a demotion or suspension.

So there he sat, unable to progress until he knew what to do. But he had to do something, tell someone. And the natural person would be Blake.

He watched her working at her computer, her face expressionless, nearly angry. He had heard of this thing called resting bitch face. One of his kids had said it at home over dinner describing a girl at school, the other had laughed. He had been angry at first. It sounded insulting and he questioned why one of his own children would use language like that. They had laughed in response, told him what it meant. A face in repose that looked angry or cruel. A part of him felt bad thinking that about her. Especially since he felt he had something like it himself.

He reached his conclusion. No choice, really. He had to talk to her. But not here, not now.

He kept working, one eye on his screen, the other on her until eventually she rose from her seat, picked up her lanyard and a box of cigarettes from her desk, made her way to the door. Sheridan rose, followed her out.

She was standing in the self-appointed smoking area, outside the back door by the vans. The gulag, it was called. An officer lit up and nodded to her. She nodded back, her expression telling him she didn't want company. He sauntered away. Sheridan took his place.

"Can I have a word?"

She looked at him, suppressed a smile. "Come over to the dark side, Nick? Didn't think your fitness regime would allow it."

She proffered her packet. He saw a cancerous mouth on the side, winced as he shook his head.

"It's about work," he said. "I didn't want to say it in the office. Thought it was best when we were on our own."

She looked round the parking lot. Officers and detectives were coming and going all the time, cars and vans on the move. "And you chose here?" she said, smiling once more.

"Better than inside." He paused. Gathered himself for what he was about to say. "Look. There's no good way to say this. The Killgannon thing. I . . ." He sighed. "Harmer hasn't been straight with us."

She froze, dead as a statue, cigarette on the way to her lips. Slowly, she turned to face him. "What d'you mean?"

"I . . . hacked his computer."

"You did what?"

"Just listen. He's got stuff on there about Tom Killgannon and Dean Foley that he shouldn't have. Or at least should have shared with us before we sent Killgannon in there."

"Like what?" She glanced sideways at anyone who might be

listening in, made the movement as natural as possible. Her face gave nothing away.

"I think he knew Foley was in Blackmoor when we sent Killgannon inside. He knew their history, what Killgannon had done, how he'd got him in there."

She took a huge lungful of smoke, let it percolate within her, slowly blew it into the air. Then let the cigarette fall from her fingers, stubbed it out casually but firmly with the toe of her boot. "I don't know what to say, Nick. I'm as confused as you are."

Sheridan looked round. Shook his head. Then looked back at Blake, mind made up.

"We've got to go and see Harmer."

"When, now?"

"Why not? We've got to know what's going on."

Blake looked unconvinced. "It's risky. Let's think about it."

"We don't have time. Come on."

He walked back into the building. Blake watched him go, then followed him.

"Come in."

Sheridan walked into Harmer's office, Blake running along behind him. Harmer sat back, regarded the pair of them.

"What can I do for you?"

"It's about Operation Retrieve," said Sheridan. "We've been doing some digging and—"

"Is this about Foley and Killgannon?"

"Yes, sir," said Blake.

Sheridan was pleased she was speaking up, backing him up.

Harmer nodded. "Sit down. And make sure the door's shut."

They did so.

"I was going to talk to you both. After your visit the other day, I looked into the Foley case. And there are some . . . irregularities. To be honest, I don't know how we didn't see this earlier. This could be a real mess."

"How so?" asked Sheridan.

"Like I said, I looked into Foley's file. And I think there's something else going on here. A huge amount of money went missing the night Killgannon busted Foley. Foley's money. And the last person to see it was Killgannon. Or Mick Eccleston as he was then."

"So?" said Blake.

"Everyone was questioned. No one saw anything. No one knew what had happened to it. Like it had just disappeared into thin air. But someone had taken it. And the suspicion was always on Killgannon."

"How much went missing?" asked Sheridan.

"Over two million."

"What?" Sheridan again. "And we think Killgannon has it?"

"We don't know. We don't know anything about this Tom Killgannon, do we?"

"He's got a good record."

"For doing underhand, dangerous things. Not always on the right side of the law either. For all we know he could be dodgy, shall we say? In fact I think he might be."

"What d'you mean?"

"As I said, I've been doing some digging. And Killgannon wasn't the only one undercover in Foley's gang. And that other one didn't have such a good ending as Killgannon."

"What, he's dead?"

"May as well be. Poor bastard."

Sheridan flinched. Harmer hardly ever swore. This must be serious. "What, Killgannon sold him out?"

"I'm trying to find out. So we've got more to go on. It's not easy."

Sheridan thought. "But none of this changes the essential job, though, does it? Whether he's taken money or not, it doesn't matter. He's there to do a job and he's been compromised. We have to get him out."

"He's safe where he is at the moment," Harmer replied, voice hardening. "He's in segregation, away from the wing, from Foley. Let's think about this."

"What's to think about?"

"This could be a major complication, DS Sheridan. We have to proceed carefully. As I said, he's fine where he is. I need to think about this." He sat up straight, looked at the door. "I have work to do."

Sheridan reluctantly stood. Blake also.

Sheridan walked slowly back to his desk, Blake to hers. Neither spoke. He stared at his screen once more and thought.

How did Harmer know Killgannon was in solitary? Who had told him? Sheridan was waiting to hear from Killgannon. And what about this other undercover officer? What had happened there? It sounded like Harmer knew more than he was letting on. And not sharing it. This wasn't how Sheridan did things. This wasn't fair play.

He tried to work. Think what to do next.

But he couldn't concentrate.

30

"GOD, IT LOOKS AWFUL," said Lila. "Like a haunted house or something."

"Or a concentration camp. Look at all that barbed wire . . ."

They had driven to HMP Blackmoor in Anju's Citroen C3, that her parents had bought her for passing her exams and to bribe her to keep studying. She had laughed as they drove off, asking Lila what they would think if they knew she was using the car to drive her friend to see someone in prison. Lila had laughed along, but apprehensively. Parents buying gifts like cars for their children and nurturing their education was completely alien to her. A world she had never been in and could never be part of.

The morning was crisp, the winter sun shining and the sky a pale robin's-egg blue. Consequently the drive had been pleasant, Lila almost forgetting the purpose of the trip, feeling instead they were just out for the day. She felt slightly guilty about Tom for thinking that.

She also felt very nervous about seeing him again. It had been over two weeks since he had set off on this assignment and she hadn't heard from him at all. While she admittedly hadn't tried to contact him, he had told her not to. If he could, he'd said, he would phone her. She hadn't expected him to, not really. And he hadn't. She knew it would be difficult for him and talking to her would make it even worse. That was the reason she hadn't reached out either. She felt he would understand. Or hoped he would. But now she was changing all that by coming to see him. She just hoped neither of them would regret it.

They pulled into the parking lot. Looked at the prison once again. It seemed to suck all the light from the sky into itself, making the day darker, colder. Lila felt her stomach turn.

"Here we are, then," said Anju turning the engine off.

The mood in the car changed, reflecting the prison, turning from light to dark. No more laughing or singing along to music, no more convincing themselves they were on a carefree day out. This was it.

"Well," said Lila, "time to go in."

She looked over at the main gate where other visitors were beginning to gather. Dressed against the cold they resembled a huddled, sad mass of broken people in Primark clothes, their urban dress at odds with the surrounding countryside. Blank-faced women, old before their time, holding on to small sullen children, their hard eyes counting down the years until it would be their turn inside, their tiny fists clenched to demonstrate how they would get there. Older relatives beaten down by time and circumstances, their prematurely aged features roadmaps of wrong turns and dead ends. A few wild-eyed, gap-toothed crackheads trying to pretend they hadn't taken anything before coming, hoping they wouldn't be turned away.

Lila knew she would have to join them. Be one of them.

"It's hard to tell," said Anju quietly, "whether they're like that because visiting the prison made them that way, or it's the end result for them being like that."

"We do sociology," said Lila, equally quietly, "I think we know the answers."

Anju said nothing.

"It's like stepping back in time, going to join that lot," said Lila.

Anju frowned, turned to her. "What d'you mean?"

A hard sigh from Lila. "I used . . . I wasn't always like this. Student, regular life, all of that. I used to . . ."

"Don't. You don't owe me anything."

"No, I . . . I feel like I should. I didn't used to have a . . . what could you call it? A life like yours. It was more like theirs." She gestured to the crowd.

Anju smiled. "So what? Doesn't matter. You're here now. You've come a long way from . . . wherever you were before. And you fought hard to get there. I can tell." She placed her hand on Lila's knee. "It doesn't matter. It's not who you are now."

Lila felt a near electric charge from Anju's hand, the warmth penetrating through her jeans. She looked up, straight into Anju's eyes. "Who am I now?"

Lila would think back on this moment, try to remember who had moved in first. She couldn't remember, didn't know. Sometimes it had felt like her, others like Anju. Most of the time it had felt mutual, both at the exactly the same time. But the result was the same. They kissed. Long and with increasing passion, hands gripping the other's body, each pulling the other toward them, getting as close as the car would allow. Lila's heart hammering like it was about to explode, shaking from everything. Fear, lust, desire, love. And things she couldn't name too.

Eventually they pulled apart. Eyes wide, chests heaving, as though they had both run marathons. Both still staring at each other.

"That's who you are now," Anju said eventually.

Lila just stared. Couldn't find any words.

From out of the corner of her eye she saw the gate open, the mass of visitors move forward.

"You'd better go," Anju told her.

Lila nodded, not trusting herself to speak. She didn't move.

"Quick, before they shut the gate."

She nodded, got out of the car, closed the door, her movements seemingly done by someone else.

She made her way to the gate. The words, questions, in her head bursting like fireworks before they could properly form.

She tried to pull herself together. Prepare herself to see Tom.

31

"VISITOR. OFF YOUR ARSE, COME ON. Lucky you're about to go back to the wing. Wouldn't normally be allowed this."

Tom was still on the seg block when the door opened and an officer stood there. He was barely squeezed into his uniform, more angry bovine than human, face like a shaved bull, ready to charge at the merest excuse of a red rag. Tom stood up slowly, not wanting to do anything that could be misconstrued as a violent attack. This guy wasn't just ready, he was hoping for it.

"Out here."

Tom left the cell.

"Face the wall."

Tom did so. The officer locked his cell door, turned to open the door off the wing.

"Go on."

Tom walked through it, waited at the other side.

"Get moving."

He did as he was told, not minding the deliberate dignity-sapping instructions. This is it, he thought. Sheridan's come through. He had to stop himself from smiling as he walked.

They reached the visitor's room.

"Face the wall."

Tom did so.

The door was opened.

"Go on, then."

Tom scanned the room. Strip lit from above and painted a color of green that only existed in institutionally depressing paint charts, it had official posters on the walls warning of expected penalties for smuggling contraband, breaking contact laws, or attempting to pass gifts. Everyone sat at tables, leaned in, hunched together, trying to create invisible bubbles of privacy. Wives, parents and children desperately trying to reconnect with increasingly distant husbands, fathers, and sons. Like the most depressing restaurant ever. Officers took the place of waiters, watched and listened. Reminded everyone where they were. Not that anyone would forget.

Tom's heart sank. He couldn't see Sheridan.

Then he saw who was there.

Lila.

And a completely different set of emotions overtook him.

She looked up, smiled. No, beamed. So pleased to see him. She stood up as he approached, attracting the attention of a prowling officer. She hugged him.

The guard broke them up. "Come on, enough of that."

They both sat down at either side of their table, just like everyone else. Tom's initial euphoria at seeing her drained swiftly away. He didn't want her to see him like this. In here. Subjugated. Powerless. It was like something had shifted inside her too, like she was experiencing something similar.

They both gave each other tentative smiles, both not wanting to be the first to speak. Unsure how to proceed.

"So here you are, then," he said eventually.

"Yep. Here I am."

"So . . . how you doing? At home. Everywhere." Like English was no longer his first language.

"Fine, yeah." A nod and a quick look around. Hoping no one

was listening in, not wanting to make eye contact with anyone else. Not sure she could believe she was actually here. Then trying for honesty. "Missing you."

The words hurt as much as he had expected. Reminding him why he hadn't been in touch with her. He tried another smile. It didn't disguise what was in his eyes. "You too." Then, before either of them could linger on that, he went on. "How's things at home? You managing?"

"Yeah. Pearl's moved in."

Tom nodded. "Good. Company for each other."

"Yeah. We're getting on OK. She's . . . OK. Yeah."

"I'm glad. I hope you two can be friends."

"She's fine." Almost a smile. "We watch films together. The kind I can't watch with you."

Tom smiled. Easier this time. "Stuff about bursting into song over dying boyfriends?"

"It's not like that."

"You know what I mean."

"Yeah. And she's managed to get the Wi-Fi set up. Got me into *Riverdale* and *Glow* on Netflix. And *Dynasty*."

"I take it back," said Tom, properly smiling now, "she's a horrible person and you shouldn't be friends with her."

Lila laughed. The moment passed and died away to nothing. Silence fell once more.

"How did you get here?" asked Tom. "Did Pearl drive you? Why didn't she come in?"

"No, I got a lift from someone at college. A friend."

Tom picked up an undertone to Lila's words. "A friend?"

Lila looked away, eyes down to the right. "Yeah. A friend."

Tom picked up on the gesture, what it meant. "What's he like?" He smiled as he spoke.

Lila glanced up, then away again. "She."

"Oh. Right."

Tom stared. So much he wanted to ask her but knew this wasn't the right time. Then arrows of sadness and regret. Anger. He should be at home with her, looking after her. Listening to her, trying to guide her. The pair of them getting ready for Christmas next month. Not here in this place.

"You look like you've been in a fight."

Startled, her words brought him out of his reverie. "Oh. Yeah. Nothing serious." Playing it down. Knowing she wouldn't be convinced.

Her look told him she wasn't.

"It's a harsh environment. It doesn't mean anything. You've just got to stand your ground. Not get pushed around."

Lila sighed. "I worry about you in here."

Tom tried to smile the worry away. "You should see the other fella."

"No thanks."

He nodded. Another silence.

"Miss you." She sighed. "It's not the same without you at home."

"But you can watch *Dynasty*."

"Yeah, but it would still be better if you were there." She was trembling behind her words. Tom realized that being here with him was hitting her harder than she had expected.

"It's not going to be long now. Don't worry. OK? I'll just . . ." He glanced round, conscious of ears everywhere. "It won't take me long now. I'm getting close. I'll get that done and . . ." He shrugged. "Come home."

She nodded, eyes down. He couldn't tell how convinced she was by his words but he could guess. Not as convinced as he wanted her to be but desperately wanting to believe.

She looked directly at him and the fear, the pain was no longer hidden in her features. Tom's heart went out to her but he had to keep it together. She was the one walking out of here, not him. He didn't want to take all that back into a cell with him. Couldn't.

"How's everything else at home?" he asked again, not sure what else to say as everything felt unsure.

"I'm still going to college."

"And you've a got a new friend. So everything's OK?"

"Yeah. Well, you know." Lila leaned forward, suspicious. "Why?"

"Has anyone been around to the house?"

"What d'you mean?"

"Remember, I told you and Pearl that I'd asked someone to keep an eye out? On the pair of you, on the house. Just in case, you know, anyone came along trying to poke holes in my story."

"So you're asking if I've seen anyone suspicious."

"Well, I—"

"Yes."

Fear came suddenly into Tom's eyes. "What?"

"This biker was at the top of the hill the other day. Said he couldn't get his bike started but it worked first time. I watched him leave. Haven't seen him since."

"What did he look like, this biker?"

"Tall, good-looking. Nice leather jacket. Big boots. Black guy."

Tom eased slightly. Sat back, a small smile on his face.

"What's wrong?"

"That's Quint. He's the old mate that I asked to keep an eye on you both. And the house."

"Well he's pretty shit at it because I spotted him straight away. Crap liar. Bike's not working. Jesus."

Tom smiled. "You're good, aren't you?"

"Yep."

A bell rang. "Time's up," shouted a guard.

They looked at each other, their faces unable to hide their respective sadness.

"Don't give you long, do they?" said Lila.

"Never long enough."

The guards walked around the tables, forced goodbyes, and checked for contraband. Some seemed genuinely sorry to be intruding in private moments, some seemed to enjoy it.

"I've got to go," said Tom. "Thank you for coming. I mean it."

"Pleasure." Lila realized what she had said. "Well not a . . . well, you know what I mean."

He smiled. "I know. It's helped me, seeing you. Thank you."

She gave a sad smile. They embraced under the watchful eye of a guard.

"Won't be long now," he told her.

Lila nodded, trying to keep tears at bay. Then turned and made her way to the door.

Tom tried not to watch her go. Instead he walked to the doorway, ready to reenter the main body of the prison, queued up alongside everyone else.

Tried, like everyone else, to keep his face as devoid of emotion as possible.

32

THE DOUBLE LOCKS INN stood on the Exeter Ship Canal. An old redbrick pub, the kind of destination cyclists and walkers made for during the summer. Accessible by foot or cycle path from the quay, an easygoing place where people would while away sunny afternoons, drink beer, eat home-cooked food, and let their dogs splash about in the canal. Still technically walkable from the center of the city but due to the silence and surrounding greenery, it felt out in the countryside, far from anywhere.

Winter nights were different. The trees and bushes denuded, now screeds of arthritic branches gnarled against the darkening sky. No walkers. No dogs. The only cyclists were those pedaling home late from work. Approaching by car spoiled the rural idyll. A drive around a labyrinthian industrial estate, then avoiding the potholes to cross a rusted, narrow metal bridge, the plates clanging and loosening further with the weight of each vehicle, down a minimally surfaced road to reach the pub.

Sheridan pulled his car into a shadowed corner of the uneven graveled parking lot and turned off the engine. Sat there, unmoving. He and Blake had arranged to meet to discuss what Harmer had told them. Somewhere neutral, well away from the eyes and ears of Middlemoor.

He never thought his career would come to this. Secret meetings in pub parking lots with his own colleagues. Yes, this kind of thing happened with Chief Inspectors and others, but not fellow officers. It just wasn't right. We're supposed to be better than them, he thought. We have the moral high ground, we shouldn't need to engage in this murky cloak-and-dagger kind of stuff.

When he had graduated from the academy he had felt bright, shining. Like the Christians would say, born again. So eager to fight crime, to make a difference, keep the streets safe, the first few weeks as a probationary constable were the happiest of his life. He might have annoyed his superiors, his peers even, with his earnestness, but that didn't matter in the long run. He just hoped some of his enthusiasm rubbed off on them, inspired them to try harder at their jobs. And he had hoped, as he continued with his career, that feeling would continue. That he would never become disenchanted.

But he soon saw things, experienced things that were so far out of his field of reference that all of his beliefs were challenged. When he witnessed firsthand as a uniform the depths to which one human being was capable of sinking in order to damage another, the shine soon wore off. Especially as he saw it repeatedly. He was then faced with a choice: go along with it, become like everyone else on the force, accepting of the status quo and develop coping strategies to get through every shift, or declare it wrong and fight against it. Keep that part of himself shining. He chose the more difficult way.

And he still believed it had been the right thing to do. Even now, sitting in this parking lot. Whatever happened, no matter how unpleasant, how repulsive, he would always find something within himself to keep going. To not accept things as they were, to use his position to make things better. He completely believed that. And to prove it, lived this personal creed every day.

A knock on his window jolted him from his reverie.

He looked up. There was Blake, leaning down. She gestured for him to get out. He did so, locking the car behind him.

"Have you just got here?" he asked.

"I saw you arrive. Came over to get you when you didn't emerge. Come on." She turned, walked toward the pub. He followed.

A corridor with bare, uneven wooden floorboards gave way to a tiny bar with a fire roaring in one corner. The few people drinking inside barely looked up as they entered. Blake looked at the bar.

"What are you having?"

"Sparkling water, please."

She gave him a quizzical look.

"I'm driving."

"One won't hurt."

He shook his head, personal credo still intact. "Sparkling water, please."

She went to the bar, returned with a glass of red wine for herself and a bottle of sparkling water for him. Sat down opposite. "Cheers," she said.

She had changed her clothes from work, he noticed, and she looked very different. Now dressed all in black; tight jeans, boots, zip-up leather jacket with a scarf coiled round her neck. Heavy makeup. He had never seen her dressed like this before. He still wore his work suit, padded anorak over the top. He looked at his watch.

"Let's talk."

She moved in, head close to his. They looked, he imagined, like a couple having an affair before returning home to their respective partners. He tried straightening up, not wanting to give that impression, but she spoke so quietly, he had no choice but to lean in to join her.

"So. What are we going to do?"

Blake sighed. Nodded wearily to herself as if she been thinking hard, reached a conclusion. "Well, first I've got something to tell you. Then we'll take it from there." She took a mouthful of red wine. His water was untouched. It was only set dressing so he could sit in a pub and not look out of place. He didn't think it was fair to come into somewhere that made a living by selling drinks and not buy one.

"I was a uniform up in Manchester when Foley was arrested."

"What? But how did—"

"Just listen, Nick. I was on the scene the night he was busted. The night that Mick Eccleston sold him out."

"You were there?" Sheridan couldn't believe what he was hearing, or why he was only hearing this now. "Why have you never told me this before?"

"I told Harmer. It was his call whether he told you or not. Apparently he didn't think you needed to know."

"But—"

"Just listen, please. I was there when Foley was arrested. And when the two million went missing. For a while we thought it was going to throw the trial, that we wouldn't get a conviction. But Eccleston's testimony was more than enough to put him away."

"And you thought it was Killgannon, I mean Eccleston? Why?"

"He was the logical suspect. The last one seen with it. But he was thoroughly investigated, and it seemed he was clean. He was at a loss to explain it as well. Claimed he had followed the chain of evidence with it back to the station. I don't know. Emotions were running high that night. It was a big bust. Would have been easy for something to slip through the cracks. Eventually we had to let it go. And it's never turned up."

"So what has this got to do with what's happening now?"

"I'm getting to that." Another sip of wine. "You see, there was another guy undercover in Foley's operation that Eccleston didn't know about."

"Witness N. I found that in Harmer's files."

She nodded, a small smile playing across her lips. "Right. And his career ended that night. He crashed the car he was driving trying to get away from the bust—on the orders of Foley's lieutenants—and *bang*. That was the end of that for him." She sighed. "He took the force to court for substantial damages but they fucked him over. He refused out of court settlements, expected a big payoff. He lost. Got nothing. Not even his pension."

"That's not fair," said Sheridan.

"Who said anything about life being fair?" Another mouthful of wine. "They dropped him. Not even a handshake. He tried to get work. But it was difficult. So long story short, he dug out all his old acquaintances from working with Foley. Went back to work with them. It was easy work, strong-arm, violence, extortion. But he got arrested and sent down. For a long, long time."

"I'm sure he deserved it," said Sheridan.

Blake smiled. "Everything's black and white to you, isn't it?"

"It has to be. There's good and bad. We're the good guys, they're the bad guys. We behave in a better way. We set an example. If an officer turns to the bad side I've got no sympathy. He deserves everything coming to him. We should be better than that. Have you read a writer called Ayn Rand?"

She shook her head, amused. "No, and I'm not about to. Anyway, this guy who, according to you, should have known better was eventually transferred to Blackmoor and reunited with Foley."

She sat back, looked at Sheridan, waited for him to speak. Sheridan just looked confused. "So . . . what does that have to do with what we were talking about?"

"Everything. Because . . ." She leaned forward once more, fingers toying with the stem of her glass, a look on her face that Sheridan could only describe as seductive. He had never seen her like this before. The straight-faced, almost angry coworker was gone. This was a completely different person who sat in front of him.

"Because," she continued, "this is where you come in. You see, that guy in prison, the one you have no sympathy for, is an old friend of mine. We came through the academy together. Even had a bit of a thing going at one time. Both wildly ambitious, both on our way to the top. We were the golden couple. And now look at us. He's where he is, I'm playing second fiddle to you."

The way she spoke that final word couldn't have sounded worse if it was the harshest swear word Sheridan had ever heard. He just stared at her.

"You play everything by the book, and that's your trouble. No imagination." The words angry, hushed, at odds with the flirtatious smile and body language she was presenting to the rest of the bar. "You believe in fair play. And because of that, you expect everyone else around you to as well. Don't you?"

"Yes, I do. You know I do."

"You would never believe another cop would go behind your back, have secret meetings with her boss. Would you?"

"No." His voice full of sadness more than anger. "No, I wouldn't."

"Well I did. You see, I moved down here to kickstart my career. I became a DC but I don't think there's much higher I can go on the ladder. Not on this force. And time's running out for me. So I went to see Harmer. Had a word. Well, more than a word, actually. He's easily flattered, our boss. Especially by a pretty young officer, telling him how brilliant he is . . ."

Sheridan's throat was dry. He wished he could drink his water but his hands wouldn't move. "You slept with him."

She nodded. "Not much sleeping went on."

"But . . . do you find him attractive?"

"That's not the point. He finds me attractive and that's enough. Way it works, Nick."

"So . . . what has this to do with our operation to get Cunningham to talk?"

"You think that's what this is all about? You poor, deluded man, Nick."

"Well, what then?"

"It was never about that. It was always about the money, Nick. That missing two million. You see, I'm a good cop. No matter what you think of me. I've got good instincts. And they're never wrong. I think Eccleston, or Tom Killgannon, or whatever he's calling himself now, has it. I've always thought that and every year that goes by and it never turns up, I'm more and more convinced. So the next step was simple. I heard about the trouble in St. Petroc a few months ago and recognized Killgannon as Eccleston straight away. So I thought, what if we can get Killgannon into prison next to Foley and Foley can persuade him to give up that money? I did my homework. Found out Cunningham was in there, wanting to confess to the right person in exchange to see his dear old mum again before she pops off. And of course Harmer came to see it the same way. The cherry on top, though, was putting you in charge. Because when the whole thing went tits up—as it's going to do— you'd take the blame, possibly a demotion, and I wouldn't have to care about my career because I'd have enough money to invest in my future. Foley would see to that. And that would have been that." She sighed. "But you had to find out about it, didn't you? The one incorruptible cop on the force. Don't suppose there's any point in offering you a cut?"

Sheridan sat there, unable to move. He felt like his whole world had been rocked off its axis. He couldn't find the thoughts, the words, to express what he was feeling.

"Thought not."

He looked round the bar, couldn't believe that the night was still going on as it had before, that nothing seismic had happened around him to match what had happened inside.

"So what are you going to do now?" asked Blake, taking another mouthful of wine.

"I . . ." What was he going to do now? He had to think. Sit

quietly, let his inner moral compass find true north once more
before he could even speak, let alone make his mind up. "I don't
know what I can do . . ."

She took another mouthful of wine and drained the glass. "I'm
empty. Time to go." She didn't move. "But before I do, I need to
know where we stand. What are you going to do about what I've
just told you?"

He just stared at her.

She shook her head, stood up. "Come on. Let's talk about this
outside. Maybe the fresh air'll wake you up."

She put her arm within his, snuggled into him as they walked
out together.

Through the door the cold wind hit them like ice. Sheridan
looked around. Confused, like he had just woken from a dream.

"Let's walk to the car."

Still arm in arm, she walked him through the dark night down
to the unlit parking lot, their feet crunching on gravel the only
sound. They reached his car.

"So," she said, looking him straight in the eye, "What are you
going to do? Have you made up your mind?"

He looked at her face, like she was slowly coming into focus.
And with that, so was his mind. "Yes," he said. "I know what I'm
going to do. There's no point talking to Harmer if you're both in
it together. I'll find someone who'll believe me. You two won't be
on the force anymore and Killgannon'll be out like a shot. I would
never have been party to this if I'd known." His voice had become
stronger as he spoke. He was finding that shining part of himself
once more. Being true to it like a good police officer should. Being
better than the bad guys. Even if the bad guys turn out to be female
colleagues.

Blake looked sad for a few seconds. "Oh, that is a shame, Nick.
I was hoping you wouldn't say that."

Sheridan had found his voice. "You knew I would never agree with you, so why tell me all this in the first place?"

"Because you found out about Foley, Nick. I really didn't want you to find out. Honestly, I didn't. For your sake, I mean."

"What d'you mean, for my sake?"

"Because there's no going back now. Sorry."

Sheridan was about to ask her what she meant by that but he didn't get the chance. Unseen by him, a tall black man wearing an expensive leather jacket detached himself from the shadows and stepped up behind him, put a restraining arm around his neck, pushed him against the car, placed a silent automatic against the back of his ribcage, pulled the trigger, and blew his heart away.

Sheridan didn't even have to time to acknowledge he was dying before his body hit the ground.

His phone started ringing.

33

Tom stood in the queue, waiting patiently. Three people in front of him, one already on the phone, turned away from the rest, trying to create what privacy he could.

He was back on the wing. He had been sitting in his cell on the seg block, staring into space, doing nothing. He had tried exercises, push-ups and sit-ups, until his arms felt useless, his stomach cramped. He could smell his own sweat soaking through his T-shirt. Sour. Just like every other inmate in the prison. *I'm one of them now.*

And he was. Like he was ticking off a list of things he expected inmates to do. Get into trouble and be put into segregation. Be constantly on the phone. Have tearful, depressing visits with loved ones. His disguise was complete. He had become his cover story.

Tearful, depressing visits with loved ones. That wasn't how it had actually gone with Lila in the visiting room, but afterward, alone in that Spartan cell designed to crush his spirit even more than the ones on the wing, he hadn't been able to stop himself. Tears came as he thought of Lila walking away from him, being able to breathe clean air and go where she wanted to. Able to go home, sit in the living room, watch TV. Go to bed when she wanted. He had come close to losing himself then, breaking down so much that he wondered whether it would be possible to pull himself back together, get into shape, and finish this job.

It would have been so easy to just give in, lie there with the walls closing in on him and let himself go, acknowledge defeat. So he tried to bring himself back, compartmentalize his emotions. He used to be so good at this. Concentrate on the task in hand. Stay alive. Get the information out of Cunningham. Gradually he had done so, pushing his feelings about seeing Lila out of his mind, but it had been a struggle. Brought the old days back again. Reminded him that this line of work wasn't something a person could do for long, not without losing themselves to it, possibly forever. He had started exercising then, pushing himself as hard as he could, hoping the pounding of blood around his system would drown out his thoughts. He kept going until he couldn't move anymore, slept that night on the floor of the cell.

And then the key in the lock, an officer looking in, telling him it was time to return to the wing.

He got up, went outside. He had expected to be told to stand and face the wall once more but the officer wasn't alone. Louisa Bradshaw was there. As was a small, balding, suited man, staring at him.

"Hello, Tom," said Louisa.

"Doctor," he said, giving a formal nod.

"We're going to return you to the wing now," she told him, "put you back in general pop. We think you've served enough of a punishment for your action."

Tom said nothing.

"Do you agree?"

"Obviously."

"But I don't want to hear of any more incidents like this one, right?" It was the small, bald man who had spoken.

Tom turned his attention to him. "Sorry, I don't think we've been introduced."

Silence froze the group. It was clear the officer, the bovine one Tom had interacted with previously, wanted to teach him a lesson in respect. Or a lesson in anything, any excuse to inflict physical pain. Even Louisa looked taken aback and Tom realized that, for all her talk and her offers of help, she would never be totally on his side.

"Warden Shelley," said the small man. "I run this place."

"Right. I've never met you and I genuinely didn't know who you were."

Shelley scrutinized Tom for any signs of sarcasm. Tom had been sincere. He said nothing more. Waited.

Shelley turned to Louisa. "You think this . . ." He searched for the right word to describe Tom. " . . . one is ready to return to the wing, then?"

"Yes, I do. I've talked to him and believe this won't happen again." As she spoke her eyes alighted on Tom's, as if asking him to agree with her. Or at least not disagree. "He's agreed to see me for sessions in how to handle his anger."

Shelley turned back to Tom, squared up to him. "You going to do that?"

"Yeah," said Tom. He didn't elaborate. Didn't feel it necessary.

Shelley appeared to be making up his mind. "OK, then. But if I hear of one incident involving you, just one, then you're back down here, busted down to basic, you got it?"

"Absolutely."

"I've got a strict no-tolerance policy for people coming into my prison and denigrating. Play by the rules and you'll do all right. OK? Don't and you'll have to be dealt with."

He's so much smaller than me, thought Tom, I could rest my arm on his head. Stretch my arm out and hold his forehead while he tried to swing shots at me. "I understand."

"Something funny?" Shelley was still staring at him.

"Just pleased to be going back to the wing," said Tom, slightly annoyed that he must have let his feelings show.

Shelley stared once more. So did the bovine officer. They both looked like they were waiting for Tom to do something so they could keep him on the seg block. Shelley looked toward Louisa, then back to Tom. And that look told Tom everything about Shelley's attitude. He was clearly a misogynist. The way he had been looking at Louisa—dismissively, disrespectfully—told him that he didn't like psychologists, especially female ones, deciding what was best for the prisoners. *His* prisoners. But he knew he had to go along with it. Perhaps, thought Tom, this doctor might actually be an ally after all.

"Doctor Bradshaw's going to take responsibility for you," said Shelley, "But you're also to take responsibility for your own behavior. I don't want to see you back here, right?"

Tom agreed.

Shelley walked off. Louisa nodded to Tom, followed Shelley off the wing.

AND NOW TOM QUEUED FOR THE PHONE. Only one person in front of him now. Not wanting to intrude, Tom looked away.

Some old faces had left the wing, new ones had arrived. And a different atmosphere. Toward him. He could feel all eyes on him as he was escorted back from the seg block. Like there was a sense of anticipation, waiting to see if he would kick off again. If they were hoping for that, Tom disappointed them. He did everything the officer told him, stood away from the doors, turned his face to the wall while they were being unlocked, everything. A model inmate. But he could still feel the eyes on him as he walked the length of the wing toward his old cell.

It was association time. Hard-eyed men standing and sitting, watching. Searching for an angle to everything, everyone, some leverage to be made, some advantage gained. Keeping up that level of vigilance was exhausting but necessary. No one could show weakness. No one could be seen to back down from a challenge. No one could show disrespect or accept it. It was a near silent battlefield, a war of attrition, of glances and muttered words, of body language and silences, all conducted under the eyes of the watching officers.

And now they were all watching Tom, taking the measure of him. Seeing what he would do now that he was back. Wondering whether to challenge his growing reputation as a hard man, like the Navajo warriors of old, believing if they defeated someone in combat they bested not only them but the souls of those the defeated had in turn bested, advanced up the rankings, became a feared presence in their own right.

Or seeing him as a potential ally, someone to get on their side. Barter favors with to keep them protected. Do whatever they could for Tom—contraband, sex—to get him to rid them of other predators. Tom ignored all those eyes, even Cunningham's, who had seen him approach, expecting him to enter their cell. Tom had nodded as he walked past. Made straight for the phone queue.

The person in front put the phone down, walked away. Tom's turn. He dialed the number by heart, waited. It was answered.

"Sheridan?" Tom asked.

"Try again." It was a female voice.

Tom froze. So surprised by not hearing Sheridan's voice, he couldn't place it at first. Then he realized. Blake.

"What's happening, Blake?" Careful not to use her rank, give things away.

She laughed. "Nothing. Nothing's happening."

Tom was more confused than annoyed at her words. "What d'you mean?"

"Nothing, Tom Killgannon. Or should I say Mick Eccleston?" Tom froze again.

"This phone line is dead. Sheridan is dead. And so are you."

She hung up. Tom was left staring at the receiver. He quickly dialed again. Nothing. And again. Nothing.

A dead line.

He stared at the receiver. Behind him, other inmates in the queue became vocal. He placed the phone back in its cradle, walked dazedly to his cell.

He was alone.

34

"Get rid of this." Blake prized the SIM card from Sheridan's phone, handed it to Quint.

"Glad to," he said, taking it from her and pocketing it.

"Not around here," she told him. "I'll deal with the phone."

They both looked at the body of her colleague slumped by the side of his car. Blood had sprayed all over the window and roof, and left smears where his body had slid down to the ground.

"What we going to do with him?" asked Quint. "You thought of that?"

"Yep. Put him in his car and leave him here."

"He'll be found."

"He will. But not till tomorrow and I'll be involved in working his case. Now go on. Get him in there."

Quint bent down, manhandled Sheridan into the driver's seat, careful not to get any blood on his clothes. Blake stood there, watching him.

"Don't bother to help," he said.

"I won't. You're off back to Cornwall after this. I'm not. I don't want his blood on me."

He finished his task and crossed to his bike, hidden in the bushes. Got on it, checked no one was watching them, then roared away.

Blake watched him go. Looked at Sheridan's car. Tried to decide what she was feeling.

He was her partner. No, had been her partner. But that didn't mean she should be upset at his passing. Yes, he had a wife and children who would be heartbroken at his death. And she would be lying if she said she didn't feel a pang of remorse for them. But it had to be done. *Had* to. Once he realized what had been going on, it was either him or her. And it wasn't going to be her. He would never understand. That was the heartbreaking thing. If he had been any other kind of cop, more able to turn a blind eye or even, for a cut, help her, it would have been different. But he was straight by the book, boring Sheridan. Well, some of the things she had planned for him in death would put the lie to that. Tarnish forever his image as the perfect cop. Yes it was sad, but again, she had no choice.

She took out her phone. Not her usual one, a cheap pay-as-you-go burner. Unregistered. Untraceable. She called a memorized number. Waited. It was answered.

"It's me. Sheridan's been dealt with. You can move on Killgannon."

She cut the call, didn't wait for a response. Pocketed the phone and walked away.

35

THE DOOR SLAMMED BEHIND LILA. She placed her bag in the hall, keys on the hallway table. Unzipped her coat, hung it up. Same routine as always. Getting used to it. Even starting to enjoy it.

"That you?" a voice called from the living room.

She yelled a reply as she kicked off her boots and entered. Pearl was sitting in the armchair, flicking through one of her glossy magazines. Lila hadn't found the point in them at first, thinking they were a waste of time and money, just full of photos of emaciated, bored, or angry-looking women in expensive clothes, and advertisements for watches and handbags she could never afford, or even want. Then an interview with some celebrity who was using their platform—or so they claimed—to make the world a better place. If that was so, she thought, their platform didn't extend to Cornwall. Then more pictures of, and advertisements for, shoes. But lately she had been picking them up when Pearl wasn't around, glancing through them at first, then looking more concertedly. Even imagining herself in the clothes, the feel of the fabric next to her skin, skipping along some tropical white beach, smiling against the sun . . .

That's how they get you, Anju had said. And then it's a slippery slope to conformity. Bit ironic, Lila thought, a rich doctor's daughter lecturing her on the perils of conformity but, as she knew from experience, finding your own path in life took many forms, regardless of your background.

"Hey," Pearl said, looking up from where she was sprawled over the armchair, legs dangling to one side. "Good day?"

"So-so." She sat down on the sofa opposite her. "Shouldn't you be at work?"

"Got Briony, the new girl, doing the dead zone. I'll pop over later when it's busier. Anyway." She closed the magazine, sat up fully. "I haven't seen you properly to talk to since you went to see Tom. How's he getting on?"

Lila thought of the visit. How Tom had tried hard to look like prison hadn't changed him, even in such a short space of time. How his wounded eyes and damaged face had given away that lie.

Or how she had fought back tears as she left. Sat in the car silently sobbing, Anju's arms around her, pulling her close. Crying on her shoulder. Anju stroking her cheeks, kissing away the tears. Feeling Tom's absence like a physical thing, but glad she had someone there to comfort her. It was a feeling she wasn't used to.

Afterward she hadn't come straight home, even though Anju had dropped her off at the front door. Instead she had walked the cliff path, ignoring the cold, persistent wind razoring through her too-thin coat, the rocks and mud underfoot making her lose her footing. Walking until it was too dark to see anything around her but the black, star-flecked sky, hearing nothing but the top line roar of the wind competing with the deep cymbal clash of the sea. Until she felt like she was alone in the universe, a tiny, galaxy-dwarfed speck clinging to a rock as it hurtled away through space. Completely insignificant yet somehow the center of everything. She didn't move, didn't cry. Just stood there. Balancing. Holding on.

"How is he?"

Pearl's question bringing her back. "Yeah, he's . . ." Lila didn't know what to say. Be honest? Be brave? "He said he was doing

OK. I don't know. He looked a bit . . . you know. Like he didn't want to be there."

"That's a given."

"He asked after you anyway."

"What did you say?"

Her question a bit too quick, Lila thought. "Asked how you were doing. How we were getting on. Told him we were watching *Dynasty* together."

Pearl smiled. "Sure he loved hearing that."

"Anyway, he says he hopes that it'll all be finished and he'll be back soon. That it won't be long now."

"I hope so. Not that I'm not enjoying being here with you and having some company . . . I'm glad you're here. I wanted to talk to you."

"What about?"

Pearl dropped her eyes. "I've had an email. From my mum and dad."

"Oh."

"Yeah. And I don't know what to do."

Pearl's parents had been two of the main instigators behind the near murderous events that put St. Petroc on the national news. Once the police had arrived, they had disappeared, leaving the pub and hotel to Pearl. It had been a rough few months for her too. Lila thought with a pang of guilt, she didn't give her enough credit for that.

"Did they say where they were?"

"No, but they wanted to meet me."

"Are you going to?"

Pearl looked straight at Lila. And Lila knew that no matter what she had thought of Pearl in the past, how she hadn't fully trusted her, their actions had bonded them. She may not be a friend by choice, but they were now bound by something deeper.

"I don't know."

"What did they say?"

"That they were sorry. That I shouldn't worry about them, they were all right. They'd taken their savings and were trying to start again. They were abroad, didn't say where in case someone was monitoring these things. But they hoped I could understand what they had done and why and forgive them for it."

Lila almost laughed. "Forgive them. They'd have killed me if they'd been allowed to."

Pearl said nothing.

"So what do they want? You to go and join them?"

"That was the impression I got."

"And are you?"

"I wanted to talk to you first before I did anything else."

Lila frowned. Thought of that night on the cliff path, balancing on the edge of the world, the universe. "Why me?"

"Because you . . ." Pearl sighed, "you've been through shit with your parents. And it's . . . I just . . . I don't know how I'm supposed to feel about it. About them." Pearl seemed on the verge of tears.

Lila paused, thought hard. Pearl was reaching out as a friend; perhaps it was time to put any lingering doubts about her aside and treat her as a friend. It's what Tom would want her to do. "Yeah, it's difficult. Conflicted. You're brought up to think you should love them no matter what. And that you should forgive anything they might do to you." Lila gave a bitter laugh. "Sometimes you have to learn the hard way that life's not like that. Sometimes you have to just say 'fuck you' and walk away from them."

"And that's what you think I should do now?" Pearl sounded like she genuinely didn't know. It felt like Lila was the older, wiser one. And maybe, in terms of life experience, she was.

"Families aren't biological."

Pearl smiled. "Spoken like a psychology student."

Lila also smiled. "I've learned that the hard way. Living here with Tom, he's my family now. Or I hope so. It takes a lot to trust after . . . you know."

"Yeah." Pearl nodded. "Part of me wants to write back, tell them how much I miss them and go and see them. Try and make things like they were before. But then I think . . . it won't be like that, will it? Because before was a lie. They were planning all this . . . this monstrous stuff that I never knew about and I was supposed to just go along with them. And I couldn't. And no matter what they say or do, it won't make up for it. But then I think . . ." She shook her head. "Oh, I don't know."

"It's up to you," said Lila after a while. "I can't choose for you. I can only tell what I did. You might be, I dunno, different."

"It's just so . . . hard. You never think these kinds of things will happen to you."

Lila gave a harsh laugh. "Tell me about it."

Pearl fell silent. Neither spoke. Pearl eventually broke the silence. "Thanks. For listening, anyway."

Lila shrugged. "What are friends for?"

Pearl smiled at that. Lila did also.

"Fancy an episode of *Dynasty*?"

"You're on."

"I'll make some coffee."

Pearl got up from the armchair, went into the kitchen. Lila watched her. Felt that balancing universe thing again. Realized she didn't have to cling on to the rock quite so hard now. That she could stand on her own.

Any further thought was cut off. There was a knock at the door.

"Can you get that?" called Pearl from the kitchen.

She got off the sofa, went to open the door.

There stood the black biker she had seen previously. He smiled at her.

"Hi," he said. "We've met before, remember?"

"Yeah."

He smiled. "I should have introduced myself properly. I'm Quint. A friend of Tom's?" His upward inflection made the statement into a question. "Anyway, he said I should look in on you. You know, see you're OK. That OK? You must be Lila, yeah?"

Lila didn't answer.

Quint laughed. "Least you didn't say no. So I reckon that must be yes." The smile dropped. "Can I come in? Want to talk to you."

Lila's first reaction, her gut instinct, was to say no. But she overrode it. Tom had told her about him. She had kind of expected him to be in touch. But something still told her she didn't want him in the house.

"Please? Freezing out here."

Lila reached a decision. She moved aside, let him enter.

"Thanks," he said, going past her.

She closed the door behind him.

PART THREE
HANGED

That same night in Manchester

"*Shit . . .*"

Foxy opened his eyes. Couldn't see anything, his vision all blurred and smeared black. He closed them and tried again. Wiped his hand across his face. That hurt, like dragging needles, but at least he could see, if not fully. He blinked again. There. Some kind of liquid in his eyes, thick, viscous. He blinked again. Put his hand to his face, looked at his palm. Realized it was blood. And something else in the pooled blood in his palm. Small, glittering shards. Glass.

He tried to pull himself into a sitting position and felt pain like he had never known before. His body wouldn't respond, his left side refusing to follow commands. Then he remembered. The crash. He looked up. Through the blur he saw the BMW wrapped around a lamppost, the windshield shattered and himself in front of it. He worked out what had happened.

When the police arrived, everyone in Foley's gang had driven off straight away, looking for any exit the police hadn't covered. They all panicked, drove any which way. Foxy tried to keep a cool head. He tried to work out which exits the police would have blocked, come up with alternative routes around them. He could still get away with this, he thought. Still convince them he was on their side. That all the easy money and pussy, the drugs and the violence, hadn't turned him. Salvage something. He just had to get out of the estate to do it.

He pulled himself up using the front hood of the car and the lamp-post. They were almost one since the crash. He gasped for breath, pain singing through his body like a choir of demons. His left arm hung uselessly at his side. His first thought: get away. Get help. He heard a noise. The passenger seat airbag had inflated, saving that half of the window from splintering. The cry came from behind it. He pulled himself around to the side of the car, looked in. The girl he had been with, Hayley, was still sitting there. Trapped.

"Oh god . . ." She began to move, coming around slowly, then faster as she realized what was in front of her face, fought with the airbag, thinking it was suffocating her.

"It's all right," Foxy said, or tried to say. His mouth didn't seem to be working well. "It's all right . . ."

She managed to fight her way through the bag and out of the car. Unsteady on her legs from both high heels and the shock of the crash, she was bloodstained but not to his extent. Her wide eyes told him that shock was setting in. He didn't have time for that. He had to get away. And her as well.

"Come on," he said, letting go of the bonnet and reaching out his good hand, wobbling as a result, "we've got to go."

The night came back into focus for her now and she realized where she was, what must have happened. Then she looked at Foxy. And started screaming.

"Shut up, you stupid bitch, shut it . . ." Anger straight away. He didn't have time for this.

"Your face, shit, what's happened to your face?"

He moved toward her, she pulled back instinctively. He could hear voices, see lights, getting nearer.

"A fucking car crash," he said, or tried to. The words sounded fine in his head, mangled as they left his mouth. "Now come on."

He made to grab her, pull her with him. She flinched away once more.

"No," she said, shaking her head, tears forming in her eyes. "No, I'm not, this is . . . not fun anymore. I'm scared, Foxy . . . I'm scared . . ."

"Come on then."

"No . . ." She refused to budge. The tears came freely now. "I want to go home. I want my mum . . ." She kept shaking her head. "This is . . . no . . ."

The voices, loud, angry, were getting nearer. He grabbed her arm, dragged her along with him. Unsteady on his feet, but determined. She refused to move.

"The fucking law's coming, come on . . ."

She didn't move. *"The law? The law . . . I'm going to tell them, Foxy. Tell them I wasn't involved, tell them it wasn't me. I'm going to tell them . . ."*

"You're coming with me . . ." Another grab for her. He didn't have the strength to compel her to move and his words weren't helping. He had to impress on her the seriousness of the situation, just how badly and quickly they needed to get out of there.

His heart was hammering, pumping blood around his body, out of his body. He needed to move. He needed attention. With no other choice, he pulled his gun out, pointed it at her. He had never been firearm trained. In fact his Glock had barely been fired, except for practice in the Worsley Woods. But he was used to brandishing it in order to get attention, to make someone follow his orders. That was usually enough.

"Now." He pointed it at her.

She just stared at him. *"Foxy, what are you doing?"*

"We've got to go. I can't . . ." Weakening now, a different kind of darkness than the night dancing before him. *"Come on . . ."*

"I'm not moving." Her voice edging toward hysteria. *"I'm staying here. I'm not . . ."* She closed her eyes, pretended she wasn't there. *"I want to go home . . ."*

Anger overtook him once more. He couldn't leave her here, she would try and control the narrative—his narrative—close down his own attempts to come out of this any kind of hero. But she wouldn't come with him. And he couldn't hang around here any longer. He made one last attempt to get her on his side.

He grabbed her once more. "Come on." Started walking, hoping he had enough strength to drag her with him.

"Get off me . . ." She shook off his grip easily.

He tried again, pulling at her. Again, she resisted.

Then came the shots from behind. The sound of bodies running toward him.

"I don't have time for this . . ."

He pulled her along beside him and she twisted her ankle, falling over her heels. She crumpled to the ground in a heap. He bent down, pulled her up.

Just as a bullet whistled past the side of his head.

"Shit . . ."

Crouching, he returned fire. Hayley dragged herself to her feet, began running. Toward where the gunfire was coming from.

"Stay here you stupid bitch . . ."

Another bullet, even closer this time. He could see bodies in the distance. Moving slowly toward him. He raised his gun, fired blindly, unable to see clearly.

Later, he told himself that it was an accident. That he hadn't meant to hit her. He had just been desperate, blacking out, even. But he did hit her. Several times. Damaged nerves from the crash, he told himself later. His trigger finger must have spasmed.

He also told himself that pulling up a nearby manhole cover in a desperate display of strength and dropping the gun down it, waiting for the splash as it hit running water in the sewer below, then replacing the cover was just his instinct as a cop kicking in. Nothing more.

With no energy left, he collapsed next to her.

It wasn't me. I didn't do that. It . . .

The questions would have to wait. The voices and those bobbing flashlights were getting nearer.

WHEN THEY FOUND HIM, HE WAS STILL ALIVE. *But he would never be the same again.*

36

FOLEY WAS ESCORTED THROUGH THE PRISON ONCE MORE. Not just by an officer but also by Baz. It wasn't that Foley didn't feel safe inside at the moment, just that he felt it best to have protection from someone he could trust. And he didn't trust the officers. They didn't just hate him, they despised him. His money paid for his life inside as well as keeping them on his side, but it also meant that a higher bidder could turn them away from him. And things had been very fucking strange recently. Since Clive had arrived inside, in fact. And Eccleston. And until he could get rid of this feeling of unease, Baz would accompany him everywhere he went.

Outside the main building, around the corner, ignoring the drizzle and mist, the dankness from the moors, the prematurely gray day. Walking the pitted, paved footpath by the perimeter fence, the razor wire creating a double obstacle before the outer wall could be reached. The space between the fence and wall was a graveyard of failed escape attempts and contraband that never reached its target. Foley had seen it so many times he ignored it. This was his everyday life. His home.

He stood outside Dr. Louisa Bradshaw's hut. Turned to face the wall, smiling, in a mockery of what the officer would have him do, waited for that same officer to knock on the door. It was opened.

"Come in," said Louisa, seeing Foley standing there. Then she saw Baz, seemed confused.

"He's with me," said Foley.

"I don't think—"

"He's waiting outside. He'll be no trouble." Foley turned to the officer. "You can go. Come back when I'm finished." Like dismissing a servant.

The officer, disgruntled but knowing where his money came from, left.

"Right," said Foley, summoning up a smile, "let's go."

He stepped inside. Louisa followed. Baz took up his sentry position. Tried to ignore the cold and damp.

Inside Foley walked toward his usual armchair, sat down. He could smell the coffee but it didn't have its usual siren call today. He had too much on his mind. A burden ready to be unloaded.

"So," said Dr. Bradshaw, settling down in the opposite chair with a notepad on her lap, coffee at her side. "How've you been, Dean?"

Foley opened his mouth to speak. He often started with wit, barbs, or charm. Only when he couldn't come straight out and say what he wanted to, had to work round it, circle slowly down. But not this time. Straight in.

"Not going to lie, things have been difficult." He squirmed as if the chair was uncomfortable. "Since I last spoke to you."

"In what way?" Pen poised.

"I . . ." He had planned what he would say as they walked across. Before that, even, the night before. Rehearsed his words and even her anticipated responses, planned what he hoped the eventual outcome would be. But sitting there, facing her, the words wouldn't come. And he couldn't think of anything to say to talk round it. "I . . . it's been difficult."

She waited, gave him time, space, to gather his thoughts. Find his voice.

"It's this . . . it's what you said to me last time. Got me thinking."

"About?"

"About . . ." He sighed, leaned forward, agitating his hands. "This ex-cop. This narc. I've thought about him for years. Wondered where he was, what he was doing, whether he was alive or not, was he fucking up someone else's business, pardon my French, you know? And I thought . . . what I would do when I got hold of him. What I'd always threatened to do. Make him pay. All of that. And like I said he's here now, right in front of me . . ."

"And?"

Foley shook his head. Looked at his hands is if expecting to find the answer there. "I don't know. Just don't know."

She waited.

"I mean, last time we were talking about revenge."

"We were."

"And how good it felt when I took it into my own hands. Administered it myself." His voice relished the word *administer*.

She nodded slowly, keeping eye contact, encouraging him to continue.

"Well . . . that's it, isn't it? Taking pleasure in punishment. Doing what's right. Letting everyone know you've done the right thing. A warning to anyone else thinking of starting. Don't mess. Don't take liberties. And, you know, the satisfaction of a job well done."

"We talked about that. You said it was the way things had to be. What was expected of you."

He nodded.

"Now you're saying you got satisfaction from it? From hurting surrogates of your father?"

Foley jumped at the mention of the name, like he had just been shocked. "Surrogates." He nodded. "Yeah." Another nod. "I suppose . . . I've said it so it must be. But it's more than that, you know? You look at yourself and . . ." He stared at her, fists raised before his eyes. "It's for its own sake."

"Can you explain?"

He looked at his fists again. Rotated them before his gaze. Saw them in another time and place, glistening with blood and gore, knuckles sore and distended. Clenched so hard he couldn't immediately unlock them. And his body pumping with adrenaline, sweat and blood on his skin, soaking his clothes from both sides, lungs burning hot as a steam engine's furnace, arms just pistons, parts of a machine. But his mind content. At the nearest thing to peace he had ever known. Justice served. The natural order restored.

"I see," said Dr. Bradshaw.

Foley looked up, startled. Had he said all that aloud? From the look on the doctor's face, it seemed he had. He said nothing, suddenly embarrassed.

"You've described a high that's certainly attractive to you," she said. "And attainable. But I suspect that violent euphoria becomes harder to attain the longer it goes on. Am I correct?"

Foley thought back again to the punishment beatings. How, even before Mick Eccleston had betrayed him, the highs were getting harder to reach, more difficult to maintain. Like they were further away and he had to grasp for them, strain to catch them. And when he did he barely held on to them. And that in turn made him even angrier. But it had been a weary anger. An unpleasant one.

"Yeah," he said. "Bang on."

"And how d'you feel about that now?"

Foley didn't answer immediately.

"You said as soon as you heard this man had entered the prison, you wanted to see him. And when you saw him you wanted revenge for everything he'd done to you. Is that correct?"

"Yeah, that's right."

"But you didn't know if you would do it yourself or get

someone to do it for you. And if you did, you feared it would sap the enjoyment from it. And now you don't know if you even want to do it at all?"

He nodded, shifting around once more. "You see, I've been having . . . dreams."

"What kind of dreams?"

"Bad ones. Ghosts, even. Like I'm being haunted. And I wake up . . . well. Not in a good state."

"Tell me about them."

Foley was reluctant to delve any further but knew that he had to. This might be his only chance to make things right with himself. To find some kind of peace. To know which way was forward. "There's me and him. And we're back in Manchester, the night it all went tits up. The night he betrayed me. And we're there again and . . ." He shook his head. "It gets weird then. Like the whole thing starts to melt away. And I'm shouting at him, *You've done this! You've taken all this away from me!* And there's cars disappearing, and money . . . all of that. Until there's just me and him left."

"And where is this?"

"I dunno. Like . . . nowhere. And it's like a western. Just me and him facing each other. And I'm armed, I've still got my gun, see. And he's got nothing. He's just standing there. And I try to raise my gun arm to take aim. I try to feel the anger inside me, let it do its job, let me shoot him, and I want to keep shooting him until there's nothing left of him and I'm all out of bullets. And I'm shouting how much I hate him and he's just standing there. And I try to bring my arm up . . ." He mimes the action. "But I can't. Can't move. Can't do anything." He sat back, panting.

Neither spoke.

Eventually Foley laughed. Unsteadily. "Just a dream, eh? Can't go around reading too much into that bullshit, can you?"

"That's for you to decide, Dean. You've been talking about how you should take revenge against this person for what he's done to you in the past. Yes, it may be emotionally satisfying for a while, but in the long term it may well cause more upset than not."

"But it might not."

"That's for you to interpret how you wish. Same with your dream. You tell me that you don't think you can take revenge anymore. That you won't get anything beneficial out of it, even though you've been thinking about him the whole time you've been in here and what you'd do to him if you saw him again. Does that sound about right?"

Foley nodded.

"And how d'you feel about that?"

"I dunno, honestly. I've got a reputation in here. Can I speak honestly?"

The question, asked abruptly, threw her off guard. "No point in being here otherwise."

"Right." He nodded, making his mind up about something. "My reputation. I know you know about it. And you maybe think of me differently because of it, I don't know. But somewhere like this, a reputation's all you've got. And if that goes you've got nothing. So I have to decide what to do. And it might not be the answer you want to hear. Or I want to hear. But I have to do something."

"You know I have to report you if you're going to—"

"Yeah, I know all that. But you don't know who this bloke is. And I haven't said anything about him to you so there's no way you could tell anyone anything. It's just . . ." He sighed. Put his head in his hands. "I get tired of all this. So tired. But I don't know what to do. What can I do?"

"I've given you all the help and advice I can. The tools to cope. You've got to make that decision on your own." She looked at her watch. "I think that's it for today, Dean. Sorry."

He looked up at her like he had been cut adrift.

"I think you've got plenty to be getting on with, though. A lot to think about before our next session, don't you?"

Foley leaned forward once more. Exasperation in his voice. "But I need to know what to do. I'm . . . I can't just go on like this . . ."

"I'm sorry, Dean, this is all I can do here. If you need someone to talk to on the wing then I'll—"

Foley stood up. "You haven't been listening, have you? I can't do that. I can't talk to anyone on the wing. Because they'd know then. They'd *know*. Everyone's going to be expecting me to do this, and if I don't, I'll be weak. And I'll have had it. So no. It's here or nothing."

Louisa sighed. "OK, Dean. Let me see what I can do. I'll juggle some things around and see you again this week. That's the best I can do, OK?"

Foley sighed. Looked round like the room was just another prison cell. "Suppose it'll have to."

"Leave it with me."

He left.

37

DC BLAKE LOOKED AT THE CRIME SCENE at Double Locks. Not the spot where her partner was murdered, not the place where she betrayed him. Nor where she had taken justified action to protect her investment. Just another crime scene.

She shouldn't have been there. By law, she was too close to the victim to be part of the investigation. But she had to find a way to control the flow of information, shape the way it was used. Guide it away from herself. So she had turned up at the scene, ostensibly to see if she could be of any assistance. Play the role expected of her.

The Double Locks crime scene was a few days old. The novelty for rubberneckers had worn off. Barely anyone gave it a second look now. The white tent and erected fence hid the parking lot from the towpath, and the sight of white-suited officers going painstakingly about their business was now deemed boring. Once onlookers realized it wasn't like on the TV, and police work was as exciting to watch as any other job in the public sector, they drifted away and left them alone. The only aggravation came from the owners of the pub who were waiting for the all-clear to reopen, complaining of lost revenue. Blake knew what they really meant: come and see the site of the latest grisly murder! Follow the signs! Read the information placards! Then stop for food and refreshment! And bring your friends and family! She couldn't blame them, they had a business to run. But the investigation would take as long as it had to.

DCI Harmer was with her. "Must hurt, seeing all this, Annie. Could get very emotional for you."

"I just want to be on the team, Dan," she said, deliberately using his first name, playing up the intimacy between them, her voice lowered, matching the words, "Part of this investigation."

His expression looked pained. "Too risky. You were his partner."

"All the more reason, then. Plus, I owe it to him."

He didn't reply, just stared at the forensics going about their business in their white tent.

She kept working on him. "Dan," seductive now, the promise-laden tone one he could never refuse, "come on. I knew him better than most."

"Maybe you didn't."

She frowned. "What?"

He looked at her then, opened his mouth, closed it, then opened it again. Deciding whether to share something with her or not. "They're going to question you, you know. This team."

"They already have."

"Another time, I mean." Again, that indecision. She knew he would talk to her though. She waited. "Listen, between you and me, there've been some irregularities discovered concerning Nick Sheridan."

She frowned, barely suppressing a smile. Kept acting. "What kind of irregularities?"

"Well . . ." He looked round, checked they weren't being overheard. Leaned in closer. "His computer was taken away, checked over. Looks like there was some . . . there's no way to say this gently. It looks like he was crooked."

She assumed a wide-eyed look. "No . . ."

"'Fraid so. It seems he was taking payments. From whom, we

don't know. Or why. But the evidence is all there. It's being examined now."

"Not Mr. By-the-Book Nick Sheridan."

"I'm as surprised as you are, Annie."

"Then that's all the more reason for me to be on this team. You need me there. Someone has to make sure findings like that don't taint the rest of us."

Harmer frowned. "You think there might be more?"

"God knows. But if that's what they've found so far, we might need damage limitation."

He nodded. "You're right."

She smiled and he looked at her as if just seeing her for the first time. "You done something to your hair?"

She smiled, put her hands to the ends, fluffed it out, arching her back as she did so. "You like it? You've always said how much you find redheads attractive." She leaned forward so he could get a good view of her cleavage. "Haven't you?"

"You remembered."

Of course I bloody remembered, she thought. Everything gets filed away for future use. "I did. I also bought something to wear to go with it . . ."

Harmer could barely control himself. "And . . ." He looked round, seemingly wishing he was somewhere more private. "Do the collar and cuffs match?"

Blake felt a bit of sick in her mouth at the words. Harmer imagined his mannish badinage was the kind of thing women loved to hear. God, it was like being shagged by David Davis.

She giggled appropriately, leaned right in to him, mouth to his ear. "Who said anything about cuffs?"

He just stared straight ahead as the meaning behind her words sunk in.

"Usual place, usual time tonight?" she whispered.

He nodded as vigorously as a cartoon dog.

"So I'm on the Sheridan investigation?"

How could he refuse?

SHE DROVE AWAY FROM DOUBLE LOCKS, back to Middlemoor. Her official title was team liaison. She couldn't be seen to be working with the investigating team directly, but was privy to everything that went on. That suited her perfectly.

They were looking for the woman Sheridan had been seen with the night of his death, focusing on her as the lynchpin of the investigation. A drinking companion, dressed in figure-hugging black, black hair scraped back. Leaning into him over the table, a suggestive smile on her face all the time they talked. No one had managed to trace her yet. Blake had been questioned, of course, but cleared. Figure-hugging black had never been her style. And no one would ever suggest an affair between her and Nick Sheridan.

Along with the Detective Inspector brought in from Avon and Somerset to oversee the investigation, she had interviewed the other drinkers in the pub that night. Most of them had barely looked at her, just took her for the female sidekick of the leading investigator. And she was happy to let them believe that. The general public, bless them, were always eager to help an investigation, believing that they might hold the clue that could unlock the whole thing, bring a murderer to justice. So they would explain what they saw on the night in question in as much painstaking, boring, unwanted, and unnecessary detail as possible. All the while never noticing that the woman they were talking about was sitting right next to them.

She should have been on the stage.

Inside Blackmoor was going to plan too.

Just the way she liked it. No surprises.

In control.

38

DOWN—HOLD—UP AGAIN. Down—hold—up again. And again. And again. Tom was keeping himself fit. Sit-ups in a cell was cramped enough, in a shared cell just about impossible. But he had to keep himself fit, keep himself sane. Keep himself ready.

Evening. Association time but neither of them had left their cell. Cunningham lay on the top bunk, singing softly to himself. He had the kind of voice Tom would have expected given his choir background, high and clear, even at low volume. Something in Latin, Tom thought. Some religious piece or perhaps even opera. Nothing he recognized. Cunningham tuned out the room when he sang to himself, and it was something he had been doing more and more since Tom came back onto the wing. So with Cunningham doing that and Tom doing his exercises, it was like two different worlds coexisting in the smallest space possible, or so Tom thought.

Everything was back to the way it had been. At least superficially. Cunningham's face had lit up when he returned. There were red marks and welts on his face and arms, they looked like they stung. Perhaps Tom's presence had stopped other inmates bullying and abusing his cellmate. Perhaps that was why he was so pleased to have him back.

Earlier, Tom had tried talking to Cunningham, with some success.

"So I hear you're looking to get out, visit your mother?"

Cunningham jumped as if he had been shocked. "Who told you that?"

"Thought everyone knew. They're waiting for you to give up some information then you can go, yeah?"

Cunningham thought about Tom's words, smiled. "Yeah . . ."

Tom saw, in that moment, why Cunningham hadn't given up the location of his bodies yet. The power it gave him. Not only over the police and prison staff, but the families of the victims themselves. He was enjoying it.

"Why not tell them? Then you can get out? Seems simple."

"It's not. Not that simple. It has to be . . . I have to see my mother when . . . when the time is right."

"What d'you mean?"

"She's still in the hospital. There's nothing they can do for her. They're going to send her home to die."

Tom couldn't work out what kind of emotion was behind the words. But he kept talking. "So you want to see her at home, right?"

Cunningham nodded.

"Why don't you tell them what they want to know, then arrange to see her when she's back at home?"

Cunningham stood up, his eyes angry little dots. "Because I'm doing it my way. *My way.* Don't tell me . . . don't tell me . . ."

Tom held up his hands. "OK, OK . . ." He waited for Cunningham to calm down. "Hey, here's an idea. Why don't you tell me? Then I can tell them when you want me to."

Cunningham looked at him, something like joy appearing briefly in his eyes.

"I mean," Tom continued, "that's what friends are for, helping each other out when they need to."

Cunningham said nothing, but it looked as though a war was

being waged behind his eyes. Like a cartoon character with a devil on one shoulder and an angel on the other. Tom waited.

Eventually Cunningham turned away, looking like he had lost his train of thought, or lost interest in the conversation. That was when he began to sing.

And didn't stop.

Tom, realizing he wasn't getting anywhere but needing to do something in that small space, started his sit-ups.

As he exercised, he thought. The phone call. Blake. Anger and fear danced within him, each vying for prominence. He tried to tame the fear but couldn't. Too overwhelming, too all-embracing. He was stranded, in prison, alone. His only contact with the outside world gone. His life in danger.

He'd walked back to his cell, numb. Laid there all night, not knowing if he slept or not. Unsure even whether he heard Cunningham's night terrors. Just letting the enormity of his situation sink in. Trapped. Stranded.

The next day had been the same. Every movement around him became a potential threat. He was ready to retaliate, his body tensed and coiled. Get the first punch in, make it count, make it dirty. Don't be fair, just win. Everyone from the inmates to the officers. They could come at him one at a time or all together. He just had to be ready.

He thought about pulling his razor apart, melting the blade into his toothbrush with a lighter. He decided not to risk it. If he was discovered with it, he'd be busted down to basic, and he didn't need that. So he started exercising.

Push-ups, sit-ups, squats, anything he could manage in that cramped space to make his body harder, stronger. Focus his mind away from the ever-present fear. As he worked out, he planned. What to do next, how to get out of there.

Just walk up to the warden and tell him who he was and what

he was doing there. And be disbelieved. With no backup and no way to find out if Sheridan was working with anyone else besides Blake, his claims would make him the laughing stock of the wing and an even bigger target than he already was. Quint? There was nothing his old commando mate could do either. He was only insurance in case anyone tried to get to him through Lila or Pearl. No. There was only one way out that didn't involve serving his whole sentence.

Get Cunningham to confess.

Dr. Bradshaw had said doing so would reduce his sentence. He wondered how sympathetic she would be to hearing his whole story. First though, he had to get results.

He finished up, having reached his number, and stared at the ceiling while he got his breath back, ready to start on his push-ups.

He didn't get that far. An officer put his head round the door.

"On your feet, Killgannon, you're wanted."

Tom frowned. "Where?"

"How do I know? Just told to come and get you."

"Not my turn for a shower, is it?" He was sweating profusely from his workout and beginning to stink out the cell. That was why aftershave was almost as valuable as tobacco in prison. "Could do with one, though."

"Come on."

Tom got to his feet. Cunningham stopped singing to himself, lowered himself down from the bunk.

"Not you," said the officer, pointing, "just him."

Cunningham wordlessly got back on the bunk. Tom frowned. That seemed odd.

"Come on."

Tom was led off the wing. He recognized the officer as one of the two who had given the art group the tour of the topping shed. And that seemed to be where they were headed now.

Tom shivered from more than just the cold. He was off the

wing, out in the open night air. The sweat dried to his body, turned suddenly freezing. This wasn't right, he thought. Something was going on. Then he realized. This is it. This is Foley's attempt on me. He steeled his body, ready for attack.

The officer reached the door to the topping shed, took out his key to open it.

"In there."

Tom turned to face him. The officer flinched. "You coming as well?"

The officer became tongue-tied. "I . . . there's someone in there who'll, who'll tell you what's . . . Just get in."

Tom stared at him, unmoving. Eyes unblinking. "How much are they paying you for this?"

The officer turned away, unable to face him.

"Pathetic," said Tom. "Fucking pathetic."

The officer said nothing.

"At least give me a weapon to defend myself."

The officer looked up. Conflict in his eyes. But he had made a decision. "Just get in there."

He gave Tom a shove through the door, locked it behind him.

Tom looked round. Or tried to. The room was in darkness. His fingers played along the wall, searching for the light switch. He found it, flicked it on. The room was illuminated by the overhead strip lights. It seemed to be as it was the last time he had been inside. Except for one thing. The makeshift noose and rope tied from the central roof beam. The chair beneath it.

Two shapes detached themselves from the shadowed piles of stacked chairs. Two huge inmates. Tom had never seen them before—or didn't think he had—but he knew the type. Prison enforcers. Big, covered in tattoos, both professionally done and prison marked, with the kind of dead eyes that only came to life when they were taking someone else's. One had a mohawk, one had a beard but a bald head. Other than that they were indistinguishable.

"Come to give me a message?" Tom asked, body already tensing into a fighting stance.

"Yeah," said Mohawk. "It's behind us." He pointed to the noose.

Beardy reached into his pants pocket, brought out a cell-made shiv. Mohawk did likewise. They began advancing toward him. "You going to give us any trouble?" asked Mohawk. "Be easier if you didn't."

Tom smiled. No humor reached his eyes. He looked around for potential weapons. Couldn't see any, except the stacked chairs. Better than nothing. But only just.

Beardy was making his way around Tom's back, attempting to come at him in the clumsiest pincer movement he'd ever witnessed. They were slow moving but he didn't believe they would be slow witted. Or that wasn't a chance he was going to take. He feinted to his right, made it look like he was going to run, put the two of them on the front foot, ready to go after him, then quickly darted to his left and the pile of stacked chairs. Before they could react, he had a chair in his hand. He brandished it at them like a lion tamer.

The two of them turned, smiled at him. "That the best you can do?" said Mohawk.

"Come here and find out."

They both moved slowly toward him. One of them had to break, he thought, make a sudden movement, attempt to get him. He just had to work out which one.

It was Beardy. He lunged at Tom, trying to get his knife arm around the metal legs of the chair. Tom brought the chair leg down onto his arm. Then again. It had virtually no effect.

Changing tactic he lunged with the chair, aiming it at Beardy's face. That produced a better result. The leg struck him just above the right eye. He recoiled. Tom struck again. This time he hit him right in the eye. Pushed as hard as he could. Beardy, hands to his face, screamed in pain and retreated.

Tom didn't have time to relish this triumph. Mohawk was now behind him, a shiv in his hand too. He felt, rather than heard, its swish and tried to dodge out of the way. The blade, small but vicious, connected with his forearm. He gasped in pain, looked at it. Blood sprayed out of his arm as it scythed away from the blade. He let go of the chair. It dropped to the floor.

Tom tried to ignore the pain, knew there were more important things to do. He could hurt later.

Looking around, he checked his options and quickly assessed the situation, looked for something that might give him an advantage. He jumped on the chair underneath the noose, grabbed for the rope and swung his body toward Mohawk. Both feet connected and the man went over. The shiv fell away. Tom jumped down, picked it up.

And felt a sudden pain across his right shoulder blade. Beardy, half-blinded, had got himself upright and swung at Tom with his shiv again. He felt the blood instantaneously soak through his sweatshirt. Tom dropped the shiv and turned, ready, trying to ignore the extra pain.

No time to think, he went in on Beardy's blind side, punching him on the side of the head. The man, already in pain, brought his hand up to defend himself. Tom kept punching, as fast and as hard as he could.

Behind him, Mohawk was getting up. Thinking fast, deciding Beardy wasn't the immediate threat, he bent down, grabbed the shiv, and turned to Mohawk who threw a fist that was more hopeful than accurate. Tom managed to grab his meaty, muscled arm with one hand and, holding the shiv in the other, twist it down and around. The man pushed against him and Tom stumbled, losing his footing. He let the arm go. Mohawk swung again.

Tom managed to get most of his body out of the way but his right shoulder took a hit. Right where the shiv had already caught him. Mohawk was so big, his blow so powerful, that Tom felt like his arm had gone dead. Beardy, battered but still going, came up behind him, thrusting his knife. Tom just managed to twist out of the way, going to the ground, feeling something in his knee pop as he did so.

He spun away out of the grasp of them both, looked around frantically for a way of escape. Couldn't see one. He turned back to them. Looked at the shiv in his hand.

"You want this? Come and fucking get it . . ."

Ready to take the fight to them and be finished, he stepped into the path of the half-blinded Beardy, swung the shiv at him. Backward and forward, as deadly and as quick an arc as he could manage, darting and dancing on his feet as much as his damaged knee would allow, becoming a hard target to hit. Beardy put his arm out and the shiv connected. He instinctively pulled his arm back as the blood started to spurt. Tom pressed forward, swung again. Connected again. Same arm. Beardy grabbed his bleeding arm with his good one. Tom went for a third cut. The blood was now geysering.

He turned to see where Mohawk had got to. The attacker was wary now, standing back from him. Wondering why Tom hadn't followed the script. He came for him.

Tom scanned the room. In the far corner was a wooden handled mop standing upright in a bucket. He ducked away from the advancing Mohawk, made a grab for the mop.

Thinking he could leave Beardy for a few seconds, Tom turned to Mohawk who had stopped his movement and was regarding him uncertainly. Dropping the shiv, he swung the mop, hard as he could, feet braced as well as he could manage. The wood connected with Mohawk's head. He actually screamed "Ow," which Tom might have found amusing under other circumstances.

He swung again, but Beardy managed to grab the shaft of

the broom. He followed through with his grip, pushing it toward Tom, forcing him back. He put both hands on the handle, ran Tom back to the wall, pinned him up against it. Wood against Tom's throat, pushing.

Tom knew he would choke if he didn't do something so, knowing one eye was already damaged, he pushed his thumbs as hard as he could into both of Beardy's eyes. The man tried to pull his head back and away from Tom, which eased his grip, making Tom in turn press all the harder. And harder still. Beardy cried out in pain. Tom kept pushing, managed to get his thumb right in the corner of his left eye. He could feel the back of the eyeball, see it beginning to pop out of the socket.

Beardy screamed and pulled away, letting go of the mop, trying to claw Tom's hand away from his eye. Tom relaxed his grip, took hold of the handle and pushed Beardy back. He stumbled, ended up on the floor. Tom, not waiting to think, just acting on instinct, swung the wood until it connected with his head. Then again. And again. Until he was sure Beardy wasn't going to get up for a while.

He turned, quickly, looked to see where Mohawk was. He had found the shiv Tom had dropped and stood up, nursing his injured head while holding the shiv out toward Tom without much conviction.

Adrenaline was killing the pain. Tom stood his ground, held the mop handle like a weapon, snarled. "What are you waiting for? Eh? Come on, then, let's be having you . . ."

Mohawk just stared. Glanced at the doorway, down to his fallen comrade who was now bleeding profusely from his arm, the side of his head and ear, cradling what was left of his eyes, then back at Tom. He looked at the knife in his hand. It suddenly seemed very small.

"Come on, you fucker, what are you waiting for?" Tom's voice rising in pitch, in ferocity.

The other man held up his hands. "Hey, mate, just a job. No hard feelings."

He turned and made for the door, dropping the knife as he went.

Tom made to follow him. Before his attacker reached the door, it was unlocked from the outside. A crew of officers in riot gear stormed in and stopped, staring at him.

Tom, blood soaked, anger in his eyes, ready to take on the world just stared back, then yelled, "Who's next then? Who's fucking next?"

And they were on him.

39

"HERE WE ARE AGAIN. We're going to have to stop meeting like this."
Anju smiled as she spoke, hands around her coffee for warmth.

Lila looked confused, distraught, even. "Why?"

Anju frowned, looked closely at her. "You being serious?"

"Erm . . ."

Her hands uncurled from the cup, wrapped themselves round
Lila's. "It was a joke. Didn't you get that?"

Lila gave a smile. It took a second or two. "Sorry. Sometimes
I . . . don't react to things the way everyone else does. It's . . . I
missed a bit. When I was younger."

Anju's smile widened, her grip on Lila's hands tightened. "Don't
worry. I'll help you get all caught up."

Lila couldn't help but smile in return.

Anju took her mind off things.

But there were things she wanted to talk to her about.

They were in Grounded, a coffee shop in Truro's artisan quarter.
It was an off-campus place where they had taken to meeting. Lila
found the coffee good, if a little pricey for a student, but Anju didn't
seem to notice. Coming from money will do that, Lila thought, but
not in a cruel way. Anju couldn't change her background any more
than Lila could. But only one of them wanted to.

They sat on the seats they always did. In front of the counter, smelling the fresh ground coffee and pastries, leaning forward together, arms on the stripped, reclaimed wood tabletop. The wooden stools were circular, their round, padded seats with holes in the center, in brown and white. Like sitting on a doughnut, Lila had said the first time they went there. I think that's the idea, Anju had replied. Subliminal advertising.

"We had a visitor," Lila said after taking another mouthful of latte.

"Is Tom home?" Anju had taken to calling him Tom too. Not Mr. Killgannon or your friend, nothing like that. She just accepted Lila's home arrangement.

"No, not Tom. Still haven't heard from him. But someone turned up saying he's a friend of Tom's."

"So he's got news from him?"

"Not exactly."

"What then?"

Lila sighed. Told her all about Quint.

"THIS IS QUINT," Lila had said to Pearl as the man followed her to the kitchen.

Pearl looked up, startled. Didn't know what to say.

"He says he's a friend of Tom's," Lila said before anyone else could speak.

"I am a friend of Tom's." Quint grinned. Cheerful, disarming. He stuck out a finger, pointed in a theatrical manner. "You must be . . . Pearl. Am I right?" Still smiling. "I'm right, aren't I?"

Pearl returned the smile. It was infectious. "Yes, I'm Pearl. Hi." She walked to him, shook hands over the kitchen table. "I was just making tea. Want one?"

"Yeah, that would be great, thanks. Cold out there." He began unzipping his leather jacket.

"Sit down. Please." Pearl's sense of hospitality kicked in.

He did so, hung his jacket on the back of the wooden chair.

"So what are you doing here, Quint?" asked Lila, staying standing.

"Well, Tom's on his . . . mission, shall we call it. And before he went, he asked me to just keep an eye on you both."

Lila said nothing. Waited for him to continue.

"I was trying to keep a low profile but after you saw me the other day, well . . ." He put his hands on the air, shrugged. "Thought I may as well come and say hello. So here I am." Another disarming smile, accompanied by a little wave this time. "Hello."

Pearl, once again, returned it. Lila didn't.

"I went to see Tom a few days ago," said Lila, face not giving anything away.

"Yeah?" said Quint. "He mention me?"

"He did, actually, yeah. I told him we didn't need anyone to look after us."

Quint shrugged. "Well, you never know."

"So why would we need someone looking out for us?"

Quint's smile faltered. Lila stared at him, watching him all the time. The smile broke, his features regrouped, ready to take another approach. "Nothing in particular, I don't think. But he and I go way back. We served together. We always had each other's backs. When he was recalled for active service, so to speak, he phoned me and like I said, here I am. I was camping first but it got a bit cold for that." Another smile. "Can't do it like I used to. So I booked into a B&B nearby. I was on the way there when you saw me the other day."

Lila nodded, said nothing.

Pearl placed a teapot on the table, three mugs, milk from the fridge and a sugar bowl with a spoon in it.

"Help yourself," she said. "Although I'd give it a few minutes to brew."

Quint thanked her. Lila sat down.

"So you were in the army, that right?" asked Pearl.

Quint shook his head. "Commandos with Tom. Or, you know. What he used to call himself. I've got to get used to calling him that now. Suits him, I think. He looks like a Tom."

"We've never known him as anything else," said Pearl, lifting the pot and pouring. "Sugar?"

"No thanks," said Quint, then hit them with another dazzling smile.

Don't say it, thought Lila. Please don't say it.

"Sweet enough, that's me."

Pearl laughed.

Prick, thought Lila.

With their mugs of tea in front of them, the conversation seemed to have wound down a little.

"So why are you here now? Tonight?"

Quint turned to Lila. "Well, like I said. You saw me, and black people in this part of the world, we tend to stick out, right? So I thought it best to introduce myself."

"So why does Tom think we need protecting? You still haven't answered me," said Lila.

Pearl gave her a warning glance, *Don't be unfriendly*. Lila pretended she hadn't seen it.

"Didn't he tell you why?"

"No. Could you tell us?"

Lila could remember exactly what Tom had said to her. She just wanted to hear Quint say the same thing.

Quint took in a breath, let it go. "Well, as you know, Tom . . ." He placed emphasis on the name, like he was saying it in italics. " . . . made a lot of enemies. In his previous life. Led him to being here. So he just wanted to know that, if anyone tried to get to him while he was . . . away, then I'd be here to help you two. That's all." Another shrug, palms open. "Nothing sinister. Just that."

"But we don't *need* protecting," said Lila.

Pearl looked at her, startled.

"Well we don't," she continued. "No one knows Tom's here, no one knows we're here." She pushed her thumb at Quint. "Except him."

"Lila, that's . . ." Pearl began but stopped herself.

"No," cut in Quint, "it's fine. It's bad enough that Tom's away doing what he's doing, that's stressful enough without some stranger popping up."

Lila said nothing. It was Tom she was angry at. She knew that. Or the police officers who had talked him into doing this. Not Quint. And she felt bad about taking it out on him. But not bad enough to apologize.

"Yeah," she said. That would be as much of an apology as she was going to give.

"So what are your plans, then?" asked Pearl. "Now that you've said hello."

"Don't know that there's much I can do. I'll give you my number and if there's anything you don't like the look of, or anyone, give me a call. I'll come round. Sort it. And I'll keep popping in." He looked at Lila. "If that's OK with you?"

Lila shrugged. She couldn't find a way back down from her earlier hostility.

Quint smiled. "Good." He drained his mug, stood up. "Well, I'll be off. Oh, one more thing. D'you mind if I just do a quick check of the house? See that no one can get in. That kind of thing."

"Sure," said Pearl. "Go ahead."

"Thanks."

He left the room. Lila and Pearl looked at each other.

"He seems nice," said Pearl. "You didn't have to be off with him."

"Couldn't help it. Everything that's happened since I came here . . . you can't blame me for being wary."

"No, but . . . he's a friend of Tom's. And Tom mentioned him. So he must be OK."

"Yeah."

They heard him moving about upstairs. It made Lila feel uneasy. She stood up.

"Just going to the loo."

"Lila . . ."

"Sorry. All that tea."

And before Pearl could say anything else, she was out the door and up the stairs. As quietly as she could go.

At the landing she didn't head in the direction of the toilet. She walked slowly down the hallway toward the room she had heard Quint in. Light was spilling from beyond the frame of the door. She peeped through. Spied. Quint had moved the bed and was kneeling in front of the fireplace, looking up the chimney, his arm in as far as it would go.

Lila didn't stop to think. She entered the room.

"What are you doing?"

Quint was startled. Pulled his arm down from the chimney. His eyes wide, then he composed his features. But just before he did, Lila was sure she saw something else flit across there. Something unpleasant. He stood up, dusted down his arm.

"I was . . . these old houses. Some of the chimneys are wide enough to get a body up. Or down. Just making sure no one could get down there. Wouldn't want that, would we?"

"And can they?"

He smiled again. An everything-was-fine kind of smile. "Nah. You're all right." He looked around the room once more. Eyes lingering on the chimney breast for longer than they should. "Well, I'd better be off."

Lila stood aside to let him out. Kept her eyes on him until he left the house.

Later, she would identify what had passed across Quint's eyes before his smile returned. Anger.

"AND THEN HE LEFT?" asked Anju.

"Yeah," she said. "Haven't seen him since."

"Wow." She frowned. "What was he looking for up the chimney?"

"I don't know. I had a look up there after he'd gone . . ." She shrugged. "Nothing there."

Anju thought for a moment. "Weird."

"Something just felt off about him. Maybe . . . oh, I don't know."

"What?"

Lila paused. "I think we should find out about this guy Quint. How would we go about that?"

Anju smiled. "Are we girl detectives now? Wow."

Lila didn't know what to say.

40

NIGHT AGAIN, AND THE WALLS OF BLACKMOOR PRISON seemed to absorb darkness, store it up, let it seep out through the crevices in the brick, the gaps in the metal, expel itself from the locks and under doors. The only thing keeping it at bay was the overhead strip lighting. Harsh, burning, and unforgiving, those fluorescent tubes lit corridors and wings, spurs and classrooms, workshops and walkways, like artificial suns whose illumination couldn't be escaped. But there were always ways. And means. The brightest lights cast the darkest shadows. And if there was one thing inmates knew how to do, it was move in the shadows.

The hospital wing was never busy. Extreme cases were taken to the local hospital, handcuffed to their beds with a guard attached. But that was expensive and a drain on man hours and overtime. So everything was either dealt with as quickly as possible with the injured inmate back on their wing or, in rare cases, left to recuperate on the hospital wing. There was only one patient there now. And he had a visitor.

The officer on the door looked quizzically at this visitor. "What d'you want?"

"Have a word with a patient. Visiting time, innit?" He leaned forward. "You know who I am."

The words had the desired effect. The officer looked scared.

Didn't want to disobey orders, but knew where the real authority lay. He looked quickly around, checked no one else was there. "Go on, then. Inside. Quick."

He unlocked the door, locked it behind him. Stayed where he was.

One patient in the whole wing. Raised leg in plaster, arm in a plastic cast slung across his chest. Head popping out of a neck brace.

Clive.

He sat on the edge of the bed, startling Clive to wakefulness.

"Well, you've been in the wars, haven't you? Look at the state of you."

Clive quickly oriented himself. Fear immediately took hold. He tried to shrink away from him. "What d'you want? Haven't you done enough? I'm in here, aren't I? I haven't said anything."

"Clive, Clive . . ." He smiled. At least he intended it to be a smile. "Just came to see how you are, that's all. Pay my respects."

Clive stared at him, wary. Said nothing.

"We go back a long way, Clive, don't we? All the way back to Manchester. Those were the days, eh?"

Clive again said nothing. Watching, waiting.

"They were good times. You, me, Mick." He sighed. "Ah, Mick . . ." He shook his head. "What a cunt he turned out to be."

"He didn't recognize me," Clive said at last. "We both came in together. And he didn't recognize me."

"Well to be fair, Clive, the years haven't been kind to you. Smack and booze'll do that."

"I'm clean now." A quivering pride, a strength in his voice.

"And well done you. No, I'm not here to talk about that. I'm here to reminisce about the good old days. And they were good, weren't they, Clive? Before that bastard took us all down."

"Yeah," said Clive, placated but still on guard. "They were."

"We lived like kings. We were kings."

Clive tried to nod. Winced from the pain.

"All in the past now. All in the past. We lost everything that night, didn't we? I mean, some more than others. I mean, you ran, didn't you? Thought you'd get away. No money, nothing. No way of making a living. All gone. So what did you do? Hit the bottle. Big time. And heroin." He sucked air in through his teeth. "Bad stuff, Clive. Very bad stuff. Never get high on your own supply. You should know that. It's all right for the users but we don't touch it."

"Yeah well, like I said. I'm clean now."

"I know, Clive. I know. And you tried to get back into the good books. Well done."

Clive tried to nod once more. Gave up. Just listened. Too tired to talk.

"But you weren't the only one to lose something that night. I lost plenty. I lost everything."

"I . . . I know . . ."

"But mentioning Tom Killgannon's niece . . ." A headshake. "That was out of order, Clive."

"I . . . I know. And I'm sorry." He tried to move his encased arm. "But I've paid for that."

"Well yes. And no. Because you've started him thinking. You've tipped him off. And when you get well again, he's going to come looking for you wanting another chat. And you with your blabbermouth, Clive, you're going to tell him more. Aren't you? Who killed her? How she died?"

"I'm not . . . I promise . . . I won't . . ."

"Well, you say that Clive, but we both know that's not true. So I'm sorry Clive, it has to be this way."

Clive started to cry.

He eased the pillow from behind Clive's head, cradled it, and placed it tenderly on the mattress. He placed the pillow over Clive's tear-wet face. Clive tried to cry out.

"Shh. Come on, Clive. Be brave. You know it has to be done."

Eventually Clive stopped crying and his body went limp. He kept the pillow on until he was sure that Clive wasn't pretending, that he actually was dead, then removed it, looked down at him. Shook his head sadly.

He let the pillow drop onto the bed, turned and left the ward.

The officer was on the door.

"I was never here."

The officer stared at him. Then looked nervously at the ward. Then back to the visitor.

"Never. Understand?"

The officer was too terrified to disagree.

He walked slowly back to his wing.

41

DR. LOUISA BRADSHAW had never fully made her mind up about Paul Shelley. As a prison warden he seemed competent but not spectacular. No standout schemes for rehabilitation or to cut reoffending. No brave trials, no particular vision, no rocking the boat. Just keeping on keeping on. Like he was only in the position for a short while and wanted to hand it over to the next incumbent as he found it. A safe pair of hands. And plenty of other clichés that he would no doubt employ when asked about his job. A remarkably unremarkable man. Or perhaps, she thought, that was just the impression he tried to give. Perhaps the truth was something else.

She sat beside him in his office, noticed just how hot it was. Not warm, hot. Uncomfortably so. Did he do that on purpose, to make colleagues and inmates alike feel ill at ease? If so, why? And how did he stand it himself? She didn't know, but wanted to shed her sweater she was so uncomfortable. The fact that she was wearing a T-shirt with the NASA logo underneath stopped her. Not work appropriate. But then she didn't think it would ever be this warm.

The office itself was as expected. Framed photos on his desk of his wife and children. All as unremarkable looking as him, she thought, mentally chastising herself for judging on appearances. Surely working in this place had taught her not to do that.

The lighting was softer than in the rest of the prison and

there were some framed certificates and photos on the wall. Diplomas and cricketing photos. Shelley dwarfed in pads and a helmet, holding the bat in an aggressive way, the ball nowhere to be seen. Shelley and others bundled up in rough weather gear, on top of a mountain, all smiling at the camera. Probably needs something like that, she thought, after spending most of his working life stuck in a place like this.

There was still something off about him, though, and Louisa couldn't quite place what it was. At one time she would have dismissed feelings and intuitions as something for the new agers, not specialists like her. But again, this place had taught her to respect her instincts. It always seemed like there was something he wasn't telling her. A secret he didn't want to share. Something to do with the way the prison was run. Her place in it. She might have imagined it, but he had seemed to be on the verge of saying something to her a few times, breaking down whatever self-imposed barrier he had erected, testing to see if she could be trusted. Then changing his mind. She had said nothing at those times, just filed it away.

The door opened. An officer brought in Tom Killgannon.

Louisa was shocked, but hoped she didn't show it. That wouldn't be professional. However, the change in Killgannon since she had last seen him was more than noticeable. His hair was wilder, beard more unkempt. Bandages and plasters covered his arms, face, and shoulder. Bruises and cuts grew round them. That was to be expected since his attack, but something in his manner marked him as different too. He seemed less like the man she had first spoken to and more like a hardened prisoner. The tattoos on his arms that she had previously dismissed now seemed more prominent. His body seemed harder, leaner. He might still have that softness, that intelligence in his eyes, but they were hooded now, hidden. She couldn't tell what was in there.

"Sit down," said Shelley.

Tom sat.

Shelley leaned forward, hands clasped together. Like an old headmaster trying to reach a bright but wayward child. Or bargain with one who was uncontrollable.

"Has a night in segregation given you a different perspective?"

Tom looked up. Louisa still couldn't see his eyes. "On what?"

"On telling me why you were attacked. On why you think you were important enough for two very dangerous criminals to take the risk of further punishment and take you on?"

Tom shrugged.

Shelley looked down at his hands, back at Tom. Trying again. "How did you come to be alone in that room?"

"Ask your wing staff. One of them escorted me there. Then locked the door after me."

Shelley looked uncertain, unsure how to proceed. "I won't hear any criticism of my staff, Killgannon."

"Then stop asking me pointless questions. Because you'll hear a lot. This whole thing should go to adjudication. Your staff led me in there. There was a noose and two ugly bastards waiting for me."

"How did your alleged attackers get into that room?"

"Ask them."

"They're not here anymore. Their injuries were quite serious. They've been moved to other institutions where they can receive better treatment."

"Color me surprised. Scared of the lawsuit?" Tom hadn't raised his voice yet. All his words were in the same flat, weary monotone.

"So what had you done to annoy them?"

Tom shrugged. "Never seen them before in my life."

"But you must have—"

"Stop fucking about." Tom leaned forward quickly, spoke sharply. There was power in both of those things and Shelley was taken by surprise. Louisa too, to a lesser extent, but Shelley actually jumped back. "You know what's going on. There was a noose in there. They were sent to either hurt me, intimidate me, or kill me. They'd been paid to do it. And you know who by."

Shelley stared at Tom. Tom returned the stare. Louisa saw his eyes for the first time. The intelligence was still there but no softness.

Shelley looked away, pretended to find something on his desk fascinating. "You're making ridiculous allegations, Killgannon."

Tom laughed, shook his head. He turned his attention to Louisa. "Why are you here?"

She was shocked at the frankness of the question. This wasn't the man she had spoken to recently. Or if it was, something very bad had happened to him since then.

"I'm . . ." she began, " . . . here to assess you. See if you're fit enough to go back to the wing."

"Fit. You mean mentally? So I can do your investigating for you without attacking anyone else who comes to kill me, is that it?"

Louisa reddened. "Something like that."

"Investigating?" asked Shelley.

"Ask her," said Tom, indicating Louisa with his thumb.

Louisa said nothing.

Tom turned his attention back to Shelley. "Just tell Foley not to send any more people after me. Then I won't have to fight them off."

"Foley?" said Shelley too quickly. "Dean Foley? Why would he take an interest in you?"

He smiled, blurted out some kind of laugh. "Ask him."

"I'm asking you."

Tom looked between the two of them. Louisa thought he was making up his mind about sharing something and was reminded again of Shelley. With Tom it seemed different. Not that he didn't want to share something, more that he was now almost beyond caring what would happen if he did.

Tom sighed. "Right," he said. "I'll tell you. Do whatever you like with this information afterward."

They waited.

"Tom Killgannon's not my real name. I'm an ex-cop and I'm here undercover."

Shelley laughed out loud. "Bullshit. Any undercover operation in my prison goes through me. I'd never heard of you before you arrived and started causing trouble."

"It was supposed to be done secretly so no one would know, especially not the target."

"Who is?" Shelley asked, amusement in his voice.

"Noel Cunningham. I'm supposed to get near him, befriend him, find out where those kids' bodies are in return for letting him out to visit his mother." He looked at Louisa who was about to speak. "When you asked me to do the same thing, I couldn't believe it."

Shelley looked between the two of them. "You asked him to do the same thing? Why?"

"Because they seemed to have bonded. And there was a good chance Cunningham would open up to him."

Shelley sat back, smiled. "So you tell us now that you're under-cover. Taking this very seriously, aren't you? Very good. Keep going."

Tom ignored him. "I was the person whose testimony brought down Dean Foley. He knew me back in Manchester under a differ-ent name. I was undercover then. He made me, sent those two men over to me."

"Is that right."

"My contact, DS Sheridan of Devon and Cornwall Police is dead. He can't vouch for me."

"Of course he can't."

"But his partner, DC Blake should be able to."

Louisa had wondered who Dean Foley's target was. Now she knew. She also noticed a change in Tom's demeanor when he mentioned the Detective Constable's name. Like saying something he didn't believe. She couldn't work out why.

"Well let's give her a call, then, shall we?"

Shelley picked up his office phone, found the number from his rolodex, dialed. It was answered. "Warden Paul Shelley, Blackmoor Prison. Could I speak to a Detective Constable Blake? Yes, I'll hold." He looked directly at Tom, still smiling. "You're in luck. There is a Detective Constable Blake. They said they'd put me through to her."

Tom watched him impassively.

"Yes," said Shelley. "DC Blake." He introduced himself once more. "I've got an inmate here called Thomas Killgannon. He says he's an undercover operative working for both yourself and DS Sheridan, is that true?"

Tom stared at him.

"Oh," said Shelley, "I'm sorry to hear that. My condolences. No . . . you haven't. Right. Thank you. Sorry to waste your time." He replaced the receiver, looked back at Tom, triumph in his eyes. "Never heard of you."

"Speak to her commanding officer."

"Who would that be?"

"I don't know."

"I'm sure you don't. You were right, though. About DS Sheridan. She says he's dead."

Tom's face changed. Sadness tinged and desperation appeared on his features.

Shelley sat back, threw his hands in the air. "Thanks for the entertainment. I suppose you're to blame for the death in the infirmary last night too, aren't you?"

"What?"

"Clive Bennett." Shelley looked at something on his desk. "Isn't that the inmate you attacked, that got you your first spell on the segregation block?"

"Bennett. Bennett. That's him. Looks different now. That's why I didn't recognize him . . ."

"I suppose you know him too."

"He was one of Foley's gang back in Manchester. You can check that. He joked about my niece. She's dead. That's why I lost it and attacked him last week."

A shadow passed over Shelley's features at the mention of Foley's name. "Get him taken back to his wing." He looked at Louisa. "Can't win 'em all, Dr. Bradshaw."

Louisa didn't want to move, didn't want the conversation to end. "I'd like to keep working with him."

"What, treat him for being delusional?" Shelley laughed at his own joke.

Louisa was beginning to think Tom Killgannon wasn't delusional. Or at least there was more to his story than he was saying. She addressed Tom directly.

"Will you feel safe back in general population?"

Tom shrugged. "As safe as I can in here."

"Fine. Then I'll take you back there."

She stood up. Tom did the same. Shelley just watched them go, the smile no longer in place.

42

"How are you feeling?"

Tom looked at Louisa, walking alongside him. She had set the pace and didn't seem to be in any hurry to get back to the wing. She seemed sincere but he still didn't want to engage her in conversation. He had just tried that and it had got him nowhere. He was aware of how much his most recent spell on the seg block had changed him, tipped him into a different character. He didn't feel like he was even Tom Killgannon anymore. He felt like he was becoming someone else. Someone harsher, harder. Even crueler, maybe.

"Are we in session now?" he said, his words virtually spat at her. "Is this therapy?"

She seemed upset by his tone. "It's a genuine question. How are you bearing up?"

Louisa stopped walking, looked round, checking for eavesdroppers. No one was in earshot. They could hear voices, cries echoing down the corridors, but no one nearby.

"I believe you, Mr. Killgannon."

"Not Tom anymore?" He couldn't take the sneer out of his voice. It seemed to have settled in permanently.

"I'll call you Tom if you like. It doesn't change what I'm saying though. I believe your story."

Tom looked wary. "Why?"

"Because . . . I shouldn't be breaking client confidentiality, but someone fitting your description was mentioned to me by another of my patients recently. Your description and background. And how it personally impinged on them and their situation. Then you say all this today and I just put two and two together. Am I right?"

"If by other patient you mean Dean Foley then yes, you are."

Louisa fell silent, thinking before speaking. "What if . . . bear with me here, what if . . . I were to get you two together. Somewhere neutral like my office, just so you can both talk to each other in a safe space? Have a conversation away from all the other pressures of this place, try and come up with some kind of, I don't know, way of going forward for both of you? Would that be worth trying?"

"What, so he can do the job himself? Kill me, face-to-face?"

"The meeting will be properly monitored. He'll know not to step out of line. He won't. I'm sure of it."

"Oh, you're sure of it, are you? You know him that well?"

Louisa reddened. "Yes, I think I do. I've come to understand him quite well."

Tom laughed. Something harsh escaping from a trap. "Really? He's playing you. That's what he does. Plays people. Tells them what they want to hear. Until he gets bored of you. And you really wouldn't want to be around him then."

"I think he's changed since he's been here."

Tom held up his arms. "I've got the scars that say he hasn't."

Louisa shook her head. "I think it's worth a try. For him as well as you. I've worked with him a lot. I don't believe he's the same person he was when he came in. People change. Especially in somewhere like this."

She looked directly at him as she spoke. He felt the truth in her words.

"Don't they?" she challenged.

Tom didn't answer.

"Tom?"

"How can I trust you? What about the other stuff? Cunningham?"

"I asked you to do that in good faith. I knew nothing about why you say you are really in here."

"'Say' I was in here. That's why I *am* in here."

"And I believe you. Honestly I do, but you have to admit, it's easy for someone like Shelley to reach the conclusion that you're delusional."

"And how does that help me?" Tom felt anger rise within him. He turned to face her, aware of how much he towered over her, how much more physically powerful he was. How much he could hurt her. "The whole point of me being here was to get Cunningham to talk. My outside contact's been killed and for whatever reason my other contact is denying all knowledge of me. I have to get out. Never mind Foley, what are you going to do to help me?" Leaning over her, dwarfing her. Hands clenched into fists, ready.

Fear on her face, Louisa shrank away from him, pushed herself into the wall. Her hand went to the pocket of her jeans.

He moved backward, away from her personal space. Unclenched his fists, averted his eyes from her. "Sorry . . . sorry. That's not me. That's not me . . ."

Her hand stayed by her pocket. She kept staring at him.

"I'm sorry. It's . . ." He looked up, around, aware once again of just how enclosed he was, how much at the mercy of someone else's timetable. How his life was no longer his own. "It's this place, it's . . ." He looked at her, briefly. "Sorry." His eyes darted away, didn't wait for a reply.

She nodded then slowly moved herself away from the wall. Her hand still hovered over her jeans pocket. "OK."

"It's just . . . I'm just . . ." He felt this new persona, the one the prison had forced upon him, the battle-scarred survivalist, crumbling away again. He was reverting to Tom once more. "I've got to get out of here. I should never have accepted this job. Should never have said yes."

Louisa made no response.

He looked at her again. "You have to believe me. I'm not delusional. I'm not a liar or a fantasist. I know that phone call to Blake made me seem so, but I swear to you I'm not. Please. You have to believe me."

She didn't answer straight away. "You seem . . . certain. And Dean Foley's told me things that back up your story, like I said. But why would she deny all knowledge of you? Especially if her partner's just died?"

"She must be up to something. And I don't know what she's after. But I'm not going to find out in here."

"Would Dean Foley know?"

Tom gave the question thought. "If he's in on all this then he might."

"All the more reason for us to arrange that meeting."

Tom didn't reply immediately. He weighed up his past, his future. Sighed. "Looks like it's my only choice, doesn't it?"

Louisa nodded, more from relief than anything else, he thought.

"I'll get it set up," she said. "In the meantime, do you want me to find out about this DC Blake for you?"

Tom looked directly at her once more. There was none of the recent prison savagery in his gaze. Just hurt and honesty. "Would you do that?"

She attempted a smile. It didn't quite come off. "I said I believed you, no matter how ridiculous it sounds. I mean, I'm not much of a detective or anything, but let me try and find her. Talk to her."

"I would really appreciate that. But be careful."

"I will."

"Thank you." So emotionally fragile was he that he felt tears threatening the corners of his eyes. He quickly blinked them away, refused to acknowledge their existence.

But Louisa caught him. Pretended she hadn't seen them.

"OK." Her voice was soft. "Get yourself sorted. And I'll take you to your wing."

Tom tried to harden himself up once more, ready to front it out on the wing.

It took him longer than he thought.

43

Louisa ushered Tom back into his cell, both of them trying not to make eye contact that could be read as significant by anyone else. Cunningham seemed to have barely moved. Even though it was well past breakfast Tom wondered if he was still asleep.

"Morning," said Tom.

Cunningham came alive immediately. Jumping up, looking at Tom like he was a ghost. Staring at Tom but not truly seeing him. Then he noticed the state Tom was in.

"You . . . what happened? Where've you been?"

Tom sat down on the rigid chair, tried to look relaxed. Compared to where he had just spent the night this was beginning to feel positively homely. It was easy to see how inmates became accustomed to it and became scared to leave.

"I seem to have made some enemies since I've been in here," he said.

Cunningham examined Tom's injuries with his eyes, let them rove all over him. Tom couldn't tell if Cunningham was excited by what he saw or appalled. Truth was, he didn't want to know.

Tom sighed, rubbed his face with his hands, trying not to reopen wounds, pull dressings off as he did so.

Cunningham was fully interested now. "Have you been . . . what happened?"

Tom sighed, not wanting to go over it again. He was about to brush Cunningham's question off but stopped. This might be it, he thought. A way of sharing something, getting him to open up. He sat back. Took a deep breath.

"I was attacked. In the old topping shed. Two blokes. They came at me with shivs."

Cunningham's eyes widened. He glanced nervously toward the door, as if expecting the blokes to come barging in.

"It's OK," he said, "they've gone now. I took care of them."

"Two of them?" Was that fear in Cunningham's voice or admiration? Tom couldn't tell. Yet.

"Like I said, I seem to have some enemies."

Cunningham nodded, his jaw slack. Thinking. He looked up. "Was this because of me?"

"How d'you mean?"

"Because you stopped that man attacking me the other day? Did they come after you for what you did to him?"

Tom was about to say no, it was something else, but stopped himself. "I don't know. Might have been. Dreadlocked Darren might have wanted me taken care of."

Cunningham's eyes were off somewhere else. "You did that for me . . ."

Tom nodded. "Could well be."

Cunningham's mind was off somewhere else. Tom waited.

"So you saved me from him and then they did this to you. Because of him. Because of me."

"Looks that way," said Tom.

Cunningham was nodding once more. "So you are my friend, then . . . you must be my friend . . ."

"Told you I was."

"Yeah . . ." Cunningham slipped back into his own world.

Tom waited. Was this the right time to ask him about the graves? Would there be a better one?

"How've you been?" he asked. "Since I was away."

Cunningham looked up again, confused by the question, not used to being asked by anyone not in a professional capacity. "I . . . I've been . . . here." His head fell, eyes darkened. "I've been . . . lonely."

Tom tried to contain his excitement.

"Well," he said, "No need for that. I'm back now."

Cunningham frowned. "Did Dr. Louisa drop you off?"

"She did. She's good, isn't she?"

"She's helped me a lot. Since I've been in here. I told her about you."

"I know. She said. Said it was good that we were friends. That we could help each other. Confide in each other."

Another nod from Cunningham.

"She knows you want to go and see your mother and she's keen to arrange that. And you know what they want to know. But like I said, if you wanted to tell me, I could let them know as and when you needed me to. If that would help you."

Tom said nothing, waited.

Eventually Cunningham looked up at him. Smiled. He opened his mouth, ready to speak.

And the cell door opened.

"Visiting time for Killgannon. Come on, mate. On your feet."

44

TOM'S HANDS CLENCHED INTO FISTS. "Me?" he asked the officer.

"Yeah, Killgannon, that's you."

Any other time, thought Tom. Any other time . . .

"Who is it?" asked Tom, getting to his feet. "Who's here to see me?"

"Scarlett Johansson. How the hell do I know? Come on."

"I'll see you later, Noel," he said, but Cunningham had already turned his back to him, was staring once more at the cell wall. Tom tried to quell the anger he was feeling, get his head around the trip to the visiting room, the visit itself.

He followed the officer out, watching all the time for attacks, ready to defend himself. Nothing happened.

He saw them straight away. Lila and Pearl. Sitting together. And they saw him. He could tell from the way their expressions changed on taking in his appearance. His bruises had started to heal but not quickly enough. Yellow wasn't any more attractive than purple. He felt so ashamed that they were seeing him like this. So ashamed that he actually looked like this.

"What happened?" asked Pearl as soon as he sat down.

Tom paused. Tell them the truth or make something up? He couldn't not tell them the truth but he didn't want to worry them unduly. "I got jumped," he said.

"Jumped?" said Pearl. "Who by?"

"There were a couple of them. I fought them off, don't worry. They didn't really hurt me. Looks worse than it is." The last sentence accompanied by a smile that became weaker as the words went on. "Occupational hazard, here. Not much health and safety in the workplace."

He glanced at Lila. She hadn't spoken, just stared at him. He couldn't tell if it was fear or disappointment on her face. Or something else altogether.

Pearl was also staring at him. He wished he had never come to the visiting room.

"It won't be long now," he said, attempting another smile. "He'll open up to me soon. Really. Soon." His words faded away.

"You said that last time," said Lila.

"Yeah I know, but—"

"About the fighting. You looked bad then. You look worse now. And about coming out soon. You said that last time. And you're still here. And now it's worse." Her voice was slowly rising, becoming shakier.

"It'll . . . it'll not be long now. Promise." Tom hated himself for saying that.

"Just come out, Tom," said Pearl. "Come home." She reached across the table, placed her hand on his. It felt like an electric shock to his body.

He locked eyes with her. Their silence said more than words could. Lila looked away, giving them a semblance of privacy.

He took his hand away in case it attracted the attention of a prowling officer.

"I will. I promise."

Silence fell between them. All they could hear were the hushed conversations around them, as families and friends pretended they were alone too, talking normally.

"Quint's been to see us." Lila, recovered, spoke again.

"Quint?" said Tom. "What for?"

"Said he was keeping an eye on us. You know, just like you asked him to."

"Yeah, but he didn't need to come and see you. Just check you were both OK."

"Well, he thought otherwise. I found him with his arm up the chimney in the spare bedroom."

Both Pearl and Tom stared at her. Then both spoke at the same time.

"What?" said Tom, more a statement than a question.

"You didn't tell me that," said Pearl.

"Yeah," said Lila, continuing. "Said he was checking to see if someone could get into the house that way. Making sure we were safe." The last sentence dripped with mockery.

Tom's features hardened, his voice flattened. "What does he look like, Quint?"

"Black guy on a motorbike," said Pearl. "Wears a Belstaff jacket. Nice one. Not cheap."

"Hair?"

"Short," said Lila. "But not shaved. No beard or anything. And in good shape. About your age, maybe a bit less, I'd say."

Pearl nodded in agreement. "Why?" she asked, "You think there's something up? He seemed fine to me."

"It sounds like him. Just seems a bit odd, that's all." He sighed. "Maybe he's just doing what he thinks is best."

"Who is this guy, anyway?" asked Lila.

"He's an old friend of mine from Afghanistan. We were on a crew together. He's a good bloke. He runs a security firm now, protecting Arabs and Russian oligarchs, that sort of thing. He doesn't get the chance to do much hands-on work anymore. When I asked him to keep an eye on you two, he jumped at it. Maybe

I should call him. He's on my list of approved numbers in here. Yeah, I'll do that."

Lila had fallen silent once more. The others followed suit.

"So," said Tom, trying to be cheerful, "anything else to tell me?" He turned to Lila. "How's your . . . friend?"

She reddened. "Fine. Going to bring her round. Introduce her to Pearl."

"Must be serious."

Lila shrugged, tried to conceal a smile. "Yeah, you know. Is what it is."

Tom smiled. For the first time in a long time feeling genuinely happy.

"Come home. Then you can meet her." Steel behind Lila's words.

He knew the subtext. Just come home. I'm missing you. Not that she would ever say it. He looked into her eyes. She knew he understood.

An officer announced that visiting time was over. They stood up, embraced, Tom clinging to them both like they were life rafts and would drift away if he let go. But he had to let go.

They left. He went back to the wing.

Still watchful, still in that tiring state of perpetual readiness.

45

"Hello, Dean. I managed to get another session for you. Make yourself comfortable."

Foley sat down in the armchair. Louisa passed him coffee. Just the way she knew he liked it. He thanked her. Took a sip. Too hot. Placed it carefully on the floor beside the chair. Looked at her. It seemed like there was something she wanted to say to him but was waiting for the right time. He blinked the thought away. Probably just being paranoid. What with everything else going on.

"So how have things been?" Louisa asked, settling back into her armchair, notepad angled away from him so he couldn't see what she was writing. "You were very agitated last time. Wanted to meet again urgently. Has there been an event of some significance in your life since we last met?"

There it was again, he thought. Her tone of voice. That sense that she had something to say to him but was waiting for him to speak first. Perhaps he would have to be wary. Even if it went against everything that these sessions were supposed to stand for. Or maybe he should just confront her head on. Get rid of all this pissing about, get it out in the open.

He sat back. Looked at her. "Go on," he said. "Say it."

She had the good grace to look confused, he thought. I'll give her that. "Say what, Dean?"

"That you think I had . . ." He paused. Didn't want to say a name, either real or assumed. " . . . That I had someone attacked in this prison. That I took revenge. Is that it?"

"I don't know, Dean," said Louisa, face as unreadable as her notepad, "is it?"

"Well you seem to think it is. So maybe it is."

She just looked at him. Didn't reply. He began to feel uncomfortable.

"Isn't it?" he said.

Again, she waited.

Foley sighed. Tired with all this. "No," he said. "Yes, I heard there was someone attacked in this prison. Like everyone did. Like you did. But I had nothing to do with it. I never gave that order."

He saw some kind of spark in her eye. She tried to hide it, he thought, but he had seen it.

"Do you know who did?

Another sigh. "Does it matter?"

She thought for a moment before speaking. "This person who was attacked. Would I be right in thinking he was the undercover police officer you previously had dealings with? The one you blame for being in prison?"

"Yes." Straight away. No point lying.

"And you didn't give the order to have him attacked?"

"I said I didn't, didn't I?" Voice rising with anger. He pushed it back down. "I didn't."

"Which implies someone else did."

"Well, obviously."

A thoughtful expression appeared on her face. "And how d'you feel about that?"

He paused. That wasn't the question he had been expecting. Although thinking about it later, it was the only one worth asking.

"I . . . I haven't thought about it. In those terms. The way you're saying."

"And what way is that?"

"Like someone else is getting my revenge. Doing it for me without me asking."

She regarded him silently once more, face unreadable.

"I'm being honest with you. I didn't have anything to do with it. I was as surprised as you."

"It didn't work."

"No, it didn't. He was too good for them. I could have told them that."

"Told who? The ones who carried it out or the ones who ordered it?"

"Both."

"But they didn't ask you. That's what you're saying."

"No. They didn't." He felt anger rise within him again. This time unsure whom it was directed at.

"And how does that make you feel?"

And there it was. The question he had asked himself repeatedly since the attack on Killgannon. And he hadn't been able to give himself a satisfactory answer either. But he had to be honest now. He had given his word. Dr. Bradshaw would expect nothing less. *He* would expect nothing less.

"Tired," he said. Then reached down for his cooling coffee so he didn't have to elaborate.

"In what way?"

He replaced the coffee mug. Swallowed the last little bit down before answering. "Just tired. Of all of it. I just want it to end, I just want some peace."

"You want all what to end?"

He thought once more before answering, trying to articulate just what his subconscious had been trying to tell him for a long time now. "You know who I am. What I am. In this prison and outside. If I was on the out I'd still be doing what I did and enjoying it. Loving it. Don't get me wrong. But I'm not. I'm in here. And I've tried to keep things going the way they should. Like they would if I was still outside. But sometimes . . ." He sighed, faded away.

"Sometimes what?" she prompted.

"I still want everything like it always was. The respect. The reverence. The fear, even. But I just want . . . quiet. To be left alone. And no amount of money or influence in here is going to do that. I just don't want . . . to do this anymore."

"I see."

"I mean, don't get me wrong, I still want everything that comes with being top dog, I'd be stupid not to. But I just . . ." He sighed. "It's hard work, keeping this up. In here, especially."

"Like *King Lear*."

He frowned. Was she insulting him? Was this a joke he didn't understand?

"*King Lear*," she elaborated. "Shakespeare. He doesn't want to be king anymore but still wants to be treated like a king. All the trappings that go with it."

Is that really me? he thought. "What happened to him?"

It looked like she didn't want to answer. "Civil war over his empire. It didn't end well, shall we say."

They sat in silence. Foley eventually broke it. "Was it worth it?"

"Was what worth it?"

"This. All of this. Ending up here. My old man. What a cunt he was, pardon my French, and all that."

Louisa shrugged.

"I was wondering what he'd have made of all this."

"I know he's overshadowed the whole of your life, Dean."

"Yeah."

"And I've suggested coping strategies to deal with his pervasive influence. To try and stop you feeling you have to compete with him all your life."

"Yeah." Unsure of the words but understanding the meaning, he nodded. "I've just been thinking a lot about him lately. And being inside. Questioning, like. Would he be proud of me for what I've achieved? You know, everything I did on the out, and that? Or would he think I was a failure for getting banged up all this time?" He fell silent once more.

Louisa spoke quietly. "And what conclusion did you reach, Dean?" Foley couldn't look up from the floor, couldn't meet her gaze.

"Failure."

She waited. Eventually Foley spoke again.

"I'm just tired. I get no joy out of any of it. Not anymore. Like the thing with Killgannon. You may as well know his name. You probably do anyway. There was a time, not so long ago, when I could have ripped him apart with my bare hands. Happily. Got right stuck in, really made him suffer for what he'd done to me. Now, when I hear that someone's had a go at doing him over I'm just . . . I don't know what to think. I mean, yeah, if anyone's going to do it, it should be me. Not someone else fucking with me."

"Is that what you think they were doing? Couldn't someone else have held a grudge against him?"

"I know it was aimed at me. I just know. Like that job on that guy in the hospital wing. Clive Bennett. That was against me too."

Louisa frowned. "Clive Bennett? That was natural causes. He was in bad shape. His heart gave out."

He gave the kind of smile that pitied her naivety. "That what they told you? Shelley would say anything to stay in charge of his little fiefdom, even getting a doctor to lie about cause of death. No, Clive was one of mine. But it wasn't me. I didn't give the order."

"So you're saying that your power is slipping, is that right?"

He smiled once more but there was no condescension in it this time. Just a kind of weary acceptance. "Civil war. And it doesn't end well . . . And before you ask, it makes me feel . . . well I should say powerless, shouldn't I? Or scared. Or furious. And I was when I first heard about both things happening. But I don't feel any of that now. I just feel tired. Like I want it all over with."

He felt Dr. Bradshaw regarding him differently. Sadly? Was that it? Or compassionately, perhaps. He hoped it wasn't pity. He had never wanted anyone's pity in his life.

She leaned forward, spoke. And before the words came out, Foley knew he had been right. He wasn't just being paranoid. There was something she had wanted to say to him. Had been since he sat down in the chair.

"Dean," she said, "Would it help if you and Tom Killgannon got together and talked?"

He just stared at her, didn't know what to say.

"I just think it might help you both if you found somewhere neutral to talk, away from everything and everyone else. Sorted out your differences. Just the two of you. What d'you think?"

"I . . ." He began to speak, because he thought it was expected of him. But he really had nothing to say. He hadn't finished processing her suggestion.

"Take your time."

He did. Tried to work out for himself what he could gain from talking to Killgannon-Eccleston. Whether he would try to kill him then and there, or if he wouldn't do it, let the opportunity go to waste.

She waited.

"What are you suggesting?"

"The two of you. In this room. Talking. Seeing if there's any common ground, if you can both find a way forward for yourselves. Put the past to rest, even."

"Steady. That's a hell of a lot to ask."

"Would you be prepared to do it, though?"

A smile appeared at the corners of Foley's mouth. "Would this count toward my parole?"

Dr. Bradshaw kept her face impassive. "It wouldn't hurt it, let's say." She waited for his answer.

"Yeah, all right," he said. "Yeah. Let's do it."

"Good. I'm glad you feel that way."

"I mean," he said with a smile that looked like it belonged to his old self, "What's the worst that can happen?"

Louisa wondered whether she had made a very big mistake.

46

ANOTHER NIGHT IN BLACKMOOR. And Tom was trying to chase down sleep.

Other inmates didn't seem to have a problem. Some would sleep around the clock if they could. With their bodies, their lives, rendered down to basics, being locked up for most of your twenty-four hours a day, alone with just the thoughts and impulses that had got you inside in the first place, then sleep was the only free, legalized oblivion on offer. And you took it willingly. But not Tom. His head was whirring too much.

The terror of losing control of his environment had dulled but not disappeared. He no longer lay awake worrying whether he would burn to death if there was a fire, whether they would forget to unlock his cell door in the morning. It had become part of the low-level, constant anxiety of negotiating prison life. He couldn't sleep because he was terrified he might never leave.

He worried that he might end up like Charles Salvador; in for something minor but his constant aggression ensured he would never be released, so he changed his name to Charles Bronson and styled himself the most violent man in prison. He could see how something like that could happen. Looking for threats around every corner, challenging anyone who stepped in front of him. He could understand how that would escalate, but he also worried he would be forgotten.

After returning from Pearl and Lila's visit, Cunningham seemed to have slipped back into his own sullen mind. The progress Tom had made now reversed. Tom knew why, even though neither had expressed it: because Tom had visitors and Cunningham didn't. He might consider Tom his friend, but having visits from his "niece" reminded Cunningham he was truly alone.

So Tom hadn't pushed it. Just waited, with as much patience as he could muster, for the time to be right.

Cunningham wasn't making his quest for sleep any easier. His night terrors playing up once again.

Tom heard the now familiar wailing coming from the top bunk, accompanied by the equally expected thrashing and punching. The crying crescendoed, the words becoming clear: "I'm sorry . . . I'm sorry . . . please, please don't, I'm sorry . . ." And yet more thrashing.

Tom lay on his side staring at the thin strip of light coming under the door, showing there was some kind of life beyond his cell, that he was still connected to it. The lack of sleep here, as well as in the seg block, had built up within him. He felt like he would never rest again. Like his body would never be allowed to recharge. And now Cunningham. He had had enough.

Anger coursed through him as he sat up and swung his legs down onto the floor. He sighed, stood up, turned to the top bunk ready to yell at Cunningham, make him shut up, just let him get some sleep for once, just once in his cretinous fucking life, just once . . .

The cell was never truly dark. There was the 24-7 light from the wing coming under the door, the glow of the perimeter lights through the smudged and filthy windows. Cunningham sat upright, staring at the wall. The shadowed corner of the room, the only true darkness in the whole cell. Tom knew what was coming. Cunningham telling him there were ghosts in the shadows, that he could see them, wanting Tom to see them also. Tom didn't want to look again.

"Cunningham, listen, why don't you—"

"Look. Just . . . look . . ."

Cunningham stared at the corner, arm outstretched, finger pointing. Tom tried to fight it but couldn't. He followed Cunningham's gaze.

"There, it's . . . there . . ."

"There's nothing there, Cunningham, now—"

Tom stopped. Stared. There in the shadows, something was moving.

Like a gas trying to become solid or a dream trying to become real. A figure taking shape before his eyes. The rest of the room dropped away, the faint lights from outside and under the door dimmed. There was only the figure in the corner.

"You can see it as well, can't you?" Cunningham's voice, quieter now, almost calming.

Tom didn't reply. Couldn't. Just kept looking.

The figure became almost recognizable then drifted apart.

"I'm sorry," said Cunningham, voice lowered, reasoning, not screaming anymore, "I really am. Please, let me make it up to you. All of you . . ."

Tom didn't know what Cunningham was seeing. He saw only one image. One person. A young woman. And he knew instinctively who it was.

Hayley.

"I'm sorry as well," he found himself saying. "I really am. I wish it could have been me and not you. I want that so, so much. Spent ages thinking that after it happened, tried to make it happen . . . but it didn't. So I'm here and you're . . . there. Wherever. And I'm sorry."

He was aware of movement at his side. Cunningham had moved his attention from the shadowed corner to Tom.

"You really can see . . . You . . . your own ghosts . . ."

"We've all got our ghosts, Cunningham."

"Mine talk to me. I tell them sorry, I'm always saying sorry. But I think they're hearing me this time. They're telling me . . ." He cocked his head to one side, listening. "Yeah, they're telling me . . . that they want to be put to rest. So do I . . . so do I . . ." Almost crying with those last few words. "Yes, yes, I'll do it, I'll do it . . ."

Tom kept staring. But he couldn't see anything now. Just shadows. Whatever had been there—or he had imagined had been there—was gone. He blinked. There was nothing. Just a sleep-deprived man looking at a corner.

Cunningham was still talking. "Yes I will," he was saying. "I will. I promise. And then everything will be all right. I'll make it all right." Nodding. "Yes. Thank you. Thank you."

He turned to Tom, almost smiled. "Time for sleep now." He lay down and within what must have been seconds was out.

Tom wondered whether he had ever been awake.

NEXT MORNING, TOM OPENED HIS EYES as the lights went on. He had slept. Actually slept. For the first time in ages.

He got out of bed. Cunningham was already up. He sat on the chair watching him. Smiling.

"Good morning, Tom."

"Morning." Tom was instantly wary.

Cunningham stretched, smiled. "This is a new day."

"Isn't it always?"

He laughed. "No. This is a real new day. The first new day in a long time. Praise God."

Tom didn't answer. He stood up, made his way to the steel toilet. Cunningham loomed behind him.

"I'm going to tell them where they're buried, Tom. All of them."
Still smiling like he had shaken hands with God.

Tom paused, turned back to look at him.

"What?"

I'm going to tell them where the bodies are. Their souls have gone, but the bodies are still there. And I'm going to show them. Show them all."

Tom just stared.

"And you're coming with me."

And in that moment, Tom saw his way out.

47

"Oh, it's you. Just passing, I suppose?"

Quint stood at the door of the cottage. Lila had heard his motorbike approach and wasn't surprised to see him. In fact she was ready for him.

"Yeah," he said, slightly taken aback at the welcome. From his expression it looked like he had expected something warmer. "Can I come in?"

Lila stepped back to allow him to enter. She managed to make the gesture seem so offhand, he hesitated, not sure whether he actually was welcome or not. That had been her plan. He followed her into the living room.

"On your own?"

"Yeah," she said, sitting down on the sofa. The TV was on. She was watching *Pointless*. It was nearing its climax. The couple had opted for the category of American Crime Writers. She made no attempt to mute it or turn it off. Nor did she offer him anything to drink or eat.

"No Pearl?"

"At work."

Undeterred he sat down in the armchair. "Everything OK?"

She shrugged. "Yeah. No problems."

"How's Tom? Have you seen him?"

He's persistent, Lila thought. And he hasn't lost his temper yet. If I'd turned up to someone's house and they treated me like this, she thought, I'd have left by now. Or at least let them know how I felt.

"Yeah," she said, "Went in the other day."

"How is he?"

She thought. This answer required some emotion. Or should have. But she didn't want to give anything away to him.

"Well as can be expected, I suppose. We talked about you."

Something passed over his face. Lila pretended not to be watching him, keeping her eyes on the TV, but she was studying him. She tried to catch what the emotion might have been. Fear? Apprehension? Something like that. Nothing positive.

"Jesus," said Quint, trying to make a joke of it, "you must have been short of conversation pieces."

"No, we chatted for quite a bit." Lila turned her attention away from the TV toward him. "He told us some stories about when you two used to be together. Back in the army, was it?"

"Yeah, that's right," said Quint, smiling. "Plenty of stories about that." The smile seemed superficial. Cracked ice on a barely frozen lake waiting for the slightest weight to break it.

"Iraq, wasn't it?"

"Yeah," he said.

Lila turned away from him, back to the TV. She didn't think this couple were going to win. They had chosen the wrong category.

Lila seemed to be about to pursue the subject, but Quint jumped in, changed it. "Did he say anything else?"

"Such as?"

"How he's coping, when he's coming out, that kind of thing."

Lila's smile was as fake as Quint's. "He's all right, I think. You know what prisons are like these days. Holiday camps, aren't they?" She forced a laugh for his benefit. "Probably having a better time in there than he would be out here."

Quint nodded in agreement even though it was clear he didn't go along with her assessment.

Lila kept watching the screen. The couple failed to win anything. They were given commiserations and that was that. The credits rolled.

"Bad luck," said Lila, pointing at the TV. "You get all excited watching something, invested in it, and it ends like that. Nothing. Hardly fair. Although I suppose fairness has got nothing to do with it, really, has it?"

"Not really," said Quint, unsure where the conversation was headed.

Lila stared ahead at the TV, not really seeing it, but trying not to see Quint either.

"Yeah well, if you're OK then I'd better be off." He stood up as if he was suddenly in a hurry to be out of there.

Lila didn't move. Didn't look at him. If she was surprised at his abrupt exit she tried not to let it show. "You know your way out, don't you? Should know your way around by now. I'm going to watch the news."

"Yeah," he said, although it seemed like he wanted to say a lot more. Lila kept her head angled away from him, feigning interest in the TV. She missed his look of angry exasperation as he left the room.

Lila didn't move, didn't dare breathe until she heard the front door closing, the motorbike revving away. She waited a few seconds, just to be sure. Then her expression changed. "You can come in now."

Pearl entered the room.

"Did you hear all that?" Pearl nodded.

"What d'you think?"

"About what in particular, Iraq?"

"Yeah."

Pearl shrugged, spoke like she was trying to convince herself. "Well they might have been in Iraq together. I mean, Tom never said that they weren't. When was Iraq? After Afghanistan or the same time?"

Lila shook her head. "Tom said Afghanistan."

"Maybe they were in Iraq as well."

"Then why didn't Tom mention that? He said Afghanistan." Lila thought. "Tom wasn't in Iraq . . ."

"But what does he want with us then? How does he really know Tom?" Pearl asked, then a sudden thought, "He's been in this house. He knows who we are, what we look like, where we go, he's been around the house, he knows how to get at us . . ."

"I know," said Lila, louder than she had expected, Pearl's fear contaminating her like an airborne virus.

Pearl stopped speaking. "What are we going to do?" Almost a whisper.

"I don't know."

And as she spoke, the carapace she had presented to Quint began to crumble.

"I really don't know . . ."

48

DEAN FOLEY LEANED BACK, eyes closed, body rigid, while Kim worked her particular kind of magic. He almost didn't hear the cell door open but he heard the voice when it spoke.

"Am I interrupting?"

Foley shot forward, sent Kim spilling onto the floor. Warden Paul Shelley stood in front of them, a smirk on his lips. "Officer Shelton. I didn't know you were so talented."

Kim pulled her uniform together and stood quickly. She turned her back on the warden who leered at her until she was fully clothed and red-faced, hair disheveled, she left the cell as quickly as possible.

Shelley watched her go, turned back to Foley who had pulled himself together and was standing up. Shelley grinned. "Well, well, well. Who knew?"

"You did," said Foley. "You know exactly what happens in here and when. And who with. You probably take a cut of what I pay her. Is that why you've decided to visit me now?"

Shelley's smirk faltered. Foley continued.

"Asked her to do that for you, yeah? Know she comes to see me so you thought you'd get a bit of it for yourself, that it? But she knocked you back so you try and humiliate her like this?" He shook his head. "Pathetic."

Shelley stood fuming. "You wanted to see me."

"I could have made the journey. No hardship."

"Neither was it to come here."

"I'll bet. And it does you no harm to be seen on the wings, does it? Reminds them all what you look like."

"What do you want?" More of a statement than a question. Shelley's voice flat, wanting this over with.

Foley sat back down, lit a cigarette. Shelley seemed about to tell him there was no smoking, but a look from Foley stopped him. He took a deep lungful, held it, exhaled slowly, enjoying every second. Even sitting down while Shelley stood he looked in command.

"Yeah," he said, regarding the burning tip, "I want to go out."

Shelley looked like he couldn't understand the words. "You— what? You—want to go *out*?"

"Little trip out. To the moors. Bit of fresh air. Good for the system." Still examining the tip of his cigarette.

"That's . . . that's ridiculous. I can't let you go wandering on the moors."

"Why not? You're letting Cunningham and Killgannon do it."

"That's different. There's a reason for that. And you know it."

"There's a reason I want to go out too."

"Which is?"

Foley took the cigarette away from his mouth, stared at Shelley. Shelley flinched before the unblinking gaze.

"I want to talk to Killgannon."

"Talk to him in here. I'm sure the lovely Dr. Louisa could arrange something."

"She's trying to. But if Killgannon's out with Cunningham I'm guessing that he's not going to be coming back. That right?"

"What d'you mean?"

"Killgannon's undercover law. If he's out with Cunningham, then that must be his job. Get him to give up the bodies. Then he'll be off on his next assignment and I'll have lost him. With me so far?"

Shelley didn't answer straight away. Just stared, slightly slack-jawed at Foley.

"So is that a yes?"

"I . . . Killgannon will be back. I assure you."

Foley smiled. "I like my idea the best."

He sat back, resumed smoking, dragging long and deep on his cigarette. Watching Shelley all the while. Knowing it was only a matter of time before the warden said yes.

Foley took his silence for agreement. "And I want to take Baz with me."

"No. That's too much. I could find a way to explain why you were out there but no one else."

"Baz is coming with me. End of story. Do whatever you have to do, I'll pick my escort, probably Chris, he's a good bloke. Dependable."

"When do you want to do this?"

"Same time Killgannon and Cunningham are out."

Shelley made one last attempt at standing up for himself. "But there might be media, TV cameras following Cunningham. I can't have them seeing you as well. What would happen then?"

Foley stood up. He wasn't very tall but he towered over the warden. "I run this place for you, Paul. I make sure there are no riots, that no one gets out of hand. That there are no fights over drugs or anything else. I keep a lid on everything. It's in your interests as well as mine to keep this place running smoothly, isn't it?"

Shelley nodded, dumbstruck.

"Well, that's the price you pay. Letting me have a few little jaunts. I mean, just imagine what would happen if you said no . . . couldn't guarantee there'd be a safe place for you and your staff anywhere in this prison . . ."

Shelley sighed. "All right, then. I'll make sure you're out when Cunningham and Killgannon are out. But please keep away from any cameras. And the police."

Foley smiled. "I made a career out of it."

Shelley turned to the door, in a sudden hurry to leave. He turned. "Why Killgannon? Why do you want to talk to him?"

"We used to be close, back in another life," Foley said. "And I've got a message for him."

Shelley left. He didn't want to hear any more.

49

DR. LOUISA BRADSHAW DROVE NORTH.

She had phoned Middlemoor police station in Exeter, asked to speak to Detective Constable Blake's superior officer. She didn't know why Shelley hadn't done that. It wasn't difficult. She was put through to a DCI Harmer, told him who she was, what the situation was.

"I'm phoning about Tom Killgannon," she had said.

Silence on the line.

"I believe he's working for you within Blackmoor. To do with Noel Cunningham?"

More silence. Louisa felt as if Harmer was deciding whether to confirm her story. She pushed on.

"His handler was Detective Inspector Sheridan? I understand he's dead now."

"And what can I do for you, Doctor?"

"You have a Detective Constable Blake working for you?" She made the statement a question. "She stated that she has no knowledge of Mr. Killgannon."

"And why would my Detective Constable want to confirm or deny that?"

"I don't know. That's why I need to talk to you to get this all sorted out."

More silence. Eventually Harmer spoke. "Can you verify you are who you say you are?"

"I think it's best if I come and see you, DCI Harmer. That way we can get this sorted out, quickly."

"Yes," he said, the reluctance in his voice unmistakable, "Why don't you make an appointment for later this week?"

"I'm afraid things have moved on and it's more pressing than that. Cunningham's confessed the location of the bodies and insists on Killgannon accompanying him onto the moor. So could I come to see you after I finish work this evening?"

They hung up and when Louisa had finished work, she got into her semiancient Mini and drove from Blackmoor to Exeter.

Shelley hadn't been happy at the idea of Tom Killgannon accompanying Cunningham out on the moors. Shelley hadn't been happy about anything.

"So he is undercover. And he's been operating in my prison without anyone informing me."

"Seems that way. And now Cunningham wants him outside with him."

"Does he now?"

"You'll get a lot of publicity from this. It'll be a vindication that your rehabilitation methods work."

Shelley almost changed personality before her eyes. Sat up straighter, favored her with what she supposed he believed was his good side. Vanity. That was all she had to appeal to in the man. Or most men, when she thought about it.

"But. We don't tell Cunningham that Killgannon's undercover. It might make him recant."

"I can see that logic, yes."

"And we don't tell Killgannon that we know either. Let him sweat a bit longer."

"Why?"

A sly smile appeared on Shelley's lips. "Because the bastard thought he could sneak into my prison and not tell me what he was up to. That's why."

Petty and vindictive, thought Louisa. But understandable.

She tried to replay the day's events as she drove. Sort through everything that had happened so she could switch off and enjoy the evening. That was what she usually did, but found it different tonight as she was still working, sort of. On a normal night she would get home to her flat in Truro, kick off her boots, stick the TV on, pour herself a glass of wine, feed the cat, and, while waiting for her partner Nicole to arrive home, put the day into context. She tried to do that now while driving and listening to Radio 2. It wasn't the same.

The main roads leading away from Blackmoor had, she thought, a nerve describing themselves as such. They could only be considered that in relation to where they were. They twisted round forests, went up and down hills, gave out on to both breathtaking scenery on precarious slopes and huge high hedges that hid oncoming traffic. She was on one such section now. Darkness had fallen so she should have been able to gauge headlights as they came toward her. She wasn't good at gauging distances in the dark. Her own fault, she had put off going to the opticians for new glasses. She was looking forward to getting on the straighter roads that were well lit and she could put her foot down.

She thought of Dean Foley and Tom Killgannon. Hoped she was doing the right thing by getting them together. Hoped she would get the chance to, if Tom Killgannon didn't disappear after Cunningham located the bodies. Dean seemed to think it was a good idea, although she was slightly unnerved by his final response to her. She just hoped that he was a changed enough man not to slip back into his persona. She liked to think that her work counted for something, that he had made progress. And Tom Killgannon. A wounded man. Looked like he was in a prison of his own making before he came to Blackmoor. Maybe he could—

"Jesus!"

The motorbike came from nowhere. Roaring out from a blind bend, bearing straight toward her. She pulled the wheel over to the left, felt the car shake and shudder as it hit the embankment, the hedge, heard the scratching of hawthorn and bramble along the side of the car. She managed to wrestle back control, stopped the car crashing into the side.

Heart hammering, she checked around to see where the bike had gone. No sign of it. Or any other traffic. She took deep breaths, calmed herself down.

Bet that bastard's caused me damage, she thought. I'll need the paintwork looking at.

She kept going. Slightly slower now, more aware of oncoming vehicles.

The road wound out of the hedges into a forested area, began to climb steadily. The denuded trees formed a canopy over the road. She looked to her left, saw a steep drop into the trees.

And heard the powerful revving of a motorbike once more.

Headlights filled her mirror, temporarily blinding her. She squinted, tried to make out the road ahead although she could still see the image of the headlights ghosting on her retinas.

The bike overtook her. She tried to look out, see who the rider was. Couldn't make out anything. Leather jacket, full face helmet, dark visor down. He drew level with her car, began to move into her door.

"Shit . . ."

Her first response was to pull the wheel to the left, get her car away from him, but that would tip her over the edge and down the slope into the trees. She put her foot down, tried to speed past him. But her Mini was no match for the bike. Without expending much effort, he pushed his bike to match her speed, an angry roar from the engine. She felt like he was actually going slower than his bike was capable of. And at the moment, he was just keeping pace with her.

That gave her an idea. She slammed on the brakes, coming to a stop with a screech of rubber. The bike kept going. At least for a few seconds before the rider realized what had happened and swung around in the middle of the road, coming straight toward her.

Louisa started to panic. The headlights were becoming blindingly huge in her windshield. She didn't know whether to pull forward or to reverse. Or to just sit there. No, she couldn't just sit there. She had to do something.

She put the car in gear. Tried to swing around, go back the way she had come. The rider anticipated her movement, swung his bike out to stop her. She stepped hard on the brake, the seatbelt pulling the air from her lungs as she leapt forward.

He turned the bike again, ready to come at her. She put her foot down and drove.

He quickly caught up with her.

Louisa was frantic now.

The bike pulled alongside her, pushed itself into her car. Instinctively she swerved again, just managing to avoid a roll down the embankment, straightening up once more.

But the bike didn't allow her to get back onto the road where she had been. It took up that position, had moved two of the Mini's wheels onto the dirt and gravel at the side of the road. The car began to skid, half on, half off the uneven surface. The front wheel hit a branch causing her to lose control. She screamed but managed to right herself again. Kept driving.

The bike pushed again. The Mini's front wheel hit a rock. The steering wheel leapt from her hands. The car began to swerve from side to side, shuddering away from her control. She tried desperately to turn the wheel, keep the car upright and on the road, but the bike wouldn't let her.

All four wheels were off the road now.

A tree loomed up ahead of her.

She swung the wheel uselessly to avoid hitting it head on.

And the car rolled down the embankment into the trees.

PART FOUR
HUNTED

TWO DAYS AFTER THAT NIGHT IN MANCHESTER

CONSTABLE ANNIE BLAKE stood at the back of the interview room, by the door, hands behind her back. Anonymous as a person, barely a presence. Just a faceless uniform. Not what she joined the force for. But observing, processing all the time.

Before her, Dean Foley, his expensive lawyer next to him, was being questioned by two detectives. Two days in custody had scrubbed off Foley's usual dangerous charm. Now there seemed less pretense about who he was or who he thought he was.

She had seen these two detectives at work before. DI Torrance and DS Sharp. Physical opposites: gravity pulled Torrance's large body downward like a full trash bag. His hair was the color of used tea bags, fingers also, from nicotine. Sharp's name was near literal, he was all bones and teeth. His elbows looked like they could cut. The only thing they had in common, she thought, was they were both midlevel careerists. Doing what they would call a good job, which for them meant crossing the "t's and dotting the i's. Putting a file together to present to the Crown Prosecution Service. And that would be that.

I won't end up like either of them, Blake thought.

In the short time she had been on the force she had grown to detest most of her superiors. They were dull timeservers, superior in name only. She was there for advancement. In whatever way she could do it.

Foley's mouthpiece droned on, making sure he was seen to be earning his fee. The detectives nodded, answered his points briefly. Foley sat so still it barely seemed he was breathing. He looked at Blake like an animal waiting for its prey to display the slightest weakness.

The detectives started the tape, cautioned him, ran through their list of prepared questions. Foley said his "no comment's" in as disinterested a manner as possible. The detectives kept going, the lawyer looked alert. Foley gave the same answer, not even changing the bored, offhand inflection in his voice. It was a charade to be endured by both sides. In TV dramas interviews were shown as violent confrontations, verbal cat and mouse games, even near-religious confessionals. Real life was nothing like that.

Or so she thought.

"So where's the money, Dean?" Torrance, the senior detective asked.

Foley paused, didn't answer straight away.

His solicitor looked at him, waiting for an answer. Before he could give it, sensing an opening, the other detective, Sharp, jumped in.

"Come on," he said, "you've got no reason to lie about that, we've got you bang to rights on everything else. What have you done with it?"

Torrance leaned forward. "Come on, Dean, what have you done with it?"

Foley paused again. Then answered. "I haven't got the money."

The lawyer started to speak. Foley waved him silent as if batting away a fly.

Torrance again. "What d'you got to lose, Dean? Tell us what you've done with it."

Foley, for the first time in the interview, displayed an emotion other than assumed boredom. Anger. He leaned forward. "Why don't you talk to Mick Eccleston, eh? Or whatever his real name is."

"Why would we do that, Dean?"

"Because if anyone's got it, he has."

The two detectives shared a glance. "And why would he have it, Dean? Why not you?"

Foley sat back again. "You'd have to ask him, wouldn't you? Maybe you don't pay him enough. Maybe he wanted some overtime. I mean, he's not earning with me anymore. He's going to be poor from now on, isn't he?"

The detectives kept questioning him, pushing. But Foley just slumped back in his chair, the flare of anger gone, indifference assumed once more.

He said nothing but "no comment" for the rest of the interview. But he didn't need to say anything more. Constable Annie Blake had heard all she needed to.

Dean Foley, she decided, was a man she would keep an eye on.

The next day in Manchester

She had to show her police ID *to be admitted to the hospital room. Even then she had to justify why she was there. The uniform on the door was following his orders to the letter. She would have to be clever if she wanted to pass and not show up on the official log. Squeeze the tears out, pretend to be his girlfriend.*

"Sorry," he said, "I can't let you in. He hasn't given his statement yet. He can't have anyone talk to him until he's done that."

Turn it up a notch. "Please, he's . . . he's all I have . . ."

The uniform checked the corridor both ways then, with a sigh that said he was charting new territory but wasn't without a heart, said, "Go on, then. But don't be long. I'm supposed to mark everyone in and out."

She gave him a smile so radiant, the red face he was left with could have been sunburn. That's how easy it is to manipulate men, she thought. They're fucking idiots.

The only time Blake had previously been into a private hospital room was when her grandfather was dying of cancer. All the grandkids were trooped in and presented, told to stand at his bedside looking suitably upset. The man had been an absolutely tyrannical bastard before the cancer had slowly crippled him and robbed him of his power. Most of them, those who had been on the receiving end of his wrath, including her, were there just to see that he wasn't coming back.

Then, the room had been bleak, like he was just place holding the bed until a proper, more deserving occupant came along. Blake had managed to squeeze tears out then too. It didn't work. He was too far gone to notice and she still got nothing from his will.

She often thought she had joined the police because of her grand-dad. Regretted he didn't live long enough to see her in her uniform. To continue his family reign of terror when she was able to physically fight back, have him arrested if necessary. Or just hurt him. A lot.

She entered the room. It was completely different from her last visit. As if she had walked onto a movie set, except in a Manchester hospital. With tubes and wires hooked up to sighing, pinging, flashing surrounding machines. Foxy lay on something more like a science-fiction life support pod than a bed. Blake was impressed. But at the center, the recipient of all the life-sustaining attention looked nothing like the man she used to know.

His face was mummified with bandages, tubes poking out of his nose and mouth. His arms and body were similarly covered with plastic casts and bandages, one arm supported. His legs were under the cover. She didn't want to look. She sat down in the chair beside the bed.

"You stupid bastard," she said, surprised to find herself crying. "You stupid, stupid bastard . . ."

Undercover, he had said. With Dean Foley's gang. This is it. This is my glory job . . .

He shouldn't have bragged about it. Could have compromised the operation. And his head seemed to be in the wrong place from the start. The glory job. You should have just done what you were supposed to . . .

All that time spent together in the academy. They had bonded straight away. Recognized something in the other that was there in themselves. An ambition, a hunger to succeed. They almost tore each other apart when their relationship started. They were inseparable.

Both posted to Manchester's inner city, Blake found opportunities for advancement harder to come by than Foxy did. And when he was posted undercover, part of her—quite a large part, if she was honest—resented him. *The way he celebrated without taking her feelings into account.*

She had watched him, preening before a mirror, trying to get his manner, his attitude, his clothing right. You've only got this job because you're black, she wanted to say. They only want you in the gang because you're officially representative of the racial mix in that area. That someone somewhere is getting a pat on the back for ticking a box on a racial quota form. But she didn't say any of that. Because that would have been the end of their relationship. And Foxy, if he stopped to think about it, might even have agreed.

At first he had been keen. Going along with the gang, delivering his reports on time, crammed with as much detail as he could manage. But he wasn't getting anywhere near the top of the organization. He had been working his way up, trying to worm his way onto the right side of Dean Foley, when this bloke Mick Eccleston arrived out of nowhere and was fast-tracked up the promotion ladder. That was the turning point for Foxy. When he saw all his hard work come to nothing, when he mentally said fuck it and decided if he was supposed to be a gangster then it was time he made some money as a gangster. That was when he went to the dark side.

Blake noticed straight away. He changed. Became harder, more callous. He brought her gifts. She rejected them.

"What the fuck is this supposed to be?" she said, throwing some expensive, trashy earrings on the sofa while he stared at her, angry enough to punch her. "I'm not some gangster's moll. And you're not a gangster. You're a cop. Remember that."

They grew apart. Blake moved out of the flat they shared, found her own place. He called fewer and fewer times, eventually stopped coming around at all. She didn't know where he was.

And then this happened. No one knew all the facts yet, but there was a dead girl involved, a crashed car, a missing gun. And, if he came around, a potentially very expensive and very ugly court case. When he came around. Keep saying that, she thought. Keep saying that.

She kept staring at him. Almost wanted to reach out, hold his hand.

She didn't know how long she sat there but after a while she realized that the room was now dark and she was holding his hand.

He wasn't going to wake up and even if he did, she had nothing prepared to say to him. So she stood up, left the room.

Thought about him lying there. Look what the job had got him. Thought of those two detectives just going through the motions with Foley. Look what the job had done to them.

Thought of what Foley had said about Mick Eccleston. The undercover cop was in the wind now, gone. But that didn't mean he was untraceable to police like her. And it didn't mean Foley couldn't play a part in finding the money either.

She knew what to do. It wouldn't be easy but it could be done.

Find a cop in Witness Protection with over two million of stolen money.

Whatever happened to her on the force, she wouldn't let it grind her down.

Because this would be her own glory job.

5Ø

IT WAS THE COLDEST, bleakest day Tom had experienced in months. And he felt it even more so out on Blackmoor.

The day was in perpetual twilight. The sun absent, the wind pricking exposed skin like a fistful of needles, heavy gray clouds scudding across the expansive sky, threatening storms. Down below, Tom stood to one side while Cunningham led a team of police detectives and forensic officers as they searched for his hidden graves.

Tom stood back with a couple prison officers who had spared no blushes telling him, and anyone who would listen, what they thought of this whole business. The whole party, leaving their parked 4x4s and heading to inaccessible places on foot, looked like the most reluctant team of ramblers he had ever seen. Except for Cunningham.

Bundled up in heavy-weather clothing, he kept looking back over at Tom, waving at him, checking he was still there, like a dog not wanting to go too far from the person who feeds it. Smiling all the while. He looked like a malevolent Michelin man. He was giddy, looking around constantly as though he could barely believe he was there.

"What's he need you for then, anyway?" asked a guard, clearly unhappy at being outside when he could be on the wing with a cup of tea.

Tom shrugged. "Hand holding, I suppose. I'm his cellmate. He opened up to me about wanting to show where the graves are. So he could visit his sick mother."

"Cellmate, eh?" said the other officer, a suggestive leer on his fat features.

"Yeah," said Tom, his tone of voice indicating that their innuendo or insinuations weren't welcome. "Cellmate. The prison shrink asked for me to be put in with him. Said he would talk to me."

"That all he's done, then?" said the first one, clearly not picking up on Tom's warning.

Tom stared at the man until he backed down, blinked.

The two officers had made a point of not sharing their snacks and flask of hot coffee with him, nor the illegal bottle of brandy they kept taking nips from when they thought he wasn't looking. They had also told him he wasn't to stray from their sight. Tom complied. He had nowhere else to go to.

At least not yet.

He was working all the time he stood there. They had parked their minibus at the bottom of the slope Cunningham and the police had walked up. It led to some rocky tor, Tom had been told. Good views for miles around. If the weather was better than this. Tom was more interested in the road they had traveled up on. He tried to get what bearings he could from the weak sunlight, tried to work out where he was on the compass, what direction his home was in. If this were going to be his only method to escape, then he would have to take it. Deal with whatever paperwork, or supposed illegalities cropped up afterward. He could cope with anything as long as he was free again.

So far he hadn't found a way. Too many police with Cunningham, the prison officers too wary. Thankfully there wasn't any media presence. Their scrutiny would have made escape impossible. He was biding his time. He would spot the opportunity when it came.

The first prison officer checked his watch. "Nearly lunchtime." He turned toward Tom. "Want yours?"

"Yeah. Sure." He was hungry, but he wasn't about to let these two know that.

The other leaned into a bag at the back of the minibus, brought out three wrapped packages. He kept one of the two biggest for himself, passed the other big one to his partner, the smallest one to Tom.

"There you go."

Tom opened it. Prison mystery meat on cheap white bread.

"Eat up."

Theirs were shop bought along with a chicken leg each and a bag of chips. They grinned as they ate.

Tom turned away, looked at the roads once more.

Made calculations.

51

DC ANNIE BLAKE waited until she heard the sound of the shower then knelt by the side of the bed, pulled something out, and opened it.

Her go bag.

Everything she had planned for led up to this moment. She had known it would come, worked for it, added to it. The bag contained everything she would need to walk out of this life, start another one. A better, richer one.

Passport, credit and debit cards with untraceable money in those accounts, clothes, even a small amount of gold that she could sell.

She had worked next to criminals her whole career. Learned from the best. The ones who never—or rarely—got caught. She had studied their methods, noted what had gone well for them, what hadn't. Vowed not to make their mistakes.

She was near to Foley's money. She knew it, could feel it. And with Killgannon now out with Cunningham, she had to move. Time for her endgame.

She took something else from the bag. An untraceable Desert Eagle XIX in .44 Magnum. It was loaded. She racked the slide. Put it down at the side of the bed on top of the bag.

The shower stopped. After a short while, DCI Harmer stepped out, toweling his hair.

"This is disgraceful, not going into the office yet," he said, not looking at her. "We should have been in hours ago."

"Didn't hear you complaining."

He laughed, threw the towel onto the bed. "No. You wouldn't."

He looked up, realized that she was standing there naked. He smiled. "Ready to go again?"

Wouldn't take long with you if I was, she thought. "No. We'd better get going."

He stood there, staring at her. "God, you're gorgeous."

"Come on. Work."

He had come around to her flat the previous evening. He had stopped bringing wine, she noticed, and other presents. Now he just came and went. Literally, she thought. And it took about that long. Maybe he was getting bored of her. That was fine with Blake, because his usefulness was very nearly at an end.

She had used him as much as she could. He was a good smoke screen for her activities. Even toyed with asking him to join in her scheme but ultimately decided not to. If he said no, she would have had to take care of him. Just like Sheridan. And that might attract too much attention. She had also considered doing something similar to his computer as she had done to Sheridan's. But something different. Kiddie porn. That would be more his kind of thing, she thought.

But no, she would just breeze out, leaving him behind. Wondering, like all the rest, where she had gone.

"You're right," he said. "Killgannon's got Cunningham talking. We'd better get ready to pull him out." He picked up his phone from on top of his neatly folded clothes. Checked the screen. "Oh."

"What?"

"That psychologist who never turned up last night? The one who wanted to talk about Killgannon? She hasn't turned up for work today."

Blake shrugged. "So?"

He kept looking at his phone, reading something. "It's more serious than that. Her car was found off the road on Blackmoor, a few miles from the prison. That's why she didn't turn up. Why she didn't answer her phone when I called."

Blake thought she should express concern. "What? Is she dead?"

"Thankfully not. She was discovered in time, taken to a hospital. Looks like someone forced her off the road."

Blake tried to mask her true feelings. Bradshaw was still alive. That fucking idiot couldn't even . . .

Harmer's voice cut through her thoughts. "I wonder if this has anything to do with Sheridan's murder?"

"Why should it?"

"One accident, one murder close together. Killgannon the common denominator. Suspicious, don't you think?"

"I've been following the investigation into his death. There's nothing there to point toward Killgannon." I've seen to that, she thought.

"Nevertheless . . ."

"What?"

"I think we should consider it. Come on. You're right. Let's get to work."

Blake looked down at the gun lying on top of her bag by the side of the bed. Harmer couldn't see it. But if he said anything else she didn't like, he might just feel it.

She felt as if she was having an out of body experience and was looking down on herself. Things were starting to unravel. She had to get a grip. And fast.

"I'll get dressed and go straight to Blackmoor. See what's going on."

"No need for that. Just give them a ring. And then when—or if—Dr. Bradshaw improves, go and see her then."

"It's still our jurisdiction. We should be—" The sound of a text came pinging from the burner phone in her go bag.

"D'you need to get that?"

"Dan, I should check this out. It might be important."

He was dressed now. He looked at her. Torn about what to say. "Go on, then. I'll see you back at the office later."

No you won't. "Thank you, sir."

He crossed to her, wanting a farewell kiss. She moved forward so he didn't see the bag, the gun. She let him kiss her. It was like having synchronized slugs running over her lips.

He left. Once she was sure he had gone she checked the phone. Saw the text:

> Out of prison on the moors. Come
> right now.

She went, taking the bag with her. And the Desert Eagle. Two million was plenty if it was shared.

But even more if it was just for one person.

52

"SO WHERE ARE THEY FROM HERE, THEN?"

Dean Foley stood in front of the car, the prison officer's own Audi, surveyed the moor ahead of him. He was dressed for the city streets, not the open countryside. Immaculate gray pinstripe three-piece suit, crisp white ironed shirt, tie, and polished, handmade shoes. A Crombie overcoat that cost more than the monthly wage of the officer accompanying him. He knew it was impractical for where he was, but he didn't care. They were the clothes he wore entering prison, his business, cocktail reception, court appearance suit, and he wanted to wear it now. Inmates were allowed to wear their own clothes when they were escorted outside the prison, and Foley wanted to feel something different than the cheap, itchy prison sweats against his skin, to remind himself of who he used to be.

Who he could possibly be again.

Baz stood next to him, shivering in his prison issue sweats and an anorak. Chris, one of his tame officers, stood with them.

"Somewhere over there, I think they said they were going," said Chris, pointing off to a mist-shrouded rocky incline over by the horizon.

Foley looked where indicated then closed his eyes, breathed deeply down to his diaphragm. Exhaled. The air was cold, harsh, with a trace of damp. But so much sweeter than the foul stuff that came from prison. That mixture of sweat, cleaning products, bad food, cheap aftershave, bad breath, and infrequently washed bodies. He would take the cold anytime.

"Wonderful, isn't it, Baz? The fresh air, the open countryside . . . You forget, don't you? Cooped up in there all the time, you lose sight of things. Forget what really matters."

Baz looked like it was anything but wonderful. His expression was miserable, his body language turned in on himself. Like he was counting the seconds until they could get back inside. Like he couldn't function anywhere else. Foley smiled to himself. That was what he had suspected about him. It was interesting. All helping him to make up his mind, come to a decision.

He turned to Chris. "How do I get to talk to Killgannon?"

Chris shook his head. "Going to be risky. We can't just walk up to them, tell him you want a word. Not with all those cops there."

"So what do we do? You realize this may be my last chance to talk to the man before he disappears again."

Chris pretended to look concerned. "Let's get nearer to them. I'll see what I can do. Depends who they've sent to look after him. Hopefully someone I can talk to." He nodded, remembering how much Foley was paying him, impressing on him his importance.

"Right," said Foley. "Let's do it then." He pointed to the rocky outcrop. "Just over there, you say?"

Chris nodded.

"Come on, then." Foley set off walking.

"Can't we take the car?" asked Baz.

Foley turned, looked at him. He seemed to have shrunk since coming outside, his whole frame diminished. Probably more than that: his identity. He could no longer cope anywhere but inside. And to think I used to hold you in such high regard, thought Foley. Pathetic, what you've come to.

"Yeah," said Chris. "Might as well. Looks like rain."

He got behind the wheel of the Audi. Baz scurried onto the back seat, grateful not to be outside anymore. Foley waited until they were both settled then slowly curled into the back of the car, like Chris was his chauffeur. Even if he did have to shut his own door.

"Right," Foley said. "Let's get going."

He sat back, smiled. Tried to enjoy the journey.

53

Night rolled over Blackmoor in a series of heavier shades of gray.

Tom felt as though a mist was rolling in, making him squint to see clearly, but it was just the darkening clouds. Like they were too heavy for the sky and were coming in to rest on land. He had spent the whole day on the moor and found the environment unwelcoming. Unnerving, even. Like the place was almost sentient and didn't want anyone to walk on it, only suffered those who came onto it if they departed quickly. Rocky outcrops loomed over them like menacing ancient gods as the darkness thickened. The woods and forests thrust spiked leafless branches against the sky while their dark black hearts were ready to absorb any unwary travelers and never let them go.

He shivered from more than just cold.

Then shook his head. He was imagining things. He had been locked in for so long, the open space was in danger of making him agoraphobic. Considering his claustrophobia, he might have found that amusing. But not right now.

"Fuck's sake," said the first officer, who Tom had discovered was called Ray. "Aren't they back yet?"

"Coming down now," said the second, who had revealed himself to be called Tony. "Look, over there. You can see the flashlights."

On the rocky hill ahead of them Cunningham and his party were returning. Cunningham, Tom noticed, was at the back of the pack now. Dragging his feet like the reluctant kid on the school trip.

With nothing else to do, they watched the party until they were there in front of them.

Ray crossed to the lead detective. "Any luck?"

The detective shook her head. "Nah. A few false alarms, but he's having trouble remembering anything." A roll of the eyes to accompany her words told them what she thought of the whole enterprise. "It all looks different now, apparently."

"What, this all used to be fields?" said Tony, laughing at his own joke in case no one else did.

The detective smiled politely. "Forensics took some readings, a couple of maybes but nothing positive. Going to be a long haul." She looked between the two of them to Tom. "Think of the overtime."

Tom said nothing. There were things he wanted to ask her, one professional to another, but he refrained. He knew how it would have sounded. And knew she wouldn't have answered him.

"Right, then," said Ray. "Back inside for you."

"And his mate," said Tony. "Here he comes now."

Cunningham was escorted over to the two officers. He was beaming, almost manic. Buzzing with excitement.

"You had fun?" asked Tom, deadpan.

Cunningham nodded.

"Found anything?"

"Not yet, but it's just good to be back out here. Makes you feel alive, doesn't it? Like it's speaking to you, telling you secrets." He nodded to himself, hearing something no one else was. "I'll find them tomorrow. Tomorrow. The moor'll not let me go without them. It wants to help."

Tom didn't look at the two officers. He didn't need to, to know what they would be thinking.

"Come on then," said Tony, "sooner we can get you two back, sooner we can go home."

Cunningham and Tom climbed into the back of the minibus. Ray took his position behind the steering wheel, Tony next to him. He started the engine, the radio blaring at the same time. Kiss FM.

"Few bangers to make the trip go better," said Ray and drove off.

Tom closed his eyes.

And opened them pretty soon. There was some kind of commotion going on.

Ray and Tony were shouting, swearing. Tom saw headlights outside the bus, coming up alongside. Looked like a motorbike. Whichever way they went, the bike was still there.

"What the fuck's going on?" said Tony.

Tom knew immediately what was happening. They were being attacked. He jumped forward in his seat. "Keep driving," he shouted. "Put your foot down."

Tony turned back to him, fear at the situation mixed with anger at Tom's interference. "Just fucking sit down, you. We'll deal with this."

"You haven't even got a gun," said Tom.

The biker had come alongside them. Ray had tried to shake him off but he was keeping pace with them.

As Tom looked out of the window, the biker drew alongside the driver and, holding the speeding bike with one hand, produced a handgun, an automatic.

"Get out of the way!" he shouted, but to no effect.

The biker fired. Glass shattered and the top of Ray's head decorated the ceiling of the bus. Tony just stared, too scared to move.

The bus sped up, began to weave all over the road.

"Get his foot off the accelerator!" Tom shouted.

Tony didn't move.

"Get his . . ."

Tom leaned forward over the front seat, ignored the blood, and pulled Ray's body back. He took the dead man's hands off the steering wheel, replaced them with his own. Tried to wrestle the bus back under control.

"Get your foot on the brake," Tom shouted at Tony but the guard didn't respond. "Get your foot on the brake!" Still no response.

Tom looked ahead through the windshield. Away from the direct illumination of the bus's beams, everything else was pitch black. He didn't know if he was on flat land or on the blind brow of a hill with an oncoming vehicle out of sight. But he would have to take a chance.

Keeping his right hand on the wheel he reached down for the handbrake with his left, pulled it as hard as he could.

Tires squealing, the bus skidded into a turn. Tom held on to the steering wheel with both hands. Concentrated. Ignored the smoke, the smell of burning rubber and electrics. Just held on tight as the bus gradually came to rest in the opposite direction it had been heading.

He sat back, breathed a sigh of relief.

But it was short lived. Headlights outside told him the biker was back.

"Get out," he shouted to Tony, but again the man didn't move.

He looked at Cunningham who had curled up into a fetal ball and was reciting a prayer to himself.

The biker pulled to a standstill, got off the bike, leaving the engine turning over. He came around to the back of the bus, ready to open the doors.

Tom got there before him. He slammed open the door, knocking the gun from the biker's hand, smashing his knuckles in the process. He didn't stop to think, just fell back into his training.

He had the element of surprise but, he knew, not for long. He kicked at the biker, aiming for his face, but only connecting with his helmet. The kick jarred him though, knocked him off balance. Tom pressed on, punching him in the stomach—once—twice—then another kick to his groin. The biker folded.

Tom looked quickly around. Assessed the situation as fast as he could.

He should find out who his assailant was, get that helmet off him. But that would slow him down. And he might get the better of him this time.

So as the biker began to come around again and search for his gun, Tom noticed his bike was standing there, still running. He made straight for it, hauled himself onto it and, without thinking or looking back, roared away into the night.

54

Blake drove her Dacia Duster over the moor, headlights full on. She was breathing so hard it felt like she was running the distance, not driving. Quint's call had just come through: Killgannon's gone, taken my bike. He had left her GPS coordinates. A good thing she was already on the way.

Everything was unraveling. She couldn't stand it. Her whole plan suddenly falling apart. She had to keep herself together. Plot. Plan. Don't give in to panic, to despair. Keep calm. Think.

It had been going so well. She had managed to keep a degree of a grip on the investigation into Sheridan's death, even from a distance. The little extras she had managed to put onto his computer pointed to a completely different kind of cop than he had appeared to be, one that had shaken plenty of her colleagues. So the team had gone off in that direction, investigating things that had no bearing on him when he was alive, never mind in death. And, with subtle—and sometimes not so subtle—suggestions as to where to look, who to talk to, it would be months before they exhausted those erroneous possibilities. If they ever did. By which time she and the money she was convinced Killgannon had been hoarding would be long gone.

She floored the accelerator of the Duster, jumping forward in her seat as if that would make it go faster. A Dacia Duster. She was embarrassed to own it but she had wanted a four by four. An SUV. A prestige car that put her—physically if nothing else—higher than the other drivers on the road. She had dreamed of a BMW or Porsche, or even a Lexus or a Jaguar at a push. But this was all she could afford. A Dacia. The budget brand. But even if she couldn't yet afford the thing she wanted—emphasis on the *yet*—then at least she could prepare herself for it by driving this thing.

She slammed on the brakes. Lost in her own thoughts, she nearly didn't see the figure in the road standing before her, waving both arms. Quint.

She pulled up before making contact. He ran round to the side of the car, threw his helmet on to the backseat, jumped in. She looked at him. He looked dreadful. Tired, dirty, his expensive jacket scuffed and abraded. Like his bike had been riding him, not the other way around.

"What happened?" she asked.

"Killgannon got away."

"You said. How did it happen?"

"He . . ." Quint sighed. It was obvious from his usual demeanor that he wasn't used to failure in his work. He clearly didn't take it well. "He overpowered me." Said quickly, the sooner the words were out there, the sooner they would be gone. "I forced the bus off the road, he . . . took my bike. Went off."

"Was he the only one in the bus?"

"Another prisoner, Cunningham. And an officer. I took the driver out."

Blake sighed. She felt like headbutting the steering wheel and punching Quint. Anything to get rid of this desperate, hopeless aggression building within her.

"He's dead?"

"Looked it. Half his head was missing."

Blake stared at him.

"Hey, lady, you hired me for this job. You know the way I work. You know what it is I do. You've been happy with what I've done so far. Don't start with any of that fucking princess bullshit now or I'll just take the rest of my money and be off."

Blake dropped her head, sighed once more. A mess. Nothing but a mess. But she would dig her way out of it, salvage something. She had to. Just keep her nerve.

"You're right. It's what I hired you for. I'm sure you had to do it."

"I wouldn't have done it otherwise."

"So where are they now? Cunningham and the other officer?"

"Don't know. I didn't hang around to find out. When Killgannon took my bike, I just got out of there. There'll be police, prison staff, all sorts there by now." He could barely contain his rage at failing at his job.

Panic entered Blake's voice. "But that must be just round here. You can't have run that—"

"I know what I'm doing. My career's been made living in terrain like this. I got away from them. They won't find me here. That's why I told you to meet me here and not nearer to where it happened."

Blake relaxed slightly. "Right." She checked her watch. This was it, the time to come up with a plan that would get everything back on track. Get her the money, get her out of here.

She looked at Quint. "You need transport."

"Why?"

"Because I want you to get back to Killgannon's house and tear it apart. No need to be nice anymore. We're way past that."

"What about the women there?"

Blake shrugged. "As you say, it's what I'm paying you for."

"Right. So any ideas on getting transport?"

She checked her phone. Received another text. Smiled.

"Might have just the thing."

Things might be falling back into place again.

55

Tom Killgannon was lost.

He had roared off on the stolen motorbike, all attempts at location and direction gone in the adrenaline rush of the attack. He didn't know which way he was heading, he only knew that he wanted to put as much distance between himself and the bus, the rest of the hunting police force, and most importantly, the prison as he could. So he kept going in what he hoped was a straight line, off the roads, bumping over stone, splashing through mud, gorse and bramble tearing the denim of his jeans, catching his legs at high speed. He didn't stop. Just kept riding on into darkness.

As he rode he thought. Tried to order what had happened, what was happening. Formulate the best way to get out of all this. The most obvious thing to do would be to head home. That was also the most obvious thing from any pursuer's point of view. So it was the last place he could go.

Also, he had to try and think who was after him. Blake. That, he believed, was a given. And whoever owned the motorbike he had taken. Who else? Foley? That didn't make any sense. He had agreed to a meeting in prison. And when Tom's job was finished, he would honor that. He couldn't think of anyone else. Not with an immediate grudge against him.

He went through his options. Find a nearby town or village,

stay there the night. Too risky. That would be the second place they would look, plus he didn't have any money to pay for a room. And he wasn't going to steal some. He almost smiled at the next thought. Break in somewhere that looked deserted, keep his head down, stay there. Just like Lila had thought she was doing, all those months ago. If he did that, he hoped she would, at some point, appreciate the irony. No. That wasn't a good enough option either.

So, by process of elimination, he knew what he had to do. Find somewhere on the moor, bed down there as best he could, find out where he was in the morning, plan from there.

That was what he would have to do.

He felt the ground rising, knowing that the higher he climbed the more he could see of the surrounding area, the sooner he would know that someone had reached him. But not yet. He was quite alone.

The bike's beams alighted on a tall, rocky outcrop before him, the kind, he thought, that sheep would shelter under during winter storms. That would have to do. He pulled the bike up alongside it, cut the engine. Wheeled it under the rock. Looked to see where he was.

On a distant horizon he could see lights. He didn't know if that was the prison, a town, a village, or even a city. Could be a band of villagers with flaming pitchforks, even, searching for him. He watched. The lights were unmoving. A settlement of some kind. Far enough away not to be a problem.

The moor itself was even bleaker in darkness. He had mistrusted it earlier in what daylight there was, now it seemed positively treacherous. Like there was something with him in the darkness, just waiting for him to make a mistake, to claim him for its own.

He tried to put thoughts like that from his mind. Walked about, swung his arms against his body. Tried to revel in his sudden freedom. All he could think was this: he was cold. Very cold. The temperature had dropped significantly since he had first got on the bike and it had been cold before that. He looked around for twigs, branches, anything he could use to make a fire. No. He couldn't do that. Might attract attention. He would just have to huddle up in his parka, get as near to the bike's engine as possible until it cooled, try to get some sleep if he could. Hope that hypothermia didn't set in by morning.

The wind blew sharply in his face. And with it something else. The near ice touch of rain.

With that, the storm clouds above made good on their daylong threat. The rain came lashing down.

Tom got as far under the lip of rock as he could. Ready to sit out the night and everything in it.

56

"THERE THEY ARE."

Blake pointed. It wasn't necessary: The only thing ahead on the moor's shingle track was a stationary car with its headlights on. She pushed the Duster harder, hoping to increase speed but in reality just rocking the pair of them backward and forward on the SUV's cheap suspension.

She pulled up next to the other car. Before she had time to turn her engine off, Dean Foley burst from the back of his car, angry and roaring. She got calmly out, closed the door.

"I don't like not knowing what's going on," he said, getting right in Blake's face. His sheer physical presence was intimidating. His anger unnerving. She could understand why he was so feared. "Baz here says we've got to wait, so I waited. Now what's this all about?"

Blake looked quickly inside the car. A confused and scared-looking prison officer was behind the wheel, Baz in the back. He smiled when he saw her. She smiled in return.

"Hello, Foxy," she said. "Long time no see."

Baz stepped out of the car. Looked at her.

"You two know each other?" Foley, his anger unabated, stared at them, suspicious.

"Yeah," said Baz, crossing to Blake, "we go back a long way, don't we, babe?"

He put his arm around her, pulled her toward him for a kiss. Blake resisted.

"What's the matter?" Anger in his voice. "Don't you fancy me no more?"

Blake hadn't known how she would feel seeing him again. Hadn't prepared herself. He looked rough. And not just because of the scars. Standing there in his prison-issue best, he emanated waves of thwarted ambition, bitterness. She barely recognized him.

"That's not why I'm here and you know it. So let's get on with things."

He stared at her, mentally adding her to the list of those who had betrayed him. She could practically feel him doing it.

"All the fucking same . . ."

Blake had tried to rekindle their relationship after the crash, more from duty or pity than anything else. But they were too different by then. She was in the ascendancy and he couldn't cope with that. He was consumed by anger and self-loathing. Blake thought he had a point to be angry with the police since they wouldn't give him the pension he thought he was entitled to. But he'd gone bad, they said. Undercover work's not for everyone. You need the right temperament. A sense of perspective. Even his union rep told him to just accept it, let it go, get on with the rest of his life.

So he took it out on Blake, initially. Shouted at her, hit her. She had never thought she would be the kind of woman to stand for that kind of abuse. Whenever she had been called out to a domestic to find a bloody, battered, broken woman crying with pain but refusing to press charges, she'd thought the woman deserved all that was coming to her. If she was too simple minded to leave, then Blake had no sympathy for her. But it wasn't like that. As she found out.

It was gradual. Baz resenting her for having a career, a job, even. Letting that resentment grow. Fueling it with drugs and alcohol. Taking it out on her. Their relationship so complicated by love and mutual desire that she didn't realize what she had become until it happened.

One of those women she had no sympathy for.

So she left him. Eventually.

"Don't start that," she said, snapping back to the present. "Head in the game. You contacted me for a reason. And we're here now so let's get on with it."

Baz just stared at her.

He had contacted her out of the blue. He was in Blackmoor with Dean Foley. Had heard she was with Devon and Cornwall Police, trying to advance her career in a way she couldn't in Manchester. Guilt mingled with curiosity. She went to see him. Having the time of his life, he said, like an old boys' club. Had she tracked down Mick Eccleston yet? Did she have the money? And if so, when could he get his cut?

His words dug into her. She had tried to find Mick Eccleston and Foley's money but with no success. And then something dropped into her lap. The events of several months ago in St. Petroc. Tom Killgannon had done his best not to get his face seen anywhere but she had spotted him. And it didn't take too long to put a plan into action.

Noel Cunningham wanted to talk. They needed someone to go inside. It was a simple matter to nudge Harmer in the direction of Killgannon. He was right in their lap. And even easier to make Harmer think he had come up with the idea himself. It was a perfect plan. She never wanted to see Baz again and wouldn't after this. She would cross him. And take great joy in doing so. Payback for all the things he had done to her.

She turned away from Baz. "Mr. Foley," she said, smiling, "a pleasure to meet you at last."

She stuck out her hand, ready for him to shake. The gesture, the smile, her words, took him by surprise, stopped his rage in full flow.

He accepted her hand, more confused than angry now. "And you are?"

"Detective Constable Annie Blake. And I'm here to help you."

Suspicious now. "Help me? How?"

"By taking you to meet Tom Killgannon. Or Mick Eccleston as you know him."

Foley looked between everyone, back to Blake. "I don't know what's going on here," he said. He pointed to Quint. "And who's this?"

"This is Quint," said Blake.

"No I'm not," said Quint.

"You are for now. I read up on Eccleston's old case files in Manchester. He often worked with some kind of backup. This, for all intents and purposes, is him."

Dan Jameson had fallen into her lap. Ex-army, ex-mercenary, trying to make a living back in the UK. She had arrested him for attempted murder in Manchester. He was trying to carve out a career as a hitman but without much success. She thought he was the kind of person she could do business with at some point so made sure the charges against him were buried in return for a favor sometime in the future. She remembered Jameson when she saw Killgannon had chosen Quinton Blair, an old friend of his. Jameson had been very thorough in assuming Quint's identity. And, as she had discovered, hadn't baulked at getting rid of anyone else.

Foley turned to Baz. "What's going on?"

"This is the friend I was telling you about in the car. The one I texted. The one I said we had to meet."

"She's law. And we should have been back in Blackmoor hours ago."

Baz shrugged. "Things have changed, Dean."

Foley stared at him. Blake felt she was coming between these two men who had some unfinished—perhaps even unspoken—business.

"I thought you'd want to get back inside," said Foley. "You weren't enjoying it out here today."

"No I wasn't. But that was then." He smiled at Blake. She didn't return it. "We're ready to move forward."

Anger came to Foley once more. "Are you fucking me about, Baz? What's going on? Tell me."

"We think Killgannon's got the missing two million," said Blake.

Foley thought for a second before replying. "You mean *my* two million."

Blake shrugged. "There'll be plenty to go round when we get it. We can all have a share. Call it a finder's fee."

Foley said nothing. Didn't have to. The look on his face betrayed the fact he didn't agree with her.

"The important thing," she told him, "is to get it first." She turned to her companion. "Quint."

"I'm not Quint."

"Don't start that again. You know where you've got to go. What you've got to do."

"Won't Killgannon be there?"

"Not if he wants to go back inside again, but you'd better be quick. The law might turn up at any minute looking for him. He'll have been missed by now."

Quint nodded. Looked pensive. "How do I get there? Your car?"

Blake looked offended at the idea. She crossed to Chris, still sitting behind the wheel of his car. Flashed him her police ID.

"DC Blake, Devon and Cornwall police. I'm going to need your car." He began to protest. "It's not a debate. My associate is taking it. Now."

He got out, stood behind the door. Looked very uncertain. Blake nodded to Quint who came over, got behind the wheel. Drove off. Chris walked toward the Duster. Made to get inside.

"Where d'you think you're going?" asked Blake.

Chris looked at her as though the question didn't need answering.

"I have official police business with these two prisoners. You're going to have to make your own way home."

"But it's miles away. I don't even know where I am . . ."

She turned away. "Right. You two. In my car."

Foley looked at her, then at Baz. His attention stayed on Baz. "I don't trust you anymore," he said.

Baz shrugged, smiled. "You'd be very wise not to."

Foley kept staring at him. "It was you, then, wasn't it?"

"What was me?"

"The attack on Eccleston. Clive Bennett's death. You did all that."

Baz shrugged, that unpleasant smile still creasing and cracking his features. "You're slipping, Dean, losing your power. Someone had to step up and replace you." He spread his arms wide. "Who better than me? Good old, loyal, dependable Baz." He couldn't keep the hatred from his voice. "Standing beside you all that time, doing whatever you told me to do, carrying out your every order. Well not anymore, Deano. From now on it's me in charge."

Foley just stared at him. "I thought you might try something like this. That's why I brought you out with me today because I couldn't trust you to stay inside without me."

"I know," said Baz. "And that's what I wanted you to think. I played you, Dean."

Foley's expression changed. He had looked like he had been about to do Baz some damage, possibly terminal. Now he wanted to listen. "What d'you mean?"

"I wanted to be out here as much as you. I want to see Killgannon as much as you do too."

"Why? The money?"

Baz just smiled.

"Well," said Foley, nodded, "It looks like we're off on a little jaunt together, doesn't it?"

They all got into the Duster. Blake started up the engine, mounted her phone on a clip on the dashboard.

"You know where Killgannon is?" asked Foley.

Blake smiled. "I know exactly where he is."

She turned the Duster around, drove off.

The rain started.

They passed Chris as he made his long walk home.

No one acknowledged him.

57

LILA LAY BACK, EYES STILL CLOSED, sighed. Smiled. Turned to Anju, found she was smiling just as broadly, looking straight into her eyes. Neither spoke. Neither needed to.

Anju hugged Lila close to her. Curled her face into the side of her neck. Lila could feel her breath on her skin and knew from her lips that she was still smiling.

Lila sighed again. She hadn't felt this happy, this relaxed, in ages. Years, perhaps. Tom was right, she thought. Things are going to be better from now on.

They had both known this was going to happen. Ending up in bed together. Both had wanted to, but neither had planned it. Like the rest of their relationship, it had happened organically, grown out of what had gone before.

Anju had driven around to Lila's house, just to spend the evening together. Watch some TV, eat Lila's attempt at pasta carbonara, chill. Be together. But as soon as she entered, they both knew what was going to happen. Looking back at that moment, both had known even before that, when the invitation was made. But neither had expressed it. Neither had needed to.

And it had felt so right. Lila didn't feel guilty. Nor did she feel like she was doing it as an act of distant revenge to spite her parents. It had been because she was falling in love with another person and wanted to express that, explore that.

She held Anju harder to her. Enjoyed the feeling of the other girl's body against her own. Could happily lie like that for the rest of her life.

Then heard a car outside.

Anju moved, made to get up.

"Don't worry," said Lila. "It'll just be Pearl coming back from the pub."

Anju relaxed once more.

And stayed that way until there was hammering on the front door.

That wasn't Pearl.

They both jumped up, looked at each other. Didn't know who it was but knew it wasn't going to be good news.

"Could that be Tom?" asked Anju.

For a split second, Lila allowed herself to hope. To think that things would be all right for him too. But that soon faded.

More hammering.

"I don't think so . . ."

They both quickly got dressed, pulled on whatever clothing they found to hand. Went downstairs. Anju not letting Lila go down alone.

They stood in front of the door. Heard more hammering.

"Who is it?" called Lila.

More hammering.

"Let me in." Muffled, urgent.

They couldn't make out the voice. Lila ran to the living room, opened the curtains, checked the car outside. She didn't recognize it. Not Quint, she thought. He would have been on his motorbike. She went back to the front door. More frantic hammering.

Lila and Anju shared a look. They both knew they were going to open it.

Quint came roaring in, gun in hand.

Anju screamed. Quint turned, knocked her to the floor with the butt of his gun. Lila ran to her.

"What the fuck are you doing?" Her anger, concern for Anju overrode her fear of him.

He slammed the door behind him. Stared down at them.

"Get her in there," he said, gesturing to the living room. "Now."

Lila helped Anju to her feet. She was bleeding from where the gun had connected with her temple.

"Move."

Lila helped Anju to the sofa and sat down next to her. "You OK?"

Anju nodded. "Yeah. I think . . ."

Lila looked up at Quint who covered them both with the gun.

"Sit there. Don't move."

Lila stared at him. "I knew you were wrong from the first moment. Knew it. Should have trusted my instincts."

"Yeah, well," said Quint, looking round the room, "bit late for that now."

"What d'you want?"

"What I've wanted all along. The money."

Lila frowned. "What are you talking about? What money?"

"The money Killgannon stole from Dean Foley. Don't play stupid."

"Haven't a clue what you're talking about. Tom didn't steal any money."

"Yeah? You think? How well do you know him?"

Lila made to stand up. Quint waved the gun at her. She sat down again. Even more angry. "He wouldn't do that. I know him. And he wouldn't do that."

Quint smiled. "We'll see, won't we?"

"What are you going to do with us?" Anju's voice was weak, wavering. She held her hand to her head, trying unsuccessfully to stem the flow of blood.

"Depends how useful you're going to be."

"Useful for what?" asked Lila, defiance still in her voice.

Quint smiled. There was no trace of the charming man who had visited them previously. Lila was angry with herself for not challenging him sooner. Letting it come to this. "Useful to me. Can't search this whole house on my own, now can I?"

"What makes you think we'll help you?" asked Anju, voice quiet, but as defiant as Lila's.

"Because I'm holding the gun. And you don't want to be on the wrong end of it if you piss me off, do you?"

They both stared at him.

"There's a stupid bitch policewoman out on the moors right now trying to track down your beloved Tom Killgannon. And she thinks I'm just going to roll over and give her whatever money I find."

"There's no money here," said Lila. "I've told you. I would know."

"We'll see, shall we?"

The gun seemed to loom even larger in front of her face.

Lila said nothing, just held on to Anju.

Her only slim hope was that Pearl would come home and see what was happening.

That slim hope.

Lila had learned, from bitter experience, not to believe in hope.

58

Tom didn't think it was possible but he was finding sleep even more elusive than in prison.

The rain and the cold hadn't let up, hadn't allowed him to sleep. That and the constant churn of his mind as he tried to understand what had led him to this situation and how he could get out of it.

He tried once again to put everything in place, give events some semblance of order. Sheridan was dead and with him, his way out. Blake thought he had stolen Dean Foley's money. He didn't know how or why she had reached this conclusion but she seemed firmly convinced of it. Dr. Bradshaw wanted Foley and him to talk, bury their differences. He didn't see that happening now. So where would he go from here, what would his future be? Assuming he had a future. Another identity since this one was compromised? Back to prison for real? Not seeing Lila or Pearl again? The last hurt the most. He had just been getting his new life established. Just about come to terms with his past, making tentative steps toward a future. That could all be gone now.

He didn't have time to think anymore. Headlights were approaching along the ridge below him.

He looked around, checked that the bike was out of sight. Hoped it was just some hill farmer checking on his errant flock.

Still, he didn't want to engage with whoever it was, so tucked himself as far back into the rocky overhang as he could.

He heard the roar of an engine as the vehicle made its way up the hill. Stayed as still as he could. If it was a search party, there would be more of them. Probably with dogs. And they wouldn't be able to cover the rough terrain as easily as this vehicle which, he guessed, must be some kind of 4x4. Must be a farmer.

The 4x4 stopped, headlights still blazing. He shrank back even further into the shadows.

Heard voices. Couldn't make out the words, but managed to identify the genders. A woman. A man. No, two men. And at least one of those voices he recognized.

DC Blake.

Incredulity washed over him. What was she doing here? This was more than just coincidence. This had been planned. But how?

He thought. A GPS tracker on the bike? That must be it. The only way she could have tracked him down. Then anger: How could he have been so stupid? He should have checked. He should have known. It was what he would have done if he had been in her situation. A necessary precaution.

He tried not to blame himself any further. Needed his mind sharp, had to work a way out of this.

He listened, tried to make out what was being said but the wind and rain carried most of the sense of the words away. He heard Blake's voice.

"Get looking. He must be around here somewhere. The signal says he is."

Tom looked round, saw the hillside illuminated once more in the glare of the headlights. Saw more outcrops of rock than he had realized were there originally. Heard footsteps approaching.

He thought of making a dash for it, trying to reach the bike, ride away before they could stop him. Quickly abandoned that idea. They had the tracker and they might be carrying guns. He had been lucky before. He might not be so lucky this time.

"Found the bike."

That was the definite end of that plan. But did he recognize the voice? He wasn't sure. Not in this weather.

He peered closer. The figure was medium height, dressed in an anorak over what looked like prison issue gear. Very inappropriate sneakers on his feet. He was examining the bike. Blake shouted something in response that Tom didn't catch.

Time to make a decision.

Tom felt around on the ground for a suitably sized rock, small enough to fit into the palm of his hand, big enough to inflict damage. He found one easily, weighed it, readied himself.

The man started to creep toward the overhang.

Tom barely had time to register the man's identity or what he looked like. All he knew was that he must be subdued, and in the most direct way possible.

He leaped out of the shadows, rock held high, and, before the other man could turn round, brought it down as hard as he could on the side of the man's head.

"Ow . . ."

The man staggered forward to his knees, hand to his head from the sudden pain. He looked up.

"What d'you do that for?"

Tom only had to time to register the blood on the man's face and how hideous he looked even without it. He didn't have time to think. He hit him again. This time the man went quiet.

Blake's voice drifted up from down below. "Baz? You OK? What's happened? Baz?"

Tom lifted up Baz's body, placed it in front of him like a shield. Made his way to the edge of the cave mouth, looked down the hill. And stared, open mouthed.

DC Blake was there, as he had expected. But she wasn't alone. Standing next to her, looking exactly like he had all those years ago, was Dean Foley. He might, thought Tom, actually have been wearing the suit he always used to wear. It was like a hallucination in the rain.

He didn't have time to be surprised, though, not if he wanted to get out of this alive. He held up Baz's body before him.

"You want him? Let's talk."

59

"So why are you doing this to us?"

Lila and Anju were sitting on the sofa. Quint sat in the armchair opposite, still pointing the gun at them. He hadn't relaxed. Lila had no idea how much time had passed. Could have been minutes, could have been hours.

"You know why," he said. "And I know what you're doing. And it's not going to work. So you may as well stop it now."

"What am I doing?"

"Trying to get me to talk. Humanize yourself in front of me. Make me feel like you matter. Save yourself the trouble. Don't bother. It won't work."

Lila said nothing in reply. Just had a momentary flashback to a similar situation several months ago where she had tried the same thing. It hadn't worked then, either. Trying not to let that thought add to her problems, she pressed on.

"So you're going to get this mythical money for yourself and double cross your partner, is that it?"

"Shut up." Almost yawning as he spoke.

"Is that your job?" asked Anju. The bleeding had stopped now but she still looked pale. Possibly concussed, Lila thought, desperately wanting to help her.

"Yeah, it's my job."

"So, what, you're a hitman? Is that right?"

"Yeah." He shrugged. "Suppose that covers it."

"How d'you get into that?" asked Anju, seemingly serious and interested.

Very clever of you, thought Lila. Ask anyone about their job and they'll always talk about it. Even people like him.

"Was in the army for a few years. Went over to Iraq, like I said. Did a few stints there. Special Air Service. The army trains you for war. When you leave all you can do is fight. So I went back east, joined up with a few private contractors."

"You mean mercenaries?" said Anju.

"You could say that. All those rich Arabs want their own private army. I was just hired help. Good thing was, if there was any trouble, they just waved money at the problem and it disappeared." He smiled, almost wistfully at the memory. "We could do whatever we liked and get away with it."

"I can understand all that, but how did you get to be a hitman? I mean, it seems like a much more specialized job."

"Suppose it is, really. I came back home, homesick, really. Tried to go into security consultancy. Got bored really easily though. Then someone asked me to off someone. And of course, I was good at it. So someone else asked. And someone else. And word got 'round. I was the go-to guy. For a price, of course."

Anju leaned forward, the expression on her face genuinely curious. "So why haven't you killed us yet?"

"Because you might be more help to me in looking round this house. Or you might not. Then I'll think again."

She sat back. Thinking. "Listen," she said eventually.

"What?"

"You said you're going to take the money you find here and cut your partner out, right?"

Quint didn't answer.

"Well, like Lila says, she doesn't think there's any money here. And neither do I, to be honest. But I'll tell you one thing." She leaned forward. Lila noticed her top was gaping and she hadn't had time to put her bra back on underneath. Quint's eyes went there too.

Anju continued. "My parents are rich. And I don't just mean rich for Cornwall. I mean very rich. They would pay you to leave us alone. Pay you really well. Honestly."

Quint stared at her, as if seriously considering it.

It felt to Lila like the room held its breath.

"Nah," he said eventually. "Too much hassle."

"What d'you mean?" asked Anju. "I'm serious. They'd give you plenty of money to get me back safe."

"Maybe they would. But I've heard that before. Even fell for it a couple of times, when I was just starting out. Always ended up messy. More trouble than it was worth. Either they didn't have the money when push came to shove, or they wouldn't pay up, or they threatened me with the law . . . It never worked. So no thanks."

"Please," said Anju, "it won't be like that this time."

"I said no." Steel back in his voice. He repositioned his gun arm. Reminded them he was still in charge.

"But there is one thing," he said.

"What's that?" asked Lila.

"I'm hungry. Make me something to eat."

6∅

"OK THEN," said Foley, smiling through the rain, "let's talk."

Tom stared at him, waiting for whatever trick he was planning. Nothing happened.

Foley behaved as if the rain, the wind, and the cold didn't touch him. Tom was certain that wasn't the case but he knew Foley. Don't show weakness in front of an opponent. And right now he was showing only imperviousness.

"Seriously," said Foley, ignoring the water running down his face. "Just you and me. Talking. Why don't you come down?"

Tom moved slightly forward, still holding the semilimp body of Baz. His human shield.

"Never mind about him," said Foley, stretching his arms out, waggling his fingers. "I'm not armed."

"No," said Tom, gesturing with his head. "But she is."

Blake was standing to the side of Foley, out of his peripheral vision, gun drawn, pointing it at Tom.

Foley turned to her. Irritation back on his face. "Put that away. We don't need that now."

She stared at him, a look of pure hatred and anger. "I'll be the judge of that."

Foley returned her glare, held it until most opponents would have blinked or looked away. Instead Blake held his gaze.

Foley broke first, looked back at Tom. Smiled. "Seems we have a standoff."

Tom knew what Foley was up to. It was another old ploy of his. Don't show weakness. Absolutely. But only show the illusion of it if you intend to show real strength later. After you've lulled your opponent—or even your assumed associate—into a false sense of security. Let them think they have the measure of you while all the while you're taking the measure of them. Tom had never seen it fail for Foley. Except once. With him.

"Fine," said Tom. "I'll talk from here." He held Baz up. "And I'll keep him in place too. Just in case your mate gets a bit trigger-happy."

Foley spread out his arms again, as if he was some genial party host and that was fine by him.

Tom, sensing no immediate threat, turned his attention to Blake. She was still holding the gun on him. Unlike Foley, it was very clear that the weather—and everything else—was affecting her. At this moment, he thought, she was the dangerous one. The one to watch out for.

"So what's all this for?" he asked her. "What's it in aid of?"

She smiled. "Money, of course."

Tom frowned. "Whose money? What are you talking about?"

She didn't reply. Instead kept staring at Tom.

Foley smiled. "She thinks you've got my money. My two million. I must admit, the question's crossed my mind over the years. So have you got it?"

Tom sighed. "Why would I take your money?"

"Because two million would set you up very nicely. You and your new identity."

Tom felt like laughing. "The case against you nearly collapsed because of that money. The case I'd spent years working on. It could have prejudiced the trial. Sent me into Witness Protection for nothing. Why would I do that?"

Foley thought. "I don't know, Mick. I really don't know. Unless . . ." He looked up, a thought having occurred to him. "Maybe you just wanted me to go free."

Tom stared at him. Wondered whether he had heard him right through the storm. "What? Why would I do that? The case . . ."

Foley continued. "Yeah, yeah, the case. I know. The case. But isn't it obvious? I've been thinking about this a lot. I mean, I've had a lot of time to think, haven't I? But how about this . . ." He pointed at Tom, as if accusing him. "You couldn't bear to see me behind bars. That was the main thing. Everything we'd been through, all those things we'd shared . . . part of you just couldn't let me go through with it, could you? You couldn't let all of that go. Am I right?" Foley smiled. "I'm right, aren't I?"

Tom shook his head. "I can't believe I'm hearing this."

"Never mind this bullshit," shouted Blake, making sure she could be heard over the storm, "just tell me where the money is."

Tom looked between the two of them. He noted Foley's reaction as she said *me* rather than *us*.

"So you're in this together, then?" asked Tom, knowing what the answer would be. Hoping he could drive a wedge between them.

"No," said Foley. "This is all her and that one."

He pointed at Baz who was beginning to stir in Tom's arms.

"He was one of your lot once too, you know," said Foley, smiling. "But he turned. Came to work for me. Properly. Not pretending. Like you." The smile faded replaced by a look of compassion.

Tom wasn't fooled for a second.

"Couldn't get any other work looking like that, could he?" said Foley. "Poor fucker."

"He was a good man," said Blake, sounding even more angry about Baz than about the money, waving her gun toward Foley. "Better than either of you two. So don't talk about him like that."

Tom heard Baz groaning, starting to move as he came around. He held him even tighter, not letting go of his bargaining chip.

Baz opened his eyes. "What . . ." He looked up at Tom, frowned. "What did you do to me?"

"Hit you on the head. But you're fine now."

"What?"

Tom stared back at him. "I've seen you on the wing, haven't I? With Dean?"

It took a few seconds longer than usual, but Baz's thought process began to work again. "Oh, you knew me long before that . . ." He pointed toward Foley.

Tom looked at him again. Tried to see through the blood and the rain, rebuild the face, scrub out the scars . . . "Jesus. Foxy?"

Baz smiled. "Yeah. Foxy. That's me. That was me. And you didn't fucking recognize me."

"It's been a long time. I also wasn't expecting to find you here. Like this."

"Yeah," said Baz, the words curdling in his mouth, "and the law looks after its own, doesn't it? Especially the white ones. The black ones can go and get fucked."

"I didn't even know you were undercover until later," said Tom. "I thought you just worked for Dean."

Baz nodded. "That's how they wanted it. Neither of us knew about the other. But we could keep an eye on each other for them when we reported. Clever fuckers."

"Foxy . . ." Tom's memory inevitably went back to that night.

He remembered sitting in the BMW with Foley, seeing Hayley in one of the other cars, with . . .

"Hayley," he said. "You were with Hayley that night."

Baz smiled to himself. "Oh yeah. She was your . . . niece. That was it, wasn't it? Didn't know until afterward."

"Yeah. My sister's girl. And she died that night."

Tom felt his heart racing. The cold and the rain disappeared. So too did Foley and Blake. All that mattered was Foxy, Baz, and the next words out of his mouth.

"That's right. She did."

"So what happened?"

"You mean, how did she die?"

"Yeah." He could barely contain himself. "They said crossfire."

Baz didn't reply straight away. He paused. "Bet that's been worrying you for years."

Tom wouldn't give him the satisfaction of admitting it. "What happened? Tell me."

Baz turned his head away. Tom couldn't see the smile on his face. "I mean, if it was me, if it was my niece, and that had happened to her and we were close, and that, it would have torn me up." He turned to Tom. "Did it tear you up? Inside? All those years?"

Tom felt anger welling up inside him. He wanted to choke Baz until he told him what had happened to Hayley. Instead he spoke with as calm a voice as he could manage.

"Yes, it did." As much as he was willing to admit.

"So you want to know what happened to her that night? How she died?" Baz not even bothering to hide the smile now, actively enjoying having the power over him.

"Yes," said Tom, still managing to keep calm, but only just, "yes I do."

Baz laughed. "Well, I'd better tell you then."

61

LILA OPENED THE FRIDGE DOOR, peered inside.

"Nothing hot," came Quint's voice from behind her, "nothing you have to cook. You might get ideas about throwing hot oil. Wouldn't want that, would we?"

"What about a cheese sandwich? Am I allowed to make you that?"

"Yeah. As long as you use a blunt knife."

She took the block of cheese out of the fridge, closed the door. Quint stood in the doorway of the kitchen, gun held on both her and Anju. She took a dinner knife from the drying rack, began to hack at the block of cheese.

She buttered the bread, stuck a few lumps of cheese on it. "Want pickle with that?"

"If it's on hand. Not if it's miles away."

Back into the fridge for the pickle, smeared a brown dollop on the cheese, slapped the top lid on.

"There you go."

Quint gestured with his free hand for her to bring the plate over and put it down on the table, near to where he stood. She did, then he waved at her to walk away to the far end of the kitchen. She did that too.

He ate. Anju glanced between him and Lila, looking like she

was desperately trying to come up with something that would get them both out of there. Lila hoped she wouldn't try anything that would get them killed.

"Shall I make us some tea?" asked Lila, mainly to stop Anju trying anything rash.

"What d'you think this is, some fucking tea party?" said Quint through a mouthful of sandwich.

"Don't you want some, then?"

He nodded, tried not to take his attention off the two of them.

Lila crossed to the kettle, filled it from the tap, flicked the switch. Arranged three mugs with teabags in, got the milk from the fridge, the sugar from the cupboard. She looked down at the sugar bowl.

And had an idea.

A pretty desperate one, and it probably wouldn't work, might even get them both killed, but she had to try it. The alternative wasn't looking too promising. She didn't believe for one minute that Quint was going to let them live after he got what he wanted. Even if he *didn't* get what he wanted. So a bad idea would be better than no idea at all, she reasoned.

The kettle boiled. She filled all three mugs with boiling water, turned to Quint. "Sugar?"

"Two," he replied.

She put two spoonfuls into his mug.

"Milk?"

"A little."

She added a little milk, squeezed out the bag. Handed it to him.

She went back to the counter top, turned to Anju. "I know how you like it." She put some milk in Anju's, took the bag out. Handed it to her. "There you go."

Anju took it.

"I'll just do mine. Then shall we go back in the living room? Better than in here."

"You'll go where I tell you," said Quint, brandishing the gun.

"Fine." Lila nodded.

She took the teabag out of her mug. Added six large spoonfuls of sugar. Anju watched her, frowning. That wasn't the way she took her tea. Lila flashed her eyes at her, hoped she remained silent. Hoped Quint didn't catch the gesture.

"Yeah," said Quint. "Get back in the living room. I'll decide what to do in there. Go on."

Anju went first, followed by Lila. Quint, gun still extended, followed behind.

As soon as they reached the living room Anju stopped dead, stared at the window.

"Shit . . ."

Lila did the same.

So did Quint.

Outside, the night was lit up. Quint's borrowed car was in flames.

"What the fuck . . ."

Lila noticed he had momentarily dropped his gun arm, was no longer pointing it at them. She looked quickly at Anju, told her with her eyes that she was going to do something and to be ready. Anju looked terrified, but nodded.

It took seconds but felt like a lifetime. Lila turned on Quint and, while he was watching his car go up in flames, threw the contents of her mug into his face.

An old prison trick that Tom had told her about. Boiling hot water to burn, sugar in it to make it stick. Make it really hurt. Lila had got him right in the eyes.

Quint screamed. Lashed out.

She grabbed Anju's wrist, made for the front door.

Quint hadn't locked it behind him when he had barged in. She had remembered that. With Anju beside her, they ran into the night.

62

Tom loosened his grip on Baz, looked at him properly. The force of the rain had turned the glare of the headlights to a grainy TV static. He regarded his face without having to squint. Baz said nothing, just smiled.

"Well?" said Tom. "Tell me."

Baz smiled. "You don't need to cling to me. I'm not going anywhere."

Tom loosened his grip. Waited.

Baz smiled. "You're not interested in me, though, are you? Where I've been, how I ended up like this." He pointed to his face. "Don't care."

"What happened to you?"

Baz laughed. It was a bitter, phlegmy thing. "Yeah, that's right. Play along, just to find out about your niece. Say what you think I want to hear. But if you do want an answer, a ton of shit. That's what's happened to me. And I ended up looking like a monster. And if you look like a monster, you may as well behave like a monster, right?"

Tom thought of Cunningham. "Not necessarily."

"Well, whatever. You're only interested in the pretty dead girl, aren't you? Why? Do you feel guilty about her? Think you should have been there for her, saved her?"

Tom now stood next to Baz but had trouble keeping his hands down, wanting to grab him, force him to speak. "Just tell me what happened to her. How she died."

Baz smiled.

And the side of his head exploded.

Tom closed his eyes as blood, brain, gore, and bone smashed into him, covering him. He wiped his face, looked round, tried to make out what was going on, body now in fight or flight mode.

Blake screamed. Stared at the dead body of Baz, changed her aim to Foley.

"You haven't got the balls, love," he said, not even looking at her, his gun still outstretched. "Anyway, you were going to get rid of him when he'd stopped being useful, weren't you? I've just saved you the effort. Don't lie and pretend you weren't."

Blake did nothing. Said nothing.

"You said you were unarmed," said Tom.

Foley shrugged. "I lied. Who'd have thought?"

"Where did you get a gun from?"

"Prison officers, eh? Pay them enough and they'll do anything for you."

Anger welled within Tom. "He was going to tell me what happened to Hayley. He was going to tell me, and you . . . you killed him . . ."

"Yeah, I know," said Foley, as casually as he could. "That's why I did it."

Tom just stared at him. Couldn't believe he could hear him say that. "What?"

Foley shrugged once more. Tried to appear as nonchalant as he could on a moor in the middle of a storm wearing a three-piece business suit and overcoat. "You've probably been carrying that around for years, haven't you? Her death."

Tom said nothing. Just glared at him.

"All those years of guilt, blaming yourself. I'm sure of it. Want to contradict me? Tell me I'm wrong?"

Tom still said nothing.

"Thought so. Like I said, I've had a lot of time to think about these things. And you never knew what happened to her, did you? Not really. She died in crossfire, but whose bullet was it? Not yours, then whose? But you blamed yourself, didn't you?"

Tom just stared.

"Now maybe— as I said, I've had a long time to think, reflect on things—maybe that blaming yourself was all part of some misplaced guilt about what you did to me, how you fucked over the one man who was closer to you than even a brother. Who became family. Maybe that was all part of it, what d'you say?"

Tom spoke. "I don't know. You'll have to ask Dr. Bradshaw that one."

"Dr. Bradshaw's dead."

They both turned toward the source of the voice. So wrapped up in their own dialogue they had almost forgotten that Blake was still there. She stood over Baz's body, the Desert Eagle pointed at both of them. She might have been crying. She might have been angry. She might have just been grimacing against the wind and rain.

"What d'you mean she's dead?" asked Foley. "How can she be dead?"

Blake stared straight at them. "It doesn't matter. That's not important. What is important is the money. Now I've stood here long enough. It's time we—"

Foley moved so fast Blake—and Tom—didn't see him coming. Like a human volcano about to explode, he crossed to Blake, pulled her roughly up by her lapels. The action caused her to drop her gun in the mud.

"What d'you mean, she's dead? Tell me about it."

"She was coming to see me. And my boss Harmer. To discuss you, Tom Killgannon. She'd worked out what was going on. Knew I'd denied you were undercover after she'd spoken to Harmer. Well, I couldn't . . . couldn't let that happen, could I? No . . ."

Foley and Tom shared looks. Foley looked as angry and upset as Tom was, if not more so.

"So what did you do to her?" asked Foley.

Tom recognized Foley's quiet voice, knew what it signified. The calm before the storm.

"There was an accident. A car accident. Those country roads are treacherous at this time of year . . . Boom . . ." She smiled. "And off the road she went." She looked between the pair of them, as if explaining something she was sure they would understand. "One less person to worry about."

Foley grabbed her with one hand by the throat. Pulled the other back, still holding his gun, and slapped her as hard as he could. Then again. And again. And again. Her head went limply from side to side, the gun butt ripping at her cheek, blood arcing from her mouth, eyes rolled back in her skull, vacant.

"Stop it!" shouted Tom. "Enough . . ."

He grabbed Foley's arm in midslap.

"Dean. Enough."

Foley stared at him and for a few seconds Tom wondered whether he had miscalculated and Foley would start on him next. And yes, he held the gun on Tom. Tom knew there was no way he would miss from this distance. But Foley just kept his eyes locked on Tom's while the rage inside him calmed down.

He let Blake go. She crumpled to the ground in a heap next to Baz. A puppet with cut strings. No longer a threat of any kind.

Foley kept staring at Tom. Eventually he smiled. Tom couldn't tell what kind of smile it was.

"Just the two of us now," said Foley.

"Then let's talk. That's what Dr. Bradshaw wanted, wasn't it?"

"All right, then. Let's talk."

63

"TRY AND KEEP YOUR HEAD DOWN. Come on . . ."

Lila ran away from the house, Anju with her. Quint reached the front door, cursing, firing blindly. Just my luck to be hit by a stray bullet, thought Lila, after everything we've been through to get this far.

They dodged and weaved, making as hard a target as possible for the half-blinded assassin. Between themselves and the flaming car, not to mention the still-burning sugar on Quint's face, he couldn't find them. But that didn't mean he wasn't trying.

"Lila!"

Lila turned at the voice. Pearl was crouched behind an old stone wall, her car parked behind that. Lila and Anju ran over and crouched down next to her.

"Was that you?" asked Lila, pointing toward the burning car.

"I didn't know what to do. When I drove up I saw a car outside that I didn't recognize so what with everything that's been going on recently, I parked up here and walked down. When I got to the house I looked in the window and saw him holding a gun on you both." She shook her head. "You were right about him, Lila. I should have listened to you earlier."

"Never mind. So it was you?"

Pearl's expression looked pained. "I didn't know what to do.

If I called the police they might take ages and he might hear them and keep you both locked in there. So I torched his car."

"Why?" asked Anju.

"To get him out of the house so you could lock it behind yourselves. Then we could call the police and get them to come and take him. I didn't expect you two to come running out first."

"Lila had a plan of her own."

"And it was pure luck that it worked. And pure luck you did what you did, too."

"I'll call the police." Pearl began going through her pockets. Found her phone.

"No signal down here," said Lila. "We'd have to get to the top of the bank for that."

They all looked back toward the house. Quint was still standing in front of it, some of his vision returning, scanning the area, looking for them. The flaming car burning through the storm, throwing off heat where there should only be freezing rain.

"Can we get away in your car?" asked Anju.

Pearl looked at the road up the hill, back to the house. "It's too risky. I'd have to drive it out of where it's parked and that'll take me near to him. He might hit us."

"Right," said Anju. "So what do we do, then? He'll find us if we stay here. Should we run for it?"

"There's a shortcut up that path to the top of the road," said Lila. "But it's on the other side to where he is. And if we get to the top of the hill, we've still got miles to go to anywhere."

"But we can call the police then."

"If we can get up without him catching us."

"So what do we do?" asked Pearl.

Lila looked at the house once more. Worked out where Quint was in relation to the buildings around him. Looked at the other two.

"I think I've got an idea . . ."

64

"PUT IT DOWN," said Tom, "it makes me nervous."

Foley looked at the gun in his hand as if seeing it for the first time, surprised it was there. "Fair enough," he said, tucking it inside his overcoat, "wouldn't want it falling into the wrong hands, now would we?"

That done, Foley looked at Tom. Taking the time to really scrutinize him.

"You look different. Well, I suppose you would after all these years. And I don't just mean the hair and beard and everything. There's something different about you. You don't look like you used to."

Tom said nothing. Foley kept staring. Eventually he smiled.

"But there's still a bit of you in there. The old you. The old Mick. You can't get rid of it that easily."

"You look just the same," Tom said. "Only more so."

Foley laughed. "Prison tends to do that to a person, doesn't it?"

The laughter stopped. Like two gunfighters, neither wanted to be the first to look away in case the other made their move.

"So you still blame me for everything that happened to you?" asked Tom.

"'Course I did. All I thought about. For years. You. What you'd done. How you'd betrayed me." No drama in his voice when he spoke that word. Just a prosaic matter-of-factness. "Used to lie awake at night, planning my revenge. Picturing it in detail, real exquisite detail. Every scream, every gasp . . ." He shook his head. "Didn't sleep for ages thinking all that. And I had people looking for you. All over the country. Even abroad. Thought you might have skipped to somewhere sunny. Spain or Florida, something like that."

Tom almost smiled. "Spain or Florida? Credit me with some taste."

Foley almost returned the smile.

"Like I said, you obsessed me. I tried everywhere. Every angle. Looking for you. Searching, hunting . . . no sign of you. Eventually, I came to the conclusion that you'd probably died. And that made me even more angry. Because that meant someone else had done you in. Or cancer, something like that. And I tried to think you deserved it but it still hurt like hell that it wasn't me who'd done it. Like I'd been robbed of that satisfaction."

Tom said nothing.

"Because, like I said, I'd planned it all. What I was going to do to you . . . Christ, you were going to suffer . . ."

"And now that I'm here, in front of you? Are you still going to make me suffer?"

Tom tensed as he spoke. He was bigger in frame than Foley, but never bigger in rage. Foley was an expert at transforming that anger into physical action. Tom knew he would never best him in a fight if it was one-on-one.

Foley sighed. Looked up at the rain. Back at Tom. "What's the point? Eh? What would it achieve?" He shook his head. "You were wrong. What you said just now. That I'm not different. That I haven't changed. The Dean Foley you knew, all those years ago . . . that's not who I am anymore."

Tom didn't know how to reply, what kind of response to give.

Didn't even know whether Foley was telling the truth. Instead he gathered his thoughts. His turn to share.

"I've thought about you over the years too. A lot. Obviously. I've been living my life in hiding ever since that night. I've been living in fear that you'd find me. And I knew what you'd do if you did."

"And here I am."

"Here you are."

"That why you came down here?" asked Foley.

"Yeah. Wanted to get as far away as possible. So I came to Cornwall. Lived on my own in the middle of nowhere."

"As far away as possible. You got that right. Still in the 1950s, round here."

"It's not that bad," said Tom, almost smiling. Despite the reality of the situation, a part of him acknowledged that it was like two old friends catching up.

"But you were right," said Tom. "Well, half right."

"About what?"

"My guilt. That's what sent me down here. Away from everyone."

"About your niece?"

"Yeah. And also about my involvement with you."

Foley smiled, triumphant. "Told you. What did I say? All those sessions with Dr. Louisa paid off." Then a shadow passed over him as he remembered.

Tom kept talking.

"I said half right. Not like you meant. You showed me a side of myself that I hated. Well, you didn't just show me, you allowed me to let it out. You indulged me, encouraged me. And it was a side of me that was cruel, heartless, arrogant. Took pleasure in hurting people in as many ways as I could. Enjoyed the power and fear that it brought. I could do anything when I was with you. Anything. You know you said once you could shoot someone in a pub on Deansgate and get away with it? Remember?"

"'Course I remember."

"Well so could I. I knew I could. That's how powerful I felt. And I wanted to do it, just to see what it felt like. You were the one who brought that out."

Foley shrugged. "Can't blame me for something that was already there in you. If you didn't like it you wouldn't have done it."

"But I did like it. That was the thing. And it was only when I was with you that I behaved like that. I would never have done it otherwise."

"So what? You want me to apologize for existing just so you can feel better about yourself?"

"No," said Tom, shaking his head. "You don't understand. I'm not explaining myself clearly. That whole side of me, all of that . . . I loved it. Really loved it. And it scared me how much I loved it. How much I didn't want it to stop. I wanted to keep going forever. Or part of me did." He paused. Took a deep breath. Another. "So when it was time to do my job, to break up the gang, I was relieved that someone made that decision for me. Because it wasn't just about stopping you. It was about stopping me as well. And I don't think I could have stopped otherwise."

Foley nodded slowly, looked down at Baz's body.

"He didn't stop. He kept going."

"And look where it got him." Tom looked back at Foley. "You see what I mean, what I've been getting at? I've lived the rest of my life trying to be a different person. The person I am now, this Tom Killgannon, it's more than just a name. It's another chance. I've lived in fear, not just of you finding me, but that I'd go back to being who I was. I've worked to get rid of that part completely."

"You managed?"

"I thought I wasn't doing so badly. Till I went into prison. Then it all came back."

"Like I said," said Foley. "Prison changes a man. Or focuses them. Makes them more of what they are."

"Don't say that."

He held his hands up, shrugged. "It's true, but . . . whatever."

Silence fell between them. Foley eventually broke it.

"We were who we were."

"What's that supposed to mean?"

"It means it was the only life we had, the only life we knew. The only thing we could do to get out of that shithole we came from."

"There were other ways," said Tom.

"The army? Doesn't suit everyone. University? Seriously, no matter how clever we were there was no chance of going there. Not when we'd been to the schools we'd been to. So what else could we do?"

Tom didn't answer.

"I wanted to make something of my life," said Foley. "And so did you. So I did it the only way I knew how. Whatever opportunities were there, I took them. Just like you did. So don't give me all that guilt and angst and shit. We did what we had to do."

"But did we have to enjoy it so much?"

Foley stopped himself before he could reply. Thought. Gave a small smile. "What kind of man would you be if you didn't take joy from your work? Take pride in it?"

Tom just stared at him. Felt suddenly tired. Like everything had caught up with him. Not just the last few weeks and months, but everything. His whole life.

"You still feel the same?"

"About what? Pride in my work?"

"About what you had to do to get where you were."

Foley thought about it. "I've got a degree, you know. Did it inside. I knew I wasn't thick. Knew it all along."

"No one ever said you were."

"It's a working class thing, though, isn't it? No matter how much money you make, how successful you get, you can never shake it. So I did a degree. Prove them wrong."

"What's it in?"

"English Lit. Hardest thing I ever did."

Tom smiled despite himself.

"You see," said Foley, "this is something else I've spent a long time thinking about. All the money, everything like that, it made things easier. Money always does. But I thought doing what I did would make me somebody else. Someone better. Get me respect."

"D'you think it did?"

"Got me feared." Foley shrugged. "Suppose that's the next best thing."

"What about now?"

Foley looked directly at him once more. And Tom saw just how much his terrifying old friend had changed.

"I'm just tired," he said. "Really, really tired."

"What are you going to do about it, then?"

Another shrug. "Change. Because I'm sick of all that."

"So what happens next, then?"

Foley smiled. Tom didn't know if it was a good smile or not.

65

"Bastard . . . bitch . . ."

Quint staggered around in front of the house, not knowing which direction to take, where Lila and Anju had gone. He was clearly torn between hunting them down and going back inside. Searching for what he had come for, then getting as far away as possible. He had to rule out the last option. And he couldn't see to ransack the house. So he searched for the girls as best he could, hoping he could find them, force them to search the house for him. And then dispose of them when they found the money. He didn't normally relish killing, seeing it only as a necessary part of his job. But in this case he would make an exception.

He didn't notice Lila as she crept back down the hill toward the house, keeping to the shadows all the time, ensuring that her path was clear, that she didn't step on anything that could give her position away.

He had found Pearl's car, was looking around for them there. Lila watched, initially scared for the other two but knowing they would have moved away by now. She saw him try to open the door, fail. Yell for them to come out, make it easy. He sounded in pain. She carried on.

The front door was locked. Lila had expected that, knew that Quint would have tried to stop them getting back in where, as Pearl had said, they could call for the police. Quietly, she crept around the side of the house to the back garden.

Tom and she had been working on it during the spring and summer, cutting back the overgrown bushes and trees, carving out a pleasant place where they could both sit, enjoy the sun, drink, and eat. She also knew that there were plenty of places where she could either trip and fall or give herself away by standing on branches or foliage. She made her way carefully forward.

The back door was, she knew, locked, but the drainpipe beside it was old, heavy. Iron from a previous century. It clung to the outside wall of the house impervious, like nothing could bring it down. Lila hoped that was the case as she clasped it with her arms, put her legs around it, and pulled herself up it.

It was heavy going. There was a time when she would have done this easily. She had always been fit, able to lift at least her body weight, but recently she had let that go. A more comfortable, settled lifestyle will do that, she thought, telling herself to get back in the gym.

It was difficult, but not impossible. She pulled herself up all the way to the first-floor bathroom window. It was open. She never properly closed it. And she could fit her small frame through. Although she was settled with Tom and had found the nearest thing to contentment in her life, there was a part of her that was still wary. Ready to run as soon as things got bad. She had planned an escape route from the house just in case she needed it. It wasn't Tom she was afraid of, just parts of her past catching up with her. And if that happened, she would be off. It was one of the first things she had done when moving in here. Sometimes, when she and Tom were having a particularly good time, she felt ridiculous for actually planning that. But now she was glad. Better to be safe than sorry.

She placed her foot on the narrow window ledge, balancing her weight between that and the pipe. Reached out for the open window, transferred all her weight to that. Pulled it as wide as it would go, and head first, slipped through.

She hung half in, half out of the window, as she cleared knick-knacks and shampoo bottles from the windowsill, carefully placing them at the side, before hauling herself through.

She stood upright, listened for a few seconds. Nothing. She was alone in the house. She went quietly down the stairs, trying to avoid the creaking boards.

In the kitchen, the keys for Tom's Land Rover were where he always left them, in a repurposed antique bowl that didn't match the rest of the crockery but held keys for the house, the pub, their bike locks. She picked them up, careful not to jangle the others there, went to the back door. Turned the key, opened it. Stepped outside.

Listened. Nothing nearby. Quint was somewhere else.

She walked slowly around to the side of the house where the Land Rover was parked. Put the key in the lock as quietly as possible, opened it. She slipped behind the wheel. Tried to pull the door closed as well as she could. It only half caught, but that would have to do.

Now for the part where she had to make some noise. It was unavoidable. She started the engine.

It caught.

She put the headlights on full beam and saw Quint come running down the track toward her, gun pointing ahead of him.

She ducked down as a crack appeared in the glass of the windshield. It was on the passenger side. Thank god he can't aim properly, she thought, as she put the car into gear and slammed down on the accelerator.

Quint didn't have time to move as it came roaring toward him. The front bars caught him on his left hip, sent him spinning away. His gun loosened from his hand, landed on the hood, bounced away into the dark.

She slammed the brakes on, got out. Looked down at him.

"Fuck . . . what've you done to me . . . fuck . . ."

His leg was twisted backward, like the bottom part of his body faced one way and the top another. His face was seared with weeping burns.

Pearl and Anju ran from their hiding place to join her.

The three of them looked down at the broken man. No one wanted to speak first.

Anju did eventually. "What shall we do with him?"

"Call the police," said Pearl.

"Yeah but what do we do with him in the meantime?" asked Anju.

Lila looked over at the concrete slipway that led into the water, back to Quint.

"I've got an idea . . ."

66

"What happens next? Good question." Foley's smile was still in place.

"You still think I've taken your money?"

Foley studied him before answering. "No. I don't. Not if everything you've just said is true about who you were, or thought you were, back then. But to be honest, I don't care. If you took it, for whatever reason, keep it. I've got plenty of money stashed in other places. It would be nice to have, but I don't need it."

No one had moved. Blake had come around, was cradling Baz's broken body with her own. Her face was now bloodied and ruined. She sobbed silently to herself. Tom and Foley still faced each other, ignoring the storm. Their world only as big as the two of them. Tom didn't think he was in any danger. But he still wouldn't let his guard down. He imagined Foley was doing the same thing.

"So what are you going to do now?" asked Tom. "Go back to Blackmoor? Serve the rest of your sentence?"

Foley laughed. "Are you?"

"I wasn't—"

"Whatever." Foley looked around, took in the landscape as if seeing it for the first time. He put his head back, closed his eyes. Opened his mouth. Let the rain in. He licked his lips, his expression approaching ecstasy. His head dropped forward. He opened his eyes. "I don't think so."

Tom waited. Knew there was more to come.

"Dean Foley's dead. He died the minute he set foot on this blasted heath." Smiled at his own words. "He might have stepped on to this moor, but there'll be a new man walking away."

"And what about me?"

"What about you? Are you going to walk away a new man?"

"I meant are you still digging more graves?"

Foley thought before answering. "I reckon there's more ways than one to suffer for your actions. You've got enough going on with your guilt and everything. You've suffered as well. Maybe not as much as me or not in the same ways, but you've not been left unaffected." Another smile. Less pleasant this time. "And I've taken away the one thing you wanted. Closure on your niece's death. Answers. You'll never get that now. You'll only be able to guess. Crossfire'll have to do. And that might even make things worse for you to bear. So I suppose that makes us even. Or even enough."

"So I'm safe from you? In this new identity?"

"You're safe. Until I decide you're not."

Before Tom could reply, or respond in any way, Foley turned, walked toward the Duster and got behind the wheel. He put the engine into gear, turned it around.

Tom just watched him drive away.

For how long, he didn't know. Eventually he became aware of the sky beginning to lighten, the clouds parting. The rain easing. He looked around. Blake still cradled Baz, talking to him, stroking his face. He walked up the hill, got the bike out from under the overhang. Mounted it, ready to set off.

"What about me?" Blake had looked up, been watching him. "What's going to happen to me?"

"Get on the back of the bike. I'll drop you off at the police station where you can turn yourself in."

"I was going to get the money and run away. Start a new life."

"I'm sure you were."

"Just like Foley's done. Just like you did." She reached her hands up to her face. "Now look at me. At what he's done to me. I'm ruined." She looked down at Baz once more. "Maybe I should have stayed with him. Maybe we belonged together . . ."

Part of Tom thought he should have been more sympathetic to her words, her situation, but the main part of him knew that she had tried to have him locked up in prison permanently. She had tried to hurt him.

"Ambition can be a fucker, can't it? Especially if you go after the wrong things."

She didn't reply.

"You coming, then?"

She gestured to Baz. "What about him?"

"Someone'll come back for the body. He won't be left behind."

She shook her head. "He was always getting left behind." She gave a sound that may have been a laugh or a sob or maybe both. "I spent years hating him. For what he'd done to me. How he'd hurt me. For the way he was. He didn't start out like that. I don't suppose any of us do, really." She looked up at Tom. "Six of one, half a dozen, isn't it? It's not just the things you do. It's the things that are done to you . . ."

"Suppose it is," said Tom. "You coming, then?"

Blake shook her head. "I'll stay here with him. Make sure he's looked after."

"Your call," said Tom.

He was too tired to argue. He turned on the engine.

67

THE SUN WAS FULLY UP by the time Tom reached home.

He was cold, soaked through to the bone, but he just wanted to get there as quickly as possible. That was the first thing. Sort everything else out after that. Just get home.

The wind and easing rain made him feel colder the farther he went.

He pulled off the main road, turned down the bank. As he got closer to his house he realized something was wrong. There was a burned out shell of a car in front of it. Pearl's car was parked halfway up the hill. And his Land Rover was parked haphazardly. It had a shattered windshield.

His heart started beating faster. He pulled up, adrenaline pumping around his body once more. Instinct kicking in. And then he saw them. Lila, Pearl, and another girl standing on the concrete causeway, looking down at something in front of them. He turned off the engine.

They had already seen him, heard the bike. Pearl and Lila were running toward him, the other girl some way behind. He guessed who she was.

"Hey," he said.

Lila was the first to reach him. She hugged him so hard, he felt he would burst into tears there and then.

No words offered, no words needed.

Then Pearl reached him. The hugging started again.

They were fine. They were all fine. There was nothing to worry about. They were all right. They were all right.

Smiles and tears from two of the women. He looked at the third. She smiled at him too. He returned it. A perfect homecoming.

He made to head inside.

"No," said Lila. "Not yet. Here." She took his arm, escorted him to the causeway.

There was the body of a man lying half in, half out of the water. Tied up with the tow rope from Tom's Land Rover.

"We're just waiting for the tide to come in," said Lila. "Or the police to arrive. See which happens first." She looked at him, rage in her eyes. "I know what I want to happen."

Tom's exhaustion was coming back.

"No," he said.

He walked down to the causeway, grabbed the ropes around the man's body. Hauled him out of the water, onto the dry concrete.

No," he said again.

Lila stared at him. "What are you doing? He killed your friend, Quint."

Tom stopped, stared at her. "What?"

"Sorry. I should have said it differently. But he did. And took his place. He was going to kill us, but we got away from him." She looked down at the prone man. "Why did you do that? The bastard should suffer."

Tom looked down at the pitiful wreck of the man before him. There was no fight left in him. Either of them.

He thought of Foley. Of the man who used to be Foley. Of the man who used to be Mick Eccleston.

"Because that's not who we are. Not now, not anymore. We're better than that. We have to be."

"But . . ."

"No. No *buts*. We have to be. We can't change today into tomorrow like that. You . . ."

He slumped down next to the man on the causeway, no longer able to stand up.

And began to sob his heart out.

PART FIVE
RENEWED

Mick just stood there, staring at the carnage. Ambulances were arriving now, their flashing lights adding to the chaos all around. He walked back to where he'd left the duffel bag. Stood beside it once more. Looked down at it.

He felt so, so tired.

Of everything.

68

PAUL SHELLEY STOOD OUTSIDE an unremarkable terraced house in Honiton, Devon, hoping that what he was about to do would save his career.

TV cameras, newspaper photographers, bloggers, and online journalists swarmed about in front of him, like some unhealthy miasma given human form. He should have hated it but was embracing it instead. He needed this stunt to work, to deflect attention away from him and what had happened at the prison under his watch. As much publicity as he could get. With himself at the center of it. The wise leader, the unassuming man behind this achievement. Play it that way, forget the rest, and see where his career would go next. He imagined his face on the TV screen. All fifty-six HD inches of him. Yes. This was going to work.

It had been a different story a couple of weeks ago.

DEAN FOLEY ESCAPES FROM BLACKMOOR—JUST WALKS OUT

One of the many headlines. He had been called before his superiors, asked to give an account of himself and his behavior. He thought the best way out was to lie, which he did. Blamed the individual officers involved in the case, particularly Chris Cartmel who had accompanied Foley on the outside. He tried to brush off questions, deflecting the blame every time. It was the staff, it was

government underfunding, lack of training, sloppy wing procedure, it was anyone and everyone's fault but his.

The only thing he did take credit for: putting an undercover
officer inside to get Noel Cunningham to give up the locations of
his remaining victims.

That had the potential to be an even bigger mess than the Foley
debacle. So when DCI Harmer of Devon and Cornwall police
corroborated Tom Killgannon's story, especially in light of the
conspiratorial behavior of DC Blake and the inmate Barry Foxton,
not to mention hiring the hit man Dan Jameson, he was more than
happy to take credit for it. The whole thing was an unmitigated
disaster. And he knew he was lucky to still have his job. However
he also knew that what had happened since, Cunningham finding
the locations of his victims, made up for a lot of that.

And now he was here. Keeping his part of the bargain. Cunningham had asked to see his terminally ill mother in return for giving
the locations of the remaining bodies. And Paul Shelley was a man
of his word.

As he was waiting, the car pulled up. Like sharks scenting
blood, the media knew this was the vehicle and gathered around
it, smothering it in their bid to be the first to get a photo, a quote,
a piece of moving footage. The police officers present held them
back, allowed the car to pull up, Cunningham to get out.

He looked terrified when he saw all the cameras, tried to get
back into the car. His police escort ensured that didn't happen.

He would look very different in the papers. They had been using
the same photo of him for years, the baby-faced, bow tie wearing
choirmaster. Neat hair, big smile. They hadn't been expecting this
disheveled, sweating, greasy-haired obese man wearing prison-issue
sweats. But, Shelley thought, they could spin that to their advantage.
Write some tabloid piece about his inner degeneracy now showing

on the outside. Wouldn't be the first time they had done something like that. And it wouldn't be completely wrong, either, he mused.

Cunningham was bundled inside the house as quickly and efficiently as possible. The cameras went after him. Shelley, spotting his chance, inserted himself between the cameras and the closed front door. This was the address he had been waiting for.

"I'm Paul Shelley," he began, in what he hoped was some kind of rousing Churchillian manner, "warden of Blackmoor Prison. Noel Cunningham is here today because of the tireless efforts of myself and my staff. And it is important that we send a message. That our rehabilitation regime works. That this is the end result of the work we do in Blackmoor. Rehabilitation. Repentance. Restitution." He smiled once more. Why had he never thought of that phrase before? It just came to him. Clearly, he was a natural at this. He smiled, but noticed out of the corner of his eye that cameras were being turned off, journalists turning away. This wasn't how he'd planned it at all. He made one last ditch attempt.

"What you see today is the culmination of all our work at Blackmoor. All my work. I think I can take full responsibility for what you are witnessing today."

He had lost them now.

"Thank you very much."

He turned, knocked on the door, went inside the house.

The house was depressing. It had the stench of the old, the dying. Shabby, undecorated for years, the only new additions were local council-supplied aids for movement and independence. Or at least the independence of getting to the toilet. Shelley couldn't wait to get out of there.

Cunningham was in the living room, alongside police officers. He looked up when Shelley entered.

"Hello, Noel," he said, as if bumping into him at a party, "Everything all right?"

Cunningham stood, nodded. "I want to see my mother now."

"Of course."

"That was the deal."

"Absolutely."

Cunningham remained standing, staring at Shelley.

"You all right, Noel?"

Cunningham moved right up close to him. Shelley could smell his unbrushed teeth. "You tricked me," he said.

Shelley was aware of the police moving toward him.

"I didn't trick you, Noel. How did I trick you?"

"You sent Tom in to see me. I liked Tom. He was my friend. And now I can't see him anymore. You sent him away."

"I'm sure he'll . . ." What? He was sure he would what? "Come and visit."

Cunningham stared at him for a few seconds longer, turned away. "I want to see my mother now."

"Come on then," said his police officer escort and began leading him upstairs.

Shelley tagged along too.

When they reached the landing, Cunningham stopped. "I want to see her on my own."

The police officer looked at Shelley, who shrugged.

"All right then, Noel," said the officer, "I'll go in and check the room's secure, then I'll let you in. Right?"

Cunningham nodded.

The officer stepped inside, checked the room. Shelley peered through a crack in the door. An elderly woman, made even older from disease, lay near comatose under the sheets. So light she was almost a skeleton.

"All clear."

Cunningham nodded his thanks, went in. Closed the door behind him.

Shelley and the officer waited.

"How long has he got?" asked Shelley.

The officer shrugged. "How long does he need?"

"Could be minutes, could be—"

Shouting came from behind the door. Crying.

The officer rushed toward it, pulled it open.

And there was Cunningham, bent over the still body of his mother, pillow over her face.

"I hate you . . . hate you . . . All my life I've hated you . . . what you did to me, how you hurt me . . . I hate you . . . hate you . . ."

Screaming, tearful, unstoppable.

Other officers ran upstairs, bundled Cunningham out of the bedroom. Shelley looked in. He didn't need to be an expert to know the woman was dead.

Cunningham, now sobbing uncontrollably, was taken forcibly downstairs.

Shelley watched him go.

Thought of the last words he had said to the TV crews.

Watched Cunningham leave the house.

Taking Shelley's career with him.

69

It's often said that doctors make the worst patients. But Dr. Louisa Bradshaw knew that just wasn't true. Besides, she wasn't that kind of doctor.

Very lucky. She heard that a lot in the first few days after she came around and found herself in Truro's Royal Cornwall Hospital. Broken arm, broken leg, concussion but no internal bleeding and no major organ damage. You should do the lottery.

She had no memory of the crash. Or the hours that preceded it. Only that she had been told she had been going to Exeter to talk to the police. That part had come back to her but she wasn't sure if it was an actual memory or whether the doctors and police had told her so many times that it had become one. She of all people knew things like that happened.

But she could remember the previous few days at work. Talking to Tom Killgannon and Dean Foley. Trying to arrange a meeting between them to settle their differences. No chance of that now. Don't dwell on your work, she had been told, again by the doctors. Concentrate on getting well.

Nicole had been to see her several times. She had woken once to find her sitting by the side of the bed, crying silently. Asked her if she looked that bad. Nicole had replied with a hug, a weak smile, and a second bout of tears.

Nicole. She had been thinking about her a lot. More so than work. About what was important in her life—who was important in her life. Despite living together neither of them had been in a hurry to make some kind of commitment. But she felt differently now. An event like this, she thought, puts the rest of your life in perspective.

So she was on the mend, trying not to think about work, when the nurse, Toni, came into the room.

"You're popular, aren't you?" she said.

She was carrying a bunch of flowers almost the same size as she was.

Louisa sat up. "What?"

"For you. Just delivered to the nurse's station."

"Who are they from?"

Toni laughed. "That's for you to find out. You've got an admirer."

She left them by the side of the bed, arranging them so they wouldn't fall over. "Oh," Toni said. "There's a note. Here you go."

She took the small envelope, opened it. Read the card.

And her heart skipped a beat.

She read:

> *I will do such things,*
> *what they are yet I know not*

She recognized the quote straight away. *King Lear*. And knew immediately who had sent it.

The signature was another quote from Lear:

> *From a man more sinn'd against than sinning*

She put the card down, lay back on the pillow. Felt like the wind had been knocked out of her.

Dean Foley. He hadn't forgotten her.

She didn't know if that was a good thing or not.

No, she told herself. Of course it's a good thing. It meant that her work had value, that she had made significant breakthroughs with him. Given him insights into himself, his psyche, that he was going to carry forward into whatever he did next, wherever he went next.

She read the card again. Studied the quote. It wasn't complete. He had only written the first half of it. Mentally she completed the whole thing:

"I will do such things, what they are yet I know not; but they shall be the terrors of the earth . . ."

She put the card down, looked at the flowers.

Her good mood suddenly gone.

70

IT HAD TURNED INTO AN IMPROMPTU PARTY.

Nobody intended that to happen. Just a few drinks at Tom's house one Sunday night. Pre-Christmas. Tom and Lila, Anju, Pearl. And some of the new staff from the Sail Makers. Not really a party. But Pearl had arrived with a couple boxes of beer, plus wine, and Tom had made a huge pan of chili, so things became more festive than perhaps expected. And no one minded.

Life was good. Tom tentatively admitted that. There had been little comeback for his exploits in prison but plenty for Blake and Harmer. Neither had jobs and one was looking at a life sentence. They had cleared Sheridan's name in the process. Tom felt it was the least that could have happened.

Shelley was no longer warden and after the murder of his mother, Noel Cunningham had been moved to Broadmoor Prison for the Criminally Insane. Tom considered sending him a Christmas card. Decided against it.

Dr. Louisa was on the mend and Dan Jameson, the fake Quint, was also looking at multiple life sentences. The body of the real Quint had been found on Blackmoor days after Cunningham had shown them where his bodies lay buried. He had raised a glass or two for his old friend Quint on several occasions, felt like maybe his death would become another burden to carry around, another ghost to haunt him.

Lila had seen what he was doing and talked to him about it.

"It wasn't your fault," she had said to him one particularly dark night after he had been released, as he was attempting to come to terms with the enormity of what he'd been through. Put his ordeal into perspective so he could carry on with his life. "It wasn't. You said yourself Quint was a security consultant. That's what he did now. You'd have paid him, wouldn't you? For his work?"

"Yeah, I was going to. Probably not as much as he usually made, though."

"There you go, then. It was a job. And it went wrong. You weren't to know. You can't blame yourself for it."

He didn't talk about Quint again. At least not to Lila.

He resumed his therapy sessions. Talked about it plenty there. But that was what they were there for.

He attended Nick Sheridan's funeral. Sheridan had turned out to be a decent bloke after all. And his decency had got him killed. Seeing the turnout at Exeter Crematorium, how many colleagues attended, how well his wife and children were supported, he felt like Sheridan would have been a man he could have enjoyed getting to know. He didn't speak to anyone, didn't stay for the reception, and drove away afterward on his own. He had paid his respects. That was enough.

And then there was Hayley. He had come so close to finding out what had actually happened to her, only for the chance to be taken away. Forever. He was unsure how he felt about that. Part of him was still in turmoil. But another part of him felt like that was the end of something. Nothing he did or could do would bring her back, so he just had to get on with life. Let her death—and his responsibility for it—go.

His inner jury was out on which voice he would eventually listen to.

And Dean Foley was in the wind. For some reason Tom didn't feel too bad about that. He didn't think Foley would come back into his life but he couldn't be sure. Foley wasn't the type of person who could be second-guessed. But he felt safe from him, for the moment at least.

Or as safe as he could ever feel knowing Foley was walking around free.

He stood in the kitchen, watched everyone enjoying themselves. Lila and Anju seemed really happy. He could tell just by watching the way they were with each other. Their happiness communicated itself. He found himself smiling.

Pearl caught him. Crossed to him.

"What are you mooning about?"

"Oh, nothing. Just how happy Lila looks."

"I know. Sweet, isn't it?"

"Yeah. I mean, just think, all those months ago what she was like. You'd never have believed she could smile like that."

"Well that's what happens when someone shows another person kindness."

He felt Pearl looking at him. Knew she was slightly drunk. He felt her body pushing against his.

Pearl was very attractive. And single, which he found inexplicable. But she was his boss. He also felt that if something started between them, it would be serious. And he wasn't sure if he was ready for that kind of commitment. So he had kept her advances at arm's length and not made any of his own. No matter how much he had wanted to.

But now, the alcohol relaxing everyone, the ordeal of prison in the past, things felt different. Perhaps it was time to move forward.

"You mean me or Anju?" he said.

"You just did what *you* always do." Slightly slurring her words, hand on his arm, leaning into him.

He put his arm around her. "Steady."

She looked up at him, her expression unmistakable.

And they kissed.

Afterward, neither would be able to say who had made the first move. It felt like it had been done simultaneously. But it felt so right. Their mouths locked, bodies pressed together. Arms held each other.

It was only the surrounding silence that made them both look up. The rest of the room had stopped whatever they were doing and were watching them.

They quickly pulled apart.

Lila was the first to cheer. Everyone else soon joined in.

Tom and Pearl looked at each other, smiled.

Pearl laughed. "Well that was a long time coming. Merry Christmas."

Tom felt himself redden. "I . . . I just need to . . ."

He slipped out of the room as another cheer went up behind him.

He made his way upstairs, stood with his back against the wall on the landing. Took a deep breath, another. That wasn't him, he thought. That wasn't him at all. Another deep breath. Or maybe it was. Maybe this was Tom Killgannon. This could be his character, his life, going forward. He smiled. He could get to like this man.

He knew they were thinking he had gone to the bathroom but that wasn't where he was headed. There was something he had to do, something he had to check. He had been avoiding it since he got out of prison and knew that now, with a house full of people, it was completely the wrong time. But the alcohol gave him courage. And it needed doing.

He went into the spare bedroom, looked round. It was

undisturbed. Good. He crossed to the chimney, knelt down before it. Put his arm inside. Fingers searching.

Found it. Pulled it out.

The plastic brick was filthy but undisturbed. Good. The fake Quint hadn't found it. He put it on the hearth, felt inside again. The others were all there. He took his arm out, picked up the first one again. Wiped the plastic clean. Saw the notes, tightly bound, the Queen's face staring off uninterested, as if financial transactions were beneath her. He knew what denomination the notes were in. Knew how many there were.

And knew where they came from.

"Tom? You coming back down? We're missing you."

Lila's voice from the bottom of the stairs. He looked once more at the bundle in his hands.

"Yeah. Be down in a minute."

He put the brick of money securely back in place, dusted his hands. Stood up.

Ready to rejoin his guests.

Ready to be Tom Killgannon once more.

ACKNOWLEDGMENTS

First of all, I should say that HMP Blackmoor is not a real place. I've worked in prisons and young offender institutions in the past and it's nothing like any of them.

Thanks as always to my agent Jane Gregory and all at Gregory and Company for always having my back.

And to Katherine Armstrong, Jennie Rothwell, Francesca Russell, and the rest of the gang at Zaffre.

To all my friends in the crime fiction world. It's the best gang to be part of.

A special thank you to all the readers, bloggers, booksellers, and journalists who enjoyed the last novel. You really help enormously and I can't thank you enough. Hope you like this one even more.

And lastly to my wife, first reader, coadventurer, and professional geek Jamie. You actually made me enjoy witness protection . . .

PRISONS AND ME

It's no secret I've been in prison. A couple of prisons, actually. I talk about it all the time at events and in interviews. Never hide it. In fact, I like saying it because it pulls people up, makes them give me a second, untrustworthy glance. Sometimes they even check their wallets or their watches. Or flinch, wondering whether I'm going to attack them. Then I go on to explain I was there for a reason. You see, I used to be a Writer-in-Residence. They relax then, a little bit. Because even though I tell people I was on the outside going in and could leave at night, there's a little bit of that word—prison—that powerful, stigmatic word that everyone has an opinion about, but most people don't actually understand, that stays there until I speak further. And sometimes, unfortunately, afterward.

Long story short, I answered an ad in the paper from the Writers in Prison Network and ended up in Huntercombe Young Offenders Institution for two and a half years. And I loved it. It may well have been the happiest job I've ever done, which sounds contradictory at least since I was behind bars doing it. I was working with kids up to eighteen. The place I was going into had just appointed the country's first full time Arts Coordinator, helping a group of inmates form themselves into a rap act—X-Konz—and perform at Capital Radio's Party in the Park that summer.

The Governor came to see me (unheard of in most prions, I later found out) and gave me a two-word brief: "Bring life." I tried my damnedest.

Another Writer-in-Residence told me before I went in that the lives and backgrounds of the kids I would be working with were the stuff of nightmares. And straight away I found that to be true. I wrote a short story, *Let's Pretend*, about a teenage rapist who's in prison because his mother sold him to a pedophile ring and who, on being let out, can't go to his terminally ill father and instead has to become a procurer of young boys for his tormentors or they'll abuse his baby daughter. My then wife said it was the most depressing thing she had ever read. My boss called it a normal day at the office.

Some of the kids I worked with were unreachable, even at that young age. I can admit that. And it was sad. I still tried to work with them, though. Their futures weren't bright because their pasts had been so damaging but they still needed help, coping strategies, even if I was just a guy trying to get them to write stories and maybe change the endings to the ones that had led them into prison. To get them to imagine, to dream. One of my class said that when he sat down to write a story, the walls just opened up and he was free.

It was a polarizing environment. There were no "meh" days. Because I was working in such close emotional proximity to these kids, (without, as Home Office rules stated, giving too much of myself away—try making that one work) getting them to open up, talk freely, relax, and know that what they said or wrote in my writing room wouldn't go back onto the wing with them and that if anyone tried to do that, they wouldn't be back again; it was demanding, full-on work. And sometimes things went brilliantly. Really brilliantly. I had the privilege of helping people to turn their lives around for the better, by using writing as a breakthrough instrument. I had great poets, rappers, story writers, and magazine editors. Kids who found something they were good at and could be valued for. Who were made to feel worthwhile for the first time in their lives. Later, I had a group member decide to get help for his alcohol addiction because of realizations he'd come to through his writing. A father took me out to lunch to thank me for helping him to reestablish a relationship with his son because all he talked about in their visits was writing class. Or the one guy who said he was having so much fun he didn't want to be released.

Like I said, great stuff. But, I always stressed, it wasn't me, it was the process. And by that same definition, good days would be followed by bad days. A combination of factors, the process not working, the prison system being what it is, any number of things, I felt like there was nothing I could do. Days like that I went home and drank copiously.

After two and half years of this, I moved to work in an adult prison. Not Blackmoor, I hasten to add, that place is entirely made up. And then after that I felt quite burned out. I like to believe— have to believe—that what I did helped though.

Unfortunately, since 2010 the prison budget has been slashed and my kind of work, along with anything broadly rehabilitative, was the first to go. Now our prisons are overcrowded, under-staffed, and we recently had a moron of a Justice Minister who banned prisoners from receiving books until he was challenged in court. A far cry from my experience. Then, I felt like I was trying to grasp something that was always almost out of reach but could be found. Sometimes I managed it, other times I wasn't so lucky. I just hope there are still people within the prison environment doing that now.

PALE GUARDIAN

PALE GUARDIAN

A James Asher vampire novel

Barbara Hambly

Severn House Large Print
London & New York

This first large print edition published 2017
in Great Britain and the USA by
SEVERN HOUSE PUBLISHERS LTD of
19 Cedar Road, Sutton, Surrey, England, SM2 5DA.
First world regular print edition published 2016 by
Severn House Publishers Ltd.

British Library Cataloguing in Publication Data
A CIP catalogue record for this title is available from the British Library.

ISBN-13: 9780727895974

Severn House Publishers support the Forest Stewardship Council™
[FSC™], the leading international forest certification organisation. All
our titles that are printed on FSC certified paper carry the FSC logo.

MIX
Paper from
responsible sources
FSC
www.fsc.org FSC® C013056

Typeset by Palimpsest Book Production Ltd.,
Falkirk, Stirlingshire, Scotland.
Printed and bound in Great Britain by
T J International, Padstow, Cornwall.

For Robin

One

'Don't go out there—'

Dr Lydia Asher turned as a weak hand plucked at her skirt.

By the light of her lantern the young soldier's face was drawn with pain and chalky with loss of blood. The single eye that had survived the shrapnel when a German shell had struck the forward trench blinked up at her with desperate intensity.

'It's all right,' Lydia whispered. 'You're safe here, Brodie.' It was astounding how many peoples' names she managed to remember, now that she wore her spectacles full-time. Around them the long tent was silent, the wounded men sleeping. For the first time in nearly a week, the road eastward from the camp was quiet, the surgical tent, across the way, dark. Northward, in the direction of Ypres, she could still hear the guns. It was March of 1915. 'We're all—'

The young man shook his head. 'She's walkin' tonight, M'am. I seen her look into the tent. The *bean sí* . . .'

'Shhh.' Lydia leaned over him, marveling that he was alive at all – she'd assisted Major Overstreet yesterday in removing nearly two pounds of wood and metal fragments from the boy's chest – and gently straightened the blanket; the night was bitterly cold. 'It isn't a banshee.'

'It is, M'am,' insisted Brodie, his voice barely

1

a breath, in his pain still mindful of others who slept nearby. 'I seen her in the trenches, just before the Germans came on. The other men have seen her, too. She wears a nursin' sister's uniform but she's none of them here at the station, her eyes is like a cat's in the dark. Wait till she's gone by, M'am. 'Tis the worst sort of bad luck to see her.'

'I'll be all right.' She made a move to disengage her sleeve from the grasping fingers, but his eye pleaded with her.

'You think I'm off me head but I'm not. I really have seen her, down the trenches, in the dead of the night. Me mates say they've seen her near the aid stations, an' the clearin' stations like this one—'

Quietly, Lydia said, 'She doesn't come into the wards like this one. You and your mates—' her glance took in the other men, shapeless lumps beneath the blankets in the frowsty darkness – 'will go back to hospital tomorrow. It isn't you she comes for.' She pushed up the white cuff of her VAD uniform – the best the Medical Corps could come up with for her, as she was neither a nursing sister nor a surgeon – and showed him the four stout lines of silver chain around her wrist. 'Silver keeps them away, you know. I'll be perfectly all right.'

His eye was slipping closed and his head, in its swathe of bandages, sagged back onto the thin pillow. 'Does she come for the dyin', then? That's a *bean sí*, isn't it? And if I seen her walkin' . . .'

'Just because you saw her,' murmured Lydia gently, 'doesn't mean she's coming for you. You

2

rest now, Mr Brodie. I promise. You'll be all right, and I'll be all right. You'll be moved back to hospital in the morning.' *If they have enough ambulances and enough petrol and enough drivers for the less desperate cases, and if the Germans don't decide to shell the Calais road again . . .*

He slid into sleep even as she stepped away from his cot. When she reached the tent-flaps at the far end of the ward, she lowered the flame on her lantern as far as she could, and adjusted a sheet of tin around the glass chimney, such as the wire-cutting parties sometimes used, or the bearers out searching for the wounded. After eleven days in the gutted village of Pont-Sainte-Félicité Lydia was sure enough of her way around the casualty clearing station to at least not bump into walls or fall into either the gaping cellars of bombed houses or the shelled-out labyrinth of abandoned German trenches that surrounded the town.

She pushed up her spectacles to rub her eyes.

She had swabbed the last of the blood from the fluoroscope table that was her charge, checked to see that the machine itself was disconnected from the generator wires, and put back in their places the clumsy lead apron and gloves that she insisted on wearing (to the annoyance of the surgeons: 'It's not a bloomin' death ray, M'am! We've got men dying in here!'). She'd sent her assistant, a slow-speaking Welshman named Dermott, to bed some hours before, when he'd started making mistakes owing to the fact that like herself he'd been awake since yesterday

3

morning. Everything that was left to do, Lydia was reasonably certain, could wait until daylight.

Except this.

This had to be done while darkness yet covered the land.

The thing that Brodie had seen (*How DARE she come peeking into the tents!*) she didn't worry much about, though nothing living stirred in the camp now except the ever-present rats.

As she had intimated to Brodie, in such proximity to the Moribund Ward, where nearly two hundred men lay irreclaimably dying – not to speak of the lines of trenches to the east – she, and he, and all the men in his ward, were almost certainly safe.

She touched the thick links of silver that protected her wrists, and the further chains that lay over the big blood vessels of her throat, and reflected with a kind of tired irony that she stood in the one place in all of Europe where she could be fairly sure that she was not going to be attacked by vampires.

The silence outside was like death, save for the not-very-far-off thunder of the guns.

With her lantern hooded, her eyes accustomed themselves to the darkness. Those who hunted the night in nearly every city of the world were well used to turning aside the eyes of the living. They would assume that she, too, believed the simple mental tricks that shielded them from human notice – that she was merely making some routine round – and would not slip away when they heard the damp scrunch of her footsteps.

But she was aware of what she sought, and so could sometimes see past their illusions. Over the past week and a half – at least before the mad avalanche of wounded had begun to pour in six days previously – or was it seven? – she had been able to catch glimpses of them, and had kept a list. *Tall dark woman, big nose. Stout man, sleek dark hair. Tall blonde man, square face. Small blonde woman, beautiful . . .*

Those were only the ones she'd seen. She knew there were others.

Hundreds, certainly. Thousands, perhaps.

Would Jamie, her husband back in Oxford with their three-year-old daughter, recognize some of them? *Probably.* He knew more of them by sight than she did, though she was certain that on her second night here she'd glimpsed Elysée de Montadour, the Master vampire of Paris.

At a guess, every vampire in Europe was here in Flanders, or further south along the line of trenches that stretched from the Channel to the Alps. Most of them would be lurking around the hospitals. With far less courage than the stretcher-bearers, they only ventured into no man's land itself in the dead hours of the night, if at all. Men and women who had chosen to murder others rather than face whatever lay on the far side of death weren't about to run the risk of encountering a raiding party, or being caught in a sudden barrage of shells, or becoming entangled in barbed wire that would hold them until the sun rose and ignited their pale and bloodless flesh.

Not when there was easier prey a few miles off.

The shattered walls of a ruined cottage provided her with concealment. Her lantern's hooded glimmer touched broken rafters, charred spills of bricks, gaping cellars. Most of the furniture – and many of the bricks – had been looted within hours of the clearing station's establishment in Pont-Sainte-Félicité (she herself had bagged a kitchen table for Dermott's makeshift developing station). She strained her ears as she moved from room to room, until she heard a flickering whisper and stepped close to one of the blown-out windows.

And there they were. Six feet from the window, themselves taking advantage of the walls of a ruined house to survey the hospital tents which glowed very faintly in the darkness, from the lanterns within. Their reflective eyes caught dim shreds of light that shone through the cracks of the hastily-erected wooden mess huts. The tall, dark woman with the big nose, and two men – the taller man strong-built, with fair, receding hair, the smaller, slender and dark. Both men wore British uniforms; the woman, a black dress that blended with the night. Their flesh was almost milk-white, and they stood so close to the window that she could see the woman's hands were armed with inch-long claws. Were it not for the stillness of the blighted town Lydia wouldn't have heard the wind-whisper voices. Flemish? Italian? Lydia knew that vampires had come to the Front from as far away as Sicily, Edinburgh, Athens.

She blinked – her eyes were aching, she had spent twenty hours out of the past twenty-four either taking x-ray photographs of bleeding men

6

or helping out in the surgical tent – and when she looked back they were gone.

'Bother,' she muttered, and moved on.

Not what she was seeking.

Still her heart quickened with terrified dread.

What she sought, she had seen seven nights ago, the night before the big push at Neuve Chapelle. Every night, every day, in the surgical tent and the fluoroscope room and in her dreams when she'd collapse at odd hours to snatch some sleep, she'd fought recurring dread – *I have to find out what was happening. I have to see if it happens again . . .*

It took her about two hours to circle the collection of medical tents, wooden huts and mule-lines, meticulously careful to look about hcr as if she were simply checking the area for spies or deserters or for Quartermaster's Storeman Pratt out making deals for the Army rations he stole and sold to civilians on the side. She saw three more vampires: one in the ruined houses of the village – the slim woman with soft cascades of light-brown hair whom she'd seen last week, Lydia recalled – and two down in the caved-in horrors of the deserted German trenches, wearing dark civilian clothes and whispering to one another in German. The language didn't trouble her. Plenty of Swiss spoke German, not to mention French Rhinelanders. In any case, she knew quite well that once a living man or woman crossed into the kingdom of the damned, they generally lost all interest in the affairs of the living.

To the vampire, the war – and the battle zone – meant one thing only.

7

The deserted trenches around the village were horrible. They swarmed with rats, reeked of the German soldiers buried when English shells had caved in their dugouts. Five months at the Front hadn't cured Lydia of her morbid horror of the vermin. Carrying her lantern low so that its light wouldn't be seen above, she had to hold up her skirts in the other hand as she picked her way down the side of a shell-crater, and into the zigzag pits. The water down there was almost knee-deep and freezing cold, and her feet groped to stay on the duckboards down under the surface. The mud beneath them would be like quicksand.

She didn't see the thing she'd seen the previous week. Stumbling with weariness – *I HAVE to find out . . . What if there's another push tomorrow and it's another five days before I can watch again?* – she scrambled up the broken trench ladder she'd scouted out the week before.

I HAVE to find out . . .

A rung of the ladder snapped soggily beneath her foot. She dropped the lantern, grabbed for support, and a hand came down from the darkness above and grasped hers, cold with the cold of a dead man's. The iron-strong fingers tipped with inch-long claws.

She was drawn up over the parapet of sandbags at the top with the effortless strength of the Undead.

'Mistress,' a voice murmured, 'when first you came to this place, for two nights did you walk thus, but I thought you had given the practice o'er. You shall come to grief at it.'

Lydia shook out her muddied skirts and propped

her thick-lensed spectacles more firmly onto the bridge of her nose. 'I thought all the vampires were out making a feast of the wounded.' Her voice cracked a little, at the memory of poor Brodie, of all the men in the ward. She realized she was shaking with weariness. 'Either here or up in the front-line trenches—'

'What would you, Mistress?' returned the voice reasonably. 'When the shelling is done, and the dying lie in the mud of the battleground where the guns have left them, where none will reach them? When men die in their blood waiting for an ambulance that will never come? We feed upon blood, lady. We feed upon death. The whole of Flanders, the whole of the Rhineland, the whole of the Front glows with sustenance such as we are, in time of peace, are obliged to ration, sip by sip, lest our existence be suspected. Can you blame those who exist by absorbing the life-force of the living, for being drawn to such a banquet?'

'Yes!' Lydia tried to pull her arm free of his steadying grip. She staggered in her exhaustion and would have fallen had cold arms not caught her, thin as whalebone and steel, and lifted her bodily. 'I can. I do. It's so unfair . . .'

'You are frozen,' said Don Simon Ysidro's soft voice. 'And spent. And I promised James that I would look after you here in Flanders.'

'He'd never have accepted such a promise—'

'Nevertheless I gave it.' To his near-soundless whisper still clung the accents of sixteenth-century Spain, whence he had journeyed, a living man, to the court of the queen whom the English

9

called Bloody Mary. He had encountered the Master of London among the stones of an English churchyard one dark night, and never returned to his home. 'And you will come to grief not from the kindred of darkness,' he went on, as he bore her toward the tents, 'but from getting your feet wet in cold such as this, or from encountering that pestilent creature who peddles ammunition and food and heating-oil to the local peasants – to the poor Germans, too, belike.'

'Storeman Pratt.' She relaxed suddenly, and rested her head on the vampire's thin shoulder. 'You're perfectly right, Don Simon, he probably *would* kill a nurse who surprised him at it. Or at least make up some frightful crime and then blackmail me about it.'

Beneath her cheek she felt the sturdy wool of an epaulet, and guessed that he, too, had adopted the uniform of a British officer – *Procured from Mr Pratt himself, I daresay!* – which no observer, if they *did* spot him, would dare question. He probably had impeccable papers, too – *Very likely purchased from the same source!* She felt beaten, her anger denied and deflected, lost in the greater rage at the greater deaths about which she could do nothing. Her mind touched briefly on the young Yorkshireman who'd died on her x-ray table . . . *Was that this morning? Yesterday afternoon?* On poor Brodie, whose x-ray had showed her that he would almost certainly have his legs amputated once he reached the base hospital at Calais. On another boy – barely seventeen, he'd looked – she'd checked with Captain Calvert in the surgical tent, sobbing for his mother and so

10

riddled with shrapnel that he'd been set gently aside, so that men whose lives *could* be saved could be operated on first.

You're dying anyway, we have no time to save you . . .

Shuttling desperately between her fluoroscope machine and the surgical tent where every trained hand was needed, she hadn't even had time to go back and see that youth before he died.

Tears that she hadn't been able to shed closed her throat. More than anything else, she wanted to be with Jamie at this moment. To be back in Oxford and out of this place of stink and death and cold. *I'm just tired,* she told herself firmly. *I'll feel better when I've had some sleep* . . .

Don Simon Ysidro was a vampire. There had been times, in the eight years of their acquaintance, when she had hated him – for what he was, for what she knew that he did and had done in the centuries since his non-death. There had been times when she'd felt herself falling in love with him – despite her unswerving love for the tall, leathery Lecturer in Philology at New College, Oxford whom she had adored with the whole of her heart since the age of fourteen.

But Jamie was back in Oxford, still recuperating, slowly, from the pneumonia that had nearly killed him in the first month of the war.

And she was here, in the darkness, feeling the thready pale spider-silk of Ysidro's long hair brush against her forehead, and hearing the guns.

She said, 'Someone else is out there looking for vampires.'

'Are they, indeed?'

The smell of latrines, of the hospital tents, of cook-tent smoke and makeshift stoves surrounded them like a fuggy embrace. Ysidro stooped and canvas brushed her face as they entered the nurses' tent, a barely-visible bulk in the darkness. One of the VAD's she shared with would be on the ward at this hour of the night; the other slept like an unwaking corpse. A tiny flicker of light as Ysidro kindled the lantern next to her bed showed her the vampire's face, thin, aquiline, pale as white silk, framed in a loose mane of colorless hair and illuminated by eyes that had, in life, probably been hazel. They'd bleached now to a cold sulfurous yellow, faintly pleated with gray – he'd told her once that this 'bleaching' occasionally happened to vampires, no one quite knew why. The mental illusion that kept her from noticing his fangs also kept Sister Violet Brickwood from waking, not that the poor woman *would* stir, after twenty hours on her feet . . .

Ysidro pulled Lydia's shoes and stockings off her, and wrapped her feet in the blanket of her cot. Then he dipped water from the jerrycan in the corner and poured it into the kettle, which he placed on the heating-stove.

'I saw her a week ago . . . no, longer . . .' Lydia shook her head. 'The second night we were here.'

'Ah.' She thought he did some mental calculation, placing the night in his mind.

'After I finished setting up the fluoroscope room I walked the perimeter of the camp. When we were back at Givenchy – before the clearing station was moved here – I knew there were vampires all around the camp, every night. I'd

12

glimpse them between the tents, and some of the men have seen them, too. They don't know what they are.'

'Did you look for me?'

'I couldn't imagine you'd let anyone see you.'

A smile touched a corner of his mouth, turned his face suddenly human, a living man's, and young. 'You had the right of it, Mistress. Yet you did not make a practice of such patrols at Givenchy.'

'Once I knew they were there, I didn't really see the point.' Lydia propped her spectacles again. 'I mean, I knew they wouldn't attack the nurses, or the surgeons, or really anyone but the dying. Why cause themselves problems when there are so many easier victims? That sounds horrible, but when I thought about it – and about how few of us there were to take care of the wounded and how terrible the casualties were – that was during the fighting at Ypres – I came to the conclusion that I could probably save more lives by getting a few hours more sleep, instead of chasing vampires whom I knew I'd never catch. I don't . . .' she stammered. 'I don't mean that, exactly, but . . .'

'You chose rightly, lady.' He held up a hand. 'And you did a hero's work at Givenchy, and here. I have watched you.'

She brushed his compliment aside with tears of shame in her eyes.

'There was no right choice,' his soft voice insisted. 'More men lie in the Moribund Ward, and in the trenches themselves, than would suffice to glut the greediest of the Undead, were there

13

five times more of us here than there are. We have no need to trouble even those men who can be saved, ere you load them into the ambulance-wagons. Our business is with the dying. 'Tis not we, these days, who deal out death.'

'I know.' She took off her glasses to wipe her tears. 'It doesn't mean you aren't monsters.'

'The vileness of my condition is old news to me, lady.' He measured cocoa from its tin (*Where would a vampire learn to make cocoa?*) into her mug, and stirred the hot water in. 'I admit, 'tis not the future I envisioned for myself when I studied my catechism with the Christian Brothers in Toledo. Yet you have not told me how you came to resume your practice of walking the night?'

'I just . . . wanted to get some idea of the local vampire population.' The thick pottery was God's blessing against her chilled hands. 'Though I knew they'd followed the clearing station down here. But the second night, in the ruins of the village, I saw another woman, moving about like me with her lantern hooded. I thought she might have been a spy when first I saw her light – I suppose there are local women, who think the Germans ought to own this part of France, or even German women who've been slipped across the lines. I closed my lantern entirely and followed her, and it became pretty clear to me that she was doing exactly what I did the first night: she circled the camp at a distance, and checked the bombed-out German trenches. She – we – glimpsed vampires twice, and she stood off at a distance, fingering something she wore at her

14

neck, a silver cross or something of the kind, I assume. She kept watch around the ward tents of the men especially. A spy wouldn't do that.'

'No.' He settled himself on the foot of Nurse Danvers's empty bed, folded slim hands around his knee.

Lydia frowned across at him in the lantern-light. He was attired, as she'd surmised, in the trimly tailored uniform of a staff colonel in the British Expeditionary Force. 'Have you seen her?'

'I have,' returned Ysidro. 'At all events I have seen a young woman with a lantern, stealing about the ruins of the village, and down in the abandoned trenches. This was ere the battle started: brunette, and smaller of stature than yourself, though broader in shoulder and hip. Her clothes were dark, and she might well have worn a silver crucifix about her neck – something silver, at all events.'

Lydia touched the chains around her own throat again self-consciously: enough silver to burn a vampire's mouth or hands, to give her a split-second in which to wrench free, to scream, to run . . .

As if anyone could outrun the Undead.

And unless the crucifix was of nearly-pure silver, it would have no more effect on a vampire than would any other pendant of similar metal content.

'Did she speak to any of the vampires?'

'Not that I have observed. She has not your familiarity with those who hunt the night, Mistress. She seeks, but cannot find. At least, 'twas so ere the casualties started coming in such

15

numbers. Since the fighting started on the tenth I have not seen her.'

'Have you any idea who she is?'

He shook his head, or came as near to doing so as she had ever seen him, a slight motion more of his eyes than his head, as if in the centuries since his death he had lost interest in communication with the living. 'Yet I saw none but yourself engaging in such behavior at Givenchy. And none of the vampires to whom I've spoken, either here or nearer the lines, have mentioned any like matter. I admit I have not joined the groups that go out into the trenches, or into no man's land in the dead of the night. Peasants.' The two smallest fingers of his right hand flicked in a gesture of concentrated scorn. 'Without manners or conversation, most of them. I shall enquire.'

'Thank you,' said Lydia. 'I appreciate it. I'd like very much to know if others – elsewhere along the Front, for instance – are also trying to . . . to meet, and speak with, vampires, or if this is just something, someone, local. I don't expect, when the battle itself was going on, that the woman I saw could get away from wherever she was. Or possibly didn't dare.'

'Given the likelihood that one side or the other might break through the lines, or that shelling might commence anywhere at any time,' remarked the vampire, taking the empty mug from her hands, 'I myself would hesitate to venture far from shelter. I understand the Venetian nest foregathered in the chateau at present occupied by the Master of Prague and his fledglings, for a session of *écarté* which lasted through three nights.'

16

'What did they play for?' A dreadful question to ask an Undead multiple murderer, but she really did want to know. 'I mean, do you play for money? Do you *have* money? The Bank of France froze all withdrawals at the start of the fighting.'

Ysidro looked down his highbred nose. 'One of the first lessons one learns, Mistress, when one becomes vampire, is never to let oneself be caught without money.' He came back to her cot-side and drew the blankets up over her. 'The second lesson one learns is how to obtain it – anywhere, and under nearly any circumstances. Those who do not learn such lessons in general do not survive. Thus under ordinary conditions, money means very little to the Undead. The gamblers at the chateau played, I understand, for credit-vowels, much like the surgeons and the orderlies play here. Had I known you sought information regarding this enterprising vampire-seeker I would have arranged to attend: such gatherings are clearing houses for gossip, and do not take place often.'

He tucked the blankets in around her, for the tent, though stuffy-smelling, was deeply cold. 'Sleep now,' he ordered, took her spectacles from her hand and placed them on the up-ended packing crate at her side. 'Morn will come soon enough.'

I shouldn't take comfort in his presence, she thought. *He's going to leave here and go straight across to the Moribund Ward . . .*

I shouldn't feel glad to know that he's near.

She stopped herself from catching at his hand,

17

and only asked, 'Where were you? I mean, why weren't you playing cards and trading gossip—? The Master of Prague has a *chateau*? *HERE*?'

'You would expect him perhaps to sleep in a dugout?' One eyebrow lifted, and through a haze of myopia she saw again – or imagined – that his face for a moment became the face of the man he had been, almost three hundred and sixty years ago. And then, more quietly, 'I was watching over you, Mistress.'

And where were YOU sleeping? During the shelling, and the confusion, and the constantly shifting dangers, any one of which could trap a vampire aboveground when the first light of dawn would ignite his flesh and engulf him in flame . . .

Instead she asked, 'Do you know what this woman wants?'

'I expect—' he turned down the lantern – 'nothing good.'

Two

Colonel Stewart shut the buff folder on his desk with a little hiss of annoyance, and scowled across at James Asher as if what he'd read there were all Asher's fault. 'Damn medicos won't clear you for service till you can run three times round Piccadilly Circus and shin up the Monument with a rope. Got no idea there's a war on and we need every man.'

Asher suspected that the damn medicos, up to their hairlines in shattered and dying men, were as cognizant of the war as Stewart was and were seeing it a damn sight closer. But he only returned, 'I can't say I'm surprised. Or entirely disappointed. Just coming down here knocked me out. I'd hoped to go back up to Oxford tonight and I'm staying in town instead.'

'You look perfectly fit to me,' grumbled the colonel, rising to show Asher from his office. 'Damnit, man, you'd only be sitting in a cell with a lot of Jerries listening to 'em talk! How hard can it be?'

Asher, who'd had three relapses of pneumonia since his return to Oxford in September – after nearly dying of it in Paris – reflected that the last thing his lungs needed was to be surrounded by forty German prisoners of war, all coughing themselves blue. He made noises of commiseration, shook hands and promised to notify the

19

War Office the minute he was fully recovered, and descended the steps of the rambling labyrinth on Whitehall feeling as if he'd personally swum the Channel after battling half a regiment of Roman gladiators, single-handed and armed with a golf club.

Definitely in no shape to deal with Paddington station and two hours standing in the corridor of an overcrowded railway car, much less a trip to the Front.

A younger man – and on that cold March night, though not quite fifty Asher felt like a septuage-narian at least – would have leapt at the chance, if not for glory then because his beautiful young wife, Lydia, was also at the Front. But seventeen years on Her Majesty's Secret Service had cured Asher once and for all of any possible craving for glory, and of even a moment's belief that if such a thing as glory existed (something he had always very much doubted) it could be achieved in war. And though he would without hesitation – even at his age (or the age which he felt) – have re-swum the Channel and fought those hypothetical Roman gladiators a second time with his seven iron in the hopes of even an hour in Lydia's astonishing company, he was sufficiently familiar with the workings of the War Office to know that were he to volunteer to gather infor-mation from captured German prisoners, he would undoubtedly be assigned to do so in Serbia, not Flanders. (Lydia's letters were censored but before her departure last November they had worked out a dot code, so he knew she was in Pont-Sainte-Félicité, near Neuve Chapelle.)

Whitehall was nearly dark. The pavement was thick with foot traffic from the government offices, though it was close to seven. Asher's years of sneaking in and out of foreign countries with information about naval emplacements, border fortifications and orders for new weaponry had given him a permanent watchfulness of all those around him, an awareness of faces and details of dress which, in Berlin or Vienna, could mean the difference between making it back to his hotel safely and being found dead in a storm drain. Thus, despite the swift-thickening twilight, he was very much aware that most of the men hastening to catch the 7:10 from Charing Cross had white or grizzled hair beneath their Homburg hats, and that the home-going crowd – thinner by half than it had been the year before – was at least a third female. Women and older men moved to take up the positions of men at the Front.

Or of the men who'd gone to the Front six months ago and were already dead.

Buildings loomed against the cinder sky like a black necropolis. Since January, when German Zeppelins had rained bombs on coastal towns, the government's orders to black out windows and streetlamps had assumed a new seriousness – Asher had read recently of a movement afoot to drain the Serpentine and the lake in St James's Park, lest the glitter of moonlight on their waters serve as a guide to the night raiders. Though the traffic – both motorcars and horse-drawn – was far lighter these days, Trafalgar Square was a nightmare of jostling dark shapes swimming

21

through the gloom, and had Asher not known the place like the back of his hand he would not have been able to locate the Underground station. Below ground the lights were bright, but the crowds were such – reduced bus service and an almost total absence of cabs more than made up for the shortage of men in city offices – that Asher had a long wait for a train to Bloomsbury.

By the time he reached the small lodging house near Euston Station his head was swimming with fatigue. He had already telegraphed Mrs Grimes – the cook back at the Oxford house – that he wouldn't be home, and briefly toyed with the notion of sending a second wire to bid Miranda a special good-night. At three, and with her mother now gone, his daughter set great store by good-night kisses, even by remote proxy. But the extreme likelihood that the Oxford Post Office wouldn't deliver the greeting until the following morning put the idea from his mind, and he ascended five flights of stairs to what had been the servants' quarters of the tall, narrow house – rooms of any kind were another thing extremely difficult to come by in London in the spring of 1915 – and dropped onto the cot in the penitential little chamber without undressing.

This turned out to be a fortunate circumstance, because twenty minutes later the landlady's daughter thumped loudly on the door with the news that a message had come from the War Office, and it looked to be important.

It was from Colonel Stewart, begging him to return. Sir Collin Hayward of Intelligence was on his way to Paris first thing in the morning, but having heard that Asher was in town, wanted very much to speak to him about assisting in the vetting and training of agents to be sent to the Continent.

Asher roundly cursed both Stewart and Sir Collin, but resumed his coat, tightened his tie (which he hadn't taken off – tired as he was, he assumed he'd have slept in it), and made his way downstairs and back to the Underground.

He spent the next three and a half hours in conference with Sir Collin, who, to do him justice, looked like he hadn't had more than a few hours' sleep in the past week.

Then because of a breakdown on the Northern line – it was past midnight, and the Underground nearly empty – Asher had to take the Piccadilly line and walk back to Grafton Place from King's Cross. And, owing to the completely unlighted condition of the streets, and a moderately thick fog which had settled over the city, he found himself, uncharacteristically, lost.

This was what he was doing, wandering among the nameless streets east of King's Cross Station, when he encountered the revenant.

The fog confused the way sounds carried from the railway yards. It was too dark, even, to see the street signs, many of which seemed to have been taken down or taped over (in an effort his landlady had told him to thwart German spies). Likewise it was difficult to determine in which direction Regent's Canal lay. In places the fog was thick enough – reeking with the smoke of the munitions factories across the river – that

Asher had to feel his way along the house walls and area railings. He could only be glad that at this hour, nobody was operating a motorcar, not that anyone in this neighborhood (if he was where he thought he was) could afford such a luxury (or the petrol to put in it) . . .

Then he smelled it. Sudden, rank and horrible, like rotting fish and the urine of rats mixed with the peculiarly horrible stench that oozes from human beings who have washed neither their bodies nor their clothing for months on end. Unmistakable.

He had smelled it in Peking, two years before. A thousand times stronger, for the things had been forty and sixty strong by the time their hive was destroyed. Don Simon Ysidro had told him that the only other place where such monsters were to be found was Prague, where they had spawned and multiplied for nearly three centuries in the old Roman sewers beneath that city. *The Others*, Ysidro had called them, though they were related, in some way, to vampires. Undead, mindless, nearly impossible to kill, they would devour anything they could catch, and presumably lived for much of the time upon rats, with whose minds they had a curious affinity.

Here.

In London . . .

Shock and horror smote him like a physical blow.

Damnit—

Horror chilled him.

In London . . .

Listening intently, he could hear it, a slow soft

24

dragging as the stink grew stronger. *The canal can't be more than a hundred yards off.* The Others hid under the bridges in Prague, when night cloaked that city. Down in the bed of the rivers, and in half-flooded sewer vaults, for their flesh would slowly dissolve from exposure to sunlight.

Their minds – if they could be said to have such things – were joined by a sort of mental telepathy, something the older vampires were adept at, though no vampire, so far as he knew, could control the actions of the Others.

And their condition, like that of the vampires, was spread by 'corruption of the blood'.

The vampires, whose mental powers of illusion were lessened by the movement of running water, kept away from them. Lydia had written to him months ago of the vampires at the Front: *Are these things there as well?*

One could reason with vampires.

Not with the Others.

The Others, one could only flee from, and the thought of such things at large in London iced him to the marrow.

Asher felt his way along the wall – the brick gritty under his fingers – until he reached the corner he knew had to be nearby. The smell nearly made him gag. A faint *plish* of water, around the corner to his left. By the feel of the broken pavement underfoot he guessed this was an alley. A few feet further on he trod in something squishy that smelled of rotten vegetables. Ahead, the slight metallic rattle as the Other brushed a dustbin.

Then the furious squeal of a captured rat, followed by the sudden pong of blood. The rat shrieked again – being eaten alive, presumably – and there was a loud clang as either another rat, or a cat, fled the scene in panic. Yellow light bleared suddenly in the fog with a man's shape silhouetted against it:

''Ere, then, what's . . . *Bloody 'ell*!'

Pressed to the brick of the alley wall, Asher was shocked at how close he stood to the thing, close enough to see it clearly through the fog once the light from the open door streamed out. It was indeed such a creature as had bred in the mines west of Peking, the human face deformed and bruised where the jawbones had elongated and the sutures of the face opened. The mouth, human no longer, was raw where its new-grown teeth had gashed the lips. It held the dying rat in one hand – still thrashing – and blood ran down its arm and its chin. The creature's eyes, as it swung toward the open doorway's light, flashed like mirrors.

It dropped the rat and sprang.

The shirtsleeved and unshaven watchman who'd opened the door let out a yell and tried to slam it again between them, but the creature already had him by the arm. It yanked him through and into the wet murk of the alleyway. Asher caught the lid off a dustbin and struck with its edge at the revenant's face. With a grunting bleat the Other struck it aside, staggered back, still holding the shrieking watchman; Asher slammed at it with the lid again and, when it was knocked away, caught up the dustbin itself and

26

rammed it at the monster like a clumsy battering ram.

The revenant hurled his quarry from him and Asher heard the man's skull crack against the brick of the wall. Then it lunged at Asher, who struck with another dustbin – *Do NOT let the thing's blood touch you, do NOT* . . . The creature made one more lunge at the watchman, who lay crumpled where he'd fallen at the foot of the wall, then doubled like a rat and darted into the blackness. Asher plunged after it, one hand to the wall to guide him, and thirty feet on collided with more dustbins, falling over them as the light of two other doors opened in the murky abyss and men's voices shouted about what the 'ell was goin' on 'ere . . . (Only one of them, the philologist in Asher noted automatically, used a Southern Indian's sharper terminal 'g' . . .)

By the time Asher was pulled to his feet the creature was gone.

'What the hell is that stink?' demanded the white-haired Indian. 'Are you all right, sir?'

'He attacked a man,' panted Asher, pointing back into the solid wall of fog. 'One of the watchmen—'

The men looked at each other – three of them, a sailor and two watchmen in this district of small shops and warehouses. 'That'll be 'Arry,' said the other watchman, a silvered bulldog of a man, and as one they all ran back along the alley, Asher thinking, *What the hell will I do if the victim is alive but infected? What the hell can I say?*

The door still stood open. A fat man, balding, with a publican's apron around his waist was just

27

moving to close it; the stouter watchman called, 'What 'appened 'ere, Tim? This gennelman says as 'ow 'Arry was attacked—'

Tim the publican's heavy-browed face creased in a frown. 'They took him away.' Sharp little blue eyes studied Asher and he added, 'You want to come on round the corner to my place, guv, an' have a sit-down. You look done up like a kipper.'

'Who took him?' Asher leaned suddenly against the wall, trembling in a wash of fatigue.

The publican's frown deepened and he put a steadying hand under Asher's arm. 'Dunno, sir. Looked like a plainclothes 'tec ter me. Skinny little feller. I'd just tied a towel round 'Arry's conk – bleedin' like a pig, 'e was – an' the feller says, "I'll take him. Cut along and get some water, 'fore we have every cat in the neighborhood lappin' at the blood." That's where I was off to now, and to get word to Weekes who owns the shop here.'

'He's right about the blood,' agreed the Indian. 'You take the gentleman inside, Tim, I'll get that water and send off to Weekes.'

Asher was led off down the alley to the back door of the Wolf and Child (which, he reflected, had no business still pouring out brandy at this hour of the night). He glanced back, his heart hammering, and he saw that, yes, the wet, black brick of the wall opposite the warehouse door glistened with a dark smear of blood. More blood was dribbled on the pavement where Harry the watchman had fallen.

I have to find him. Find where he was taken.

28

If the creature too was wounded, and its blood found its way into Harry's open flesh, in a few days he'll begin to change . . .

The Indian guard emerged from Harry the watchman's door with a bucket of water, and doused the blood in a soapy torrent.

When Asher returned to the place on the following morning, slightly light-headed and shaky from the fatigue of the night before, and inquired of Mr Weekes – the owner of the silk warehouse Harry had watched – the shop owner had no idea to which hospital Harry had been taken. Nor had Tim the publican, just washing down the front steps of the Wolf and Child and readying to start the day's business, after seeing Asher back to his room in Grafton Place the previous night. 'No, he's got no family here in town.' The fat man shook his balding head. 'Lives in lodgin's somewhere in Camden Town, I think . . . No, I never did hear the name of his landlady. Not that it sounds like she'd care tuppence if he was brought back home cut to pieces in a sack . . .'

'If you do hear of where he might be found—' Asher handed the man his card, containing his Oxford address – 'please telegraph me here at once. I have reason to believe that the man who attacked Harry suffered from a contagious disease – spread through blood contact – and it's imperative that I at least make sure Harry wasn't infected.'

Which in its way was the truth. Neither Weekes nor Tim had been contacted yet by the police,

29

and when Asher inquired at the Holborn Police Station later in the day he learned that the attack had not been reported. Though it was now four in the afternoon and he felt as if his bones had been ground down to the snapping point with weariness, Asher made his way to the Foreign Office.

Langham, to whom he'd reported in his days of mapmaking and rumor-sniffing in the Balkans in the 1880s, was delighted to see him. He clucked worriedly over his haggard appearance ('They told me you'd dashed nearly gone to join the choir invisible in Paris, old fellow – Stewart's an idiot for saying you should be passed as fit for a listening post . . .'), and poured out for him some indifferent sherry from a cache in the bottom of his office bookcase. He listened to Asher's carefully-tailored account of the events of the previous evening: that there had been an attack in the service alley behind the Wolf and Child in Chalton Street, that Asher had heard repeated rumors of German plans to spread an infectious disease in London, that he had reasons to suspect that the man attacked – Henry Gower – had been so infected.

'The men who work in the same street tell me that someone came, almost at once, and took Gower away, presumably to hospital.' Asher sipped his sherry – it didn't help in the least. The thought of trying to deal with the train back to Oxford that night filled him with sickened dismay. 'But it turns out that as of this morning, neither Weekes – Gower's employer – nor any of the witnesses were contacted by the police, and no report was filed. Yet we must find Gower, and more than anything else we must find the – man – who is potentially spreading the disease.'

'And what are the symptoms of this disease?' Langham spoke calmly, but his weak blue eyes were fixed on Asher's face.

Asher felt himself go perfectly cold, with a chill that had nothing to do with the onset of fever.

'High fever,' he replied promptly. 'Rash and virulent irritation, especially around the mouth. What appears to be bruising of the capillaries of the face.' Keeping his face bland, he observed that his former boss was watching him closely, with an expression of studied nonchalance.

He knows about it already.

'Hm.' Langham folded his ladylike hands. 'I'll get a report out to the hospitals, of course . . . and thank you for reporting this, old man. I'm sure it's nothing – some men are being sent home from the Front with quite gruesome cases of shell shock lately – but would it be asking too much for you to write up a report when you get back home? You are going up to Oxford this evening, are you not? That's good,' he added, when Asher nodded as if the matter were a foregone conclusion. 'You look like the very devil, old man. By all means, go to bed and stay there . . . And don't worry.' He permitted himself a secret, and slightly patronizing, little smile. 'Think no more about it. The matter is in hand.'

Asher felt the hair prickle on the nape of his neck.

'I'm glad to hear it, sir.' He smiled, rose, donned

31

his hat – it took all his remaining strength to do so – and got out of the office, and the building, as casually as he could.

And kept an eye out behind him, all the way to Paddington Station.

Three

'Well, thank God Jerry's taking a breather anyway.' Captain Niles Calvert dunked his hands in the tepid wash water and chivalrously handed Lydia the only dry towel in the wash corner behind the surgical tent. 'We can get some of this lot mopped up . . . God, I hate doing surgery under lights.'

'I keep wondering what we'd do if the generator went out.' Lydia carefully removed her spectacles to wipe the bridge of her nose. Rice-powder was another thing she'd given up when she'd signed her contract with the Army, and without it she felt like a schoolgirl: a blinky-blind, goggle-eyed golliwog (as the other girls at Madame Chappedelaine's had called her), a carrot-topped skinnybones with a nose like a parrot. On the other hand, it was very nice to see the faces of the men she worked with, to say nothing of not falling into shell-holes.

'And what I keep wonderin',' put in Captain Horatio Burke, straightening his own glasses, 'is how I can be sweatin' when I'm freezin' half to death.' Like Lydia, prior to the war the lumbering, grizzle-haired surgeon had had far more experience with the academic side of medicine, and after a long day of work on men deemed critical – but not violently urgent as yesterday's had been – his features sagged with fatigue.

'Different set of glands,' Lydia replied promptly. 'It's part of the fight or flight reaction.'

'You mean it's to do wi' why I don't run outen here screamin'? Aye?' he added, as a tall figure appeared in the darkness of the tent doorway.

'Message for Dr Asher.' The young man carried a hooded lantern, and by its upside-down glow, and the reflected glare from the surgical tent where the orderlies were cleaning up, Lydia automatically noted the square-jawed earnestness of his features, the brilliantined sleekness of his dark hair and the freshness of his uniform. *From Headquarters* . . .

Her heart turned over in her chest.

Oh God, Jamie . . .

Or Miranda . . .

Her hand shook as she took the note.

It was Don Simon Ysidro's handwriting. *I have found those who have seen the woman.*

She raised her eyes in startled alarm to the face of the messenger – he was taller even than Jamie's six-foot height – and he merely said in the plumiest of aristocratic accents, 'If you'd come with me, please, Doctor Asher.'

Don Simon was sitting in a staff-car some twenty feet from the lights of the camp. The young officer – he wore a captain's uniform but God only knew if he was entitled to it – helped Lydia into the vehicle, saluted the vampire and retreated. Lydia could see his broad-shouldered, slim-hipped figure silhouetted between the car and the soft glow within the nearest tents.

It was a still night. The only shelling was miles away, around Vimy, Captain Calvert had said.

34

Shadows moved within the tents as the nursing sisters saw to their charges. When the night wind stirred it brought the stink from the incinerators where the orderlies were burning amputated limbs.

'Is that young man actually in the Army at all?' Lydia asked, and there was a whisper of amusement in Ysidro's usually expressionless voice as he replied.

'*Dios*, no. John – Captain Palfrey – resigned his commission in the First Dragoons last November, under the impression he was being recruited by a branch of the Secret Service so secret that not even the rest of the Department was aware of it – a hoax which has been embarrassingly easy to maintain. Spare me any expression of indignation on his behalf, Mistress: I have certainly saved that young man's life thereby and most assuredly the lives of at least a quarter of the men who might have found themselves under his command. He is a deplorable soldier. Will you come with me, and speak to those who have had converse with this seeker of the Undead among the Dead?'

'Converse?'

'After a fashion.' The glimmer of lights from the camp had lit the cloud of Lydia's breath when she spoke; no such vapor proceeded from the vampire's lips. 'Seeing them, she called out to them, but any vampire in his senses is wary of overtures from the living. They seldom end well. Will you come?'

'It will take me about half an hour to finish with the fluoroscope room. And I'll need to find something to tell the matron—'

'John will deal with that. Get a stouter cloak. 'Tis cold where we're going, and wet.'

Lydia guessed what he meant, and shivered. Under Captain Palfrey's respectful escort, she swabbed and tidied the x-ray table and made sure the fluoroscope was disconnected and that her own protective garb was laid out where she could find it on the morrow. The lecturers at Oxford's Radcliffe Infirmary had been fairly blithe when demonstrating this new miracle equipment, but Lydia's own researches – including at least one article in an American medical journal – had prompted her to encumber her machine with lead shielding (which made it difficult to maneuver and maddening to move) and herself with a lead apron and gloves. Major Overstreet – who handled the most serious cases – would snarl at her for taking too long, when a soldier's life was at risk on his table, but Lydia was convinced that the dangers of exposure to Röntgen rays were not imaginary.

It was nearly eight o'clock, and pitch-dark, when she finally returned to the staff-car. It made a lurching turn and set off eastward; a moment later the hooded headlamps splashed across the stones of the bridge that crossed the Lys River. After that Lydia could see nothing beyond the ruts of the road, water gleaming in potholes, and the occasional gleam in the eyes of a rat.

Most days, one could smell the trenches from the ruins of Pont-Sainte-Félicité, no mean feat, Lydia was aware, considering the olfactory competition from the camp itself. In time the car stopped, and Don Simon stepped down, helping

36

Lydia after him with a gray-gloved hand. Through a break in the clouds the gibbous moon showed her a tortured landscape of what had been, up until last year, some of the most fertile farmland in Europe. Now it was a wasteland of mud, standing water and shell-holes, slashed across and across with trenches, deadly with tangles of barbed wire. Cold as it was, the stench was terrible. From the muffled sounds around them, Lydia guessed these former German trenches were in use now as Allied reserve trenches, with the front-line trenches and no man's land a few hundred yards further to the east. Ysidro steadied her down a ladder into the maze of communication trenches that connected the reserves with the firing trench: far safer, but hideous with icy water just beneath the half-submerged duckboards. The hands of corpses projected from the mud walls. Once she saw a skull face, flesh entirely eaten away by rats. The rats themselves were a constant scuttering movement, amid a broken debris of battered helmets (both German and British), rusting tins and broken entrenching tools that littered the shadows.

Her companion, with his courtly manners, was a vampire. A creature from horror tales.

This was nightmare.

'Ah.' A deep voice spoke from the darkness *'C'est la belle rousse qui patrouille dans le camp.'* A lantern-slide was cracked. Lydia made out, in the black angle of the communication trench, the two men she'd seen last night who'd been talking in the ruined village to the woman in black. The taller, fairer man bent and kissed her hand, and

37

even through her glove his lips were warm on her frozen fingers. *He's fed.* Lydia knew it had been on some poor soldier who was dying in any case – quite possibly a German, whom she knew she was supposed to *want* dead (*Or why else are you here?*).

I shouldn't have anything to do with these people. Any of them . . .

With the preternatural quickness of perception that many vampires possessed, the fair man must have read her thoughts in her face, because when she looked back up she saw understanding in his dark eyes, and pity for the dilemma in her heart.

'We have asked ourselves, my friends and I, what it is that you seek with your lantern each night.' His French lilted with an Italian intonation – *Jamie would tell me exactly what part of Italy he comes from.* 'It is this woman, then? This dark-haired nurse—'

'She's a nurse?'

His nose wrinkled in half-comic distaste. 'She smells of carbolic and vinegar, Madame. Her dark cloak covered her dress, but the greatcoat she had underneath it was brown.'

'She could have borrowed it,' put in the slim dark youth behind his shoulder, whose face reminded Lydia of the statue of the degenerate Roman Emperor Heliogabalus in the Capitoline Museum of Rome. 'Or stolen it. Or bought it from that slippery English clerk at Pont-Sainte-Félicité . . .'

'And in fact,' agreed Lydia, taking a deep breath to steady her nerves, 'I can't see what other woman *would* be wandering about so close to the front lines.'

38

'Ten thousand pardons.' Ysidro bowed. 'Madame Doctor Asher, may I beg the favor of presenting to you Antonio Pentangeli, of the Most Serene Republic of Venice? And this is Basilio Occhipinti.'

'*Madama*,' murmured the dark vampire, and Antonio bowed again.

'I kiss your hands and feet, beautiful lady. As for this dark-haired nurse, wherever she acquired her greatcoat, she called out to me in French, saying, *I would speak to you*. And when we said nothing – Basilio and I – she called again, *You have nothing to fear. But I need to speak with those who hunt the night. I have a proposition, a partnership, to offer you*.'

Lydia said, 'Drat it.'

'Do not distress yourself, dear lady. Neither Basilio nor I – nor, I think, any of us who hunt the night in this appalling place – are so foolish as to think that such an offer from the living means anything but their desire to lure us into imprisonment and servitude. Don Simon will have spoken to you of the game of fox and geese that children play – and at which he himself cheats like a Greek – and it is true that it resembles the relations between the Living and the Dead. We – like the fox – have the power to easily kill any goose. But let the geese organize themselves to surround us, and it is we who die.'

'Not all of your brethren,' returned Lydia, 'have the wisdom to realize it.'

'What can the living offer us?' Antonio Pentangeli spread his hands. Like most vampires he extended his mental powers of illusion so that

Lydia had to look very carefully in order to notice his claws and fangs, and the fact that he did not breathe. 'The moment the shooting began, both sides lost their power over us: the power to give us what we crave. They are like nursemaids trying to bribe a child with a peppermint, when that child stands knee-deep in a pile of sweets.'

'Was that all she said?' asked Lydia after a moment. 'Just that? A proposition – a partnership?'

''Twas all we lingered to hear.'

'Where was this? And what time?'

'Between midnight and morning. The moon was on the wane, and rose late – two nights before the battle started at Neuve Chapelle. This was south of here, near – what is the name of that village, Basilio? Haut-le-Bois?'

The slender vampire nodded, and after a moment, added, in a much thicker accent than his friend's, 'She spoke good French, nearly as good as your own, *Madama*. Yet with some accent.'

'Could you tell what sort?'

He shook his head. And indeed, reflected Lydia, one had to be very fluent indeed in a language to be able to tell whether a speaker had an accent, and where it might be from. (*Damn Jamie . . . HE could probably do it . . .*)

'Would you do this for me?' Lydia raised her eyes to Antonio Pentangeli's face. *A predator*, she thought, her heart pounding. *Who knows how many people he killed in Venice, since he himself was killed by its Master, and brought into the world of the Undead?* 'If you hear of this woman again – if you meet others who have been

40

propositioned by her – might I beg it as a favor, that you tell Don Simon about it?'

By Basilio Occhipinti's grimace he found the idea of taking such trouble grotesque – like her Aunt Lavinnia would look, if one of the scullery maids asked her to pass along love notes to the butcher's boy. But Antonio nodded, his dark eyes grave. 'I will, *bella donna.*'

'*Antonio*!'

'Think, dear heart.' The taller vampire laid his palm to Basilio's cheek, but his eyes, Lydia observed in the lantern-light, were flat and cold, doll-like as a shark's. 'Whoever she is, the little nurse, she has some scheme in mind and we know not what it is. Whoever she finds to help her, it will be someone who wants something that isn't blood. We don't know what sort of bargain will be made.'

He bent again over Lydia's hand. 'We shall keep our ears to the ground, Madame, like cowboys in an American dime novel, and will send you word of what we hear.'

Then they were gone.

They seemed to melt into the shadows, but Lydia was prosaically aware that in fact one or the other of them had simply used the same psychic aura that older vampires developed, to make her not notice them walking off down the communications trench, or scrambling inelegantly up its wall. Jamie practiced, diligently, keeping his mind focused when he was in the presence of the Undead, and could sometimes see them move. Lydia knew she should have done so also but had been simply too exhausted. In any case she knew Don Simon would not permit harm to befall her.

Nevertheless she trembled as the Spanish vampire led her back along the trench in the direction of the motorcar, her head aching and her heart beating fast. They were vampires. Charming and polite and well-dressed . . .

She recalled again the warmth of Antonio's lips on her hand. Stolen warmth. Stolen life.

Creatures of evil . . .

Yesterday she'd received a letter from her Uncle Richard, which had mentioned in passing (after lamentations about the difficulty in obtaining coffee and petrol) that two of the footmen who had enlisted last September – men whom Lydia had known since childhood – had been killed at Festubert. A third – Ned – had been returned, blind and crippled, to his family, who would have to support him for the remainder of his life.

So where lies the greater evil? She didn't know.

A thousand tales and warnings about supping with the Devil flooded to her tired mind, but she honestly couldn't think of any way of quickly tracking this other night-prowling nurse who had a *proposition*, a *partnership*, to offer the Undead . . .

And when she stumbled, there was Simon's hand – cold as marble through his glove and the sleeves of her coat and frock – supporting her arm.

Simon, whom Jamie had sworn he would kill, along with every other vampire who crossed his path . . .

42

He stopped, swung around. 'What's—'

A man flung himself down on them from the top of the trench. Lydia had an impression of uniform, but his head was bare. He was without rifle or pack, clutching a bayonet like a dagger. He slashed at her, seized her arm to drag her into the blow. She saw the gleam of reflective eyes, gasped at the fishy stench of him as Simon yanked the man away from her, tried to twist the weapon from his hand. Instead the soldier pulled his arm free of the vampire's grip – the grip that Lydia had seen bend steel – and flung Simon against the wall of the trench as if he'd been a child.

Lydia ran, stumbling in icy water and broken duckboards – *There has to be a ladder somewhere . . .*

But the soldier was fast. Hands gripped her waist, the reek of him clogged her throat; as she tried to wrench free she glimpsed the slimy glister of a fanged, deformed mouth gaping to bite. Then the man jerked, head falling forward, and Lydia yanked free as the filthy stink of her attacker's flesh was drowned in the sharp stench of splattering blood. Ysidro raised the entrenching-tool with which he'd struck the soldier's neck for another blow.

She sprang clear as Simon chopped down again with the metal blade, but soldier was still trying to rise, still trying to come at her. The third blow severed the head.

The body continued to crawl.

Methodically, Simon chopped with the pointed end of the tool into the spine – with all the horrific force of a vampire's preternatural strength – severing it, Lydia estimated, just below the first thoracic, and again below the first lumbar, vertebrae. The arms and legs were still moving as Simon caught her hand and dragged her along the trench. He kept firm hold of the bloodied entrenching-tool.

There might be others.

She knew from experience that they hunted in packs.

Four

'It was a *yao-kuei*, wasn't it?' Lydia whispered the name by which she'd first seen the revenants, three years previously in Peking. She pulled her tent-mate Nurse Danvers's greatcoat more tightly around her nightdress and dressing gown. Despite the small oil-stove beside which she sat, the tent was freezing. 'Jamie says *draugar* is the Icelandic word for creatures like that.'

'James would know such matters.' Don Simon brought her another cup of cocoa, as he had last night. There were times that Lydia felt the whole clearing station lived on cocoa.

Nurse Danvers had been coming off her rounds when Lydia returned, had helped her wash off all trace of her attacker's blood and had reaffirmed that Lydia had no cuts or scratches through which that blood could possibly have entered her system. The moment she'd finished this chore she had inexplicably (to her, at least) sunk down, fully dressed, on her own cot and dropped into Sleeping-Beauty-like slumber. Lydia had just been tucking a blanket over her when Don Simon had appeared, silently, at her side.

'I find it distressing,' the vampire went on, 'that the Scandinavians would *require* a word for, as you say, "creatures like that". Yet neither Antonio nor Basilio – nor indeed, any of the Undead to whom I have spoken, on either side

45

of No Man's Land – have mentioned seeing these Others.'

Lydia set the cup on the tent's wooden floor beside her cot, frowning. 'You're right.' A moment before, her revulsion at the thing that had attacked her, had consumed her – the deeper terror that she might somehow have been infected by the revenant's blood, that her own body might distort into a misshapen horror while her mind disappeared into the collective semi-consciousness of the brutes . Now that revulsion vanished before the puzzle of where this particular revenant had come from.

'I haven't heard the men in the wards speak of them, either,' she added. 'And they *do* speak of the vampires.'

She frowned, remembering poor Brodie (*He goes to hospital in Calais tomorrow, I'll have to bid him good luck before he leaves . . .*). She glanced across at Don Simon, warming his thin hands before the stove. She assumed he'd also examined his own flesh for any possibility of transfer of blood, in the three-quarters of an hour since he'd set her down outside the dim lights of the camp. *Did he make poor Captain Palfrey check his back? How did he explain matters to that well-meaning young man?*

She wondered if Palfrey could see, as she did, the glassy claws that the vampire state caused to grow in place of the fingernails. If Simon had used the psychic skill of the Undead to block from the young man's mind the huge scars that crossed the left side of his face and neck, where the talons of the Master vampire of Constantinople

46

had raked him in a struggle, five years before, to save Lydia's life.

She herself couldn't always see them.

She went on, 'My assistant, Mr Dermott, tells me some of the men say they've seen a ghost ambulance-wagon, or ghost stretcher-bearers...'

'That's Antonio and Basilio.' Don Simon's slight gesture was a dismissal. 'They often hunt in an ambulance-wagon.'

Lydia turned her face away, for a moment too shaken to speak. Tears flooded her eyes in spite of the fact that she knew, as he had said, that they preyed only on those dying already...

I should hate them all. I should hate HIM.

Don Simon watched her face without expression, a pale shape in the dark of the tent.

How can he be both things to me? Both friend and monster?

She was well aware how meticulously careful he was, never to let her or Jamie see him kill. *And it works*, she thought despairingly. *If we don't SEE it, part of our minds can pretend it isn't happening.*

Good heavens, maybe we DID see something of the kind and he made us forget it. Can he DO that?

She wouldn't put it past him.

She tasted over on her tongue the words, trying them out. *I don't want your protection. I don't want you watching over me. I want you to go away.*

She guessed that he wouldn't. *I'll just never see him at it again ... or maybe now and then, a glimpse from the corner of my eye ...* 'We

47

need to go back there.' She looked back at him once again in the dim glow of the stove. 'Now, before first light destroys its flesh. Jamie says sunlight doesn't burn them as quickly as it does vampires, but it will crumble their flesh and their bones to dust. Is that true?'

'It is, Mistress.'

'Then I need one to study. The blood on my frock is too mixed up with mud to examine clearly, even with Major Overstreet's microscope. And I should talk to men in that part of the trenches.' She opened her locker at the foot of her bunk and brought out her spare uniform (*I'll need to talk to Storeman Pratt tomorrow about another one – I am NOT putting the bloodied one on again no matter HOW many times it's boiled!*). 'Someone else must have seen it. We can at least get some idea of what direction it was coming from. Or, if it was German . . . Even if there were others with it, they'll have moved on by this time . . .'

'It shall be as you command.'

He vanished – or seemed to vanish, momentarily blocking her perception of his movement. Shuddering in the cold, Lydia dressed herself again quickly (*And God bless the woman who invented the brassiere!*) and gathered up the bloodied, mud-slathered garments in an old pillowcase. Handling them gingerly, she took a few minutes to cut swatches from the least-contaminated bloodstains, which she stowed in a candy tin at the bottom of her locker. By the time she checked her watch and buttoned on Danvers's borrowed greatcoat, and slipped from the tent with the incinerator-bound pillowcase clutched at arms-length in one hand, it was quarter past two.

Lydia recognized – vaguely – the place where the staff-car lurched to a stop. The damp night, though windless, was very cold, the far-off crashing of the guns to the north like metallic thunder. The effects of the cocoa were wearing off and Lydia felt tired to death and chilled to the marrow of her bones. She leaned forward to the front seat to glimpse Captain Palfrey's wristwatch – her own was the old-fashioned kind, pinned to her breast under a layer of greatcoat – and saw that it was past three.

'Will you be all right?' she whispered to Don Simon. First light would be in two hours. She estimated it was nearly two muddy, slogging miles from where they halted – in a welter of shell-holes and barbed wire – to the communication trench where they had been attacked.

'John has orders to return you safely to the clearing station, should circumstances separate me from you.' He took her hand in his own gloved one and led her toward the remains of the reserve trench, the glow of the shuttered lantern he carried swinging again across the glisten of mud, shattered steel and the red spark of rat eyes in the dark. As they descended the ladder once again she hoped Simon's sense of smell was more discerning than her own in the quagmire of stench: rotting flesh, old blood, cordite, feces, smoke . . . *A whole pack of revenants could be just around the bend of the trench and I'd never smell them.*

The communications trenches were dug in a series of angles to protect against blast, resulting in the sense of being trapped in a wet, filthy labyrinth. On the walls of the trench boards had been roughly fastened, arrows drawn in chalk or paint with directions written above: *1st Scots*, *2nd Lancs*, or, simply and more prosaically, *Rear. Bogs* . . . Without them, Lydia couldn't imagine how anyone could traverse this maze of head-high walls, zigzagged defiles and caved-in dugouts.

She found herself clinging to Don Simon's hand.

'Did you see his uniform?' she asked. 'Whether he was British or German? If these things are multiplying in the German trenches . . .'

'I would have heard,' returned the vampire. 'Many of us haunt both sides of the lines. In any event, what use would such creatures be? Unless their minds could be directed and controlled the danger would be too great. No general in his senses would take such risk.'

'But that may be why this woman – this dark-haired nurse – is seeking a vampire, don't you see?' Lydia glanced quickly across into her companion's face. 'You've said – many times – that a vampire can govern the actions of a living mind. Can summon at will those whose eyes he has looked into, can . . . can even some-times put himself literally into another's mind, if his victim is drugged, or insane. They're seeking a vampire . . .'

'Then they are fools,' returned Don Simon calmly. 'An old vampire, whose strength has waxed with time and who has been taught to manipulate the minds of the living, perhaps. A master vampire, or someone like Antonio, whose master instructed him in these ancient skills . . . Not all masters trust their fledglings to that extent. And so old a vampire will have doubtless learned not to put faith in the living – leaving aside the fact that no vampire, of any age, cares the purchase of a button about the wars of the living. We do not care, Mistress. As Antonio told you earlier tonight: *we do not care*. Not about our homelands, not about our families, not about those whom we loved in life. Nothing exists for us but the hunt. We know any other ties to be dangerous, and ties to the living, most dangerous of all.'

He paused for an instant where the communications trench in which they now picked their way branched, then turned right (*Welches*, said the sign), his strength helping Lydia find her feet where the duckboards were broken and the icy, filthy water soaked through her shoes.

'The Master of Prague, where these things have long bred, and the Master of Peking, have both affirmed to me, that even the strongest master vampire has no dominion over the minds of these things. If this nurse you have seen— *Carajo*!' He flinched at the sudden, earth-shaking thunder of an explosion that sounded nearly on top of them. Orange glare filled the sky. Another roar followed, and the splattering of torn-up earth, followed by the shouting and cursing of men.

'We're almost there!' Lydia seized Don Simon's hand again, her heart in her throat but her mind still calculating: *That shell was at least a hundred yards away . . .*

Around the corner ahead . . .

She snatched the lantern from his hand and slammed back the slide – no further need of precaution against snipers, not with what sounded like a full-on barrage starting – and ran, digging in her pocket for the rolled-up empty sandbags she'd brought to carry her prize. The ground jerked and the duckboards underfoot suddenly erupted with fleeing rats, swarming from their holes and pouring in a gray river up the side of the trench, as if the Pied Piper had blown his horn somewhere in the hellish cacophony of the darkness. *If there's a push on I'll lose this thing, or it'll be buried in a barrage . . .*

She heard Don Simon swear in Spanish behind her, and a shell went overhead with a noise like an oncoming train.

Am I being intrepid or stupid?

Her heart in her throat, not giving herself time to think, Lydia whipped around the angle of the trench and her lantern-light fell on the huddled black mass of the revenant, and a smaller form leant over it. A woman.

Lydia stumbled to a halt. A shuttered lantern stood near the revenant's severed head, and by its dim light Lydia saw the woman bend over the hacked and bloody body, doing something she couldn't see. As the figure raised its face, she had a momentary vision of a heart-shaped countenance framed in pulled-back dark hair, a rich mouth twisted in resolution and shock. The gleam of a silver cross, dangling around her neck.

Something else by the lantern, a satchel . . .

Another explosion shook the ground, closer this time, and the woman grabbed for something in her pocket. Don Simon's hand closed on Lydia's elbow and Lydia was dragged back around the protective angle of the trench. She saw the woman rise from beside the corpse – it was still aimlessly clawing around it with one hand – and flee down the trench, turning to throw something . . .

Don Simon yanked Lydia along the trench, and she realized what the other woman had flung instants before they ducked around the next angle and the massive shock wave of noise, oily heat and flying debris almost knocked her off her feet. *Grenade* . . .

Men surged, shouting, out of another communications trench, as the barrage intensified over their heads. Yells of 'Get out of it, boys!' mingled with the screaming whistles of officers and bellowed commands to re-form ranks. Don Simon's arm circled Lydia's waist and he dragged her along, slithering expertly through the struggling bodies. He froze as a shell howled overhead and pulled her back, judging the sound of it, Lydia thought . . . And sure enough, some dozen yards ahead of them the crash of its explosion made her head reverberate, and dirt and mud splattered her as the trenches caved in under the blow.

The noise hurt her bones, and the mud splattered on her glasses made it nearly impossible to see. Men formed up around them again into ranks, which flowed through the communications

53

trenches, Don Simon swimming against the tide. They came into a clear space of trench, the walls broken into craters by shells and the duckboards shattered underfoot. Men clattered past them, bearers carrying rolled-up blankets or the new-style litters, feet sinking – as Lydia's sank – into bottomless mud. Twice she stumbled, and glancing down saw she'd tripped over corpses. But every new explosion filled the air above the trenches with flying shrapnel and splattering bits of red-hot metal – *I hope Captain Palfrey has taken cover somewhere . . .*

He evidently had. His hands reached down from the trench-ladder as Lydia was helped up out of the darkness, and it was he who half-guided, half-carried her toward the road down which men were already rushing toward the trenches, to re-enforce the existing troops against the German 'push' that everybody knew was going to come the moment it was light.

I have to get back to the clearing station. The wounded are going to be pouring in any minute . . .

'I'm afraid the car was commandeered, M'am,' gasped Captain Palfrey, as they stumbled over the broken ground. 'I got their names, and units. The colonel's going to have words to say to their commanding officers—'

'The colonel?' Lydia stumbled, and sought in her pockets for some piece of cloth sufficiently un-soaked to make headway against the muck that smeared her glasses. The shell-fire was some-what behind them now, except for the occasional strays, and men still raced past them, packs

54

clattering, rifles in hand. Minds focused on what lay ahead.

Four miles back to camp . . .

'Colonel Simon.'

The first threads of daylight had not yet begun to dilute the darkness. Don Simon presumably knew how long it would take him to get to a secure shelter – *God knows where!* Reaction was setting in, and Lydia had to cling to Palfrey's arm to keep from falling as they plowed through the wilderness of mud and old shell-holes, her wet skirts slapping and tangling her feet. Rats still swarmed. Once the fighting stopped, the creatures would stream back, to feed on the dead.

Lydia thought she glimpsed, away in the darkness, the pale shape of an ambulance-wagon jolting, and wondered if it was really an ambulance-wagon or just Antonio and Basilio.

Passionately, cold and exasperation and despair overwhelming her, Lydia cried, 'Don't you know what he really is?'

Captain Palfrey took both her hands in his – warm and strong, like Jamie's, the capable hands of a man who understands horses and guns and tools – and his blue eyes held a gentle understanding. From his pocket he produced a clean – *clean!* – handkerchief, and stood while she took off her glasses and wiped the lenses.

Then with a little smile he tapped the side of his nose and said, 'Well, M'am, it's all a deep dark secret, of course . . . And he's warned me that all kinds of the most ridiculous stories are circulated about him. Nursery-tale stuff you'd hardly credit, like a combination of Count Dracula and Bluebeard. But I've guessed the truth.' His eyes shone in the first whisper of the coming dawn. 'He – and his Department – are probably England's best hope of winning the war.'

Five

In his tidy back room on Grafton Place, James Asher sat on the end of the bed and looked down into the narrow yard, glistening under gray morning rain.

And thought about the Others.

Hideous memories, most of them. Shambling figures in the dark of ravines, in the hills west of Peking. Red eyes gleaming in the tunnels of abandoned mines.

Lydia sitting on the muddy shore of one of Peking's artificial lakes, red hair glinting with the fires that consumed the last of the Peking hive, weeping . . .

Miraculously unhurt.

He'd known she was walking back into danger, just a little over two years later – back in November, four months ago, now. He'd said goodbye to her, his first full day on his feet after recovery from pneumonia. He'd gone to the train station with her, the sixth of November, the gray mists that drifted over the station platform still smelling ominously of leftover gun-powder from Bonfire Night. Lydia in her VAD uniform: the single small trunk beside her wouldn't even have contained her cosmetics before the war. After the porter took it away she'd clung to him, gawky and thin and stork-like, her cheek pressed to his (she had carefully removed her spectacles, as she always did before they embraced). Wordless.

He knew she might never come back from the fighting. Seventeen years on Her Majesty's Secret Service – and another decade and a half of following newspapers and reports – had made him sickeningly aware of what waited at the Front: machine guns, artillery that could kill at a distance of miles. And the White Horseman, Pestilence, more terrible than either.

Danger from the revenants, whom they had last seen in Peking, had been the farthest thing from his mind.

Looking back at their parting he couldn't believe he'd been that naïve. *Of course some government was going to hear about them sooner or later.*

Of course they'll try to make them into a weapon of war.

His studies had unearthed almost as many examples of similar beings in folklore as the study of vampires did: *draugar, haugbui,* the Celtic *neamh mairbh.* African and Caribbean zombies. Greek *vrykolak,* Chinese hungry ghosts, the barrow wights of ancient English legend. Things that came staggering out of their graves to feed – insatiably. The vampires of Prague, Don Simon Ysidro had told him, had been trying for centuries to get rid of them, to no avail.

And now one of them was in London.

Mrs Taylor – who rented out rooms in this tall, narrow house near Euston Station – had brought him up tea and bread and butter, rather to his surprise and unasked ('I seen yesterday as you was poorly, sir . . .'). He had spent nearly eighteen hours, since he had returned from his abortive visit to the Foreign Office yesterday afternoon, lying on the bed looking at the ceiling wondering if this was any of his business or not. He ate without much appetite, though he no longer felt feverish. Only deeply fatigued.

What he most wanted to do was pack up his slender belongings, take a cab (if he could find such a thing) to Paddington Station and be in Oxford tonight, playing hide-and-seek with Miranda and deciphering Lydia's latest letter from the Front.

What he would do instead, he already knew, was send another telegram to Mrs Grimes, and then go to the Wolf and Child on Chalton Street, to talk to publican Tim.

Think no more about it. Langham's confidential, between-you-and-me smile. *The matter is in hand.*

Asher moved his hand toward the now-cold teapot to see if there was another cup left in it, but instead lay down again. Two years previously, he had sworn enmity to the vampires of London and had destroyed most of the London nest . . . only to discover that those he had killed were the unreliable members whom the Master of London wanted to be rid of anyway.

Twelve years prior to that, at the end of the African war, he had tendered his resignation to the Foreign Office, being unable to put from his mind the young Boer boy he had killed – a good friend, so far as a spy living under cover is able to make actual friends – in the line of what the

Department considered duty. Even then he had known that swearing enmity to the Department would be futile and absurd, though he knew what they were. When he'd left Langham's office on that occasion, his chief had shaken his hand and said – with that confidential little smile – '*Au revoir*.' The words had been deliberately chosen. Nothing about Langham was accidental. *Until we meet again.*

Think no more about it . . .

Go back to Oxford and shout '*A plague on both your houses*!' from the window of the departing train.

A revenant was hunting in London. It was only a matter of time before the infection began to spread uncontrollably.

A knock like a siege engine hammered the door. 'Mr Asher, sir,' trumpeted young Ginny Taylor's adenoidal voice in the hall. 'There's a lady come t' see you.'

Asher levered himself from the bed, astonished at how much energy this took, and slid into his jacket. 'Thank you, Ginny,' he said to the girl – fourteen, clean-scrubbed, with a face that reminded him of the roan cob that used to pull his father's gig – as he stepped out into the corridor. 'Please tell her I'll be right down.'

'Professor Asher!' Josetta Beyerly sprang to her feet from the threadbare chair in the parlor window, strode across to grip both his hands. 'I didn't mean for them to drag you down here—'

'This is a respectable house,' replied Asher gravely. 'As Mrs Taylor would no doubt have

60

told you if you'd even thought about suggesting the possibility of coming up to a gentleman's room. I take it Mrs Grimes telegraphed you with her conviction that I'd taken ill again?'

'Why "good society" leaps to the automatic conclusion that every interaction between a woman and a man is of necessity immodest—' began the young woman indignantly; then she caught herself, and shook her head. 'It's all of a piece,' she sighed. 'A way of making women their own jailers . . . And yes,' she added, with her beautiful smile. 'Mrs Grimes wired me last night. Please.' She drew him back to the chairs by the window. 'Sit down, Professor . . . *Are* you all right?'

Bright brown eyes looked across into his as he took the seat opposite. Even in the blue-and-white uniform of a volunteer at First London General Hospital, she wore a little rosette of purple, green and beige ribbons that marked her as a suffragette (*And I'll bet she fights every day with the ward sister about it . . .*). He smiled a little, pleased by her stubborn adherence to a cause that many women had set aside at the start of the war because *we must all stick together . . .*

Strident though she was about her politics, Josetta had been Lydia's close friend since 1898, the year his wife had spent at a select finishing school for girls in Switzerland, where Josetta, five years the elder, had been the English mistress. And Josetta had been the gawky, bookish young heiress's only friend. Eighteen months later in England, it was Josetta who had secretly coached Lydia through the examination to get her accepted to Somerville College – an acceptance which had resulted in Lydia being disowned by her outraged father. A small legacy had enabled the one-time English mistress to remain in England, where she took day pupils in French and music to make ends meet, and now, at thirty-seven, she was active in a dozen causes, from votes for women, Irish independence and settlement houses to 'rational dress', the elimination of the House of Lords, and vegetarianism.

'I'm quite well,' Asher reassured her, though her dark brows plunged over her delicate nose at this. Evidently, he reflected, it was obvious he was lying. 'I was kept later than I'd planned by meetings, and in fact I was on my way to the post office to let Mrs Grimes know that I won't be home today either, nor probably tomorrow.'

'Is there anything I can do for you?' she asked. 'Do you have board at this place, or are you eating at one of the frightful cafés hereabouts? Come to dinner with me at my club, if you'd care to – the menu isn't much, but at least it would be an improvement on fried chips and sausage.' She smiled, reached across to pat his hand, still slim as a girl. 'Lydia did tell me to look after you.'

'Thank you.' Asher returned her smile, though he suspected that, to earn even the utilitarian Josetta's disapprobation, the food on offer at the Grosvenor Crescent Club must be mediocre indeed. 'I should like that.'

'Have you heard from her?'

'Not since before I left Oxford. But I know the fighting in Flanders has been heavy, so she may not have had time to write.'

62

While the former English mistress spoke of her own experiences with the casualties of the spring's first great 'push', and of her outrage against the propagandist posters which plastered the hospital (and indeed, two virulent examples of the genre glared from the wall of the parlor: *Women of Britain say 'Go!'* and *Lend your Five Shillings to your Country and Crush the Germans*), his mind sifted her words automatically. '. . . And of course they don't know any better. Most of those poor boys haven't been outside their own neighborhoods in their lives. The women who'd come into the settlement houses could give you chapter and verse about each others' grandfathers and great-aunts, but would regard Kensington as foreign soil . . .'

'There is something you can do for me,' said Asher, when Josetta finished her account of procuring books and magazines for the wounded men in London General. 'If you would be so kind. Do you still have connections with the settlement house in Camden Town? I have heard—' It was a bow drawn at a venture, but he guessed the query would at least bear some fruit – 'that there's been a . . . a mugger, or a slasher, working along the Regent's Canal. A man who attacks at night, and who stinks of dirty clothes and fish. It would help me enormously if you could ask some of the people down at the settlement house, or people in that neighborhood, if they've heard of such a thug making the rounds.'

Josetta regarded him curiously – like himself, he realized with a smile, sifting what he said, tallying in her mind what his purpose might be. 'And does this have something to do with these "meetings" that are keeping you in town?'

Though Lydia – Asher was fairly sure – never spoke to anyone of his former life as one of Her Majesty's Secret Servants, he guessed also that his wife's concerns for him, particularly in the years since he'd become drawn into the affairs of the vampires, had communicated themselves to her friend. Josetta may well have developed suspicions that he wasn't the retiring Oxford don that he appeared, though God knew what interpretation she'd put on his comings and goings. Exactly as he would have, had he been recruiting a political semi-radical for the Department for one of his networks abroad, he replied, 'It's just a matter of personal interest.' With a raised eyebrow and a look that said, *I know perfectly well you're not fooled, Miss Beyerly.*

She returned his secret smile. 'I'll see what I can find. Dinner tonight at seven?'

'Seven it is.'

The Wolf and Child stood at the corner of Chalton Street and Matilda Court, three doors from Weekes and Sons, Importers of Fine Silk, where the unfortunate Harry had been employed. A woman passed Asher in the doorway of the long, wood-paneled taproom: her electric-blue jacket faded and four years out of style, with the telltale mark pressed into her left sleeve by the frame of a sewing machine. The taproom was as quiet today as it had been the previous morning, with only a couple of neighborhood men consuming

64

a pint and a laborer's lunch of bread and cheese. But the lunchers avoided one another's eye, and there was worry in the face of the old man behind the bar as he watched the woman depart. 'Y' maun excuse us, sir,' he said as he fetched the pint of mild that Asher ordered. 'We're a bit moithered just now. Our man didn't show up to open—'

Asher made a gesture of casual acceptance, though cold stabbed him behind the breastbone, and the shock worse because it was unattended by much surprise. 'I'm in no lather.' He kept his accent rural, Shropshire, as he had yesterday morning when speaking with Tim . . . 'Hard lines on you, gaffer, him droppin' his work on you, though. Must be a chore findin' help with all these lads joinin' up.'

'Nay, Tim's not one to scarper, think on. That was his missus just now—' The old man nodded toward the door. 'Never come 'ome las' night, he didn't, and poor Masie at her wits' end over it. 'Tis not the same,' he added worriedly, 'since the start o' this war.'

No, thought Asher, laying his three-penny bit on the counter and looking thoughtfully toward the street, at least in part to conceal the anger that he knew was in his eyes. *No, things are not the same.*

He dreamed that night of Pritchard Crowell, a man he hadn't even thought of in nearly a decade.

Crowell was something of a legend in the Department. Asher had worked with him only once. In Mesopotamia in the early nineties they'd scouted

65

out opposition to Ottoman rule, and put together a network of sleeper agents in the Caucasus and in the desert country beyond Palmyra. The villagers often worked for German 'archaeologists' who coincidentally searched for their buried cities along proposed railway routes where troops might later be moved.

He recalled a wiry small man in his fifties, dark-eyed and dark-haired and absolutely unobtrusive. A wrinkle-threaded face, a hawk-bill nose and a touch with picklocks that half the professional burglars in London might have envied, and a chilly ruthlessness which, at that time, Asher had sought to make his own. The job, and the job only, existed, and everything else, including one's own survival, merely facilitated whatever one had been ordered to do.

'We are weapons . . .' Asher heard again that low voice – a middle-range tenor and like everything else about him, expressionless and unremarkable – against the Mixolydian wail of voices outside the inn at El Deir where they sat. Even through his dream he smelled the burnt languor of coffee, the stink of dust, camel dung, harsh tobacco and *ras el hanout*. 'If one is in a fight for one's life, one wouldn't thank a knife that turned round in your hand and asked questions. One does what one has to, my lad, and forgets about it afterwards . . . Clean as you go, and don't look back.'

This applied, Asher recalled, to the members of one's own network – one's friends among the Bedu or on the Turkish Army supply staffs in Constantinople. They were warned ('When feasible,' Crowell had qualified, casually) that Higher Purposes might require them to be cut adrift. Asher remembered the occasion on which Crowell had let the population of an Armenian village which had sheltered them be massacred by the sultan's tame bandits, rather than give them a warning which would have revealed that the Turkish Army codes had been broken.

One does what one has to . . .

The pragmatist in Asher's soul had admired Crowell's uncanny expertise in the sheer craft of spying – of getting into places, of winkling shards of information from men and women wholly committed to Britain's enemies. He always had an astonishing plethora of information at his fingertips, and was eerily expert at slipping through shadows to escape and bring the 'goods', whatever they were upon any given occasion, back to Langham and the others at the Department. He was an uncannily brilliant guesser. The patriot in Asher had striven to emulate what he saw, both the cold virtuosity and the single-minded loyalty to his Queen. In his dream now, Asher saw him as he'd seen him in those days: clever, cold, unobtrusive and ruthless.

Forget about it afterwards. Clean as you go.

Someone paused for a moment in the doorway of the little *meyhane* where they sat: Asher caught the shadow out of the corner of his eye, and his glance went to the silver coffee pot on the low table between them to see who it was, so he would not be seen to turn. The man was gone before Asher made out the image in the round belly of the polished metal.

But he thought it was Langham.

And just as he woke he thought he smelled the fishy, greasy reek of the Others, that the visitor had left behind.

Over supper, earlier in the evening, at Miss Beyerly's club – mutton every bit as bad as Asher had suspected it would be – Josetta had told him that yes, she had heard rumor among the laborers who worked nights along Regent's Canal, that there was a bludger afoot, mostly in the hours between midnight and three. So far he'd killed a whore and a seven-year-old pickpocket who'd been sleeping in a doorway and had, so the story went, eaten some of their flesh. Hungry Tom, he was called in the neighborhoods, or Tom the Ogre, though nobody had seen him nor knew whether his name was actually Tom or something else. The police were claiming that no such person existed.

'*The matter is in hand,*' Langham had said, with his sly little secret smile.

Langham wants the thing 'for King and country'. Asher knew it as he knew his own name. *He may not know precisely what it is. Only that it can be used.*

And that its use will redound to his credit.

Looking across the coffee table at Crowell in his dream – though Asher knew that in fact, after a lifetime of hair-breadth escapes and false rumors of demise Pritchard Crowell had succumbed to a lucky shot by a Bosnian merchant's blunderbuss in 1899 – he thought, *Crowell would have put Tim the publican out of the way.*

'Of course the police would rather that such a

68

person doesn't exist,' had sniffed Josetta after dinner, stirring coffee like diesel oil in the old-fashioned gaslight of one of the club's small parlors. 'Both the victims are the sort of people the government has been pretending for years are criminals who deserve what they get, or who no longer live in the up-to-date London of the twentieth century . . . Certainly not worth avenging, with the cost of slaughtering Germans to be thought of. And there are no reliable witnesses . . .'

Except Tim, thought Asher, in his dream of Mesopotamia. *Tim, who saw the body of the creature's most recent victim, in the fog of the alleyway behind the Wolf and Child.*

'It pays to be tidy,' Crowell was saying to him, emphasizing the point with one tiny forefinger: he had hands like an eleven-year-old boy. His wrinkled eyelids puckered. 'You never know who's going to talk to whom; what blithering postman is going to remark to his friend who works in Army Intelligence some day, "Ach, that man who's calling himself Martin and drawing pictures of ships in the harbor, I knew him in Strasbourg three years ago when he was named Schmidt . . ." And then it will be you for the high jump, my lad, and the whole show we've set up here blown to kingdom come. And nobody would ever associate the disappearance of the local postman with some traveling artist who'd scarcely even met the man . . .'

Clean as you go.

Crowell might be gone, reflected Asher, waking in the darkness of his rented lodging. But Langham remained.

He turned the dream over in his mind.

And there were a dozen or a hundred fledgling Crowells in the wings, waiting to take his shape, and continue his business.

After killing his young friend Jan van der Platz, Asher had quit the Department, when he'd realized that he was one of them.

Then he smelled blood, quite close to him, and knew suddenly he was in mortal danger.

His eyes flew open to darkness and a cold hand crushed down over his mouth, almost smothering him, while another had him by the wrist even as he snatched for the knife under his pillow.

The hand released its grip an instant later and Asher heard a curse of pain, and knew that his assailant had been burned by the chains of silver he wore.

Vampire . . .

Six

Lydia didn't even stop at her tent, just went straight on to the fluoroscope chamber and was setting up the apparatus when Captain Calvert barged in looking for her. 'Good, you've heard, then— Good God, woman, where've you been?' was his only comment on her muddy and disheveled state, and he was out the door and into the surgical tent before she drew breath to reply. 'Brickwood, I'm devastated but I'm going to have to ask you to stay,' his voice went on as his steps retreated across the tent. 'Go in and wake up Danvers, would you? Matron, can you get me . . .?'

The tidal wave of wounded didn't slacken for another thirty-six hours. The Germans had hit the line hard, over a front of two miles: first came the men wounded in the preliminary shelling, then the thousands who'd been mowed down, like standing wheat before a reaper's scythe, as they'd scrambled up out of the trench to meet the onrushing line of the enemy. The situation was not helped when four German shells landed on the village of Pont-Sainte-Félicité itself, turning the marketplace to rubble and killing two orderlies. Colonel St-Vire wired furiously up and down the line for more surgeons, more nurses and more orderlies, and later Thursday morning Lydia found herself administering chloroform at

71

the tables of surgeons she'd never seen before, Captain Glover from the First Lancashire and Captain Bryce-Bayington who looked young enough to be one of Jamie's students back in Oxford. Matron – Sister Flavia – came as close to cursing as Lydia had ever heard her do over the three extra nurses who arrived ('Nurses! I shouldn't hire a one of them to make tea for a proper nurse!'), and just before the Germans started shelling Pont-Sainte-Félicité a second time – as Lydia was on her way out of the fluoroscope tent – Lydia recognized one of the new nurses as the young woman she'd seen in the trenches last night, bending over the corpse of the revenant.

The young woman who had tossed a grenade at the corpse, either to destroy it or because she'd seen Lydia and Don Simon.

The young woman who was looking for a vampire with *a partnership to offer you* . . .

For a moment Lydia only stood in startled surprise. But there was no mistaking the wide forehead, the sturdy shape of the shoulders, the dark widow's peak and snub nose. And like her own, she noted, this younger girl's blue-and-white VAD uniform was blotched and splattered with mud – *She must have been bundled straight into a truck and ordered to come here just as she got back to . . . to wherever it is she's assigned, with . . .*

With what?

The revenant's blood? One of its still-flexing hands?

Then Burke bellowed from within the surgical

72

tent 'Asher! Where t' bloody 'ell's them snaps?' and Lydia dashed to his side with the films that she had been taking between filling in as an assistant in the surgery. A few minutes later she glimpsed Captain Palfrey helping the orderlies carry men in from the pre-operative tent, working alongside the Indian motor-mechanics and the cook. Then German shells hit the village again, close enough that fragments of brick and wood clattered like rain on the canvas walls of the tent.

She sponged the other woman from her mind.

She worked on into the night, existing on hot tea and the biscuits Danvers's grandfather had sent her yesterday, which her tent-mate gamely divided among the surgical staff. It occurred to her that she ought to be terrified, when a shell struck particularly close, but she found that associating with vampires for the past eight years had had the salutary effect of making her less inclined to panic: *I can run away screaming anytime I want, which wasn't the case when I was dealing with that horrid Rumanian count or whatever he was in Scotland . . . and if I get killed here, nobody else is likely to suffer.*

James was safe, wherever he was.

Miranda was safe back in Oxford.

These men need help.

She stepped out once, around two in the morning of the nineteenth, and thought she glimpsed the pale shape of Don Simon, standing in the doorway of what was left of the town church across the green from the surgical tent, like the Angel of Death in his trim brown uniform.

73

To make sure he's on hand if I need rescuing, if one of those shells hits? Or just waiting for the next man to be moved into the Moribund Ward?

How many others of them are around, where I can't see them?

Not many, she reflected, *with shells still striking the village . . .*

Bearers passed her, carrying a man from the drop-off point by the road into the pre-operative ward. *I'd better get back.*

When she looked again the vampire was gone, if indeed he ever had been there. She was sufficiently tired now that she wasn't certain of what she saw.

At least the surgeons got to sleep most of last night.

The next time she emerged, toward dawn ('There's tea in the mess tent,' Captain Calvert had said, 'and you *will* go and have a cup and sit down for ten minutes'), she passed the door of the clearing tent, the flap tied open so that bearers could carry men in. She saw the little dark-haired nurse kneeling beside one of the cots, her arms around the shoulders of a man who lay there, freckles starring like spattered ink in his waxen face and covered with mud and blood.

'You're alive!' the young woman cried, covering the man's hands with kisses as he raised them to touch her hair. 'Dear God, I thought I'd never see you again—'

'Tuathla,' he murmured. 'Well you know there's no Jerry livin' that's yet forged the gun that'll shoot the shell that'll end my love for you, *mo chroí,* so don't you be thinkin' it.'

74

'*Miss* Smith!' Matron materialized like a ghost from the dense gloom of the lantern-lit ward. 'If you will *kindly* come over here and lend us the assistance you presumably volunteered to give to your country—'

The dark-haired nurse scrambled to her feet. 'Yes, M'am. Of course, M'am.'

Educated English. Little trace of the graceful Irish drawl that lilted her red-haired lover's speech. Miss Smith . . . Tuathla Smith . . . or was *tuathla* some kind of County Liffey endearment? Lydia's mind seemed to be turning things over very slowly, and she started as a firm hand took her elbow and Captain Calvert said, 'I told you to get into the mess tent and *sit down* for ten minutes, Dr Asher. Bearers are still coming in and we're in for a long morning of it.'

She and the captain were still in the mess tent – Captain Calvert turning to give orders to Trent, the head bearer, to marshal the walking wounded to help carry from the drop-off point – when a shattering explosion sounded from the direction of the river, and not only fragments of dirt and stone rained on the clearing station, but water, as if it had been flung from buckets. Instants later Storeman Pratt raced in, white-faced – the stores tent stood only a dozen feet from the stream – and cried, 'Bugger it, Captain, Jerry's blown the bloody bridge!'

Calvert said something worthy of neither an officer nor a gentleman and sprang to his feet. The surgeon at the other end of the table – a saturnine French Colonel pulled in from God knew where – cursed quietly in his native

75

language and added, 'What they've been after all along, *en effet*. To cut the medical help off from the lines.'

'Finish your tea,' ordered Calvert, as Lydia began to rise. 'You, too, Colonel Lemoine, sir. Be back in the tent in fifteen minutes. The men can rig a causeway out of the rubble . . . God knows we've got plenty of that,' and went tearing off in quest of Colonel St-Vire.

'At least now they've got it,' added Dr Lemoine – Lydia tried to remember what the collar insignia on his pale-blue greatcoat denoted – 'let us hope they leave off wasting shells on men already incapable of harming them, and let us get on with our business. Before last year,' he went on, holding aside the tent-flap for Lydia to pass through before him, 'I gave thirty years of my life to my country's army. But as I learned more and more about the monstrous "improvements" in weaponry I always wondered in my heart: how can we loose such horrors upon living men? Shells that can reduce men – men with wives and children – to blots of jam from five miles away. Airships to drop bombs on women and children minding their own business in their own homes. Battleships to bar food and medicines from our enemy's country, so that all will starve together – old men, women, children.'

In the dust-choked morning haze Lydia saw his jaw work with fury and pain.

'And yet I swear to you, Madame, when I see such things as they do – shelling the hospitals where the wounded lie, torpedoing passenger ships when they know full well that the innocent

76

will perish – I think nothing is too savage to do to them in retaliation. No action of ours is too horrible, if it but makes them throw up their hands and cry, *I quit!*'

His dark brows pulled together, a handsome man of about Jamie's age, with gray flecks in his pencil mustache and the features of a sorrowing king.

Then he glanced across at her – he was taller than she by three or four inches – and made himself smile. 'And you, Madame? I had heard the British Army refused to accept female surgeons—'

'Well, they do. And even if they didn't, I'm not a surgeon, you know. My research was on glandular secretions, so I just signed on just as a regular volunteer. But when Colonel St-Vire heard I knew how to operate a fluoroscope apparatus he had me reassigned to the unit and put me in charge of the x-ray photography, and they pull me into the surgical tent whenever they need to. I couldn't remove a splinter on my own, but I do know how to administer anesthetic, and what all the equipment is for, and the sight of blood doesn't bother me. Here,' she added sadly, 'that's enough.'

Every spare orderly and bearer, along with the ambulance drivers and the walking wounded, were streaming down to the river. In the horse-lines, the animals squealed and milled in panic. Lydia heard a motorbike roar away into the iron-gray morning, to get the Engineers from Headquarters. Now that the profile of the town was considerably flattened she could see the line of ambulance-wagons – both motorized and horse-drawn – lined up waiting on the far side of the river, while their drivers scrambled to pull free the men and horses from those who'd been hit on the bridge itself. The screams of dying mules mingled with the brutal roar of the guns.

I was in that. Lydia felt a sort of distant, tired wonder at the fact. *Simon and I. I tripped over a corpse, and the hands of other dead men were sticking through the walls where dugouts had collapsed . . .*

She thought she glimpsed Captain Palfrey in a group of mechanics, black with soot and mud and carrying beams from the ruins.

'And Monsieur Asher?' asked Lemoine gently.

'In England.' Lydia's throat closed at the recollection of the misty train platform: the strength of his arms, the warmth of his body against the gray of that bitter morning. At the thought of Miranda at the nursery breakfast table, solemn with a goodbye that she thought was only for a day or two. ('I'll see you when I come home, darling . . .') It was a moment before she could speak. 'With our daughter. I try not to think of them, at times like these.'

She turned, to go back into the charnel house of the tent.

'And for that—' Lemoine's quiet voice turned grim, 'the Boche deserve whatever we can do.'

By eleven in the morning, when the surgeons finished the last of the desperate cases, the Royal Engineers arrived with planks, beams and struts to repair the bridge. Captain Calvert ordered Lydia back to her tent and to bed. She could see

78

at least a dozen motor trucks, and twice as many other vehicles – horse-drawn farm carts, milk floats, staff-cars – waiting on the far bank and all overflowing with wounded. The drivers, and many of the walking wounded, waded out into the Lys to fasten beams to the broken foundations of the stone bridge's arches. 'When they're done,' said Violet Brickwood, falling into step with her, 'they'll all come across at once and it will be all harry in the surgery again. I hope somebody's making the surgeons rest.'

Once in their tent, Lydia lay down in her clothes and passed out as if she'd had a pipe of opium.

And dreamed of the revenant. Dreamed of being tied to a pillar in that horrible lightless room in Peking, listening to the creatures – the *yao-kuei* – smashing through the doors and windows only feet away from her. Dreamed of whatever-his-name-was, that colleague of Jamie's who'd been infected with the creatures' blood, his eyes gleaming like a rat's in the dark and his grip brutally strong on her arm, gasping *Extraordinary. Never been here in my life but remember it . . .* as the last of his mind dissolved into the dim hive of the revenants' collective consciousness, as he touched her face with his bloody and reeking hand.

Simon, she thought. *Simon came and saved me . . .*

And through her dream she heard his voice, like silk chilled from winter midnight, *Mistress . . .*

In her dream she was back on her cot in the nurses' tent, Simon's hand gentle on her shoulder, shaking her. She sat up, and threw herself into

79

his arms, weeping: wanting Jamie, wanting Miranda, wanting to be back in Oxford researching pituitary secretions and wanting the world to be the way the world had always been. No shell-fire. No terror. No watching young men die under her very hands, no cold calm x-ray pictures of shrapnel lodged in organs that couldn't be mended . . .

She whispered, 'I want Jamie . . .'

The tent was silent. No camp noises, no gunfire. Just afternoon sunlight, indescribably sweet, filtering through the dirty white canvas, and the smell of grass and roses, which told her this was a dream. Don Simon, perched on the side of her cot, wore his colonel's uniform, brass buttons winking in the light.

Does HE dream of afternoon sunlight and the smell of roses, lying in his coffin in the daytime hours?

His grip on her was strong and reassuring, the slender shoulder and steel-hard arm within the sleeve as real as anything she had ever felt. His face, in its frame of cobweb-pale hair, was the face of the living man he'd once been, save for the eyes.

His hand stroked her hair. 'Would you have me set him before you?'

She wiped her eyes. In her dream, though she wasn't wearing her glasses, she saw perfectly well. 'It wouldn't be the same,' she said. 'I mean, I should know it was just a picture . . . a very, very accurate one, since you can walk in his dreams, the way you walk in mine . . . The way you're walking in mine right this minute.'

''Tis the best I can give you, lady.' He moved

to put his hand to her cheek and then, as if he had seen the horror of her nightmare, drew it back with the gesture unmade. 'I would fain do more, were it in my power.'

He is in my mind, thought Lydia. *Right at this moment. Asleep in his coffin, wherever it's hidden . . .*

This is how he convinced that poor imbecile Captain Palfrey of his bona fides. I'll bet Palfrey's positive he's seen Don Simon by daylight, positive that he showed him unimpeachable proofs of the genuineness of this Secret Department of his . . . Positive of God knows what else! All because at some point Simon looked into his eyes, and later walked in his dreams – as she knew the old and skillful among the vampires could do – *and convinced him that these things really happened. That those dreams were real memories.*

I really should hate him.

But he was an old, old friend, and there was infinite comfort in the strength of his arms.

'I just want things to be the way they used to be,' she said at length. 'Living in Oxford, I mean, with Jamie and Miranda, and the worst one would see in the newspapers would be bunfights about who actually reached the South Pole first. I know it can't be that way again.' She sat up a little, and Don Simon handed her a perfectly clean white linen handkerchief, to blow her nose. 'I just – this is so hard.'

'Did you not weep for the dying,' replied the vampire in his soft voice, 'and fear for your life, and curse the stupid uselessness of it all – did you not pray that the world will somehow heal before your daughter grows to be aware of its horrors – you would be no more human than the fools and monsters that let this war begin. I have had centuries of watching war and stupidity, Mistress, and they grow no better, I am sorry to say. Your courage is the wine of hope to the men you work with, as well as to those you save. To James as well, I think, and to your child. It keeps their hearts beating. I am sorry you are in pain.'

She wrapped her hand around his, pretending (*I shouldn't . . .*) for a time that he was the living man he had been . . .

Although goodness knows as a living man he was probably a bigoted Catholic and a friend of the Grand Inquisitor and an enemy of England and a firm believer in the humoral theory of medicine. He probably beat his valet, too.

'Thank you,' she said simply, and raised her head from his shoulder. 'I've seen the woman – the one who was hunting the vampires, and looking for the revenant last night. She's one of the extra VADs who came in last night, her name is Smith – Tuathla Smith, I think . . . Oh, bother,' she added, as the tent-flap opened and Matron came in, and suddenly the light changed and Don Simon was gone and the sound of shelling, though no longer close enough to shake the ground, pounded the air with a constant, terrible roar. She heard men shouting above the grinding roar of a fleet of motors . . .

Lydia sat up, and fumbled for her glasses, on the plank floor beside the cot. By the light it was about four in the afternoon. For one moment she recalled that she'd dreamed about roses . . . roses and sunlight . . . then she picked up her much-creased cap from beside the pillow, pinned it on, and said, 'How many of them are there? Should I go to surgery, or the fluoroscope room?'

'Fluoroscope.' Matron spoke over her shoulder as she leaned over Violet's cot. 'Come on, Miss Brickwood, they've got the bridge fixed and the ambulances are coming in. There's tea in the mess tent, and sandwiches,' she added, as Lydia ducked through the flap.

For the next fourteen hours Lydia alternated between working the fluoroscope and assisting whichever of the three surgeons needed help: dripping chloroform with a steady hand, retracting the edges of wounds so that shards of metal could be fished out, clamping off blood vessels and stitching shut flesh and organs so that Captain Calvert or Captain Burke or Colonel Lemoine could get on with the next man. Well after sunrise on the following day – the twentieth – the last of the urgent cases was finished, though the hammering of the German guns had eased many hours before. A dozen of the last group in the ambulances were German prisoners, muttering confusedly: *Haben wir gewonnen?*

Lemoine retorted, in the same tongue, 'You have lost – as you will lose all in the end.'

But Captain Burke only patted his patient's hand and said, 'Nowt t'worry reet now, lad,' as Lydia signed the orderlies to carry the shattered man into the fluoroscope room to see where the shrapnel was buried.

When they were finished at last Colonel St-Vire ordered the whole surgical staff, save for himself, to their tents: 'And I'd better not see one of your faces for the next eight hours, understand? I hear we held the line and pushed Jerry back. It'll be awhile before they try again.'

'Sir, can you tell the neighbors to keep it down?' Captain Calvert pointed east, in the direction of the Front and the thunder of the guns. 'I can't see *how* I'm to get my beauty rest with that *frightful* din going on . . .'

''Ud take more'n eight hours' kip, think on, to render – hrrm! – *some* people beautiful . . .'

Lydia returned to her tent without the slightest thought for Miss Smith, lay down again, and was asleep within moments, dreaming of arteries and kidneys, of pancreatic ducts and lobules, with a sensation of walking in some wonderful garden without anyone's life being at stake, only to view these wonders at her leisure.

When she woke up, and washed (*finally!*) and brushed her hair and had bacon and porridge and tea in the mess tent, and felt herself again ('Be ready to be on at six, Dr Asher . . .'), she went to the ward tent in quest of the little dark-haired volunteer with the heart-shaped face.

And found that she was gone. Nor was there any sign of the red-haired, freckled soldier she'd sat beside, though two men recalled seeing them ('She bust out weepin' like a babe, M'am, an' cried out his name . . . Danny? Davy? Harry? Su'thin' like that.') While Lydia had been sleeping, trucks and ambulances had been departing steadily, carrying the most stable of the men back to the base hospital at Calais. Hundreds had already gone.

Matron – unsurprisingly – had barely had time to scribble down the names of the men as they were brought in, and the nature of their wounds. She thought the extra volunteers had come in from the Friends' ambulance station at Neuve Chapelle, and possibly – she wasn't sure – from the base hospital.

There was no Nurse Smith listed anywhere.

Seven

'Lay thy crest,' growled a voice like chains stirred in a pot of blood. 'An' I wanted ye dead I'd have had the throat out o' you ere this.'

Asher sat up in his narrow bed. He could see nothing in the darkness – the room's shutters were fast – but he could smell where the vampire sat, and feel the weight of him on the side of the mattress. A stench of graveyard mold and dirty clothing.

Lionel Grippen.

The Master of London.

The weight shifted and a match scratched. As Grippen turned up the gas Asher saw the familiar form, tall and heavy-built, clothed in a frock coat ruinous with age and a waistcoat of Chinese silk spotted with old blood. Greasy black hair, thick as a horse's tail, spilled from beneath the brim of a shallow-crowned beaver hat and framed a face fleshy and thick, a nightmare of centuries of uncaring murder.

The vampire flexed his hand a couple of times and dug a kerchief from his pocket, to wrap on over the burn the silver had left.

'You're seeking this revenant,' said Grippen. 'What've ye found?'

'That someone's screening his movements.' If the master vampire's aim was to hide the revenant himself, Asher was fairly certain Grippen would, indeed, have killed him – or had him killed by the living men in London whose debts he paid, whose affairs he protected, whose dreams he read and who followed his orders without asking who he was or why he wanted things done.

Two years ago, after Asher had killed most of the London nest, Grippen had broken up the ring of henchmen centered on the East End tavern called the Scythe. Asher guessed he'd put together another.

'Germans, you think?'

'There's a nest of the things in Prague.' Asher reached for the shawl he'd spread over his blankets and dragged it up around his shoulders, for the room, though stuffy, was bitterly cold. 'It's certainly a more effective way of destroying civilian morale even than Zeppelin raids. And it could be easily done, by infecting a man and bringing him across immediately, before he starts to transform. In a way I hope it's that, rather than that the condition has developed spontaneously, for God only knows what reason—'

The vampire growled, with the first display Asher had ever seen from him, of uneasiness or fear. 'That can't happen, can it?'

'So far as I can find out, nobody knows how these things first started. They spread through contamination of the blood, but the original source has to have developed it somehow. Which means, it can develop again.'

Grippen whispered, 'God save us, then.'

'I've been saying that for a long time,' returned Asher. 'However the thing came here, the Foreign Office – or men in the Foreign Office – are hunting it, not to destroy it, but to capture it . . . to use it for their own purposes. If that hadn't been the case already I think my former chief, Langham, would have recruited me, instead of warning me off.'

'Faugh! There's the Quality for you.'

Asher couldn't quarrel with him there. 'When did you first see him? And where?'

'Limehouse. Candlemas, thereabouts.' His English had a flatness strongly reminiscent of American, even after three centuries; as a philologist Asher could not help his mind from marking it as Elizabethan. 'Killed a newsboy that was sleepin' rough. Tore him up somethin' savage. Later I smelled him in the fog, near the hospital in St James Road, and I think he killed a whore in the Canal Road near the Kingsland Basin. Leastwise that's what Gopsall tells me, that runs the Black Dog near there. I never actually seen the thing.'

'And it killed a man in an alleyway behind Chalton Street, between King's Cross and Euston, Monday night. The body disappeared. So did the only positive witness. If German agents were behind it, they'd publicize it. They'd see to it that its victims were found – and they might well see to it that its victims were more than prostitutes and homeless newsboys. The Department is covering its tracks.'

'Faugh,' said the vampire again. 'And you look down on *us*, for killin' a whore here and there. You're not sayin' they're lettin' the thing rove free?'

'I don't think so.' Asher shook his head. 'I think they're hunting it – or someone *in* the Department

88

is using the Department's resources to hunt it, while keeping it quiet.'

'For Christ's sake, why?'

'To avoid panic. And, I suspect, to capture the thing to see if we can use it ourselves . . . And the man who captured it would, of course, get a fat promotion and maybe a knighthood if it turns out to be useful.'

The vampire grimaced in disgust – not, Asher was certain, from any moral objection, but at the unworkable stupidity of the idea. Though susceptible to destruction by the light of the sun, the Others, Asher knew, moved about underground for a few hours longer than could vampires, who fell unwakeably asleep with the sun's rising. Like their cousins the vampires they were tremendously strong, and would devour vampires in their coffins if they found them.

'I've been warned off. Unless the condition *has* somehow developed spontaneously – which I pray to God isn't the case – this creature was brought to this country and somehow got loose, which tells me that whoever brought it here has no idea what they're dealing with.'

Grippen snarled again. 'So what do we do?'

Asher stifled the surge of anger at *we* from a walking corpse that had drunk the blood of the living, that had used their deaths to fuel its unholy powers, for over three hundred years. A creature that had kidnapped his child two years ago. Though he had recovered Miranda safe he had sworn to kill it, and all those like it . . .

I am no more part of WE with you than I am with Langham . . .

But, of course, he was.

That was why he was angry.

The revenants were a plague a thousand times worse than the vampire, for they multiplied without conscious volition. And they could not be negotiated with.

The contagion of their being had to be extirpated before it spread.

And whomever it was who had brought one to England – for whatever purpose – had to be found. And destroyed.

He was aware that Grippen was watching him with cynical amusement. In addition to smelling his blood, the vampire had felt that flush of heat that had gone through him and knew – from centuries of observing humankind – exactly what emotion had kindled it.

'How large a network do you command in London these days?' asked Asher after a moment. 'How many observers can you call on?'

'Pah.' The vampire scowled, a horrible sight. 'Damnéd war. Run by a damnéd crew of rabbit-sucking pimps. Half the men in London have turned their backs on their families and homes, to go slaughter cabbage-eaters in Flanders muck, and for why? Because of lies these pribbling whoresons have conjured about country and King, making a man ashamed to tell 'em he'd rather not go die so England can keep its grip on a passle of colonies oversea!'

'Instead of sending them dreams in their sleep about how worthy of trust *you* are? And how they owe *you* their lives . . .'

Grippen jabbed a clawed finger at him. 'None

o' your backchat! You whored for 'em yourself, by what Simon tells me. And pimped others to give you what help you sought.'

'I did,' replied Asher quietly. 'I did indeed. I apologize for my words.'

'Hmph. What help d'you seek? 'Tis mostly women and street brats I command these days, and Papist Irish who refuse to sign up 'cause they're too busy runnin' guns from the Germans to the Irish Volunteers. Scum.' The vampire shrugged, as if he spoke of roaches on the wall.

'I'm surprised to see you here,' remarked Asher, changing the subject, rubbing his wrist where the vampire's grip, however fleeting, had driven the silver links hard into the flesh. 'I thought all the vampires were at the Front.'

'And so they be.' Grippen seated himself again on the edge of the bed. Nearby in the darkness the bells of St Pancras chimed two, and even with the shutters and curtains tightly closed the night smelled of dank fog and the soot of trains. 'The more fools they and bad cess to the lot of 'em, swillin' like piggins at a trough. Those that're masters of the cities they rule'll find their error, when they come back to find some upstart's moved in on Paris or Munich or Rome and set up housekeepin' . . . I thought I'd stay here and watch my patch. And a damn good thing, with this clammy wight that should be in its grave prowlin' about spreadin' its contagion. Fine homecomin' that'd be, to get back and find London eye-deep in the things. Has that sneaking Papist whoreson—'

Meaning, Asher knew, Don Simon Ysidro.

91

'—got anythin' to say of it?'

Asher shook his head, and the vampire's eyes glinted, as if he guessed where Ysidro was and why.

But Grippen kept his peace, and after a moment Asher said, 'Find out if you can where this thing has been sighted or smelled, where rumor has placed it. If it's staying by the canal it can come and go through fog, and through the sewer outfalls. You say you learned of it first six weeks ago – find if there's any word of sightings before that. And keep your ear cocked for word that anyone else is seeking it, or that any who've seen it have disappeared.'

'There's enough disappear in this city without help of revenants, or them as seeks 'em. Christ, you think vampires could dwell anyplace where the poor was kept track of? Where'll I find you?'

'I'm going up to Oxford in the morning.' The thought of the train journey made his bones creak like an overladen bridge, but if he were to stay in London for any time there were things he wanted to fetch, to say nothing of seeing Miranda. 'I should be back Sunday, I'll be staying—'

He paused on the words, as Langham's jowly face and watery, penetrant eyes flashed across his thoughts and he remembered what his old master Pritchard Crowell had taught him, about making things look like accidents. *The wicked flee where none pursueth*, Holy Writ (and Asher's pious and long-deceased father) declared . . . and, frequently, Asher had found, the same could be said of the deranged. Yet it was a truism in the Department, particularly 'abroad', that in some circumstances it was better to flee and be thought deranged (or wicked) than to stop and be picked up by the opposition and shot as a spy.

In other circumstances, of course, flight could be just what the opposition was waiting for you to do.

'I'll put an advert in *The Times*,' he said. 'You still go by the name of Graves?'

The vampire's smile widened unpleasantly. 'That's me.'

'Mine'll be under the name of Scragger.'

'Dr Asher, M'am.' Eamon Dermott laid aside the film plate and turned to Lydia as she came into the fluoroscope tent, still puzzling over Matron's notes and the absence of Nurse Smith. The murmur of voices and clink of metal on china drifted faintly through the wall from the surgical tent, but held nothing of the frantic note of the 'big push' of yesterday and the day before. Down by the river, the Engineers were nearly finished clearing debris to start properly repairing the bridge. This evening, Lydia guessed, would be what Captain Calvert called 'cleanup'.

Men whose wounds could wait a little. Men who wouldn't die from not being seen to at once.

Outside, vehicles of all sorts were still leaving for the base hospital at Calais with wounded. Constant in the distance, the thunder of the guns continued.

'These orders you had from Captain Palfrey Thursday night . . .'

Oh, drat it! Lydia pushed her spectacles up more firmly onto the bridge of her nose and tried

93

to look like Miranda did when questioned about the disappearance of sugar from the sugar bowl . . . *Oh, that? They merely wanted to consult me about training in the use of the fluoroscope* . . .

'Yes?'

'Did it have anythin' to do with taking German prisoners away?'

'German prisoners?'

Dermott nodded. He was a stocky young man a few years Lydia's junior, a Quaker who'd worked in his father's photography studio and assisted the local doctor in his North Wales village. 'Yes, M'am. I know 'tis not my place to be askin' questions, but some of the prisoners— That is, I speak a bit of German. And one of the prisoners said this mornin' as how both here and at the Front when they was captured, there was an officer separatin' out some of the men, puttin' 'em in a truck and away they'd go. He said he was captured with his cousin, and looked to see him here, but instead it was this same thing. A half-dozen men separated out from the rest and took away, M'am. And he asked me, was this usual, and how would he get in touch with his cousin again? He was a lawyer, see, this German, and had spent some time in England. He said it wasn't anything the British would do.'

'It's certainly nothing I've ever heard about.' Lydia frowned. 'Not with the wounded, at any rate. Seriously wounded?'

'No, M'am. Mostly walking wounded, he said. I did ask Captain Calvert about it, M'am, and he said he'd never heard of it neither, not here nor anywhere else, but if the officer had papers for

94

it – which he did – it must be pukka. But it didn't seem quite right to me still, and I thought about this Captain Palfrey that came the other night with papers for you, and you going off as you did . . . Well, there might be other things going on that even gentlemen like Captain Calvert aren't told about. But I was only asking, and I wouldn't wish to cause trouble.'

'No,' said Lydia thoughtfully. 'No, it's nothing I've heard of, Mr Dermott. Captain Palfrey was simply relaying a request for me to consult about training in the use of the fluoroscope.'

The vampires Antonio and Basilio, driving their ambulance-wagon all along the trench lines? A shiver went through her: anger, helplessness, frustration. Had some other enterprising ghouls, braver than the rest, started a delivery service for the convenience of those Undead who didn't want to risk getting that close to the Front?

How easy it was, to prey on the helpless. The wounded, and prisoners . . . .

She closed her eyes for a moment, sickened. *Every vampire in Europe is here. Feeding at will. Killing at will.*

And nobody notices.

In the momentary silence, the crashing of the guns sounded very loud.

And why would they notice?

She looked at Dermott again. 'Could I speak with this man?'

Eight

'Rhinehardt?' Nurse Danvers checked the note-book she carried, close-scribbled with hundreds of names dashed off in a hurry between cleaning, bandaging and the endless ancillary chores of making beds and ironing sheets. Lydia was burn-ingly aware that she herself should be in the fluoroscope tent at that moment, sorting through films of the men waiting for surgery, instead of snooping around the prisoners' compound . . .

'A fair-haired man.' Lydia repeated the descrip-tion Dermott had given her. 'Broken nose and shrapnel wounds in the face.'

Across the small tent where the wounded pris-oners had been kept under guard last night, Matron called, 'Danvers—'

Danvers peered at her notes, turned the book sideways, pale brows crumpling together.

'Danvers—'

'Just coming, M'am! Oh, aye, he's been taken on to Calais. A whole lot of them went this afternoon.'

BOTHER! 'Thank you!' As Lydia hurried from the prisoners' tent – jammed with men last night, nearly vacant now save for a handful of the worst cases down at the far end – she cursed herself for not waking earlier. Yet she was aware she needed the sleep, and by what Dermott had said of this man Rhinehardt's wounds, she doubted whether

96

the man she sought would have been able to talk to her much earlier. A dozen finger-sized fragments of shell-casing and wood from the trench re-enforcements had been taken out of his face, throat and chest last night. That morning, Dermott had said, he'd still have been under morphia.

To her left, by the road that led westward to Calais, a line of soldiers caught her eye, rifles ready, and before them, men in gray-green uniforms, seated on the ground. A big wagon, drawn by two exhausted-looking farm horses, was being loaded under guard.

This afternoon, she said . . . but these things always take forever . . .

Lydia caught up her skirts and nearly ran. 'Excuse me, Sergeant Waller, but is there any chance I might speak to one of the prisoners? There are some details about his injury I didn't get last night before he was operated on . . .'

'Well . . .' The sergeant frowned. A friendly soul, he had several times traded encomia with Lydia about the perfections of their respective children. 'We're not supposed to, M'am. But if it's in the way of medical information . . .'

Sure enough, Captain Rhinehardt lay on a stretcher, waiting for a place on the next wagon or (Lydia did a hasty calculation) probably the next but one . . .

Now if I can just remember enough German . . .

'*Bitte* . . .' she said hesitantly, and the young man turned his head, blinking up at her with his one undamaged eye.

'*Gnädige Frau Doktor . . .*' His voice sounded like dry mud being scraped off tin.

97

'Do you speak English?' *If he's visited England* . . .

He was haggard with pain and still sleepy from the morphia, but answered her in that language. 'Please forgive me for not rising, Madame . . .'

'Good Heavens, Captain, it's I who should be asking *your* forgiveness, for troubling you at such a time.' She knelt at his side. 'My assistant, Mr Dermott, said you were seeking your cousin, who had been . . . taken away from the other prisoners. Things were so confused for the last few days we're still not certain what happened, but I will try to trace him. Was his name Rhinehardt also?'

An infinitesimal nod. 'Oberleutnant Gleb Rhinehardt.'

'And he was also wounded?'

'Not so badly as I, Madame. How do you say it? Walking wounded. A bullet had broken his arm.'

Lydia flinched. Flanders soil, manured for crop-lands for centuries, was incredibly virulent in cuts. Even the smallest wounds went septic within hours.

'And men were being taken away from the main group of the wounded?' A glance along the line of the prisoners showed her at once that over a dozen of them were on their feet and able to help their comrades.

'So they were, Madame. A French officer – a surgeon – with two British soldiers, and a nurse, or a nursing sister – dressed as you are, in light blue with a white apron. Gleb was sitting with me – he could have escaped, fled when the remainder of our unit did, but he was captured

98

when he saw that I could not walk. I heard our officer calling to him to do so and he would not let go of my hand. At the dressing station he asked the sergeant in charge of guarding us, could he fetch me some water, and the sergeant permitted him to do so; there was a water butt nearby. Gleb walked over to it with his cup and this French officer saw him and pointed to him, the two soldiers stopped him and took him away with five others, in a big ambulance-wagon. A long chassis Sunbeam, I think it was. Gleb was a motor mechanic in Dresden, Madame. There was no vehicle in our lines that he did not point out to me and tell me about, inch by inch.'

Something that might have been a smile twitched one corner of his mouth at the memory of his friend, then quickly faded.

'I saw Gleb trying to talk the soldiers into letting him come back to me but they put all six of those men into the ambulance truck. He got one of the regular guards to bring his cup to me with the water. I asked this man, where had they been taken, and he said he didn't know. No one I have spoken to knows anything about it. But one of the other prisoners here told me the same thing: that this French surgeon and his nurse took away ten men, only lightly wounded, from the dressing station where he, and they, had been held before coming here. The French surgeon looked at him – the man who told me this, a sergeant in the Uhlans – but said he was too badly injured and would not do.'

Lydia frowned. This didn't sound like anything Don Simon had told her, but of course considering the other vampires abroad along no man's land, there was no way of telling. However, if this young man had been able to identify the make of an ambulance . . .

'What time of day was this?'

Rhinehardt shook his head. 'The assault started just after sunrise. I was hit before we reached the English lines, and I was unconscious when Gleb found me. I know it was daylight when we were at the English dressing station – an hour, two hours, before dusk began to fall, perhaps? It is hard to judge, Madame . . .'

'Of course,' said Lydia quickly. *Not vampires, anyway. Unless they've got the living working for them – like poor Captain Palfrey – but why on earth would they want the walking wounded?* 'Thank you,' she added. 'I'll do everything I can to see if I can locate your friend . . .'

'*Danke*,' he whispered, and closed his eye.

'Is there anything I can get for you? Do you need more morphia? Or cigarettes?'

'*Danke*, Madame, but I am well for the moment.'

Lydia started to rise, then knelt again and asked, 'One more thing, if I may ask, sir. How did you know the French officer was a surgeon?'

The young captain blinked up at her, his brow tightening as if the pain were returning, and his voice was a little slurred with weariness. 'He was here,' he said. 'I saw him pass through the tent last night, before I was taken to surgery. I was afraid . . . He and his nurse were both there. I was afraid they had come to search for others.'

'Was it Nurse Smith?' asked Lydia. 'Short and young, with black hair and a heart-shaped face, a . . .' What was the German word for a widow's peak? She sketched a downward-pointing arrowhead from her hairline, hoping he understood, and he nodded.

'Yes, this was her,' he murmured. 'The one who loved the Irishman.' His eye slipped closed again, and after a moment, he said, 'If it would not be a trouble to you, *Frau Doktor*, yes, I think I would like some morphia, if I am to go in the ambulance.'

Lydia stopped at the ward tent, and made arrangements with Matron for a syrette of morphine to be sent to Rhinehardt, on her way to the fluoroscope room. Subsequent inquiry however, that night in the mess tent and at intervals the following day, yielded nothing out of the ordinary about Colonel Lemoine. As far as anyone knew, Captain Calvert told her, Lemoine was with the Second French Army somewhere near Nesle. He'd only happened to be at Haut-le-Bois down the line when word came of the German attack. Further queries over bully beef and stale biscuits the following evening elicited only the information that no Nurse Smith was assigned to the nearest clearing station south of Haut-le-Bois, at Orchies-le-Petit, at least as far as Captain Calvert knew.

Before bed that night Lydia took a jar of Aunt Lavinnia's marmalade to the stores hut, and ascertained that Storeman Pratt had never heard of her there, either – and due to his wide-flung network of graft and trade, Pratt knew pretty much everyone on the Front.

'Tell you what, though, Mrs A—' The rangy,

101

curiously angular-looking storeman unscrewed the jar lid, and without breaking the bleached white wax of the seal inhaled the faint scent of oranges and sugar with the half-shut eyes of a connoisseur – 'I'll hold onto this 'ere jar, and ask about a bit, y'know? Tiny Clinkers, what looks after the motors at Headquarters, got a list of just about every woman on the Front, how old they are and if they're pretty and will they or won't they, if you'll excuse my French, M'am. Pretty, you say?'

'I think so. Black hair, widow's peak, short, retroussé nose. What my nephews call a pocket Venus. I heard that young Irishman with the freckles call her Tuathla . . .'

'That's just one of them Irish fairy-tale names.' Pratt shook his head at the entire heritage of Celtic civilization. 'Readin' too much Yeats an' seein' leprechauns, an' handloom weavin' their own skirts. Last couple years, every coal-'eaver's daughter in Holborn been changing 'er name from Nancy and Mary to Eibhlhin and Nuala. I've never heard of a nurse looks like that in this part of the Front, much less one that'd be at Headquarters t'other night when the balloon went up. Home-made, this is—' He gestured with the jar – 'There's men at Headquarters – them as don't have relatives that could afford to stock up on sugar before the war – would trade me any amount of petrol and cigarettes for this, and I'll see you get the worth of it, M'am.'

'Thank you.' Lydia put as much warmth as she could into her voice, though she wanted to stamp her foot at him. The petrol and cigarettes were of course being stolen from motor pools that were to take the wounded to hospital, and the slender rations of comfort that were supposedly being sent to the men. But her mother, and the fearsome Nanna who had reigned over the nursery in her childhood, had drilled her in the art of sounding friendly no matter what she thought or actually felt, and this training served her in good stead now. As she was turning to leave a thought came to her, and she turned back. 'And does Corporal Clinkers have a list of all motorcars on this portion of the Front?'

'Lor' bless you, M'am, we all of us got those. What might you be interested in?'

She had the impression that if she'd pulled thirty pounds from her pocket he'd have sold her Commander-in-Chief Sir John French's personal vehicle.

'A long-chassis Sunbeam lorry ambulance. Can you find who has them, and where?'

'Nuthin' simpler, M'am. Just gi' me 'arf a day.'

The warmth in her voice was genuine when she said again, 'Thank you.' Technically she supposed that getting information from – and fraternizing willingly with – Storeman Pratt was probably less dreadful than getting information from vampires . . . Unless you counted Pratt as a vampire himself.

'Am I on this Corporal Clinkers' list?'

'Oh, absolutely, Mrs A.' Pratt saluted her. 'Right up there with Matron and seventy-eight percent of the nuns at Calais. Under 'D', for *Don't Waste Your Time On It, Boy-O.*' He screwed the jar shut, and stashed it under the counter. 'And if you should 'appen to be sent any other little thing you might want to spare – or if there's anythin' *you'll* be wantin' in the way of sweets or smokes or silk stockin's . . .'

'You are a disgrace.' Lydia did her best to sound severe but couldn't keep from laughing, and his own grin widened.

'I do me best, M'am.'

'No luck, Mistress?'

Without a sound, Don Simon Ysidro had materialized at her side.

The night was now pitch-dark, the tent-canvas once again dimly aglow with lanterns, though owing to a failed delivery (or perhaps, Lydia speculated darkly, theft by Storeman Pratt and his spiritual kin) there were fewer of these than there had been five nights ago. Someone had tried to rig barriers of twine and fragments of bandage, to mark the new shell-holes, and the trees blown out of the ground by the German bombardment now lay strewn about the camp, half sawn-up to fuel the extra furnace that was being constructed (*In the bearers' abundant spare time!*) for the amputated limbs. The air was gritty with smoke, and reeked of spoiling meat.

The smell of someone's cigarette, momentary in the darkness. In one of the tents, someone with a beautiful Welsh tenor was singing 'Keep the Home Fires Burning', against a thready harmonica and a soft chorus of bass.

Jamie . . .

She pushed the thought of her husband aside.

Miranda . . .

'You heard all that?' She nodded back in the direction of the stores hut.

'I know you have been seeking word of this woman we saw in the trenches, as I have been, among those who hunt the night. So far as I have learned, these revenants do not wander at large in the German lines. Nor yet have any seen any such thing in the wasted lands between the lines, nor wandering in the abandoned trenches on either side.'

'They might have.' Lydia removed her spectacles, and polished them with her handkerchief. Her head ached, from an afternoon of concentration in both the x-ray room and the surgical tent. 'If a man had taken a head wound, and was wandering about in confusion; or a wounded man in no man's land trying to make his way back to the lines . . .'

'We are cowards at heart,' said Don Simon. 'Seldom do we actually venture into no man's land. Aside from the issue of shelling, too many men on both sides use cocaine to stay awake at their posts, and there is greater chance that we will be seen and shot at. If any saw such a man, either in the wasteland or in a bombed-out trench, we – my kindred and I – would take him, for such men seldom reach safety in any case. None that I know of have said to me – nor to any to whom I have spoken – "*I saw a man whom I thought merely wounded, and when I went to take him, found he was such a creature instead.*" Personally,' he added, tilting his head in a gesture curiously mantis-like, 'I find this very odd.'

'That means there aren't a great many of the Others about—'

'Yet.'

'Yet.' Lydia resumed her spectacles and frowned. 'How are they created, Don Simon? I mean, the ones Jamie told me about, in Prague . . .'

'I know not, Mistress. Nor does the Master of Prague . . . Who is, I think, vexed and distressed at the news that one such creature has unquestionably appeared here. With all of no man's land a labyrinth of old trenches and buried dugouts and sapper's tunnels, 'twere too easy for these Others to move about. They can cover themselves from the awareness of the Undead, and find us where we sleep, in the crypts and cellars of ruined churches and manors, devouring us in our coffins. And if, like the revenants of Prague and Peking, those breeding here can control rats, the situation is more dangerous still.'

Lydia flinched in disgust. In the mines northwest of Peking she had seen men swarmed by rats, when they'd attempted to invade the *yao-kuei* hive there.

'As I once told James – and as it is also written in the Book of the Kindred of Darkness – the Others first appeared in Prague just after the Great Plague, five and a half centuries ago. But whether it is a virus that transforms their flesh – or if such virus is a *mutation*, as de Vries calls such changes, of the virus that transforms the flesh of a man into that of a vampire – if *that* be a virus – I know no more than do the messenger dogs in their kennels.'

'Has any vampire ever . . . ever killed one? A

106

revenant, I mean. And not just trying to get away from it.'

'Never that I have heard of. Would you drink the blood of such a thing, knowing that to mix its blood with your own might pass its condition along to yourself? How much less would one try to drink its life, the energies of its death? The mere thought appalls.' He put his hand beneath her elbow, and helped her across rough and squishy debris around a shell-crater. It had rained that day, and cloud still veiled the moon.

'But you drink the blood of syphilitics, and consumptives, and drug-takers,' pointed out Lydia, a little diffidently. 'The blood and . . . and the life . . .' She glanced across at him, wondering at the same time why on earth she felt she needed to be tactful: *He's certainly aware of what he is . . .*

''Tis not the same.'

Lydia stumbled on a flooded wagon-rut, and became aware that they were leaving the tents and huts behind them. 'Where are we going?'

'To meet Antonio and Basilio once more. They have seen this ambulance-truck with the walking wounded, and know now where it went.'

Antonio Pentangeli and Basilio Occhipinti were, as before, in a dugout in what had been a German reserve trench before the English had retaken Pont-Sainte-Félicité, playing picquet – an antique card-game much favored among the older vampires – at a broken-down table to the music of a gramophone with a cracked horn. A couple of candles burned on shelves – Lydia saw

107

the lights flare up as she and Don Simon came around the last corner of the revetment – and, of all things, a small pot of tea sat keeping warm on the makeshift stove: ''Tis a cold night, *bella donna*.' Antonio poured some out for her into a teacup that had to have been looted from the village. 'You seek a long-chassis Sunbeam ambulance with a French officer, who visits the dressing stations in search of the walking wounded?' He brought up a chair for her, cushioned with a folded blanket.

He was dressed, Lydia observed, in an officer's uniform as before; the beautiful Basilio was costumed as a driver, with the armband of the Red Cross. She tried not to think of Uncle Richard's footmen – Charles and William – bleeding in some shell-hole watching the approach of their ambulance-wagon with hope.

'Have you seen him?'

'Twice. Most recently the night before last, when all the German prisoners were brought from their attack. But again before that, three weeks ago, just after the fighting at Neuve Chapelle. This same officer, with the brow of Saturn and the little black mustache—'

'Colonel Lemoine,' said Lydia at once. 'That's what the German prisoners said, too.'

'I know not.' Antonio shook his head. 'But he had papers which he showed to the guards. He selected from among the prisoners, men not badly hurt. I am not, you understand, much concerned about such men, nor do I understand how prisoners are dealt with in this war. In my day the captains simply ransomed them back to one

108

another, if they were gentlemen, or killed them if they were very angry, or hadn't enough food, or if the prisoners were Protestants.' He shrugged. 'And I thought perhaps this was an ordinary thing.'

'It may be.' Lydia propped her spectacles, and sipped the tea. Basilio offered her sugar in a Limoges dish, and, of all things, fresh milk. 'But I've never heard of such procedure. There are several very queer things happening hereabouts: between the revenant we saw, and this nurse whose name isn't Smith offering deals to the Undead . . . and people disappearing whom everyone is too busy and too tired to look for. You told me once—' she looked back at Don Simon, who had resumed his seat, hands folded, on a sort of earthen bench that had once been a bunk, his yellow eyes narrowed – 'that the Undead feed primarily on the poor: on people whom no one will trace and no one cares about. Like that song in *The Mikado*, about, "They'll none of them be missed". And that sounds like a description of those poor prisoners. As if someone wants the living – in reasonably good shape – rather than the dying.'

'Doing in fact with human beings,' remarked Don Simon, 'what the despicable Storeman Pratt does with petrol and cigarettes and morphia, I daresay. As war is waged now, things get mixed up and lost and mislaid all the time, and nobody thinks a thing of it. Where is this Lemoine posted, know you, lady?'

'Nesle, Captain Calvert says. But he's often in the camp at Haut-le-Bois.'

'I think a journey thence might profit us all. I shall arrange for the proper papers to be made out to release you from your duties for a time, and the good Captain Palfrey will call for you in the morning.'

Nine

The casualty clearing station at Haut-le-Bois lay some twenty miles south of Pont-Sainte-Félicité, where an outcrop of the Artois Hills made a long promontory above the farm country around it. In Sussex it would have been considered 'a bit of a rise', but in Flanders it amounted to 'heights.' Rain began just before sunup, and 'Colonel Simon's' staff-car jolted cautiously over roads deeply rutted by military traffic and cratered with shell-holes. 'It reminds me of the fen country, when the floods are out,' said Captain Palfrey, with affection rather than annoyance in his voice which made Lydia inquire, 'Are you from there?'

Rain streamed off the brim of his hat as he looked up – he'd climbed from the car to mend their second puncture of the trip. His smile alone answered her query. 'Can you tell?'

'Well, my husband probably could spot you from the way you pronounce your words – he's an expert at that. But my uncle always says that the only people who really love the fens are those who're born there.'

The young man lifted one hand, ruefully owning his guilt. 'Wisbach. Actually Deepmere, about ten miles from Wisbach; my grandfather's place, really, but I was born there. My grandfather is Viscount Deepmere.'

111

Lydia said, 'Good Heavens!' having danced in her brief debutant days with several young men who had probably been Palfrey's older brothers or cousins – 'good society' in England being actually rather small. (And the 'good society' admissible to parties in the home of her own grandfather, Viscount Halfdene, smaller yet.)

As they resumed their careful progress, Lydia learned from him, by degrees, the difficult but not surprising tale of the younger son of a younger son, raised on the fringes of 'good society' with no prospects and no greater ambition than to return to Norfolk and raise cattle, horses and sugar beets – a niche already solidly occupied by his elder cousins. 'And Father was in the Twenty-Fourth Bengal Cavalry, so it was the Done Thing that I'd follow in his footsteps. Grandmother put up the money for me to get into the Guards rather than an India regiment. Father was her favorite. When he died Grandmother got it into her head that India's a horribly unhealthy climate – he and Mother both died of cholera – and wouldn't hear of me going there. It's where he met Colonel Simon,' he added, a little hesitantly, and a frown puckered his brow. 'At least I think . . .'

'Tell me about Colonel Simon.'

'Well, a great deal about him falls under the Official Secrets Act, you know,' Palfrey warned her. Shy pride glimmered in his blue eyes, and a trace of hero worship. 'But I think – I *know* – my father knew him in India. I remember his name in letters father wrote me . . .'

Or he's put it into one of your dreams that you remember . . .

'Father died when I was just six, but . . . I remember the name. Mother, too.' He sounded uncertain, as if sorting clear memories from things he felt he knew from somewhere without being able to quote specifics.

'Wouldn't he be a much older man,' probed Lydia, 'if he knew your father?'

'He is . . . older than he looks, he says. But he must have known Father, because he knew my name when he met me. And he spoke of Father like one who knew him.'

Or like one who has practiced the art of 'reading' people and telling them what they want to hear, for three hundred and fifty years . . .

'He introduced himself to me at the Guards' Club, and said he had a proposition for me, if I were willing to do it. A few nights later we met, very late, and I was interviewed by the chief of his Department—'

'And where was that?' asked Lydia. 'What Department?'

'The Foreign Office.' Palfrey frowned, concentrating on maneuvering the staff-car off the bombed-out road and around an enormous morass of shell-holes. This was an area which had been retaken, Lydia guessed, fairly recently – the whole length of the drive (it was now mid-morning) the booming of the guns sounded very close, and the crackle of rifle-fire. Two or three miles off, Lydia calculated. What had once been farmland lay all around them in a waste of shell-pitted mud, crisscrossed with abandoned trenches and entanglements of barbed wire still bright and sharp in the rain. Once the road had brought them

113

close enough to the reserve trenches that Lydia could see the men piling sandbags along the lip of the cut, and the smoke that rose from the cooking-fires. Twice lines of men passed them, marching in from St-Omer. Stoic faces, empty and sunk into their own thoughts. Supply-wagons followed the men, mules slipping and straining against the sheer weight of the gray mud. Mostly the land was empty, desolate under the pattering rain.

'Somewhere in Whitehall,' the young captain continued, the uncertainty in his voice telling its own tale. 'It was hideously late at night, as I said – I'd dozed off in my digs waiting for Colonel Simon to call for me. When I got back it was nearly morning and I fell straight to sleep when I came in, and woke up still dressed in my chair. And then, what with the black-out and Colonel Simon's caution about letting me see where we were, I'm not sure I could find the place by daylight anyway.' His eyes sparkled boyishly at being part of such a hush-hush operation. 'I know the officer I spoke to told me the official name of the Department, but I've forgotten it. Mostly we just call it the Department.'

As Jamie does . . .

Only Jamie's Department is REAL. Not something Don Simon caused this poor young man to dream about . . .

Palfrey chuckled. 'It's all rather like a blood-and-thunder novel, really. My pay just magically appears in my bank account, so I think they must deposit it in cash. But the officer told me, at Whitehall that night, that what Colonel Simon is doing in France is of vital importance to the War.

114

Without his work – and of course I have not the slightest idea what it actually is – our armies here might very well be overrun and wiped out by summer. Colonel Simon has a network of agents in France, and some in Germany. Mostly what he needs – what he needs *me* for – is as a bodyguard, a driver, a man to make arrangements for things when he's called elsewhere. And I've tried to give satisfaction,' he added shyly. 'I realize I'm a complete fool about the brainy stuff – I was forever being caned at Harrow for not being able to learn Latin or history or how many x's you need to make a y – but I *can* get things done. That's done it,' he added, pleased with himself, and nudged the car back up onto the crazy road again. 'I'd feel a complete fool if we went through all that to avoid a puddle a few inches deep, but on the other hand, those craters could have been deeper than the top of this car and quicksand at the bottom, you know, and then where'd we be?'

'And your grandmother wasn't horrified that you quit the Guards?'

'Well, she was,' admitted Captain Palfrey. 'I told her a little about Colonel Simon – though he'd warned me not to speak of his having known Father. She's the only one I've told . . . she and Aemilia, of course.'

'Aemilia?'

'Aemilia Bellingham.' His fair-skinned face actually blushed. 'We hope – that is . . . I hope we're to be married when the war ends.'

Lydia closed her gloved hands, and looked out across the sodden wasteland toward the reserve trenches. Don Simon had come here, she thought,

115

to watch over her; and because of the terrible fragility of vampire flesh, he had needed a living servant. Like a *'shabbas goy'*, Jamie had once said: the Gentile servant whom pious Jews would hire to open windows or start kitchen fires on the Sabbath, so that their own piety would remain unblemished. She wanted to shout at this young man, *Have you ever seen him by daylight? He's a vampire, Undead . . . he lives on the blood and the energies of the dying . . .*

Only he wouldn't believe her. *He's warned me that all kinds of the most ridiculous stories are circulated about him . . . a combination of Count Dracula and Bluebeard . . .*

Precisely the sort of thing, Jamie had told her, that he – Jamie – had done in his spying days, when he was setting up a network somewhere abroad: German shopkeepers or Syrian peasants or Russian factory workers, who would provide him with information about their country's roads or local rebellions or how many of what supplies were being ordered. Who would cheerfully do so under the impression that they were actually helping their country rather than giving that information to enemies.

If anything went wrong, it was the dupes who would be punished, not the spymaster.

'And here we are!' Captain Palfrey guided the long-nosed vehicle carefully off the main road again, and toward a cluster of tents. 'According to my map, that should be Haut-le-Bois.'

Lydia had been provided not only with papers requesting her presence ostensibly in Arras, several hours further down the Amiens road, but with a convincing story of why they were stopping in Haut-le-Bois (a faulty map and a can of petrol so badly watered that, once Palfrey had poured it into the gas tank, the staff-car barely ran at all). As this portion of the line was fairly quiet at the moment, while Palfrey and the dark-faced, cheerful Algerians of the motor pool drained the tank and replenished the jerrycans, Lydia had sufficient time to walk around the whole of the camp and ascertain that there were no German prisoners anywhere in it, walking wounded or otherwise.

Colonel Lemoine invited her to join him for lunch in the officer's mess, and entertained her – over appalling coffee – with accounts of his various postings in the farther corners of France's overseas empire: Indochina, Algeria, West Africa and the 'concessions' in Shanghai and Peking.

'We were there in October . . . three years ago?' said Lydia. 'Nineteen twelve . . .'

'I had left by then,' said the physician. 'I came up the previous year during the uprising, and left when peace was restored to the city. It must have been in August or September of '12.'

'What was your impression of the hospitals?' asked Lydia, to deflect the man's attention from any possibility that she herself might know that at that time the little hive of revenants had been festering in the coal mines in the arid hills west of the city. She longed to mention Dr Krista Bauer – the German missionary whose account of finding the body of one such 'hill demon' had brought Jamie and herself (and Don Simon)

117

to Peking – to see what Lemoine's reaction would be.

But caution closed her lips.

Only when Lemoine had walked her out to the motor pool, where Palfrey waited for her with the car, did she glimpse, among the other vehicles, a long-bodied ambulance, clearly a converted truck, though even wearing her spectacles she couldn't have told a Sunbeam from a governess cart. She let the colonel help her into the staff-car, and as he walked away turned casually to one of the several motor mechanics still loitering nearby and said, 'Do you think Colonel Lemoine might be here when I come back this way? I had ever such a delightful time.'

'Alas, Madame, that is very much the luck of the day,' replied the man in his singsong French. Lydia had observed that the cook in the officer's tent had been African, and recalled what Captain Calvert had commented some days ago: that the government of France was bringing in more and more men from its overseas empire, both in the Army and in the factories and farms, to free native Frenchmen to join the fight. 'He comes and he goes, the colonel, and now that this section of the Front is quiet he is gone more than he is here. Myself—' He tapped the side of his enormous nose and looked wise – 'I think he is employed by the government on some other matter that he does not tell us. The other Big Ones—' he nodded toward the officers' tents – 'make no comment when he disappears.'

Lydia turned the matter over in her mind as the staff-car made its slow, lurching return journey

118

north to Pont-Sainte-Félicité, with the rain falling again, and the desultory spatter of machine-gun fire like the clatter of Death's bones in the gathering darkness.

Everything innocuous and clear.

Reaching the clearing station, she had to help Dermott clean up the fluoroscope room and develop films for nearly two hours before she was finally able to return to her tent.

A letter lay on her pillow, addressed in James's firm, jagged black writing. Three straggly hearts on the envelope were from Miranda. A fourth, more firmly drawn, could only have been from James.

Her eyes filled with tears so it was a moment before she could read the small news of familiar things – of the sweet stillness of Oxford during vacation, of rain pattering on the Isis, of her maid Ellen's shy suitor, Mr Hurley, from down the King's Arms.

She read these innocent tidings first, like a forbidden sweet, having seen immediately the dots beneath certain letters that told her of coded matters. Only when she'd pretended to herself for a few moments that the price of sugar was all anyone had to worry about did she get out a pencil and decipher what couldn't be shown to the censors.

One revenant at least in London.

Asher took the train up to Oxford on Friday afternoon, the 19th of March. He ached in every joint when he woke, and by the time he reached Oxford his chest burned and his skull buzzed

119

with fever. Ellen and Mrs Grimes put him to bed, and Mrs Grimes – in between making blancmange and gruel – told him in no uncertain terms that this was his own fault for gallivanting off to London when Dr Hoggett had told him to rest, and that if he came down with pneumonia again she was going to throw him out into the road to die and would tell Miss Lydia that he'd run off with a drover's widow from Dorset.

Dr Hoggett – one of Asher's very small circle of intimate friends – when he came to see him on Saturday, added to this that he himself would then marry Mrs Asher, and it would serve Asher right. Hoggett returned Sunday evening, by which time Asher was well enough to beat him in two games (out of four) of chess after dinner: 'But if I hear you speak again of going back up to London tomorrow I'm going to break out my grandfather's phlebotomy knives and bleed you to keep you in bed.'

So Asher remained in the old brick house on Holyrood Street, rereading *Bleak House* and Lydia's letters and reflecting upon how ridiculous it was for a man approaching fifty, with gray in his hair and mustache, to feel moved to sing silly songs ('*Tho' the road between us stretches/Many a weary mile/I forget that you're not with me yet/When I think I see you smile . . .*') at the sight of his wife's handwriting.

He checked the Personals column of *The Times* daily, but saw no message from Dr Graves. The revenant was lying low.

On Tuesday he was well enough to play hide-and-seek in the garden with Miranda – who was still of an age to believe that if she put her head in a cupboard in the potting shed that she was concealed – and to have tea with the Warden of his college. It was good to talk philosophy and ancient history with the old man, and to forget for a time what they both knew was happening in Europe: when Professor Spooner digressed indignantly on an undergraduate who had 'missed every one of my mystery lectures and was actually caught fighting a liar in the quad!'. Asher, long used to his conversation, merely inquired as to why the young man in question had chosen so public a place to light a fire.

Dr Spooner's kindly and erudite hospitality was a welcome contrast to dinner Wednesday evening with Lydia's Uncle Ambrose, the Dean of New College, who spent the evening complaining about the price of bread (*Who does he think is growing crops, with twenty thousand men a day being slaughtered in Flanders?*) and the influx of female servants at the colleges – 'They've actually hired a woman as a cook in the college kitchens! A *woman*! And I must say the quality of the men they're getting in these days is nearly as bad . . .' remarks which immediately segued into a fussy diatribe about how more men – 'decent, skilled, intelligent men' – should be volunteering for the Army instead of staying home.

'Honestly, between you and me, Asher, I'm ashamed to see who they're getting into the Army these days! I don't mind the Canadians so much, but the Australians . . .! And as for the idea of bringing in a lot of Indian wogs and niggers from

121

Africa . . . How on earth are we going to keep a proper attitude back in the colonies when this is all over, I ask you, when they've been encouraged to kill white men? And for God's sake, when I see them fraternizing with white women here . . .!' He shuddered. 'And as for the officers . . .'

What the hell did you think is going to happen? Where do you think those men are coming from? You spill them like sand into the wind – send them with rifles in their hands against German machine-gun nests – and you think there will always be more?

His one attempt to divert the conversation onto Lydia resulted only in an angry speech about how hospitals were no place for a woman and how Asher should never have permitted Lydia to become a doctor in the first place. 'What's a woman know about medicine, anyway? All that suffragist nonsense . . . God made them women, and they should be content to be so!'

He returned to the dining room after seeing Uncle Ambrose off, to find that Ellen – who took over a footman's job of serving when they had company, now that Mick had joined the Ox and Bucks Light Infantry – just setting a cup of cocoa at his place: 'I thought you might need it, sir. And this came for you this afternoon while you were resting.'

It was a letter from Lydia.

The letter was long, and merely glancing at it, he knew there was something greatly wrong. A moment's mental calculation told him it had been sent before his own letter could have reached her, telling her of the revenant – or revenants

122

– in London. But there were three times the usual number of little code-dots sprinkled over and around the text: some in ink, some pricked with a pin, some looking like flecks of the mud in which the Flanders trenches were drowning.

He carried the letter and the cocoa into his study, put on his reading glasses, turned up the gas and began to decrypt with a cold weight on his heart.

P-S-F – A (The simplest of the code: *still at Pont-Sainte-Félicité, and well.* Sometimes the coded portions of her letters consisted only of that)

Other in N-M-L x volunteer nurse seeks vampires x says has proposition a part-nership to offer x seen here CCS 16-3 x same nurse sought found body of Other, did ?? then destroyed it x alias Tuathla Smith no such person x German prisoner says Fr officer taking prisoners away not to HQ x Sunbeam ? ambulance no markings
DSY here

The following morning he took breakfast in the nursery. ('Grown-ups don't eat in the nursery, Papa!' objected Miranda, though delighted with his presence; she was at this time much invested in everything being in its proper place. 'It's my house, best beloved, and I can eat wherever I want.')

He had spent yesterday morning in the garden with her, listening to her explanations of where

123

fairies hid when it rained (which it had, on and off, for several days), and now produced Lydia's letter, of which he read to her the plain text: expurgated of Lydia's weariness, her anger at the war, and some of her more ironic comments, even those she'd deemed mild enough to go through the censors. Miranda, a grave little copper-haired princess, was aware of such things as the war and that Mummy was away taking care of the men who were fighting it. She asked for clarification of things like x-rays and trenches, and made sure in her own mind that Mummy wasn't going to be hurt and would be back for Christmas.

After that he kissed her goodbye and returned to the railway station, stopping at Blackwell's for a large-scale Ordnance Survey map of London. He reached London shortly after noon, took rooms under the name of Edmund Hocking in Pembridge Place, Bayswater – he'd had papers made up for Hocking when last he'd been in Paris and the Department knew nothing of them – and put an advertisement in the papers asking for a meeting the following night with Mr Graves.

The advert was signed 'Scragger' – the old name for the public hangman.

Then he went to the British Museum, where at this time of day he was almost certain to find Osric Millward.

Osric Millward was a vampire-hunter.

Entering the vast, hushed space of the Reading Room's dome, Asher spotted him without trouble. He sat at his usual place at the end of one of the long desks, amid a welter of catalogs, manuscripts

124

and ancient black-letter books on the occult: a tall, thin man whose raven hair was shot now with silver and whose dark eyes peered at the pages before him like those of an Inquisitor probing a heretic's lies.

When Asher had first met him, back in the eighties, Millward already had a reputation of being something of a crackpot, a profound believer in the beings whom Asher at that time had regarded as mere creations of folklore, like broom-riding witches and Miranda's fairies at the bottom of the garden. By the time Asher had returned from his first excursion 'abroad' on the business of the Department, Millward's study and belief had turned to obsession. A respected scholar of proto-Judaic Middle Eastern religious texts, Millward had gradually ceased to publish, and his lectures at King's College were more and more frequently cancelled because he could not be found. He'd be off on unexplained trips to London or Cornwall or Edinburgh, following up clues about vampire nests or suspected vampire kills. Eventually he lost his stipend from King's. In despair, his wife had returned to the home of her parents.

Watching him from the Reading Room's doorway, Asher reflected that Millward was everything that he himself dreaded to become. *'To hunt us would be to hunt smoke,'* Don Simon Ysidro had said to him once. *'You could hunt us down eventually, were you willing to put the time into it, to give your soul to it, to become obsessed, as all vampire-hunters must be obsessed with their prey . . . Are you willing to give it years?'*

125

I should have been willing, Asher thought. *And I wasn't.*

In the eight years since that night in Harley Street, Ysidro, and Grippen, and those fledglings that Grippen had begotten, had killed who knew how many men and women, the poor whom no one would miss or avenge. Asher didn't know whether, in that eight years, if he'd given his heart and his time and all of his attention to hunting vampires – instead of the hours of his mortal happiness with Lydia and Miranda, with the students he guided and the research into languages that gave him such joy – whether he'd have been able to find and destroy them or not.

And if he had, he reflected despairingly, there would only have been more.

'*We have what you do not have,*' Ysidro had said. '*We have time.*'

Looking at that shabby, graying figure, with his threadbare jacket and his unshined shoes, Asher could not keep the thought from his mind: *At least he has tried to rid the world of evil. While I, like the vampires, have traded the lives of all those unavenged innocents in the London slums for the peace and the joy and the happiness of these past eight years. Knowing they existed, and turning my face away.*

So far as Asher knew, Millward had never destroyed a single vampire.

As Asher circled the space between the shelves and the desks a young man emerged from the shelves carrying a couple of very fat, yellowing volumes that Asher recognized as the 1867 reprints of a Georgian collection of Scots witchcraft

126

lore: there was mention in them, he recalled, of the 'Cauld Lad' that used to walk Graykirk Close in Edinburgh, whom it was considered death to meet. The young man, though shabbily dressed, wore a blue-, brown-and-red school tie from Winchester, much faded, and he bent over Millward with the same fanatic eagerness that the vampire-hunter himself had shown towards his books. His face glowed when Millward showed him something in the pages, and he dove away into the shelves again with the air of Sir Percival on the track of the Grail.

When he was out of earshot Asher approached the desk. 'Millward?'

The scholar turned in his chair. At the sight of Asher his eyes widened for a moment – their most recent meeting had involved Millward breaking Asher's ankle with a rifle butt and leaving him as bait for a vampire in the buried crypt of a Roman temple under Covent Garden – and then slitted in suspicion.

'What do you want?'

'Information.' Beneath Millward's frayed shirt-cuff Asher could see the other man also wore chains of silver around his wrists. 'What do you know about the Regent's Canal vampire?'

'Have you seen it?' Millward seized his sleeve, as if afraid that being questioned, Asher might run away.

'I've smelt it. And I saw the man it killed in Chalton Street, on the night of the sixteenth. I'm trying to track its appearances, to find where it's centered. And most specifically, who's protecting it.'

Ten

Millward had a room in Bethnal Green, near the goods yard. The threadbare curtains on its single window were dingy with soot and even the dried ropes of star-like white garlic blossoms that festooned them couldn't counteract either the stink of the gasworks nearby, nor the smell of mildew that took Asher by the throat.

Cardboard boxes stacked every wall head-high, protruded from beneath the bed and ranged under the cheap deal table. A hob the size of a shoebox accommodated a kettle, and tins of crackers shared the shelf over the table with yet more, smaller, cardboard boxes; the table itself was stacked with newspapers, as was one of the room's two wooden chairs. Millward moved the papers aside onto the bed, poured water from the jar by the door into the kettle, and fetched a handful of newspaper from what was evidently the discard box to kindle beneath a couple of knobs of coal. 'My true work's in the library,' he said as he scratched a lucifer match on the box. 'This place is no more than a pied-à-terre, so to speak.'

His breezy tone made it sound as if he still had his oak-lined study back at King's College, and the comfortable little house on Star Street that he'd shared with his long-suffering wife. Asher said nothing. He'd inhabited far worse, for months at a time, in the course of what the Department called 'cover'. But it had always been with the knowledge that his own rooms at New College were his true home.

To hunt us is to hunt smoke . . . to become obsessed, as all vampire hunters must be obsessed . . .

Since the night he'd lain, half-freezing in the damp, in the crypt where Millward and his disciples had pinned him as bait for the vampire they were trying to trap, he had hated the man – a hatred revived every time his ankle hurt him in winter. Now the hatred washed away in a wave of pity, seeing what the scholar had made of himself. He'd heard – he'd forgotten from whom – that the parents of Millward's wife still made him a tiny allowance.

This was what it was, he thought, looking around him, to be obsessed.

For years he'd seen Millward as an ageing Don Quixote, tilting at windmills invisible to sane eyes. But now, strangely, the person that came to his mind was his old teacher, the master-spy Crowell. The single-minded hunter in pursuit of his prey. A weapon in the hand of the Cause. Everything geared and tuned, like the engine of a motorcar, for one purpose and one purpose only.

And something else . . .

The box that Millward set on the table before him was fairly new, and labeled neatly – all the boxes were labeled – *Regent's Canal*. The clippings – Asher noted automatically the typefaces of *The Times*, the *Telegraph*, the *Sun*, the *Daily Mail* and the *Illustrated London News* among

129

others – were arranged chronologically; among the papers on the table at his elbow he identified *Le Figaro*, *l'Oeuvre*, *der Neuigkeits Welt-Blatt* and several German, Italian and American journals as well.

'It killed first on the thirtieth of January.' The vampire-hunter plucked a clipping from the envelopes within the box. 'A prostitute in Lampter Street near the Southgate Road. People said it was Jack the Ripper returning to his old haunts – if the Ripper's under sixty nowadays he must have been little more than a schoolboy his first time round! – but the details of the crime weren't the same. And the Ripper, whoever he was, never made the attempt to hide his victims. A frightful deed.' He laid the article on the table before Asher – barely two paragraphs, an afterthought to the German submarine attacks in the Irish Sea. Asher glanced over the specifics of the horrible remains and shivered.

'The body of a man was found – or what remained of one – on February eighth, on Dee Street near the gasworks. Police estimated that he hadn't been dead more than twenty-four hours. An elderly man was reported missing at about that time near Victoria Park—'

'By the Union Canal.' Asher mentally identified the place. 'And Dee Street is where Bow Creek joins the river. Water, both times.'

'I noticed that.' Millward laid out his clippings with a slow flourish, as if proving Asher wrong somehow or vindicating himself. Asher reflected that the man had fought so long to be believed – by his wife, by the police, by the King's College

130

authorities when challenged about his disappearances – that the faint, arrogant look of defiance had become habitual, though Asher was one of the few men in England – or probably in the world – who understood that Millward was in fact telling the truth.

Those windmills really *were* giants.

'I thought it curious,' the vampire-hunter added. 'They usually avoid running water. And it is more savage than the other vampires. They kill, but do not molest the bodies afterwards, even when they conceal them. I can show you—' He turned back toward the stacks of boxes, and Asher lifted his hand.

'You don't need to,' he said. 'I know this one is different.'

Wary contempt gleamed in the other man's dark eyes. *Aye, YOU would know, who consort with such beings . . .*

Asher sorted the little squares of newsprint, moving them around on the tabletop, as he had with the bits of information about the time and place of German so-called 'archaeological' expeditions in Mesopotamia back in the eighties, or where all those extra Legation 'clerks' had been seen, and at what times. Ysidro had surmised that Millward's brother, who had died young and unexpectedly, had been the victim of a vampire (*Carlotta?* Asher wondered. *The Lady Anthea Ernchester? Grippen himself?*) It was this, in the vampire's opinion, which had turned the scholar's already-extant belief in vampires to obsession . . . But sometimes Asher wondered whether it was Millward's belief in vampires that had caused

131

him to probe into matters concerning the world of the Undead – possibly with his brother's help – and thus bring that young man into peril in the first place.

As he himself had brought Lydia. And their daughter.

Enough to drive a man a little mad.

But he was not wrong, to seek those silent killers . . .

He took one of his Ordnance Survey maps from his pocket, and with his pen marked the places where kills had occurred. He marked also neighborhoods where people had been reported missing, often vagrants who slept rough, little regarded by the police. 'Nothing further south than Dee Street,' he commented after a moment. 'Nor further north than Leyton Marsh. Nothing more than a dozen yards from navigable water: creeks, canals, basins.'

'It's where the fog gathers thickest.' Millward sank into the other chair, leaned to look over his shoulder. 'Legend has it that they can summon fog . . .'

'They actually can't.' Asher moved another two-line clipping, put another X on the map. 'But there's waste ground along the canal, and buildings that stand deserted for days at a time: gasworks, the India docks, Hackney Common. The goods yards and tracks of the Midlands Railway. The pattern of this thing's hunting is different. It's an animal we're tracking, not a man.'

'It's a man,' retorted Millward grimly. 'A woman in Canal Road glimpsed it in the fog. Or it was a man once. The Undead—'

132

'This isn't one of the Undead.' Asher tilted his head a little to one side, still intent on the map. 'The pattern is similar, as the thing itself is similar. It's a revenant, what the early English called a wight: nearly mindless, and hungry. The vampires call them the Others. Like the Undead, it can to some extent fool the perceptions of the living. And like the Undead, it can transmit its condition through contamination of the blood, like a disease.'

'You're sure of this?' The scholar's silver-shot brows drew down. 'How do you—?'

'I'm sure. I have seen them cut to pieces, and the cut pieces continue to crawl about with what appears to be conscious volition. Sunlight destroys them; more slowly than their cousins, I'm told, but I've never seen it. But the thing is alive, and it can be killed. Vampires hunt all over the city – or they did,' he added with a grimace, 'until most of them left for the Front. This revenant – this Other—'

His finger traced the gray line of the Regent's Canal, with its myriad of auxiliary cuts and basins, curving through the East End like an old-time moat among a patchwork of industry and building yards. 'It hunts along here. And I intend to find it – or them. By this time there may be more than one.'

'You will have whatever help I – and those who help me, who believe in this war that we wage against the forces of Evil – can give.'

Asher thought about the young man in the Winchester tie in the Reading Room.

And about Crowell leaving his agents to die.

'But where did it come from?' Millward turned the map around, frowned over the neat X's. Then his sharp dark gaze cut back to Asher. 'And how did you learn of it? Did the Undead create it, then? Do they control it?'

'Not that I know of. I understand the vampires of Prague have tried for centuries to exert mental control over the Others that haunt the crypts beneath that city, without success.'

Millward's silence made Asher glance at him. He read in the dark eyes loathing and distress, tinged with admiration. Almost the same feelings, he reflected, that he himself had felt towards Pritchard Crowell.

'Prague . . .'

'The only city I've heard of so far,' said Asher, 'where these Others nest.'

'How did it come to England, then?'

'That,' said Asher, 'is one of the several things I intend to find out.'

Millward saw him down four flights to the door, through a front hallway whose dirty lino was cluttered with bicycles, coal scuttles and baby prams. The sun had just dipped behind the smoke-grayed line of brick houses opposite. It was a long walk to the nearest bus stop, and Asher guessed few cabs cruised these dismal streets. Dank fog was already rising from the river. On the way downstairs, Millward spoke of the young men who believed, as he did, in the Undead, who worked for him as secretaries and gatherers of information – 'Only Donnie's left of them. The rest are at the Front.' (Presumably Donnie was the young man in the Winchester tie.) 'Donnie isn't strong, but he and I will patrol the canal—'

But when Asher stepped across the threshold and the door shut behind him, he automatically cleared every thought from his mind, and scanned the street: wide flagways bustling with house-wives, children running home from school, voices shrill in the air. A woman brought a birdcage and a wicker basket up from a nearby areaway, chir-ruping to her canary in alternation with some of the most hair-raising oaths Asher had ever heard – *Islands Scots, what's she doing here?* An old man with an elaborate cart and equipment for the repair of umbrellas called 'Brollies to mend!' in a quavering voice. Asher's eye touched the area-ways of the houses nearby, the bleared windows across the road, as if he were in Berlin or St Petersburg, seeking anomalies or . . .

There.

He didn't turn his head. His sidelong glance passed across the sunken kitchen entry where he thought he'd seen a man's face, but there was nothing, and he turned away at once. One of the first rules was, *If you think you're being followed, don't let on. Maybe later you can see who it is, and take a guess at what they want.*

He thought he'd seen something, some anoma-lous shadow, outside the Reading Room.

And now here.

The Department? He trudged down Charlotte Street toward the Great Eastern goods yard where the omnibus would stop on its way to Charing Cross. *Or someone who, like Millward, has his own freelance disciples?*

135

Someone who thinks Millward may know some-thing . . . About the Other? Someone who, like me, knows that Millward will at least have infor-mation about where the Other has been?

If it is the Department, he reflected, taking into account that he'd barely gotten a glimpse of Millward's watcher, *shame on them. If Stewart wasn't lying, and they need every man to gather information in the battle zones, why waste a good agent keeping an eye on a vampire-hunting crank who isn't even aware that every vampire in London is now at the Front?*

Unless of course, Asher thought – without looking back – *I'm the one who's being followed.*

Lydia saw the vampires outside her tent in a dream: Antonio and Basilio, Red Cross armbands pale against the dark rough coats of stretcher-bearers, Don Simon in his British Army khaki. In the gibbous moonlight, their eyes gleamed like the eyes of the bloated trench rats, and Lydia was at once aware that the sporadic gunfire in the distance had stilled.

In her mind she heard Simon's voice whisper, 'Mistress . . .'

Waking, she knew they were there still.

Waking, the sound of the guns seemed very far away. The fretful cluck of the Lys over the remains of the broken bridge came startlingly clear.

In the next cot, Danvers slept like a dead woman. Brickwood's cot was empty. Lydia pulled on as much as she could of her clothing under her nightgown – brassiere, chemise and blouse – before getting out of bed in the freezing cold.

Hastily pulling on skirt, boots, petticoat and coat, she put on her spectacles and stepped quietly to the tent's entry, and looked out into the night.

And there they were.

Simon touched his lips for silence, and took her hand. The other two vampires soundlessly following, he led her to his staff-car at the edge of the camp – no Palfrey this time, she noticed – and helped her inside; Antonio took the wheel and drove off in the direction of the Front. Just short of the reserve trenches they stopped, left Basilio with the car and, as they had before, went on afoot, descending first into an abandoned reserve trench and then following the half-flooded mazes of the communications trenches: icy water underfoot, scuttling rats, the stench of death and latrine holes. Sometimes Simon or Antonio would lift her bodily in their arms, with the preternatural strength of the Undead, and carry her swiftly, like being borne by angels in a dream.

The stillness around them was the hush of nightmare. Her arms around Antonio's neck, as Don Simon clambered like a colorless spider up the side of the trench to look over at the hideous wasteland above, Lydia thought, for the thousandth time, *I shouldn't be doing this . . .*

Yet she felt no fear.

And, after a very short time, she understood that it was the silence that lay on this portion of no man's land that had drawn their attention, which had sent them to fetch her. Such absolute tranquility wasn't natural. No crackle of rifle-fire. Not a murmur from the front-line trenches, though they lay within yards. Once they passed a dugout, where half a dozen Indian infantrymen slumped around a makeshift stove and a tin of still-steaming tea. Not dead – she could see them breathing – but dozing. This was often the case with men in the trenches, but she understood that someone had put that illusion of inattention, that haze of sleepiness, on the sentries of both sides, and on the men hereabouts, for a reason.

And that someone has to be a vampire.

Simon scrambled up onto the fire step, looked over the sandbags. Lifted his gloved hand. *Come. Carefully.*

When she cautiously put her head over the sandbags – something that could get one killed, even at night – Don Simon passed her binoculars. The moon was a few days yet from full, but gave enough light to let her see the nurse Tuathla Smith – or whatever her name really was – crouched on the lip of a shell-crater, less than thirty feet away.

Nurse Smith wore the khaki coat of a British soldier, and had, like Lydia, left off her cap. Dark curls twisted into a loose knot at the back of her head, and framed the pale blur of her face as she looked around her. Aboveground in no man's land was not the place to be, even on a quiet night . . . and perhaps she also was aware, thought Lydia, that the silence hereabouts wasn't natural.

That someone had laid this silence on this small portion of the lines for a purpose.

And that purpose was to meet her without either of them getting shot.

And if a vampire were coming to speak to this

young woman, thought Lydia, that vampire would be listening, with the uncanny sharpness of Undead perceptions, for the smallest whisper of sound.

And thank goodness that even in the cold like this the whole place stinks so that a vampire can't smell living blood.

She felt rather than saw Don Simon glance sidelong at her, nodded very slightly: *Yes, it's she.* And squeezed his cold fingers: *Thank you.*

Movement in the moonlight. Walking, like the *bean sí* of poor Corporal Brodie's nightmares, as lightly as a ghost over the torn soil of this unspeakable hell.

As Corporal Brodie had said, she wore the uniform of a nursing sister under a dark cloak. Her hair, like Smith's was uncovered, the flaxen hue of raw silk in the moonlight and lying, like silk, loose over her shoulders. Her face was an exquisite oval.

'Meagher,' she said, as the young nurse stood up.

'I'm she.'

'You seek me?'

'If you truly are one of the Undead – one of the vampire kind – I do indeed.'

The vampire looked around her, scanning the ruined landscape with those darkness-piercing eyes. Lydia remained perfectly still, her own eyes cast down, praying Don Simon and Antonio were vampires of sufficient age and power to turn aside this woman's glance.

'I am called Francesca Gheric.' The vampire's voice was a soft contralto, with an accent to it that Lydia guessed would have told Jamie of some other time, some other place. 'By some called Francesca Brucioram, or Francesca the White. And I am what is called a vampire.'

'Tuathla Meagher.'

The vampire merely looked at her extended hand, then back to her face, one butterfly-wing eyebrow atilt. 'That isn't the name your father calls you, when you dream.'

Meagher straightened her shoulders, chin lifted defiantly. 'It's the name I took for myself when I left his house and his chains forever.'

Francesca the White's mouth flexed a little, like a birdwatcher identifying the whistle of some rare species. *Oh, one of those . . .*

'It's true, then,' Meagher went on, 'that you can touch the dreams of the living? Can weave spells in them to control their thoughts, and guide them where you will? That you can control the thoughts of certain beasts – the wolf, and the rat, and the bat – and command the actions of the mad?'

Through the binoculars, Lydia saw the vampire's red lips curve . . . (*Red, she has fed, she has killed once, or several times, tonight . . .*) 'You seek a demonstration, pretty child?'

What Francesca Gheric did then, Lydia didn't see, but Nurse Meagher jerked as if at some startling sound, and threshed the air before her face with her hand. Then she fell back a step, staring at the vampire in shocked respect.

Francesca raised one eyebrow again: *Satisfied?*

'Will you help us?' said Meagher eagerly. 'In return, we can—'

'I know who you are,' the White Lady cut her off. 'And I know who you work for, and what

140

you do in that compound of yours. Don't think I haven't watched you, walking about these deadly lands in the darkness, and speaking to my brothers and sisters of the night. This man Lemoine, this physician, this dabbler in chemicals and blood. I would speak to him.'

'I'm here,' said Meagher, barely able to contain her triumph, 'to take you to him.'

And with a sudden move she raised her hand to her throat, tore loose the silver cross she wore, and cast it away into the mud.

Eleven

'Francesca Gheric.' Antonio Pentangeli gazed thoughtfully into the distance as Basilio guided the staff-car down the shell-holed road in the moonlight. 'Well, well.'

He now shared the back seat with Lydia and Don Simon, and spoke barely to be heard over the growl of the engine. Basilio, Lydia guessed, had located Meagher's motorcar while she, Don Simon, and Antonio had been in the trench, and was following it now by the sound of its motor, audible to his Undead senses over the rumble of the guns to the south. *Unless of course he's just reasoned they can't leave the road at this point.* The land on both sides was a pitted ruin, laced with the water that had leaked from demolished drainage canals and stitched across and across with barbed wire.

They were headed south on the Arras road.

It is Lemoine . . .

'What about Francesca Gheric?'

'She dwelt in Strasbourg.' Antonio's dark eyes narrowed as he cast his memory back. 'For years and years, when Arioso was master of that city. Arioso had a network of living servants over the whole of the countryside between Strasbourg and Nancy. Very clever with illusion and dreams, but all said the White Lady was the stronger vampire. She was the elder in any case, and he never could

142

control his fledglings and was forever having trouble with them. I always thought that with little effort she could have taken control of that whole district. But she didn't.'

'Is that so odd?'

'You would think so had you ever encountered Arioso.' Don Simon folded his narrow, gloved hands.

'He demanded absolute control over those he made vampire,' explained Antonio. 'And unfortunately he was drawn to people who lived untidy and dramatic lives. A non-entity himself, he loved the excitement, but then had not the strength to bend them to his will. The Strasbourg nest has always been a snake pit of internal feuds. Francesca quarreled constantly with Arioso, and had she made even a few fledglings she could have driven him and his from the city. But in the end it was she who left. She dwelt for many years in Prague. Later she had a palazzo in Venice, just across the Campo di San Silvestro from Basilio and myself.'

Lydia reflected that should she ever have the opportunity to vacation in that city – or any city in Europe, for that matter – she would consult Don Simon first about potential neighbors.

'Hieronymus – the Master of Venice – tolerated her but never trusted her. She wouldn't obey him, either, but killed as she pleased. I know he feared she would contest his mastery.

'She is not like Simon,' Antonio added, seeing Lydia's sidelong glance at the older vampire. 'Simon has chosen to live like a shadow on the wall. I'm told he dwelt in Rome for two years

143

before the nest there even knew of his presence. Francesca disobeys the masters of the cities where she dwells, forms cliques among their fledglings and networks of servants among the living – Hieronymus was forever killing them. But she would never move to take genuine power.'

'Maybe she preferred just to be a trouble-maker?' Lydia recalled girls she'd gone to school with, and debutantes who had come 'out' in the same year as she, who simply delighted in malicious gossip and the stirring-up of trouble between friends, while seeming to lack, it appeared to her, genuine friends of their own.

'She was made vampire by the Lady Chretienne,' remarked Don Simon after a time. 'A master who taught her fledglings the finer arts of the Undead state, and selected them with some care. At the time I encountered them during the Wars of Religion 'twas my impression Chretienne intended Francesca to succeed her as master of that whole region. Then later she made Philip Berengar vampire, who succeeded her, and he made Arioso his fledgling and master of Strasbourg in his turn. I thought it curious, that La Dame Blanche, as Francesca was called, was bypassed. Now she seeks the help of this Lemoine, this "dabbler in blood and chemicals". What know you of this Lemoine, lady?'

'Only what I mentioned before.' She shook her head. 'That he's with the French Sixth Army, and served in Algeria, Indochina, West Africa. He was in Peking in early 1912, where he might easily have heard of the revenants in the Western Hills.'

144

'More than that, I think.' A tiny line scratched itself between Simon's colorless brows. 'I have made a study of the vampire state over the years, and have read a good many articles on the composition and maladies of the blood.'

On Lydia's other side, Antonio Pentangeli shook his head, with an expression, attenuated as it was, that in a living man would have been an eyeball-rolling wave of exasperation. 'Were you this much of a pedant as a living man, Simon? I keep abreast of the world, but I swear this for the truth, *bella donna*, he writes sonnets about the composition of blood! Never would I bore a beautiful lady into a lethargy by—'

'Oh!' interrupted Lydia, and then, realizing that up ahead of them, Francesca might be listening for sounds of pursuit, she whispered, 'You think Colonel Lemoine might be *Jules* Lemoine, who wrote that article the year before last about viral mutations of red corpuscles?'

'I confess I did not completely understand his argument,' murmured Don Simon. 'Yet something of the way he spoke of blood made me wonder if he had ever had occasion to study the blood of the Undead.'

'And he was in Peking in 1912,' finished Lydia. 'He might have actually encountered the revenants, or someone who had fallen victim to one. He did say when we lunched together on Monday, that he never passed up an opportunity to study the pathologies of the local people, wherever he was stationed.'

The staff-car picked up speed as the road improved and the hammering of the guns faded a little to the east. For long periods now, stands of trees bordered the road, unshattered by shell-fire, and in the darkness she smelled the green scents of early spring. When she opened her mouth to speak again Don Simon gestured her quiet: the drone of a pursuing engine could be lost in the noise of one's own motor, but even the quietest of living voices might easily register to Undead ears. They had passed the turning to Haut-le-Bois some time ago, and in the weak moonlight the low swell of hills that sheltered that clearing station lifted a little against the western sky. Lydia had no idea how long it was until dawn, or if, and where, her three companions had a safe place to go to ground at first light.

Evil mingled with good, she thought, looking from Antonio's craggy profile to Don Simon's aloof, half-averted face. *But can't that be said of all human beings? I should hate them for what they are, for what they do.*

But at least, she thought, they believed her, and would understand the significance of the fact that it was Lemoine who was kidnapping German prisoners of war.

Men who weren't severely wounded, but who legitimately could be restrained. Men who had no power to protest, and no one to protest to. Whose disappearance would be greeted with a shrug: *They must have got the papers mixed up . . .*

Like petrol and cigarettes and morphia.

Basilio switched off the engine, and let the car glide to a stop. Silence lay on the land, save for the intermittent boom of the guns. *We must have swung east again, or the Front curved west . . .*

146

Antonio climbed out over the door (*So there won't be the sound of it opening, in the stillness of the night?*) and held up his hands for her; Don Simon lifted her over, with the casualness of a man picking up a kitten. Basilio remained where he was, and Antonio touched his hand where it lay on the car door, lightly, as they walked away.

Distantly, Lydia heard an engine start up again. 'A gate,' Antonio murmured, leaning close. 'Guards. French.'

Leaving the road, they climbed a hill's shoulder that gave a view onto the next rise of ground. In ancient times a wide-spread cluster of gray buildings had covered that rise, half of them in ruins now and the whole area studded with French Army tents and a half-dozen rough-built huts. A deep ditch surrounded the whole, fenced on both sides with a hedge of barbed wire.

Old trench works, Lydia thought. The dark slots went right up the slope behind the buildings, and she could see where the woods that surrounded the place had been cut back to let the 'moat' completely encircle the place.

Those buildings that remained whole, though simply built of gray stone, had the look of profound age.

Don Simon's voice was barely louder than the rustle of the leaves. 'The nunnery of Cuvé Sainte-Bride.'

'You know it?'

'Only the name on maps. 'Twas naught to speak of, even when I was in France years ago.'

A few tents glowed from lantern-light within. A window in one of the huts brightened, then dimmed as a shadow crossed it. Breeze brought the smell of latrines and cooking-fires, stinks familiar from the clearing station. And another smell that lifted the hair on Lydia's neck.

Her hand closed hard on Don Simon's fingers.

'Best be gone.' His whisper brushed her ear. 'She'll come out soon, if she's any wits at all. Dawn's coming, and we're twenty miles from Pont-Sainte-Félicité. We shall convey you home, lady, unless you'd wish a few hours' sleep at the chateau of the Master of Prague. You'll be granted little enough rest at your camp.'

'Thank you,' said Lydia. 'I'll take my chances at the clearing station.' She already had a headache from lack of sleep, but the thought of calmly bedding down in a vampire nest – though she knew to the marrow of her bones that Don Simon's influence would keep her as safe – was more than she wished to contemplate.

Both vampires bowed, like courtiers of some bygone world, and guided her back toward the car.

When night was fully come after his encounter with Millward, Asher took a cab from his hotel in Pembridge Place to Paddington Station, purchased a return ticket for Bristol, packaged up his Burberry and hat in the gents' room and paid a porter there to quietly mail them back to Oxford for him. Then he donned the cap he'd had in his Burberry pocket, and slipped down the stairway to the Underground, watching the platform behind him as he stepped at the last minute onto the train for Hammersmith. At

148

Shepherd's Bush Market he got out – again leaving it till the last moment, and still feeling somewhere in the back of his thoughts the prickling wariness that had touched him outside of Millward's – and took the omnibus for the East India Dock, switching to a cab in Oxford Street and backtracking along the Edgware Road until he came – at almost midnight – to Regent's Park.

His meeting with Grippen wasn't until tomorrow night, but he guessed the Master of London knew perfectly well where he was.

Freezing damp rose from the grass as he followed the graveled path toward the boating lake. At this hour the stillness was such that he could listen behind him for the telltale scrunch of a stealthy foot on gravel, the wet squish of someone treading last autumn's dying leaves.

He heard nothing, and didn't think he'd seen that whisper of shadow, that itchy hint of a half-recognized silhouette, since the Underground station.

But he heard nothing – not a thing – in the moments before a heavy hand closed on his shoulder and he smelled stale blood and foulness.
'Mr Scragger?'

'Mr Graves.'

Grippen seemed to form himself out of shadows, congealed darkness in an old-fashioned greatcoat. 'Who's your friend?'

'He still with me?'

'Narh.' Even as a scarce-heard whisper the vampire's voice was harsh as lava rock. 'I turned him aside in Commercial Road. He'll not be back.'

'You get a look at him?'

'Dark coat. Great nose. Winkers and spinach. He was across the street.'

Glasses and a beard, Asher knew, could also be easily wadded into a Burberry pocket. He'd done it himself, more times than he could count. 'Short? Small?'

'A rat in an overcoat. Know him?'

Asher hesitated, then shook his head. 'If you see him again, let me know. I want to know who put him on me.' Although he had a strong suspicion that he knew already.

The vampire made a sound like a dog snarling. 'Crafty cove. I'll swear he saw me, and not many as can do that. You figure him for a beak?'

'Could be,' said Asher. 'He's working for someone, and I think he's looking for the same thing we are. So chances are good we'll meet him again.'

They turned north, to where Regent's Canal bordered the park's wooded fringes in its West End guise.

'Aye,' rumbled Grippen. 'I'll have a word wi' him then, and see what he's got to say for himself.'

They followed the canal into the maze of locks and bridges among the railroad yards, surreal tangles of sidings, sheds, coal bunkers and basins. Moving slowly and without light, Grippen sniffed, probing the darkness with those dark gleaming eyes. Asher listened, and watched for movement within the blackout abysses around them. It was like picking one's way through sightless and jagged Hell.

At one point, near the horrible old workhouse of St Pancras, when they stopped to let Asher rest, he passed along in a whisper what he'd gleaned from Millward's obsessive collection of newspaper clippings: that the revenant seldom strayed far from the canal, and that in the two months it had been at large in London it had killed only half a dozen times. 'It may be living on rats.' Asher perched himself on the bollard of a half-sunk wharf across from the vast blackness of the Midland Railroad goods yard, and wished as he shivered that he hadn't sent his Burberry away. 'The Others have a collective mind – like a hive of bees – but how much mind a single one of them has, away from its nest, I'd be curious to know. Or how far away it can be, and still be under their influence. The nests of them that I encountered in China could summon and command rats to defend their hiding places, or to swarm an intruder . . . or presumably, to let themselves be caught and devoured.'

'Don't speak ill of it,' rumbled Grippen. 'We drink rat blood, at need. It's hot and it's red, and it's living – aye, and there's a little dark sparkle to it of fire, like the fire of a man's death, or a woman's. Many's the vampire that's lived on rats, if he found himself where the living were suspicious, or too few to kill without drawin' down attention. Wolves we can call sometimes, too, and foxes, though precious few o' them you'll find about these days. Aye, and bats, like that silly caitiff Stoker wrote. Small use they are, though, save to flush a quarry from hidin' with a good scare.

151

'Ye've never thought of it yoursel'?' he added after a moment, with a sidelong glance at Asher.

'Thought of what?'

'Livin' forever.'

The silence lasted a long time after that. Asher found himself curiously unsurprised by the question.

And – he noted this with abstract interest – not in the least offended that the question had been put to him.

He supposed the proper reaction would be *How dare you think I would even for a moment entertain such a notion?* though he couldn't think of a single one of his former colleagues in the Department who would have made such a reply, either. Or who would have meant it, if they had spoken the words.

When at length Grippen spoke again his voice was soft, like a monster's purr. 'Never tell me you haven't wondered, what it'd be like not to get old? Rots you, don't it, that you've had to ask to stop and breathe a bit like a spavined horse after but a mile along the canal? That for all you know, you may never get back the strength you had five years ago? That you may always have that pain in your chest, that weakness in your legs? I need a fledgling, Asher. A good one, a strong one, that's got a brain in his skull; that knows this city and this land as I know 'em. That knows mankind as I know 'em.'

'If you need a fledgling,' Asher reminded him, 'it's because I killed yours.'

Grippen waved the objection aside. 'You was in a flame, and frighted for your brat. Think on

152

it,' he urged softly. 'You get used to drinkin' blood, that's nuthin'. And what 'tis like to take a soul . . . Ahh, the heat of it, and the glory of it . . . And I know you miss it.'

Asher looked sharply sidelong at him.

'Huntin' as you used. The life in darkness, the life beyond the wall. You wouldn't have spied all those years for that cold little snirp of a queen, if it hadn't been in your blood, to see how you could move through the world whilst stayin' outside of it. Teachin' whey-faced rich-boys that Englishmen used to say "fall" when they meant "autumn", an' "ah" when they meant "ay" – tcha! An' havin' tea with them lack-wits at your college.' The dark eyes narrowed. ''Tis no life for a man and you know it.'

The big hand closed, thick black-furred fingers, tipped with inch-long claws pale and slick as glass. 'We could hold London, the two of us.'

'And you would hold me,' returned Asher quietly. 'Having given you my soul, to guide it through the body's death and transformation, you would keep a piece of it, always. If nothing else, I don't want you to have a piece of my soul. I've seen the Master of St Petersburg make one of his fledglings kiss my feet, and Don Simon Ysidro force a fledgling he'd made to remain outdoors as the sun came up. It's not a power I'd hand to anyone on this earth, let alone one who's lived by murder for three hundred and fifty years.'

'Well, that's the trick, i'n't it?' The vampire's grin was a horrible thing to see. 'You pay for what you get. And who knows but that I might run afoul of your little friend Millward some

153

night and wake up with a stake through my heart? Then you'd be Master of London. Why not?'

Why not?

Asher rose from the bollard, not refreshed but at least able to continue; knowing they had the whole of the night yet to walk.

'If I change my mind,' he said, 'you shall be the first to know.'

'We have to go back there, you know,' said Lydia, when Don Simon helped her back into the staff-car. 'I mean, I think we all know what's going on there, and what Colonel Lemoine wants Francesca's help with, though I can't see that he's going to get it. As far as I know, no vampire can control the minds of the Others unless he – or she – has actually been infected with their blood.' She shivered at the recollection of the thing she'd discovered in that hidden vault in Peking, lying like a gruesome worm, laughing insanely in the dark. 'And what could Lemoine offer her that would get her to take that kind of a risk?'

'Lemoine,' murmured Antonio, 'or whoever is behind him.' He shrugged, and glanced over his shoulder – he was in the front seat now beside Basilio – and by the sound of his voice Lydia could tell that the whole matter was to him no more than a means to while away the night. He'd probably taken two lives before he and Don Simon ever came to her tent, when in other times he'd have spent the whole of the night hunting.

Helping her was simply an entertainment, like the opera.

He went on, 'Though surely the French government—'

'The French government is desperate for soldiers,' returned Don Simon calmly. ''Tis now no mere matter of spies and secrets. They seek soldiers to throw at their enemy – men who will walk without question into machine-gun fire. Who better than the mindless, if they can be controlled from afar off? Men moreover who can be taken from the enemy himself and rendered to such a state without consequences and without questions being asked, not even by this Lemoine's own conscience, assuming that he has one. Who has not read a thousand posters on every street corner and hoarding in Paris, on the walls of every hospital and railway station and officer's mess from here to the sea? *Crush the Germans, Destroy This Mad Brute.* Pictures of German nurses pouring water on the ground rather than moisten the lips of wounded British prisoners.' His dismissive shrug was barely more than a movement of one finger. 'Of course they deserve it. Your king has said so, so it must be true.

'What think you then, Mistress? Walking into that place alone puts the White Lady at this Lemoine's mercy. He has but to hold her until sunrise – not far off now, as I have said. Once she sleeps, he can take from her as much blood as he will, upon which to perform his experiments. Or he can inject her with the blood of these revenants, making her one of their communal mind, willy-nilly. For what would *you* put yourself in such peril?'

Antonio, looking over the back of the seat,

155

raised his fair brows, his opinion of the ridiculousness of such a question clear on his face.

To any vampire, thought Lydia, the answer to that question would be, self-evidently, *Nothing* . . .

But she knew that to be not quite true.

Slowly, she said, 'If she is human – if she remained human, through her transformation to the vampire state – she might do such a thing for love. You say she has been a vampire for a long time . . .'

'She had become one not many years before I visited Strasbourg during the great Wars of Religion – 1610, perhaps?'

'So it isn't likely she would be protecting her child, for instance. I know . . . I have met . . .' Her voice faltered and she found she couldn't look at the thin pale figure beside her. 'Some vampires do retain the capacity to love . . .'

Not being able to look at Don Simon, she was gazing straight ahead of her, and saw, at her words, Antonio's gloved fingers tighten, very slightly, on Basilio's shoulder. The fair vampire agreed quietly, 'Some do, indeed. I know not if the Lady is one of them. For all our years of proximity I do not know her well. In Venice, she would carry on long courtships with living men, sometimes for years – alluring them, bedding them . . . For you are no doubt aware, *bella donna*, that while the organs of generation in the male vampire become nonfunctional, a woman can of course receive a living man, provided she feeds beforehand so that her flesh will be warm to his touch. And indeed, this was how these

156

courtships ended, for her. Her favorite sport was to kill her lover in the act.'

'Unlikely, then,' remarked Don Simon, 'that she would put her mind, her life and her freedom into anyone's hand, for the sake of a man she loved.'

'And yet,' mused Antonio, 'the lady has proven herself indifferent to the sweet seductions of power—'

'And whatever her reason for going in there was,' added Lydia, with a frown, 'I expect she *could* get out, as long as it was dark. *Would* barbed wire stop a vampire?'

'We are flesh and bone, lady.' Don Simon spread his hands. 'And that is what barbed wire is designed to catch. A frightened vampire would be less likely to let the pain of the barbs stop him – or her – but they would be able to tear their flesh free only a little more quickly than a living man. And though we can survive the loss of blood better than the living, it renders us – as it does you – weak, and in time unable to flee or seek shelter. Of a certainty barbed wire would hold them, until their captors could come up to them with stouter bonds . . . if capture is the aim of their enemies. Did you see what was in those trenches, which surround the whole of the camp and the convent?'

Lydia shook her head, though the recollection of the smell returned to her, horrible and with echoes more dreadful still.

'They are floored with barbed wire, as well as fenced with it on both sides. From which I can only deduce the presence, somewhere in that

157

camp, of a hive of revenants sufficiently large to permit the formation among them of group-mind, group-thought. A group will be capable,' he concluded, tenting his thin fingers, 'of controlling the local population of rats for their own defense. And I should imagine this close to no man's land, there is no shortage of those.'

Lydia thought that one through, and said, 'Oh, dear.'

Twelve

26-3
Jamie
Cuvé Sainte-Bride x Former nunnery x
Nord x nr Haut-le-Bois x Dr Jules Lemoine
infecting German POWs x Others x work
w vampire Francesca Gheric of Strasbourg
x How ?? x Tuathla (not real name)
Meagher x heavily fortified x how get in?
x any information x promise I will be
careful x you be careful too
    All my love

The letter was postmarked Paris, Friday 26 March, at the Gare St Lazare. The hand was undoubtedly Lydia's, though Asher guessed Ysidro had posted it. It was topped and tailed by addresses and names not Lydia's own, encoded as a rambling complaint about the difficulties in obtaining sugar and decent coffee in Paris, and the cipher it contained raised the hair on his scalp.

He was still working on an innocuous missive whose coded text read *Don't you DARE investigate ANYTHING until you hear from me* (knowing full well that this wouldn't reach her for three days at least) when a brisk rap sounded at his door, which he recognized as belonging to Josetta Beyerly.

Late-afternoon sunlight lay across the foot of

159

his bed from the room's single window. He knew Lydia's friend had pupils, most mornings – French language, or piano – and on those she didn't, she drove an ambulance-wagon from the docks to First London General Hospital. This was just as well, for through the past three nights he had hunted with Lionel Grippen, following Regent's Canal and its ramifications into Hackney Marshes and Hampstead Heath. They sought as much for the places where a revenant might be hiding, as for sight of the thing itself, and so far had found little. Most of those evenings had been foggy, as well as pitch-dark from the blackout, and Asher could feel his energy seeping away from night to night, never returning, after sleep, to quite what it had been before. Hoggett would flay him alive if he knew.

Josetta wouldn't have come to Faraday's Private Hotel like this unless it was important.

'There's something very, very queer happening over in Brabazon Street.'

'His daughter won't call the police,' the teacher explained, when she and Asher stepped from the overcrowded bus at the junction of East and West India Docks Roads. Men – women, too, now – crowded the flagways at this hour, and the bus had been jammed, for the docks, the chemical works and the gasworks all lay nearby. The raw air was rank with coal smoke and the sewery smell of outhouses. The flat-fronted brick rows of two-up two-downs were nearly black with years' accumulation of soot, and Asher had to stop beside a lamppost and cough for some

160

minutes. Josetta took his arm worriedly, and he waved her off.

'I'll be fine.' This was a lie. 'Is there some reason he doesn't want the police searching the house?'

'The neighbors think he receives stolen goods,' she replied matter-of-factly. 'He may well – he owns a pawnshop in the Limehouse Road. But I think the main reason is that he's involved with buying guns for the Irish Volunteers.'

Asher's jaw tightened grimly. On the omnibus from Kensington he'd picked out, as was his habit, the different accents of his fellow-passengers, and ever since they'd crossed the Regent's Canal he'd been swimming in a sea of elongated vowels and dentalized t's. In the shabby jacket and down-at-heels shoes he'd changed into when Josetta had spoken of their destination, he guessed he wouldn't stand out, and the VAD uniform of his companion would pass pretty much anywhere in London. Depending on how deeply the Mayo family was involved with those willing to use violence to obtain independence for Ireland, this probably wasn't a neighborhood in which to be heard asking questions.

Josetta climbed two steps – washed two or three days ago, by the look of the grime accumulated since – and rapped at the door, her sharp one-and-two characteristic knock. The house smelled of cooked cabbage and poverty, the areaway below, of decaying vegetables and piss. *No alley behind.* Areaways usually meant back-to-backs. *In this neighborhood, probably a yard . . .*

161

The woman who opened the door a crack looked as if she hadn't slept in several nights.

'I've brought someone to see Bert,' said Josetta simply.

The woman closed the door a few inches, her eyes like shuttered windows. 'Nuttin' wrong with Da.'

'There is,' said Josetta. 'You know there is, Katie. This man can be trusted.'

Tears flooded the woman's eyes and she clamped her lips hard.

Grieved, thought Asher. *And scared for her life.*

'His mouth?' he asked softly, and hardened the final 'th' just slightly, a whisper of the accents of Katie's own land. *You can trust me . . . I'm one of your own . . .* If the danger hadn't been so desperate he'd have been ashamed of himself. 'His teeth? Bruisin' here—' His fingers traced on his own head where he knew the sutures of the skull would be deforming – 'an' here?'

Katie began to cry, and opened the door.

A younger woman, still dressed for factory work, put her head out of the kitchen door at the back (and yes, by the window behind her there was a yard). From the other door on the narrow hall two tow-headed boys peeked, in their early teens and also, Asher noted, still in the grimed overalls of dockhands. None of them looked like they'd slept.

Katie led them up the stair without a word.

Asher had seen before what greeted him in the tiny rear bedroom. The figure huddled in the room's darkest corner was a man in his sixties, balled together with his arms around his knees and his body leaned against the wall. Sheets and blankets had been stripped from the bed and draped over the single window, packed tight in every cranny in a desperate attempt to shut out all light. He winced and made a sound of protesting pain as Katie lit the old-fashioned gas: 'Da, there's a man come to see you. We'll be needin' a bit of light.'

He made a strangled sound, as if clearing something out of his throat. Then, 'Don't want to see nobody, Kate.'

'He knows what's wrong wit' you, Da.'

Looking at the bruises on the face where the skull was elongating, the bloody smears on the old man's hands and mouth where his teeth were starting to grow, Asher knew exactly what was wrong with him, and his heart turned sick inside him. Sick with pity and dread.

Damn it, he thought. *Damn it*.

And damn whoever brought the first of those things over here. Damn them to the bottommost smoking crevice of Hell.

Gently he took Katie's arm, led her back into the hall and shut the door.

'Does this door lock?' he asked softly. She shook her head. She looked to be in her forties, though hard work and childbearing had aged her face. She stood no higher than his shoulder, thin as a twig-doll. Her hair was streaked with gray and she'd lost several of her teeth.

'You need to get a bolt and lock it,' he said. 'I'll come back—' He calculated times, and of course there wouldn't be a shop in town open

163

at this hour . . . 'I'll come back tomorrow, wit' your permission, and put it on, if you've no one else—'

'Terry'll do it.' Katie seemed to pull herself together a little. 'Kerr. Next door. He's a foreman at Lavender Wharf.'

'Do it tonight, if you can.' He kept his accent the one she'd unconsciously connect with home, South Ireland: those predominantly Catholic counties where resentment burned strong against the Empire which for centuries had shut the Irish themselves out of owning or ruling their own land. 'An' get your boys – them two I saw downstairs? – out of the house, find somewheres else for 'em to sleep. Your da's ill,' he went on, seeing her shake her head, as if disbelieving that such a thing could be happening to them. 'And he's not gonna get better. I'm sorry to be the one tellin' you this, I'm so sorry, but there's nuttin' to be done. He's gonna go off his head soon, an' try to harm anyone he sees. Katie—' He tightened his grip, gently, on her shoulders as her face convulsed with tears, and he glanced quickly at Josetta.

'Reilley,' she mouthed back at him, knowing what he sought.

'Mrs Reilley . . . I'm sorry, but I need to know this. When did this happen, and where? Somethin' attacked him, didn't it? Tom the Ogre? Bit him? Tore him up?'

The woman nodded, clinging now to his arms and shaking with her effort to control her sobs. 'Comin' home. Last Tuesday night. He'd been at the Green King over in Tildey Street—'

164

On the other side of the Limehouse Cut. He'd have had to cross it, coming back, late and in the fog . . .

'Will he eat? Drink?'

'He ain't all day. He did, up to yesterday—'

'Do you have laudanum in the house? Good—'

'I'll ask Polly for it downstairs.' Josetta clattered off, to return a few moments later with a substantial square black bottle in one hand, a smaller green one in the other labeled 'Infants Quietness Elixir'.

Quietness indeed, reflected Asher grimly. *Will opiates work on one of Them?* They certainly didn't on vampires, not unless they were mixed with some of those ingredients inimical to vampire flesh: silver, aconite, tincture of Christmas rose. He'd seen nothing concerning the Others in the medieval text which seemed the most accurate, the notorious Book of the Kindred of Darkness. From what Don Simon Ysidro had told him, that volume had supposedly been written in Spain only a few years after the first of the Others had appeared in Bohemia. As little as anyone knew about vampires, the knowledge was vast compared with what anyone knew about these filthy cousins of theirs.

'We're goin' to try to sedate him.' He turned back to the terrified woman beside the shut bedroom door. 'Put him to sleep. He'll be a danger to you, Mrs Reilley, an' soon. I'm sorry, but that's what this is, this sickness that he caught from the thing that tore him up. It spreads by blood, so don't let him bite you or tear you, don't let one drop of his blood mix with yours. That's

165

why I'm tellin' you, get your family outen this house. I wish I could make it different—'

She was weeping again, his hands strong on her arms.

'—but I can't. You got to be strong, M'am. There's nuttin' can be done for him now but keep him asleep if we can. You got to be strong.'

Shuddering, she wiped her nose and her eyes. 'I'll be strong.'

'Good lass.'

He glanced at Josetta again.

'I got the rest of the family out of the house.'

'Wait for us—' he turned back to Mrs Reilley – 'down the foot of the stair. I swear to you we'll do him no harm, but by the saints, there's nuttin' to be done for him. And I swear,' he added, turning to Josetta as the little woman slowly descended the stair to the darkness which had now gathered thick in the house below, 'I wouldn't ask this of you, Miss Beyerly, if I had any choice in the world about it.'

'That's a pip of a brogue you've got there, Professor,' she returned, unruffled. 'Better than the halls.' Then her expression darkened, and she said softly, 'What's happening to him? What you were asking about – looking for . . . How did you know?'

'Don't ask.'

For a moment the young woman stared at him in the dimness of the narrow hallway, as if she couldn't believe what she saw in his eyes.

'We have to get him to hospital. I can get an ambulance-wagon—'

'Let's get him sedated first.' Asher's mind was

racing, Langham's complicit smile returning to him: *The matter is in hand . . .*

You bastard. You know that thing is in London and you're watching the hospitals, aren't you? And if you get hold of this poor sod . . . What? 'Infecting German POWs . . .'

Use them against the Germans? And then later against the Irish who demand rule of their own lands, or riot against the threat of conscription for England's war?

Use them against Indians who want independence?

Sick cold went through him, like the onset of fever. (*And maybe it IS the onset of fever . . .*)

First things first.

He signed to Josetta to remain in the hall, stepped into the bedroom.

The gas was out. There was no smell of it in the room, so presumably Bert Mayo retained enough recollection of who and what he was to have turned the gas off rather than just dousing the minimal flame. A weak reflection of light from the hall picked up a red glint from the corner where the man had been huddled earlier, and, near him, the tiny, vicious sparks of the eyes of rats.

Four or five rats, all within a few feet of him.

Damn it . . .

Asher struck a match. Mayo hid his eyes. The rats fled.

So far, so good.

'Get out of it,' whispered the stricken man, the words dribbling from his lips like the mutter of delirium. 'Put out the bloody light. Make 'em shut up. Katie . . .'

167

'Make who shut up, Bert?' Asher lit the gas and turned it down as far as he safely could.

Bert covered his face with his arms, then scrabbled to the bed and grabbed the pillow to further block the light from his eyes. The walls around him were smeared with blood where his mouth had touched; the mattress, and the bedclothes hung over the window, streaked with it.

DO NOT let that blood touch you . . .

'Rats,' whispered Bert Mayo hoarsely. 'Chatterin'. Voices in me conk. Make 'em shut up!' He lurched to his feet. Seen full-on for the first time his face was a horror, the flesh a mass of bruises where the mouth and jaw had lengthened out like an ape's, blood from his bitten lips stringing into the gray stubble of his chin. Behind him in the doorway Asher heard Josetta gasp, and he reached back and took the laudanum bottle from her hand.

'This'll make the voices shut up, Bert,' he said. 'Then we'll make the rats go away.'

'Rats'll never go away.' Slowly, Bert began to circle toward the door. 'Crawl in an' out o' me skull-bones whilst I sleep. I hear their squeakin' an' it sounds like words.'

'This'll shut 'em up. Guaranteed.' *How many revenants constitute a hive mind? Is he controlled by the colony – good God! – that this Lemoine is growing in France, or by Hungry Tom out in the fog of the canal? Or – Jesus! – is his mind controlled by the rats, rather than the other way around, given that they outnumber him?*

He held out the bottle. 'Drink it,' he offered. 'You'll be the better for it.'

168

Bert's lips pulled back from the bloodied mess of fangs and he lunged at Asher, clawed hands outstretched. Asher yelled 'Door!' and, thank God, Josetta had the wits to slam it without any wailed vacillation about *I can't shut you in there with it . . .!* If he knew Josetta she had one sturdy shoulder braced against its panels, not that that would do any good—

He flung himself at the window, ripped down the wadded blankets, and hurled them over Bert's head as Bert reached him. The stricken man was strong, but it was still human strength, the strength of a man of sixty who's worked hard all his life, not the hideous abnatural strength of mutated cell tissue and altered muscle. Asher rolled him in the blankets, shouted 'Josetta!' and she was in the room, striding to help him—

'Asher, there's—'

Feet thundered in the stairwell. Men slammed into the room, half a dozen of them, as Asher grappled with the blanket-wrapped thing that had been Bert Mayo. Three of the men – laborers smelling of sweat and beer and very cheap tobacco – grabbed Bert and wrapped him still tighter in the blankets, and in the same instant one of the men seized Asher's arms from behind, pulled him out of the fray, and held him while another whipped from his pocket a weighted rubber sap.

'Get him outta here,' commanded the sixth man, who held Josetta's arms behind her – Asher automatically placed his accent within a few miles of Cork, like his round Celtic face and the thick shoulders in their meal-colored jumper. 'These two—'

That was as far as he got. Josetta stomped hard on the man's instep, dropped her weight, twisted in his shock-loosened grip and gouged for his eyes. In the same moment Asher kicked the man with the sap in front of him, performed the same classic stomp-drop-twist on his own captor before smashing him across the face with the laudanum bottle, grabbed Josetta's wrist – it did not appear to be the time to ask questions – and used the pillow round his fist to smash open the window. There was a shed outside – there was always a shed, in tiny houses like this one – and he swung Josetta out the window and dropped out after her himself, into a yard the size of a dining-room table and choked with rubbish. He pulled Josetta into the outhouse and closed the door. Through its tiny judas he saw two of the men drop through the window, dash to the rear fence of the yard and scramble over it: the logical direction of pursuit.

They stood together, in black and stinking darkness, for nearly ten minutes, long after the house itself grew silent and still.

No light returned to the windows of its kitchen. No one opened its rear door.

Josetta made not a sound, though he could hear her breathing fast and hard and could feel her trembling where her body pressed his.

He himself was shaking, as if his legs would crumple if he tried to walk.

Hirelings of whoever it was – that flickering shadow that he'd thought he'd glimpsed in Charlotte Street? The bewhiskered and bespectacled 'rat in an overcoat' that Grippen had seen?

170

Bert Mayo's pals in the Irish Brotherhood, concerned that Katie had taken a stranger into the house? (*And God knows what was hidden up in the attic . . .*) The local Brotherhood of Light Fingers, if the enterprising Bert was in fact a fence as well as a gunrunner?

Dear God, what were they going to do if Bert tore into them with those bloodied teeth?

The matter is in hand, Langham had said, with a twinkle and a smile.

In time Asher slipped out of the outhouse, crept shakily across the yard – it was now pitch-black – and listened at the back door of the house.

Nothing.

The yard of the house behind the Mayos was tidier, when Asher clambered over its fence. By the feel of the dirt underfoot, and the way plants brushed his groping hands, he guessed the neighbors had a garden (and wouldn't thank his pursuers for trampling it). He went back and fetched Josetta, offered her help (which she turned down indignantly) over the fence, and over three more, moving laterally parallel to (he calculated) Ellesmere Street, the next street over from Brabazon, before finding a house that sounded vacant. With a mental apology to its tenants he broke the kitchen window, and let himself and Josetta through kitchen and hallway and out at last into Ellesmere Street indeed.

Since no cabs ever cruised anywhere near the grimy purlieus of Brabazon Street – and the busses had long since ceased running – they had a walk of nearly a mile to the cluster of pubs

171

around the East India Docks where such a thing could finally, by chance, be obtained.

Lying awake in the darkness, Lydia thought about blood.

She'd dreamed about it, as she often did, especially since her expedition – nearly a week ago now – to Cuvé Sainte-Bride. In her dream she'd seen the vampire Francesca Gheric attempting to flee from the convent of Cuvé Sainte-Bride, getting caught on the barbed wire that half-filled the trenches which surrounded it like a toothed steel moat, trying to tear herself loose from the barbs. (These were longer and far more thickly wound on military wire, Captain Calvert had told her, than they were on the mere stuff that Americans used to pen their cattle.) *'We are flesh and bone, lady,'* Don Simon had said, and in Lydia's dream Francesca had struggled, tearing both flesh and bone in an attempt to get out of the trench before the heaving gray tide of rats reached her.

Blood had glistened on the steel barbs and, standing on the brink of the trench, Lydia had tried to figure out how she was going to obtain a sample of that blood.

She'd eventually decided that the best way was to have Don Simon transform himself into a bat and go fetch some for her, and they were in the midst of a rather convoluted argument about whether or not this was possible (*'Were it possible for a vampire to transform into a bat, Mistress, the Lady Francesca would not now be in the difficult situation that she is . . .'*) when she woke.

172

Why did I want her blood? She frowned over the question.

I've already SEEN vampire blood under a microscope. Simon had donated some a few years ago, and had been as curious as she herself, to compare it with the blood of the living.

She had written up her findings, and had handled the sample with the greatest of care, well aware that if the vampire state were in fact connected with some unknown virus – and were related to the hideous pathology of the Others – no chances could be risked of contamination. When finished with her study (which had taken place by gaslight) she had set the sample outdoors, and had been queasily disturbed to see it spontaneously catch fire, and burn up at the first touch of morning sun.

So why did I want HER blood?

A thought, like the echo of her now-fading dream, came at once: *Because the blood is the answer.*

But she had no idea what that meant.

By the sound of the camp it was three or four in the morning. The guns were stilled; there wasn't even the grind of motors from the road, or the hollow rumble of lorries on the makeshift wooden bridge. No sound had yet begun from the camp kitchen, nor was there smell of smoke. In the pitch-dark tent Lydia heard the stealthy scrabble of rats, and bit her lips to keep from screaming: in four months of living daily with the vermin she had never lost her terror of them. She should, by all rights, be sunk in the sleep of exhaustion – keeping company with vampires, on top of her duties in the fluoroscope tent (*And if we have another quiet day tomorrow I'll take the apparatus apart and give it the cleaning it needs . . .*), meant she was constantly short of sleep. *Thank goodness Colonel St-Vire insists on the surgical crews getting all the sleep they need during the quiet times . . .*

When she closed her eyes she felt as far from sleep as she was from a hot bath or Mrs Grimes's batter-cakes. But she saw, as if it were printed on her eyelids, the dreamworld moonlight glistening on Francesca Gheric's blood, dripping from the twisted spikes.

Saw Don Simon's blood under her microscope, the altered, queerly elongated corpuscles motionless and cold.

Her favorite sport was to kill her lover in the act, said Antonio's beautiful, velvety whisper.

And her own hesitant voice, *Some vampires do retain a capacity for love . . .*

She was still awake when first daylight outlined the tent-seams, and above the wasteland of blood-soaked mud and tangled wire, the guns began to pound.

'What happened to that man?' Josetta's whisper barely carried over the rattle of the cab's iron tires on the brick streets of the Limehouse. 'His face . . .'

'Don't speak of it.' Now that Asher was sitting down and more or less warm and in no immediate danger of being killed or worse, waves of exhaustion threatened to drown him. 'Not to anyone. For your life, Miss Beyerly; I'm not joking . . .'

'For my life?' At least she didn't laugh. The moon had set, and the blackness of the blacked-out streets was absolute. God alone knew how the cab driver – the only one to be found in the Wise Child, and arguably not sober – saw to steer . . . *Maybe he has a sober horse . . .*

'I don't know who is behind this,' he said wearily. 'It may be that our government brought those things – that infection – to England as a plan to win the war . . . as a cheap alternative to conscription. To get men to fight who won't ask questions, who won't even know what they're doing or why.'

He heard the harsh draw of her breath. At least, he reflected, having battled Parliament for years over votes for women, she wouldn't automatically assume that the government a) was always right, or b) knew what it was doing.

'Or it may be someone who wants to spread chaos and panic here, so that we can't produce enough food or munitions to effectively keep an army in the field. And I suspect we'd do it to the Germans quick enough. It may be someone who wants to raise a private army, for their own purposes. Someone who knows they'll be outnumbered and outgunned by the police . . .'

'I know one of the men,' said Josetta quietly. 'One of those who took the thing away, I mean. I've seen him at the settlement house. His name's Teague, he's part of the Irish Volunteers. Someone told me he's one of the men who's buying guns from the Germans and smuggling them into Ireland.'

Asher heard the hesitant note in her voice, the

175

admission of the secret she was breaking, and shut his mouth hard on his first, embittered exclamation. With Irish independence tabled 'until the war is over', – and, worse, used like a hostage to lever Ireland into accepting forced conscription – he could understand the anger of those who had waited for years for a political solution to Ireland's self-rule. The fact that armed militias had formed among the Protestants, who didn't want to be governed by the Catholic majority – and were *also* smuggling guns in from Germany to arm themselves – and the Catholics, who in the face of violence in the countryside, were responding in kind, did not help the situation any.

'Thank you,' he said quietly. 'Whoever is behind this – and there's no reason to think this Teague is working for one side or the other in particular – please remember that we have no idea who is passing along information to whom. If you value your life, tell *no one* about what happened tonight. The last man who was a witness to the existence of these things vanished without a trace on the sixteenth of March. Promise me.'

She gripped his hand as if to emphasize what she was about to say, but he was unconscious before her words were spoken.

Thirteen

'Is the offer still open,' inquired Lydia, 'for me to pay a call on the Master of Prague?'

Don Simon regarded her for a moment with raised brows. Had he been like any of the men she worked with – both here in Pont-Sainte-Félicité and in fact back in Oxford – he would probably have greeted this volte-face with *And this is the woman who thinks we're monsters?* and similar chaffering, but this was evidently another of the things he'd outgrown (or gotten tired of) in three-plus centuries of being Undead. He merely inclined his head and replied, 'Graf Szgedny will be honored and flattered, lady. Am I correct in my guess that this concerns the Lady Francesca and her bargain – whatever it may be – with Dr Lemoine? Then might I suggest that the visit itself be kept secret?

'E'en in the best of times,' he added, when Lydia almost protested that she'd never in any case mention to Captain Calvert that she was going to tea with a vampire, 'the Undead are frightful gossips. With eternity before us and little enough of each night required for hunting, I do not see how it could be otherwise, given the human material of which the vampire is formed. Caution warns me against bringing your inquiries to the Lady Francesca's attention.'

'I think that's wise.' Lydia glanced back over

her shoulder at the lights of the clearing station. The purposeful bustle among the tents would soon die down. Another day was done. A few dozen men had been brought in – even when there was no 'push' on, constant sniper-fire took its toll. Shells were always falling, sometimes close enough to the front-line trenches to blow men into fragments on their way back from the latrines. Trench foot, pneumonia, hideous and fast-spreading sepsis from the smallest of cuts . . .

When things grew quiet, did poor Brodie's *bean sí* still walk among the tents? (*And is there a German equivalent, over on the other side of no man's land? I'm sure Jamie would know . . .*)

'What about Antonio and Basilio?' she asked worriedly. 'They know I'm asking questions. And they're friends – or at least neighbors – of Lady Francesca.'

'I spoke to them when we parted Thursday evening. Antonio at least shares my alarm at the Lady's meddling in human affairs: such involvements never end well. Then again, merely the suggestion that someone is experimenting with the Others – let alone producing them – is enough to incline them to my will. The Others shock and repel us as much as they do you, lady. Perhaps more so, for those of us who are aware of them at all recognize a kinship . . . and fear the further connections that may exist. Do not look to them for aid in this matter, but at least they will keep their silence.'

Shouting near the bridge, and the rumble of engines. 'Bother,' said Lydia. 'I'd hoped it would

be a quiet night . . .' *Not noisy enough for a push.*
A local attack . . .

'I must go.'

He bowed over her hand. 'Until tomorrow, then,
Mistress. 'Twere best we pay our call early, while
the rest are out. I shall send John in the afternoon
with papers, and come for you when darkness
falls. 'Tis a dozen miles.'

'I'll be ready. You haven't heard—' She paused,
half-turning back from the lights of the camp.
'You haven't heard anything concerning Jamie,
have you? Mrs Grimes wrote that he'd gone down
to London. The last I heard from him was that
one of these . . . these things . . . is in London
itself.'

The startled widening of his eyes was the
greatest display of shock she'd ever seen from
him. But all he said was, 'Is it so, indeed?'

'That means that either someone was infected
here – one of Lemoine's assistants, perhaps,
or one of those poor prisoners who escaped
– and developed the condition when he got to
London. Or else someone shipped or carried
one of Lemoine's subjects to Britain, and it
escaped.'

'Or that the vector of the infection is asymp-
tomatic, and does not manifest the physical
changes of the condition himself.' Don Simon
folded his arms, and leaned one slender shoulder
against the corner of the smashed-in wooden hut
that stood between the last of the disused German
trenches and the first houses of the village. From
its shadow Lydia knew they were nearly invisible
to the hurrying figures in the camp. 'Rather like

179

that woman Mary Mallon, who spread typhoid a few years ago in America . . .'

Lydia shivered, and pulled her greatcoat more tightly around her body. 'I've asked Jamie to send me whatever information he has. If I know Jamie . . .'

She looked aside, unable to go on.

'I do indeed know James,' returned the vampire. 'Thus I feel sure that when you do receive a reply to your reports of these creatures – and recall that any letter of yours to him must be forwarded from Oxford – 'twill contain the words *Do NOT pursue this matter*. Lionel is in London still.' He named the Master vampire of London. 'But to attempt to touch his dreams in quest of what he may know of this is like playing the lute before a rooting pig. If you will it, Mistress, I shall seek out James's dreams in the depths of the night, and at least endeavor to learn if he is well.'

Then he was gone, as if he could – as the legends said – dislimn into mist, and melt away.

Feeling rather like the corpse at a funeral in morning dress better suited to London than to Wendens Ambo, James Asher stepped from the first-class railway carriage and handed his companions out, reflecting for the hundredth time on the usefulness of 'connection' with the aristocracy. The son of a Church of England rector, he'd always been aware that the folk up at the 'big house' at Wychford had the power to make life easy or difficult for his parents and sister – interference which Sir Boniface's family seemed to regard as part of 'keeping them in their place'. Four years at Oxford in close prox-imity to the scions of nobility hadn't much improved his opinion of the breed. But he had discovered at Oxford that the purpose of Oxford was as much to meet people as to actually learn anything. One could learn as much or as little as one chose, depending on the ability of one's parents to keep one there. (Or, in Asher's case, one's diligence at any number of tutoring jobs.) But being in Balliol or Merton or King's would be, ever after, a passport to a degree of acquaint-ance, rather like sharing a seat in a lifeboat with total strangers.

After four years, men of one's year or one's staircase or one's college were strangers no more. His Oxford connections had certainly been as much of a factor in his employment in the Foreign Office as had been his fluency in Czech and Persian.

And by marrying the granddaughter of a viscount, he had quadrupled the number of people to whom he could acquire an introduction on the grounds of casual proximity. Lord Halfdene's four surviving sisters might look down their elegant noses at the mere New College lecturer their beautiful niece had married, but when push came to shove, one of them at least could be counted on to know the person whom Asher sought to meet.

So it had proved in his quest to locate – and speak to – the Comte de Beaucailles, whose prop-erty in the Département du Nord had included the old convent of Cuvé Sainte-Bride. Once Josetta's suffragette friend in the government

181

purchasing office had found mention of the money Britain had lent to the French to refurbish the place as a research laboratory – after the French Army had acquired it in November – it had been easy to identify the former owner. Lydia's Aunt Lavinnia, though she habitually referred to Asher as 'that person poor Lydia married', wasn't immune to being taken out for a criminally expensive tea at the Northumberland (Lydia's income deriving from American bonds and real estate in four major cities, and not farmland). In the course of consuming two cups of China tea and a single cucumber sandwich, Aunt Lavinnia had divulged the fact that the Comte de Beaucailles had come to England (as Asher had suspected: who in their right mind would remain in Flanders, or even in a Paris shorn of sugar, coffee and entertainment?) and was residing, with his family, as the guest of Lord Whitsedge at Whitsedge Court.

Lydia's Aunt Harriet, while deploring her niece's education, current occupation and husband (her own was the younger son of a duke, and a well-regarded barrister), knew everyone in Debrett's and was sufficiently good-natured as to write to Lord Whitsedge (whose Aunt Claire had married a Halfdene cousin) on Asher's behalf (though she referred to him in the course of a single paragraph as Ashley, Ashford and Ashden). And Lydia's Aunt Faith, who even now shed tears over the way in which her dear sister's child had 'thrown herself away' after being 'the most beautiful debutante of her year' (Lydia still had nightmares about her single 'season'), was so ecstatic at the idea of a weekend away from acting as companion to Aunt Louise down at Halfdene Hall that she had even agreed to accompany Asher (and Aunt Louise's official companion, Mrs Flasket) down to Whitsedge Court and introduce her plebeian nephew-in-law to Lord Whitsedge and his guests.

The Comte de Beaucailles proved to be an elderly, fragile man who took Asher to his bosom on the grounds of the perfection of his French. It was a joy, he said, to listen to after the tomcat squawking of 'ces Anglais', the gesture of his yellow-gloved hand dismissing the hosts without whose hospitality he would have been living on cabbage soup in Hoxton. He nursed a profound hatred of Germany and all Germans, as if the Battle of Sedan (in which he had fought) had been yesterday instead of forty-five years previously, and could still be reduced to shouting outrage over the Dreyfus Case. But he recalled with tender vividness the France of his childhood, the France of the days of empire, and every detail of the convent which had stood only miles from the family chateau.

'The good sisters were still at Sainte-Bride when I was a boy,' he reminisced, to Asher's question after dinner. 'It was much larger in the days before the Revolution – quite a substantial foundation – but my cousins and I were always welcome there. My great-grandfather provided the money for a new chapel in 1773, and many of our aunts and great-aunts had taken the veil there. Its cellars were famous—' He chuckled softly, and made an ironic little half-salute with

Lord Whitsedge's indifferent sherry – 'and there had been a healing well there, oh, centuries ago. Standing as it does on a ridge of hills, there is a veritable labyrinth of catacombs beneath it, far exceeding the present size of the convent.'

The remaining servants had pulled shut the draperies of slightly faded mustard velvet over the Regency drawing room's long windows. One of Lord Whitsedge's other guests was playing the piano, a Mozart dance whose effervescent serenity echoed bittersweet in the quiet room. Whitsedge Court was an old-fashioned country seat in which gas had never been installed, let alone electricity; Lady Whitsedge's booming voice could be heard from the card table, bemoaning the absence of the footmen, and the butler's replacement by his venerable and stone-deaf predecessor. In London Asher had been conscious of the number of women hurrying along the sidewalks at the close of factories and shops, and of the hoary heads of bus conductors and ticket clerks on the Underground. Here in the depth of Essex, with the cold spring wind blowing spits of rain from the Channel, the sense of loss, of men missing who would never return, was more poignant, despite Her Ladyship's evident belief that the entire war had been concocted by God to inconvenience her daughter's coming-out.

'*Honestly*, if the fighting goes on for another six months – and *what* those generals are thinking, I can't *imagine* – Alice will be nineteen. *Nineteen*! I could *flay* Mother for talking me into delaying her debut last spring . . .'

'When was the convent abandoned?' Asher inquired.

'Oh, heavens, when I was ten or eleven, I think.' The Comte seemed to bask in the belief that the most casual of acquaintances found his childhood in the long-vanished France of Empire as fascinating as he did himself. 'Yes, because that year I was enrolled in the Lycée Notre-Dame in Lille—'

'I remember there was a sort of ruin across the field from my father's rectory,' reminisced Asher mendaciously. (He'd been packed off to school in Scotland at the age of seven and his father hadn't been a believer in bringing young James home for those few summers before his own death in 1874.) 'I have no idea what the place was – monastery or a small castle or just an ancient inn – but my sister and I found a way into it from the crypt of a sort of little chapel in what had been its grounds . . .'

The old nobleman laughed. 'Nothing nearly so romantic, I'm afraid! The convent at Cuvé Sainte-Bride had in a manner of speaking died by inches, so there was a huge zone of deserted farms, chapels, bathhouses and storage-buildings all round the cloister, even in the days when the good sisters were still in occupation. My cousins and I played hide-and-seek – risking our lives, I'm sure, for some of those old crypts were none too stable, and the roofs were always falling in! – in the unused portions, so as not to disturb the nuns. But after they were removed we ran about them underground like wild Indians.'

The old man's eyes sparkled at the recollection,

and he leaned forward, decades melting from his lined face. 'After my cousin Etienne was caught in a cave-in and nearly drowned – because, of course, the deeper crypts flooded in the wintertimes – my grandfather had most of the outbuildings torn down and the ways into the crypt sealed. But still we'd get in. There was a well by one of the old barns, on the hillside behind the convent, and if one of your friends would lower you by bucket to just above the level of the water, there was a little door leading into what I think used to be a drain from the old baths . . . Ah, the smell of that tunnel, all green and damp! And our girl cousins used to stand at the top and cry because none of us boys would let them go down with us. And one of the young men of the district, Henri Clerc his name was, unblocked the entrance that led into what had been the nuns' old wine cellar, and would use the place to tryst with the village girls . . .'

A young footman, walking carefully on a wood-and-metal leg encased in the livery's old-fashioned silk stockings, brought them a tray of drinkables and a soda siphon. At the other end of the too-long, lamp-lit room Aunt Faith meekly nodded while Lady Whitsedge continued her monologue on the shortcomings of maids who would quit and go to work in factories, and Mrs Flasket listened in intelligent silence to Lord Whitsedge's account of his spaniel bitch's latest confinement.

Asher kept the old Comte talking, and, when he finally retired to his small chamber (which looked down on an inner courtyard of the rambling old Court: Aunt Faith, though regarded throughout her family as little better than a paid companion to Aunt Louise, still rated a room in the main part of the house), was able to put together a rough description of five different ways to enter the crypts of Cuvé Sainte-Bride undetected. He spent the remainder of the night encoding a letter to Lydia, which ended with a further admonition not to investigate anything herself. *If Don Simon is there, and willing, he is far more likely to enter and leave in safety than you are. I will put in train arrangements to come there myself to follow up on his reconnaissance.*

The thought of going to Colonel Stewart for the necessary papers – and of the concessions he'd have to make to get himself assigned to that area of Flanders – made him groan, not to speak of the hazards of crossing the submarine-haunted Channel and making his way from Calais to Pont-Sainte-Félicité and Haut-le-Bois. Then there was the issue of leaving his ill-assorted 'network' of information-gatherers on their own in London, seeking for word of this second revenant, and for the Irish gunrunner Teague. *I'll have to brief Grippen*, he thought, *without telling him who's collecting the information.* Josetta and Millward could communicate with the master vampire via newspaper. It wouldn't be the first time he'd run a network in which no member was aware of the identities of the others.

And God knows what Grippen will do with the information when he gets it.

Damn. He leaned back in the leather armchair beside the tiny grate, and drew his dressing-gown – and a paisley cashmere shawl – tightly around his shoulders. Despite the fire, the room was freezing cold and there was no coal left in the scuttle: guest rooms at Whitsedge Court were not supplied with fuel to burn all night. The clock on the mantelpiece chimed a tiny silver reminder that it was quarter to three. Around him the house was silent, with the darkness of centuries.

For eight years I've tried to keep the governments of both sides from employing vampires. He closed his eyes. *And I might as well have saved myself the trouble, since once the fighting started, both sides are giving the vampires, gratis, the only thing they'd have accepted as payment.*

And after swearing to kill them I'm working on their side.

He thought about going back to Oxford. Or taking Lydia and Miranda and emigrating to America, which was quite sensibly keeping out of the war while selling ammunition and supplies to both sides. But he knew there was no question of doing so. If one side or the other – *Or both, God help us!* – found a way to control the revenants, to use them as soldiers, God alone knew where that would end.

Not well.

He made a move to rise to compose a note to be placed in the Personals column to Grippen for a meeting – and the next thing he knew it was broad daylight and a maid was coming quietly into the room to open the curtains.

Fourteen

'We who hunt the night have long memories.' Don Simon Ysidro's gloved fingers, grasping Lydia's, were cold as they steadied her over the broken ground; cold as the iron of the unlit bull's-eye lantern she bore. The moon, four days past full, hid behind its bank of clouds, though the rain had stopped half an hour ago. The darkness smelled of wet trees and farmland. Somewhere an owl hooted. 'Yet being human, we are no more comfortable looking back on the road we have travelled than are other men. Among us it is held to be a sign of weakness and advancing age. Most look neither forward nor back.'

They had left the car with Captain Palfrey, in blackness so thick Lydia could only form the vaguest ideas where she might be. Having been taken to vampire lairs before, she had half-expected to be blindfolded – or at least have her glasses taken away, which would have amounted to the same thing – and had formed her protest ready: *What if something happens to you and I'm left out all alone in the dark?*

But the cloud-smothered blackness of the night had made any sort of blindfold supererogatory. Don Simon had taken the wheel ('He's a marvel, isn't he?' had enthused Captain Palfrey, in the back seat beside her), and in addition to driving the staff-car, Lydia suspected her guardian of using his mental influence on both her and her living companion in the back seat. Even now, barely sixty feet from the car, she found she had only the dimmest recollection of the drive: of how long it had been, or of any feature of sound or smell, or of the number of turnings or the condition of the road surface, that might have identified where they were. She remembered chatting with Captain Palfrey, but couldn't call to mind a single word. Had he been likewise beglamored? she wondered. And if so, was he even aware of it?

Damn Simon . . .

'Graf Aloÿis Szgedny, like the Lady Francesca, became vampire in the days of the great Wars of Religion,' the vampire's whispering voice continued, as they walked on through what smelled, and felt, like woods. 'The master who made him – Odo Magnus Matilorum – was a very old vampire, who recalled clearly when first the revenants were seen in the days when plague made its terrible harvest through Christendom. The city of Prague was not hit so hard as other regions, yet it is a pious lie to say that 'twas spared through a vision of the Christ Child. Szgedny does not speak of this matter often. Indeed I am surprised that he has consented to do so to you. Remember when you speak to him that he is a very great nobleman, of ancient lineage, long used to deference.'

Wet leaves rustled in the stirring of breeze, and droplets pattered on Lydia's cloak and hair. She had the dim impression of looming walls ahead, and her feet gritted on what felt like gravel. Then her thought slipped away, to the memory – tiny and perfect, like something in those miniature Austrian snow globes – of walking up to the garden door of her house in Holyrood Street in Oxford, with her shoes crunching on the gravel of the path and James and Miranda standing in the lighted doorway . . .

She found herself, with a sensation of waking up, in a damp-smelling corridor, candlelight ahead of her outlining a partly-opened door. *DAMN you, Simon* . . .

She was aware that her heart was pounding. She was in the house of the vampire, and, for the sake of good manners, had left her silver wrist and neck chains back at the clearing station. *If anything goes wrong* . . .

She caught his sleeve. 'Goodness, I didn't think . . . does the Graf speak English?'

'German, Latin, French and Polish, as well as his native Czech . . . which in his time one only used to address one's servants or one's horses.'

I work and eat and sleep, daily, in a place within range of German guns. They've shelled the clearing station more than once. Why should I worry about paying a call on a deathless multiple murderer?

Her knees were still shaking.

He led her up a short flight of stone steps, and pushed open the lighted door.

'I trust Madame was not chilled on her journey here?'

Like most vampires Lydia had seen, the Graf seemed to be in the prime of life, though his long hair and his abundant mustaches were

191

silvery-gray. His face was heavily lined, and beneath grizzled brows his gray eyes were level and cold, catching the firelight like mirrors as he rose from his seat beside the hearth. When Lydia sank into a curtsey (thanking her governess and the instructors at Madame Chappedelaine's School for the ability to do it properly and with grace) he took, and kissed, her hand.

'Thank you, my lord, I was most comfortable. It's kind of you to ask.'

He conducted her to a chair, and Don Simon took Lydia's cloak (and the lantern), and fetched tea from the small spirit kettle on a marquetry table nearby. Lydia could not help noticing that only one cup stood ready, and beside it, a small plate of chocolate biscuits (*and I'll bet he got THOSE from Storeman Pratt!*)

She was infinitely glad of Don Simon's presence.

'And I'm most grateful to you, sir, for consenting to see me. I appreciate it very much.'

Beyond the reach of the firelight Lydia made out the dim shapes of a long salon: card tables, a harp, the flicker of gold leaf on an elaborate clock. Deep-set windows opened uncurtained to the night. Closer, flame-glow outlined the carving of the hearthside chairs, the marble angels, lizards, lilies and foxes that twined the fireplace itself.

'Simon informs me you seek information about the Lady Francesca Brucioram.'

Lydia took a sip of tea, and nibbled on a biscuit. After a full day in the fluoroscope tent and the surgical theater she felt she could have devoured

192

the entire plateful without denting either her exhaustion or her hunger. 'In a manner of speaking, my lord. About her, and also about the revenants, the Others, to which I understand you can attest at first hand. Don Simon will have told you what we believe is happening at the old convent of Cuvé Sainte-Bride?'

'He has told me.' The wrinkled lids lowered over eyes devoid of expression: intelligent, cynical, and cruel. His powerful fingers rearranged themselves on his lap.

'Francesca the White is a woman with a great store of anger inside her,' he said at last. 'From what cause I know not.'

The slight movement of his head caused the fire-glow to pick momentarily at the strings of the distant harp: Lydia wondered if it was in tune, and if any of the vampires played.

'In most lamia – as you doubtless know, Madame – the capacity for feeling dwindles quickly. Loyalty, and the affection for one's family, become as the recollection of sugarplums loved in childhood: an objective awareness that such a craving once existed, coupled with a mild distaste at the thought of gorging oneself now. Given the opportunity to slay one's enemies with near-impunity, one finds no real desire to put oneself to the trouble. They will die . . . and we will not.'

The gray brows pinched slightly over the broken aquiline of his nose. 'For La Dame Blanche, the hunt is about cruelty. Many enjoy chasing a victim, the game of cat-and-mouse in the darkness: seeing a man piss himself with terror, hearing him squeak and plead at the touch of claws on his throat. The taste of his hope when he still thinks he can get away.' The tiniest smile tugged one corner of his mustache.

'For her the game is more elaborate. More personal. And the pleasure she takes in it has seemed always to me – for she left Prague, as most of us did, when the Prussians attacked under King Frederick – to come not from the kill itself, but from a sort of spite. As if every victim were the one who had done her ill. As if every kill were vengeance. I had many occasions to speak to her, when one of her "games", as she liked to call them, would involve three or four members of the same family or a circle of friends, pursued over a time long enough for word of their misfortunes to spread. In a city barely a tenth the size of London, of older beliefs and different organization, this can cause serious danger to others of the nest.'

'Did she ever try to command your fledglings, my lord?'

His lips compressed in an anger that she hoped wasn't directed at her. 'She did.'

'Forgive me, my lord—' Lydia ducked her head and looked as humble as she could – 'did it ever impress you that she would have taken command of the Prague nest, if she were able?'

His deep, soft voice remained level. 'There were times when I thought as much.'

'Yet she never actually made an attempt to supplant you? Or began a conspiracy to have you killed?'

''Twould have been fairly easy to arrange,'

194

added Don Simon from the shadows. 'In those days, much of Bohemia believed in the *vampìr* more certainly than they believed that the earth circles the sun.'

'Not so easily as you might think,' retorted Szgedny. 'I had – as I still have – eyes and ears throughout the city, among the living as among the Undead. In any case, she did not.'

'Did you ever ask yourself why?' Lydia took another sip of tea.

He sat for a time like a cat watching birds. When he said, 'I did not,' there was, instead of irritation in his deep voice (in so far as it displayed anything), a kind of curiosity at himself for this omission.

'Because it sounds to me,' said Lydia diffidently, 'as if the Lady Francesca might be incapable of creating fledglings. And that's what she thinks Lemoine can give her.'

In his dressing-gown and his paisley shawl, before the faint warmth of the tiny hearth in the room at Whitsedge Court, Asher dreamed of the echoing vastness of the Liverpool Street Station. Streaming mobs of people, as he helped Aunt Faith and Mrs Flasket from the cab, paid the driver, mentally identified the man's speech as originating from around Shepherd's Bush; his ear caught the sing-song cry of the girls selling violets around one of the cast-iron pillars near the platform steps. Two girls and a woman, in the black of mourning . . . Beyond them, a worried little man (from Devon, by his accent) fussed with his Scots servant about the cat he carried in a basket . . .

Faces in the crowd. The smell of smoke from a cockle vendor's barrow and a child's frightened wailing. Clouds of steam rolling from Platform One as the express from Norwich ground to a halt. A flicker of shadow, a characteristic movement near the bookseller's – a ragged dark mackintosh . . .

When he turned it was gone.

Dreaming, he returned to the scene. Aunt Faith clung again to his arm – she was the only one of Lydia's aunts who would treat him with more than chill civility – and prattled in her gentle voice of the letters she'd gotten from the family of one of the Halfdene footmen who'd come back, blind and crippled, from the Front, while his own attention moved like a gunsight, trying to identify that flicker of a half-familiar shape.

Like spotting Lydia, or Dr Hoggett, or any of his scholastic colleagues at a great distance off in a crowd . . .

Who was that?

He knew, but the knowledge slipped away.

And in his dream he remembered – not entirely illogically – Josetta Beyerly, when she'd let him off at his lodgings Tuesday night after their adventure in Brabazon Street. Exhausted and shivering a little with what he suspected was a low-running fever, he hadn't waked until the cab had reached the door and then he'd been simply too tired to insist that they go round the corner so that he could slip in through the old mews that had been one of his reasons for choosing Faraday's Private Hotel in the first place.

196

When she'd seen him to his door, and walked back down the shallow step to the cab, he'd thought, as her heels clicked on the flagway, *I hope she's keeping safe . . .*

He'd looked up and down the dark street before closing the door behind him, and had seen no one.

''Twould make sense,' said Don Simon at length, 'of her own master's decision to make another her favorite in Strasbourg, lesser in strength by all accounts than the Lady. One does not bequeath one's estates to a gelding.'

For a long time Szgedny said nothing, but Lydia had the impression, almost, of hearing an abacus click behind those colorless eyes. 'And 'twould make sense,' he said at last, 'of her anger. 'Twas clear as day she considered herself a law unto herself, and entitled to be master of Prague in my stead.'

'And if Lemoine is working with the physical pathology of the Undead,' Lydia continued, 'which it sounds like he is doing, from what I've read of his work – she might well trade her assistance in controlling the Others for a cure for her own condition.'

'Children trading pebbles by the seashore.' The Graf's nostrils flared in irritation. 'A thousand imaginary ducats to pay for an imaginary horse. Best of luck to them both.'

'Are you sure?'

She saw Don Simon's yellow eyes move sidelong, to touch the Graf's snow-gray ones.

'I at least am sure,' returned the Master of

Prague, 'that the Lady Francesca is incapable of commanding the revenants. Three hundred years I have watched them, and my master before me. Years will go by – decades, sometimes – between sightings of them, beneath the bridges of the Vltava and on the river's islands when the moon has set. But they are there, in the crypts beneath the old city, the forgotten cisterns and drains. The sub-cellars of the old town palaces and the ossuaries under churches ruined and built over and erased from the memory of the town. Never more than a few handfuls of them, living on rats in the darkness.

'My master, Odo Magnus, tried to gain command over them, when first they began to appear. One of his fledglings made the attempt also, Odo believed in order to gain control of the city and to drive Odo out. Or else to kill him and those loyal to him – such schisms, lady—' He inclined his head to Lydia – 'are uncommon but by no means unheard of, among those who hunt the night. This fledgling ended by being torn to pieces and eaten by the Others, who will it seems devour anything.'

'So we have observed,' murmured Don Simon.

'I have myself, like Odo before me, tried to control them as I control the minds of the living.' Stirred to the point of forgetting his calm dignity, the Graf leaned forward, gestured with one powerful hand, and his French became harder to follow as it slid back into the language as he had first learned it, centuries before. 'Looking into their eyes I saw naught: no mind, no memories, no dreams. Not even the most rudimentary

198

sensations of hunger and fear by which one commands the actions of beasts. Meditating—' He glanced at Don Simon, as if making sure that he understood whatever mental technique that was, that each had learned from his master to control the perceptions of men – 'I could touch nothing of their thoughts, either singly or en masse. The effort only revealed my hiding place to them, and I was obliged to flee.'

'And there's no chance, my lord, that you were trying this too close to running water? You said they live in the channel of the river.'

A wolf's smile lifted one corner of the long mustaches again. 'Clever little lady. I was inland, well enough.' The silvery eyes met hers, and Lydia glanced quickly aside. To meet a vampire's eyes opened your own mind to the possibility of its tampering with your dreams. To the danger that one day it would summon you . . . and you would go.

'And the fact that the Lady Francesca didn't take the opportunity to enlist the Others herself, against you,' she concluded, 'seems to confirm that she probably couldn't. If she dwelt in Prague for – how long?'

'Seventy years, or thereabouts. And you are right, Madame.' He sat back, like a bleached cobra recoiling upon its rock. 'I doubt not that she made the attempt, more than once. She would have used them, if she could.'

'But Dr Lemoine doesn't know that.'

'And if her goal be merely to get of him some cure for her incapacity,' went on Don Simon, 'I cannot see her taking any pains to make sure these things remain under control. Lemoine's experiments are sufficiently irresponsible as they stand – God knows how they acquired the first of their revenants, upon which to found their efforts, though I can conceive several ways in which 'twere easily done. But Lemoine at least is a living man, with a living man's loyalties to his own. So far as I can ascertain, the Lady Francesca has none.'

'Tell me one more thing, my lord, if you would,' said Lydia, as Don Simon fetched her cloak and they prepared to leave. It was, by the exquisite goldwork clock, nearly ten, and for several minutes she had seen her escort listening carefully, for the sound of returning feet. By the look of the card tables, there was every chance the Graf's fledglings would foregather in this room, or wonder why they were excluded from doing so.

Whether their fear of her companion would keep the vampires at bay in a group she didn't know, though she was aware that most vampires held Don Simon Ysidro in considerable awe. In any case, the thought of that many of the Undead knowing who she was, and what she looked like, and that she was tampering in their affairs, frightened her a good deal. They gossiped, Don Simon had said, like schoolgirls, and there was no guarantee that one or more of them weren't bosom-bows with Francesca.

'And what might that be, Madame?' Graf Szgedny bent over her hand.

'Has there ever been occasion on which a vampire has tried to make a fledgling of a revenant?'

'The condition of these things is spread by the blood. I know of no vampire, no matter how inexperienced, who would take such risk.'

'But so far as I understand it, at least, it is the *death* – the absorption of the mind at death – that is involved in the transformation to vampire, not the blood itself. Might a vampire take in whatever mind exists in the revenant, and return it to the creature's body after it's dead? And then control it, as a master vampire controls its fledgling?'

'There must be an exchange of blood, lady. The blood is what transforms the living man into the vampire, once he has passed through death. The risk would be simply too great.'

Lydia heard nothing, but Don Simon turned his head a little, then bowed deeply to the Graf. 'That sounds like Elysée de Montadour's voice, and those execrable fledglings of hers—'

'Flee.' Szgedny made a slight gesture, as though flicking water from his fingertips. 'Your visit shall be as if it never occurred.' For a moment – as sometimes happened with Don Simon's – his face turned briefly human when he smiled. Tired – and amused, perhaps, at being able to step for a moment out of the society of the Undead and provide information to the quests of the living. But the cynical cruelty in his eyes remained.

Asher returned to London on the Saturday afternoon train from Saffron Walden, though Aunt Faith chose to remain at the Court until Wednesday, with Mrs Flasket to bear her company. 'I'm sorry you have to return,' said the Dowager Lady Whitsedge, as she poured out tea for Asher in the bright sunlight at breakfast that morning. 'Thursday night was the first time I've seen the poor old Comte so cheerful. I do quite worry about him, losing his home as he has, and his son and both of his grandsons. I think it quite took him back, to tell somebody about his home, and the way things were when he was a boy.'

Once, on the four-mile drive to the station, Asher caught sight of a bicyclist following the Court's pony-trap at a distance: too far to easily make out details of the rider under the striped shadows of the new-leafed trees. The man was wearing a shabby Fair Isle sweater rather than a mackintosh, but something in his outline, even at that distance, rang alarm bells in Asher's mind.

Fifteen

'Is all well, M'am?'

Lydia looked up quickly from the corner of the makeshift table, which, in daytime (and through more nights than she cared to think about) served Eamon Dermott as a workbench. The tiny root cellar beneath the ruins behind the fluoroscope room was barely large enough for both it and the tin basin he used as a developing bath, its rafters so low that during the daytimes (and through more nights than Lydia cared to think about) she and her assistant had to duck and weave about, to avoid the films hanging as they dried.

It was the only place in the clearing station where she knew she could work undisturbed.

She turned Jamie's letter face down beside her candle, and crossed to the door.

VAD Violet Brickwood stood on the stair. Listening, Lydia heard no clamor of voices and motors in the camp, no rattle of the fluoroscope being moved in the building above.

Only the guns.

She propped her glasses on her nose. 'I'm well. I just—'

The young volunteer's glance went past her shoulder, to the papers that strewed the table. 'I couldn't help seeing, M'am, that that nice Captain Palfrey brought you that letter today. I hope it's nothing amiss with your husband, or your little

203

girl?' The earnest brown eyes returned to Lydia's face in the lantern-light, seeking – Lydia realized – the marks of grief. 'I'll sometimes go read my letters in the stores tent,' the girl added. 'If they're from my sister, about Mama, I mean. I just . . . Please don't think I'm meaning to pry, but you've been down here a long while. I just hoped you were all right.'

Lydia smiled, and gave the younger girl an impulsive hug. 'Thank you,' she said. 'All is well. There's nothing amiss.'

Except for a MONSTROUS scheme to dissolve the souls from out of men's brains, that their bodies may be enslaved because the governments find they're running out of good Frenchmen or good Englishmen or good Russians to kill.

Lydia returned to Dermott's worktable as Violet's shoes patted gently up the stair again, and stared at the letter.

It was on the stationery of Whitsedge Court (*What on EARTH is Jamie doing there?*) and ran to many pages – *It must have taken him HOURS to write it all!* – so that the minuscule dots, blots and pinpricks wouldn't be obvious as a code. Even though the letter had been sent to Don Simon's accommodation address in Paris, Jamie didn't trust anyone. The letter before this one, which she'd received through regular (censored) Army channels, had contained the terse warning *??? home team screening*, after the alarming information that there was a second revenant at large in London.

??? home team screening.

Monsters. She closed her eyes, leaned her

204

forehead on her knuckles. The King's own government – or at least the Department that worked for them – was hiding the existence of those things she had encountered in China. Protecting them.

How that was worse than simply killing those poor Germans she wasn't sure, but it turned her stomach.

And chilled the blood in her veins.

A quick scratch on the door behind her. A whispered voice. 'Mistress?'

She turned in her chair and managed a half-smile. 'Well, you were right,' she said, as Don Simon slipped into the tiny cellar, closed the door without a sound. 'Jamie does indeed say *Do NOT investigate this yourself.*' She held out the decryption to him, her hand shaking with exhaustion. 'He suggests you do it.'

'Does he?'

The vampire scanned it. Four possible entrances to the sub-crypts and drains beneath the convent of Cuvé Sainte-Bride. Heaven only knew where Jamie had acquired the rough map, which according to the plain text of the letter was her Aunt Faith's house in Little Bookham (Aunt Faith had no such thing and had been Aunt Louise's pensioner for decades). One entrance was in the ruins of a chapel near lilac trees; another, thirty feet down the side of a well in a farmyard a mile from the Amiens road. And Heaven only knew if any of the four would still be usable.

'He says he's coming here himself, as soon as he can get the military clearances he needs.' She tried to keep her voice calm and decisive. The labored shakiness of Jamie's handwriting had told its own story. *Don't do it. You'll kill yourself* . . .

'Does he?' The vampire's pale brows lifted.

'It would help things,' said Lydia hesitantly. 'Speed things, if we knew at least whether those entrances are still open or not, or how dangerous they are. Obviously they're difficult of access, since none of the other Undead have spoken of revenants wandering about the back roads and battlefields—'

'Yet one at least got through.' Don Simon refolded the decryption, drew it thoughtfully through his long fingers. 'Whether that was one of ten, or one of fifty, we know not – nor yet why our Nurse Smith would have risked her life getting a sample of its blood or its flesh, when she has access to ample at Sainte-Bride. Curious.' His glance shifted sidelong to her. 'If I read this description aright – and the map also, though 'tis clearly not to scale – the crypts and catacombs beneath the convent at its height extend far beyond the walls as they currently stand, and presumably beneath the trenches that surround it. And given the habit which the living have, of judging situations to be "under control" when they very much desire them to be, 'twould little surprise me if one or more of these things is hiding in the far corners of these crypts, unbeknownst to this Lemoine.'

'Which would mean—' Lydia regarded him somberly by the candle's flickering light – 'that it's only a matter of time before they start to multiply beyond the convent walls. And once they start to spread . . .'

'E'en so.' He folded up the paper. 'Though if they exist in any substantial number, how they are to be destroyed, with the French Army and, it seems, the War Department of England shielding them, 'tis another matter.'

He picked up Lydia's cold hand and kissed it. 'As for James's coming, if I have learned one thing since last September, lady, 'tis the oriental leisure of official conduct with regards to these "military clearances" of which he speaks. I should refer them all to the forgers who work in Montparnasse and Pigalle: 'tis a wonderment to me that none has ever questioned "Colonel Simon", on how speedily he seems to acquire documents.'

And taking up her candle, he followed her up the crumbling stone steps to the ground above.

On the following day the British First Army made a determined probe at the German lines, principally (Captain Calvert opined, spattered bicep-high in blood and cursing like a very quiet and well-bred Australian sailor) to pull potential German attacks from the French around Arras. From first light Wednesday, when the casualties began coming in, until midnight Thursday night, Lydia took x-ray photographs, administered chloroform, held retractors and sponges, and irrigated wounds, in between taking tea out to the men queued up on stretchers outside the pre-op tent where Matron was grimly sorting them into those who would live and those who wouldn't. Lydia saw not so much as the glint of reflective eyes in the darkness on either night, but knew they were watching. She didn't know whether she was more furious at them or General Haig.

Colonel St-Vire finally sent the last members of the surgical crews to bed at three o'clock Friday morning with orders not to stir until teatime.

'Captain Palfrey's been to see you twice,' reported Nurse Brickwood worriedly, coming into the nurses' tent Friday evening while Lydia was sponging down with a flannel. Lydia felt her stomach sink, at the thought of what Don Simon might have found. Nevertheless she finished washing, brushed her hair, dressed and went to the mess tent (*Does this headache have anything to do with not having dinner last night?*), and was picking at a rock-hard biscuit soaked in a bowl of lukewarm Maconochie when Palfrey's voice exclaimed 'Dr Asher!' from the twilight of the doorway.

He dodged between the tables to her, and Captain Burke – with whom she'd been eating and commiserating about the upcoming evening's work – heaved his bulk from the bench and shook a facetious finger at her. 'Any more meetin's wi' that captain, lass, and I'll be writin' Professor Asher of you.' Everyone in the clearing station knew by this time that Lydia was involved in 'something for the brass' – presumably concerning x-ray photography – and had come to recognize Captain Palfrey as the liaison.

She thankfully abandoned the tinned swill before her and rose to meet the young captain, who guided her swiftly from the tent.

But instead of handing her a note – and enough

light lingered in the sky that she knew Don Simon hadn't come himself – Palfrey inquired worriedly, 'Have you heard anything of Colonel Simon, Dr Asher? I'm dreadfully sorry to interrupt you, as I know you've had a rough time of it these past two nights – everyone has, all the way up to Festubert . . . But Colonel Simon didn't meet me last night.'

'He is very much a law unto himself . . .'

'I know.' The young man grimaced at his own concern. 'And he'll joke me sometimes about being a mother hen. But . . . Wednesday we drove down as far as Haut-le-Bois, and he ordered me to wait for him, with the car, in a lane a few miles beyond the village. I had orders, if he didn't return by sunrise, to go back to Aubigny and wait. Aubigny is where we're staying. Where *I'm* staying,' he corrected himself. 'I honestly have no idea where Colonel Simon stays. He had me rent a sort of accommodation address for him there, but he doesn't seem to use it.'

The young man's brisk calm cracked then, and for a moment his mouth tightened, and distress pulled the flesh around his eyes. 'But he . . . He never came to my lodgings last night. I sat up nearly all night for him, and I – in my heart I feel something terrible has happened to him, M'am. Dr Asher. Every time I fell asleep – and I did nod off three or four times – I thought I heard him calling for me. I must have gotten up and gone to the door a dozen times! And I wondered—'

And I was so tired when I finally lay down last night I wouldn't have waked if Miranda had stood

209

next to my cot and screamed. Her heart turned chill inside her. *He went to investigate the crypts under Sainte-Bride.*

Because I asked him to.

And he didn't come out.

Asher told himself, as his train pulled out from Saffron Walden on Saturday afternoon, that the man on the bicycle couldn't possibly have anything to do with the glimpse of what might or might not have been a half-familiar shadow in Brabazon Street Tuesday evening. Nevertheless he changed his own jacket in his second-class compartment and stepped off the train on the last foot or so of platform as it was leaving Epping, and after a considerable hunt for a cab, found one and took it to Pembridge Place. There he paid his bill, changed his jacket and hat yet again, and sought new lodgings in Kensington, after two more cabs and an excursion to Holborn on the Underground, just to make sure that he wasn't being followed. Descending to the Underground troubled him, for its tunnels were the logical place for the Others – two of them, now – to hide.

How long before they added a third to their number?

Does Teague the gunrunner have the slightest idea of the danger of blood contact? Did the man or men employing him?

Tomorrow, he told himself, he'd need to consult both Millward and Josetta, Sabbath or no Sabbath.

After a slender tea at a café, which he was far too exhausted to eat, he composed a telegram to

Josetta, another to Miranda (care of Ellen and Mrs Grimes) and a Personals message to 'Dr Graves', then retired to bed, where he lay, shivering with fever, for the next four days. Between bouts of coughing he hoped Mr Fair Isle had been struck on his bicycle by a lorry and squashed flat.

On Thursday he felt sufficiently recovered to venture forth to the British Museum.

Osric Millward was precisely where Asher had found him first, at the end of one of the long desks beneath the great rotunda of the Reading Room. The shabbily-dressed Donnie was still helping him, assisted by another – stooped, a little rat-like, wearing no tie at all, but a kerchief knotted around his throat under a battered frieze jacket – whose intense eyes remained on Millward's face with every word he spoke.

Millward's 'network'. Asher wondered if they had had brothers, sisters, sweethearts, friends who had become victims of a vampire. In their unprepossessing faces he read not only hunger for revenge, but a kind of eager gratitude to have someone who believed them.

The posters Asher had passed in the hallway leading to the great room – garish colors, looming figures – seemed aimed at those two young men, the only men under the age of forty-five in the room: *Come Along, Boys, Before It's Too Late! Will You Answer the Call? YOU are the MAN we want . . .*

How much courage did it take to say *No, I need to stay in London and hunt for vampires*?

Millward sprang to his feet as Asher approached,

211

seized him by the hand. 'When I didn't hear from you I feared they'd gotten you.'

He meant the vampires of London, not their own government departments, but Asher shook his head. 'I had to go down to the country to see a man about a dog.'

The older man studied his face, his brows drawn together in concern. Asher reflected that he probably looked more like someone who'd been attacked by vampires than like one who had an appointment to meet the Master of London in Piccadilly at midnight for a chat. Millward steered him into a chair, murmured to his two acolytes, 'Would you excuse us . . .?' and sat down himself. When the young men had gone he whispered, 'I've found where they're hiding.'

Sixteen

'Shouldn't we wait until it gets dark?' Captain Palfrey braked the staff-car to a halt. 'Colonel Simon always does.'

Scanning the description and instructions she had recopied from Jamie's original letter, Lydia wondered how complicated it would be to explain to this young man that 'Colonel Simon' only appeared at night, Palfrey's convictions to the contrary. 'It'll be dark soon,' she said instead. Indeed, sufficient twilight had gathered to make reading difficult, in the shadows of the leafless trees. 'And if anything goes wrong and we get separated and have to run for it, I'd feel much safer trying to do so with at least a little daylight.' She added, 'I don't have Colonel Simon's night-eyes,' and Palfrey, turning in the front scat, grinned understandingly.

'Lord, isn't that the truth! I don't think any man living does.'

You're quite right about that. She went back to studying the paper. Their visit to Cuvé Sainte-Bride two weeks previously had revealed nothing about picket guards, and Lydia wondered how great a staff the French Army was willing to pay for.

How many men could be trusted not to blab about what was going on inside, either from horror and outrage or simply in their cups in the

213

estaminets of Haut-le-Bois? Lemoine had a couple of soldiers to help manage the prisoners when they were selected, and certainly at least one man on the gate, but how many more? And how many was too many?

Three people can keep a secret only if two of them are dead. Wasn't that how the old proverb ran?

Lydia propped her glasses on her nose, and took a deep breath. '*Old farm near Amiens road,*' she read aloud. '*Well.* Is there rope in the car?'

'Yes, M'am. I had some Wednesday night, also. Colonel Simon took it with him.'

'*Sub-crypt of chapel* . . .' She lowered the paper, scanned the silent woods around them. They stood a little above the lacerated road, where a lane led to the bullet-riddled shell of what had been a farm. '*Near lilac trees*—'

'There are lilacs two miles down the main road from here, and up the ridge a little. I noticed them because there are lilacs at Deepmere. They're Aemilia's favorite.' Palfrey looked shy at the mention of his sweetheart's name. 'They won't be in bloom for two months yet . . .'

Lydia smiled. *And you probably keep them pressed in your book of the King's Regulations . . .*

'We'll go through the woods.' She turned back to judge how well concealed the staff-car was behind them. 'If we keep the road on our left we shouldn't get too lost. You don't happen to have anything like a tarpaulin or a gun-cover in the boot?'

He shook his head. 'I have a billhook, though. It won't take but a few minutes to cut brush.'

214

Lydia strained her ears for the sound of another vehicle on the road as she helped her escort pile cut saplings and shrubs of hawthorn over the vehicle ('You might want to not cut them all from one area . . .' 'Oh, right! Excellent thought, M'am!'). They were still, by her calculation, several miles from the old convent, and though the vehicle couldn't be seen from the main road, anyone who *did* see the rough camouflage-job would be bound to guess that somebody was up to something.

Of course, simply the sight of a staff motorcar sitting out here would cause them to guess that.

It was quite clear that fighting had passed over these woods the previous autumn. As they trudged through the shredded rags of undergrowth, the shrapnel-blasted trees, Lydia caught occasional glimpses of weather-faded khaki or gray under the winter's dead beech leaves, and the brown of exposed bone.

Wednesday night. Lydia shifted her grip on the unlit lantern she carried, her heart beating hard. *Did he get in? Was he trapped below ground?* The earth would block most of a vampire's psychic connection with the living. Even had Simon tried to make mental contact with her Wednesday night, she'd been awake, concentrating on taking x-ray photographs and administering anesthetics. Last night she'd slept so deeply she doubted anything could have waked her. *Oh, Simon, I'm sorry . . .*

If he were underground she suspected she'd have to be standing at one of the entrances to the

215

crypts to hear his voice whisper in her mind. Even then it mightn't reach her.

Or will I reach the chapel and find only a heap of ash and bone?

The chapel lay in the center of a zone of shell-craters and scratched-out, makeshift shelters, scrabbled with entrenching-tools by men who had no time to do more than scrape gouges in the earth to lie in and pray. All around the pulverized walls, branches, trunks, shrubs and earth bore the appearance of having passed beneath the teeth of some frightful harrow that had stripped everything in its path. The lilacs of which Palfrey – and Jamie's informant – had spoken had survived only because they lay far enough from the chapel itself to be on the edge of the death zone.

This near the road, any building that could have given shelter would have been bombed out of existence by the other side. She didn't need to slip and scramble into the chapel itself to guess what she'd find there, though she had to check: a pit some twenty feet deep, where bombs had repeatedly fallen on the sub-crypt, caving it out of existence. The graveyard smell of incompletely buried bodies lingered over the ruined earth.

She whispered, 'Drat it,' though it was just as well. The fewer holes for stray revenants to get through the better. 'How far are we from the Amiens road?'

Hiking over the ridge took the remainder of the fading daylight, though there was very little (*Thank Heavens!*) barbed wire in the shell-torn underbrush of the woods. Palfrey led the way, with a map of the area and a compass; full darkness was closer than Lydia cared for, when they finally glimpsed the charred stones of the farmhouse. There had been fighting here as well, but it didn't look as though the shattered cottage had been shelled.

'Mills bombs, it looks like.' Palfrey lowered his map, and frowned through the gloom at the ruin. 'Look how much of the roof is undamaged.'

The well stood halfway between the house and what remained of the barn. The windlass was gone, as was most of the well-curb. Palfrey found an unburnt section of beam, lit the lantern and laying the beam across the hole, stretched himself out on it to lower the light on his rope. 'We're still fairly high above the local water table here,' he reported, and Lydia, kneeling to peer down, saw the yellow reflection of the light some fifty or sixty feet below.

'Is that a hole, or a door, in the side of the well shaft?' she asked. 'Or just a trick of the shadows?'

The young captain lowered the light as far down as he could, the shadow clearly outlining a roughly rectangular mouth of shadow in the wall.

'Look,' she added, pointing, 'those are iron staples in the wall leading down to it.'

'Good,' returned Palfrey grimly. 'Because there isn't anything to tie this line to closer than twenty feet from the well. It should just get us down to the first of the staples.' He pulled up the rope, untied the lantern and carried the coil to the remains of the barn door. Lydia undid her belt – she wore a holstered Webley service revolver at her waist – and kilted up her stout linen skirt above her knees.

I really should get a man's trousers, to do things like this. They can't be less modest than a pair of bicycle bloomers. She checked the safety and the cylinder of the Webley, actions she'd performed half a dozen times in the car already. *Though it would be impossible to sneak out of the camp unnoticed in them. I wonder if Storeman Pratt would sell me a pair?* Captain Palfrey, returning with the end of the rope in his hands, halted in startled alarm at the sight of her calves and ankles: 'Oh, come, it can't be worse than a bathing costume, surely?' she answered his blush.

'No, of course—' He looked away from her as he dropped the end of the rope down over the edge. 'That'll reach,' he said. 'I'll go first.' He threaded his belt through the lantern's handle, wrapped the rope firmly around his forearms (Lydia watched carefully and hoped she remembered from her schooldays how it was done), and climbed down, leaning out on the rope and bracing his feet on the wall.

I think I can do that . . .

She wondered breathlessly how deep the water was in the well, and if there would be rats in the tunnel.

If there were people at Cuvé Sainte-Bride, there would be rats.

And revenants, of course . . .

The rope ended a few feet below the first of the iron staples. She saw Palfrey shift over to the staples, and continue the descent, testing each before he put his full weight on it. She saw three of them jar and

218

shift, and heard the patter of bits of stone as they fell into the water below. With the disturbance of the surface the smell of it came up to her, a sickening whiff of rotting meat. *What'll I do if a staple breaks and he falls in? I'll never be able to get him out.*

When he drew near the entry hole she saw that the last few staples had been broken off – *Did they rust quicker because they're closer to the water?* – and Palfrey had to wedge his boot-toe on the tiny stubs that remained. One of these broke, and he swung himself deftly into the narrow slot. Lantern-light outlined the doorway's edges, then dimmed as he moved a little into the passageway beyond. For an outraged moment Lydia thought he was going to go in alone ('This is no task for a fragile little woman . . .') but an instant later he put his head out again, and signed for her to descend.

I have Josetta's word for it that there's scientific proof that women are just as strong and enduring as men . . .

And Simon got himself into this because I asked him.

She took a deep breath, wrapped the rope around her forearms and began her descent.

Jamie . . . Miranda . . . if I get killed I'm so sorry . . .

Oh, dear, which staples were the weak ones . . . ?

Rope to staples. Staples – there were nineteen of them – into the blackness, with barely a feather-brush of yellow light on the wet stone against which she pressed her face and body as she descended. The horrible suggestion of the

219

charnel reek below her, like a kitchen garbage pail too long neglected.

Nineteen. Her groping toe extended down, found nothing. Shifting a little sideways, she found the nubbin of the broken staple, but Palfrey whispered, 'I'll get you, with your permission,' and his hand – with that male gripping power that always surprised her – closed firmly around her calf. 'Lower yourself down . . .'

His arm circled her hips and he swung her down into the doorway with him.

Inside in the tunnel, the fishy, ratty stink of the revenants mingled with the acrid whiff of carbolic soap. Lydia was aware that she was terrified and aware also that there was no time for it, and no turning back. And of course, no guarantee that Simon had ever passed this way . . .

Palfrey slid down the cover of the lantern till it was barely a glimmer, and unholstered his own gun. From his tunic pocket he produced a silencer, which he screwed onto the barrel. Lydia observed he'd also brought the billhook from the car, hanging in a leather sheathe from his waist. *As if any of that's going to do any good . . .*

The tunnel was barely five feet in diameter, and went on for what felt like miles, though Jamie's map had assured her it was not quite three-quarters of a mile from the well to the convent's crypts. It dipped and rose, the low places sheeted with water, sometimes knee-deep, that stank like a sewer. A few yards before the end, it dropped off into what looked like another well, and another ladder of iron staples on a sort of pillar led up to what appeared to be the pierced cover of a drain.

The smell from above was almost unbearable. Revenants.

Lydia held her watch close to the lantern and saw that it was just before eight. The sun had set some forty-five minutes before. The Master of Prague had told her the revenants were awake and moving about well before full dark: some vampires were astir that early also, Don Simon among them, though they could not venture out into the deadly sunlight. Her heart pounding so that she felt nearly sick, she listened, but heard no sound.

Palfrey moved her gently aside, slipping up the lantern-slide the tiniest crack, mounted the ladder and shifted the cover aside. Nothing attacked him, and the next moment he climbed through, and lowered one hand down to her.

The room above had been a chapel; it was a storeroom now. Above the tops of crates (*Lait en poudre* and *Legumes sec*) the walls showed whitewash. To the right an archway had been barred across, and the lantern-gleam flashed on silver. Shapes stirred beyond. Chains clinked; Lydia saw the flash of reflective eyes. She heard Palfrey gasp and read the shock on his face, but gripped his wrist, bringing him back to himself. Touched her own lips. *Not one sound . . .*

One of them, she thought, *is poor Captain Rhinehardt's cousin, who was captured because he wouldn't leave his kinsman*. Brain gone, soul gone, as casually as students in a biology laboratory would pith a frog.

She wondered how she had ever considered Simon and his brothers and sisters in Undeath the worst monsters at large in Flanders.

221

And in making those judgments, will I become a monster, too?

She touched her companion's elbow, moved softly toward the chapel's shut door.

A door opened somewhere beyond, and footsteps retreated on a stone floor. Echoes implied a corridor . . .

'—tell her the equipment is ready,' said Lemoine's voice beyond the door. 'And make her understand that we could not set it up in any other place.'

'There's still a little light in the sky,' returned a woman's voice. The footfalls paused upon the words, then started again, and died away.

'You're a fool if you think this will help you,' said Don Simon Ysidro's voice.

Lydia shut the lantern-slide, opened the door a crack. There was indeed a short corridor beyond. Reflected light – the strong glare of electricity (*They must have a generator somewhere*) – flowed through a half-open door a few yards along, showing her the same ruinous medieval masonry, roughly plastered and whitewashed.

'Oh, I think that remains to be seen.' Dr Lemoine, standing in the doorway, turned and re-entered the room behind him as he spoke, a sort of keyed-up cheerfulness edging his voice. Lydia signed for Palfrey to follow, crept toward the lighted door.

'If the Undead could increase their power by killing the Undead, they would have been preying upon one another for thousands of years.' Don Simon's whispering tones held nothing but a kind of tired patience, like a mother pointing out to a

222

child that no matter how much that child wanted to fly, those cardboard wings would not do the job. 'To drink the blood of another vampire only renders a vampire desperately and incurably sick—'

'Ah, but she's not going to drink your blood.' Something in the room ahead clinked softly, metal on metal. 'Only absorb your energies, at the instant of your death.'

'The instant of my death,' sighed Don Simon, 'was in 1555.'

'And how many deaths have you absorbed since then?'

Lydia felt Palfrey halt, threw a quick look back and saw his face, in the reflected glow, transformed with protesting shock. This transmuted to unbelieving horror as they looked around the jamb of the door, to the room beyond.

The laboratory was a small one. Lydia guessed that the straps that held Don Simon to a sort of steel gridiron at one end of the room must be plated inside with silver. Either that, or simple stress and exhaustion prevented him from using any illusion to conceal his true appearance: silk-white, skeletal. His own claws – his own fangs – were clearly visible from the doorway, as were the scars that ripped across his face and continued down onto his throat, to where the open neck of his shirt fell away from it, gouged by the Master of Constantinople six years ago, when Simon had saved her life.

Beneath the grid on which he lay were arranged cylinders of oxyacetylene gas, their valves linked together so that a single switch (so far as she could tell) would ignite them all.

Don Simon's right arm was strapped close to his side; his left was extended to a small metal table – of the type Lydia was familiar with from the surgical tent – and likewise held by a strap at the wrist. The fingers of this hand Dr Lemoine grasped in his excitement, his voice almost trembling with eagerness. 'Your death – their deaths – is what she needs. Not your blood.' He nodded toward a couple of gleaming gallon jars on the floor, and a small array of scalpels on a nearby table. 'We know that draining all the blood from your body wouldn't kill you. But your death, your real death—'

'Will gain you nothing. If alliance with the Lady Francesca is your goal, 'twill thwart you of it, for 'twill drive her mad—'

'No,' insisted Lemoine. 'No, it will simply complete her transformation to the vampire state. Her power is incomplete, it has always been. Once we—'

At that point Palfrey produced his revolver and shot Dr Lemoine in the back.

Even equipped with a so-called silencer, the report was loud in the underground silence – Lydia wondered, as she strode into the little room, how many soldiers were in the crypts and if the weight of the earth and the tangle of the small rooms and chapels would stifle the sound. She'd already seen a small ring of keys on the table with the surgical equipment and snatched them up, Palfrey still standing in the doorway, as if hypnotized with shock, dismay, betrayal.

Good, at least he won't turn on the oxyacetylene himself in a fit of heroism . . .

224

Would Jamie?

She didn't know.

'There is a guard in the hall above,' said Don Simon, as Lydia unlocked the straps. ''Twill take them a moment, but – *cagafuego*,' he added, as the revenants in the nearby chamber began to howl.

'Can they control rats?' She caught his arm as he rolled off the gridiron, turned toward the door, which was still blocked by Palfrey, staring at him as if he could not believe what he saw.

Don Simon's wrists and forehead, Lydia noted automatically, were welted and bleeding where the straps had touched – a glance confirmed that, yes, the leather was sewn inside with silver plates.

'You knew.' Palfrey's revolver pointed at both of them, perfectly steady though his whole body was trembling with shock. 'Mrs Asher, you . . . you *knew* . . .' The blue eyes turned pleadingly to Don Simon: pleading, anger, disbelief. 'What *are* you?'

Boots clattered on the stair, a man's voice yelled, 'Colonel Lemoine—?'

And against the wall where he had collapsed, Lemoine raised himself to one elbow, blood seeping across the left shoulder of his lab coat. 'Spies!' he gasped. 'Germans!'

Palfrey reacted automatically, ducking back to the door and firing into the passage; Don Simon grabbed Lydia's arm, as she would have taken the moment to dodge past him. A gunshot in the passageway, unmuffled by a silencer, it rang like the crack of doom, and Palfrey buckled and collapsed. There was another unsilenced shot and Lemoine groped his own sidearm from its holster; Don Simon dragged Lydia out the door, stooped to snatch up Palfrey's revolver and fire another shot at the guard – who lay, Lydia now saw, a dozen feet away in a spreading pool of blood.

'Dressing,' Don Simon ordered, ripping open Palfrey's tunic. Lydia whipped her clasp knife from her pocket and cut a four-inch strip from the hem of her skirt (*I couldn't have done THAT if I'd been wearing trousers!*). The vampire tore the tough linen into two pieces as if it had been paper, wadded up the larger piece over the bleeding hole in the young captain's chest and used the shorter to bind it into place, with shouting and the thunder of feet sounding somewhere in the darkness of the stair. 'Stay close.'

'*I have a constitutional dislike of losing those who serve me,*' he had said to her once, and with a single swift movement scooped the taller man up over his shoulder as he rose. Lydia picked up Palfrey's revolver, reached back into the laboratory behind her to switch off the electric light there – Lemoine was on his feet, stumbling towards the door. She heard him crash into something as she caught Don Simon's hand in her own free one. In pitch darkness she followed the vampire at a run down the uneven corridor back to the chapel-cum-storeroom, while the guards shouted and bumbled in the stair.

She felt rather than saw when they passed through the door into the chapel, and heard the revenants howling and baying in their cell, and the clash of their chains. (*Do they chain them to*

226

keep them from eating one another?) Now and then one of them yelled a German word. Iron scraped – the cover of the drain. She groped for the staples on the wall, dropped down into the darkness, and the ice-cold fingers closed around hers again.

'Thank you, Mistress. She'll be in the hunt—'

No need to ask who 'she' was.

'We've a motorcar on the other side of the ridge, up the lane about two miles from the chapel with the lilacs. Did you try that way in first?'

'I guessed 'twould have been a target for artillery.' They were striding along the uneven passageway, Lydia stumbling where the floor dipped, cold, smelly water freezing her feet where the way was flooded. 'Is there a rope?'

'Only near the top. There was nothing to tie it to.'

The vampire swore again. 'Mine I left in the farmhouse, rather than have any man find it hanging down the well. 'Twill be but minutes to fetch it—'

Lydia thought of trying to leap from the threshold of the little doorway in the well's side, up to the first broken stub of iron, and shuddered. Even hanging onto the vampire's neck or shoulders had only to be thought of, to be discarded – vampires didn't weigh much, but she knew the double weight would crumble the rusted remains of the metal. 'All right. How badly is Captain Palfrey hurt?'

' *'Tis not so deep as a well nor so wide as a church door*,' the vampire quoted grimly. 'Can I but bring him to help, 'twill be well.'

227

Lydia shivered, recalling the young man's horri-fied face. *You knew . . .*

She said no more, but kept hold of the vampire's hand, and in time smelled the contaminated water of the well ahead of them, and the wet pong of moss on its stones. She listened desperately to the silence behind them, trying to determine if she could hear footsteps or not. And wondered whether anyone there would be smart enough to deduce that they'd have to escape via the well, and be waiting for them at the top.

Or didn't they know about the well?

And did Simon shut the drain-cover in the chapel—?

He stopped, and she felt him put Palfrey down. Holding Lydia's hand, he signed her to kneel, then led her, feeling the floor, to the edge of the doorway, to show her where it lay. Then he kissed her hand and released it, and she felt the sleeve of his shirt brush her cheek as he stood. There was the faintest whisper of scratching as he jumped – she was glad there was no light, for she didn't even like to picture it – and, presum-ably, seized the broken nubbins of iron above and to the right of the doorway, for she didn't hear a splash. A moment later the faint pitter of dislodged stone fragments falling into the water.

She crawled back to Palfrey, took his hand. It was cold with shock. She put the back of her wrist against his lips, and felt the warm thread of breath. His pulse, when she felt it a moment later, was fast and thready: *He HAS to be got to help . . .*

'*You knew,*' he had said.

228

And how will I explain to him that vampires can bend and ensorcel human perceptions? Particularly the very old, very skilled vampires like Simon? How will I explain – how will I make him believe – that all those times he thinks he met Simon by daylight, all those 'impressions' he had of reading mention of him in his father's letters – were only thoughts implanted in his dreams?

EVERYTHING – resigning from the Guards, and coming here to France, and leaving poor Miss Bellingham – EVERYTHING was based upon a lie. Everything he undertook was only because Don Simon needed someone to work for him in the daylight hours.

Her hand tightened involuntarily on Palfrey's, and – a little to her surprise – she felt the pressure feebly returned.

She listened into the darkness of the tunnel behind them, seeking again for the rattle of soldiers' boots, the creak of belt leather. *How much do the guards know? How many of them are there? And do THEY know the kind of thing Lemoine is up to, with his enslavement of German prisoners who are stripped of their own minds?*

Do they know how deadly it is to come into any contact with these things that might result in blood transfer? Do they—?

Something brushed her face.

She realized her thoughts had been wandering an instant before she smelled blood and cold hands seized her around the waist and throat.

A woman screamed, cursed, in the blackness beside her – silver burning a vampire's hands . . .

Lydia tried to wrench free and fell over Palfrey's

body, cried out in pain as those steel hands grabbed her again, around the waist and by the hair, this time, and a woman's voice hissed in her ear, '*Rogneux puteresse!*'

She was dragged away into the tunnel's reeking darkness.

Seventeen

Asher knew the place when Millward described it, a vast zone of waste ground beyond London's East End, where drab dockside merged with marshes, gorse and woodland. Rough land blotched around its edges by turpentine works, phosphate plants, varnish factories and sewer outfalls, before one came to the market gardens of Stratford and West Ham. Brown with factory waste, the River Lea and assorted creeks and cuts wound their way toward the Thames, and the bodies of vagrants and outcasts turned up periodically in the dirty margins of those streams, unmourned and not much regarded by the Metropolitan Police.

'There's a pub about two hundred yards from where Carpenter's Road ends in the marsh,' said Millward. They had retreated to the Reading Room's vestibule, with its garish recruiting posters, and the intermittent comings and goings of scholars, journalists, students and cranks. 'A stone's throw from the waterworks reservoir . . .'

'The Blind King.' Asher saw the grimy red-brick box in his mind: nailed-up shutters, padlocked door. The ground was marshy but the steps up to the door, and the narrow window slits at ground level, told him there was a cellar of sorts beneath it. 'It's been shut up for years.'

'Well, the police found a body near the outfall

embankment Tuesday morning. Donnie and I went out there—' Millward nodded back toward the Reading Room – 'when we heard about the state in which it was found. A man we met there spoke of some boys playing along the City Mill Creek and in the marshes finding rats . . . You said these things can control rats? Dozens of them, torn to pieces and partially eaten, they said, lying all of a . . . all of a heap, as if they'd been dumped from a basket. He said it wasn't dogs.'

The vampire-hunter's silver-shot brows tugged together, oblivious to a tweed-clothed woman who was trying to get past him with her arms full of notebooks. Millward always planted himself in the center of any room.

'He said he'd seen rats after a ratting, and it was nothing like. Nothing like anything he'd seen. And a man who lives in Turnpike Row said he'd seen a thing, twice, in the fog, late at night, a thing like what you described.'

Asher spread out his ordnance map against the wall and located the Blind King, and then Turnpike Row, City Mill Creek and the embankment of the outfall. His recollection of that end of Hackney Marsh included no other buildings nearby isolated enough to permit concealing any creature that size in a cellar.

'Good man.' He folded his map, gripped the former scholar's shoulder. 'It sounds as if one of them's being kept there and is feeding itself on rats. The other may be lurking near. Any sense that anyone else thinks it might be the Blind King?'

Millward considered the matter, and Asher guessed he had pursued enquiries no further.

Guessed that with his instinctive upper-class reticence, it hadn't even occurred to Millward to go down to the nearest pub on Carpenter's Road – the Dolphin – and further his researches. But he only shook his head, and didn't – as many people did when faced with such a question – elaborate or surmise: 'I wouldn't know, no.'

'Good man,' Asher said again. 'I'll go have a look at the place this afternoon.'

'Will you need help?'

'Probably later, yes, thank you. At the moment I think one man will be less obvious than two.' And particularly, Asher mused as he listened and mentally sorted through the rest of Millward's researches and newspaper cuttings from the past five days, if one of those two was as striking in appearance as the handsome raven-and-silver vampire-hunter. Nor did Millward possess the professional spy's quality of what Asher mentally termed *unvisibility*: the trick of blending into a crowd, of making himself look like nobody of importance. All his colleagues in the Department had had it, whether they were dressed as dons or coal-heavers. Pritchard Crowell, he recalled, could 'doze off' so convincingly that village chiefs of police had been known to interview local informers in his presence, and never be able to give a description of 'that fellow in the corner' when the informers (or in one case the village chief of police) later turned up dead.

It was – Asher reflected, as the suffocatingly overcrowded bus clattered its way out to Hackney that afternoon – one of his few reservations about Doyle's Sherlock Holmes tales: the fact that

233

Holmes, though repeatedly touted as a master of disguise, was also described in terms of being a man of distinctive appearance.

But then, there was a streak of actor in many of the best agents, himself, he suspected, included. He stepped from the bus at Old Ford Road, glad of the stick that – with the flour in his hair and mustache, the long, grizzled side-whiskers that formed part of his little disguise kit, and a pair of steel-rimmed spectacles – contributed to the addition of twenty years to his age. And indeed he felt like a man in his sixties, as he hobbled his careful way across the Five Bells Bridge and then along the railroad right-of-way through that grubby world of empty fields and straggly market allotments. The hot rawness in his chest and the swiftness with which fatigue descended on him were whispered reminders of the previous week's fever. *Don't mess about with this, Jimmy!* Hoggett had insisted, the last time – just after Christmas, it had been – that Asher had been felled by low-grade fever, crippling fatigue and paroxysms of coughing. *Once you've had pneumonia it lingers in your body for years . . .*

Like the infection that had been devouring poor Bert Mayo in that tiny back room on Brabazon Street: once contracted, there was nothing that could be done. He was, he knew, lucky.

The most pneumonia would do was kill him.

He reached the Dolphin public house at about three. It was the dead hour in business, before all the local mills and factories let out. The Dolphin was of the old style of public houses, literally a house, with beer and ale served in the front parlor and more private quarters in the back. The place was empty when Asher reached it and he presented himself as a Liverpudlian on the tramp, looking for some kind of easy work, having had pneumonia in the first days of the fighting. The landlady, with a husband and one son dead and another son still at the Front, was sympathetic, and Asher's offer to 'help with the washing-up' to pay for a second glass of beer and a sandwich earned him a full account of the two mysterious heaps of dead rats (one Sunday and the next only yesterday), and the condition of the vagrant's body found in the Lea Tuesday morning.

'Myself, I think it was an accident at the railway workshops, or the mills up past Bully Fen,' Mrs Farnum insisted, dipping hot water from the copper on the stove (the interview had moved into the kitchen) and spreading towels on all but a corner of the kitchen table. 'They're short of men there to work and they push them to all hours of the night – no, Mr Pritchard, I won't have you lugging great buckets of water about, I know how that pneumonia sticks to a man's bones!' (*I should introduce you to Hoggett* . . .) 'You just stand here by the sink and do the washing and I'll bring the glasses up to you . . . My father worked in the Houldsworth Mill in Reddish and had his hand taken off and all the flesh skinned off his arm – clear down to the bone! – by the belt on a ring frame, and the company claimed he was drunk and it was his own fault, but when you've worked fifteen hours – let alone where you'd even get the

235

liquor to get drunk on – you're that tired, as the men are, working now, those that're left—'

But by the sound of it, once Asher had sifted through the long circumlocutions of her tale, the man had not been ripped up by machinery, but by a beast.

'Looked like poor Dandy did, when that brute mastiff of Ted Clavering's tore him up last Michaelmas two years . . .'

A beast, he thought grimly, which had once been a man.

The sightings in the fog by Mr Sawyer of Turnpike Row were both confirmed as well, and both between the so-called Channel Sea River (actually a drainage creek) and the equally narrow Waterworks River – both within a few hundred yards of the Blind King, Asher estimated – and had been accompanied by a smell. 'I think that was the worst of it, you know,' said the Widow Farnum. 'Evil, that smell: fishy, and greasy, and ratty – not like nothing I've smelled before . . .'

'*You've* smelled?'

She nodded with a grimace. 'Near the old boarded-up pub out past the end of Carpenter's Road. He's lurkin' around there, whoever he is – You can't get anybody here on the street, nowadays, to walk out on the marsh at night. Even them as works in the phosphate plant, they'll walk in groups back home . . .'

In the late afternoon's harsh chill Asher walked out along Carpenter's Road itself, where it petered out into the Stratford Marsh, and hobbled as slowly as he dared along the railway embankment as if following the Great Eastern line northwest

236

to the cluster of factories in Hackney Wick. *Always look as if you've got good reason to be where you are* had been the first thing he'd learned when working in the Department, and it was a caution he'd never forgotten. And the Blind King – sitting like a dropped brick in the midst of those brown wastes of clay and grass, now thinly filmed with the first of spring green – was the choice of a professional. You couldn't get near it without being seen. But from the railway embankment, Asher identified the path leading to it which continued the roadbed of Carpenter's Road, and noted that the straggly assortment of sheds around the original pub seemed to have been put into some kind of order. They all had doors, and the grass around the walls of the pub itself looked beaten-down, as if there'd been activity there in the two weeks since Bert Mayo had been dragged away from the upstairs room on Brabazon Street.

Wind swept over the marshes, smelling of the estuary. A gull cried, rocking on black-tipped wings. Asher kept moving stolidly, leaning on his stick and prickling with the sensation of being watched – the awareness that the red-brick house wasn't empty. The feeling pursued him, all the long trudge back to Hackney, and on his bus ride home.

The negotiation with Colonel Stewart that evening was a long one, but Asher emerged from it at last with a temporary commission as Major, orders to report to General Finch in Flanders, an ambiguously-worded mandate to 'undertake such independent investigations as will further the war

237

effort, at his own sole discretion', and a place on the Channel steamer *Eleanor* on the fifteenth. Stewart had wanted him to depart on Monday, but there remained the problem of the Blind King, and the thing that dwelt beneath it.

For that, Asher guessed, he was going to need Grippen's help.

He took a circuitous route back to Warwick Place, dropping out of the last bus on Holland Walk amid a beery crowd of pub-goers and walking through the deserted, blacked-out, misty streets to the mews that served all the houses on that block. Since that afternoon on Stratford Marsh he had been plagued with the uneasy sense that Mr Mackintosh had picked up his trail again, though he had never been able to form a clear proof that this was or wasn't so. It was probably this suspicion that saved him. As he counted doorways with his left hand he listened behind him and before him, mind sorting every drip and whisper of the night, and something made him turn even as a cosh cracked a terrific blow on his shoulder. The next second a man's weight slammed him to the pavement and he barely got his hand up in time to catch a garrote slipped around his neck. It cut into his fingers as his attacker dragged it tight, cutting off Asher's breath as he twisted to get some kind of purchase against his assailant.

The man was an expert, grinding him into the pavement with elbows and knees as the silk line tightened. His fingers under the noose distributed the strain but didn't alleviate the pressure; his ears were ringing and he was losing consciousness when he felt the man's grip slack suddenly, greater weight crushing him at the same moment he gasped, and heard a man's hoarse voice behind him curse.

Only half-conscious, he felt rather than heard light footfalls fleeing, and his second gasp filled his nostrils with the stink of old blood and dirty clothing as he heard Grippen snarl, 'Dogs spit your arse, whoreson!' The Master of London continued in that vein for some minutes, using terms that even Asher – a trained etymologist – had never heard, while Asher lay face-down on the wet bricks, trying to breathe through a bruised throat and wishing he had a notebook and pencil.

At length he felt Grippen's coat-skirt brush his hand and the vampire turned him roughly over. 'Live you?'

Asher started to reply, but could only cough, and the vampire dragged him to his feet.

''Twas the suck-arse clot that followed you to the park,' said Grippen. 'Hogs chew his lights— argh! Damn!'

Asher lit a match (*To hell with the blackout*) and saw, to his startled alarm, the whole side of Grippen's face was blistered, one eye welted almost shut and both blood and pus oozing from the skin. 'What the—?'

'The whoreson had silver – a chain of it wrapped round his fingers, or plated onto the back of a glove, devil burn him! Worms eat his—'

'He had it ready?' Asher offered him a clean handkerchief.

'He was too goddam occupied wi' skraggin' you, wasn't he, to go diggin' about for it in his pockets!'

'In other words,' said Asher, 'he knew he might be dealing with a vampire?'

Grippen was silent for a moment, daubing his injuries and thinking that over. Then he said, ''Od's cock.'

Asher said, 'Yes,' quite softly, with the sense of things coming together in his mind: glimpses, like the fleeting sense of a familiar outline half-seen from the corner of his eye, that slowly coalesced into a half-recognized form.

'Will you come with me?' he added after a moment. 'I've found the revenants – and something tells me they'll be moved elsewhere by tomorrow, and all this looking will have to start again. I think it's best we deal with them – and the man who's seeking them – tonight.'

The protesting squawk of chickens rattled in the misty night. A man cursed: Asher placed his vowels within ten miles of Cork.

Teague.

After a moment the faintest creak from the dark ahead of him spoke of a shed door opening. He hoped to Heaven that Grippen was listening behind them, around them, in the salt-smelling blackness for the squishy tread of feet, sniffing for the fishy, rat-piss foulness of their quarry. But like the vampire, he knew that the Others could, upon occasion, conceal their stink and their sound and their presence, until they were on top of their prey.

240

In a voice that living ears wouldn't have picked up, even had the listener stood – as Grippen stood now – shoulder-to-shoulder with him at the foot of the railway embankment, Asher breathed, 'How many in the house?'

And that bass rumble softer than a gnat's whine murmured back, 'Four above stairs. If the thing's in the cellar no man'll be down with him. I wouldn't be. I smell smoke an' beer.'

Enough thready moonlight pierced the mists to show Asher the vampire's turned head, and the distant, grimy mustard seed of lamplight leaked from the house's shutters caught a reflection in his half-shut eyes. Asher knew what he was doing.

Two years ago, in the spring of 1913, Grippen had stood thus in the alleyway behind Asher's own house on Holyrood Street in Oxford, and had put the household to sleep, so that he could walk in and steal Asher's child. Even retrieving Miranda, safe and unharmed, had not shaken Asher's resolve, taken at that time, that he would kill them: Grippen, Don Simon, the London nest. Every soul of the cursed Undead who crossed his path.

And here he was at Grippen's side, watching him do the thing that the old vampires, the skilled vampires, the vampires who had absorbed thousands of lives over hundreds of years, could do.

He heard the man Teague, in the shed, mutter, 'Jaysus . . .' in a voice thick with sleep. Then long silence, broken, in time, by the soft, slithering bump of his body sliding to the floor from whatever bench or box he'd sat down on when drowsiness overcame him. The chickens continued to squawk frantically, desperately, and on the still air Asher caught the faintest whiff of blood.

Grippen said, 'He's all yours, Jimmy.' Taking Asher by the elbow, the vampire led him toward the shed, not to risk even the faintest flicker of lantern-light on the marsh until they were within the shed itself. As they approached it, Grippen rumbled, 'You given further thought to my offer?'

To become vampire.

To acquire just precisely those qualities that would be most useful to a spy: the mental power over other men's perceptions, the ability to turn their eyes aside, to cause them to think you looked like someone who belonged where they glimpsed you. In time, to bend their dreams so that they were sure they'd met you before and that you were trustworthy.

To become a thing of illusion and shadow, apart from the world and its pain.

Abilities and qualities he had worked for years to acquire. He had sought to perfect them in himself, having seen them in Pritchard Crowell. 'I've given it thought, yes.'

He edged up the slide on the lantern as they entered the shed, showing two chickens, tied by their feet at the back. Blood made dark splotches on their white feathers. To Undead senses, the smell would permeate the fog for miles. The beam of his light traced wires from their bound legs up the corners of the rear wall and across the rafters of the small loft that covered half the shed's width, to a mechanism that would drop a steel grille, like a portcullis, down over the door. He could see where coins had been welded onto the steel, enough silver to burn the hands of a vampire – or a revenant.

Beside an old milking stool at one side of the shed the man Teague lay: Asher recognized him from the confused struggle in Brabazon Street. A heavy pug chin and a broken nose, the tight, nearly lipless mouth sagging open like a child's in stuporous sleep.

Asher climbed to the loft and found rope there. Rope, and a dozen long crates labeled Ludwig-Loewe, one of the largest arms manufacturers in Berlin.

Grippen stood just outside the shed door, barely more than a shadow. Asher guessed that if the grille had fallen and trapped them both inside the rickety roof wouldn't have held out against the vampire's strength. But wariness was the core of the vampire's soul – they understood themselves to be both predator and prey.

He dragged Teague to one of the supports that held up the loft, tied his hands together and then sat him up against the beam and tied him to it, in such a way that he could cut him free, and drag him from the shed, without loosing his bonds. He roped his ankles together as well – the man didn't stir – then crossed to the terrible shadow by the door. 'Anything?'

'Narh. But you don't always hear 'em. Or smell 'em, much as they stink.'

Nerves prickling with watchfulness, Asher shut the lantern, slung the remainder of the rope over his shoulder, and followed Grippen to the shut-up pub itself. Unlike the Dolphin, the Blind King had been purpose-built as a pub, with a large taproom facing the road and kitchen, storeroom and private parlor behind. The four men dead asleep in the parlor, with drinks before them on the table and cigars smoldering in a cracked Queensware dish, were those who'd helped drag poor Bert Mayo from his daughter's house on Brabazon Street – it had for years been part of Asher's business to remember even faces glimpsed once and under trying circumstances.

Even through the dusty fetor of a building shut up for decades, and the heavy odor of cigar smoke, the smell of the revenant stained the air. Asher found the cellar door in the kitchen, re-enforced with makeshift metal, and triple-locked. His ear to its panels, he could hear a kind of groaning bleat down below.

Not just 'a revenant', he thought. *Not just 'one of those things'*. A man named Bert Mayo, whose daughter loved him enough to take care of him and shelter him though what was happening to him terrified her.

Every one of the revenants started out human.

As did, he reminded himself, every one of the vampires.

Grippen came in and listened, too, then looked around the kitchen by the light of Asher's lantern, and grunted. 'Whoreson cullions.' He nodded toward the crates stacked around the walls, more long boxes of rifles, and smaller metal containers of ammunition, likewise bearing the mark of German manufacture. 'The Papists, is it, taking the

244

chance of this greater war to rise up 'gainst the King?'

'It could actually be either side,' returned Asher quietly. 'Either those who seek to free Ireland from English domination, or those who don't want to be ruled by a Catholic majority. Who want Ireland to continue as a part of a greater Empire. And are willing to stamp out anything they consider rebellion.'

'I've no quarrel wi' killin' Papists.' Grippen's fangs glinted in the shadows, and he shrugged. 'Either way 'tis naught to me. But they're fools an' worse than fools if they think making revenants'll gain 'em anything. As well loose a cage full of wolves and tigers onto a battlefield. They'll kill your enemy, sure, but devour as many of your own in doin' it.'

'They think they have someone who can control them,' said Asher. 'For the sake of humanity I hope they're wrong. Does the name Francesca Gheric mean anything to you?'

'The White Lady?' The piggy dark eyes narrowed. 'What of her? A troublemaker in every city she's dwelt in, I hear tell, but when all's said she's proved no great threat to any.'

They passed through the taproom on their way out, the four men lying, bound hand and foot by Grippen, on the floor. 'When I give the word,' Asher added, 'get these men out of here. Is the revenant in the cellar chained?' He found he couldn't use Bert Mayo's name.

'Aye.'

He couldn't say, *Good*, either, knowing that a bullet wouldn't kill the thing that that poor old

245

Irish fence had become. That the only way out for him – and for any future victim of his insane hunger – was through fire. Fire, or the burning corrosion of the sun.

All he could say was, 'Let's do what we have to do, then.'

Eighteen

Teague was awake when Asher and Grippen returned to the shed. The chickens still chattered and clucked, though softer, resigning themselves – as animals do – stoically to their pain. The Irishman, Asher noticed, hadn't cried out, and it interested him that the man had enough on his conscience to keep him quiet even in a pitch-black shed on the Hackney Marshes with a revenant somewhere out in the darkness . . .

And the smell of fresh blood close by.

Asher unhooded the lantern. 'So is this something you're being paid for, or were you the ones taking delivery on that first package from France when it got away in London?'

Teague spit at him. Asher sidestepped the wad.

'We know about that French doctor trying to cook these things up for their army, and it doesn't really make a lot of difference whether it was the French who sent that poor Fritzy over here and he went astray, or whether one of your people lifted him from them, either on-site in France or on the way. What I need to know is, who are you working for, and do they – or do the French – have some way of controlling these things?'

'Sod you.'

'I see you mistake me for someone in the Department.' Asher slipped one of his knives from his boot, set the lantern down and slashed

247

the buttons from Teague's shirt, then ripped the garment back over his shoulders. With precise care he cut a large, shallow X in the Irishman's chest, only deep enough to bleed. Copiously.

Teague's eyes flared in horror. 'Damn it, you can't . . .'

'I told you I'm not in the Department.' Asher wiped the blade on Teague's shirt and replaced it in his boot. 'Even if I were, I suspect you underestimate them. I think the smell of that'll carry more than those poor chickens.'

He stepped back, and watched his prisoner thrash in a violent effort to twist free of the ropes. The man didn't curse, as he would have, Asher thought, had he been less utterly terrified.

At length Asher said, 'That's not going to help you, and it is wasting your time. I think you know none of your men is in any state to help you and I think you know what's going to happen when that revenant gets here. Even if you do manage to break free and get away during its attack, I think you know what happens to those whose blood gets mixed with Fritzy's. So why don't you—'

He turned his head sharply as, from the door, Grippen said, 'It's out there.'

'You're lying—' Teague's voice was hoarse with shock. 'I been setting chickens out here three nights now—'

Asher retreated a step or two up the ladder to the loft, his eyes warily on the door.

'I don't know anythin'—'

'Too bad.'

'I swear it!'

Asher said nothing. He'd been perfectly prepared to have Grippen impersonate the revenant – the night was coal-sack dark and the vampire perfectly capable of imitating the random, bleating groans that had come from the cellar – but he knew this wasn't the case.

Damn it, he'd better not hold out . . .

He dropped from the ladder, walked to the door to listen, to breathe the damp air— '*Don't!*' Teague screamed, clearly thinking he was going to go through the door and keep on going.

Outside in the blackness Asher neither heard nor scented a thing. But the whole night seemed to whisper of it.

He turned back, his face a calm blank.

'They got one they say'll be able to command 'em—'

'Name?'

'I dunno. Some woman.'

'*Would* or *does* command them?'

'I dunno! She said *would be, will be . . .*'

'Who said?'

'Meagher. Oonah Meagher. Calls herself Tuathla. Let me out of here, for the Lord's sake—'

'I thought finding these things was the thing you most wanted in the world, Teague. Bringing them over to England, so they could walk about—'

'For the love of God, man, it's business! Meagher and her friends, they heard talk of a risin' against John Bull, while England's army's away in France an' half the Ulster volunteers with 'em! Meagher works over there for this Frenchie, says he's come up wi' a scheme to make soldiers out o' nuttin', men who'll walk straight into machine-gun fire an' won't care. I dunno the whole of it, they just hired me an' my boys to meet 'em on the Calais beach in a motor launch: two hard Armagh lads an' a Fritzy that just huddled under a blanket an' shivered. We put 'em up in a safe house in Brunswick Road an' that's where he broke out from . . .'

'Names of the friends?'

'For God's sake—!'

He could still smell nothing, hear nothing, but backed from the doorway toward the ladder. Grippen was nowhere to be seen, and Asher knew better than to think that the master vampire would tackle a revenant. Keeping his voice expressionless, he replied, 'No. For the sake of the men – and women – who won't be either killed by these things or transformed into them; who won't have to be killed like murrain cattle to keep this plague from spreading. For the sake of this country – of the world, if you will – if these things start roving at large. And for your own, of course.'

'Jimmy Darcie, Nan Sloan, Joey Strahan . . .' He almost babbled the names. 'Uh— Jerry Dwyer . . . Ned Mulready . . .'

'Any of them hurt when the thing broke out?'

'No! 'Twas down the cellar, an' broke a window. I'm to tell 'em when we catch it – then we heard it got Bert . . . Please, man, please, what d'you want me to say? If it's comin'—'

Asher heard – or thought he heard – the soft crunch of a step on the wet gravel outside, and his heart turned sick with shock. 'Any more of them come over, or just the one?'

'Just the one – dear God—!'

'Who else is in on this?'

'Nobody— Just us! Meagher, an' Joey—'

'Safe house, bunch of hard lads,' mused Asher. 'That's a lot of money invested, for just a couple of rebels.'

'Nobody else knows!' Teague screamed the words. 'Not a livin' soul, I swear it—'

Asher tested the ladder that led up into the loft, made sure that it wasn't attached and could be pushed down easily. He pulled the knife from his boot again and mounted a step or two, to check whether the cord that would release the trap on the shed door could be easily cut. It could. He mounted another step and Teague shrieked, 'Butler, a chap named Butler! He paid for it all! Sets up deliveries of the guns wi' the Germans! We told 'em we had a way to get fighters is all! He gave Jimmy Darcie a hundred pounds and paid us besides! I swear that's all! I swear it!'

Asher sprang down from the ladder, bent to cut the cord that held Teague to the beam, and in that instant was surrounded by the stink of the revenant: blood, rats, urine, filth. He swung around, aghast to see that it was inside the shed with them, coming at them in the dim glow of the dark lantern, *How could I not have seen it? Not have heard it . . .?*

With a hideous crash the steel-and-silver grille dropped over the shed door, but the revenant didn't slow its rush by a second. Asher made to dive to cut the rope on Teague's feet, but like a nightmare darkness surrounded him, and he

251

had a vague awareness of being dragged literally off his feet. The next second, it seemed, he
fell with a crash on the plank flooring of the
loft and by the lamplight reflected from below
saw Grippen hurl the ladder down into the shed
beneath them.

Teague screamed.

'You've more bollocks than brains,' snapped
Grippen, and ripped open the lid of one of the
crates. 'Could have got yoursel' killed, an' who
knows how many of these godless things yet to
deal with.' As Asher had guessed, the crate was
full of rifles, brand new and still thick with factory
grease. The vampire pulled one out and used it
to smash a hole in the flimsy wood of the roof
between the rafters. 'Don't bother,' he added, as
Asher moved toward the edge of the loft. 'The
man's dead.'

Teague was still screaming, but Asher knew
what the vampire meant.

Grippen sprang lightly up to the hole and pulled
himself through it, reached down – brutal, strong
hands in their black gloves – to draw Asher up
after him, then slid down the roof to the edge
and dropped off, a bare eight feet to the ground.
Asher followed, and walked with him to the
boarded-up pub, where, more by touch than
anything else – for no gas was laid on in the
building and Asher guessed, now, that it would
be deadly dangerous to light a lamp – they
dragged Teague's compatriots out and into one
of the other sheds.

'There's paraffin in the kitchen,' said Asher.

'Stay here, then,' growled the vampire. 'I'll

252

make sure the place is good an' doused – an' you look like hell.' He shoved Asher down onto something – it felt like a barrel – in the smaller shed, and turned back, a dim shape of black in the blackness, toward the pub.

Realizing that he was, in fact, almost too tired to stand, Asher caught the dirty wool sleeve of his coat. 'Did you ever hear that thing coming?'

'Nary a peep.'

'Did you hear anyone else? See anyone?'

The vampire turned back, stood over him, a dark presence more sensed than seen. 'There's someone out there, aye,' he said. 'One of these Irish or one of your lot, I don't know. Followin' old Hungry Tom in there—' he jerked his head toward the larger shed – 'I'm guessin'.'

'The Department knew one of their subjects had been taken,' said Asher wearily. 'They had a man looking out for him, the moment he landed in England. Trying to trace him – and trying to keep those who'd stolen him from recapturing him before they did.' He rubbed his throat, where the bruises of the garrote still smarted. 'By whatever means they could.'

The matter is in hand, Langham had smiled . . .

And somebody in Germany was doubtless saying the same thing to his superiors, and basking in anticipation of promotion.

He added, 'Thank you. That's twice tonight you've saved my life.'

'Huh.' The vampire set his hands on his hips. 'I ain't given up hope you'll come round to my way of thinkin', Asher. I need a man like you. And you're a natural for it. But I warn you now.

I'll kill you mesel', ere I let that Papist whoreson Ysidro make you a fledgling of his.'

Grippen scattered paraffin over both the Blind King and the shed where the first revenant – Hungry Tom, Tom the Ogre, some poor nameless German soldier picked at random from among prisoners in a war he might never have wanted to have anything to do with – gouged and tore at Teague's body. Then Asher and the Master of London sat down to wait until it was almost sun-up, Asher to make sure that neither revenant would escape the flame into night's darkness, Grippen listening for 'our little pal' in the darkness, though Asher was, by this time, fairly certain of who it was out there. Certain, and a little disgusted with himself for not having guessed it sooner.

Shortly before the first whispers of daylight, Asher became aware that Grippen had gone, and tossed burning screws of paraffin-soaked newspaper through the broken windows of the pub, and the hole in the roof of the shed. Then he went back into the smaller shed, to inform Teague's henchmen that the police would be on their way. With the first stains of light, he discovered that the smaller shed also contained boxes of German rifles.

And that it now contained only two bound Irishmen, when he knew that there had been four, asleep around the table in the pub.

Grippen had brought them out to the shed in darkness.

Grippen, who'd had a severe burn from the

254

silver wielded by Asher's attacker earlier in the night; a burn that vampires had only one way of healing.

He closed his eyes. Yes, the men had been smuggling guns from Germany to Ireland, a hanging offense in time of war. And yes, they'd been part of a plan for even greater horror: greater still, had the plan progressed to the point where Germans could get involved. And yes, they'd have killed him two weeks ago if he hadn't gone through that window and gotten away.

But they'd been prisoners. And bound.

And the house would burn over their bloodless bodies and no one – not the police, not Osric Millward and his hunters – would know how they died.

And Grippen wants me to become part of that world. Because I'd be a useful fledgling. A good vampire.

He walked away from the burning buildings, back toward the railway embankment. With the destruction of the two revenants he was fairly certain that he was now safe from further attack – Langham certainly wouldn't care about the fates of a couple of Irish rebels – but frizzling in any case with the sense of being watched as he went.

But if I'm right about who it is who's been watching me—

The thought snagged at his mind as he started the long trudge across the Marshes toward St Paul's Road, where the busses would begin running for the city.

—why doesn't Grippen try to recruit HIM?

255

Nineteen

'My dear Madame Asher!' Lamplight bobbed on the stone of the walls. On the other side of the archway – filled in with bars which gleamed with tarnishing silver plate – the revenants muttered and jerked at their chains, their eyes catching the light. Lydia's cell had been, she guessed, a burial chapel built off the long catacomb that had been adapted for the revenants. One archway – the one barred with silver – opened into it. Another, also barred, led back into the main round chapel that served as a storeroom.

When the Lady Francesca had dragged her back up out of the tunnel to the well and had thrown her in here, she'd left the cover off the tunnel. In the ten or fifteen minutes that Lydia had been in the cell, with only one of her pocket candles for light, she'd seen half a dozen rats emerge, either from the tunnel, or from the hall which led to Lemoine's laboratory, and trot straight into the catacomb where the revenants were chained.

There they were torn to pieces, and devoured raw.

So thirteen revenants constitutes a community large enough to have a hive-mind capable of controlling rats.

Lydia was fascinated, despite her horror of the rats and her fear that the next person who entered

256

the storeroom would throw her into the catacomb as well.

I am wearing silver but how long would I be able to stay awake even if three chains' worth is enough to get them to back off?

Palfrey, bleeding to death back in the tunnel . . .

Unless Francesca went back and finished him?

Poor Palfrey—

Colonel Dr Jules Lemoine strode into the chapel, his left arm in a sling (Palfrey's aim, Lydia now saw, left a great deal to be desired), pale in the light of the lantern he carried in his good hand. This he set down, and drew a key from his pocket.

'What are you doing?' Nurse Meagher appeared from the shadowy hallway at his heels. 'You can't mean to let her out, sir! She tried to kill you!'

'Nonsense.' Lemoine held up Lydia's Webley. 'This weapon hasn't been fired. It was her companion – like her,' he added gravely, 'under the delusion that the vampire we took was their friend.'

'She is the pale vampire's *mignonne*.' Lydia didn't see her enter, but Francesca Gheric now stood beside the chapel door.

Seen closer, and in the lantern-light that was marginally better than the shreddy moonlight of no man's land, she was indeed beautiful. But maybe that was only a vampire's illusion. Like Meagher, she was dressed as a nurse – *In case any of the guards sees her?*

Any Matron on the Front would tell her to put her hair up . . .

Facing the three of them, with the revenants

stirring and growling on the far side of the silver bars, Lydia had to struggle to keep her breathing steady.

She clutched at the bars of the smaller archway that separated her from Lemoine, made her expression as earnest as if she were trying to convince her Nanna that she'd only been seeking a book of sermons in her father's library, and cried, 'He is indeed my friend, sir! He has long ago given up preying upon human-kind, and has pledged his loyalty to the British crown!' *Which I'm sure was precisely what he told poor Palfrey* . . .

The colonel's gaze melted from sternness to pity. 'Madame, Madame, do you truly believe that?' and Lydia let her eyes fill with tears.

'Who told you about the passageway that you used?' Meagher walked up to the bars, planted herself at Lemoine's side.

'Colonel Simon.' Lydia took off her spectacles, wiped her eyes and tried to sound as if she were struggling against the inner suspicion that she had indeed been betrayed. 'He said the fate of Britain depends on his mission here—'

Meagher rolled her eyes impatiently. 'Of course that's what he told her! And probably his driver as well.'

Lydia reached timidly to clutch Lemoine's sleeve, and threw a glance of terror toward the darkness beyond the silver barrier. 'Colonel, what *are* those . . . those *things*? Captain Palfrey wouldn't tell me anything, only said things like, "Dark forces are at work . . ."'

'Why did he bring you?' demanded Meagher.

'He said he might need a second person to drive the motorcar, if he were injured.' She sobbed, and bit her lip in what she hoped was a touching display of wan and ignorant courage. 'I wanted to help—'

'It's all right.' Lemoine put a strong hand over hers. 'You've gotten mixed up in things that are no business of yours, Madame. Deeply secret things. And you *can* help.'

Meagher's blue eyes flared wide and she grabbed the edge of Lemoine's sling, dragged him from the bars to the far side of the little storeroom chapel. Francesca watched them for a moment with cynical cerulean eyes. *Probably telling him he can't trust me and that Don Simon's going to read my mind first thing, if they let me go . . .*

Then the vampire turned her mocking gaze back to Lydia.

Lydia hastily looked away, and fumbled in her pocket for a handkerchief. But she felt the tug on her mind of cold power, power from outside herself. James had told her that picturing a door shutting, or a blank brick wall, worked, but she remembered also that both Antonio and the Master of Prague had described Francesca Gheric as overwhelmingly powerful – *Can she see through that brick wall?*

What will she see if she does?

And will thinking of it tip her off that I'm not as ignorant as I pretend?

Lydia called up images to her mind of what it would feel like to be swept into Simon's arms, passionately kissed (*What about those teeth?*

259

Never mind . . .), overwhelmed by a torrent of ecstasy (*Was that Mr Stoker who'd said that? Or Mrs Radcliffe in* Romance of the Forest*? Or was that someone else . . .?*). Hoping for the best, she yielded meekly to that terrible cold grip on her will, and raised her eyes timidly to the vampire's. (*And I hope this works . . .*)

(*Oh, wait, if I were passionately in love with Don Simon why would I be wearing all this silver . . .?*)

Francesca's lip curled again at whatever she saw in Lydia's thoughts, and she put her hand through the bars to pat her cheek, patronizing as a duchess handing a farthing to an orphan while her friends are watching.

Lemoine jerked from his conversation with Meagher and reached the bars in a stride. 'You will not touch her!'

Francesca raised her brows – *YOU'RE saying this to ME?* – and the physician hurriedly collected himself.

'It's clear she's only this Colonel Simon's dupe,' he amended. 'She has nothing to do with either the Germans or the British government, or my own.' He turned back to Lydia. 'I'm very sorry, Madame,' he said, 'but you're going to have to stay here for a time. And I'm afraid you'll have to remain underground—'

Drat it, Simon won't be able to speak with me in my dreams—

'—since the men on guard in the compound know only as much as they need to know, to accomplish their duties.'

'I wouldn't say a word to anyone.' Lydia gazed

260

up at him with brimming eyes. 'It's just that—' She glanced at the revenants in their long, niche-lined cell. 'Those things . . . And . . . And the rats—'

'The rats won't bother you.' Lemoine thought hard for a moment. 'I'll have you moved as soon as a place can be readied for you. You have nothing to fear, Madame. Our work here – our work with these . . . these men—' He nodded toward the catacomb – 'is nearing its conclusion. In a day or two I may ask you to help us—'

Meagher's nostrils flared, like a horse about to kick.

'We need trained personnel, and I can promise you, Madame Asher, that whatever this Colonel Simon told you, the work we're doing here will indeed make the difference between victory over the Germans, and defeat.'

Behind her, Lydia heard one of the revenants speak, in a dazed mumble yet completely comprehensible: '*Wo bin ich? Welcher Ort ist das?*'

Where am I? What is this place?

Her heart clenched in rage and grief, *Dear God . . .*

'*He could have escaped,*' Rhinehardt had said of his cousin. '*Fled when the remainder of our unit did . . . but he would not let go of my hand . . .*'

Without waiting to hear what Lemoine had to say next, or plan her own strategy, she pulled away from him, stumbled to the farthest corner of the cell, curled up on the floor and wept as if her heart would break.

Lemoine put her in a storeroom off the laboratory, formerly the cell of some anchoress, Lydia assumed, since it had a judas window in the door. The bars of that little window had been wrapped in silver wire, and a hasp and padlock hastily screwed onto the door. Both, Lydia saw, were plated with silver.

'I am truly sorry for the crude amenities, Madame,' said Lemoine as he led her in, past boxes of laboratory glassware and light bulbs, spools of wire and packets of silver chain now stacked up in the hall. 'Please understand that my hesitation to release you stems from the desperate importance of what we do here.'

There was a cot in the cell, an empty box for a table, a tin pitcher of water and a chamber pot behind a screen. When he'd locked her in and crossed the lab, Lydia heard Meagher say, 'That's all very well, Colonel, but the fact remains that thanks to that girl, we've lost the vampire. God only knows how long it'll be before we trap another! That puts our work back two days, three days, maybe a week—'

What Lemoine replied Lydia didn't hear, but after his footsteps had died away down the hall, Francesca's voice said, very softly, 'Don't trouble yourself, my sugarplum. He'll come back for her.'

It was a long time before Lydia could sleep. The electric bulb burned permanently in the laboratory: dragging the lightweight screen from the chamber pot to cover the judas in the door only dimmed the glare. For many hours (specifically, from 3:10 until 6:25 by her watch) she could think of little but poor Captain Palfrey, lying in the tunnel on the lip of the well in the darkness:

deluded, dying, dreaming perhaps of Don Simon's lies about aiding King and country. *I'll have to write to Aemilia Bellingham*, she thought at one point . . . *But say what? That he was chosen because he was stupid, and died because he tried to do his duty to a hoax?*

And what makes me think I'll live to see daylight again?

She wondered if Francesca had gone back through the tunnel to finish him, before Don Simon could return.

She wondered if the man who'd cried out in German – whether it was Gleb Rhinehardt or some other poor soldier – had done so because he actually had some dying flicker of his own mind left, or whether it had been merely a spasmodic firing of the nerves in the brain, the equivalent of the galvanic twitching of a frog's severed legs in the laboratory.

She wondered if Tuathla Meagher was planning to kill her the moment Lemoine's back was turned, and what would happen to her if Lemoine's gunshot wound – which seemed to be in his shoulder – turned septic.

Not as long as Francesca thinks she can lure Don Simon back here, using me as bait.

Cold comfort.

One thing Dr Lemoine was right about was that there were no rats. Presumably all were lured into the catacomb of the revenants – a frightful thought, considering how many rats swarmed every shell-crater and trench in no man's land.

'As you've seen, they're not mistreated in the least,' Lemoine told her, when he returned later in the day (10:15, by Lydia's watch) with a tin mess kit top holding a quarter-cup of bully beef, two rock-hard biscuits and a sloshy quantity of Maconochie, the ubiquitous tinned stew of the field kitchens. 'Nor are the other German subjects we're still keeping above ground. Those who have been—' he seemed to hesitate over a euphemism for *infected* '—*converted* are fed quite well, but half of them refuse real food and kill and eat rats instead.' (Lydia felt inclined to take issue at his definition of Maconochie as 'real food', but didn't.) He had locked the door of the laboratory behind him, and opened that of Lydia's cell, to allow her to eat at one of the laboratory tables. He had gained some of his color back, and the slight difference of his tone told her he'd injected a little morphia for the pain.

'They're only kept chained because I'm afraid they'll attack one another.'

'But what *are* they?' asked Lydia again, guessing that such a question – whose answer she already knew – would not only add to the impression of ignorant harmlessness she was trying to give, but tell her how many people above Lemoine in the French Army and government were in on the secret.

??? home side screening, Jamie had written.

So at least someone in the British government might know of this hideous scheme as well.

And probably – like Colonel Lemoine – thought it was going to be perfectly safe.

And that it was perfectly acceptable to mind-strip, enslave and kill German soldiers for the purpose. They had, after all, asked for it.

She widened her eyes and kept her mouth shut. Men, she had learned back in her days as a debutante, loved to explain things to women. And Lemoine especially wanted to make sure she understood how right he – and the French Army – was in undertaking this terrible project.

'Hundreds of thousands of men have died.' Lemoine leaned across the corner of the table, the tea he had made for them both on a Bunsen burner forgotten before him. He hadn't taken enough morphia to be dopey, but the impression Lydia had was of a man after two glasses of wine.

'Hundreds of thousands more are dying daily in a bloody stalemate that cannot be broken. Already France struggles to fill its ranks. You've seen the colonials, the native troops of Algeria and Senegal and Indochina, fighting white men whom they should be taught to respect. You've seen them in Paris, learning to treat white women as they treat the whores of their own countries. And they have not the courage, the *élan*, of the white race! The men of France – yes, and of Britain, too! – bleed away their lives in the mud, and what kind of world will we win, if this goes on? What sort of world can we bequeath to our children? There must be some other solution.'

Lydia nodded, with an expression of shaken horror. 'But where does the Lady Francesca come into this?' she asked timidly. 'And what were you going to do with . . . with Colonel Simon? He said you were going to kill him . . .'

Gravely, Lemoine asked, 'You know what Colonel Simon is, do you not, Madame?'

She turned her eyes away as if distressed, and

265

rotated her tin cup of now-cold tea in her hands. 'He – I – It isn't how it is in all those silly books,' she stammered. 'He told me that . . . that people like him . . . They only need to drink a little bit of blood to survive. Just a sip . . . mostly those they . . . they *take from* aren't even aware of it . . .'

She had no idea whether this was something Francesca had told Lemoine, and if it was, whether Lemoine had believed it or wanted to believe. But he looked troubled, and nodded. 'But the fact remains that many of the Undead do in fact kill their victims,' he replied gently. 'I have made a study of them for some years, Madame. At first – like yourself, I daresay – I was unwilling even to believe in their existence. Later, as I studied them further, I came to realize that these revenants, these Half-Dead, are, as it were, cousins of the true vampire, and that like the vampire they have a psychic – a mental – component of their state.'

Lydia nodded. 'I know that Colonel Simon can . . . can communicate with me in my dreams.'

'Even so, Madame.' Lemoine would have grasped her hands, she thought, in his eagerness that she should believe and agree, had she not been married. 'I believe – and I shall very shortly accomplish it, I hope – that vampires can learn to control the minds of these revenants.'

Lydia forcibly stopped herself from protesting *Not according to the Master of Prague, they can't*, and only exclaimed, 'Oh, my goodness, how?'

'By absorbing the mind – the life – the soul – of one of the revenants, before his mind entirely dissolves into the group-mind of their kind. Once

266

she – the Lady Francesca – can control the mind of one of them, she can participate in, and guide, as it were, the whole of the group.'

'And she's agreed to do this?' Lydia hoped she sounded wondering rather than totally disbelieving, or completely aghast. 'Isn't it terribly dangerous?'

'Not if there is no blood exchanged. The disease – the state of the revenants – is in the blood,' the Frenchman assured her. 'The control is in the mind.'

'And she'll do this for you?' Lydia gave an exaggerated shiver. 'She seems so . . . so *sinister* . . .'

'She will do this,' agreed Lemoine. 'For a consideration.'

Twenty

By Lydia's later estimate, it was two days before the next stage of the 'project', as Lemoine called it, could be undertaken. Both Meagher and Lemoine saw her daily, Meagher tense – *screwed*, as Lady Macbeth would have it, *to the sticking-place* with frustration and dread that something would go wrong – Lemoine dreading likewise but quiet and calm. Lydia saw no one else, and gathered by degrees that, as Lemoine had said, none of the fifteen guards aboveground knew what the project was nor why a dozen or so German prisoners were being kept in the upper area of the compound . . . nor what had happened to the further dozen who had disappeared into the catacomb.

In the face of Meagher's sharp-tongued impatience, Lemoine increasingly turned to Lydia, vastly to the Irish nurse's irritation. Lydia bit her tongue and pretended that she was her Aunt Faith – book-learned intelligent but absolutely uncritical and accepting – and by nodding and unconditionally agreeing with whatever the Colonel said, gathered that no one in the French High Command knew the exact nature of the means by which the hemato-bacteriologist (for such was Lemoine's area of study) proposed to 'convert' German prisoners of war to men who would fight for France. 'Most of them assume

I'm using a combination of drugs and hypnosis,' he confided, one afternoon while Lydia was helping him sweep the laboratory. 'I cannot reveal the true nature of my work until I have something to show for it – until the Lady Francesca is actually able to demonstrate her control over the revenants. The British government paid for much of this.' He gestured around him with his good arm at the whitewashed crypt, with its line of electric bulbs hanging from the ceiling and the grinning, horrible apparatus of the burning-grille to which Don Simon had been lashed.

Lydia plied her broom and looked fascinated.

'I understand they've been putting pressure on Commander Joffre for information,' Lemoine went on. 'I am curious as to how much our High Command will disclose, even as we prepare to mobilize our new weapon. It is one reason for my concern about this Colonel Simon of yours, provided he was telling you even a little of the truth: the British do not even yet appreciate how desperate things are here in France.'

'Is that why you're keeping me here?' Lydia paused in sweeping, and straightened up. Lemoine was always careful to keep the door of the laboratory locked, and even with his injured shoulder she wasn't at all certain she'd be able to overpower him and take the key. And if she did, if she'd be able to find her way out. But in the meantime her body craved exercise, and she swept and washed tables and – with the hot water Lemoine brought her – washed her own chemise and linen when he, rather shyly, presented her with a second set, almost certainly borrowed from the grudging Meagher. Anything to keep moving.

'It isn't that I mistrust your intentions,' the Colonel assured her. 'But Nurse Meagher is right. At this point we cannot afford even the smallest whisper of rumor regarding what we do here.'

In addition to food and hot water, in those two days Colonel Lemoine brought her reading material: issues of the *Lancet*, containing his own articles on disorders of the blood and their effect on the brain and other tissues, volumes of several Russian occult publications which contained his articles on the nature of vampires, the Ossian Poems (Meagher's – her name was in the front cover), Yeats's *Fairy and Folk Tales of the Irish Peasantry* (from the same source) and four numbers of the *Irish Literary Review*. Between reading all of these works cover to cover, Lydia paced her cell, back and forth, aching with inaction, and when she slept, her dreams were broken and troubled.

Once, waking, she saw Francesca looking in through the judas at her, a speculative smile in her heaven-blue eyes. And once, jerked from sleep by some noise in the laboratory outside, she went to the judas and saw two revenants there, slimed and filthy and smelling of sewage and rats. The laboratory door stood open. By the stillness outside, it was clearly deep in the night.

Some of them have got away, and are hiding in the crypts.

Lydia withdrew to the farthest corner of her cell, almost ill with terror. They came to the door of her cell but drew back in pain from the silver

270

lock. The incident expanded, horribly, the possibilities of what might have become of Captain Palfrey in the tunnel. *Dear God, poor Palfrey* . . .

If something went wrong – if Lemoine and all his men were arrested or killed or pulled out of their barbed-wire fortress of Cuvé Sainte-Bride – would the revenants in the catacomb break free in hunger and find some way of tearing through the door? The thought returned to her in nightmares.

Escape – if and when the opportunity presented itself – would be horribly dangerous, and the chances that Don Simon would come back for her – if he had managed to get away at all – dwindled to almost nothing.

When she told Lemoine of the revenants' incursion the next day he looked shocked and troubled – though the outer door actually hadn't been locked properly – and asked her several times if it might not have been a dream. 'Because we've been very thoroughly over the crypts below the convent, right down to the foundation vaults, and haven't found any evidence whatsoever that any of them have gotten away . . .'

Lydia knew it hadn't been a dream.

She felt safer sleeping during the day, and that evening was just finishing cleaning the laboratory after supper and tea with Lemoine, when the lab door rattled on its hinges, and Meagher's face appeared in the judas window that led to the corridor. 'Colonel!' she shouted, her voice jubilant, 'Colonel, we've got him! Lock that bitch up, Colonel, and open the door—'

271

Lydia lunged for the door and Lemoine caught her arm. She whispered, 'Simon—' as Meagher called out again, triumphant,

'Francesca got him! Get the gridiron ready—'

Lydia tried to pull free of his grip but as she'd guessed, even one-handed, Lemoine was strong. 'I'm sorry, Madame – but you do understand that he was deceiving you? He was deceiving you all along—' he insisted, as he pulled her, as gently as he could, to the door of her storeroom, thrust her inside and slammed it.

If I call out his name I'll give myself away . . .

She threw herself against the door, face pressed to the silver bars of the judas, as Lemoine unlocked the door of the laboratory and both Meagher and Francesca entered, their prisoner borne slung over Francesca's shoulder.

Lemoine gasped, 'Good God! What did you do to him?'

'Broke every bone in his body,' returned the vampire calmly, and flung her prisoner down on the grille above the gas cylinders. 'This time there'll be no running away.'

The captive vampire sobbed in agony as Meagher and Francesca dragged his limbs straight, and screamed as they buckled the straps over his arms, his ankles, his forehead. When Francesca stepped aside, Lydia saw that the man's hair was black, not white.

It wasn't Don Simon.

It was the beautiful Basilio.

She rapidly calculated the number of people that the handsome vampire must have killed – between thirty and sixty thousand, not counting the dying whose lives he had devoured since the start of the war – but it didn't make what she watched less horrible. Francesca bent over him, held the left hand that was fastened away from his body, at a ninety-degree angle to his side, gripped his chin in her other hand, forcing his eyes to meet hers. Basilio began to sob, '*Prego, prego, per favore—*' and Francesca smiled, and kissed his mouth, like a lover, murmuring in whatever Renaissance form of Latin or Italian that both had learned, centuries ago. On the other side of the grille, Lemoine stepped close, and cut Basilio's throat with a scalpel, catching the blood – which oozed slowly rather than spurted, Lydia observed (*of course it would, if his heart doesn't beat*) – in a glass laboratory jar.

He had no pity on any of his own victims . . .

Her eyes still locked on Basilio's, Francesca stepped back, gripping his hand, and with her free hand signed to Meagher. Lemoine turned a switch and the roar of jerry-built fans in the old air-passages filled the room.

Basilio screamed, 'Antonio!' as flame engulfed him.

Francesca's head snapped back, her face convulsed with ecstasy. Greasy black smoke rolled up under the low vaults of the crypt, but the fans could make little headway against the hideous stench.

Basilio screamed for ten minutes and thirty-five seconds (Lydia timed him). It was another eight minutes before Francesca released his hand – still jutting from the flame and still, as far as Lydia could see, attached to the bone of the arm – and

stepped back. Her eyes were shut, her face transformed, like Bernini's statue of St Teresa in the
Vatican. Across the flame that still swathed the
blackening corpse (*If it IS a corpse – how long
WOULD it take a vampire to die in flame?*),
Meagher and Lemoine watched the White Lady
with shocked and fascinated eyes.

Then – and this interested Lydia almost more
than all the rest – she saw both colonel and nurse
lose the focus of their gaze, and stand as if in
trance as Francesca walked to the door and left.
She knew this was what vampires did – put people
in that half-dreaming state of inattention, so they
couldn't see the vampire move – but it was the
first time she'd seen it done, Francesca obviously
having forgotten that Lydia was present on the
other side of the storeroom door.

I'll have to write all this down for Jamie.

Under the grille the gas cylinders still spouted
flame, the vampire's singularly tough tissues
slowly dissolving into ash. Smoke choked the
whole of the room, as if the underground chamber
were in fact Hell. Lydia realized she was
trembling.

If I get out of this alive . . .

The train from Calais to St-Omer was vile. Even the
corridors were crowded with men coming off their
leave or shipping in from their training, tense,
harried, half-drunk or dog-tired, and all of them,
it seemed to Asher – in a first-class compartment
with a dozen officers – smoking like chimneys.
He'd acquired the uniform of a major in the Second
Army as a matter of convenience – everyone would

look askance at civilian mufti – and dozed most of the way, wrapped in his army greatcoat. But his dreams were troubled.

He had, after all, taken passage yesterday, as Stewart had originally wished. He'd turned in the names of the Irish Brotherhood clique who had been in on the revenant scheme, and that of Butler, the German agent who'd bankrolled them; had wired both Josetta and Millward to watch for further sign of new revenants. So far as he could tell, British participation in Lemoine's project was financial – at a guess the French Army hadn't told them where they were getting their 'special troops' and possibly didn't know themselves. But with a man like Langham sniffing for a way to take over the project 'for the good of the Empire' – and given the agent he was using – that situation could alter in less than a day to something far more deadly.

How many times, Asher wondered wearily, had he heard men say, 'It's perfectly safe,' or, 'It's actually much safer than it looks,' preparatory to destroying themselves and everyone around them? Including the idiots who'd gotten Britain mixed up in the war to begin with. *It's perfectly safe*, in Asher's mind, ranked right up there with *I don't really see what else we can do*, and *It will all be over by Christmas*.

His own experience of serving the Queen had been that most things were a great deal more dangerous than people wanted to think – or say – they were, and that anything could go wrong.

Even in twilight, the streets of the medieval town of St-Omer teemed with men in uniform.

275

VAD nurses in blue and white brushed shoulders with British khaki, French blue, men in the darker 'hospital blues'. Horse-drawn ambulance wagons and drays of supplies rattled from the train station: tinned beef, crates of biscuits, box after box of ammunition, rumbling field guns. Asher had the horrible sensation of seeing goods going in at one end of some nightmare factory – men, food, weapons – and coming out at the other, discreetly bundled in bandages and dribbling blood. Did vampires haunt the railway station, he wondered, silent in the shadows behind the volunteers who brought hot tea to the men on stretchers being loaded for Calais?

Or are they all at the Front?

At Divisional HQ Asher presented his papers, pointed out the 'at his sole discretion' and 'please render all and any assistance requested' clauses to a harassed clerk and then to an equally exhausted colonel. The colonel ran a jaundiced eye over the letter and said drily, 'You're another one of them, then, are you?' and Asher raised his brows.

'Has he come through, then?' he asked. 'I heard he would.'

The colonel's mustache bristled irritably and he rubbed a tired hand over his eyes. 'Don't ask me. Didn't see him – didn't read his papers – don't know a thing about him . . .'

'Small chap?' Asher put a note of sympathy into his voice. 'Silver hair, though of course he may have dyed it . . . beaky nose. Face like a raisin and a voice you can't hear across the room. Hands like a schoolgirl.'

The officer's grimace answered his question and Asher thought, *He always did get across men in authority* . . .

And he wondered at himself that he wasn't surprised to have his suspicion confirmed.

'And I suppose,' Asher went on, 'he bagged the best of the motorcars in the pool, didn't he? Always does.'

'Not my business.' The colonel sniffed. 'Good as told me so. And where'll you be off to, with your precious "at his own discretion"? I suppose you'll want it first thing in the morning? And a driver?'

'If you'd be so kind.' Asher inclined his head, and took the requisition the colonel shoved at him across his desk. 'I'll be going to Pont-Sainte-Félicité.'

Because of the weight of the earth that surrounded the crypts of Cuvé Sainte-Bride, Lydia guessed that whatever psychic outcry had poured from Basilio's mind at his death had gone no further than the stone walls of the laboratory.

The following night they took Antonio Pentangeli as well.

Twenty-One

'Be careful out there.' Captain Niles Calvert touched Asher's sleeve, staying him in the doorway of the wooden hut designated 'officer's mess'. 'Jerry's getting ready for something – you've been hearing that since you landed at Calais, haven't you? But every wire-cutting party, every listening post, up and down the line as far as Langemarck, reports the same thing: fresh troops coming up, supplies laid in, artillery moving about behind their lines.' He glanced out past the dim glow of lantern-light through tent-canvas, the glimmer of illumination leaked between cracks in the rough board shanties that had been built over Pont-Sainte-Félicité's shattered foundations. A machine gun chattered – a German MG-04, by the sound – for the sixth time in an hour, and the rumble of the guns vibrated the ground under Asher's boots. 'Can't tell when they're going to hit.'

'I'll be careful.'

The surgeon's eyes narrowed as he studied Asher's face, as if he'd have preferred a reply more along the lines of, *Heavens, perhaps I'd better stay indoors* . . .

'Mrs Asher goes out like that as well – as I'm sure you know. And she won't be told either. It always worries me sick,' he added, 'even before . . .' He hesitated, then lowered his

278

voice. 'I don't ask you to tell tales out of school, but . . . I take it you're from Headquarters?'

'I passed through Headquarters, yes.'

Like the colonel in St-Omer, this foxlike little surgeon clearly had his own opinions about people who moved about the battle zone with things like 'at his sole discretion' and 'please render all and any assistance requested' written on their papers. His mouth twisted a little and he drew a last breath of smoke from his cigarette – the air in the mess behind them was blue with it.

'You didn't happen to hear anything about these . . . these whatever-they-are. Madmen—' His red-gold brows dived down over the bridge of his nose. 'Only they're not . . .'

'Not mad?' Asher felt cold to the marrow of his bones.

Calvert's voice was a whisper. 'Not men. Not mankind, though they seem male enough. You haven't heard tell of 'em?'

'Tell me.'

For a moment Asher was afraid Calvert would balk. It was clear from his eyes that he read absolutely no surprise in Asher's face, and was angry at it, and no wonder.

Then he said, 'Night before last a lone Jerry attacked a listening post near Loos. Didn't even seem to feel the barbed wire. They shot him, but he wouldn't die, they said. Just hung there in the wire sort of bleating at them like a dying goat, and the smell of him – *it* – was something fearful, they said, something the like of which they'd never smelled, and after six months in this

279

section, believe me, Major, that's something. They doused their lantern and didn't dare put their heads up for fear of his *kameraden*, but two of them – good men, I know them, and not easily funked – swear his face was more like an ape's, or a dog's, than a man's. By daylight he was gone. There was blood all over the wires, and over the ground. Their bullets had hit him, all right.'

Calvert shook his head. 'Then yesterday Trent, the head of the stretcher-bearers, came to me saying they'd been attacked out in no man's land, just before dawn. They go out then, if there's been a dust-up; less chance of Jerry potting at them. They had a hooded lantern with them. Trent said—'

He winced, and seemed to back himself up on his tracks: 'Trent's a good man. Conchy, and steady as a rock. Trent said they'd found a . . . they'd found a dead Tommy in a shell-hole, and with him what he first thought was a dead Jerry, crumpled up where a shell fragment had hit him. But when they got close, Trent says the Jerry sat up, and came at them – crawling because he'd been blown nearly in half, and his face, when he described it, was like this other thing that Guin from the listening post had seen: ape-like, dog-like, and smelling like Hell doesn't have words to describe. Trent and his boys were about to go after this . . . he called it a Jerry . . . with clubs, when another of 'em came over the lip of the shell-hole. They shot it, but it just got back up again, and I can't blame 'em for running for it.

'*What is it*? What's out there?' Calvert's face

280

had such intensity that Asher almost felt the surgeon was about to grab him by the shoulders and try to shake the truth out of him. 'Trent and his boys went back just after daybreak – and got shot at by snipers for their trouble – and found the wounded Jerry . . . not just dead. Half-burned-up, Trent said. He said his sister used to work in a match factory, and had got burned once by the phosphorous there. He said these burns looked like that. He said that by the look of him, the dead Tommy had been torn open and partly eaten.'

'Did you report this?' *Shit, bugger, damn . . .* Had Asher not been blessed with ears that didn't turn red with anger, he knew he would have been scarlet to his hairline. *Bastards . . . BASTARDS . . .*

Calvert's mouth twisted. 'Oh, aye.'

'The matter is in hand . . .'

When Asher said nothing, Calvert pitched his cigarette stub to the mud and ground it with his heel. After a time, in a calmer voice, the surgeon asked, 'Did Mrs Asher see any of these things?' He held up his hand, as if to stay Asher's reply of *I don't know*, and said, 'I just wondered. The way she started getting these "special orders" to come and go, and drivers taking her off down to Arras and Amiens, and I never did quite believe it was all about teaching others to use a fluoroscope, although God knows we need that, too . . . And I know you can't say. But looking back, she'd take these walks late at night, like you're off to do. So I just wonder.'

Keeping himself outwardly calm, as he had

long ago learned to do, Asher felt, inwardly, that he was shaking in his whole being like a plucked guitar string. *They're getting out . . .*

What the hell did those idiots THINK was going to happen, if they started farming these things, growing them like a Hell-crop of monsters . . .?

'I wonder also,' he said. 'And I don't actually *know* anything. But tell your stretcher parties – and tell your surgeons – that if they encounter one of these things again, *do not* make contact with its blood. The condition is transmitted by blood contact, and is irreversible. Those who are infected lose their memories and their minds, and yes, they will eat not only the dead but the living.'

Calvert stared at him: hardened at everything he had seen and done on the Front since the previous autumn, he was still knocked aghast.

'I hope to catch up with Mrs Asher in Amiens,' Asher went on. 'And to find out – I hope – a little more about what's going on. She may in fact be teaching fluoroscopy.' He pushed his hat back, and rubbed his face. The thought of fifty miles over the shell-holed roads tomorrow was already a nightmare. 'If she's already on her way back – if we miss each other – please let her know that I'm here and I'm searching for her. Don't let her go off on another of these "special assignments" before she talks to me. And in the meantime,' he added grimly, 'I think I need to have a look at whatever she saw out there in the dark.'

The man they got – the revenant they got – had just begun to turn. Looking through the judas into

282

the lighted laboratory, Lydia thought he looked barely twenty, desperately trying to keep his fortitude in the face of his captors and clearly on the verge of vomiting with terror. She saw him reach up repeatedly to finger his face, his mouth, the sides of his skull where the sutures would be just beginning to deform. He looked wildly from Lemoine's face to Francesca's, horrible in their absolute impersonality, as if he were indeed nothing more than the chicken they were going to have for dinner, once they'd wrung its neck.

Had Lydia had a gun she'd have cheerfully shot them both.

It was worse, she thought – as the young man balked at the last moment, at the sight of the gas cylinders beneath the grille – knowing that even if he did escape, even if both Lemoine and the White Lady were to drop dead (*and go straight to Hell!*), he was doomed, damned, infected already with the condition that would eat his brain into nothingness, that would turn him into a walking appetite that spread its horror into any that it wounded but did not kill. *Even if I shot them, and Nurse Meagher* – who was absent from the laboratory and whom Lydia had not seen all day – *I would have to kill him, too.*

She leaned her head against the edge of the judas, and discarded the idea of going to hide her head in the pillow of her cot. *Jamie's going to need to know exactly what happens and how long it takes. And I want to know, too.*

I'm so sorry, Hans or Gleb or Heinrich – even if you were the person who shot Uncle Richard's poor footman Ned, I am so sorry . . .

She timed it. Nearly seventy seconds elapsed from the moment that the White Lady took the young soldier's hand – gazing into his eyes, whispering to him in German – and the moment that she signed Lemoine to turn on the flame. Longer, Lydia thought, than it had taken for poor Basilio to surrender his mind into hers. But it was less than a minute before he ceased screaming, and only two and a half, before Francesca let go. Her shoulders relaxed just before she did, and her head dropped back a little, as Josetta's sometimes did when she'd sipped really, really good champagne.

Nothing of the paroxysm that had shaken the whole of her body, with Basilio's death.

'How do you feel, Madame?' asked Lemoine.

Francesca looked at him, and smiled. 'Not bad at all.' She moved her shoulders, as if readjusting to the decrease in tension. Ran a hand through her flaxen hair. 'Certainly I'm not hearing voices in my mind, if that's what you mean. To be honest,' she added, ''twas a concern of mine as well. Let me—' Her smile widened. 'Let me adjust . . . digest . . . contemplate . . .'

'Of course.' Colonel Lemoine's stiffness spoke worlds for his own impatience, his own barely-concealed apprehension that something might still go wrong with his mission, his project—

He turned his head, regarding the burning corpse on its bed of blue flame. 'And there will be no trouble – no danger – in destroying these things, once the fighting is over?'

'Mmm . . . I shouldn't think so.' She made a little rippling movement of all her muscles, like

284

a cat stretching, as if feeling for some change within herself. 'If I am able to control them – as I feel, I think, I must be . . .' Her velvety voice was barely audible over the roaring of the ventilator fans. 'What can be simpler than ordering them all into a walled enclosure open to the sunlight, and waiting for dawn? If in fact,' she added casually, 'you *want* to get rid of them when the fighting is done. Someone in your government might want to keep them around a little—'

Lemoine's eyes flared wide. '*Never!*' By the horror in his voice the idea – obvious to Lydia – had never crossed his mind. 'These creatures – these *monstrosities* – will be used for one thing only! When we have achieved that victory, we shall ask you to destroy them – all of them!'

'Oh, peace!' She lifted one clawed hand. ''Tis your endeavor; I'm only your . . . *condottiere*. Your helper. You have paid me . . . *amply*.' Smug satisfaction oozed like cream from her words. 'I am in your debt, I am indeed, Colonel. And I am – agog – to see if in fact your supposition about how these things can be controlled is in fact correct.'

'Tomorrow night?' The voice of a man who is trying hard not to nag.

'Tomorrow night.'

'I don't suppose—'

And Lydia, incredulous, realized that the issue of whether or not someone in the government would want to keep a mob of tame revenants when the war was done had already dropped completely out of his thoughts. As if he truly imagined that saying *Never* and *You must destroy them* was going to be the end.

As if the truly important thing – the only thing – was victory over the Germans, and not other uses to which such a horror might be put.

He really is thinking no further than that.

'No.' The Lady smiled to take the sting out of the word, and reached with a forefinger – with its long, glass-like claw – to flick the surgeon's cheek. Lydia saw – and she was positive the Lady saw as well – Lemoine stiffen, as if he would have twitched away from the contact, detesting the woman even as they bargained for the victory of France. 'I will return tomorrow. Ah,' she added, practically purring as she turned toward the laboratory door. '*There's* our wandering girl!'

Meagher stood in the doorway.

She'd become a vampire.

Lemoine turned his head, saw her, startled . . . then Francesca glanced at him, that eternal, pleased smile still broadening her lips, and he relaxed. 'Would you finish up here, Nurse Meagher?' he asked, and Lydia realized, shocked, *He doesn't see it. HE DOESN'T NOTICE.*

And he hasn't noticed that she's probably been missing since last night.

No wonder Graf Szgedny, and poor Antonio, and Don Simon said she was strong . . .

Lemoine left, probably, thought Lydia, to write up his notes. Francesca and Meagher stood looking at one another in the electric glare and stinking smoke of that charnel house crypt, the light of the dying flame playing across their faces.

'Is it done?' Meagher asked, as if she were no longer certain of her voice,

'Well, *he's* done, at any rate.' The White Lady shrugged peerless shoulders. 'As for whether I'll be able to control the whole swarm of them . . . truly, it remains to be seen. I certainly feel no ill effects. But as for coming to Ireland with you . . .'

'I wouldn't ask you to.' Meagher put up her hands, to push her black heavy hair from her face, then looked at them, turning them over in the light. Her nails had already grown out to claws. She opened her lips a little, ran her tongue over her fangs. 'Thank you,' she added. 'I can . . . if you will but teach me how . . .'

Francesca Gheric regarded her, hugely amused. Like an adult, thought Lydia, listening to a four-year-old's plans to slay dragons or find buried treasure.

Does Meagher really think she isn't this woman's slave now?

Or that, having been deprived of the ability to make a fledgling for the whole of her Undead existence, Francesca's going to let her new-wrought fledgling go?

'In time,' purred Francesca. 'In time.'

'When you do,' said Meagher, her speech still a little fumbling, 'perhaps we can – we should . . . The revenants are getting out, you see. I've counted them, and . . . I knew there were a few, hiding in the foundation vaults below the wine cellars, and the drainage passages. But now . . . I think they're finding ways outside. Will we be able to . . . to summon them back?'

The master vampire chuckled. 'Old Stiff-Rump will have a seizure if we don't, won't he?' She shrugged again. 'They come back ere daybreak, you know. 'Tis where their hive is. In the meantime—' She put out a hand, and stroked her fledgling's cheek. 'Let me look at you. My pretty, pretty child . . . You do know that our condition, our state, is one of perfection, don't you? Physical perfection. The prime of life, if I may so term it. The prime of health.' She reached up to finger the girl's black, curling hair. 'Your handsome soldier – whatever his name is – won't be able to keep his hands off you when he gets here—'

Meagher shook her head uncertainly, and stepped back from the caress. 'It's not . . . It's not important what I look like.'

'Oh, but it is, my sugarplum.' Her voice turned warm and crooning. 'We look as we always knew in our hearts that we look – as we look in our sweetest dreams. And we gain strength – we maintain our strength – by the kill. How are you going to get anyone to walk up a dark alley with you if you aren't the prettiest thing he's ever seen in his life? We maintain our ability to make the living see what we wish them to see, only by the lives we drink.'

'I know that.' The girl spoke unwillingly, as if bracing herself for a horror – like Lemoine facing the burning of that young German alive – that must be got through, to attain the goal. 'And I will do whatever I need to do, pay whatever price needs be paid—' The words stammered, learned by rote in another lifetime, and Francesca laughed again, and again patted Meagher's cheek.

288

'And so you shall, my blue-eyed angel. So you shall. But right now, how do you feel?'

Meagher's eyes met hers at last, and she whispered, 'Hungry.'

'I, also.' Her smile turned dark, gleaming and terrible, and she put a caressing arm around her fledgling's shoulders. 'Let us go forth, then, sweet child. And I'll teach you how to hunt.'

Twenty-Two

Moving among the charred ruins of what had been a small French village, a willow pole in one hand like a blind man's cane and a lantern, sheathed down to its tiniest thread of yellow light, in the other, Asher was aware of the Undead. Since the night in 1907 when he'd come home to find the household in near-coma slumber and Don Simon Ysidro sitting at his study desk, he had dealt with enough vampires to spot them in the darkness. There were techniques of mental focus that improved one's chances, though this didn't always help, and he had the bite scars to prove it. Revenants were abroad, and some at least shared their vampiric cousins' ability to go unnoticed until they were almost on top of their victims.

By what Grippen had told him in London, he guessed himself almost safe from the vampires here.

But the reeking network of old trenches, gaping cellars and shell-craters – black as the abyssal pits of hell – could conceal any number of revenants.

Still he walked, whispers of moonlight glimmering on the ruined land.

If Lydia had received 'special orders' to go down to Amiens – and he guessed that Amiens wasn't her actual destination – she was almost certainly with Don Simon Ysidro, and curiously, the thought brought him comfort. He had for years watched the relationship between his wife and the vampire and was virtually certain that Ysidro would not let harm come to her. '*I will keep her safe*,' the pale vampire had said, on the night before Lydia's departure for France: the night Asher had waked to see a light burning in the upstairs hallway of their house on Holyrood Street, and had gone down in his dressing-gown to investigate, nearly certain what he would find.

He had been, at that time, barely three weeks recovered from his most recent relapse of pneumonia and had just begun to be up and about for a few hours a day, readying himself to begin teaching the Hilary term. The weather had turned cold at the start of November; the house was freezing. As Asher had expected, the vampire Ysidro had been sitting in Lydia's green velvet chair before the banked ashes of the study grate.

'*Will you be going to France?*' Asher had asked him, wanting to hate him and not able to do so; and the vampire had inclined his moonlight-colored head.

'*Look after her.*' It was as if they continued a conversation already begun, and the vampire nodded again.

'*I came here tonight on purpose, James, to reassure you that I would.*'

'*Have you told her this?*'

Ysidro made the slight movement with his eyes that passed for a headshake, even as his nods were barely perceptible. '*Best not. Yet I thought you would wish to know—*'

291

Movement in one of the half-caved-in trenches; a fugitive glint of the feeble moonlight in animal eyes. The scrabble of rats among the bricks of a fallen chimney. Beyond the shattered stumps of what had been an orchard, past the makeshift bridge, the ruined country swelled, plowed by shell-fire into a sodden wasteland of darkness, barbed wire and wrecked wagons, stinking of the carcasses of horses and mules. Asher stopped, heart beating hard. Then, after a moment, moved on.

'Promenading oneself', Ysidro called this. Vampires did it, when newly arrived in the territory of a nest not their own, to ask permission of the master vampire to hunt on his or her grounds. Vampires always knew who walked their domains of darkness. If they wanted to speak to you, they would.

A white flicker in the bitter night.

The glint of eyes.

Asher kept walking, old instinct forbidding him to let any adversary know that he was capable of detecting them. He even made himself start when she laid a soft little clawed hand on his arm and said, 'James!' in a pleased voice.

'Madame.' He bowed. Lydia had told him she thought she had seen this woman, among the many who haunted the vicinity of the hospitals behind the lines. 'A long way from Paris.'

Her French was modern, though it slipped now and then into the old-fashioned idiom of Napoleonic times. Moonlight made her green eyes nearly transparent. Scorning disguise, she wore a simple white dress, her black hair loosed about her shoulders in thick curls. Blood and mud spattered her hem and her sleeves, but this he only noticed later. It seemed to disappear from his consciousness as he spoke to her, even as he was only intermittently aware of her claws and fangs. She appeared to him to be the most beautiful, most desirable woman he had ever seen.

'Dare I surmise you have come out in the hopes of a rendezvous?'

Elysée de Montadour was insatiably curious and vampires were the worst gossips in the world. She'd have accosted him if he'd had a whitethorn stake in one hand and a silver crucifix in the other.

'The merest recollection of your name in one of my wife's letters was enough to bring me forth.'

'Brave soul.' The next moment, the green eyes narrowed. 'As for your wife, she's gone off with Don Simon . . . and when you meet her again, tell her for me that spectacles *never* improve a woman's appearance! *Outré*!' She gave a theatrical shiver. 'Like a great bug! Not that I mean to disparage—'

Of course you do, you witch. 'No, no . . .'

'Purely for her own good, as woman to woman—'

'Of course.' He kissed her hand. Warm. Even in the wasted moonlight there showed a flicker of color in her cheeks. 'Do you know where they've gone? The surgeons tell me she had orders for Amiens.'

She made a sly little moue. 'Maybe after they left Cuvé Sainte-Bride, they did. I hear that's where Simon was seen, five nights ago, Johanna tells me . . . You know Johanna Falknerin, that horrid harpy from Berlin?'

'We've met.' Asher had no desire to encounter the hawk-nosed Rhineland vampire – or indeed any of the Berlin nest – again.

'Dreadful woman! And tells tales . . .' Elysée shook her head. 'And speaks French like a goat! One can barely understand a word she says, not that one would wish to . . . Disgusting. But she says she saw Simon emerge from Cuvé Sainte-Bride with his minion – I presume your pretty little wife – and go off in a motorcar. So they may well have gone to Amiens for all I know.'

She shrugged, the gesture extravagant, as if playing to some far balcony packed with admirers. 'So they're not back yet? Only to be expected. Simon is the most *extraordinary* creature in his taste for the company of the living.'

'What about the revenants?'

She startled, swung about and swept the shapeless landscape with those darkness-piercing eyes. 'The Boche,' she said softly. 'Only cabbage-eaters, gone off their heads . . . They have to be, don't they? Oh, I know about those awful things that are supposed to exist in Prague, but how could they get here? Even the Germans can't be such fools as to—'

'I doubt there's anything,' returned Asher, softly and from the bottom of his heart, 'that either side in this wretched war would consider too foolish to contemplate. Have you seen them?'

'Not close.' She drew nearer to him, like a frightened woman seeking comfort in a male

294

embrace; Asher retreated a step. Her glance flickered at him, half-reproachful, half-amused. 'And not near here. South, five, perhaps six miles, towards Arras. I saw one the night before last, shambling among the shell-holes in the moonlight. Looking for wounded, I suppose. And I have seen the bodies of the wounded they have found and fed upon. Last night I came on – I don't know, I suppose one had got himself caught in barbed wire, and the flesh burned away off his bones when the sun came up. But it could have been a living man, you know, caught too close to a bomb-blast.'

'It could.'

'These things . . .' Elysée looked over her shoulder again, her beautiful face taut with dread. 'I have heard – from the Prague vampires, I have heard – that they devour the Undead in their coffins. That they live in the sewers, and the crypts below old churches . . . I have thought of fleeing back to Paris, but what if these things come to Paris? What if they make their nests there, like rats, like wood beetles that no one can ever quite root out? Who among us would be safe?'

'Are there any of you, left in Paris?'

She waved, as if to chase away a subject unpleasing to her. 'There isn't a city in Europe, where we who hunt the night linger. The cities are full of soldiers, and spies, and people looking for spies, and for what sort of pickings? And my boys – dear boys . . .' She smiled at the mention of her nest of fledglings, chosen – in Ysidro's opinion – for their looks rather than their brains.

'On their own, without me, they'd get themselves killed inside a week.'

'And is there another man,' Asher asked, 'a day ago, maybe two, who has promenaded himself as I did? A smallish man, and slender? Large nose, gray hair, dark eyes? Possibly – probably – in uniform?'

The delicate brows puckered, and again she shook her head. 'None save you and your wife, and that little fool of an Irish nurse . . . Whom I haven't seen, now that I consider it, in weeks . . . Did she ever meet with the Undead, do you know? Did the pretty Lydia encounter her?'

'I sincerely hope not.'

'And this man—' Elysée, who had once been an actress, made a mime of mocking a man with a large nose. 'He too is seeking us? La, so popular as we have become . . . Is he a friend of this Irish *poule*?'

'I don't think so,' replied Asher. 'But I suspect they have acquaintances in common.'

In the deep of her dreams, Lydia heard the lock click.

Simon, she thought. *Simon came back for me . . .*

She struggled to shake off sleep, to surface from a black well fathoms deep. *Why can't I wake up? I sleep so badly in this place . . .*

To the very walls, the blanket on her cot, clung the stink of charred flesh.

I shouldn't be asleep anyway. It's night. It's dangerous to sleep at night. But if Simon just unlocked the door of my cell, it HAS to be night. It can't be Simon, the lock is silver . . .

Fear jolted her awake. A bar of the laboratory's electric glare fell across her face. The cell door stood open, about an inch.

Beyond it, the laboratory was tomb-silent. Even the constant, distant groaning and yowling of the revenants in the crypt was stilled.

Simon?

Lydia got cautiously to her feet. She was still dressed – *It IS still night, I DIDN'T go to bed*. Heart hammering, she tiptoed to the door and looked through the judas.

Nothing. The lab was empty. The burning-grille, steel-bright where Lemoine had scrubbed it that afternoon, gleamed under the harsh string of bulbs. The door to the corridor stood open, like this one, an inch or so.

This is a trap.

She knew it to the marrow of her bones.

But what kind of a trap? They've already GOT me.

A trap for Simon? She remembered Basilio screaming as the flames poured over him. Remembered Antonio crying in that thundering bass voice, '*Oh, God, oh God, have mercy on me, a sinner . . .*' The look of shuddering ecstasy on Francesca's face.

DON'T GO NEAR THAT DOOR.

Slowly, the gap in the outer door widened, and the reek of the revenants flowed into the lab.

Oh, dear God . . .

Even before the door opened sufficiently to reveal them Lydia knew they were there, and they were. She ducked back into her cell, looked desperately for some way to lock it from the inside – there was neither keyhole nor handle on that side of the door, and the door itself opened outward. Slowly the things shuffled into the lab, half-crouched and unbelievably hideous in the too-bright glare of the electric lights. Faces still bruised where the jaws had grown forward, mouths bloody from the unaccustomed length of new tusks. Eyes blank. The nostrils of their deformed noses flared, sniffing; heads thick with matted, uncut hair swinging back and forth; the remains of their uniforms stinking of bodily waste unregarded.

(*Why on earth don't they die of their own infections? They must after a time . . . CAN they die in this state?*)

At the same time the other half of her mind screamed in panic *NO! NO!* as they suddenly turned, sniffing, toward the cell door.

NO!

Get past them? The door was narrow and there were four of them in the lab.

The cell was barely six feet by ten. *I can use the cot as a shield . . .*

She unfastened the silver chains from her wrists, wrapped them around her hands. *How badly will that amount of silver burn revenants? Enough to let me get past them?*

The cot weighed something over twenty pounds and she was barely aware of it as she up-ended it, flattened against the wall beside the door, holding it in front of her body. *The legs are going to tangle in the door so I have to wait till they all get—*

The reek smote her like a hammer as the door

298

was yanked open. Lydia shoved the cot at them, slithered past and out the door and almost into the arms of two more revenants that had entered the lab behind the first group. She flattened back to the wall, threw a fast glance at the door . . .

And saw Francesca standing, smiling, against the dark of the corridor.

Lydia twisted, dodged to another corner as the revenants came at her. One of them, still more man-like than bestial, sprang at her like a panther; she looked for something loose to throw and there was nothing. *If I strike at it and miss, it'll grab me—*

She dodged past and the other four emerged from the cell, surrounding her—

'Stop this!' Lemoine's voice shouted from the hall. 'What the hell are you doing?'

The revenants stopped in their tracks.

Stood swaying, scratching themselves, looking about them as if she, Lydia, had suddenly become invisible and odorless.

Francesca's smile widened. She stepped out of the doorway, angelic eyes glittering with delight. 'We're only having a little test.'

Lemoine pushed past her into the laboratory, in shirtsleeves, clutching his aching arm. *He must have been in bed and asleep.*

Lydia began to shake so that she could barely stand. She felt as if she would vomit, as much from sheer terror as because the six revenants stood only a few feet from her – even Lemoine hesitated to approach her, his eyes darting from the creatures to the White Lady, still standing beside him in the doorway. Lydia could almost see his struggle, knowing he should stride over to her and bring her out of the circle of the things and not daring.

Meagher slipped into the lab behind him, blue eyes sparkling with the mischief of Hell. 'And here we thought you'd be pleased,' she teased, and Lemoine swung around to face her. This time he saw what she was, and his eyes bulged with shock.

He whispered, 'What have you done?'

'Well, I was hardly going to risk touching those things—' Francesca gestured toward the revenants – 'before I'd made sure you were paying me in genuine coin.' She put an arm around Meagher's shoulders, and the Irish vampire stepped into the embrace like a cat asking to be stroked. Like sisters. Like school friends. 'And I'm pleased to say your procedure passed the test, dear man, with flying colors. You should be well pleased.'

She turned her attention – Lydia didn't see how exactly she did it, more than just looking at the revenants – back to the creatures, and they shambled into one corner of the lab.

'It is . . . an extraordinary sensation,' the White Lady went on. 'Feeling their minds. Look.'

She fixed them with her gaze. After a moment a huge gray rat emerged from behind the boxes in one corner of the lab, then another. They ran toward Lydia, who stepped back with a sickened cry. Lemoine said again, 'Stop that!' and the rats stopped.

'Go ahead,' said Francesca after a moment. 'Hit one. It won't run away.'

Lemoine stood still for a long moment, then

300

looked around him for something to strike the rat with, but as Lydia had observed a few moments before, there was nothing loose in the lab to use for a weapon. With a laugh, Meagher stepped forward, picked up the rat – which made no move to resist – and grabbed it by head and body, and with a twist broke its neck. In the brightness of the laboratory lights, Lydia could see the rosy pinkness of the Irish girl's face, the red of her lips: only by the reflective gleam of her eyes, by the fangs that showed when she smiled and the long claws that tipped her fingers, could anyone have said she was vampire. She'd clearly fed.

Meagher turned her mocking eyes on Lydia. 'Why don't you go back into your cell now, dear?'

'They won't hurt you,' added Francesca, when Lydia tried to step past the revenants without touching any of them. It wasn't possible to do, but Francesca was right: they didn't even turn their heads when Lydia's shoulders brushed against them as she slipped by.

'You see,' said the White Lady to Lemoine, as Lydia closed the cell door behind her. 'Everything you wished to achieve. I stand ready to complete your plan.' She curtsied elaborately.

Lemoine drew a deep breath and let it out slowly. Accepting – Lydia could see the shift in his shoulders. Accepting that sometimes evil must be done that good may come . . .

'I am . . .' he began, and then paused. 'This is astounding. First we must test— How many of these creatures can you control, and at what distances? Not,' he added warningly, 'with a test

301

such as this, which, if you will permit me to say so, was inexcusably cruel—'

'And I am *inexcusably* sorry.' Francesca curtsied, without an atom of contrition in her voice. 'I assure you, it will not happen again.'

Even from the judas of her cell, Lydia could see the White Lady and Meagher exchange a wink.

A wink which Lemoine didn't even see. *Isn't he even aware that they can tinker with his perceptions? That they're altering them – blinding him – even now? Making him see what he wants to see?*

Or doesn't he even need a vampire's delusion for that?

'When we have tested – when we have documented what is possible – I will inform the Ministry,' Lemoine went on, as the revenants filed from the laboratory. 'No one – NO ONE – knows the extent of what I have sought here: the Germans have spies everywhere. And not the Germans only,' he added darkly. 'Even the British poke and pry, and try to find out what isn't their business—'

He started to follow the revenants from the lab, when Meagher touched his arm and said, 'Lock?'

'Ah.' Lemoine crossed to the door of Lydia's cell. In one quick stride Lydia was huddled in the corner, knees drawn up to her forehead, arms wrapped around her shins, shaking and sobbing.

'Madame,' said the French surgeon urgently, and hurried to her side. 'Madame, be calm. You must be calm. You can see – you *have* seen – that these creatures are now completely under control. Believe me, I swear to you that what we do here, shocking as it may seem to you, is necessary, for the defeat of Germany and the salvation of France . . . and of your own country, of course.'

He knelt on the floor before her, grasped her hand in his. 'Sometimes one must use shocking methods, to bring about the good of all,' he said. 'Germany *must* be defeated. France – the French people – *must* prevail. Once this war is won, these things will be utterly destroyed, never to be used again—'

If I go on shuddering like this he'll give me a sedative.

And does he actually believe that seeing what I have seen, the French government is going to let me go and tell people about all this?

Lydia looked up and straightened her glasses, and tried to give him an expression of dewy-eyed trust. 'Do you . . . do you swear it?' she managed to whisper – *Not bad*, she thought, considering how badly she wanted to scream *YOU IRRESPONSIBLE WRETCHED IDIOT!!!*

'Upon my honor, Madame,' said Lemoine. 'And upon my honor, as soon as it is safe to do so, you will be released . . .'

Lydia gave a sniffle or two (*Do NOT scream . . .*) and, a little to her own surprise, succeeded in forcing herself to her feet, and crossing the cell to pick up and right her cot. 'I just want to go home,' she whispered, like a beaten woman, and, spreading pillow and blanket back into place, lay down with her back to the door. 'I just want to go home.'

She heard the click of the silver padlock, and the creak of the laboratory door.

Rising swiftly, she crossed to the judas in time to see Francesca leave the lab in Lemoine's wake. Meagher turned, and with a casually savage stomp, broke the back of the surviving rat that still sat in the midst of the laboratory floor.

Twenty-Three

'*Mistress . . .*'

Lydia jerked awake, as the voice whispered, like a thread of pale mist, at the edge of her dreams.

She immediately checked her watch. Four thirty. The first threads of light would not yet have begun to stain the sky outside. She hadn't meant to fall asleep that early and, given the events of the night, hadn't thought she would. But the fact that Simon's mind could touch her dreams meant that he was somewhere close by, underground as she was and near enough that he could read her dreams.

Damn it, she thought. *Damn it, revenants or no revenants, I have to sleep . . .*

Her heart was hammering and she debated about getting changed for sleep – she had fallen asleep again fully dressed – and then decided against it. *If he's down here it may be that he has a plan to escape now, before sunrise*, and she wasn't about to undertake it in a pair of French Army pajamas.

She lay down again, closed her eyes, tried hard not to see the laboratory door opening, the circle of revenants closing around her. Tried not to see the tickled delight in Francesca's eyes, like a child at the cinema waiting to watch Ben Turpin get a custard pie in his face. '*There was a kind of spite to her*,' Szgedny had said . . .

305

Fall asleep! Simon will have to retreat, will fall asleep himself soon . . .

Miranda sleeping in her tiny cot back on Holyrood Street, silk-fine red hair spread over her pillow. Princess, the nursery cat, sleeping at Miranda's feet. Jamie asleep . . . Jamie . . . the recollection of waking somewhere in the deeps of her wedding night and lying there looking at the shape of his shoulders in the moonlight, the way slumber smoothed the lines of his face and left it like a young boy's . . .

'Mistress . . .'

In her dream (*Do NOT wake up . . .!*) she sat up (*Aunt Lavinnia would FAINT if she knew I dreamed about Simon standing at the foot of my bed . . .*) and caught him against her as he perched on the cot's edge, cold and skeletal in uniform trousers and braces, the sleeves of his shirt wet with dirty water: 'Simon, where *are* you?'

'Hush – near. Near enough to see what happened tonight. Forgive me, lady – I would have come from hiding had things gone any further. But I heard Lemoine coming and gambled that he'd be able to stop her. Had I shown myself—'

'Don't be silly,' said Lydia. 'We would both have been killed, and you at least have to get out of here and warn somebody – Jamie, if you can do it—'

'Hush,' he said quickly, and the cold, clawed fingers pressed her lips. 'I'll sleep soon. Have you still your picklocks?'

She nodded. 'I can't use them on the padlock . . .'

'Do you still aid this Lemoine in the cleaning of his workroom? Good. Leave them behind the storage boxes where the rats came from tonight. The Irishwoman has a key to the laboratory but regards it little now that she has ceased helping him with his work. I can take it from her room when all have gone out to this test of theirs tomorrow. Revenants—'

His head nodded suddenly, and the thin white brows buckled over his nose.

'Revenants haunt the crypts.'

'Simon—' *Good Heavens, don't fall asleep before you can get yourself hidden—!*

She was sitting up in bed, alone.

His voice whispered, like an ectoplasmic scratching at a dark windowpane: 'Can't get out . . .'

True waking came then, and the clammy stuffiness of the underground. The smell of the revenants, and of greasy smoke, absorbed into blankets and walls.

It was late afternoon when Asher reached Army Headquarters at Amiens. The road south of Pont-Sainte-Félicité had been shelled Monday night, and was blocked with supply-trains waiting for the digging parties to get duckboards on the surface. Beyond Haut-le-Bois it was impassable, necessitating Asher's driver to backtrack half a dozen miles and take a muddy track over a shallow range of hills, to a more protected route.

Before they reached that point, Asher was able to get a glimpse of the old nunnery of Cuvé Sainte-Bride.

He didn't dare stop, but the state of the road and the heavy traffic of mule-drawn wagons allowed him ample time to train his field glasses on the square gray buildings on the slope above the road, the dense snarls of barbed wire that rimmed the trenches around it, the lone sentry at its gate. According to the records unearthed by Josetta's friend at the War Ministry (*Who could easily have been interred under the Official Secrets Act for her trouble*, he reflected), there were five French soldiers and five British assigned to the place, as well as Lemoine and five members of 'staff', some of whom were almost certainly local cleaners and a cook. But the requisitions for rations were too high, and even without Lydia's messages Asher would have deduced its use as a prison of some kind by this time. Presumably Lemoine had the French equivalent of 'at his sole discretion' and 'please render all and any assistance'.

I wonder what he told them back in Paris?

The truth?

Or just, I have a plan to win the war.

He wondered how far Lydia and Ysidro had gotten into the place before they'd slipped out again, and what they had discovered. Was a coded letter even now lying on his desk in Holyrood Street?

Two miles down the wider road after crossing the hills, the car broke down.

'I don't blame you for wanting to get a shift on, sir,' confided the young captain in charge of Field Artillery Battery Twelve, while Asher waited in the makeshift hut for horse-drawn transport to be arranged. Asher had given him a cigarette and expressed his genuine admiration

308

for the battery – four BL-60s that dated back to the Boer War and a number of Woolwich Mk-IX naval guns mounted on railway carriages. Beneath a careful public-school English, the glottalized t's and disappearing l's of the West Country still lurked through. 'There's weird stories going about this countryside at night – things people see in the woods just lately, or things they've found. It's not some form of shell shock, sir, or nerves. There's not a man in the battery'll venture past the perimeter when the light goes.'

'An' I don't care what Colonel St-Vire says,' added Asher's driver, 'beggin' your pardon, sir, I'm sure, an' no disrespec' an' all . . . But it's Jerry. It's got to be. Nick Frampton – my mate back at Félicité – 'e swears the thing 'e saw shamblin' about the old trenches one night, wi' a face on it like God's nightmare, 'ad on a Jerry uniform, an' eyes glowin' like a cat's. The men are spooked, sir.' He drew on the Woodbine Asher had given him. 'I'm glad that axle went out 'ere, an' not further on down the road where we might be stuck when it was growin' dark.'

'Have you reported this?' asked Asher. 'How long has this been going on?'

'A week?' The driver glanced inquiringly at the captain. 'Ten days?'

'A week,' said the captain. 'And I think it's growing worse. As for reporting, what can we say, really? Things somebody says he saw – the state bodies are found in, or that poor horse the lads found in the woods, torn to pieces by God knows what . . .'

'Me dad's a gamekeeper,' put in the driver. 'An'

I never seen an animal what could do that. But beyond that . . .' He spread his hands.

'You write a report, you send it to your colonel,' went on the captain, 'who's got his own plate full of grief just keeping shells coming for the guns and food for the men, and he sees it an' thinks, *Hrm, well, somebody going a bit shell-shocked, this'll wait*. But if you were to know anyone, sir . . .' His casual finger brushed the War Ministry papers, which, Asher was well aware, had 'Spook' written all over them.

'I might have a friend or two who'd be interested in this.'

'I'd appreciate it, sir.' The captain touched his hat brim. 'Because God's honest truth, sir, it's giving me the jim-jams.'

A corporal came in then, with word that transport had been found, and Asher did the last ten miles to Amiens in a wagon-load of wounded drawn by two of the beautiful copper-bay Shire horses that a year ago – like their owner, Asher reflected – had been peacefully plowing some Shropshire rye field. Conscripts who would lay their faithful bones in foreign earth. As they jogged toward the great cathedral city Asher turned the problem over in his mind, reflecting that the young captain of Battery Twelve was right. '*You write a report, you send it to your colonel . . .*' and the revenants slipped from the crypt beneath Sainte-Bride, a danger not because of who they killed, but because of those that survived an encounter.

And say Lydia and Ysidro did find something, some proof utterly damning, in their visit to the half-ruined convent – proof that presumably had sent them hotfoot to Amiens . . . What then? What if he himself added to the report the contention that the Irish Brotherhood – and who could tell what other groups within the Empire, or what other groups they'd talked to – once means of controlling them was found – were seeking to breed up their own? Would that stand up against Langham's bland assurances that 'everything is in hand'?

Would everything lock up in some committee or other until it was too late? Until some wounded survivor of an attack was simply sent home to Britain with the infection in his veins?

No, thought Asher.

Simply, *No*.

No one at Headquarters in Amiens had seen or heard anything of Lydia, with or without a companion whom Asher was fairly certain was masquerading as a British officer. (*If the Undead can tamper with human perception he can probably make them believe he's Sir John French and none of them would think to question the impression . . .*) As a major rail hub and supply depot immediately behind the front lines, the ancient cathedral town was swollen with troops and short on everything: coal, food, petrol, transport and most especially housing. Nevertheless, Asher's papers got him a somewhat elderly Silver Ghost (plus driver) for the following day, and a garret room on the Rue des Tanneurs near the cathedral, to which he repaired after a sketchy dinner of bread, charcuterie and what he privately suspected was mule meat in the officer's mess.

311

Coming down the steps of the mess, he was just reaching for the handle of its outer door when the door was opened and Pritchard Crowell came in.

Asher was in the act of putting on his cap and didn't pause or turn his head, simply brushed past the man who was a legend in the Department – the man who had supposedly died in 1895 – the man who had instructed him in the finer points of running networks 'abroad' – stepped out into Rue des Trois Cailloux, and ducked into the blackness of a shop doorway where he waited for ten minutes. When he was fairly certain that Crowell wasn't going to emerge and follow him, he made his way – cautiously – to his lodgings, but wasn't terribly surprised, an hour later, to move his blackout curtain aside and, after long waiting, glimpse against the darkness on the far side of the canal a flicker of movement, a suspicion of moon-glint on uniform buttons.

Crowell had been in uniform at the mess.

Pritchard Crowell.

Why did it never occur to me years ago that the man had to be working with a vampire partner?

Probably because I'm not insane, he reflected after a moment's thought. *It's the sort of conclusion Millward would have leapt to immediately. When I knew the man – extricating himself from impossible situations, slipping past sentries and guards like a combination of Leatherstocking and Bulldog Drummond – I disbelieved in vampires, though I had studied their lore for years. And by the time I came to understand that the Undead*

312

were more than legends, Pritchard Crowell was – supposedly – dead.

And I had rebuilt my life in Oxford.

Is Crowell a vampire himself?

A flicker of dark mackintosh in the corner of his eye, a shadow seen from the railway embankment on Stratford Marsh . . . A half-glimpsed figure on a bicycle on an Essex lane. *Grippen would know.*

Or is that why Grippen tried to recruit me?

He recalled the night Ysidro had recruited him, to search for the day-killer that was slaying the vampires of London in their coffins – after first drinking their blood – eight years ago: *We need a man who can move about in the daylight.* Twice since then, he'd encountered attempts by governments to recruit vampires, back in the days of that intricate chess game of information and preparation, before war had shattered all schemes.

Crowell was working with a vampire. He's been hiding, for twenty years, waiting . . . for what?

Yet it's HE who's watching ME. It's he who tried to kill me back in London. Not his vampire partner.

What does that mean?

Is he waiting, tonight, for a vampire partner to appear at his side, so that he can direct him or her up here to make sure of me?

Or is he waiting for me to come out, so he can follow me to Lydia?

Lydia, who's the one who knows . . . whatever it was she and Ysidro had found out about Cuvé Sainte-Bride.

Damn it . . .

313

And of course, rooms in Amiens being scarce as hen's teeth, he had been forced to take one in a building that had only one way out – a room that had only one window, so he couldn't even take the expedient of leaving over the roof. Not that that was anything he wanted to try at the moment. Exhaustion made him feel as if he were wearing the lead-imbued apron Lydia had rigged up to protect her from the supposed danger of invisible rays from her fluoroscope; his lungs felt on fire and all he truly wanted was to lie down and sleep.

Not possible, he told himself. He simply hadn't the strength. *Think of something else.*

A fingernail scratched at the door of his chamber. Like the gnawing of a mouse, barely to be heard.

He slipped up the shade on his lantern the tiniest fraction, and crossed to the door.

'Simon?'

'A friend of his.'

Asher unhooked the silver chain from around his wrist, wrapped it round the fingers of his right hand. Opened the door and stepped to the side, fast – though that, he knew, would make no difference against a vampire's attack.

The vampire standing in the dark of the attic corridor had the curious appearance of an old man. A seamed face framed with long gray hair; eyes that had probably once been dark gleamed on either side of a broken hook of a nose. Like most vampires at the Front (according to Lydia, anyway) he wore a uniform, this one French. But his face, like Ysidro's, was not a twentieth-century

314

face. Pale gloves hid the clawed hands, one of which he extended to Asher.

'Permit me.' His French was eighteenth-century, but kept slipping back to an older form. 'I am the Graf Szgedny Aloyïs, of Prague.' He stepped into the garret, like a Slavic god, and handed Asher a card. The address lay near the Charles Bridge in the Bohemian city, almost certainly an accommodation. 'And you are the *Anglus* – the English – whom Simon has made his friend? From him I understand that you and I have another acquaintance in common, Solomon Karlebach, the Jew of Prague.'

'Did Simon send you?'

'I have not seen Simon since he escorted the most charming Madame Asher to visit me for the purpose of learning about the woman Francesca Gheric, who has now taken employment with this French madman, Lemoine. It is on that subject that I have sought you out, *Anglus* – that we must speak.'

At Asher's gesture he took the room's single chair, and Asher seated himself on the end of the narrow bed, and unapologetically refastened the silver chain on his wrist. Szgedny's odd, dust-gray eyes followed his movements, and one corner of the long gray mustaches lifted in an ironic half-smile. 'Elyséc de Montadour tells me you seek to destroy the things that breed in Cuvé Sainte-Bride. Evil is being done there – I see you try not to smile, to hear me say such a thing . . . An evil I do not fully understand. But Hieronymus, Master of Venice, tells me that three nights ago his fledgling Basilio Occhipinti perished, in

315

horror and in flame – this he felt, he knew, as masters sometimes do feel the deaths of their get. Yet afterwards he said he felt the young man's mind, his awareness, still stirring, in a way that he had never encountered before. As if thought and brain had been pulped, Hieronymus said, and yet the soul were trying to speak out of the bleeding mush.'

Like Ysidro, the vampire showed little expression or change of tone in his deep voice, yet his eyes burned somberly. 'Basilio and his lover, Antonio, slept in the crypt of a ruined church, ten miles from Cuvé Sainte-Bride.'

'Mrs Asher wrote me of these two.'

'But ere Hieronymus reached me with this tale, Antonio had come to me in great consternation saying Basilio had not returned to the crypt the night before. Yet, he said, he knew his friend was alive – if you will excuse my use of the term. After Hieronymus's visit I sought for Antonio, for whom I cherish great respect, but could not find him. He had not taken the ambulance-wagon in which he usually hunts. Then, on this Wednesday past, Hieronymus came to me again saying he had experienced, the previous night, the same sensations concerning Antonio: first the horror of death by fire – only it was not death, exactly. Fragmented dribbles of his thought, his self, remained somewhere, weeping and screaming . . .'

He shook his head, deeply troubled. 'It is Sainte-Bride,' he said at last. 'The evil there. It is breeding these things, these revenants . . . And in my bones I feel that it has taken both Basilio and Antonio. This Lemoine – or rather his minion,

316

the Irishwoman Tuathla – has sought for many weeks to find a vampire willing to work with him, willing to become his partner in some enterprise. It can be nothing but to give him a way to control the revenants whose numbers have grown so quickly of late.'

Asher said, 'I agree.'

The vampire considered him beneath the long gray brows, as if waiting for him to add, *But what has this to do with me?*

When he did not, Szgedny went on, ''Twas the White Lady who came forward at last and entered this man's service. When your beautiful lady spoke of her to me, she surmised that the White Lady was incapable of getting fledglings. The reward, she surmised, that La Dame Blanche asked of Lemoine was that he find some way to alter her condition. To permit her to pass along her own condition to others: to beget fledglings of her blood.'

'Slaves, you mean.'

'Children are – or should be – slaves to their begetters. E'en the Commandments so order it.' The gray vampire inclined his head. 'But this . . . This is an abomination. I am convinced she has drunk the lives of Basilio and Antonio – and indeed used those bleeding fragments of Basilio's thought to call Antonio to her. Whether this will give her what she seeks—'

Asher thought, *Ah*, with the sensation of seeing the pieces of a puzzle drop into place. No great cry of triumph, but an awareness of what had been before him, like a half-filled-in decryption of a cipher, all along.

317

'Can she control the revenants?'

'As I told your lady, I have never found it possible. But who knows what means this Lemoine has found?'

'According to Mrs Asher, who has read his work, he has studied the vampire state for many years,' said Asher thoughtfully. 'And he had the chance to observe them in China, where for a short time a hive of them flourished near Peking.'

'They must be stopped,' said the vampire. 'This Lemoine must be stopped. Say what you will, *Anglus*, of me and of my kindred – and yes, I know you have made a vow to destroy us, as your master Karlebach has vowed. But though the revenants hunt us in our crypts, through the brains of the rats that seek out our scent, in this you must aid us. For the sake of all the living, as well as the sake of the Undead, these things cannot be permitted to spread. Though they would kill us all, yet the harm that would come of making them your slaves – if you can do it – would be an ocean, a cataclysm, compared to what little harm we do when we hunt the night.'

Asher closed his lips on the observation that 'little harm' was a generous way of looking at the matter. But he remembered that small band of furious Irishmen, who thought they had found an unstoppable weapon to make their land free. And Lemoine, who similarly believed that he had found a way to defeat the Germans before the war could shred away the willing manhood that had – in his eyes – made France great. And Langham who doubtless believed the same, when Crowell went to him with the information that such a useful creature had gotten itself loose and could be captured and put in British hands . . .

In exchange for what?

Protection? Another 'letter of instruction' like his own, to carry him here to France?

And meanwhile each night brought closer the moment when a wounded man would be sent home from the Front, with the infection in his veins.

He left the lantern on the corner of the dresser, and walked back to the window to peep out.

Cloud had shifted across the moon, but even had the light been a little better, he doubted that he could have seen anything in the blackness below. 'Is there anyone there?'

Behind his shoulder, close enough to the back of his neck to make his flesh creep, Szgedny's deep voice replied. 'I see none.'

Which doesn't mean he isn't somewhere near. And doesn't mean that he won't dog me tomorrow, if he thinks I'll lead him to Lydia . . .

'Aid us.' The vampire's hands rested on his shoulders. 'Simon speaks of you as a man capable of such a feat.'

'I hope I am,' said Asher slowly. 'But I will need your help.'

Twenty-Four

The clink of a chain.

The flat, grunting '*Unnh . . .*' of a revenant – a creature, thought Lydia miserably, who had once been able to say things like *Take care of Mother* to a younger brother, or *Whatever happens, I will hold you always in my heart* to a weeping fiancée.

For two hours she had heard the thing moving around in the laboratory on the end of its short chain. 'Devil on you, you stupid gobshite,' said Meagher disgustedly. 'Ain't you got brain enough to hear through dirt?'

Lydia could have told her that any mental instruction that the White Lady might have given, in the ruined trenches just north of the old convent compound, would be unlikely to penetrate the depth of earth that surrounded the convent crypt, but didn't. And in fact she wasn't certain of this. Lying on her cot feigning sleep, she was profoundly curious as to whether Francesca's commands to the rest of the group of revenants *would* be perceptible to an isolate chained in the lab.

So far, to judge by Meagher's *sotto voce* cursing, as she sat on a lab stool with a pocket watch in one hand and a notebook (*time-synchronized commands?*) in the other, it didn't look promising.

'*Bitseach*,' added the Irishwoman, something

320

Uncle Richard's head groom had occasionally called Aunt Isobel's high-strung mare.

'Eleven,' said Meagher. 'Time for dinner, and let's see if the *raicleach* upstairs can teach you some manners.'

Lydia's heart lurched within her, at the terror of last night's 'experiment', but the next moment she heard the soft clang of a wire cage, and a rat's frantic squeaking.

Simon is out there somewhere, she thought desperately. *Waiting for the moment to come in – please, God, don't let Meagher start poking about and find the picklocks! – and with all the revenants out of the crypt, this one remains.*

And Meagher.

A hoarse grunt from the revenant, and the rat's squeals turned to shrieks. Meagher said, 'Ah, you disgusting maggot!' and there was a metallic rattle, as if she'd dropped the cage. The revenant howled, clashing its chain. If exposure to food had been scheduled for eleven, followed immediately by the command to desist from pursuing it, Lydia guessed that poor Gobshite had failed the test.

Or Francesca had.

And if that were so, and her control of the revenants wasn't complete (*Why not?*), would they simply scatter in the trenches, rove the battle-fields, until one of them managed to wound a man but not kill him? Wound him badly enough to return to England or Paris with the contagion growing in his veins . . .

I have to get out.

What would Jamie do?

321

Poison them? Burn the place down? Blow the place up . . .?

'Tuathla!' The voice outside was a hoarse cry. Lydia heard the legs of the stool scrape, and risked the vampire's distracted attention to roll to her feet and cross the tiny cell in one long stride. A soldier stood in the lab doorway, staring into the room – yes, the revenant was standing over the torn-apart cage, greedily devouring the rat – and Meagher had sprung down from her chair . . .

I know him . . .

It was the freckled soldier Meagher had been bending over in the pre-op tent, on the night of the big push.

'Joey—!'

He won't be able to keep his hands off you, Francesca had predicted.

Joey's eyes were stretched wide, seeing her for what she was – changed, Undead, vampire – and trapped, aghast, fascinated, literally enchanted by what he saw. He whispered, 'Dear God in Heaven . . .'

Meagher crossed to him, slid her arms around his waist – he was over six feet tall and her head barely topped his breastbone – and as if against his will he bent to receive her kiss. Lydia heard him groan, in ecstasy and grief.

'You did it,' he breathed, separating his mouth from hers at last. 'Oh, *mo stór, mo chroí*, I never thought . . . I prayed and hoped another way could be found. For freedom . . . for Ireland . . .'

He shook his head, stunned, and Meagher put one small hand up to stroke his red-brown hair from his brow. 'Goose,' she murmured. 'Silly lamb.'

'And is it true?' He pulled himself together with an effort. 'This creature . . . She can control these things? You've found a way? A way you can learn now? I got word from Teague in London, they got the thing again, got it chained up good now, with silver as you said. Is there anythin' I can—?'

She said, 'Poo,' and waved her hand. 'Teague's a fool. And Francesca's a bigger one.'

He put up his hand to her cheek, but she turned away with a shrug.

'To do this,' he whispered, tears in his voice. 'To make yourself into such a creature, for the sake of our country . . . When can you—?'

'Don't be an imbecile,' Meagher snapped. 'I'm not going to do anything of the kind. To spend my time with those things?' She nodded toward the revenant, tugging at its chain and reaching now and then toward Joey, whose face convulsed with pity at the sight of it. Dirty, bestial, blood-smeared and stinking, it still wore the remains of a German uniform, a dim reminder that it had once been a man. 'Even if I could do it, without goin' mad myself—'

'Goin' mad?'

The girl laughed shortly. 'Isn't that a joke on her, with all her petting ways, and speaking to me as if I was a child? And her just hugging herself, that she can bid these things come and go: it's enough to make a cat laugh. She took one of those things into her mind, *mo chroí*, so she could get a grip on the minds of them all.

And now it's *their* minds that are getting a grip on *hers*. I can see it in her eyes.'

She looked back at him, twinkling with delight, and saw the look on his face as Lydia saw it in the glare of the laboratory lights: heartbroken, disappointed, shocked, crushed.

'But what are we to do?' he stammered. 'There must be some way you can get control of these things, without . . . without riskin' of yourself. Are you sure? Teague's got the creature, and others can be made from it: *and* the thing's hand you sent along! We can't let this go now! We're so close! We can't let what you've done – my darling, my darling, how you've become – we can't let it go all for nothing . . .'

'Goose.' She stretched out her arms to him, and Lydia saw the change in his face as desire swamped all his horror, all his desperation at the shattering of their long-held plan – a desire whose insane intensity confused him all the more. Her husky voice was a caress as she stepped close to him, wound her arms once more around his waist. 'Silly goose.'

She put her palm to the side of his face, stroking ear and cheek and neck. Then with a flick she brought her hand down, and with her claw-like nails slit the veins of his throat.

Joey Strahan stepped back with a gasp but Meagher had him fast. Lydia saw him thrusting, struggling with all his strength to break her grip. She sprang up on him, literally climbed him so that her mouth could fasten on the squirting artery, and he sobbed and cried incoherent pleas and prayers as his strength gave out and he fell to his knees. Meagher dropped with him, his hair locked in one hand and the other arm still round his waist, ignoring the blows he rained on her back – by the time he realized he had to strike with all his strength, Lydia guessed that his strength was half gone.

The revenant jerked its chain, groaned and howled, smelling the blood. Lydia flinched when the young soldier started to convulse, as the blood drained from his heart and organs. His hands flailed helplessly; Meagher's dark head bent low over him as he slipped to the floor. A final spasm arched his back like a landed fish and he made a thin, protesting noise, and went limp.

Meagher sat back on her heels, her head tilted back, mouth glistening with gore. Lydia reached her cot in a soundless rush and lay down, her back to the door, and took care to breathe deeply, mimicking the rhythms of sleep. Whether the vampire came to the judas or not, Lydia didn't know – and she breathed a thousand thanks for the silver plating on the lock and bars. But she heard Meagher laugh, the thick chuckle of sated lust.

Count down from sixty ten times . . .

Fifty-nine, fifty-eight, fifty-seven . . .

A clash of chain, and the revenant's howling moan, followed by thick noises that could only be tearing flesh.

Meagher had shoved Joey's body into its reach.

. . . fifty-six, fifty-five, fifty-four . . .

'Mistress . . .'

She rolled off the cot and was by the door as Simon, in shirtsleeves as he had been in her

325

dream, his hands wrapped in three laboratory towels and clumsy as a drunken man's, bent gingerly to the silvered lock.

'Watch behind me—'

The door was open behind him, into the blackness of the corridor. There wasn't the slightest hope that she would hear the approach of either Meagher or Francesca before it was too late for Simon to flee, but she watched nevertheless.

Has he been hiding down here . . . for how long? If there were escaped revenants still wandering in the crypts – and how far do the crypts extend? – they must sleep in the daytime, as he did, but the risk was hideous . . . Not to speak of the rats . . .

Was that a sound in the corridor?

The lock clicked. Doubling and trebling the towels around his hand, Simon pulled the padlock loose and Lydia plunged out, and into his arms. The revenant howled again, poor Joey's blood covering its hands and chin. Simon steered her, not in the direction of the round chamber where the well was (*They must have blocked it after Simon's escape . . .*) but further up the corridor, to a narrow door and a stair that led down, barely wider than Lydia's shoulders. The darkness stank of rats, excrement, decaying flesh and the fishy reek of the revenants; cold water slopped and squished under their feet. Simon held her right hand in his, his left arm around her waist, guiding her in absolute blackness.

'They're in the vaults of the foundations,' he murmured in her ear. 'Half a dozen. They move in a group, and seem to have disregarded the Lady's summons to their brethren to go out to military exercises this evening—'

'Meagher says – Meagher told Joey—'

'The young gentleman whose liver Corporal Schultz was devouring back in the laboratory?'

'Meagher told him Francesca is beginning to – to be absorbed into the mind of the revenants. That may be the reason . . .'

'Is she, indeed?' He stopped, placed her hands on what felt like a pillar some eighteen inches in diameter, then gripped her waist in a firm hold. 'Pardon me while I execute a gavotte of joy. Keep your hands on the pillar, just as they are, while I lift you. You should feel handholds and footholds. There's a loft about five feet above the first of the footholds. Watch your head as you go through the trapdoor. The loft contains bones, but there's room to sit and to lie. *Hop-la*!'

He boosted her up as if she'd been a bunch of daisies. Lydia felt the holes in the pillar, scrambled up, as he had said, and felt the rough wood of a square trap around her, then damp wooden flooring as she pulled herself through. Her hand encountered something hard that rolled when she touched it: a human skull. She slid herself out of the way of the trap and the next moment Don Simon's sleeve brushed her as he came up through.

'Bone loft.' Lydia heard the slight grit of a cover being slipped over the trap. 'I judge 'twas formerly used for the store of food. The roof of the natural cavern is but a few feet above our heads, were we to stand. The wine vault was below us.'

'Is the way out through the well blocked?'

'With a great tangle of barbed wire. From the wine vault beneath us, a passage leads—'

'What about poor Captain Palfrey?'

'I brought him up out of the well and stanched his wound as best I might. I then put him in the motorcar, which I left at the edge of the camp, where he would be found. And I told those that loitered about the Moribund Ward, to stay away from the car and tell the others so as well. 'Twas near dawn then. I returned here the following night to find the tunnel from the well already blocked.'

'And you've been here since?'

'Where else would I be, lady? Hush,' he added softly, as she threw her arms around him again. 'Hush, lady. James will call me out, should harm befall you – or should you go on clinging to me in this fashion.' But his hands grasped hers, strong and cold. 'Listen to me now. 'Tis deep night still, and the Others still wander the crypts, in such force that 'twere peril to try to get out through the old chapel above the Arras road. There are sufficient among them that they can summon and control rats, at least some of the time.'

One hand let go of hers, and a moment later two candles, and a brass tube that rattled with the dry sound of matches, were put into hers.

'At daybreak I shall sleep. Wait a little time after that – for the Others move about longer than we – then climb down from here. From the pillar you can move in any direction and soon or late will find the wall of the wine vault. Follow this until you come to what was the great door of this place; the door itself is gone, and the stair beyond nearly filled in with rubble. You can climb past the rubble, squeezing against the wall to your right. 'Tis a short climb to another crypt, in whose floor you'll find a trap with an iron grille over it, an old drainage conduit. 'Tis wet and nasty, but leads to the caved-in crypt of the chapel, at a distance of something over a mile. Do not wait for me. Make your way back to Pont-Sainte-Félicité as quickly as you might. If James wrote two weeks ago that he was seeking military clearances to come here he might well be at the clearing station now. Tell him all and see if he can come upon a way to destroy this place utterly. Knowing James—' she heard the slight, chilly smile in his voice – 'I place great faith in his ability to do so.'

'Oh, yes,' breathed Lydia. 'Jamie's very good at that sort of thing. But you—'

He put fingers like Death's over her lips. 'I've no intention of making a martyr of myself for the good of humankind. There are other ways yet, out of this place. Now tell me of what this *Irlandésita* had to say of our fair Francesca . . . and speak soft. The Undead cannot hear so clearly through the weight of earth as they can in the night overhead, yet their ears are sharp.'

In an undervoice she related all that had taken place in the laboratory that night, not only Meagher's words to Joey, when she had casually turned her back on the scheme for which, it seemed, they had both come to the Front, but the fact that Francesca's signals to the revenants under her control had evidently not worked on

329

the creature chained in the lab. 'It might just be the thickness of the earth, as you say,' she whispered. 'Or the distance – I don't know where exactly they've taken the revenants for this test. But if what Meagher said is true, and Francesca is becoming *absorbed* into their minds, from taking the mind of that single revenant into hers . . . *Would* one of her fledglings be able to sense this?'

'Without a doubt. No master vampire I've ever heard of has made the attempt, to take the mind of one of the Others – with or without the pollution of their blood. I am indeed curious as to whether this pollution of the mind – the influence of the hive of the revenants themselves – will spread from Francesca's to Meagher's, through that link alone.'

'How horrible!'

'Horrible indeed,' murmured the vampire, 'if the mind and strengths of the Undead come to be added to the hive. As Graf Szgedny told you, we who walk the night conscious and aware know surprisingly little of our unspeakable cousins. If either of us be so fortunate as to emerge from these crypts undevoured, we must add this information to that store of knowledge concerning the Undead – and the Unliving. As for Mistress Meagher, it surprises me not that after going to the pains of sending one of these things to her rebel compatriots in Ireland she would abandon the whole scheme, once she became vampire herself. 'Tis what most vampires do.'

'Forget the things they loved?'

'Lose their capacity to love.' There was long

silence, and when he spoke again his voice seemed barely louder than the scratch of an insect's foot passing over bone.

'Love, as I understand it, is founded in hope, and in the faith that one's soul can at length be at peace in the embrace of another soul. For the damned, there is neither hope nor faith – nor any reason not simply to take one's pleasure in the kill, which is what gives pleasure to the highest degree.'

'Not all of them,' said Lydia, remembering Basilio, screaming his friend's name.

'No,' returned the vampire. 'Not all.'

Light drifted from below, lantern-glow almost painfully bright after hours of utter darkness. Lydia saw that indeed she and Don Simon were in a sort of loft built over what could have been storage space below. Francesca said, 'Brainless *putain*,' and Lemoine, 'It matters not whose doing this was. What we must do is find her, before she encounters revenants down here –'

'I thought there *were* no revenants down here,' jibed Meagher.

'In the event that there are,' amended Lemoine quickly. 'And it may be that there are some that have broken free.'

Lydia worked her way, flat to the floor and soundlessly pushing herself with her toes, to the edge of the loft, and looking down, saw that thin spots had developed in the White Lady's shimmering primrose hair. The color of the hair itself had faded, streaked with the hue of dust. Through it the scalp showed rough and slightly warty. By the way Francesca's hands moved, restlessly fingering her jaw and her elbows, Lydia guessed that physical changes were beginning to overtake her as well.

We look as we always know in our hearts that we look – as we look in our own sweetest dreams.

And her dreams were being devoured, as she had devoured the souls of how many thousands over the centuries . . .

She can still use her skills of illusion to keep Lemoine from noticing – maybe even to keep Meagher from seeing changes. Maybe she's still telling HERSELF that what she feels is only her imagination. Or some effect of controlling the revenants that doesn't really matter.

Her hand closed around Simon's, as the lantern-light bobbed back the way they'd come, up the narrow stair to the corridor outside the lab. After a short time, Lydia heard the wet *splish* of shuffling footfalls, and smelled revenants, moving through the chamber below.

When Don Simon fell asleep, his hand still in hers, Lydia estimated that it must be close to six in the morning, but dared not strike even the light of a single match to check. Revenants had come into the chamber below, and for a time Lydia had heard the shriek and squeal of the rats they summoned to their hands, and the horrible noises of the revenants feeding. *I'll have to tell Jamie that there seem to be TWO hives down here, one under Francesca's control, and one independent.*

Bother! I don't suppose I'll EVER get access to Colonel Lemoine's notes, to see how that might have come about . . . Maybe one is the German prisoners and the other is guards they might have infected? Or soldiers from the front-line trenches? Have the lines moved while I've been down here? They were only a few miles away . . .

And what do the uninfected guards up top think about all this? What do they think is going on?

The noises below died away. Lydia began to count.

When she reached sixty for what she hoped was the sixtieth time – she got distracted, retracing Simon's instructions and what she remembered about the road back to Pont-Sainte-Félicité – she lit a candle, opened the heavy trapdoor, and peered down to make sure there wasn't a revenant sleeping directly at the bottom of the pillar. Then she turned back, and took a long look at Simon, lying on his back with his neck pillowed on a femur, a great heap of brown bones rising behind him: skulls, pelvises, long bones, with ribs and vertebrae scattered about him like dried flowers. His face was peaceful, a young man's face, white eyelashes lying on the fine-grained white skin of his cheek like a child's.

He chose to be what he is.

If he hadn't, I would never have met him.

Or have met the thing he's become.

She propped her spectacles more firmly onto her nose, blew out the candle, and first climbed – then slid – down the pillar.

At the bottom she lit the candle again (*I do NOT want to trip over a revenant . . .!*) and made her careful way around the wall. She found, as Simon had said, an archway and the first two shallow steps of a wide stairway whose next step was buried in rubble. The narrow space to the right of the rubble was barely visible, even at close inspection, and thin as she was, scarcely admitted her body. Had she not had the vampire's assurance that it was indeed the way which led to the surface she would not have dared to squeeze herself in, for fear of getting stuck further in. But even when it narrowed to a crawl space, she could see the faint movement of her candle flame with the current of air, and this kept her going.

Jamie, PLEASE be at the clearing station when I get there . . .

She tried to calculate the days since Francesca had caught her in the tunnel by the well. Jamie's letter from Whitsedge Court had been dated the second of April. How long would it take him to convince the Army to give him transport to France? And if he was assigned to go to some specific place far from Flanders, how long would it take him to wangle his way out of it, acquire a motorcar (*I HOPE he isn't going to cadge a ride on a train!*) and reach Pont-Sainte-Félicité . . .

I should have left a message for him . . .

Oh, God, what if they start shelling the chapel again before I get out?

The blackness around her opened out. The dank air smelled of rats and death and revenants, but more faintly; she saw none in the low crypt into which she wriggled from the caved-in doorway. It took all her strength to wrestle the iron grille from the drain in the floor, and the stink of the

334

old passageway beneath – it was ankle-deep in water, and too low even to stand in upright – made her queasy.

The thought of encountering a revenant down there was enough to make her understand, to the marrow of her bones, why Don Simon had put off the escape until daylight.

'*There are other ways yet, out of this place,*' he had said.

She wondered whether he'd been telling the truth.

Something over a mile, he had said. The thought was horrible, but there was no going back. She tucked her skirt more firmly up under her belt, lowered herself down and dragged the grille back into place.

The last five yards were the worst. The tunnel had been caved in, choked with rubble and mud; had she been attempting the escape by night Lydia wasn't sure she wouldn't have simply put her head down and wept. But the candle flame still leaned toward the scraped, narrow crack in the mess, and, more glorious still, pallid daylight leaked through, so Lydia simply shoved her head and shoulders into the gap between two boulders, and began to wriggle and push her way. She was conscious that the stones around her were actually stones, not earth. They'd been cut. Once she even saw the broken remains of a carven saint's face.

The daylight was almost painful.

The smell of the fresh air, when she crawled forth from a hole in the steep bank of rubble that rimmed what seemed like an enormous shell-crater, made her want to fall to her knees and weep.

She had emerged at the bottom of what seemed to be a cellar, whose vaulted roof had been shattered. Fragments of stonework littered the brick floor, and a huge spill of rubble hid the whole of one end of the chamber. Clambering up this, with much slipping and backsliding, she reached a second crypt, above which, she saw, rose the remains of the church itself. It was the same chapel near the lilacs she and Palfrey had visited – *How many days ago was it?* – and had ruled out as impossible.

Exhausted, shaking and dizzy with thirst, she scrambled up a half-ruined stair to the pounded remains of the chapel itself, and from there into a caved-in labyrinth of trenches and sandbag walls. *Just get to the road*, she thought. *SOMEBODY should be along, and I'll come up with some tale to get a lift back to the clearing station.*

German spies? Black-marketeers? She glanced down at her clothing, gray with mud and torn from two long crawls through rubble: *I came to be buried in a caved-in dugout and have no recollection of how I got there . . .*

An ambulance-wagon came rattling from the direction of Arras and Lydia stepped out and waved. *Colonel Simon and I were on our way back from Amiens and were attacked last night by a German reconnaissance party . . .*

The ambulance-wagon pulled up and a slender man in a dark mackintosh sprang from the cab:

civilian trousers and shoes. At the same moment two French soldiers leaped from the back, hurried toward her. They had almost reached her when Lydia realized that the vehicle was a long-chassis Sunbeam.

Oh, damn . . .!

The civilian produced a pistol and even if he hadn't, Lydia knew she simply hadn't the strength to run away. She staggered, put one hand to her forehead, and collapsed in what she earnestly hoped was a convincing faint.

Twenty-Five

'She's shamming,' said the little man in the mackintosh as the ambulance-wagon lurched into gear. Even with her eyes shut Lydia could tell he bent over her, and she caught the whiff of smelling-salts as he uncorked the bottle of them. By the nearness of Lemoine's voice, the colonel pulled the little civilian away from her cot.

'Can't you see she has been through hell, man?' Then, closer and more gently, 'You'll be all right, Madame Asher.'

'Asher?'

'Madame James Asher.' By the sound of Lemoine's voice he – and his companion – had taken a seat on the opposite cot. Very sensibly, Lydia thought, since it was pretty clear that the Arras road had been shelled again, and the ambulance-wagon bucked like a Wild West bronco. 'Her husband lectures on folklore and linguistics at New College.'

'Her husband—' Mr Mackintosh's soft, slightly nasal voice sounded amused – 'worked for seventeen years for the Foreign Office, if it's the same James Asher I worked with in '93 in Mesopotamia. And her husband, so far as I could tell when I was back in London, knows perfectly well what's going on in your research station, Colonel – which I think answers all those questions you had about how she'd gotten mixed up with the

338

vampires. These days he works for the London nest.'

Oh, damn . . .

'I . . . She . . . *What?*'

'This woman,' sighed Mr Mackintosh patiently, 'has been lying like Ananias. You didn't even search her for picklocks, did you?'

'Of course not! And in any case, there is no lock on the inside of that door.'

Mackintosh sniffed. 'I'd say then that the woman Meagher let her out – having killed that young idiot Strahan, the kill might easily have gone to her head. Or she had some idea of shoving Mrs Asher into the arms of that abomination chained in the lab, to test her own control over it, since that's obviously been the plan from the moment Nurse Meagher figured out what you were doing with these things.'

'Nurse Meagher has been selflessly loyal! Even after she . . . she was transformed . . .'

'Cock. One of your prisoners was smuggled to London by a group of Irish gunrunners, with the intention – I should think – of holding him somewhere safe until Nurse Meagher figured out how these things can be controlled. I understand she's also been pinching tissue, which is less conspicuous to send. I have no idea what instructions she sent about safety precautions but obviously her boys botched it, because the thing got away – something a detached hand wasn't about to do. My friends at the FO got wind of it and asked me to bring it in—'

?? home side screening . . . Evidently Jamie was right . . .

339

'Probably put two and two together with what they may have already guessed about your show here. Whether Asher – his name was Grant, when I worked with him – is also working for the Department or for someone else, including the Irish Brotherhood, I don't know, but he clearly knows all about you. He's in Amiens now. I lost track of him last night, but I'd suggest you send one of your young ladies to make sure of him. He killed three gunrunners and the revenant in London, and his vampire partner near as dammit killed me.'

'Does anyone else know?' Lemoine sounded utterly aghast. As well he might, thought Lydia, considering how much of a secret he thought this was.

Jamie, she thought in the same moment. *Jamie here* . . .

'God knows.' Mr Mackintosh didn't sound terribly concerned about it. 'I'm only here to . . . *assist* . . . the Lady Gheric. But if I were you I'd finish that assessment of the Lady's abilities to control your little pets quick smart, and put the whole thing on an official footing. Otherwise you're going to find the entire circus taken away from you, and everyone shaking their fingers and telling you how naughty you were even to think of it. I'd also have a little chat with Nurse Meagher, as soon as she's up. And not believe a single word she says.'

Asher spent Friday in the cellar of a house in St Acheul, close enough to the old church there that he suspected the building's third-century crypt

340

was one of Szgedny's daytime hiding places. The cellar was so jammed with sacks of wheat and sugar, flitches of bacon, packets of coffee, cans of petrol and boxes of cigarettes that there was barely room for a cot for Asher to doze on. His hosts – three of the biggest, toughest women he'd ever seen – cheerfully fetched him bread, cheese, pâté, tea and clean linen: 'From which army would be your preference, sir?'

Arriving in company with the Master of Prague shortly before dawn, he slept most of the day. If Lydia was in Amiens, he guessed that to hunt for her would only serve to give Crowell – if he was still in the town – time to find (and attempt to kill) him. Or, worse, would lead Crowell to Lydia. He studied again the Comte de Beaucailles's descriptions of the old convent's crypts, and with the aid of a prewar map of the Département du Nord, worked out the exact coordinates not only of the convent, but of the farthest extent of its crypts.

It would be, he guessed, a long night.

His hostesses fetched him upstairs after dark, where a handsome staff-car waited in the little courtyard ('From which army would be your preference, sir?'). 'The Boche, he's getting ready for a big push,' one of them said to him, and offered him a cigar. 'All up and down the line they're saying so. We've given you an extra pistol – there in that box on the seat – a flask of coffee, some chocolate biscuits and two Mills bombs.'

'It is as well to be prepared,' added her sister kindly.

Szgedny appeared shortly after that, paid off

341

Mesdames and rode at Asher's side as he drove back through the dark countryside, the hooded light of the headlamps barely flickering on the desolation of mud, torn-up railway tracks, broken carts, dead horses and bombed-out villages. Again and again the car was held up by lines of wagons, struggling through the mud. Asher tried both staying on the road (deep mud and the necessity of levers and duckboards to pry the wheels clear) and veering carefully off the road through the fields (deep mud and flooded shell-holes).

It was nine o'clock before they reached Field Artillery Battery Number Twelve.

'You sure about that, sir?' The young captain in charge looked like he had neither slept nor shaved since Asher had conversed with him the day before – certainly not changed his clothing, possibly not eaten either. On the road outside the half-repaired cottage a shouting match had developed in the darkness between men driving wagon-loads of food and those offloading crates of ammunition; the guns sounded far off, a distant thunder broken by rifle-fire like lightning. 'I've heard there's some kind of Frenchie hospital station up there.'

'Our men will be cleared out by morning.' Asher touched his own orders – *sole discretion, all and any assistance* over some very formidable signatures – and the neat table of coordinates. 'The Germans have been running their own show in the crypts, using the boffins there as a blind. Believe me, it's devilish clever and I wouldn't have believed it myself if I hadn't seen it with my own eyes. This is our only way to eradicate them.'

342

It sounded gossamer-thin to him, but the captain frowned, looked from Asher to Szgedny. The vampire met his gaze, held his eyes quietly for a time. 'I—' the captain stammered. And then, as if remembering earlier orders, turned smartly back to Asher and saluted. 'Of course, sir. Just at sunrise.'

'Will you keep an eye on the place?' said Asher, when he and the vampire stepped out into the night once more. 'On the off-chance that the man who was waiting outside my lodgings in Amiens will appear and try to stop it? Which I wouldn't put past him,' he added, when Szgedny lifted his gray brows. 'Crowell was always an uncannily good guesser. When he realizes I gave him the slip he may work out that my next move might be—'

'*Crowell*?' It was the closest Asher had seen to the Graf looking truly surprised.

'You know the name?'

'Dear me, yes. He went by others – Jourel was one, Grassheart another. Thirty years ago, forty years ago, he was very much La Dame Blanche's minion, much as you are to Simon, and to others of the London nest. It amused her—' And his own eyes glinted as Asher opened his mouth to protest that he worked neither for Ysidro nor Grippen.

When, after all, Asher did not speak he went on, 'I think she loved the game as a form of hunting, though she hadn't the slightest interest in your Empire nor mine. There was a time when I wondered if she meant to make him vampire,

343

to serve her. He would have been a dangerous one. So that was he?' A corner of the Graf's long mustache lifted in his one-sided grin.

'Forty years ago.' *She must have been lurking somewhere in the background all the time we were in Mesopotamia.*

'He's old now,' observed Szgedny. 'I begin to think your lady wife correct in her surmise that the White Lady's bite is sterile. She can kill, but cannot give the semblance of life in death. Like those rare queen bees whose eggs produce only drones. Well, well . . .'

'Will you watch for him?'

'I can remain until an hour before first light. This young man will sleep before then—' He nodded back to the captain's rough shelter. 'That I shall see to. Spent as he is, it should be no trouble. I will speak to his dreams a little, to hold by your orders with good will. By sunrise, all the revenants should be in the crypts. And where do you go?'

For Asher had turned toward the staff-car again.

'Cuvé Sainte-Bride. I suspect if I handed in a note at the front gate, when light is in the sky,' he added, seeing the vampire's silvery eyes widen, 'that will give Lemoine and his staff just enough time to run for it, and to evacuate any uninfected prisoners. But it will be impossible for any of the Undead – or the Unliving, as you call them – to follow.'

The vampire's brow clouded. 'They will be far more inclined to clap you in irons—'

'It's a risk I'll take. Don't fear that I'll go there a moment before there's enough light in the sky to destroy a vampire,' he added, seeing thought and suspicion flicker across the Graf's face. 'I must – we must – see those things destroyed. But I won't have the innocent destroyed with them.'

'I would hardly describe this Lemoine as innocent.'

'His guards are. Without Francesca Gheric, and the revenants themselves, Lemoine can do no harm.'

Szgedny's eyes narrowed. For a moment Asher wondered if the vampire had enough power of illusion to kill him in front of half the men of the battery and every mule-driver in the British Expeditionary Force. But the Master of Prague only gestured toward the black east, and the red flashes of fire over no man's land: 'He can do no harm until the next thing he thinks up; or someone else thinks up. There are no innocent in this war, Professor. Not Lemoine, not me, not you.'

That night Mr Jourel – which was what Dr Lemoine called Mr Mackintosh, though Lydia suspected that wasn't his real name either – came and took Lydia from her cell at gunpoint, and led her to a smaller room deeper in the crypts. Deeper underground, she thought, and more thickly insulated by the weight of the earth: *So Simon won't know I'm still down here? (Does he guess that Simon's still hiding somewhere in the crypts?) Or so Francesca won't know?*

As Jourel was leading her from the laboratory he paused in the doorway, and Lydia needed no

345

threat from his gun, to stand quiet beside him. The first of the revenants bound for the surface passed them, stinking to heaven and walking without looking around them, or seeming to notice their surroundings. Those Lydia had seen elsewhere – in the crypts, in the Peking mines, or, horribly, in the laboratory two nights ago – had moved with a peculiarly shuffling gait, heads swinging from side to side, nostrils flaring as they sniffed for prey.

These weren't looking for prey – or for anything. They had almost the movement of marching men.

Francesca Gheric walked among them. Her awareness sharpened by years of discreet cosmetic use, Lydia noticed the White Lady's carefully powdered cheeks and chin, through which faint bruises still showed, where the shape of her face was beginning to alter. The Lady's head had begun to have that slight characteristic side-to-side movement, and once or twice she could not keep herself from picking at her own collarbone and wrists.

And more than anything else, there was an indefinable change: in her posture, in her step, in her eyes.

Maybe if she hadn't been among the revenants, it would have been less obvious.

Lydia counted twelve revenants, each an ambulatory reservoir of further infection.

There had been thirteen in the long crypt.

Lemoine followed, notebook in hand. He was making notes as he walked, keeping a sharp eye on his charges, so that he – no more than had Francesca – didn't see his guest and Lydia,

346

standing in the laboratory door. Jourel's childlike left hand, resting on Lydia's shoulder, tightened slightly and she wondered if Lemoine knew she'd been taken from her cell and what the old man beside her would do if she cried out.

But the thought of what the revenants might do if Francesca's concentration on them broke closed her throat. Without a sound she watched them pass along the corridor and ascend the stair into darkness.

The lower level of the crypts, entered through a winding stair at the far end of the reeking chamber in which the revenants had been kept chained, was flooded a few inches deep in water that reeked of soured decay. A small lantern hung at the bottom of the stair, its light just sufficient to show her rats: living ones crawling along the stonework, chewed carcasses littering the stair and bobbing in the dirty water. Thirty feet away, among the squat arches of the convent's deepest foundations, a chair stood ready, with a larger lantern on a goods box beside it and two pairs of handcuffs locked, one on either side, to the chair's frame. Lydia wondered in panic if she could kick Jourel and flee, but she knew from the stink, and the floating carrion, that revenants hid here.

He's going to ask me about Jamie . . .

She hadn't seen Meagher with Francesca and Lemoine, and wondered when she'd put in an appearance. Was Meagher still asleep? It was early. Did Francesca, like the revenants, now wake a little earlier than sunset?

They can't kill me. Lemoine will be furious.

347

But Lemoine isn't here NOW.

But when they reached the bottom of the steps, Jourel pushed her back against one of the niter-crusted archways, turned her roughly to face him and demanded, 'What's happened to Francesca?'

'She took the mind – the soul – of an infected man into her own.' Lydia was astonished at how calm her own voice sounded. 'That's how she's controlling the revenants. It's how she gained access to the . . . the group-mind, I suppose you'd call it. Control of the revenants was the price Lemoine asked, you see, to help her make fledglings. But now *it's* starting to control *her*.'

'You're lying. She'd never have touched the blood of those things.'

'She didn't.' Lydia tried to sound matter-of-fact, as if there were no gun digging into her left seventh rib. 'She absorbed its soul without drinking its blood, at the moment of its death. I was there. They burned it up in acetylene flame, the same as they did the two vampires whose deaths – whose souls – she absorbed, in order to let her make fledglings in the first place.'

His bead-black eyes narrowed, though the lined features remained expressionless – as Jamie could go expressionless when he was thinking – in the dim glow of the smaller lantern near by them. 'You know a great deal about it, young lady.'

'Well, as you said yourself,' she pointed out reasonably, 'my husband and I have been dealing with the London vampires for the past eight years. Think about it,' she added. 'Vampires look how they think they looked in life. That's why most of them look young, you know. But it seems to

348

work both ways now. She's starting to *think* she looks like a revenant. She is becoming one in her own mind. Becoming what they are: appetite, with the mind that controls it eaten away. And maybe the minds of the two vampires she devoured are still alive, after a fashion, within hers. Alive and welcoming the revenants in, as a way of destroying her. Maybe that's why vampires don't devour their own kind. She didn't drink their blood, either. Ask Meagher,' she began to add, but her captor's eyes had shifted past her, gazing into the blackness of the sub-crypt.

In a voice hoarse with rage he whispered, 'Bitch.'

His hand tightened painfully over Lydia's arm and the barrel of his pistol pressed into her side. But it was not of her, she realized, that he spoke.

'Stupid, lying bitch. All these years of waiting—'

The black eyes snapped back to her and he said, 'What does your husband know of this?'

Nothing, not a thing . . .

How much can he reasonably have learned?

'He knows about the revenants,' she said, hoping she still sounded as if she weren't making this up as she went along. 'I don't know whether he knows about this place or not.' *Has this man deciphered my letters to Jamie?* 'He knows Lemoine has been using German prisoners—'

'How did you know how to get inside here?'

'Don Simon – one of the vampires – showed me.'

'Who is your husband working for?'

'I don't know,' said Lydia simply. 'I haven't been home since November.'

349

'How did—?' He turned his head sharply at a noise. Movement in the blackness of the crypt and the faint, almost soundless whisper of stirred water. Then eyes gleamed in the lantern-light. Lydia's heart was in her throat at the thought of a revenant, but it was Tuathla Meagher, her nurse's uniform damp and dirty now but her face deathlessly beautiful, framed in the blackness of her hair.

Jourel shook Lydia roughly, demanded, 'Is what this bitch says true? About Francesca?'

'You've noticed, have you?' The jewel-blue eyes smiled briefly, amused, into Lydia's, like a child speaking to a puppy. Then her glance returned to the old man. 'And noticed a great deal more than that, I see. You must be Crowell. I'm Meagher. She's spoken of you.'

'Has she, now?' Jourel – Crowell, and Lydia hoped that actually was his name – gave a single, snickering laugh. 'The one who was going to raise an army of revenants and free Ireland?'

Meagher waved her hand, like a coquette dismissing the recollections of a schoolroom passion. 'Guilty as charged, my lord.' Lydia remembered poor freckled Joey, whispering of freedom for their homeland. 'I calculate – at the rate she's deteriorating – it's going to be about two more days before she loses the ability to keep Lemoine from seeing anything's wrong. Another beyond that for her mind to disappear. Nasty *cailleach* . . . I'd have left last night,' she added, with the sidelong, alluring grin she'd given poor Joey, 'but I heard you were coming.'

Their gazes locked, and held.

350

Understanding one another.

Meagher went on, 'She planned to go to Paris. The master there's weak, she said. A fool. Moreover, the Master of Paris is *here*, someplace on the Front.'

'That's what she said to me,' returned Crowell. 'That she and I would rule Paris, forever, between us. But as for laying my life into the hand of a woman I've just met two minutes ago . . .'

'What choice do you have?' Meagher stepped closer, sinking her voice though there was no one (except herself, Lydia noted nervously) to hear. 'Whatever contamination she avoided in her blood, it's in her brain now. If she made you vampire, it would pass to you. You'd be scratching in a corner eating rats and liking it inside a week. She said you were the best, Crowell: clever and strong and ruthless. With you, she said, she could rule half Europe.'

'And she would rule me.' Crowell's voice was equally soft. 'But I knew her. We knew each other, worked together, for long, long years. I knew what I'd be getting, as her . . . partner. And so I waited, while she sought for a way to overcome her barrenness, like a biblical matriarch rooting for mandrakes. But you . . .'

The vampire smiled again, and shook her head. 'What choice have you, *mo grá*? All those years of waiting . . .' Her voice teased, as if savoring his bitterness. 'And now 'tis gone, because of her impatience for it . . . Or was it yours? How many more years would you have waited? *Could* you have waited? How many more years before your own brain started to go, along with your eyesight

351

and your bowels and the heat in your loins?' Her fingers brushed his body as she spoke of it. 'How many years till you were too weak to hold onto the hand she stretched out to you, to carry you across Death? She put you at that risk, remember, for the off-chance of having you be *her* servant and no other's.'

Crowell said nothing, and they stood like lovers, hesitating before a kiss from which each knows there will be no going back. But, Lydia noticed, his grip on her arm did not slacken one bit. Nor his grip on his revolver.

'And when she comes back,' whispered Meagher, 'she'll want you. She slapped me like a housemaid, only for looking hard at the bruises on her face, where her jaw's growin' out into a snout. She wants you for her own fledgling and if you don't go to her of your own you know she'll take you. Then the pair of you can sit and eat rats together.

'This is your last chance.' The vampire swayed closer to him, blue eyes glowing like sea jewels into his. 'And you know it. Or do you know another vampire, whom you trust more than me?'

'You're something of a *cailleach* yourself,' murmured Crowell, '*acushla*. Here?'

'I've been through the whole of the vault. Even the strays and runaways are gone out; they won't be back till near dawn. You'll fall asleep for a few hours . . .'

Her glance went to Lydia, and her smile widened.

'And wake hungry.'

Twenty-Six

From the hillslope above the Arras road, James Asher could look east across to the ruined land where the French Second Army had driven back the Germans in January.

He'd hiked these roads as a young man, tramping through Picardy during one of his vacations from Oxford, picking up strange old legends and half-forgotten words, tales of Celtic gods or of peasant girls who achieved good fortune from fairies by woodland wells. The well and grotto – the *cuvé* in question – at Sainte-Bride had long been sacred to the goddess who had later been adopted into the Catholic church as a saint, and Asher recalled the scene before him as it had been back in the early eighties: lush meadows dotted with black-and-white cattle, fields hip-deep in growing wheat. Lines of elms, an echo of the back lanes of Kent in his boyhood. Birdsong, and the whisper of wind.

A ghastly wasteland of mud and shell-holes and caved-in trenches under the sickly moon. And – not clearly visible from the road that ran along the feet of these low hills – a hideous suggestion of movement in the abyssal shadows of those trenches.

The Front lay three miles to the east, but the supply-routes to the firing line did not cross these lands. There had been no traffic on the road for

353

hours. A glance at his watch showed Asher that it was a quarter to four. An hour until the first glimmerings of light.

He trained his binoculars on the two figures at the side of the road. A broad-shouldered man in the gray-blue uniform of a French officer, his left arm in a sling. A pale-haired woman in white, like a spirit in the moonlight. He saw her raise her arms, and the man looked out with his own field glasses, over the mud and the darkness.

All along the line of one trench, shadowy forms emerged from the earth. As they shambled toward the road in a ragged line Asher saw movement around their feet, as if the earth squirmed, and he shivered at what he was pretty sure that was. In a way, he thought, Lemoine scarcely needed the revenants, if through them Francesca the White could achieve control over the rats. While he watched, one of the revenants stumbled, staggered and fell, entangled in the remains of the barbed wire that both sides had stretched across no man's land. Like an insect caught in a spider's web it thrashed, kicked, and the creatures nearest it swung around, converged, almost certainly at the smell of its blood. But at the roadside Francesca the White raised her hand, and the revenants turned away, and kept moving in the line of their march.

Asher estimated the distance. A good half-mile – *Can she operate out of line-of-sight?*

Can she see through their eyes? Their minds?

Vampires could walk in the dreams of the living. Could, under certain circumstances, control their bodies, ride them like rented horses,

354

see through their eyes, speak through their mouths. Single individuals, but what about the collective mind, formed of individual conscious-nesses whose self-awareness was gone?

A sound in the trees behind him. Momentary as a thought, the filthy smell that disappeared almost at once . . .

So not all of them were down across the road. Some, at least, escaped her control. An effect of distance? Or was her control not absolute? Asher listened behind him, heard nothing. Nevertheless, he began to move down slope, to where he'd left the motorcar, concealed by the broken ruin of what had once been a farmhouse.

He moved carefully, knowing he'd be visible to someone across the road in the flatlands, if they happened to look his way. The rise of land where he'd stood had commanded a view of the convent, on the next slope of ground. What little remained of the moon was sinking in the sky, and even shot to pieces and winter-barren, the woods would be pitch dark. He could only hope that Francesca the White and Dr Lemoine were too preoccupied with their observations – and their control – of the revenants to see him.

How much of her mind does she need, to control them? he wondered. *And how is Lemoine going to phrase this, in his report to the French High Command? 'I have turned German prisoners into mindless monsters which I'm paying a vampire to control for us. They're cheap to feed and don't mind being killed and oh, by the way, be very careful about contact with good Frenchmen . . .'*

And how long is it going to be before we run

355

*out of prisoners and start looking for 'volunteers'
in our own ranks?* He could think of a couple of
his scholastic colleagues – not to speak of
Marcellus Langham, hungry for his promotion
– who'd be perfectly happy to see 'niggers' from
India or Algiers pushed into the ranks of mindless cannon fodder. *Ah, well, 'dulce et decorum
est' and all that, old boy* . . .

His mind briefly conjured the fifth year of the
war, when the Germans had adopted the same
method of fighting – *and surely there's a German
vampire who wants something badly enough to
strike the sort of bargain the White Lady struck*
– and no man's land had spread across half the
world, revenants mindlessly fighting revenants
in the shell-cratered ruins of Paris, London,
Berlin . . .

The revenants broke from their line, and began
to move toward the road.

Damn it.

He'd been seen.

He left off the cautious smoothness of his
walk and ran for the car, weakness clutching
his chest and limbs like a leaden shroud and
terror searing him. *Do NOT let yourself be
caught, do NOT* . . .

He stumbled, scrambled up, dizzy and gasping
– the foremost grabbed his arms and Asher
shucked out of his greatcoat, turned, and fired
his pistol point-blank between the creature's eyes.
The thing stumbled and Asher didn't look back,
knowing it would be on its feet and after him
but blind. He reached the car with ten revenants
from across the road lumbering toward him – two

emerged from the woods behind the car: no thoroughfare in that direction, it would take too long to turn . . .

He snatched up one of the Mills bombs and flung it at those in front, far too close to the front of the car but he was past caring; crammed himself behind the dashboard and felt the car jolt in the blast, fragments of steel (and of revenants) spattering against the vehicle's sides. *Now if only there's enough left of the road to drive on . . .*

He came up from behind the dash, yanked the self-starter and got nothing. Half a dozen revenants were only yards away and even those that had been shattered by the blast were crawling in his direction. He turned with his pistol as those behind the car scrambled onto its back . . .

Then they sprang off, as if the metal were hot.

At the same moment those in the road before him stopped, and turned away. As if he'd suddenly become invisible, or someone had blown a magic whistle.

They started to stride off down the road, in the direction of Cuvé Sainte-Bride.

Asher looked back, automatically, toward where Francesca had stood beside the road, some fifty yards from the car, pale in the moonlight. She was still there, Lemoine grasping her arm – Asher heard him shout something at her but could not make out words. He saw the woman pull against the Frenchman's grip, with a curious, swaying movement that reminded him eerily of the revenants themselves. Lemoine jerked his hand towards Asher – *Asking something? Ordering something?*

357

Francesca lunged at him, twisting her arm free and seizing the officer around the neck. Lemoine was taller than she, and built like an old-time warrior; still she twisted and shook, in a single, vicious gesture, and Asher saw the colonel's body spasm and his knees buckle, and knew she'd broken his neck.

Then she was running across the road in a swirl of white: ivory gown, pale hair flowing like a cloak. She moved with the curious light swiftness, faster than any human speed, which the vampires usually hid from living eyes, and the remaining half-dozen revenants stampeded around her.

The roar of a motorcycle made him swing around. . . .

Chest burning, knees shaking with exhaustion, Asher was too flattened with weariness even to feel surprise at the sight of Don Simon Ysidro on a dispatch rider's 550 Model-H Triumph. 'Get on,' said the vampire.

Asher obeyed, though Ysidro showed no sign of turning the bike around and evidently proposed to head straight past the last of the revenants. 'Where's Lydia?'

'She has to be at the convent. I felt no trace of her when I woke—' They were already careening up the road, weaving past the gore-littered crater left by the Mills bomb, gaining on the revenants – 'but she's not at the clearing station—'

Asher didn't ask what the hell Lydia had been doing at Cuvé Sainte-Bride in the first place, when Ysidro and his *mignonne*, as Elysée had said, had been reported getting clear of the place : . .

*Unless he has another living assistant that he
was seen leaving with . . .*

They swept past the revenants. Francesca had
outdistanced them, and was now nowhere in
sight.

'They're going to shell it out of existence at
sunrise.'

'Good,' said Ysidro. 'Then we'll have to hurry.'

When Meagher came down the narrow stair again
Lydia knew it must be shortly before first light.

The small lamp by the stair arch had gone out:
Lydia knew they burned for about six hours on
one filling, but had no way of knowing how long
it had been kindled before the man Crowell had
dragged her down to the vaults. Sick horror filled
her at the thought that the larger lantern at her
side would go out before Crowell woke, leaving
her to listen in the darkness.

For revenants. For Crowell. For rats.

For death . . .

Oh, Miranda, I'm sorry! Jamie, I'm so sorry . . .

They'd left her handcuffed to the chair while
they'd gone upstairs again, to fetch down a cot
and a chain. Lydia thought, given time, she could
have done something to break the chair – which
was a common, wooden kitchen chair – before
Crowell woke, but they'd fixed the handcuffs to
the chain and the chain around one of the squat
Romanesque pillars that held up the groined roof,
and she knew there was no getting out of that.

Meagher had drunk Crowell's blood, and he,
dying, hers, as she'd laid him down on the cot a
few feet from Lydia. Then Meagher had smiled,

359

and with the old man's blood on her lips had come over and given Lydia a playful kiss, enjoying her dread, before disappearing up the stair into the darkness. Lydia had wiped the blood off on her shoulder the moment the vampire was gone.

Then for several hours – as nearly as Lydia could estimate it – she had alternately pulled and twisted at the handcuffs, to utterly no avail, and had watched, with a deep interest that at times overcame her dread, the changes passing over Crowell's dead body.

His eyes didn't settle, as the eyes of corpses do after about thirty minutes. In between bouts of digging and scratching and scraping at the chain where the handcuffs were attached (and which she could not quite reach owing to the chain's tautness around the pillar), she tried to see whether Crowell was developing hypostasis on his shoulders, buttocks and the back of his head. *Probably not*, she thought. *And of course he won't develop rigor either, even in this cold.* She wished the light was better, and that she could examine him more closely. (*And while I'm wishing, I wish that I could run away . . .*) His face had gone the horrible, bleached, waxy yellow of a corpse's face, and his mouth had dropped slightly open.

His mind, Lydia was well aware – while wondering what that was actually like – was alive, tucked in some corner of Meagher's consciousness.

Some part of it would always stay there.

There's got to be SOME way out of here . . .

Does Simon know about this sub-crypt? She didn't know. *I don't see how he could. While he's awake the revenants have been down here, and when they're asleep, he's asleep.*

Because they are of the same order of being. Unliving and Undead. Terrifyingly similar . . .

Now and then she'd lash with her foot at exploring rats, but she noticed that the rats – which, she had observed in the clearing station, were very quick to ascertain when a human being was helpless – went nowhere near the vampire.

In time, even the waxed leather of her stout shoes grew wet, and her feet got numb from cold.

Miranda, she thought, and to her mind came again her last sight of her child, by the nursery fire. Smiling, thinking her mother was only going down to London for a day. *Oh, my poor baby, I hope Jamie gives you all the love I would have done . . .*

Then Meagher was there, standing on the edge of the lantern-light at the bottom of the stair.

She gave Lydia a smile and stroked her cheek as she passed; her hand, Lydia observed, was warm. She'd fed, either out in no man's land or in the trenches, scavenging the deaths so freely harvested by war. Looking back at Crowell as Meagher crossed to his cot, Lydia observed that the wrinkles had all but disappeared from his face, and that his hair had darkened, from white to a deep, sable brown. A young man's face. The nails on his childlike hands had become glassy and thick, lengthened to half an inch or so beyond the fingertips. In his half-open mouth Lydia glimpsed the fangs. Meagher stood for a moment

361

looking down at him, smiling, and her smile wasn't one of tenderness.

It was a smile of triumph. Of pleasure, and the anticipation of pleasure to come.

He was the best, according to Francesca. The living man who would make a very, very good vampire. Lydia had the uncomfortable feeling she'd met others who fit that description – her stepmother leaped to mind. What had Meagher said? *Smart, strong and ruthless . . .*

Appetite that cares about nothing but itself.

Francesca had worked with Crowell, for years, evidently, in something of the same way Simon had worked with her and Jamie . . . *Is that what Simon would say of Jamie? Is that what he'd see in him?*

Exhausted, terrified, it was hard to tell, or to think clearly.

You'll wake hungry . . .

Meagher knelt in the shallow water at Crowell's side, and bent over him, her black hair framing his face as she pressed her lips to his. Lydia shivered, but couldn't look away. Couldn't mentally keep herself from taking notes. For some reason she thought of the vampire-hunter Osric Millward – *He'd want to know this kind of thing . . .*

And I'll need to tell Jamie . . .

But I won't be seeing Jamie again, ever. Or Simon. Or my child . . .

Crowell's hand twitched, and Meagher covered it with her own. His whole body shivered, and he pulled his hand free, grasped her arm, clung to her for an instant. Their lips still locked, as

362

she released back into him the consciousness, the soul, that she'd carried in her own mind while his body died.

Released it back . . . but not all of it. She kept part of it within herself.

Then Crowell turned his head, as if denying that his first instinct had been to seek protection, and opened his eyes. They caught the lantern's reflection, like a cat's.

Lydia thought she should probably pray for her own soul but couldn't come up with any words.

'Pritchard?' said Meagher softly, and his hand returned to her arm, stroking this time. '*Mo chroí . . .*'

'Forty years,' he murmured. 'Forty years I've waited. I always wondered what it would be like. She made me wait . . . Just so that I would be hers, and not someone else's.'

'And now you're mine.' She nodded toward Lydia, without taking her eyes from Crowell's. 'Are you hungry? Will you play for a bit? Unchain her and blow out the lantern? They're still out with the Others, we have a little time. They won't be back till just before—'

'Whore—' The word came out of the darkness of the stairway like an animal's bleat, hoarse and bestial, as if formed with difficulty and pain. 'Swill-bellied stinking whore—'

Meagher and Crowell swung around like guilty lovers, staring into the darkness.

A white blur shimmered beyond the lantern-light. A huge clawed hand grasped the lintel of the narrow door as Francesca Gheric lurched into the glow.

363

'You dared. You *dared*—'

Crowell rolled off the cot and darted away into the darkness; Meagher sprang in the opposite direction, as Francesca lunged at her, snatching with her claws. *And now Crowell can get up the stair and away . . .*

It's what Jamie would have done . . .

If the woman he was leaving behind wasn't me.

A flicker near the stair – *Yes, that's him, all right . . .*

Crowell froze with his foot on the lowest step, light and thin and active, a young man again. In the dark of the stair above him, eyes gleamed. Stench rolled into the room like the black exhalation of Hell.

In the darkness Meagher shrieked, and Lydia had to shut her jaw hard to keep from screaming, too. She flattened back against the pillar, watched in terror as the revenants piled into the room. Six of them, mouths stretched open, howling and reaching—

—and running right past her as Francesca shouted, 'Kill them! Kill them!'

Water splashed, dashing about in the blackness as Meagher had moments ago suggested as a game. Meagher screamed again—

The next instant another pair of eyes flashed in the stairway and Simon and Jamie were beside her. Lydia choked back her husband's name as Simon made short work of the chain with a pair of bolt cutters. Behind them Crowell and Meagher screamed, but the two men ran her to the stair and scrambled up the slippery, crooked steps. *If I say anything Francesca will hear me—*

364

Will she care if we get away?

Probably not – she seemed MUCH more interested in making sure the revenants chomped up Meagher and Crowell – *but let's not take chances . . .*

She clung to the arms that held her in the darkness, Jamie's lanky with muscle, Simon's like a dancer's, leading the way through the abysses. She was aware of it when Jamie stumbled – *Good Heavens, he shouldn't be running around breaking into vampire lairs anyway . . .*

Through a doorway and into the storeroom with the drain in the floor, and the electric light of the laboratory pouring from the corridor. Jamie – as sheet-white as a vampire but looking far less healthy – rushed her along that hallway toward the stair and Lydia straightened her glasses and gasped, 'What about the guards?'

'Gone,' he panted. 'The prisoners, too. The Twelfth Field Artillery Battery is going to start shelling this place in eight minutes— Sunrise—'

Lydia looked back in panic, but Simon was gone. Stumbling, Jamie dragged her up the stair, through an old stone room and then through a modern wooden one, and out into a courtyard gray with misty dawnlight. *If they shell it as they did the chapel by the lilacs even the deepest vault will be laid bare. The light will consume Francesca, destroy the revenants . . .*

Burn Simon to ashes . . .

NO . . .

There was a motorcycle in the middle of the courtyard and Jamie flung himself onto it, Lydia straddling the carrier *à l'Amazone* and clinging

365

around her husband's waist. The morning air was freezing and she barely felt it. Rooster tails of liquescent mud splattered up around them in all directions as they roared toward the open gate, between the lines of barbed wire and the defensive trench, past the empty guardhouse and along the rutted track toward the Arras road.

Simon, she thought. *Simon can get to the tunnel that leads to the well, hidden in the darkness . . .*

Will that be protection enough?

She knew she shouldn't hope that it would be. Pressed her cheek to Jamie's back, and hung on tight.

Distantly – five miles at least – heavy guns began to sound, and in moments she heard the shattering freight-train roar of shells overhead. The road beneath them lurched, making the motorcycle jerk like a terrified horse, and even at this distance Lydia felt the shock wave of the first explosions, and the vicious spray of rocks and hot dirt pelting her back.

By the time they stopped to breathe, four or five miles down the road toward Pont-Sainte-Félicité, Lydia had stopped crying.

Twenty-Seven

Lydia got two weeks' leave, to go back to England.

Jamie didn't.

'This is what I traded to Stewart,' he said, 'for that "at his sole discretion" and "any and all assistance" on my papers.'

Against the glowing lights of the clearing station's tents shadows moved, preparing men for surgery, ascertaining how much damage had been done, writing tickets for the next stage of care. Now and then, in one of the wooden buildings – or the additions built onto the charred ruins of Pont Sainte-Félicité – a door would open, and men's voices would be heard. Storeman Pratt walked by the bench where they sat, outside the officer's mess, with what looked like an entire crate of cigarettes casually tucked under his arm.

The wet, grievous stink of mud and smoke and decaying flesh mingled with the smell of the river, and the April green of a few ruined trees.

'The understanding was that I'd have a free hand – a *completely* free hand – in gathering information, even if it meant shelling a French Army research project on the grounds that it was actually being used by Germans. I had to commit myself to gathering information.'

He coughed, deeply and painfully. He'd spent forty-eight hours in the Isolation Ward with a low fever and Lydia thought he still looked haggard and shaky. It was good only to sit beside him, to hold his hand.

Near the makeshift bridge, ambulance-wagons rumbled in and bearers clustered around with their lanterns, and from the corner of her eye Lydia thought she saw two shadows – the dark woman with the big nose, and a gray-haired man like a Slavic god – flit in the direction of the Moribund Ward.

Far off, the guns boomed like thunder.

'Is that what you told them? That it was really the Germans behind that project?'

Jamie had spent most of the afternoon – when he should have been sleeping – writing up a report about why he'd instructed the men of Field Artillery Battery Twelve to shell Cuvé Sainte-Bride into a crater of sunbathed dust.

'With Colonel Lemoine dead I could say anything I wanted. I said that the whole project was a German plan to spread plague among our troops. I wasn't that far from the truth.'

'He meant well.' Lydia shook her head. 'So did poor Meagher. I wish I could feel towards them something other than horror at the means they proposed to use. At their blindness to the devastation it would cause.'

'They meant well,' agreed Jamie quietly. 'And too often, people who mean well find it hard to believe that the thing that will win them their victory is too dangerous to use, or might have consequences that they don't foresee. And don't want to hear arguments to the contrary.'

He lifted his hand to return Captain Palfrey's

368

salute as that young man walked past in hospital blues. It was Palfrey's first day on his feet; the young man had asked Lydia, daily, when she'd gone in to visit him, if she had heard word of 'Colonel Simon'. He clearly had not the smallest recollection of the scene in the laboratory. Or he recalled it quite differently.

Jamie had surmised – when he and Lydia had talked it over – that it was Don Simon bringing Palfrey out of the well that Johanna of Berlin had seen and told Elysée about. With the woman's bad French it was not surprising that Elysée had mistaken the sex of the reported 'minion'. He had also filled in for her his recollections of Pritchard Crowell: 'Had I still been working with him, once I came to know the London nest, I think I would have spotted at once that he had a vampire partner. At least I like to think I would.'

'And your Mr Langham covered for him, when he faked his own death . . . What was it, twenty years ago?'

Jamie had nodded. 'I suspect if I'd continued much longer in the service I'd have been obliged to do the same,' he said. 'It isn't uncommon in the Department. You go into hiding, you make a new life, where those you've wronged and those you've betrayed and those whose loved ones you've killed won't find you. But the Department knows. And the Department can always come calling, if they need you.'

As Simon had, thought Lydia, eight years ago, when the London nest found itself in need of a day man.

'Or members of the Department,' he'd added,

369

'who have some little scheme of their own going, in hopes of a promotion or a knighthood.'

Lydia hoped that in time Captain Palfrey would return to his grandfather's estate and 'wait for orders' that would never come. That he'd marry his lovely Miss Bellingham and live happily ever after without ever returning to Europe again.

Now she asked softly, 'Will you be all right?'

Jamie nodded, and coughed again. 'Mostly what I'll be doing is listening,' he said. 'Dressing up in German uniform and sitting with prisoners. Finding out about troop movements, and conditions in the Fatherland. Looking at pictures and newspaper articles, deducing the conditions of their economy from toffee wrappers. Letting the boffins back in England guess where we need to apply pressure, and what kind of inducements to hold out if they ever get round to negotiating for truce.'

'Will they make you go to Germany?'

He was a long while silent. Then: 'I don't know.'

'I'm committed to another year here,' she said after a time. 'Ellen writes me that Miranda is well and happy with Aunt Lavinnia, but asks after us. I think when my year is up I'll ask for my papers, depending on where you are in your work. It must have been hard for you,' she added, 'signing up . . .'

Another silence. James, Lydia had learned, was a man who didn't speak easily of could-be's or might-have-been's. Like herself, he dealt with the world as it came at him. At length he said, 'They had to be stopped.'

370

He'd spoken to her of getting help from the vampire-hunter Osric Millward. In times past they'd made the man a figure of fun, but she knew that in his heart Jamie understood him. And understood that he was right.

'It's all very well to talk about doing evil that good may come, best beloved,' he went on. 'But the problem about evil is that the line is seldom clear, how evil is evil. And how much evil will bleed into the good you're trying to do – like the virus of the revenants, spreading in one's veins.'

'Not to speak,' added Don Simon Ysidro's soft voice, 'of the difficulty one can have in distinguishing when evil is masquerading as good.'

He stepped from the darkness, his uniform new and trim and looking as if he'd never gone crawling through old drains or cut his way through barbed wire, or done whatever he'd done to get himself to safety. He took Lydia's hand in his own gloved one, and bent over it.

'I am glad to see you well, Mistress. And yourself, James.'

With an ironic twist to his mouth, Jamie saluted him, which the vampire calmly returned.

'You will be pleased to hear that the matter of the shelling of Cuvé Sainte-Bride is being hushed up under the Official Secrets Act,' he reported. 'And that those of us who hunt the night have passed across no man's land for two days now, and have encountered no sign of revenants. I understand Colonel Lemoine's body was recovered after the destruction of Cuvé Sainte-Bride, and returned to his family, with no stain on his record.'

371

'Thank you,' Jamie said quietly. 'That means a great deal, to families.'

'It did to mine.'

The vampire turned to Lydia, and again took her hand. 'And you are returning to England, lady?'

'For two weeks.' She spoke around a sudden tightness in her throat. 'I'm taking the evening train from St-Omer Thursday. I'll return to finish out my year—' She fought back the grief she felt, the concern about all those young men in the surgical tent, the hundreds – thousands – who had passed beneath her hands since November. 'But I don't want you watching over me when I return. Nor ever again.'

He said nothing, and there was neither grief, nor question, nor surprise in his yellow eyes.

Beside her, Jamie was silent also, though she felt his eyes touch her.

'I don't care how much trouble I get in,' she made herself go on. 'Or what's happening around me, or whether I need help or not. I can't . . .'

He inclined his head. 'As you will, lady.'

'And I release you,' added Jamie quietly, 'from whatever promise you made to me, Don Simon.'

'I understand.' His glance returned to Lydia, and she knew that he did.

She turned her hand in his, and holding it, drew off his silk-fine, gray kid glove, and felt his fingers, clawed like a dragon's. They were warm. He'd fed.

Probably over in the Moribund Ward . . .
With the others of his kind.

Fed on young men dying, men she'd cared for that afternoon. She remembered their faces. Their wounds. The names they'd whispered in delirium, friends and sweethearts and children they'd never see again.

She couldn't speak.

'I chose to be as I am,' said Simon quietly. 'Not the best decision in my life, but one from which there is no going back. No more than these men—' He nodded towards the soft glow of the tents – 'can go back from the choice they made. I can be nothing but what I am, lady: a killer who devours the lives of others. I do not ask you to forgive me either my choice, or my current state.'

She couldn't look at him, either. Only sat, looking down at the long, slim hand in hers.

A demon's hand.

He saved my life at the risk of his own. And . . . She shut her mind on the further thought: *And I care for him . . .*

How can I go on accepting that he kills people, regularly, for his own benefit?

There could be no condoning what he was – what he did, and the side of his existence that he hid from her – no matter how convenient it was for her.

Gently he withdrew his hand, and she was desolate at the thought of never hearing his voice again.

Asher and Lydia got a ride on an ambulance-wagon to St-Omer the following afternoon. They had dinner in a small *auberge* near the cathedral,

373

then walked to the station in the damp cold of the spring night: Lydia had some twenty minutes to wait for her train to Calais; Asher's, to Amiens, would leave in an hour. They were standing together, handfast, marveling in one another's presence, speaking softly of Oxford and Miranda and what codes they'd use to defeat the censors, when shouting started around the telegraph offices at the end of the platform: Asher heard someone yell, 'Ypres!'

Another Jerry push, he thought. The one everybody had been expecting.

People crowded in that direction. Military police and railway officials began to work their way along the platform, stopping people from getting on the trains.

''Strewth!' exclaimed a young man in a sapper's uniform close by, to a friend on a stretcher. 'They fookin' better not be confiscatin' these trains—'

Lydia's eyes widened in protesting dismay, and yes, the officials were getting on the trains, herding people off, soldiers mostly bound for leave, a few civilians complaining vociferously that they had their papers, by God . . .

The crowd mobbed tighter around the telegraph office, and Asher heard someone shout, 'Poison gas—'

He caught the arm of one of the military police as the man moved toward Lydia's train. 'What is it?'

'Jerry's hit Ypres. Chlorine gas – four miles of line – thousands of the French dead in minutes—' The man's voice shook a little. 'Most of 'em drowned in the fluid in their own lungs. Or had their eyes burned out. We're gonna need every train.'

The shouting was growing louder, as crowds of soldiers jostled on the platforms. Bearers were already coming to carry the wounded back to waiting rooms. People called questions, cursed, groaned. A delicate little VAD, bringing tea to the waiting men on the stretchers, swore like a sergeant of the Marines.

'—still fighting – Canadians holdin' the line, some of the Frenchies as well. Damn bloody bastards—'

Asher didn't mention that the French had also experimented with poison gas.

Behind her thick spectacles, Lydia's eyes filled with tears.

She said quietly, 'I have to go back.'

'I know.'

'Please . . .' She stayed the sergeant, as he would have gone on. 'Transport back to the Front . . . I'm an expert at fluoroscope. I should get back to my unit . . .'

'Bless you, M'am.' The man saluted her. 'Where'll that be?'

'The clearing station at Pont-Sainte-Félicité.'

'There'll be a convoy of ambulance-wagons outside the City Hall at ten. But they may take you on up to Ypres instead . . .'

'That's all right. Thank you . . .'

She turned back to Asher. 'If they cancel your train—'

'I'll find another.' He took her in his arms, kissed her gently. 'And I'll wire Ellen, and your aunt—'

Her arms tightened hard around him, pulling back only a moment to remove her spectacles before pressing her face to his shoulder. 'I'm sorry—'

'Go.' He kissed her temple, then, when she raised her face to his, her lips. 'I'll write to you there, and let you know where I am.'

It was ten minutes to ten. He watched her walk away along the platform, tallish, skinny, her gray nurse's cloak billowing slightly around the carpetbag she carried, her red hair screwed tightly up under her nurse's cap and already working itself loose from its pins . . .

The most beautiful woman in the world.

And the flame that had warmed his heart back to life, from beneath the cold ash that the Department had left of it. With lucid certainty he knew that she was the reason he hadn't turned into Pritchard Crowell.

'*Why not?*' Grippen had asked.

There was the reason.

As she disappeared into the darkness outside the station's doors, he thought he saw a slim figure in a British colonel's uniform – a flicker of pale hair like cobwebs – follow her into the night.